If sexy heroes who know how to kiss you senseless
are on your wish list,
Silhouette Books knows where to find them!

A chilly air force base, secrets and an incendiary
passion set award-winning author Rachel Lee's
AN OFFICER AND A GENTLEMAN
cuddling before the fire.

For reader favorite Andrea Edwards,
THE MAGIC OF CHRISTMAS is enough to make
pigs fly, snow fill Death Valley and a grumpy single
father discover true love....

Even Santa would quail at a houseful of kids before
Christmas! But in bestselling author
Cait London's THE PENDRAGON VIRUS,
it takes more than that to keep this would-be
family man away....

RACHEL LEE

wrote her first play in the third grade for a school assembly, and by the age of twelve she was hooked on writing. She's lived all over the United States, on both the East and West coasts, and now resides in Florida.

Having held jobs as a security officer, real-estate agent and optician, she uses these experiences, as well as her natural flair for creativity, to write stories that are undeniably romantic. "After all, life is the biggest romantic adventure of all—and if you're open and aware, the most marvelous things are just waiting to be discovered."

ANDREA EDWARDS

is the pseudonym of Anne and Ed Kolaczyk, a husband-and-wife writing team who have been telling their stories for more than fifteen years. Anne is a former elementary school teacher, while Ed is a refugee from corporate America. After many years in the Chicago area, they now live in a small town in northern Indiana, where they are avid students of local history, family legends and ethnic myths. Recently they have both been bitten by the gardening bug, but only time will tell how serious the affliction is. Their four children are grown; the youngest attends college, while the eldest is a college professor. Remaining at home with Anne and Ed are two dogs, four cats and one bird—not the same ones that first walked through their stories, but carrying on the same tradition of chaotic rule of the household nonetheless.

CAIT LONDON

lives in the Missouri Ozarks but loves to travel the Northwest's gold rush/cattle drive trails every summer. She loves research trips, meeting people and going to Native American dances. Ms. London is an avid reader who loves to paint, play with computers and grow herbs (particularly scented geraniums right now). She's a national bestselling and award-winning author, and she also writes historical romances under another pseudonym. Three is her lucky number; she has three daughters, and the events in her life have always been in threes. "I love writing for Silhouette," she says. "One of the best perks about all this hard work is the thrilling reader response and the warm, snug sense that I have given readers an enjoyable, entertaining gift."

Mistletoe Kisses

Rachel Lee
Andrea Edwards
Cait London

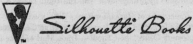

Silhouette Books

Published by Silhouette Books

America's Publisher of Contemporary Romance

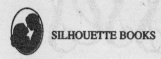

SILHOUETTE BOOKS

ISBN 0-373-20153-2

by Request

MISTLETOE KISSES

Copyright © 1998 by Harlequin Books S.A.

The publisher acknowledges the copyright holders
of the individual works as follows:

AN OFFICER AND A GENTLEMAN
Copyright © 1991 by Susan Civil
THE MAGIC OF CHRISTMAS
Copyright © 1993 by EAN Associates
THE PENDRAGON VIRUS
Copyright © 1990 by Lois Kleinsasser

Printed in U.S.A.

CONTENTS

AN OFFICER AND A GENTLEMAN   9
Rachel Lee

THE MAGIC OF CHRISTMAS   255
Andrea Edwards

THE PENDRAGON VIRUS   465
Cait London

Dear Reader,

Christmas has always been the most special time of year for me. For one thing, it actually starts to cool down here in Florida, which causes me to yearn for the sparkling white drifts and cold, muffled winter mornings of my past.

But it's not weather that makes Christmas—it's family and friends. I'm blessed with a large, wonderful, loving family with whom to share the holidays, and on Christmas, more than any other day, I recognize my blessings.

Christmas is also a time to be shared with those less fortunate. My mother set the example when I was a child. Just before Christmas a family of six in our town was burned out of their home. We didn't have much at the time and we didn't even know the family, but Mom asked each of us four kids to give one of our Christmas gifts to the children whose home had been burned. I felt so good about that, and ever since have found that my greatest joys and my best memories of the holiday season are memories of giving.

There are many ways to share the joy of Christmas with those less fortunate, everything from donating food and toys, to visiting nursing homes. The spirit of Christmas truly is in the giving and it can last the whole year round.

Happy Holidays!

Rachel Lee

AN OFFICER AND A GENTLEMAN

Rachel Lee

To Mom,
with thanks for nagging me into it.

Chapter 1

"**Y**ou okay, cowboy?" The voice was cool, light.

Alisdair MacLendon's eyes snapped open. Blue lights flashed intermittently, giving an unearthly look to the youthful face that was bent over him. Too young to shave, MacLendon thought groggily, and nobody calls me cowboy, least of all some snotty kid.

Moving was a mistake. Shooting stars slashed across his vision, and some idiot with a jackhammer started trying to take a chunk out of the side of his skull.

"Hey! Cowboy!" The kid's light voice became sharper. "Open those eyes. Tell me where it hurts."

"My head, damn it!" His eyes flew open again. *Nobody* called him cowboy.

"Sergeant!" The light voice took on authority as the kid called to someone Alisdair couldn't see. "We've got a head injury over here. What have you got?"

"This idiot wasn't wearing his seat belt. He's got the windshield in his face. Can't tell about the rest."

"Radio the hospital."

The youthful face turned back to MacLendon, who was thinking that if he puked now it would be perfect. What had happened? Oh, yeah, some turkey in a blue hot rod had run the stop sign at about ninety miles an hour. He remembered the sickening thud as his head slammed into the door stanchion.

"Just going to check you out a little, cowboy," the kid said, voice pitched soothingly. Fingers moved through his hair lightly, feeling the side of his head.

"Ouch!" The fingers found the place where the jackhammer was working.

"You're gonna have one hell of a goose egg," the kid said. "Does anything else hurt?"

"No."

The kid backed off a little, squatting. For the first time MacLendon was able to identify the components of an Air Force security police uniform: nylon winter jacket, beret, holstered gun. Captain's bars winking at the shoulders. Captain's bars? This kid was too young.

"You cold?" the too-young captain asked. "I'm afraid we don't have any blankets, but the ambulance will be here in a couple of minutes."

"I'm okay." If okay was a knife in the brain, spots before the eyes, and a heaving stomach. "What's a captain doing on patrol?" he asked. Anything to keep from thinking about his discomfort.

A grin, a one-shouldered shrug. "Keeps the troops on their toes if I show up at odd hours. Midnight on Friday seemed like a good time to pull a little inspection."

This baby-faced captain was a man right after MacLendon's own heart. And God, he must be getting older than he thought if a captain looked like a baby to him. He closed his eyes against a sudden wave of nausea.

"Hey, cowboy!" The voice sharpened. "Stay awake. Talk to me!"

"I'm not a cowboy, damn it!" His sudden glare was convincing enough to cause the captain to blink.

"Sorry. Sure are dressed like one, though." Cool eyes took in his jeans, boots, and shearling jacket. "Could've sworn that was a Stetson over there on the seat."

Spunky young idiot, MacLendon thought, and in spite of his irritation and pain and wooziness, a corner of his thin mouth twitched. He wondered if he should tell this youngster who he was, then decided against it. He would enjoy it a whole lot more when he felt better.

The young head tilted. "I hear the ambulance, *sir*. Two more minutes." Leaning forward over him, the captain reached to release the seat belt.

Something soft pressed against MacLendon's chin, and he drew a sharp breath.

"Did I hurt you?" The captain's concern was swift.

Ever afterward, MacLendon wondered what had caused him to say something so outrageous and could only conclude that he'd been more rattled by the accident than he thought. He said, "You have breasts."

The captain blinked, and then a quirky, humorous grin spread across her face. "Yes, *sir*," she said smartly. "Standard female issue, one pair."

God, MacLendon thought, closing his eyes. This captain was going to be a handful. He could see it coming.

Suddenly a radio crackled. "Alpha Tango Niner."

The captain stood up and reached for the radio that hung on her left hip, its weight a balance to the pistol on her right hip. Security cops called those radios "bricks." They ate with them, slept with them, and all but showered with them.

"Alpha Tango Niner," she said.

"Intruder alert at Zulu Bravo," said a tinny voice.

"Charlie? This is Captain Burke. Alert the team. What have you got?"

"An alarm. No visual yet."

"Roger. I'm tied up at a traffic accident for a couple more minutes, but I should reach Zulu Bravo in fifteen to twenty minutes. You know the drill."

Flashing red lights joined the flashing blue ones of the security truck. Captain Burke turned and was saying something, but MacLendon couldn't make it out. The nausea in his stomach suddenly roared into his ears, and the last pinprick of light disappeared into utter darkness.

The row of B-52 bombers were hulking eerily in the pinkish light of mercury vapor lamps that turned their camouflage colors into muddy shadows. Looking like monstrous science fiction mosquitoes, their sleek bodies faced the runway. The long wings sagged beneath their own weight, saved from touching the tarmac only by the wheels attached to the undersides of the wing tanks. As the planes rolled down the runway, however, those wings would lift and the planes would no longer look awkward. Soaring, these birds became elegant creatures of the air.

Captain Andrea Burke never ceased to marvel that anything so ungainly could fly. The B-52 pilots claimed utter faith in their planes. Like the Flying Fortresses of World World II, the B-52s could limp home even with massive damage, and having seen some of that damage, Andrea Burke could well believe the stories she'd heard. More than once during her Air Force career, she'd seen one of these bombers land safely with an injury that would have toppled a commercial airliner from the skies.

They were old, they were creaky, many of their parts now had to be manufactured by their repair crews, and they were being replaced with the technical marvel of the B1-B. Like old horses about to be sent to pasture, they had served well and faithfully. With their passing, Andrea thought, an era would end. Since earliest childhood, she'd watched these babies fly. Soon they would fly no more.

"It has to be a fault in the sensor system, Captain," Sergeant Halliday told her, breaking into her thoughts. "There's absolutely no evidence that someone crossed the perimeter."

Andrea's men had searched every nook and cranny of the controlled area in the last three hours, and she was inclined to agree with Halliday's assessment. An optical sensor had been tripped, setting off an alarm at the monitor station, but a lot of things could trip a sensor, from debris blowing in the ceaseless North Dakota wind to a voltage drop.

It was nearly four in the morning, and Andrea very badly wanted to rub her eyes. Refusing to let her growing fatigue show, however, she repressed the urge. "What if someone was leaving the area, rather than entering?"

Sergeant Halliday was Andrea's electronic security expert. A man around her own age of twenty-eight, Halliday had joined the Air Force at seventeen and promptly displayed an awesome genius for anything through which electricity flowed. He was tall, painfully thin, and even more painfully shy—except when he talked about electronics. Then, and only then, he acknowledged no superior.

"Well, ma'am," he said easily in his lazy Georgia drawl, "if that's the case, we've got serious trouble. That means someone gained access to a controlled area without tripping any of the security systems. To do that, they'd either have to know the system inside out, or they'd have to pass the sentries. Either way, it's not good."

"That's what I figured." Andrea leaned back against the wall and looked out again at the hulking B-52s. "Well, I think we're safe in saying there're no unauthorized personnel in the area now."

"Yes, ma'am." Halliday's eyes were faded-looking behind his thick glasses.

"So find me a fault in the system, Halliday. Pin it down so I can get my butt into bed." She tempered the words with a faint smile, and Halliday returned it.

"You got it, Captain." Bending again to his terminals and displays and oscilloscopes, Halliday continued his diagnostics.

"Do you know anything about the new commander the Bomb Wing's getting?" he asked as he worked.

"Only what everyone else has heard, I guess," Andrea replied. "I hear he flew bombers in Nam, that he's some kind of hotshot jet jockey—some even say he was in the Thunderbirds—and that he's up for brigadier general."

"That's what I hear, too. I suppose he'll stick his nose into everything."

"That's his job," Andrea replied noncommittally. Privately, she wasn't looking forward to the change of command any more than anyone else.

The commander of the 447th Bombardment Wing was the commander of the base's host organization, and as such he was very definitely top dog. It was a fact that the personality of the man on top had repercussions all the way down the ladder. As commander of the 447th Security Squadron, Andrea reported directly to him, as did all the other commanders on base except the Missile Wing commander. The current Bomb Wing commander was a man content to let his subordinates do their jobs. The new man might have very different ideas.

"We'll survive, Halliday," she said after a moment.

"Frankly, I'll start surviving a heck of a lot better when the change of command ceremony is over. I hate those affairs."

Halliday glanced up with a grin. "You could always get sick."

"Great first impression." Returning her gaze to the planes outside, she fell into uneasy reflection. Not everyone would be pleased to find one of his commanders was a woman. Command opportunities were limited, and despite the equal opportunity environment of the Air Force, those opportunities were even more severely limited for women. Because the Air Force had made some public relations hay out of her appointment two years ago, Andrea understood her uniqueness. She wasn't the only woman in her position, but the others were few and far between.

"Captain?" Once again Halliday's voice called her from thought. "I think I found it. We're measuring an intermittent voltage drop on that same circuit. Unless somebody's jumping back and forth through the beam at intervals, it's an equipment failure."

Andrea straightened and pulled her beret into place. "Thanks, Halliday. How long will it take to pinpoint?"

He shrugged. "Maybe a couple of hours."

"Okay. I'll tell the sentries to look sharp in the meantime. Call me when you've got it repaired."

"Yes, ma'am."

When, Andrea found herself wondering, was the last time she'd gotten a decent night's sleep? Being a squadron commander was something like being a mother, a priest, a judge, and a jury all rolled up in one, and there was no such thing as an eight-hour day or an uninterrupted night. She loved her work, but sometimes she thought she just ought to move a cot into her office and catnap round the clock in fifteen-minute snatches.

The predawn air of late October was cold, presaging the coming North Dakota winter. Almost time for survival gear again, she thought. Not since she graduated from the Academy six years ago had she seen anything approaching a warm climate. The wind nipped at her ears and tugged at her beret as she trudged to her blue security patrol pickup truck. Always the wind. She couldn't remember when it had ever stopped.

When Andrea Burke finally collapsed on her bed in the BOQ,

Bachelor Officers' Quarters, it was five-thirty in the morning. She spared just enough time to shed her jacket, boots, and pistol, and then fell fully clothed across the blankets. Like it or not, she was going to have to go to the office today and write a report. So much for Saturday. But first a couple of hours of blessed sleep.

She was just spiraling down into the reaches of a warm place where alerts didn't exist when the phone rang. Cursing vigorously, she rolled over and considered not answering it. Business would come crackling over the radio on her night table, not over the phone. Groaning, she picked up the receiver anyway. You never knew.

"Burke."

"Captain, this is Sergeant Nickerson."

Nickerson. The auto accident. She'd sent the sergeant to the hospital to clean up the details while she raced over to the airfield.

"Shoot," she said, rubbing her eyes.

"I thought you should know," he said. "That guy who was in the vehicle that was hit?"

"Yeah, the cowboy. What about him?"

"Ma'am, he ain't no cowboy. He's a bird colonel, name of Alisdair MacLendon. Captain, he's the new Bomb Wing commander."

The expletive that escaped Andrea's lips was both unladylike and expressive. Nickerson chuckled.

"Thought you should know, ma'am," he said again, and rang off.

For the moment, all hope of sleep was forgotten. The new commanding officer, so of course she had called him cowboy. And naturally she had managed to shove her chest into his face, making it unalterably certain that he was aware of her sex, which was one thing she absolutely didn't allow to intrude on her job.

Well, she was just too damn tired to worry about it now. That knock on the head would keep him cooped up in the hospital for a couple of days, anyhow. In the meantime, she *had* to sleep.

The groan that escaped her this time was satisfied, as her head landed on the soft pillow. Nor was sleep shy. It caught her instantly in a warm embrace.

* * *

Noon found Andrea staring at her bleary-eyed face in the mirror. She'd always looked a little like Huck Finn, with her reddish blond hair and the smattering of golden freckles across her nose and cheeks. Her short haircut did nothing to dispel the illusion.

Sticking her tongue out at herself, she turned from the mirror and headed for the door. Today she was off duty, and dropping by the office to write a report didn't mean she had to wear a uniform. The people in her squadron had gotten used to the sight of her in her Air Force Academy sweat suit and jogging shoes. She'd grown up as the middle child in a family with six boys, and it was easier for her to be one of the guys than anything else. Pretty soon, everybody who was around her for a while realized she was just that: one of the guys.

Picking up her radio, which was exactly the size and shape of the brick for which it was nicknamed, she stepped through the door and set out at an easy jog.

The front office at the Security Police Headquarters building was at its usual Saturday afternoon ebb. The radio crackled with quiet static: two cops sat drinking coffee and looking bored. Andrea trotted past them with a nod.

As commanding officer of the squadron, she had the largest office in the building. Entering it still gave her a thrill, even after two years. Here the majesty of the United States put on a moderately impressive display, ensuring that anyone who entered was reminded of the authority residing in a commanding officer. The floor, elsewhere tiled in nondescript beige, here was carpeted in Air Force blue. To the rear and either side of her massive, polished desk, on stands topped with brass eagles, hung the U.S. flag and the squadron's flag. Large, framed photographs of historic Air Force planes adorned the walls on either side of the room. On the wall directly behind her desk hung the emblem of the Strategic Air Command, an iron fist holding crossed lightning bolts and an olive branch. Beneath it was the motto: Peace is our Mission.

Actually Saturday and Sunday were the best days to take care of paperwork, she thought as she settled behind her desk in her deep leather chair and pulled out a report form. Distractions were few, if any, and heaps of paper disappeared as if by magic.

She was scribbling away industriously when she became aware that she was no longer alone.

"Just a sec," she said and poked her tongue out between her teeth. "How do you spell circuit?"

"C-I-R-C-U-I-T."

"I-T, huh? Sure doesn't sound like it." Suddenly her head snapped up. She knew that voice.

Colonel Alisdair MacLendon stood on the other side of her desk. He was resplendent in a Class A blue uniform, rows of ribbons on his chest. There was something about broad shoulders, a wide chest, and narrow flanks in Class A blues that made Andrea feel not at all like one of the guys.

Up, up her eyes traveled—good grief, he was tall—and finally reached a face that was craggy, weathered, and set in an expression of patience. His eyes, however, did not look patient. The color of blue ice, they were at this moment narrowly assessing.

"Ah..." The sound escaped her like a strangled sigh, and she leapt to her feet. Throwing back her shoulders, she snapped to attention with a ramrod stiffness she hadn't needed since the Academy.

MacLendon opened his mouth to put her at ease, then stopped, a glimmer of amusement in his cool blue eyes. When she stood at attention in that sweat suit, there was absolutely no question that the captain had a pair of standard female issue breasts. In fact, he thought, a little better than standard issue. He rather liked the view.

He also found he rather liked the way her hair was tousled. Not quite red, not quite blond, it was almost exactly the color of a new penny. Was it strawberry blond?

"Captain Burke, I presume," he said. The name was on a plaque on the front of her desk, but he couldn't resist giving her a hard time.

"Yes, sir!"

"Do you always come to work in civvies, Captain?"

"No, sir. I'm off duty."

He glanced at the inscription on the shoulder of her sweatshirt. "Academy graduate?" He still had some difficulty adjusting to the idea of female service academy graduates.

"Yes, sir."

"At ease, Captain," he said, finally relenting. Amusing as it was to watch her respond like a plebe on parade, the workaday world of the Air Force was a relaxed one, in most ways exactly like its civilian counterpart. He understood why Burke had resorted to military formality, but he wasn't the kind of officer who required it.

Andrea at once slipped into parade rest, feet spread, hands clasped behind her back. The view thus provided was no less disturbing. MacLendon sighed.

"I'm Alisdair MacLendon," he said. "Monday morning I'm taking over command of the Bomb Wing."

"Yes, sir." Something flickered in her hazy green eyes. Humor? Doubt? He couldn't tell.

"From the moment I take command, Captain, I will be grateful if you refrain from addressing unknown persons as cowboy. *Sir* or *ma'am* are the appropriate forms of address." Was that laughter twitching the little minx's lips? he wondered.

"Yes, sir," was her only response, however, and a clipped one at that.

"Sit down, Captain. I want to talk to you."

Andrea immediately plopped into her chair. MacLendon followed suit, taking one of the three chairs that faced her desk. He crossed his legs loosely, right ankle on his left knee.

"How long have you been in security?" he asked.

"Since graduation, sir. Over six years." Andrea found herself wishing his eyes were any color but that particular icy blue that seemed to see right through her. She hadn't felt this nervous since her plebe days at the Academy. Of course, she'd never gotten off to quite this kind of start with a new commander before, either. Worse, she had the feeling that her excessive use of military formality was amusing him rather than soothing any ruffled pinfeathers he might have.

"So you're career law enforcement?"

"Yes, sir."

MacLendon rubbed his chin. Clearly she was an exemplary officer or she wouldn't be sitting where she was. Why, then, was he so convinced she was going to be a handful?

"Did you ever finish your unannounced inspection last night?" he asked.

"No, sir. We had that intruder alert out in the Zulu Bravo

section. It took us until almost 5:00 a.m. to locate the cause of the alarm.''

"Not a faulty circuit, by any chance?" he said drily.

Just the faintest tinge of color came to her cheeks. It was so slight he almost missed it.

"Yes, sir, it was. I plan to perform my inspection tonight."

"How often do you do this?"

She gave that one-shoulder shrug. "Whenever the mood takes me. Often enough so that my troops know I can show up anywhere at any time. Sometimes I hit everybody, sometimes just a few. I try to keep it random, so they can't predict."

"What time are you going tonight?"

"About nine."

He stood up, and Andrea immediately rose with him.

"Pick me up when you leave," he said to her. "I'll go with you. I'm in room 221 at the BOQ." He narrowed his eyes slightly. "Unless you object."

She did object, strenuously. This was something she always did by herself, or with one of her noncoms. But this damn cowboy was going to be her CO in less than forty-eight hours, and even though she had every right to refuse him, at least until he took command, it wouldn't be politic.

"I recommend you wear field dress, Colonel MacLendon," she said coolly.

He turned quickly so she wouldn't catch the sudden glimmer of amusement in his eyes. "I'll be ready." He headed for the door.

"Ah, Colonel?" Her cool voice halted him and he looked back. "How's your head?" she asked pleasantly.

His lips twitched appreciatively at her veiled implication that the blow to his head had affected his judgment. "Just fine," he answered in an equally pleasant tone. "You were right, though. I did get one hell of a goose egg."

Minx, he thought as he walked away. He had the strongest feeling that with Captain Burke most people never knew what hit them. Or even that they'd been hit. A handful indeed.

Slowly, Andrea released her white-knuckled grip on the arms of her chair. Inside, she had that same slightly fluttery, slightly edgy feeling she always got before she did something danger-

ous. It had to be because he'd gone out of his way just to reprimand her about her conduct last night. What a great start!

After drawing a deep breath, she expelled it through pursed
lips and closed her eyes, only to stiffen anew as she recalled
with unexpected vividness exactly the way his eyes had settled
on her breasts. Back in the Academy she'd had a drill instructor
who'd had a problem with his female cadets. Sergeant Harrison
had been so obvious in his refusal to let his gaze stray that some
women had taken to teasing him mercilessly by thrusting their
breasts out as prominently as they could manage. One girl in
particular had possessed the ability to render Harrison nearly
speechless.

"Oh cripes," Andrea groaned, gifted with a sudden insight
as to just how she had looked standing at attention like that. Not
once but twice she'd thrust her chest to MacLendon's notice.
Was she doomed to do everything wrong around the man?

Just as MacLendon reached the front office of the squadron,
the glass doors opened to admit three men. The two in front
looked as if they'd been through one heck of a barroom brawl.
Their cheeks were bruised, one had a rapidly blackening eye,
and the other had dried blood in a streak from the corner of his
mouth down his chin. Bringing up the rear was a Master Sergeant, the man MacLendon remembered from last night in the
emergency room. Nickerson? Yes, Nickerson. Just a little above
average height and whipcord lean, Nickerson exuded tough
competence.

"Move it, Butcher," Nickerson said, his voice a whispery
rasp, when one of the men ahead of him appeared to hesitate.
"The CO's gonna hear about this even if you pretend to be
molasses."

"What's up, Sarge?" asked one of the men at the desk.

Nickerson opened his mouth as if to answer when his eyes
fell on MacLendon. "None of your business, Schuler," he said,
and in one sweeping glance he took MacLendon in from head
to foot. MacLendon knew that look. An experienced noncom
could take a man's measure in a single glance.

"Ten-hut!" Nickerson barked, bringing everyone in the room
to attention.

"As you were," MacLendon said immediately. "Carry on with your business, Sergeant Nickerson. You're obviously occupied." And you just as obviously don't want me to know what's going on here, he thought. Stepping aside, he watched the man urge the two others down the corridor toward Captain Burke's office. Well, it was a good sign that Nickerson was loyal to his CO, and that spoke well of Andrea Burke. He didn't imagine that Nickerson had found it easy to accept a woman in command. Few thirty-year veterans did.

Alisdair MacLendon was a man who liked to get the measure of his officers, who liked to know what was happening in his bailiwick. It might not be his bailiwick yet, but he had a very good notion he could get the measure of Andrea Burke if he poked his nose into this affair.

So he followed Nickerson back down the corridor at a discreet distance. By the time he reached the open door of Andrea's office, she had risen from her desk and come around it.

"So," he heard Captain Burke say, very, very softly. She stood before the two battered airmen, several inches shorter than either of them. Her feet were splayed, her hands clenched into fists behind her back, her narrow chin thrust out like a bulldog's. But her voice was calm, deceptively cool. As he moved into the room, MacLendon could see the white lines of fury stamped around her mouth, and her hazy green eyes were sparking with fire.

"So," she said again, quietly. "You couldn't have waited until you got off duty to act like a couple of animals in rut?"

"Ma'am," one of them started to say.

"Zip it, Butcher," she said coldly. "I don't give a hooker's damn if that woman sleeps with one of you, both of you, or half the men on this base. I don't even care if the two of you want to go off base on your own time and beat each other to a bloody pulp like a couple of overgrown roosters. What I do give a damn about is the security of this site. You two were assigned to protect the weapons depot. You were assigned to protect *nuclear weapons*. You were entrusted with the security of the United States of America."

A short silence followed her words. The two men's heads sank lower.

"Did you hear me, Butcher? Frankel?"

"Yes, ma'am," two voices mumbled.

"I said entrusted, and I meant entrusted. You were trusted by the people of this country to stay awake and do your job for a few lousy hours. You have betrayed that trust. You have disgraced yourselves, and you have disgraced your uniforms. I don't particularly give a hoot about your personal disgrace, but when you disgrace your uniform, you disgrace *my* uniform, too."

"Yes, ma'am."

"I want you back here at 0800 tomorrow morning. In the meantime, maybe the stockade will cool you off. Maybe *I* will cool off. Nick, take 'em out of here."

Never taking his eyes off Andrea Burke, MacLendon once again stepped aside to let Nickerson and the two airmen pass. "What will you do?" he asked her.

Only then did Andrea become aware of MacLendon's presence in her office. *Damn!* she thought, feeling her face tighten even more. Wouldn't you know every blasted thing in the world would go wrong with MacLendon there to hear about it?

MacLendon watched her face tighten, watched her back stiffen, saw Andrea Burke vanish behind a cool, expressionless facade.

"I'll hang their hides out to dry," she said flatly. "It's dereliction of duty."

"Demotion?" Under Article Fifteen of the Uniform Code of Military Justice, a unit commander had the right to summarily dispense nonjudicial punishment for infractions of regulations. The stiffest penalty allowed was demotion by one grade in rank.

"Probably." Unfolding the fists that were still clenched behind her back, she consciously relaxed her posture. "Was there something you needed, Colonel?"

"No." He regarded her steadily for another moment, thinking that he'd learned what he'd come to learn, and that he liked what he saw in this spunky young woman. "No, Captain. I got what I came for. I'll see you this evening." With that reminder, he nodded his head and left.

Chapter 2

Andrea was still objecting strenuously when she walked up to MacLendon's door that night and rapped smartly on it. She couldn't escape the conviction that if she'd been a man he wouldn't be proposing to observe her in the field. What annoyed her even more was the feeling that he had every right to question her professionalism. Whatever had possessed her to call him cowboy?

If Colonel Alisdair MacLendon was imposing in Class A blues, he was intimidating in field dress. The loose cut of the green field jacket added about four inches to his shoulders. His pistol was strapped to his waist, accentuating its narrowness. The rakishly tilted field cap had surely been designed just to give his face a dangerous look. In all, Andrea thought irritably, he made every other man she'd ever seen look like a wimp. At five foot six, she'd never felt small, but just now she felt positively diminutive. The feeling annoyed her to no end.

"Ready, sir?" she asked, managing to keep her voice expressionless, although her chest seethed with hot emotions.

Looking down at her, MacLendon wondered if he was losing his marbles. There was no way on earth he would ever have believed a woman could look appealing in fatigues, but some-

how Andrea Burke managed to look *cute*. Impossible. That con-
cussion must have unbalanced him. There was nothing cute or
feminine about the way she looked at him, however. Her gaze
was straight and steady, man to man.

"Ready." He closed the door behind him and followed her
down the stairs to the dark blue Air Force pickup truck.

Andrea left rubber on the asphalt of the parking lot. Mac-
Lendon looked quickly out the window so she wouldn't catch
the suppressed laugh on his face. She was furious with him, he
knew, but before the night was out he figured he'd have her
measure. He always got the measure of his officers.

After her quick, hot-blooded start, which embarrassed her a
little, Andrea settled down to the speed limit. What the heck,
she told herself. He's stuck with me, too. And she had it on the
best authority that she wasn't great to be stuck with.

"What's on the agenda tonight?" he asked.

"I figure on poking around the perimeter of the weapons
depot. Sir." She added the last word punctiliously.

"Do you ever have a problem with the men passing the word
that you're on the prowl?"

"Communications are monitored. The first idiot who tries to
pull that stunt is going to answer to me."

"I see." Tough little cookie, he thought. "By the way, Captain, I'm here tonight strictly as an observer. Anything I see or
hear won't go any further."

There was a moment's silence. Finally Andrea answered, hating having to say it, "Thank you, sir."

MacLendon half smiled into the dark. Spitfire, he thought.
"Mind if I smoke?"

"No, sir. My whole family smokes."

"You?"

"No, sir."

"How'd you miss it?"

Again there was a pregnant silence. Turning, he saw the struggle on Andrea's face. It was over quickly, but he caught it.

"Girls," she said finally, "don't smoke."

"Oh." He lit his cigarette and cracked the window to let the
smoke trail out. "But they go to the Air Force Academy and
become regular officers?"

"No, they don't do that, either. But if you want something badly enough, that doesn't hold you back."

"I guess not." He felt another inkling of real respect for her. It didn't mean he was necessarily going to like having her around, or that she wouldn't be a headache, but it gave him some of her measure. "Married?"

"No, sir. Are you?"

She turned the personal question back neatly, and he decided it was time to change tacks. "No," he replied. "How long have you been at the base?"

"Two years come December." She paused, then decided to make an effort to be friendly. Only God and Uncle Sam knew how long she was going to have to put up with this cowboy. "December is a wonderful time to arrive in North Dakota. No chance to acclimate. Winter hits you like a ton of bricks."

"This is my third tour here," he offered. "There's something about surviving a North Dakota winter that leaves you feeling a little smug."

"Smug?"

"Like you went eyeball to eyeball with Mother Nature and came away whole."

She surprised him with a throaty chuckle.

"Where are you from originally, Captain?" His question was a traditional military icebreaker, a perfectly legitimate query from one transplant to another.

"All over. I'm an Air Force brat."

"Who's your father? Maybe I know him."

"Charles Burke. He retired four years ago as Chief Master Sergeant."

MacLendon suddenly swiveled to look at her better. "Charlie Burke. Was he air crew chief at Mather in '74?"

Such coincidences no longer surprised Andrea. Everywhere you went in the Air Force you met old friends or friends of friends. It was, at heart, really just a large family. "Yes, sir."

MacLendon's brain clicked. He hadn't spoken to Andrea Burke at Mather, but he'd seen her. A teenage girl in a ridiculously frilly dress at chapel on Sundays. Thin, leggy, coltish. He'd seen her a couple of times rough-and-tumbling at football and basketball with a gang of boys who all had her hair and freckles. He'd noticed her because she'd struck him as out of place in both those situations. And he knew Charlie Burke. No girl would have found it easy growing up under his thumb. Another piece of the puzzle fell into place.

He stubbed his cigarette out in the ashtray and let the subject drop. Pursuing it any further would require getting more personal than he chose to get with his officers, or than she would like to get with her CO. Nonetheless he could still recall some of Charlie Burke's more outrageous statements about God's whys and wherefores in creating women. The worst of it was, the man hadn't been joking.

So he knew her dad, Andrea thought. She waited to hear all the hearty male things men always said about her father and was surprised when they didn't come. Could it be that somebody in the world didn't think her father was the best mechanic, the best sergeant, the best good ol' boy, in the Air Force?

Everything MacLendon learned about Andrea Burke raised his opinion of her another notch. A pretty remarkable young woman, he thought, as she turned off the truck's headlights and proceeded slowly down a narrow access road toward the perimeter of the weapons depot. She was approaching from the base side of the huge, hangarlike building that sat near the Main Gate, the side from which security would least expect an illegitimate approach.

Turning the truck to one side, Andrea pulled onto the grass and switched off the ignition. In front of them, to the right, lay the alert shack where B-52 crews spent a week at a time waiting for the war they all hoped would never happen. In the old days of the cold war, they often hopped aboard those planes and flew to the Fail-Safe line. These days such alerts were much rarer, but from time to time, when a chip failed in the computers at Cheyenne Mountain, or when international tensions raised the country's defense status to a war footing, they raced to their planes and took to the air.

To the left was the weapons storage building, where nuclear warheads from both missiles and bombs were stored and repaired. Most warheads were in place on their launch vehicles or in the bellies of the bombers, but maintenance had to be performed on a rotating basis, and it was here the work was done.

Unarmed, those weapons were safe, but MacLendon always felt a swift clenching in his gut when he was near them. More than once in his career he'd taken to the air with his bomb bay full of these weapons and his blackout curtains drawn, not knowing if this was the big one.

If Andrea Burke felt a similar reaction to the destructive forces nearby, her face betrayed nothing. She looked at MacLendon. "How are you on stealthy approaches, Colonel?"

"I used to be fairly good. After I was shot down in Nam, I evaded the Vietcong for six weeks."

Andrea didn't want to be impressed. For some reason she didn't understand, she didn't want to like this man. She didn't want to respect him. She was impressed anyway.

"Well, sir," she said, "the idea is to get up to the depot without being detected."

"And if you get that far?"

Andrea's expression turned grim. "I damn well better not. If I do, there'll be hell to pay." At the back of her mind was the belief that tonight, of all nights, she was going to make it through security. Why not? Everything else had gone wrong since Alisdair MacLendon had set foot in her life. And what kind of name was Alisdair, anyway? Did people actually call him that?

"What kind of security is there inside the building?" MacLendon asked her.

"None. Once you get inside, it's assumed you have a right to be there." Seeing the dubious look on his face, she explained. "I didn't set up the security arrangements, Colonel, but I assure you they're excellent. There's only one way in or out, and as long as you guard the access adequately, you don't need internal security. The inside of the building is entirely open. The warheads sit on high platforms that allow them to be viewed clearly from any place within the hangar. It also makes it impossible to move them surreptitiously. Maybe you should arrange to take an escorted tour."

"Maybe I will."

Andrea pulled off her beret and opened the glove box. Taking out two black ski masks, she tossed one to MacLendon. "Terrorists are a big concern," she said automatically, as she pulled a mask over her head. "They'd love to get their hands on one of those little babies." From behind the seat she brought out an M-16.

MacLendon looked at the ski mask in his hands and then at Andrea, who sat, M-16 in her hands, head tilted questioningly. He'd trespassed far enough, he decided abruptly. He'd learned what he needed to know about her, and he had no business involving himself in her actual functioning.

"I'll wait here, Captain," he said. "I'd just increase the chance of alerting the sentries."

After the briefest hesitation, she nodded. "Yes, sir." So the man knew when to back off. Well, that would make the next few years a lot easier to take. Moving silently, she climbed out of the truck and closed the door without a sound. A moment later, she'd vanished into the shadows.

MacLendon lit another cigarette and settled back to wait. Beyond any doubt he liked the cut of Andrea Burke. He'd been known to pull just such stunts as this one to check on his troops, was in fact doing precisely that by accompanying her tonight. Unless he unexpectedly found evidence to the contrary, he was pretty well convinced he could leave her to run her squadron and not worry about it. He hoped he was as fortunate in his other officers.

The door at his elbow suddenly flew open, and MacLendon found himself looking down the business end of an M-16. Lifting his eyes higher, he looked into the face of a young, somewhat nervous security policeman.

"Please step out of the truck, sir," the airman said. "And don't try anything. My partner has you covered."

Over the airman's shoulder, MacLendon saw another SP, his rifle also at the ready.

"I'm not doing anything wrong, Airman," MacLendon said easily. "Sitting in a truck, smoking a cigarette, isn't a crime."

"No, sir. Please raise your hands and step out of the truck, sir."

Shrugging, MacLendon climbed out of the truck, keeping his hands in plain sight. The second SP, balancing his rifle in his right hand, raised his radio with his left and called for backup.

"I need to see your identification, Colonel," the airman said, focusing on the eagle on MacLendon's cap. "Where do you keep it?"

"In my right hip pocket. I'll get it."

"No, sir, keep your hands high. Jerry?"

"Go ahead. I've got him in my sight."

MacLendon suffered the indignity of having his right hip pocket invaded and his wallet pulled out. At the same time, the airman removed his sidearm from its holster. With a flashlight, the airman examined his ID.

"It looks valid," he said after a moment. "Sorry for the inconvenience, Colonel, but this isn't a good place to stop for a smoke. You're sitting on the edge of a controlled area."

"Is it all right if I lower my arms?"

The airman hesitated just an instant. "Go ahead. Colonel, I don't recognize you."

"I just arrived on base on Friday. You'll be seeing quite a bit of me from now on."

"Well, sir, you'd better take the truck and park someplace else."

"I can't."

Both cops stiffened. "Sir?"

"I'm waiting for someone."

The muzzles of two M-16s rose again. "Perhaps the Colonel will explain who he's waiting for at this time of night beside a controlled area," said the second cop.

MacLendon smiled. These kids were good, and he was beginning to enjoy himself. "I don't want to spoil her surprise."

"Her—holy cow! Burke's on the prowl again."

"Something tells me she won't find anything she doesn't want to," MacLendon remarked. "You two are clearly doing your jobs."

For an instant pride showed on the younger man's face, and MacLendon realized that Andrea Burke had successfully instilled in these men a recognition of the importance of their work. His respect for her took another upward hike.

"Sorry, sir," said the elder airman, a staff sergeant, "but we'll have to ask you to come with us to the security station."

"But why?" Annoyance flared in him. A colonel wasn't used to this kind of treatment. "I showed you my ID, and I wasn't doing anything wrong."

"No, sir, but you *are* acting suspiciously," the sergeant replied.

"Suspiciously? Smoking a cigarette?"

"Refusing to move on, sir. That's suspicious."

Much as he disliked to, MacLendon had to admit they were right. This was a SAC base, Strategic Air Command, and he *had* been sitting at the edge of a controlled area right between nuclear weapons storage and the airfield where battle-ready B-52s stood waiting. Refusing to move on *did* constitute suspicious behavior, and these men clearly didn't know who he was beyond his ID. Frankly, if he hadn't been personally involved in the situation, he would have wanted the hides of these SP's for doing anything else.

Sighing, he shrugged. "Which way? And do you mind if I light another cigarette?"

"Just move slowly, sir, and light it now."

So he moved slowly, pulling the pack and lighter from the breast pocket of his field jacket. Then, with two M-16s pointed at his back, he marched toward the security station at the front of the weapons depot. Behind him the staff sergeant spoke into his radio, announcing that he was bringing in a suspect and requesting someone to cover his leg of the patrol. All very efficient and correct.

Just as they reached the front of the depot, Andrea stepped out of the front door, M-16 slung over her shoulder. She caught sight of MacLendon and the two SP's at his back, and a grin split her face.

"Well, well, well," she said slowly, the grin deepening. "What have we here?"

"You know perfectly well what 'we' have here," MacLendon snapped, his patience flying out the window at the sight of her amusement.

Andrea blinked slowly, and while she wanted to continue teasing him—his annoyance made it almost irresistible—her brain advised her it would be foolhardy. Her grin vanished.

"It's okay, Stewart. Colonel MacLendon was out there waiting for me. The Colonel is the new Bomb Wing commander."

The rifles were lowered instantly, and the two men snapped to attention.

"Actually," Andrea continued, her entire demeanor growing cool, "you made an excellent decoy, Colonel. These men were so busy moving in on the truck that I slipped right past them in the dark."

A quiet, dismayed oath escaped the sergeant. Andrea's eyes flicked over him.

"However," she continued just as coolly, "the backup you radioed for caught me, Stewart. You and Mallory get a six-pack, and so does the backup."

Six-pack? MacLendon wondered. She awarded six-packs for a job well-done? Well, it was certainly a unique command style, but he wasn't entirely certain he approved.

"Make it Coors, please, ma'am," said Stewart, relief drawing a grin from him.

"Coors it is." Andrea returned her attention to MacLendon. "Shall we go now, sir?"

"Not without my ID and sidearm," MacLendon said.

"Oh! Right, sir!" The younger airman—Mallory, he guessed—became awkward in his embarrassment, but he managed to dig MacLendon's wallet out of his pocket and the pistol from where it was tucked into his belt.

"Thank you," MacLendon said, his humor rapidly returning at the sight of a very good cop reverting to an awkward, embarrassed young man. He doubted the kid was older than nineteen. "You men did a very good job."

He was immediately rewarded with two under-arms salutes: arm straight across the chest, palm down, hand opened flat. He returned them and then looked at Andrea. "Captain?"

Not until they were in the truck and headed back to the BOQ did MacLendon speak.

"I'm favorably impressed, Captain Burke," he told her, watching her in the dim glow of the dash lights.

"Thank you, sir."

A cool customer, MacLendon thought. A very cool customer indeed. He wondered if she were naturally cool or if the glimpses of annoyance and humor she permitted to show from time to time were a more accurate clue to her nature.

For the very first time in his life, MacLendon found himself wondering what price a woman paid to succeed in a man's world. Andrea Burke was clearly succeeding, but perhaps she'd had to sublimate herself to do it.

And maybe this was really who she was and what she was. He didn't think he would ever find out, but for some odd reason he'd sure like to know.

"It's not very late," he heard himself say. "Shall we stop at the O-Club for a drink?"

Not very late, and it was Saturday night. It crossed Andrea's mind that she was leading a very unnatural life. She didn't think one other woman in the entire country spent Saturday night skulking in the shadows to check up on her subordinates.

Because she was a woman, she hesitated before answering. A man in her position would have accepted immediately, recognizing the political necessity and recognizing also the honor inherent in being asked to share a drink with the future CO. But she *was* a woman, and she had to consider appearances and the possibility of gossip. Still it was the Officers' Club, not some night spot in town. Deciding it was safe enough to accept, and wise to do so, she agreed.

"Thank you, sir."

"You're welcome, Captain." His tone faintly mocked her punctiliousness. "Loosen up, will you? I'm convinced you're an excellent officer, so relax a little."

"Yes, sir."

MacLendon sighed. "Have it your way, Burke. Maybe a couple of beers will help."

Andrea fully intended to drink ice tea, but she didn't tell him so. A wise junior officer didn't get drunk in front of bird colonels who were up for general. Heck, a junior officer didn't dare loosen up even a little bit.

Her uneasy concern that they might be alone at the bar was vanquished the instant they set foot in the club. Better than twenty years in uniform had won MacLendon a lot of friends, and he was hailed immediately by a group of colonels and majors who were playing cards at a large, round table. He moved immediately to join them.

"I'll just leave," Andrea whispered to him, starting to turn back.

MacLendon looked down at her with those icy eyes as if he could see to her soul. "Chicken," he mocked softly.

It was like pushing a button, he thought with amusement. Captain Burke's chin took on a pugnacious, determined set, and she marched toward the table. Lips twitching, MacLendon followed. He'd figured anybody raised among a gang of brothers would have an automatic response to that challenge. Someday, he decided, he was going to find out what happened when some-body double-dared her.

Andrea had met all the colonels and majors at one official function or another and was greeted pleasantly enough, albeit a touch coolly. She was perfectly aware that she would never have been invited to join them under other circumstances. Some pop-ular male captain, perhaps, but the subtle lines of sexual dis-crimination still existed in social matters.

"Captain Burke is showing me around," MacLendon said in answer to a question as he took his place beside her. "So far I'm very impressed with her handling of security."

Andrea shot a surprised glance at him. His blue eyes regarded her blandly.

"In fact," he added, "I predict that she has a very bright future."

Something shifted at the table. To Andrea it was an almost audible thunk as this group of men regarded her in a new light.

"You're an Academy graduate, aren't you, Captain?" asked the Missile Wing Commander, Colonel Adams.

"Yes, sir," she said, meeting his gaze forthrightly. She was floored by what MacLendon had just done for her and thor-oughly puzzled by why he had done it. She was equally puzzled by the way his opinion was accepted. He must have one heck of a reputation.

"Shall I deal you in?" asked Adams.

"What's the game?" MacLendon asked.

"Five-card stud, for chips only, no money. You know regu-lations."

"Can't pass that up."

"Captain?" Adams's gaze settled on her. "Do you play?"

"Yes, sir."

"Deal her in, Hal," MacLendon said. "If Burke plays poker the way she runs the security squadron, we're all in for a run for our chips."

Laughter rippled around the table, and the uncertainty that had accompanied her arrival vanished.

When a white-coated waiter appeared at MacLendon's elbow, he looked at Andrea. "What'll it be? I'm buying."

"Beer, sir," Andrea said, gritting her teeth. No way was she going to blow this chance by looking like a prissy female. She'd just drink real slow. "Thank you."

Hal Adams pushed her a stack of chips. "Do you go by any name besides Captain Burke?"

"Yes, sir. Andrea, sir."

"Well, Andrea, let's see if you play poker as well as MacLendon thinks."

Picking up her cards, Andrea wondered if it would be wise to beat MacLendon, because she was looking at a royal flush.

"Andrea?" Colonel Adams was waiting for her bet.

What the heck, Andrea thought. The hand was one in a million and wouldn't happen again. "I'll see and raise ten," she said coolly, pushing her chips in.

By midnight Andrea was on her third beer and was holding her own in the poker game. A number of officers had departed, and there were only four players left: herself, Hal Adams, MacLendon, and a major named Lew Brimley, Adams's deputy commander. She was holding her own, Andrea thought, looking at her cards but wishing desperately for her bed.

The conversation around the table had been desultory but enlightening nonetheless. From it, Andrea had learned quite a lot about MacLendon. He'd served two tours in Vietnam and had ended the second one by being shot down. When he crawled out of the jungle after six weeks, he'd lost forty-five pounds and was suffering from so many parasites that it had taken the military doctors six months to get him back into fighting trim.

He'd never flown with the Thunderbirds, as rumored, but he'd test-piloted at Edwards Air Force Base for a few years and had flown SR-71 Blackbirds, the high-altitude spy planes, for three years. This would be his third stint as a wing commander. In all, MacLendon sounded like an ideal selection for general.

Andrea, her eyelids heavy from fatigue and beer, almost sighed. If she were a man, she'd be shooting for those stars, too. As a woman, however, she was aware she'd be doing well indeed to make full colonel.

"I'm folding," MacLendon said suddenly, putting down his cards. "It's been a long day. Burke?"

"Yes, sir." Relieved, Andrea laid down her cards. "It's been long for me, too." Mainly because of MacLendon.

He bid her good-night at the door of the enclosed walkway

that connected the Officers' Club with the BOQ, and Andrea watched him walk away with a sigh of relief at being once again alone. She didn't tell him that her quarters were only two doors down the hall from his, even though it might create misunderstanding when he discovered it himself, as he inevitably would. At the moment she didn't especially care if he took it the wrong way. Right now she could even wish for preequal opportunity days, dinosaur days, when men and women had been relegated to separate floors. Rubbing her neck to ease the tension, she waited until she was certain he would have reached his quarters, and only then did she follow.

Shower and bed, she thought wearily. The radio on her hip reminded her that the night might be interrupted, but for once she allowed herself to believe that fortune would favor her.

Just as she was entering her room, however, she remembered Butcher and Frankel, the men who'd been arrested for brawling on duty. Damn and double damn! All sleepiness fled as she realized she had to deal with them first thing in the morning.

After flinging clothes this way and that in her annoyance, she stepped into the shower and turned her face into the hot spray. With her eyes closed, however, it was not Butcher and Frankel she saw, but Colonel Alisdair MacLendon. Why did he have to be so almighty attractive and virile? She couldn't afford to be attracted to him. He was her commanding officer, her superior, her...

Nemesis. The word floated into her weary mind like a whispered warning. So much for sleep.

Chapter 3

"**H**ow'd it go?"

Andrea turned from the window where she'd been staring out at the leaden sky and found Colonel MacLendon standing in her doorway, leaning against the doorjamb. This morning it was she who was decked out in blues, her tunic and skirt sculpting a lean figure, and MacLendon who wore civvies: gray slacks and sweater.

Irritation flared in Andrea. Couldn't the man leave her alone? He was sticking to her like a burr. What the devil was going on? She turned back to the window, folding her arms beneath her breasts, just plain not caring that tomorrow morning he was going to be her CO.

MacLendon saw her irritation, but before that he had seen her loneliness. There was nothing quite like the isolation of command, and when the decisions became tough, the isolation was virtually absolute. For a little while, when Andrea hadn't known she was being observed, her shoulders had slumped and her head had drooped. Just now MacLendon was feeling a little sympathetic.

"Demotion?" he asked.

"Yes."

"No other way?"

She turned, green eyes blazing, furious that he was questioning her judgment. "Does the Colonel see another way?"

"Is the Captain requesting my opinion?"

Her lips thinned. Funny, MacLendon thought, he hadn't noticed just how soft and appealing her mouth was until she made it thin and hard.

"Yes, sir," she said, the words falling into the room like a thrown gauntlet. The sharp lift of her chin defied him to criticize her decision. She'd lain awake half the night agonizing over this, well aware that she was about to stigmatize the careers of two young men. That enormous, frightening power was hers by virtue of her command responsibility, a duty to protect the security of the United States. No amount of sympathy or understanding could permit her to abrogate that duty. It sure hurt, though, she found herself thinking as she braced for MacLendon's answer. And all of a sudden she realized that it *mattered* what he thought of her decision.

"In my opinion," he replied quietly, "there was nothing else you could do. It wasn't the brawl, it was the situation they were in."

Something in her relaxed, and she turned back to the window to conceal her relief from him. She hardly knew the man, and it unsettled her to realize that his opinion was important.

"That's the devil of it," she said presently. "If they'd been on almost any other kind of duty..." She left the sentence incomplete. The military put up with a lot of things because many of its members were very young males. A brawl in the barracks would at most earn a reprimand. A series of brawls might lead to a day or two in the stockade. A brawl between two guys who were guarding nuclear warheads was something else altogether.

"Is there something I can do for you, Colonel?" she thought to ask, wishing he would just go away. She needed solitude to sort out her strangely tangled feelings. Worse, his presence seemed to be tangling those feelings even more.

"Actually, no," he answered, stepping farther into her office. "The fact is, I've been exactly where you are. Not every commander faces a decision like this, but too many of us do. I figured you wouldn't be feeling any too happy about it, so I dropped by. I realize I can't say or do anything to make it easier. Doing your duty isn't always easy."

"No, it's not." Why was he being so sympathetic? Andrea wondered. Yesterday he'd seemed determined to drive her crazy.

Staring at her rigid back, MacLendon decided this visit hadn't been one of his better ideas. "You know where to find me if you want to talk."

"The colonel is very kind," Andrea said stiffly.

MacLendon laughed. "Minx."

Andrea spun around. "I beg your pardon?"

MacLendon's lips twitched. "Just so you know, Captain, your little zingers don't pass me by unnoticed."

Hot color started to flood Andrea's cheeks, but MacLendon had already begun to turn away.

"Oh, Captain Burke?" He glanced back.

"Sir?"

"I also stopped by to tell you that I always thought your father was a horse's ass."

Andrea's mouth was still hanging open when MacLendon's footsteps had faded from the building. Only then did she start to grin. "A horse's ass?" she repeated out loud, and decided she liked that description a lot. In fact, merely imagining how Charlie Burke would have looked if he'd heard himself called that by a man of MacLendon's stature was enough to make the day a whole lot brighter.

Throughout the following week, winter edged more deeply into North Dakota. Monday morning there was the change of command ceremony for MacLendon, followed by a formal luncheon at the Officers' Club. That night there was a Hail and Farewell reception for the incoming and outgoing commanders. Colonel Houlihan, MacLendon's predecessor, practically danced through the whole thing, excited about his new posting to the Pentagon and eager to be off.

Andrea hated this kind of stuff and trudged her way through it grimly, hoping her radio would rescue her. For once the damn brick was utterly silent, issuing not a single squawk.

All week long her brick remained uncharacteristically silent.

It was as if the fight at the depot had infused her sometimes reckless troops with a new sobriety. The pall of the demotion hung over everything.

MacLendon had left her alone all week, except to nod when he saw her. He was interested in other elements of his command, and the rest of the base's units had the dubious honor of his undivided attention. Evidently he had made up his mind about Andrea.

Friday night she worked late. Darkness arrived early in North Dakota in early November, and the temperature had edged down into the teens. Outside, the ceaseless wind moaned, a forlorn sound that suited her mood perfectly.

"Do you work all the time?"

Andrea looked up and found MacLendon standing in her doorway. The sight of him both surprised and amused her. She was glad of the distraction from her gloomy thoughts.

"Do I make you feel guilty, Colonel?" she asked.

His lips twitched. This time she saw it, and a small answering smile came to her face.

"I've been wondering," he said, "what you do with your free time." Actually, he'd been wondering a whole lot more than that about her, but this was the only question he felt certain wouldn't make her snap his head off.

"Free time?" Her tone was enough to answer the question.

"Captain Burke," he said, "I'm giving you a direct order."

"Yes, sir."

"Find somebody to replace you this weekend and leave that damn brick on your desk."

"If I can."

He straightened. "You do have a deputy commander."

"Yes, sir."

"Then call him. Now."

Standing there and waiting for her to obey, he left her no alternative. Mildly irritated, she picked up the phone and called Lieutenant Dolan. He sounded as thrilled as she felt. Then she called Operations and informed them. How the devil, she wondered, was she going to stand a weekend cooped up in the BOQ with nothing to do?

When she hung up the phone, there was a spark of defiance

in her green eyes. MacLendon was glad to see it. It had been missing all week. He began to zip up his parka.

"I'm going to the mall," he said.

She studied him in silence, wondering why he'd told her that. It was none of her business, surely, where he chose to go. There was something personal in his presence here, she realized with a fluttering sensation in her stomach. When he finished zipping his parka, his blue eyes locked with hers, and she saw something that made her feel oddly edgy, as if she were craving something but couldn't tell what.

"I have thirteen nieces and nephews," he remarked, "and it's almost Christmas."

"Don't you like Christmas, Colonel?"

One corner of his mouth lifted. "I like the idea of Christmas. I always think of roaring fires and brandy and good company. In my entire career, I haven't spent one Christmas like that. I've eaten more chow hall Christmas turkeys than I want to think about. The worst of it, though, is buying gifts for the kids. I just don't seem to know what they'd like. It's hell, Captain."

"It sounds like it," she managed to answer steadily, although the fluttering in her stomach now felt like rising bubbles of laughter.

He regarded her with an elevated brow. "Are you laughing at me, Captain Burke?"

"I wouldn't dream of it, Colonel." But she could feel the corners of her mouth tugging upward and knew he saw it by the smile that suddenly creased his cheeks and crinkled the corners of his eyes. It was, she thought with a swiftly indrawn breath, an unfairly devastating smile in a man who was already unfairly attractive.

"What about you?" he asked. "How many nieces and nephews do you shop for?"

Andrea ran a rapid mental check. "Nineteen."

"A fellow sufferer, I see. Do you find it difficult?"

"No, sir."

He looked at her steadily for a moment. "I don't suppose—" He bit off the sentence and turned to leave. "Good night, Captain."

"Colonel?"

Her cool voice caught him before he took his third step away. He walked back.

"Yes?"

Her face felt odd, and her stomach certainly felt odder, as she said, "My car's been acting a little funny lately. Could I possibly hitch a ride to the mall with you?"

He allowed himself another smile. "On one condition, Captain. That you help me figure out what to buy for all those kids."

"I'll be glad to help. I enjoy shopping for children."

The remark surprised him. He'd figured that Andrea avoided anything that sounded even remotely feminine, as if femininity were a plague.

"I'll pick you up in an hour, then," he said. "What's your room?"

"225," she answered.

Two doors down from him, he thought as he walked away. Interesting.

Andrea had learned enough about the loneliness of command, particularly in the past week, to recognize it in MacLendon when she saw it. He'd been about to make a simple, friendly request for her assistance, then had dropped it because she was his subordinate officer and under no circumstances could he make such a claim on her private time. Particularly when that request might be viewed as sexist, although it had been perfectly natural when she professed herself an experienced shopper for nieces and nephews.

Andrea sighed and picked up her parka. Sometimes being a woman in a man's world could be a royal pain. Most of the time she managed simply not to think about it, but other times it reared up and stared her in the face. Why did this tension have to exist? It had always been present with her father, but with her brothers it had been completely absent. Most of the time it stayed out of her relationships with her troops and fellow officers. Every so often, however, she was reminded that she was an anomaly, that what she was and what she wanted to be were not always how the rest of the world viewed her.

Damn! she thought, and slammed her office door behind her. Double damn!

When MacLendon knocked on her door an hour later, she was ready to go. Dressed in jeans, wool shirt, and a commercial survival parka that was considerably warmer than government issue, she wasn't surprised to find MacLendon dressed similarly. Stepping outside with him, she pulled up her hood and tugged on her mittens.

"There's another cold front coming through tonight," he remarked as he turned onto the highway toward town. "Supposed to get down to around zero."

"That's warm for this place. Or would be, if it were January." The car's heater was beginning to catch up with the chill, and she pulled her hood off.

"What's wrong with your car?" he asked.

"Choke's sticking, I think. It stalls at stop signs and other convenient places."

"I'll take a look at it tomorrow."

Andrea swiveled her head to look at him. "Colonel—"

"Dare," he said patiently. "We're off duty, and you can call me Dare."

"Oh. I wondered about Alisdair. It's a mouthful."

"Old Scottish name," he chuckled. "There's one in every generation of MacLendons."

"About my car—"

"If it's a sticky choke," he interrupted, "I can fix it in about thirty seconds. No problem."

"No, it's not a problem," she agreed. "I can fix it myself. I just haven't gotten to it."

There was a pregnant silence. They seemed to share an awful lot of those, for some reason, Andrea found herself thinking irritably.

Finally he spoke, his voice silky. "Did I just step on your feminist toes, Andrea?"

"No, sir. It's just that I can't see letting my CO do something I'm perfectly capable of doing for myself, especially when it involves his free time."

"And I suppose you think your CO is incapable of deciding for himself how to spend his free time?"

"No, sir." Her cheeks were growing warm. "It never entered my head." She seemed to have an absolute genius for saying the wrong thing to this man.

"Did it occur to you that since you're doing your CO a favor he might want to return it?"

"I thought you were doing me a favor. You're giving me a lift to the mall."

"Andrea..." His voice had grown dangerous.

"Sir?"

"Shut up."

"Yes, sir."

And damn it, he thought, if she didn't stay silent as a clam all the way to the mall. It wasn't until they were strolling to the toy store that he realized she was going to stay quiet all night because he'd told her to. He glanced at her with frustration.

"Andrea."

"Sir?"

"Talk."

"Yes, sir." She cocked her head, and he caught the gleam in her eye. "About what, sir?"

"Anything that takes your fancy. And stop calling me 'sir.'"

"Yes, sir."

A muffled sound escaped him. She was utterly unable to tell if it was rage or laughter. Certainly the ice in his blue eyes was suddenly replaced by fire.

"Andrea," he said, drawing up short to face her.

"Sir?"

"Has anyone ever told you that it can be dangerous to drive your CO crazy? He just might be tempted to make your life miserable."

Her expression became one of perfect innocence. "I'm only trying to follow orders."

"We're off duty, Andrea."

"Yes, sir."

"Act like it."

"Yes, sir."

He took a menacing step toward her. "I told you to stop calling me 'sir.'" Her mouth opened, and for an instant he thought the imp in her would drive her to say 'yes, sir' anyway, but suddenly a laugh escaped her, and humor filled her hazy green eyes with warmth.

"Okay," she said.

"Thank God," he said with exaggerated relief. "I was beginning to think I'd have to strangle you to get you to stop that."

"No, sir," she said, and darted away laughing just as he

turned on her. "I promise," she said, grinning, holding up a hand and backing away from him. "Not again. I won't do it again!"

"If you do, I'll leave you to walk back to base," he growled, his anger belied by the twinkle in his eye.

"Scout's honor. I won't say the s-word again this evening."

Her eyes sparkled, her cheeks glowed pink, and for the first time since he'd met her, Andrea Burke didn't look like a woman who was trying her damnedest to be someone else. No, he corrected himself, she'd also been herself the night she aided him after the accident. Her imp had come out then, too, and her concern for him had been genuine and warm. Too often, however, she appeared to be inhibiting her natural liveliness in favor of some sexless, sterile image of her role. But then, he reminded himself sternly, how well did he really know her? Just because he'd spent the better part of his evenings for a week wondering how to get behind that facade...

Andrea's attention was suddenly caught by the sight of a small artificial Christmas tree in a shop window.

"Maybe I should get one of those for my quarters," she said almost wistfully. "I really miss having a tree."

"Just once I'd like to get out of having to put one up."

Andrea glanced up at him in question.

"I'll be moving into family housing in two weeks," MacLendon explained. Rank had its privileges, like a three-bedroom house for a bachelor colonel. "I'll be expected to do the usual holiday entertaining, so I'll have a tree and all the rest of the trimmings."

"Don't you like Christmas trees?" He was beginning to sound like Scrooge, Andrea thought with amusement.

"The trees are okay. All of it's okay. It's just that it's a pain to do it alone, and it always makes me so damn blue."

"Couldn't you spend the holidays with your family?"

"I could, but then my deputy would be stuck here. He wants to visit his family in Georgia."

Andrea nodded, understanding. As a bachelor officer, she'd always felt obliged to work through the holidays so men with families and others who wanted to go home could do so. She sent Dare MacLendon a glance from the corner of her eye.

"You need a wife. Then *she* could do all the decorating and plan all the entertaining."

"That's usually how it works, isn't it?" he agreed, never missing a beat. "A woman who marries an Air Force officer might as well enlist herself."

"I hear it's the same in corporate America," Andrea said after a moment.

"Is that why you haven't married?" MacLendon asked, taking her by surprise.

Andrea blinked, speechless.

He looked down at her, smiling faintly. "Yes, I asked a personal question. Are you going to answer me?"

Andrea glanced down at the terrazzo floor and then back up. "Truthfully, I just haven't *wanted* to get married."

Dare thought he could understand that, considering how Charlie Burke had treated his wife, like some beast of burden.

"What about you?" Andrea asked unexpectedly, her cheeks pink again.

"A personal question for a personal question, huh? I was married once, long, long ago. It didn't survive my second tour in Nam. Maureen discovered that the reality of being a pilot's wife didn't live up to the imaginings." Deliberately he returned his gaze to the artificial tree in the window. "Come on, Andrea," he said, "let's go get you your tree."

"But I—"

Icy blue eyes glanced her way. "You want it, don't you? Then buy it."

Once again annoyed, Andrea followed him. She didn't like being maneuvered into something, even if it was something she'd been about to do anyway. The man was clearly so used to ordering everyone around that he did it even when he was off duty. He most definitely needed a wife, one who didn't have a docile bone in her body, to keep him in line. Overbearing, that was what he was.

Dare thoroughly enjoyed the next half hour. Watching Andrea trying to remain cool and distant because of her irritation with him, while at the same time she was so clearly enjoying herself, amused him. She kept her remarks to monosyllables, but her hazy green eyes sparkled with pleasure as she selected delicate ornaments.

When her purchases were made, MacLendon insisted on carrying them out to his new Bronco himself and told Andrea he'd meet her at the toy store.

She was hovering over the stuffed animals, trying to decide which one would most thrill a two-year-old niece, when a hesitantly cleared throat drew her attention. Looking up, she saw a young man in jeans and a military survival parka, the one uniform item that was permitted to be worn with civvies. Focusing on the young, nervous face, Andrea struggled to identify him.

"You're Jones, aren't you?" she said after a moment.

"Yes, ma'am." He shifted nervously from one foot to the other.

Andrea smiled. "Are you Christmas shopping, too?"

"No, ma'am. I'm here with some friends to see a movie. I saw you come in here and—" He licked his lips and looked down at the floor.

"Do you need to talk to me?" Andrea asked gently.

"Yes, ma'am." The airman looked relieved. "I know you're off duty, but..."

"But it can't wait till Monday."

"I don't want anybody to know I talked to you," he said miserably. "I heard some things."

"Where are your friends?"

"They just went into the movie. I said I had to use the latrine."

Andrea nodded. "Can you talk here?"

Jones glanced around. "I guess...."

He sounded so nervous that Andrea decided they'd better find a more private place. "You know the coffee shop around the corner? The one that's so dimly lighted you can't see the menu?"

Jones nodded.

"I'll meet you there in a few minutes. I'm here with somebody, and I'll have to tell him where I'll be."

"Yes, ma'am." Looking immensely relieved, Jones scuttled off.

MacLendon had entered the store in time to see the encounter and, recognizing the young man's nervousness, had hung back at a discreet distance. When Jones vanished around the corner, he approached Andrea.

"What's up?" he asked.

She looked at him, her smoky green eyes puzzled. "I'm not sure. He's got something to tell me, but he doesn't want anyone to know about it. I said I'd meet him at the coffee shop."

MacLendon nodded. "Go ahead. I'll potter around here."

"Thank you."

Was she never going to call him Dare? he wondered as he watched her stride away. She walked with a boy's easy gait, he noticed, but because she was a woman, it made her rear sway in a fashion that was definitely not boyish. Sternly, MacLendon called his eyes to order and turned them to the stuffed animals. Maybe little Jenny would like a stuffed koala.

Jones had picked the coffee shop's darkest corner, and in his olive drab parka he was almost invisible. Andrea took a moment to locate him. When she slid into the booth across from him, he started like a frightened deer.

"Relax, Airman," she told him. "I almost couldn't find you, and I was looking for you. Nobody else will ever notice you." Glancing at the waitress, she ordered two coffees and two crullers.

"What happened, Jones?"

He looked up, his expression anguished. "I feel like a rat fink."

"Sometimes we have to be rat finks. It's never fun."

He nodded and drew a deep breath. "I heard a couple of guys talking at the barracks. They weren't sure what to do about it, but I remembered those security briefings we get, about how it's not up to us to make decisions about things, but to follow the rules."

"That's right," Andrea said encouragingly. "If everybody makes up their own rules about the handling of classified information, pretty soon there are no rules at all. That's why you always have to report a violation. Has there been a violation?"

"I think so."

"Tell me about it," Andrea prompted.

Just then the waitress brought the coffee and crullers, and Jones sat back, obviously still waging his internal battle. When the waitress left, he seemed to make up his mind.

"As near as I can tell, it happened at a missile site last week during the change of crew. The crew in the hole came up and were on the helipad before the relief crew even got off the chopper.''

Andrea drew a long, deep breath and expelled it slowly. "So the code book was unguarded during that time."

"Yes, ma'am."

Cupping her hands around her mug, Andrea looked down into the dark brew. Missile crews, two-man teams, spent a week at a time buried deep beneath the earth in the command capsule, or hole, as their crews called it. While there, they waited for the code from Cheyenne Mountain that would tell them to turn the key and launch their Minuteman missiles. In that hole with them was the so-called code book, a highly secret document that contained the active launch codes for each day of the year. Andrea didn't even want to think about what could happen if those codes were compromised and no one knew about it.

The book, it was true, was kept locked in a safe, but because of its extremely high classification, mechanical safety measures were considered insufficient. In fact, the codes had to be guarded continuously by persons with an equally high security clearance. The missile crewmen themselves fulfilled that function, which meant that one crew could not leave the capsule until the relief crew entered to take over.

"Jones," she said, "you did absolutely the right thing in telling me. Now I've got to know who was talking about this so I can pinpoint the missile crew that was involved."

Ten minutes later she rejoined MacLendon in the toy store. He didn't ask what had happened, and she didn't volunteer.

"I'm afraid I need to get back to the base, Colonel," she told him.

"Let's go, then."

Walking quickly beside him, trying to keep up with his much longer legs, Andrea flirted with the thought of how nice it was to be out with a man who didn't question the demands of her job. On those rare occasions when she dated, she avoided military men simply because she couldn't afford to stir up any kind of gossip in the tight-knit community that was an Air Force base. While she wasn't dating MacLendon—that was out of the question—it was still a pleasant experience not to get any arguments.

Falling a little behind, she got a good look at his tight backside and long legs in those snug jeans, and it caused the oddest tightening sensation in her belly. She blinked and missed a step, astonished by her reaction to the view. She'd never looked at a man like that before. In fact, she'd always believed only men looked at women like that.

"Andrea?"

MacLendon drew up short and looked back.

"Sorry, I'm walking too fast for you," he apologized when she caught up.

"No problem, Colonel," she answered expressionlessly, thinking she was glad he had, because she wouldn't have missed that view for the world. On the other hand, the world would have remained a distinctly more comfortable place without that sudden, unwelcome awareness.

Halfway back to the base, Andrea became aware that MacLendon was talking and she hadn't heard a word he'd said.

"—always invite a group of bachelor officers," he was saying.

"Colonel? I'm sorry, I was woolgathering and didn't hear you."

"I was talking about Thanksgiving."

"Oh."

"I was saying that I always invite bachelor officers from my command who don't have other plans for the holidays."

"Yes, s—I mean, yes."

"Will you join me for Thanksgiving, Andrea?"

Something flickered in her hazy green eyes, and she looked quickly away. Her heart had just developed a disturbing tendency to leap into her throat.

"Andrea." His voice had grown quiet. "Bachelor officers do what they can to get through the holidays. That's all I'm saying. I've always made it a policy to share the holidays with any of my officers who don't have family and aren't going home. I expect there'll be a half-dozen or so this year."

She managed to look up, her Huck Finn face composed. "I like to cook Thanksgiving dinner, but it seems like so much trouble just for me."

And impossible in the BOQ, he thought. "Then let's cook Thanksgiving dinner together and tell war stories so we don't get blue and lonely. Deal?"

She smiled suddenly. "Deal."

Chapter 4

"What I want to know," Andrea said to the two security policemen who sat across her desk from her later that evening, "is why you didn't tell me the missile crew left the hole and came above ground to the helipad before the relief crew went down."

Sergeant Nickerson stood off to one side, his lean, lined face expressionless as he watched the two young airmen exchange unhappy looks.

"Well, ma'am," said the elder of the two, a buck sergeant named Wilson, "the book was unguarded, but nobody went into that hole. We were both at our posts, and nobody could have gotten past us to go down into the hole. So nothing happened, not really."

"Except that the missile crew violated security, several regulations, and their orders. Who set you two up as judge and jury, Wilson?"

"No one, ma'am," Wilson answered miserably. "But you gotta understand."

"I have to understand what? Make this clear to me, Wilson, because you're skating on very thin ice right now."

Wilson shifted uneasily in his chair. "Well, ma'am, it's about Lieutenant Cantrell."

"Who is Lieutenant Cantrell?"

"The commander of the crew that was in the hole, Captain."

"The man primarily responsible for this escapade, I take it?"

"I guess so. You see, his wife was in an auto accident just a couple of hours earlier. I expect he was half out of his mind worrying."

"Very likely," Andrea said coolly. "I have to question his fitness to be in a missile crew if he can't think any more clearly than he did in this instance. I imagine he reached his wife's side all of five minutes sooner by leaving the hole before being relieved. And during those minutes the code book was uncovered, and all the Minuteman missiles he was responsible for were effectively out of action, as surely as if they had been sabotaged."

"Yes, ma'am, but Hart and I was there. Nobody got to the codes."

"That brings me to another point," Andrea said sternly. "You two aren't cleared to guard that book, yet you were effectively responsible for it during that time period. While I don't doubt that you would have protected it with your lives, right now I'm doubtful about *your* judgment, as well as Cantrell's. You should have told me about this *immediately*."

"Yes, ma'am," two voices mumbled.

"I'm afraid you're both going to receive a written reprimand under Article Fifteen for this. Don't give me cause to write you another one."

After the two SP's left her office, Andrea looked up at Nickerson. "You have something to add?"

Nick shook his head. "No, Captain. You're absolutely right about the gravity of what happened. I'll see that those two yo-yos write a complete report on this."

"And now," Andrea sighed, "I've got to call Colonel Adams. Boy, is he going to love this."

"Better him than us," Nick said with a faint smile. "Are you still leaving Dolan in charge for the rest of the weekend?"

"What weekend? I think this little mess just put paid to that. How much do you want to bet Adams wants to handle everything right now?"

"I'm not a betting man, Captain."

"Smart, Nick. Really smart." Sighing again, she reached for the blasted phone.

Andrea was right: Adams wanted to handle it immediately, and his mood wasn't improved by the fact that he'd just climbed into bed when Andrea rousted him out. She had to escort Wilson and Hart over to Colonel Adams's office and wait while he questioned them. Then they had to wait again while he radioed the relief crew, who were still out in their hole somewhere in the barren reaches of wintry North Dakota, to confirm the cops' story. Once he had the confirmation, Adams asked Andrea to send out a truck to pick up Lieutenants Cantrell and Morrell from their nice warm beds so they could personally explain their actions.

Though it was well past three when Andrea at last tumbled into bed, sleep stubbornly eluded her. She told herself she was just keyed up from all the activity and excitement, but some part of her acknowledged that she was more frustrated than excited. The simple fact was that she'd been enjoying herself immensely at the mall with Dare MacLendon. For the first time ever, she resented the intrusion of her job into her private time.

What might have happened if the evening had drawn to a normal close?

Aw, cut it out! she told herself, and pounded her pillow into a more comfortable shape. She'd avoided any entanglements of that kind in favor of her career for a long time now. Besides, nothing could or would happen, given that Dare was her commanding officer. It wasn't that such things were forbidden by regulation, because they weren't. Andrea was acutely conscious, however, of how a relationship with her commanding officer would appear. A woman simply couldn't afford such appearances.

But a woman could, and did, lie in the dark and wonder what it would feel like to be held by a certain pair of strong arms against the warmth and strength of a certain body. And she could wonder just how much a person was supposed to sacrifice for a career.

By Monday morning the entire base was buzzing about the missile crew that had abandoned its post and was facing a general court martial. A good month for the legal business, Andrea thought glumly as she trudged her way over to the Bomb Wing for the Monday morning staff meeting. The Judge Advocate General's corps, or JAG, were probably tap-dancing with delight. If so, the lawyers were the only ones. It never ceased to amaze her how drastically a whole life could be altered by one moment of foolishness. It also never ceased to amaze her how fast gossip could pass among fifteen thousand people. Military communications should only be as effective as the base grapevine.

The officers around the conference table all sprang to attention when MacLendon entered the room. He looked gorgeous again, Andrea thought sourly, as she watched him make his way to the head of the table. This morning he wore the long-sleeved light blue shirt with dark blue shoulder tabs and necktie, and there was no question in Andrea's mind that he'd had that shirt specially made to fit his broad shoulders and narrow waist. Nobody else in the room had a fit like that. Of course, nobody else had quite his build, either.

As she'd expected, her unit's conduct in the affair of the missile crew was the first item on MacLendon's agenda. His icy blue eyes showed no hint of warmth as he questioned her closely about how events had unfolded and how she had handled them. And finally he asked the question she'd been dreading.

"Why didn't you tell me about this Friday night, as soon as you knew what was happening, Captain?"

Her chin lifted. "When I had ascertained the facts in the matter, sir, Colonel Adams was the commander most directly involved and the one who most immediately needed to be notified. As soon as that was taken care of, I wrote a report, which was on your desk by 0830 Saturday morning, detailing the conduct of my troops and my actions. I did not imagine that a couple of Article Fifteens needed your immediate attention."

Dare leaned back in his chair, rubbing his chin, never taking his eyes from her. Not another soul at the table stirred, sensing a confrontation.

"I suppose," Dare said presently, "that Colonel Houlihan would have agreed with you?"

"I believe so, sir."

"Ordinarily I would agree that an Article Fifteen doesn't need my immediate attention. In this case, however, something greater was involved, namely the possible compromise of the launch codes and the related conduct of airmen under my command. I don't expect to hear about every brawl and AWOL, but a matter of this nature should be brought to my attention immediately."

"Very well, sir." Her gaze met his steadily and unwaveringly.

Dare nodded. "Other than this very minor complaint," he continued more pleasantly, "I commend your handling of the matter, Captain. Now, on to other matters."

For the next half hour MacLendon listened to reports and fielded complaints from his staff. Most of the matters under discussion had little to do with Andrea, so she listened with only half an ear, the rest of her longing for an end to this meeting so she could get back to her own office and away from Dare's disturbing presence. Why the devil had she been stupid enough to agree to spend Thanksgiving with him?

It was with relief that she heard her radio squawk. Since the squadron knew where she was, it must be urgent.

"Alpha Tango Niner, this is Bravo One, do you read?"

Andrea looked up at Dare. "By your leave, sir?"

"Go ahead, Burke."

She started to rise to leave the room, but MacLendon motioned her to remain, so she answered the call.

"Bravo One, this is Alpha Tango Niner, go ahead."

"Alpha Tango Niner, we have an electronic security system failure—repeat, system failure—at Delta Three Zulu."

"Roger, Bravo One. Who's out there? Over."

"Sergeant Nickerson, ma'am. When the call came in he took a squad out. Over."

"Tell Nick I'll be there in twenty minutes. Alpha Tango Niner out."

Andrea looked up at Dare. "With your permission, sir."

"This needs your immediate attention?"

"Sergeant Nickerson evidently thinks so, sir."

"Evidently. Go ahead, but this time I want a report as soon as you know what's happened."

"Yes, sir." Steaming and barely able to conceal it, Andrea hurried from the room. Damn the man! she thought. Houlihan had trusted her enough to handle things her own way. Why did

MacLendon have to be so damn nosy? Nosy and attractive. The combination was going to drive her out of her mind. Maybe she ought to put in for a new assignment at a base far, far away. Like maybe the moon.

By the time she reached Nickerson, who was on the far side of the airfield alongside the perimeter fence that separated the flight-line controlled area from acres of open land, Andrea had decided Alisdair MacLendon was a jinx. In the entire two years she'd commanded this squadron, she hadn't had as many major problems as she'd had in the weeks since Dare arrived. Just when she didn't need a nosy CO, she had one. There had to be some kind of cosmic connection there.

"What's up, Nick?" she asked the master sergeant as she climbed out of her truck.

The lines in Nick's face deepened. "Did you get roasted?"

"Only as much as I expected. What's wrong now?"

"You're feeling that way, too? Well, ma'am, somebody cut the fence."

"Last night?" Andrea scanned the chain-link fence but couldn't see the damage. "Where?"

"That's the thing, ma'am. Whoever did it is planning to come back. He fixed it so it wouldn't show, and none of the pressure sensors, trip wires or infrared detectors were triggered at any time, so we have to assume he didn't try to go any farther."

Andrea cursed under her breath and followed Nickerson to the fence, where he showed her the careful cuts in the links and the way they'd been wrapped with lead wire so the weight of the fence didn't pull the links apart, exposing the hole.

"If Lattimer hadn't been paying close attention," Nick said, "he'd never have spotted this. Frankly, this could have been here a while." Pulling his hat from his head, he ran his fingers through his hair and peered up at the barbed wire that topped the fence.

The fence wasn't electrified, because its purpose was not so much to keep an intruder out as to prevent anyone from stumbling accidentally onto the carpet of sensors that lay beyond, and to leave physical evidence if someone crossed the boundary. Security experts had long ago realized that it was impossible to stop a skilled, determined intruder. What had to be avoided at all costs was the possibility that an intruder could gain access and leave no sign of his presence. As long as the intrusion could be detected, the damage could be controlled.

"I don't believe this," Andrea muttered. "I absolutely don't believe this." Looking past the fence to the airfield where the B-52s stood in their hulking line, she shook her head. "Why would anybody want to get in there?" The question was purely rhetorical; offhand she could think of twenty or so reasons ranging from sabotage to intelligence collection to sheer curiosity.

"Unless we've become a terrorist target, I can't imagine," was Nick's sarcastic response.

"Gee, Nick, what a great thought."

He gave her a humorless half smile. "You got a better one, Captain?"

"I wish I did. Kids. I like the idea of kids playing a stupid game."

"Me, too. I ain't buying it."

"Me either." Andrea gave in and rubbed her neck. "Kids wouldn't have wired up the cuts that way. I'm beginning to wonder if I'm going to spend the rest of my life standing on Colonel MacLendon's carpet trying to explain things. Hellfire. Now I've got to recommend that he make sure those planes are checked out real good. He's going to love this!"

"About as much as you do, ma'am."

"Well, post a couple of sentries out here, get somebody out to repair the fence, and send a squad to check the rest of the perimeter."

"Yes, ma'am."

Andrea, already on her way to the truck, looked back. "And, Nick, say a prayer that that cut isn't just a decoy."

Nick's faint smile faded. "Gee, Captain, what a great thought."

"Yes, I think so, too."

Thirty minutes later, Andrea stood at rigid attention on the carpet in front of MacLendon's desk and watched the frown form on his rugged face as she explained what Nick had found. When she fell silent, Dare remained silent, too, so long that she began to get uneasy.

Finally he stirred and waved a hand. "Sit, down, Andrea. Is life here always this exciting?"

"Only the last few weeks," she replied as she perched on the edge of a straight-backed metal chair.

"Well, we're batting close to a thousand, aren't we."

Relieved that he was shouldering the responsibility along with her, rather than trying to place blame somewhere, Andrea nodded. "Yes, sir, it seems that way."

"Well, I'll send the maintenance crews out to look for anything suspicious, and I guess I'd better cancel the generation scheduled for this afternoon."

A generation was an exercise when the entire bomber fleet took off at thirty-second intervals, as they would have to in time of alert. Andrea always found it impressive.

"I think that would be wise," she agreed.

MacLendon, who'd been staring thoughtfully at a pencil he was rolling between his palms, suddenly looked at her. "You don't think there's any connection between this and that intruder alert you had the night I arrived?"

"That was a faulty circuit."

"But what caused it?"

Andrea shifted on the chair. "We don't know. We never did manage to pin it down."

"It wasn't a component failure?"

"No, sir. Halliday—he's my electronics expert—said a PCB, printed circuit board, had come loose from a connector. It's impossible to determine how that happened. It may never have been seated correctly, and a small jar could have loosened it."

"Or *someone* could have loosened it."

Andrea said nothing, merely met his gaze steadily.

Dare leaned forward, tossing down the pencil and resting his elbows on the desk. "In light of this incident, maybe we'd better consider the possibility that that board didn't come loose by accident. I'm not paranoid, Andrea, but I think it's time to assume the worst until we find out what's going on."

"Yes, sir." She wished he wouldn't lean forward on his arms like that. The posture pulled his sleeves tight across his upper arms and revealed some very respectable biceps. For the first time she realized that Dare not only had a great shape, he had great muscles, as well. Once again she experienced that odd tightening in places she seldom thought about.

"Andrea?"

Blinking, she raised her eyes from his arms to his face. "Yes?"

"Are you with me, Andrea?"

No, but I'm beginning to wish I were. "Yes, sir." For an instant, she had the horrifying feeling that he knew where her thoughts had strayed, but he stood up and continued talking business, so she dismissed the notion.

"You're tired," Dare said with unexpected kindness. "I imagine you worked all weekend again. Look, for now just bring your squadron to a higher readiness level and let me know about anything unusual that happens. And take some time off, Andrea. You won't be a damn bit of good to me if you work yourself to death. Let Dolan handle things for the next few days."

"But, sir—"

MacLendon came around the desk, perched on the edge, and looked down at her. "I know, Andrea," he said gently. "I've been there, too. You want so badly to prove yourself that you're afraid to leave anything to anyone else. But you're only one person, and you'll kill yourself this way. Or, worse, you'll get so tired you'll screw something up. Let Dolan earn his keep. Tell him to let you know if there's any more funny business, but otherwise just let him handle it. Let *him* deal with the fist-fights and AWOLs and personal problems. That's what you have a deputy for. How will Dolan ever learn to be a commander if you don't give him a chance to practice?"

"Yes, sir." He was right, of course, but she didn't like it.

"You're a damn fine officer, Andrea. I know that already. I'll hardly think less of you if you delegate. Now, go take care of your readiness level and then let your subordinates do what they're here to do."

Standing, he indicated that the interview was over. "You know, Andrea, the hardest thing a commander has to do is trust a subordinate to do the job right."

Rising, Andrea looked him right in the eye. "Yes, sir, it seems to be a common failing."

Dare astonished her with a laugh. "You're wrong, Andrea. I

trust you to do things right. I just prefer to be informed. Now, go handle it.''

At eight Thanksgiving morning, Andrea pulled up to Dare's house as prearranged. His house was on a quiet, tree-lined street in the older section of base housing. Snow had still not fallen, although the skies kept threatening it. It wasn't unusual, though. North Dakota didn't get much snow, maybe twenty inches over an entire winter. The same twenty inches, however, stayed dry and continuously blew in the wind, rearranging themselves into huge drifts that had to be shoveled almost daily. Twenty inches might as well have been two hundred.

Dare opened the front door to her just as she stepped onto the stoop.

"I saw you drive up," he said with a smile. "Come on in."

She stepped into an entry hall that opened into a large living room. Wood floors gleamed with polish and were decorated with Navaho rugs. Sandy colors, accented with blues and an occasional touch of sunset and terra-cotta, brought the desert Southwest to North Dakota.

"It's beautiful," Andrea breathed, completely forgetting herself as she stepped into the living room. And it *was*. Not decorator beautiful. Home beautiful.

Dare was pleased. "Glad you like it." He took her coat and hung it in the hall closet. When he turned around, the wonder was gone from her face. She once again looked brisk and efficient. He felt a pang of loss but swept it aside.

"Kitchen's in here," he said, leading the way.

"Where are the others?" Andrea asked as she followed him.

"They'll be coming later."

Later? Her pulse shifted into high gear as she realized he had deliberately arranged for them to be alone together. Why had he done that? Only one reason occurred to her, and it made her mouth go dry. Surely he couldn't be interested in her as a *woman*. And if he were? Oh, God! She nearly bolted at the thought. Only years of self-discipline kept her moving after him into the kitchen.

It wasn't a very big kitchen, but it was adequate. A turkey sat in a roasting pan on the counter, waiting to be stuffed. Bags of bread cubes sat beside it. Andrea pulled an apron out of the bag she'd brought with her and tied it over her slacks with hands that trembled slightly. Together they went to work.

In a very short time Andrea realized that Alisdair MacLendon knew his way around a kitchen. Without the least difficulty, they worked in an intricate, silent ballet that yielded mince and apple pies by ten o'clock. When the pies came out of the oven, the stuffed turkey went in.

Suddenly there was a hiatus in the activity. Andrea was at once relieved that she didn't have to be constantly on guard against bumping into him and worried about how to fill the time. Where were the others?

Dare disappeared for a moment and returned with two glasses of wine. "It's early, but it's Thanksgiving," he said. "Sit down at the table and relax a minute."

So she sat at the kitchen table and watched while he cleaned up the baking mess. Her offer to help was refused. Andrea thought back to all the Thanksgivings she'd spent in the kitchen with her mother while her father and brothers watched football and lazed around, and decided that her commanding officer was a pretty unique guy.

And that wasn't necessarily a good thing, she found herself thinking ruefully. What she needed were reasons *not* to like the man, reasons to quell the growing attraction she felt. This was almost as bad as—no, it was worse than—her one and only high school crush. Not since the age of fifteen had she followed a man's every movement with her eyes, as if she could somehow physically satisfy her hunger just by looking, yet here she was filling her eyes with Dare's every movement. He'd always been attractive to her, but when had he started to look perfect?

When the last of the mess had disappeared, just as rich aromas of turkey were beginning to issue from the oven, he joined her at the table with his wineglass.

"To future holidays," he said, raising his glass.

Andrea lifted her glass and managed what she hoped was a casual smile. "No football?"

"Do I have to?"

"Don't you like it?"

"Sometimes. I can take it or leave it. Why? Is there a game you want to see?"

Andrea shook her head, the faint smile still on her lips. "I watch it because it's expected. I have to be able to talk football with the guys. I'd rather scan the sports section in the morning and pick up the highlights so I can sound intelligent."

He chuckled. "Me, too. But don't ever tell anybody."

"Personally, I'd rather play it."

"Don't tell me you were on the Academy squad."

She laughed then. "Not likely! Equal opportunity didn't go that far. I fenced."

"You're very good at thrust and parry," he said.

Their eyes locked, and something happened. While some corner of her mind acknowledged the thrust of his teasing remark, the ground seemed to shift beneath her. She blinked quickly and looked away, feeling panicky.

The conviction formed in MacLendon then that, although he was going to wrestle with himself about it all day, some time before he said good-night to Andrea Burke he was going to kiss her. Only as the idea took root in his mind did he realize that he'd been wanting to kiss her for weeks.

Looking down at his wineglass, he considered the idea. It would be dangerous, no question of that. They had to work together every day. He wished the thought had never occurred to him. He liked Andrea, damn it. He liked her and respected her and felt that they had arrived at a uniquely comfortable working relationship. She was, in fact, among the best of the officers he had worked with in his career. She took her job seriously and was unquestionably skilled at both security and command. Her no-nonsense approach to matters kept her unit running like a well-greased machine. Unlike so many other female officers of his acquaintance, her femininity never came to work with her. She was a good man.

So why the hell was he proposing to upset what surely must be a delicate balance for her? Because he had to know what she tasted like? What she felt like against him? What his name sounded like on her lips? Never yet had she called him Dare. It was beginning to look as if she never would. So for the sake of a little male curiosity, he was going to risk it all?

He looked up and found her misty green eyes watching him warily. He could have sworn she knew what he was thinking. He wished he could read her mind. Was she sitting there wondering how she would handle the sexual harassment if he touched her? Because it could be considered sexual harassment. Off duty or not, he was her CO.

"Damn," he said suddenly, startling them both, and rose from the table. He couldn't touch her. They would never, ever be off duty enough for it to be all right for him to touch her. One of them would have to get a transfer first.

"Dare?"

The sound of his name on her lips for the very first time drew him up short halfway across the kitchen. "It's okay," he said, not daring to look back. "I just remembered something. Won't be a minute."

When the other guests, four very young lieutenants, arrived that afternoon at two, they were obviously nervous at the prospect of having dinner with the CO. All four were ROTC graduates, summer soldiers who were just getting their first taste of the real Air Force. Dare took pity on them and poured them all a stiff drink. By the time they sat down to dinner an hour and a half later, the alcohol was doing its work, and Dare kept it flowing freely, figuring he could sober them up over dessert.

Talk and laughter began to flow just as freely, and Mac-Lendon told a few of his funnier war stories. Around five, when they cut into the pies, Dare cut off the alcohol and Andrea started pouring coffee. After pie, they settled onto the living room couches and somebody noticed that a light snow flurry had started.

"We had that briefing last week," one of the lieutenants said. Davis was his name. "The bad weather briefing, about carrying supplies and blankets and things in your car. It really gets that bad?"

"Absolutely," Andrea and Dare answered in one voice. They looked at each other and laughed.

"This is my third tour here," Dare said, "and I still take it seriously. We get these storms called Alberta Clippers, which are breakthroughs of polar air. Inside of twenty minutes the temperature can drop sixty degrees, and the wind kicks up so bad that if there's a quarter inch of snow on the ground, you get what's called a whiteout. You can't see the hand in front of your face for the blowing snow."

Hardy, another of the lieutenants, whistled softly.

"You know that saying about thirty-thirty-thirty?" Dare asked. "At thirty degrees below zero in a thirty-mile-an-hour wind, exposed flesh freezes in thirty seconds. When we're talking about an Alberta Clipper, we're talking about temperatures that can be sixty degrees below zero, with forty-to sixty-mile-an-hour winds. If you're out in one without shelter, you can expect to be frozen to death in under five minutes. It happens. It *has* happened. So you carry survival gear in your car, and if you go off the road, you stay put until rescue comes.

"And even on a sunny day in February, it's dangerous. There are about six weeks every winter when the daytime high doesn't get over thirty below. And the wind here never blows less than thirty miles an hour. Believe me, you want that stuff in your car."

"I guess so," said Davis.

"And come March," Andrea said, "when the daytime highs rise above zero, you'll be outside in sweaters talking about how warm it is."

The lieutenant gaped, and Dare chuckled.

"This reminds me of a funny story," Andrea said. "A funny *true* story that happened my first winter here. A couple of my cops were on their way out to the missile fields when they got caught in a whiteout and went off the road into a ditch. In almost no time at all they were buried in drifting snow. We found them, of course, but it took a good twenty-four hours, and all that was showing when we located them was their radio antenna."

"My gosh," said Davis. Coming from Florida, he really couldn't imagine it.

"Anyhow," Andrea continued, "they were okay except for being thoroughly chilled and thoroughly scared. After they were released from the hospital, I called them to my office to see how they were doing. One of them, I can't tell you his name, said to me, 'I'm scared to death, Captain.' I thought he was joking, but he shook his head and said, no, he was even more scared than he had been when they were trapped. So I asked him why, and he said, 'I keep remembering all the promises I made to God.'"

When Dare walked the lieutenants out to their cars around seven that evening, Andrea went to the kitchen and started doing dishes. It had been a nice day, she thought, a very nice day, except for that one awkward moment this morning where something had happened. She wondered what it was, then shrugged it aside. She was getting used to awkward moments around Colonel MacLendon.

"Andrea, leave those dishes alone. I'll do them tomorrow."

He had returned to the kitchen, and as he came up beside her, she could feel the outdoor cold that clung to him.

"I can't do that," she answered. "I was raised to believe that leaving dishes overnight is a sin."

"Then I'll do them, and you go sit down."

"No, sir."

"Are you refusing to obey a direct order?" His voice was teasing, but there was another element, one that disturbed her. She looked up at him and green eyes met blue. The world stood still.

"Andrea."

"Yes?"

He closed his eyes. "If you don't get the hell out of here now, I'm going to do something unforgivable."

"Sir?" Her voice took on a note that made him open his eyes. She was looking up at him unwaveringly, the mist in her eyes deepening, swirling.

"Andrea, it is unforgivable of a superior officer to make a pass at a subordinate."

"A pass?" Some corner of her mind registered that she was sounding incredibly stupid right now, but it hardly seemed important when indefinable feelings were flooding her in alternating waves of heat and cold. A pass. The notion at once thrilled and terrified her.

"A kiss, Andrea. I want to kiss you."

"Oh!" The word escaped her on a sharply expelled breath, and she cocked her head, straining to find some vestige of common sense in a mind that had turned to mush. "Why?"

Damn, he thought, she was going to take this right to the bitter end, by which time he'd probably be a raving lunatic. "Why what?" he asked.

"Why do you want to kiss me?" Somehow the answer to that was incredibly important.

"Curiosity. Sheer male curiosity."

"Oh." That was safe, she told herself. Curiosity could be

appeased quickly, and then they could get back on a safer footing. She refused to analyze the strange pang of disappointment his answer had given her. All she knew was that she had to kiss him. Something deeper than thought drove her. "I guess it would be best to get rid of that curiosity before it affects our working relationship," she said finally.

It was the best rationalization he'd ever heard. For a moment he let it resound through him as the mist in her eyes darkened, as the ice in his melted to the warmth of a blue fire. She was forthright always, he thought, and realized how much he admired the honesty with which she approached life.

He walked right up to her until their bodies almost touched, and not once did her gaze leave his. There was trust there, he realized. She trusted him not to do more than kiss her, not to let this come between them at work. And, surprisingly, he trusted her just the same.

Looking down at her elfin face, it suddenly crossed his mind that he was about to kiss a woman who was utterly without experience in these matters. There was something in the wideness of her eyes, in the rapid way her breasts rose and fell, that spoke more of nervousness than excitement. Surely she couldn't be inexperienced. He dismissed the notion as ridiculous. She was twenty-eight, after all, and a liberated woman.

You're crazy...crazy...crazy. The word pounded in Andrea's head in time with the thud of her heart. This was playing with fire of the worst kind. This man was her commanding officer! She watched him step nearer, and the whole focus of the universe suddenly narrowed to that tiny kitchen, to the hammering of her heart, to the blue of the eyes that moved closer...closer....

He bent slowly and closed his eyes only when his lips settled on hers. Her mouth was soft, warm, welcoming, as he had known it would be. There was no artifice or coyness to her, and she would have scorned such things even had she known about them. She simply received his touch as if it pleased her as much as it did him.

With his mouth nestled on hers, he very carefully brought his arms around her and drew her against him in a gentle embrace. His big hands traced soothing patterns on her back as his tongue traced her lips, tasting brandy, apples, cinnamon.

Oh, God, it felt so good! Andrea moaned softly at the sheer

pleasure of his embrace. The pressure of his hands on her back and the strength of his arms around her satisfied an ache so deep it was rooted in her very soul. She could have luxuriated forever in the sensation and warmth, except that the flick of his tongue against her lips shot ribbons of fresh hunger toward her center. She wanted, needed, a deeper possession.

And then came the heart-stopping moment when her lips parted for him, separating as if they had just discovered something new and wonderful and couldn't wait to try it.

Dare drew her closer, deepening the kiss. He found smooth teeth and then, at last, her tongue, a trembling, shy tongue that didn't quite know what to do. Blazing across his mind like a meteor was the realization that she was genuinely inexperienced, and that he'd better stop now. Inexperienced women were too easily hurt.

But at that instant, just as he decided to break gently away, Andrea's tongue found his bravely in a coiling stroke that just about deprived him of reason. Inexperienced, yes, but instinctively skillful, with a thirst that suddenly seemed to match his own. And against his better judgment, Dare met her stroke for stroke, thrust for thrust, teaching her an erotic rhythm that caused her to go weak and trembling in his arms. It was complete and total surrender to the moment, and Dare recognized it with a sense of male triumph and an aching sadness.

Gently, regretfully, he raised his head. Her eyes opened slowly, hazy and heavy-lidded. Sparks of passion glowed there like green fire. His own passion was undeniable, pressed between them. Unconsciously her hips made an instinctive seeking motion, and he almost lost control. Almost, but not quite. Closing his eyes a moment, he drew several deep breaths. The kiss hadn't ended anything, he realized. It had only started it.

When he was able, he stepped back a couple of inches. Andrea opened her mouth as if to say something, but he stopped her with a finger on her swollen lips.

"Hush," he said. "I know."

Andrea's eyes became unreadable. She turned and went to the hall, taking her coat from the closet.

"Good night, sir," she said, betrayed by the faint quiver of her voice, and then she was gone.

Chapter 5

Andrea understood masculine curiosity. Her brothers had always talked freely around her, and on more than one evening she'd shared an illicit beer with them while they frankly discussed some girl's charms. In a way, back in the teen years, they'd proved their mother's warning to Andrea that guys were out for only one thing.

On the other hand, she'd seen them sweat over asking some girl out for the first time, had seen them heartbroken when a girl dumped them. Before she left for the Academy, she'd even watched two of her brothers fall in love and marry. She'd seen them moon-faced and starry-eyed, hangdog and desperate, and had long ago concluded that when you chipped away the macho veneer, you could often find mush. In spite of her parents' best efforts to convince her to the contrary, Andrea figured that, underneath, men and women weren't a whole lot different.

The sexual curiosity part was one of the differences, however. Unlike her brothers, who mentally undressed every attractive girl in the high school, Andrea had never wondered what was in a guy's jeans. Having six brothers, she'd concluded at a very early age that all men had pretty standard equipment. No curiosity in that. Men, however, looked upon women as a series of greener pastures, unexplored territory to be conquered. Her brothers had roared with laughter when a sixteen-year-old Andrea had told them she couldn't see what the big deal was: all cats were gray in the dark. Over the years she'd dated casually, kissed because it was expected, and found not one reason to change her mind on the subject.

Until Alisdair MacLendon. He'd aroused her curiosity, although she wasn't quite sure how or why. At odd moments she'd caught herself wondering what his chest looked like. Was it hairy or smooth? Was it flat or rippled with muscle? His thin, hard mouth that could look so dangerous when he was annoyed, did it feel warm and soft? How did it taste? Would the invasion of his tongue repel her the way all others had? Once, at a staff meeting, he'd been writing on a chalkboard, and she'd found herself staring at his hard, flat buttocks.

But such thoughts were fleeting and easily dismissed. Just curiosity, she told herself, and having grown up with six curious boys, she gave the matter no further importance.

But then he'd kissed her. Mountains moved, the earth trembled, and Andrea Burke stood shaken by the realization that the simple touch of lips and tongue could halt the planets in their courses. Just curiosity, but she knew how Pandora felt when she opened the forbidden chest and unleashed all the woes of the world.

By the time she went to work the following morning, Andrea had put a huge mental off-limits sign on Colonel Alisdair MacLendon. He didn't need it, and she certainly didn't, either. She had her career to consider, and any kind of involvement with her commanding officer would hang a vicious label on her that would ruin her future. Nor did he need people whispering that he took advantage of subordinate officers. Had he been in any other unit, there would have been no problem. As it was, the incident must never be repeated.

Firm in her decision, Andrea wondered why she felt so sour. Sitting behind the large desk that was a symbol of her achievement, between the flags she served, with life for once quiet, she ought to be feeling pretty good. In a couple of years she would make major, and there was no doubt in her mind that eventually she'd be selected for lieutenant colonel. That was what she wanted, wasn't it? To do all the things she'd always been told a woman couldn't do, instead of all the things she'd been told a woman should do?

Of course that was what she wanted. So why did she feel so restless and irritable? It was with relief that she greeted Nickerson when he showed up with the incident report.

"Morning, Nick. Help yourself to coffee and grab a seat."

When he'd filled a white foam cup, Nickerson sat, crossing his legs loosely, and gave her a knowing look. "If I didn't know better, ma'am, I'd say you were out of sorts this morning."

Andrea couldn't prevent a grin. "But you know better."

"Sure do." Nick set his cup on the edge of her desk and opened the folder in his lap. "Well, Captain, Airman Greene tells me she's three month's pregnant and she wants to separate."

"She's sure about that? Has anyone counseled her?"

"I tried." Nick looked wry. "Captain, I might as well be honest. I started in the Marines back when women in the service belonged to a separate corps and any who got pregnant were out. Now, I think I've done a passable job of adjusting to this equal rights business, but counseling pregnant females is about the hardest task I have as First Shirt. Heck, I ain't ever been married or pregnant myself, so what do I know? I can counsel a recruit about condoms and social diseases, I can handle domestic quarrels, but a pregnant female—well, I'm not real sure I'm very convincing. Thing is, Greene is a good cop. Pregnant or not, I'd *like* to see her stay in. Maybe you could ask somebody else to counsel her."

"I'll think about it, Nick, but I'm sure you did just fine."

"I'm not. I haven't blushed so much since I lost my ch— since before I shipped out to Nam."

Andrea felt her own cheeks heat. "You never told me why you transferred out of the marines into this outfit, Nick."

He shrugged. "I wanted to fly. And I did. And I discovered I get airsick, so here I am."

Andrea had to grin at his forthrightness. "I, for one, am glad you're right here."

Nick looked faintly embarrassed. "I'm not exactly upset about it myself. Anyhow, back to business. We got six new and very raw recruits in this morning, fresh out of Law Enforcement school. I looked 'em over, and I figure we got the bottom of the class."

Andrea had heard that before. "I guess you'll just have to break them in right."

"Well, I sure won't let 'em carry a gun until they know the barrel from the butt." He flipped a page in his folder. "We had a little to-do in the dorm last night, and I had to knock a couple of heads together. Nothing out of the ordinary.

"Hanson got picked up off-base for DWI last night," Nick continued. "The local mounties dumped him back on us. The usual?"

"Of course. That can't be tolerated."

Nick nodded. "What else? Oh, yeah, Mitchell phoned from Syracuse and said he's snowed in and won't be back from leave until tomorrow or Sunday. I called out to Rome Air Force Base, and sure enough he's lying. They haven't had a fresh snowfall since last Thursday. I told 'em to go pick him up and ship him back." He closed his folder and looked up. "That's it."

"That's enough. Drink your coffee, Nick, and take a break. How's Dolan been doing?"

Nick sipped his coffee and smiled faintly. "We-e-ll," he said, drawing the word out, "for a first looey who's never commanded anything except a latrine detail, he's okay. He has enough sense to know what he doesn't know, which is more than I can say for some lieutenants."

Andrea chuckled. "Hey, Nick, we were all green once."

"Sure. I guess you just spoiled me."

Andrea didn't quite know how to respond to that. When she'd first taken command of the squadron, she'd feared Nickerson was a man cut from the same cloth as her father. Instead, he'd proved to be a bulwark and a friend.

"No more intruder alerts or suspicious events?" she asked, needing to change the subject.

"Not since you walked out the door Wednesday afternoon."

"So maybe that fence business was just kids."

One corner of Nick's mouth lifted. "You a bettin' man, skipper?"

Andrea flashed a smile, then leaned back in her chair, sighing. "I'm uneasy, Nick, like I'm waiting for the second shoe to drop, but I don't know why. I just don't like it."

"Me neither. That fence is buggin' the sh—beg pardon, ma'am. That fence is buggin' me." Draining his cup, he stood. "Time for a little look-see tonight?"

"Maybe." Andrea thought about it. "Yeah, Nick. Let's wander around the perimeter tonight. Around midnight."

"On foot?"

Andrea nodded. "On foot, with sidearms. We won't see a thing, but..." She shrugged.

"At least we'll know the beefed-up patrols are doing their jobs."

Shortly after midnight, Andrea and Nickerson split up and began to work their way silently from opposite ends of the perimeter fence around the airstrip. Andrea enjoyed this kind of activity, had enjoyed it ever since playing hide and seek with her brothers after dark. All the boys had admitted she could sneak more quietly than an Indian and blend into shadows better, and they always credited it to her small size. She liked to think she was just good at it. For her it was a challenge to step on the frozen ground soundlessly, to press so gently and carefully down on brittle grass and twigs that they bent rather than broke. And it was even more of a challenge to do that and still move swiftly through the dark.

When she'd worked her way along a third of the fence, she paused to tug up her parka sleeve and look at the luminous dial of her watch. She'd been moving for thirty-five minutes now. Surely a patrol should have come along?

Annoyed, she tugged down her sleeve, and it was then that she heard the sound. At once she crouched and grew perfectly still. It couldn't be Nick. Even if he'd moved faster than she had, which she doubted, he would still be too far away for her to hear his stealthy sounds. Well, if anyone was along the fence somewhere, they would be silhouetted against the lamps that lighted the area of the field where the alert planes waited.

Keeping low, she began to move at an angle to the fence, farther out into the empty fields. Where the devil was the patrol? When she felt she'd moved far enough from the fence, she again crept parallel to it, watching for a shadow against the lights. It was probably just some kind of animal, she told herself, but she didn't believe it. By now just about anything in the state had gone into hibernation.

Inside her parka she was perspiring, but her nose was beginning to grow numb from the biting cold, in spite of the black ski mask she wore so she wouldn't have to obstruct her vision with the snorkel hood of her parka. Pausing, she rubbed her nose vigorously and felt it tingle, then burn. Not frozen yet, she thought with satisfaction, and crept forward again.

She heard the sound again. Freezing into immobility, she held her breath and listened intently. Again. A quiet, stealthy sound, like a man's footstep. It was still too soon for Nick, she thought. Filled with tension, she very slowly and carefully released the snap on her holster, folding the flap in behind the belt.

The lights from the airstrip kept trying to draw her attention, but she forced herself to focus on the fence, following its crosshatched length from left to right.

And then she saw it, the crouched shadow of a man against the fence. Rising, she put her hand on her pistol butt.

"Halt! Who goes there?"

The crouched figure spun about into a marksman's stance, and simultaneous with a loud crack, Andrea felt a hammer blow to her left shoulder. Without a thought, she yanked her pistol from its holster and fired at the fleeing shadow. She hit it. She saw it stumble just before darkness claimed her.

Alisdair MacLendon couldn't sleep. He'd reached the conclusion that it was wiser to keep clear of Andrea, more for her sake than his. He was perfectly aware that his attentions could destroy her career, and he had no wish to do that to her. None of these wise, mature, intelligent thoughts could prevent him from thinking about the way she'd felt in his arms, however.

In fact, he thought irritably, he felt as if he were on fire. He hadn't felt like this since he'd been fool enough to get the hots for Maureen and marry her. Then he'd had the excuse of youth. What was his excuse now? Andrea was twelve years his junior, for crying out loud. She was much too young, much too inexperienced, much too set on her career for his taste. Oh, he liked her and had a great deal of respect for her, but if he got involved with anyone at this late stage of his life, he wanted all those things he'd never had: home, hearth, and a couple of kids. Andrea most definitely wasn't in the market for that kind of thing. Yep, it was better for everyone if they kept things impersonal from here on out.

He was standing before his bedroom window in his skivvies, grateful that it was 2:00 a.m. Saturday and not a weekday when the phone rang. He reached for it with something akin to relief. Anything was better than a cold shower.

"MacLendon," he said into the receiver, already reaching for his pants.

A woman's professionally calm voice responded. "Colonel MacLendon, this is Sergeant Danton of the Security Squadron. I'm calling to inform you that Captain Burke was shot this evening and is presently undergoing surgery. Shall I patch you through to Sergeant Nickerson?"

"Yes!"

The line went temporarily silent as he was placed on hold, giving Dare an opportunity to envision the worst. Vietnam had taught him what a bullet could do to human flesh, and he needed little imagination to heighten his anxiety. Eyes closed, mouth drawn in a thin line, he stood beside his bed, phone in one hand and pants in the other as he waited for the patch to be effected. This wasn't the first time in his life that time had slowed to a crawl, but it was one of the worst. Surgery. Damn it, she was in surgery, and that could only mean the worst. A fist squeezed his heart.

"Colonel MacLendon," said the expressionless voice of Sergeant Danton, "you're patched through to Sergeant Nickerson."

"Nickerson here, sir." Nick's voice sounded tinny, and wind could be heard whistling in the background.

"What the hell happened?" Dare demanded. "How bad is Burke?"

"Well, sir, I can't rightly say how the Captain is. She was wounded in the left shoulder. Entry wound and no exit wound, so I reckon it was a small calibre firearm that shot her. I was still a good half mile down the perimeter from her when it happened, but it sounded like a .22 report."

MacLendon, who was intimately acquainted with the effects of an M-16, none of which could be termed minor, let his head fall back and released his pent-up breath as the size of the disaster scaled down a little. At least Andrea was still in one piece. "What about the perpetrator?"

"We're still looking." Nickerson went on to explain that when he reached Andrea he'd been unable, by the illumination of his flashlight, to see any sign of the assailant or to determine in which direction he'd fled. Given no sign to guide him in a pursuit, Nick decided to await the backup he'd radioed for as soon as he heard gunfire. "We still haven't found anything, sir, but we're setting up floodlights right now. If there's anything to find, we'll find it."

Dare approved Nickerson's actions and disconnected. A call to the hospital revealed only that Andrea had gone into surgery a half hour before and the operation was expected to take several hours. For lack of any more useful activity, Dare decided to go over to the Security Squadron and keep his fingers on the pulse of matters. No way was he going to sleep until he knew Andrea was all right.

It was nearly dawn when MacLendon had everything pieced together. Nickerson and Andrea had gone out to pull one of their inspections and had separated. Forty minutes later, Nickerson had heard the report of a .22, followed rapidly by the report of Andrea's .38. He'd found Andrea out cold about twenty feet from the perimeter fence, a bullet in her shoulder. Investigation of the area with floodlamps showed that Andrea had grazed her target. A trail of relatively infrequent drops of blood led toward the highway, indicating that the intruder had fled by auto.

As for the patrol that should have passed through the area, they'd been held up at the other end of the airfield by evidence of an attempted break-in, clearly a diversion. Nickerson had advised area police and hospitals to be on the lookout for anyone with a bullet wound. Beyond that, there wasn't a damn thing anyone could do.

Rubbing his eyes, MacLendon glanced at the clock on Andrea's desk. Five-thirty. Too late to go home, and too early to start the day. The gallon of coffee he'd drunk while questioning the parties involved in tonight's fiasco had left a hole as big as the Grand Canyon in his gut.

Suddenly he stood and reached for his parka. He would go over to the hospital and check in on Andrea. If rank had any privileges, he was going to use them to look in on her. Damn it, he couldn't stand another minute of wondering.

Snow was falling lightly, and the sun was nowhere near rising yet. The wind had lightened, though, and it felt odd to step out into the bitter cold and not feel the wind claw at him. That wouldn't last. This little bit of snow would probably be whipping up a ruckus before the day was over.

Andrea was out of surgery but still in recovery when he arrived. The charge nurse hesitated only momentarily before leading him down the hall. Just as he thought, colonels who were commanding officers got what they wanted.

"She's recovering very nicely, Colonel," the nurse said. "Don't be afraid to wake her. It helps her shake off the anesthetic faster."

He was left alone with her, and for a long time he simply stared down at her, relief warring with worry. How fragile she looked, he realized suddenly. She was always so calmly confident and competent that he'd never really noticed just how small and delicate she was. The smooth shoulders, one bandaged heavily, which peeked above the sheet looked small and defenseless. She was so pale that her smattering of freckles stood out like beacons on her face. In the worst way he suddenly wanted to gather her close and assure himself that she would be all right.

"Andrea?" He contented himself with clasping her cool, soft hand.

Her head stirred restlessly, and she licked her lips.

"Andrea?"

Her hazy green eyes opened a little. She mumbled something.

"I can't hear you, Andrea." With his thumb he stroked the back of her hand.

Suddenly her eyes opened wide, and she reached full consciousness. "Is he dead?"

"I don't know, and I don't give a damn." He only gave a damn that *she* wasn't.

"I do."

"He got away, so the bastard is probably okay. You're going to get a commendation for this."

"I don't want a commendation for shooting a man."

"Andrea, you're a cop and a soldier. You were doing your job. You had to defend yourself."

"Then maybe I don't want to be a cop or a soldier." Her eyelids were drooping again. "Dare..." Her voice trailed away.

His grip on her hand tightened at the sound of his name, and the urge to hold her close became nearly overwhelming. So, he found himself thinking, when her guard was down she thought of him as Dare, not as her CO, not as Colonel MacLendon. Only awareness of her injury made him keep his distance. "Andrea, do you want me to notify somebody?"

"If you notify anybody in my family, I'll never speak to you again." Sudden tears sparkled on her lashes. "It hurts," she mumbled, and then sank back into the sleep induced by the dregs of anesthesia.

Disturbed, MacLendon straightened. Shooting somebody was never an easy thing to live with, even when it was done in self-defense. Andrea would probably remember that instant, relive it right down to the way the trigger had felt when she squeezed it, for a long, long time. Sighing, he went looking for a doctor to give him all the details.

It was the hospital commander, an old friend, who finally gave him the information he wanted. Andrea would recover without permanent damage except for a scar. She would probably get out of the hospital on Thursday, but full function wouldn't be restored to her arm for six to eight weeks.

But she *would* regain full function. Incredibly relieved, MacLendon stepped out into the halfhearted light of the North Dakota dawn and realized that just as it was too late to go to bed, it was too late to have all those wise and mature thoughts that had kept him awake in the first place. He cared what happened to Andrea Burke. He cared a lot more than was wise.

Andrea returned to work Friday morning. She didn't have a single uniform blouse big enough to button over the arm that was strapped to her side, so she wore her academy sweats as a temporary measure. When she walked into headquarters, the two cops at the front desk sprang to their feet and saluted. It surprised her, but she managed a wan smile. All the way down the long corridor, similar things happened. Enlisted men saluted; noncoms snapped to attention. In spite of herself, she was touched.

And then she opened her office door and stepped into a flower garden. Flowers everywhere. She started to sniffle.

"The men took up a collection for flowers," Nickerson said quietly behind her. She turned slowly, and he saw her reddened eyes and heard her sniffle. "Skipper, are you crying?"

"No." She gave a watery chuckle and then unleashed a huge sneeze. "I'm allergic to flowers!" She started to laugh, and after a moment Nickerson joined her.

A crowd of grinning faces had gathered at the door. Wiping her eyes on her sleeve, she said, "Gee, thanks, guys. They're beautiful. But next time, send a picture, huh?"

A chorus of laughs answered her as she gave vent to another sneeze.

"I hate to do it," Andrea said. "They really are beautiful. But—" She sneezed again. "Get rid of 'em, Nick. Take 'em to the pediatrics ward or something."

Nickerson grinned from ear to ear. "Yes, ma'am."

While the flowers were being removed from her office by grinning cops and Andrea was unleashing one chain of sneezes after another, MacLendon arrived.

"How the devil did I know you'd show up this morning, Burke?" he groused as he sidestepped a huge bouquet of pink azaleas, covering his concern with irritation. "Didn't the doctor tell you to take it easy? What's with the flowers?"

Andrea loosed another sneeze and pawed around her lower desk drawer for the box of tissues she was sure she'd stashed there during a cold last winter. Finding it, she scrubbed her itching nose until it shone red.

"Thank you, sir," she said, and sneezed again. "It's great to see you, too."

"She's allergic to the flowers, Colonel," Nickerson said as he carried a double armload out.

"Oh. It looks like you guys must have bought out every florist in the state."

"Had 'em shipped in special," Nick said as he disappeared around the corner.

MacLendon returned his attention to Andrea, who was hiding behind a wad of tissues.

She was pale, he noted. Too pale. And a fine sheen of perspiration covered her face. With a quick glance, he saw that her right hand was trembling. Damn it, she was trying to do too much too fast.

"My office is polluted," she muttered in an undertone into the tissues. "It'll be months before all the pollen is out of here."

MacLendon looked down at her and saw that in spite of her grousing mumble, there was a smile on her lips. She was neither as tough nor as gruff as she pretended. Feeling faintly amused by her predicament, he crossed to the coffee maker she kept on the file cabinet and started a pot brewing. At last the final flower was gone and the door closed, leaving them alone.

"You shouldn't be out of bed yet, Andrea." He sat in the armchair facing her desk and crossed his legs. Guessing she wouldn't want his overt concern, he masked it behind what he hoped was a professional interest.

She merely looked at him without arguing, an indication of just how weak she was feeling. Her smile was tight, her green eyes empty.

"You may be right, sir. But my own company is driving me crazy." She sneezed again, then sniffled. "Damn!"

"The man you shot got away, Andrea. Considering what a .38 slug can do at that range, you must have just grazed him."

"They told me." Her eyes were dark, unreadable.

"And you're going to get a commendation whether you want it or not."

"Yes, sir." She sounded hollow, uncaring.

MacLendon suddenly longed to seize her, shake her, force the tears out of her and then soothe away her pain. His knuckles turned white as he gripped the arms of his chair. He couldn't do it, couldn't bridge the gulf that had to remain between them for her sake. He'd known this woman was going to be a handful. He just hadn't guessed what kind.

"Andrea, you can't come to work in a sweat suit." It was a dumb remark, but all he could think of to say.

"No, sir. Monday I'll be in uniform. One of the nurses at the BOQ offered to help me dress until I can do it myself." Please, she thought. Please don't order me to take sick leave. Don't lock me away all alone with the memory of the way the revolver kicked in my hand. Don't leave me with the way I sighted him with perfect calm and deliberation. The way I never even hesitated.

His icy blue eyes were watching her, assessing, measuring. She really did feel as if he could see through to the barrenness of her soul, and she wondered what he thought of her, really thought of her.

"Captain," he said quietly, "you're not the first cop to shoot a man in the line of duty, nor will you be the last."

"No, sir."

"It's not easy to live with. I know. But we do learn to."

"Yes, sir."

"Moreover, you didn't kill anyone, so at least you don't have that on your conscience."

"But I do," she said grimly. "I aimed to kill."

"That's what you're supposed to do, damn it!" He jumped up in frustration. "The man had just tried to kill you! If he'd had something bigger than that peashooter, we'd be burying you in little bloody pieces. You had no choice."

"No, sir. And that disturbs me as much as what I did."

"I see." He rubbed his chin and studied her. There was no argument for that. Deeply troubled, he asked, "Will you resign?"

Her chin came up, a welcome spark of her old self. MacLendon was so glad to see it that he could have done a jig.

"No, sir," she said coolly. "I'm not a quitter. I'll get over this, or around it or under it, somehow."

"I'm sure you will, Captain." Thank God, he thought. Thank God.

"Well," he said when he had his relief under control, "I'll let you come back to duty on one condition."

"Yes?"

"That you take off and go home when you get tired. And that you don't take that damn brick with you. Give Lieutenant Dolan a chance to discover the joys of command responsibility."

She cocked her head. "That sounds more like two conditions."

"So it's two. Do you agree?"

Andrea smiled faintly, glad to know her recent escapade hadn't raised her to a level of holiness that prevented MacLendon from showing his irritation with her. Good grief, a couple of times he'd even looked at her as if she were *fragile*.

"I agree, sir."

"Now, promise me you'll take off when you get tired."

"I just agreed—"

"Agreeing and promising to obey are two different things. I want your word on it, Captain."

"Yes, sir."

"Andrea," he said silkily, "say it. In so many words."

She glared at him, then gritted out the words. "I give you my word to go home when I get tired and not take my radio with me."

"Thank you." One corner of his mouth lifted, and the fan of laugh lines by his eyes deepened. Rising, he went to pour himself some coffee. "Can I pour you some?"

"Yes, thank you."

He set a cup in front of her, then returned to his chair. "Now to the part that you're really interested in."

Stifling another sneeze, Andrea looked up quickly at him. "Sir?"

"The part about what we know and what we don't know, and what I've done about it. You know the intruder got away. There was actually no evidence that he succeeded in crossing the perimeter, because none of the electronic alarms were triggered. At first we assumed that you scared him off before he achieved his purpose. It appears, however, that he either evaded the electronic systems somehow, or he wasn't working alone, because something *did* happen."

Andrea was all ears now, aches and pains and sniffles forgotten. "What, sir?"

"On Monday, one of my bombers returned to base with a six-foot diameter hole in the cockpit. The pilot figures he hit a goose."

Andrea nodded. It happened frequently in the kind of low-level flying B-52s did, when they practiced bomb runs, or practiced flying into Russia beneath the radar beams. A goose might not be terribly big, but it packed one hell of a wallop when it collided head-on with a plane traveling at five hundred miles per hour. "So?"

"So, Andrea, I seem to remember the geese flew south quite a while ago."

So they had. She sat up straighter and winced when the

wound in her shoulder pulled. "But...maybe there was a crazy goose, like that whale that got lost in Alaska."

"No goose feathers. No blood. I called in the OSI."

The Office of Special Investigations was the Air Force's FBI. Nobody liked the OSI. Andrea liked least of all the thought of them tramping around in her domain. Anger flared in her green eyes. "Was that necessary, Colonel?"

"I think so." MacLendon rose, sighing, and began to pace. "I figured you'd be furious, but I'm afraid I can't let that matter. If you're honest, you'll admit that they're a hell of a lot better trained and better equipped to conduct an investigation of this sort than the Security Police Squadron. It's no reflection on you, Andrea. None at all. It's just the truth. You know damn well that if something like this happened to a civilian plane, federal investigators would be called in simply because they've got the expertise and equipment local authorities lack. We're in the same boat here, and I expect your full cooperation."

Andrea eyed him grimly. "Yes, sir."

Dare came to a halt and looked across the desk at her with a faint, humorless smile. "And they're here undercover. Only you and I know about it, and only you and I and a couple of aircraft mechanics know it wasn't a goose that goosed that plane."

Andrea tried to smile at his attempted humor but failed miserably.

"Aw, Andrea," he said, his voice dropping. That valiant attempt at a smile was his undoing. He had just enough sense left to ensure that the door was tightly closed before he came around the desk to her side.

The next thing she knew, he'd caught her by the waist, lifted her from her chair, and gently tucked her right side against him. His left arm wrapped snugly around her back, and his right hand caught her chin, lifting it. He looked down into her startled green eyes.

"I swore," he said softly, "that I wasn't going to do this again. Tell me not to, Andrea."

But she didn't say a word. Instead she stared steadily up at him, and once again he saw the hazy mists swirl in her green eyes, drawing him down, closer and closer, until his mouth nestled against hers.

"Sweet Andrea," he muttered against her lips. "God, you haunt me."

She needed no coaxing this time. Her lips parted at once to his questing tongue, and he was drawn into a whirlwind of passion as smoky as her eyes. We're both too lonely, he thought, and then he stopped thinking.

Her mouth was warm, tasting of coffee, her tongue as eager as his. Right within the circle of his arms, as if by a wizard's magic, she was transformed from a cool, collected officer into a wild and wonderful woman, hungry, wanting, needing, and his hunger grew apace with hers.

He lifted his head briefly, drinking in her eyes, her swollen lips. He smiled, and she smiled back.

"Andrea," he murmured. "Delightful, wonderful Andrea." And then his lips sought hers again, wanting more and more.

"I wish I could hug you back," she sighed against his mouth, her right arm trying to find its way around his waist. She wanted, needed, to hold him, to press closer. He shifted so that her arm could slip around behind him, and groaned softly as he felt its pressure close around his waist. It had been so long since a woman had held him. So long.

His hand left her cheek, beginning a careful, gentle journey downward, wary of her injuries. The thick bandage and strapping guided him until, at last, he cradled her breast in his palm. Through her sweatshirt he felt the nipple harden instantly. She arched into the touch, her moan swallowed by his mouth.

"Andrea," he murmured, stroking lightly over her nipple, back and forth with his fingers. "You feel so nice, so soft." He dropped kisses on her eyelids, her cheeks, the tip of her freckled nose.

Andrea couldn't believe this was happening, hoped it would never end. He smelled so good, tasted so good, and his hand was wreaking havoc with her, sending shafts of pure delight racing to her core until she thought she would die if she didn't feel his weight on her, pressing against her, covering her. Never had she dreamed this was possible. Never. "Dare," she whispered, her mouth seeking his, hungry to taste him again. "Dare, please."

"Please what?" He lifted his head and smiled at her, his blue eyes warm now, so warm that they seemed to cover her with heat. "I want you, Andrea. I want you desperately." A shuddering sigh escaped him, and he bowed his head lower, his scratchy cheek coming to rest against hers. Reluctantly he moved his hand from her breast, bringing it to rest gently on her waist.

"It's the wrong time and place," he said, and the regret was so sharp in his voice that she knew he felt it as deeply as she did.

A breath almost like a sob escaped her. "Yes, sir, it is," she said presently. "The wrong time and place."

She straightened. His arms slipped from her. Blue eyes glittered down into sad green ones.

"Someday, Andrea," he said. It was a promise.

Turning, he headed for the door. With his hand on the knob, he paused and looked back.

"You look like death warmed over, Burke," he said frankly. "Get your butt home before noon."

"Yes, sir!" There was enough irritation in her voice to make him grin as he walked out.

Chapter 6

Andrea awoke in the morning furious with Dare from the instant she opened her eyes. He had held her, kissed her and touched her, and aroused feelings she had never dreamed existed even in her wildest imaginings. He had created longings and desires where none had existed before. Sleeping Beauty was awake, unfulfilled and mad as the devil.

MacLendon, four blocks away, drank coffee and tried to read the morning paper. He was mad as the devil, too—at himself. He'd felt Sleeping Beauty wake in his arms and had a pretty good idea just where he'd left her standing. If he had seduced a virgin he couldn't have been any angrier with himself.

But he felt a kind of wonder and awe, too. Not even his young wife of five miserable years so long ago had ever blossomed under his touch as Andrea had. He couldn't help feeling a little as if he had been touched by magic.

Giving up on the paper, he carried his coffee into the living room and stared out the window at the bleak North Dakota winter morning. What had he done? What was he going to do about it? He'd acted like a damn—

—cowboy, Andrea thought as she walked into Dare MacLendon's office Monday morning. A damn cowboy. Her shoulder ached miserably, perfectly in tune with her mood. She still felt as if most of her energy had slipped down a black hole somewhere. Anger sustained her and drove her in to work, determined to show that damn cowboy just what he deserved for toying with her like that. She was going to—

—freeze him, Dare realized when his gaze met hers across the conference table that morning. The little minx gave him a look glacial enough to cause frostbite. While the other officers wandered into the room and poured themselves coffee, he met her stare for stare and allowed himself to imagine her lying naked and trembling on his bed, reaching out for him—

—touching his chest, Andrea thought, stroking her hands downward to grasp his buttocks and pull him—

—into her, Dare imagined, deeper and deeper.

Suddenly they both blinked, and reality returned with a crash. Major Francis was pulling out his chair at the far end of the table, the last one to arrive. Dare glanced around, taking attendance mentally. No one missing.

"Good morning, people." Since arriving here, he'd given up on the word gentlemen. It always left that awkwardness of what to do about the one lady. Gentlemen and ma'am? Lady and gentlemen? Gentlepersons? Screw it.

"First item on the agenda," he continued, drawing his pad closer and scanning it. "General Hamilton is coming next Tuesday on a routine visit. He heard about last week's events and specially requested to meet Captain Burke. We'll have a formal luncheon at the Officers' Club, and I need a volunteer to supervise arrangements."

As Dare's gaze swept around the table, he caught an absolutely adorable look of confusion on Andrea's face. Their earlier eyeball-to-eyeball session had evidently driven all her resolutions from her head. It tickled Dare to realize he could fluster his cool Captain Burke so easily, and he began to think it might be a lot of fun to have Andrea angry with him.

"I'll handle the arrangements, sir," Captain Bradley said after a perceptible hesitation. "I've done it before, and I know the ropes."

"I hate this kind of stuff," Andrea said. "It's one of the two things that make me wonder why I ever joined the Air Force."

Dare's lip twitched. Zinged again, he thought. From the gleam in her eye, he gathered he was the other thing. Mercifully, no one asked her what the second thing was.

"Well," he said pleasantly, "you were wounded. You can always claim weakness, Andrea."

Now she was glaring again, not obviously, just enough for Dare to pick up on it. "I'm not a chicken, sir," she said icily, accenting the I.

And I am? Dare wondered. The corner of his mouth twitched again, still with amusement. People were going to start thinking he had a tic if Andrea kept this up.

"Item two," he continued. "It's almost January, people. Time to make our pledges to the United Way. Pledge forms will be distributed this afternoon to all units. I respectfully request that we attempt to surpass this year's average of five dollars per month per person. Now folks, most of us can squeeze out a little more than that. Talk to your people, and get the forms back in no later than fifteen December."

He glanced around, saw the bored nods. "The pledge thermometer will be put out in front of our building again this year. I will see it every morning."

Chuckles ran around the table.

"Next item. Toys for Tots is still looking for toys. The drop box is by the base exchange. Remind your people. The Aid Society says we have several enlisted families that aren't going to make Christmas dinner without some help. Information will be posted on the bulletin board."

He looked up. "Now, I want all staff requests for Christmas leave in my office by the tenth. We'll follow last year's general holiday schedule through January third, unless we run into some kind of problem. The Wing Christmas party is scheduled for the NCO club on December twentieth. Lieutenant Tubbs is handling it. Lieutenant?"

Tubbs stood up and began to talk about tickets and menus and bands, and Dare allowed himself to tune out for a while. His own holiday schedule was so packed with invitations that he figured he'd be running in a continuous state of semihangover from the tenth through New Year's. What would Andrea be doing?

Andrea was thinking grumpily that maybe this year she would go visit one of her brothers rather than spend her holiday season sitting in the BOQ, attending an occasional party thrown by people she hardly knew, and sitting in the Officers' Club in the evenings, drinking with the other bachelors. She wouldn't, though. She always felt that as a bachelor it was only fair to stay on duty through the holidays so the married guys could be with their families.

Just as the meeting was breaking up, it occurred to Andrea that she wasn't usually this grumpy and gloomy, and that it couldn't all be her wound. MacLendon, she thought irritably. It's that damned cowboy's fault.

Ready to growl at the first person who glanced her way, she stalked back to the Security Police building and pulled out the troop schedule. It was all very well to say they would follow last year's schedule, but that provided only a general outline. A lot of her staff had changed during the year, and their marital status had to be taken into account. She'd have to prepare a blank schedule and then send it out to her various units to fill in the blanks. It was the last thing she felt like doing.

"Let me handle it, skipper," Nickerson said when she mentioned it to him. "Me and Lieutenant Dolan. In fact, I think it's a perfect job for the Lieutenant. He might as well learn that this job isn't all glamor. And didn't you promise Colonel MacLendon you'd go home when you got tired?"

Andrea glared at him. "Did he tell you that?"

"As a matter of fact, he did, and you're looking pretty peaked to me." Nickerson gave her his most inscrutable expression.

"Don't coddle me, Nick."

"Wouldn't dream of it, ma'am. I'd as soon coddle a two-headed rattler. I'm going over to the chow hall to pick up something hot for lunch. Anything sound good to you?"

Andrea forced herself to consider the question. "Soup sounds good. And maybe a sandwich or two."

Nick nodded. He was accustomed to Andrea's appetite. "How about dessert?"

She shrugged. "If you see anything that looks decent."

"Okay. Back in a jiff."

He *was* coddling her, and she knew it, but much as it annoyed her, it touched her, too.

Her shoulder throbbed steadily, and her stitches itched maddeningly, but the wound was still too tender to scratch satisfactorily. The worst part of being shot, she decided, was being unable to get comfortable no matter what she did. That and the troubling dreams that plagued her. Getting shot at made a person aware she wasn't immortal.

And Dare MacLendon, damn his blue eyes, had made her just as aware that there was more to life than a career. Never had she dreamed that it could feel so good to be held, or that it could be so wonderful to lean against someone else's strength. Not only had he awakened desires she didn't want, he'd awakened a need to be held. For those few brief moments he'd made her feel safe, secure and cherished.

She hated to admit it, but more than anything in the world she wanted to dive into those strong arms and let them shelter and protect her. Female foolishness, she told herself irritably. It had no place in her life or plans. She'd be damned if she'd let a man interfere with her future. No, henceforward she wouldn't let Alisdair MacLendon within arm's reach.

Her mind made up, she forced herself to sit forward and reach for the paperwork on her desk. Andrea Burke had more important things to do with her time than moon over a man.

For the next ten days she was quite successful in keeping her resolution, nor did Dare test her resolve. She told herself she was glad he appeared as eager to avoid her as she was to avoid him, but in a small corner of her mind there was a sad, nagging ache of disappointment.

And then, just a week before Christmas, she answered her telephone to hear a familiar voice.

"Good afternoon, Burke," said Colonel Alisdair MacLendon.

Andrea told herself that her heart was *not* doing a silly little tap dance at the sound of that voice. No, it was just a muscle twitching, a delayed effect of the wound in her left shoulder.

"Good afternoon, sir," she managed to reply coolly.

"I need a favor, Burke," he said. "I want you to take me out tonight or tomorrow and show me how security is handled at the missile sites."

It was the last thing on earth she felt like doing. Did he lie awake nights thinking up ways to annoy people? "Why?" she demanded bluntly, and never mind protocol. "Why this sudden interest?"

"Because I'm responsible for those sites just as I'm responsible for everything on this base. It behooves me to know how it's handled." His tone lay somewhere between sarcasm and exaggerated patience. "Well?"

Well, if she couldn't get out of it, she didn't want to postpone it. In fact, the thought of spending some time alone with him caused her traitorous heart to leap and her blood to rush. "This evening," she said when she felt she could trust her voice. Weak, Burke, she scolded herself. You're really weak. "Say seven?"

"Good. Pick me up at my house. I'll be looking for you." He disconnected with a click.

Leaning back in her chair, she eased her arm from the sling and began the limbering exercises the doctor had given her. What the devil was going on? She winced as her healing muscles pulled. Well, if he really wanted to go all the way out to Romeo, the nearest missile site, he could damn well do the driving.

Dare was watching for her, and as soon as the blue truck pulled up in front of his house, he trotted down the walk and came around to the driver's side.

"I'll drive," he said. "Scoot over."

Andrea was glad to. It had been a long day—too long, really—and her shoulder was aching just about as bad as it ever had.

"Are we really going out to the Romeo site?" she asked. The more the afternoon had waned, the more difficulty she'd had in believing he was really interested in security at the missile sites. It was possible, of course, given his predilection for sticking his nose into everything. Still, something felt odd about the request.

"No. We'll drive up the road a dozen miles or so and have coffee someplace."

All her good resolutions faltered as something inside her went liquid and weak. Had he gone to all this trouble just to steal some time alone with her?

"How's your shoulder doing, Andrea?"

"You want the real poop or the polite answer, sir?"

"That bad?"

"That bad, sir."

He was genuinely sorry to hear it. "I thought by now it would be considerably better."

"It's better than it was." She wanted to change the subject. "I heard we're getting a storm tonight."

"Four inches of snow and a twenty-degree temperature drop," he agreed. "We'll be back before it gets bad."

She nodded. The storm wasn't supposed to hit until between eleven and midnight. She wondered, though, why he was heading away from town along a less traveled stretch of road. Did he think someone might follow them?

"Ah, Colonel?"

"Hmm?"

"Is there a point to all this James Bond stuff?"

MacLendon chuckled quietly. "Actually, yes. We'll talk about it over coffee."

Resigned, Andrea settled back and tried to find a comfortable angle for her shoulder. If there was one, she hadn't yet discovered it.

Dare pulled over at a truck stop about fifteen miles west of the base. The place was pretty well deserted, boasting only one interstate rig and a couple of pickups out front. Inside there were a counter and numerous booths with ragged plastic-covered seats. Dare chose a booth at the far end of the diner, away from the other patrons.

An elderly waitress with a Swedish accent hurried over to take their orders. Dare wanted coffee and apple pie. Andrea settled for coffee and tried not to think about how badly she wanted to be standing beneath a hot shower, letting the warmth steal the stiffness from her muscles.

Only when they'd been served did Dare speak.

"Well," he said slowly, "it wasn't a goose that put the hole in that bomber. It was plastique."

Andrea's head jerked up. Shock overrode her fugitive disappointment at learning he'd brought her here to talk business. For a moment she was simply speechless. "My God. But why? What could anyone possibly hope to accomplish?"

Dare shrugged. "Who knows? Simple terror? Something more complex? We won't know unless we find the culprit, which brings me to the point of all these James Bond tactics you asked about. Andrea, the OSI investigators say the perpetrator had inside help. Or that someone on the inside used someone on the outside as a diversion. Either way, we have big trouble."

For a long moment Andrea made no response. Dare saw the shock in her eyes, then saw her control it rapidly.

"Why," she asked finally, "do they think it's an inside job?"

"You're the security expert. You tell me what it would take for a terrorist to get into the nose of that B-52 to plant plastique. Hell, that's the easy part, I guess. The hard part is getting into the controlled area so he had access to the planes. OSI is very impressed with you and your squadron. You're doing a marvelous job, one of the best they've ever seen. And that's why they're convinced that the culprit had inside help. They believe that's the only way he could get past your security."

"A uniform. A badge. It's simple."

"Not that simple. OSI tried four times in the past two weeks to gain illicit entry to the area. Your guys stopped 'em every time."

"Since the shooting—"

MacLendon silenced her with a shake of his head. "Sure, everyone's on his or her toes, but they were on the alert even before you were shot, because of that business with the fence. You beefed up your patrols long before that incident."

Andrea shifted restlessly and winced as her shoulder pulled. Finally, frustrated by her own discomfort, she propped her chin on her right hand and stared glumly into her coffee. "An inside job. Damn. Who do they suspect? My people? The mechanics? The pilots?" It gave her a queasy feeling to realize she might actually know someone capable of such an act.

"Right now everybody's suspect. Everybody except you and me. You because of the shooting incident, and me because I called OSI."

Without moving her head, she raised her eyes to his. "What do we do about it?"

"Stay alert and pay attention. What else *can* we do? Plastique pretty effectively wipes out fingerprints."

Sighing, Andrea lifted her coffee cup and sipped.

"Andrea?"

"Mmm?"

"I've been meaning to tell you; you're one damn fine officer."

Color rose in a deep flush from her neck up. Dare watched in fascination. He wouldn't have believed Andrea could blush so profusely. The rush of color canceled all resemblance to Huck Finn, not that he had any problem with her looks. Her green eyes flickered and lowered, avoiding his gaze.

"Andrea?"

"Sir?" She retreated swiftly into formality, and his eyes gentled, although she was too busy fiddling with her coffee spoon to see it.

"We need to talk."

"I thought we were talking, sir." Her heart accelerated slightly. Instinctively she knew the direction he was taking.

"I know you're angry with me."

"Angry, sir?" She kept her face blank. Why the devil couldn't he leave this alone?

"I can't leave it alone," he said, as if he read her mind. "It's like a toothache. You keep poking it with your tongue."

Her hazy green eyes took on that gleam he knew so well. "I believe, sir," she said smoothly, "that this is the first time I've ever been compared to a toothache."

"Cut it out, Andrea. And drop the 'sir' business."

"We've tried that, sir," she reminded him. "You may have noticed it only works for a few minutes at a time. It also strikes me as being about as wise as playing catch with a live grenade." And if her heart pounded any harder, it was going to burst from her chest.

The mistiness was gone from her eyes, he noted. While her cheek still rested tiredly on her hand, her gaze had grown clear and unwavering. If he chose to pursue this, he was going to get the unvarnished truth from her. He wondered suddenly if he were up to it. Alisdair MacLendon had never been a chicken, however, so he advanced into the fray.

"What are your career plans?" he asked bluntly.

She ran her tongue along her upper lip, considering. "Two weeks ago I would have said I wanted to retire at the rank of colonel. I'm not sure now. I mean, I knew that if I played with guns there was a distinct possibility I might have to use one. I guess I didn't really believe it." She straightened and took a sip of coffee. "I just don't know anymore. I have to be able to live with myself, one way or the other." Suddenly her gaze transfixed him. "What about you, sir?"

"Me? I'm a year away from retirement, if I want to take it. And I'm thinking about it, Andrea. I'm thinking about it very hard."

"But you're up for general."

"I can retire as a general just as easily as a colonel. There are a lot of things I never got around to doing, and I find myself thinking about them."

She was softening. Captain Burke was slipping away like a veneer. Taking advantage of the moment, Dare charged ahead.

"About what happened between us, Andrea..."

Her head jerked up, and her eyes were suddenly snapping. "Yes, sir, let's talk about that. It's high time we cleared the air on that subject."

Uh-oh, thought Dare with amusement.

She saw the resignation pass over his face but didn't relent, even though she was tempted. She'd been having this argument with herself since Thanksgiving, and now that she was wound up, she wanted to cite all her reasons, to make him understand what she felt he'd failed to.

"I'm not sure you fully understand my situation. The simple fact is, my entire career can be destroyed by a single indiscretion. You're a man. You're expected to chase skirts. If the skirt happens to belong to a subordinate officer, it doesn't matter in the least unless she chooses to make some kind of fuss about it.

"On the other hand, I'm a woman. In these liberated times it's okay if I have an affair, but it will never be okay for me to have a personal relationship with my commanding officer. One whisper of something like that will label me forever as a woman who uses her body to get ahead. I can forget the whole idea of a career if that happens."

"Whoa, Andrea. Easy."

She shook her head, and her green eyes met his forthrightly despite the color that climbed up her throat. "It's not that I don't want to kiss you." Which was one heck of an understatement, she thought. It was about all she seemed to want anymore. "I think, however, that the price may be a whole lot higher than I'm willing to pay for a casual affair."

It was the last two words that got to him: casual affair. Was that how it looked to her, as if he were toying with her entire future for a few casual couplings? Casual was not the word for any of the things Andrea made him feel. He hadn't really examined those feelings, but he guessed it was time to do so. Before they decided how to settle this thing between them, he owed her that much, at least. And, he decided, he owed her equal honesty.

"Andrea, this isn't casual for me. I'm not sure what it is, but it's definitely not casual."

Her eyes widened; then she blinked in that way she had when she was momentarily taken aback. "Oh." Suddenly all her arguments fled from her head. *Not casual.* The admission at once terrified and elated her. She didn't want his interest to be casual, but she didn't know how she would handle it if it wasn't. Lord, she'd turned into a dithering idiot!

"I'm not sure you'll be grateful when you think about it," he said drily. "A casual affair is a lot easier to dismiss." Reaching inside his parka, he retrieved a pack of cigarettes and lit one. For a guy who'd nearly quit a couple of months ago, he was starting to smoke an awful lot.

"What are you saying, sir?"

"I've been where you are, Andrea. I know better than you think just how you view things and what you want out of life. Maybe in ten or twelve years you'll understand where I'm coming from. When you devote your whole life to an institution, you get very few personal rewards. You wake up one morning and find you've missed most of what life is about. It's not a happy experience. So I've reordered my priorities. That's why I kissed you, and that's why I'm going to kiss you again."

Andrea drew a sharp breath. Something deep inside her clenched pleasurably, but she tried to ignore it. "Sir…"

"Quiet, Captain. Don't worry. I have absolutely no intention of damaging your career. There won't even be a whisper of impropriety. But I *will* kiss you again."

Andrea found herself fascinated by his hands. Large, strong, long-fingered hands. Their backs were thinly sprinkled with fine black hairs, and it took no great leap of the imagination to picture that hair elsewhere. She swallowed. The truth was, she wanted him to kiss her right now, and it was getting harder and harder to remember why that was wrong.

"Andrea." One of his hands reached out to cover hers.

She looked up, and there was such an unconcealed wealth of longing in her eyes that MacLendon felt as if he'd been socked in the chest. Never had anyone looked at him that way.

He withdrew his hand and deliberately pushed up his parka sleeve to look at his watch. "What time would you get back tonight if you really had gone to Romeo?"

"About ten-thirty." The moment was shattered. Her answer was businesslike.

"We've got time for more coffee, then." He stubbed out his cigarette and signaled the waitress.

Andrea nodded, dropped her chin into her hand again, and let her eyelids droop. The day had been too long at two-thirty that afternoon, and now it was nearly nine. Her shoulder throbbed in time to the beat of her heart. How long would it be before she got her old energy back? And how long would it be until the sight of Dare's face stopped hurting worse than her shoulder? It was an almost physical pain that pierced her each time she looked at him.

When they stepped outside, it was immediately obvious that they had made a big mistake by staying so long. Snow whirled wildly everywhere, and the wind had strengthened considerably. Visibility was reduced to about ten feet.

"We've got a problem," Dare remarked when they were safely closed up in the cab of the truck. "Still, it'll be easier to explain what we're doing in a ditch five miles east of here than what we're doing out of our way at a roadhouse."

"We won't go into a ditch," Andrea said wryly. "There isn't a single bend in the road between here and the base. You could tie a rope around the wheel and we'd get home all right."

The corners of his mouth moved upward, and he turned on the ignition.

The state highway engineers had taken advantage of the state's flatness and unceasing winds. The road was somewhat elevated above the surrounding fields, so that the never-ending wind swept away the snow and kept the roads clean. Drifts and ice were not the danger; whiteout was. When they set out, it was still possible to see the white stripe at the edge of the road. Dare drove a cautious thirty miles an hour.

Before long, however, they were in a full whiteout, unable to see even as far as the front end of the truck's hood.

"Damn," Dare muttered. He slowed to five miles per hour, hoping their reduced speed would improve visibility. It didn't.

"Maybe we should pull over," Andrea said.

"Pull over where? I don't even know where the shoulder is now." He considered stopping right where he was, but even as the thought was forming, the truck tipped toward Andrea's side. They were off the road.

Chapter 7

The situation was quite simply one of survival. They radioed the base that they'd gone off the road and were told that visibility was zero and all travel had been stopped by order of Dare's deputy commander. No rescue would be forthcoming until the storm passed—around dawn, it was hoped. Neither Andrea nor Dare had expected anything else. Anybody who tried to come after them would probably wind up in precisely the same predicament.

Dare ventured out briefly to get the survival gear from the back of the truck, and soon he and Andrea were wrapped in wool blankets and staring at each other by the light of a single candle set safely in a tin on the door of the glove compartment.

Dare shifted suddenly, wedging himself into the corner between the door and the seat. He insisted that Andrea lean back against him and try to sleep.

"You're pooped," he said. "It's been obvious all evening. Just lean back, shut up and sleep."

Covered by layers of winter clothing, he made a comfortable pillow, and Andrea fell asleep with her back to his chest, fatigue taking her by surprise.

Dare didn't sleep. Sleep was dangerous in these subzero temperatures, and there was no guarantee you'd ever know that you were freezing to death. Instead he remained watchful. His right arm closed about Andrea's waist, covering the left arm that was strapped just below her breasts, and he let his chin rest on the top of her head.

Several hours later, Andrea came instantly awake. She was shaking, but she didn't feel more than a little cold.

"Dare?"

"I'm here." His rumble was reassuring, right above her head.

Suddenly she realized why she was shaking. "You're shivering!"

"I'm losing a little body heat through my back. It's right against the door."

Andrea shoved herself up immediately and looked at him in the light of the guttering candle. His teeth were clenched.

"I suppose you thought it would make me feel wonderful in the morning to find you frozen to death under me!"

"I'm not in any danger of freezing, damn it." He sat up and tried to pull the blanket around his shoulders. "I'm just a little cold. Shivering will warm me up in a minute."

Andrea made a disgusted sound and reached for the candy bars that had come with the survival kit. "Eat one of these. Eat them all. Damn, where are the candles?"

"In the glove box."

"You really amaze me," she scolded as she pulled out a fresh candle. "You know better than this. Every bit of body warmth is essential. You can't afford to let yourself get cold." After lighting the candle, she stuck it onto the stub of the old one. "Here. Take off your mittens and hold your hands right over the candle."

He tried to comply, but he was shivering so badly that he was unable to get much good from the flame. Andrea made a disgusted sound and opened the two middle buttons of her parka.

"Come on, cowboy, put your hands in here."

"Don't call me cowboy," he grumbled as his hands found their way inside the parka, inside her regulation cardigan, and into a nest of warmth and softness. If he hadn't been so cold, he might even have enjoyed it.

Andrea pulled the blankets up and over their hooded heads,

sealing in the heat of their breath, wrapping them in a dark cocoon. The light from the candle was dimly visible through the tight weave of the wool blankets. She made a small sound as her injured shoulder bumped into the seat back.

"This isn't going to work, Andrea," Dare said through chattering teeth. "You can't get comfortable."

"I'll get comfortable when you stop shivering. Until then, I'll survive."

But the shivering didn't stop. He'd gotten more hypothermic than he'd suspected. Gritting his teeth to stop them from chattering, he pulled his hands away from the warmth of Andrea's body and struggled to unfasten his parka. When it fell open, he reached for the buttons of hers. She helped him as best she could, and then his frigid hands slipped up her back, inside the stored warmth, and their chests came together, sharing heat. Shifting slightly, he managed to maneuver them so that Andrea rested comfortably against him, all pressure off her shoulder.

Gradually his violent shuddering began to taper off, and feeling began to return to his fingers, toes, and nose. He still felt cold, deeply, internally cold, but his body signaled that the worst was over by letting his muscles relax between bouts of shivering.

"Dare?"

"Hmm?"

"What have you got against cowboys?"

He almost smiled. "Nothing. I just don't like to be called cowboy. My ex-wife used to call me that when she was in one of her bitchy moods."

"How long were you married?"

"For five endless years way back when. Maureen wasn't cut out for either me or military life. She was a city girl, a socialite. Being a lowly lieutenant's wife drove her crazy. She should have married a general."

"Was she pretty?"

He considered. "I guess. I thought so at first. Later I thought she was pretty ugly. I got so I hated the sight of her, the sound of her. To this day I can't stand the perfume she used to wear."

"Must've been rough."

"There's nothing quite like the ugliness that can happen between two people who know each other well. You get so you know what really hurts and how to use it. Maureen was especially good at it.''

"I'm sorry." Andrea's voice was soft.

"I recovered a long time ago. It's a mistake I'll never make again, though."

"Marriage?"

"Not marriage. Marrying somebody without thinking about just what they'll be giving up. If I met Maureen now, I'd know better. I'd know it would sour her. Love doesn't conquer all, you know. It doesn't conquer anything. Sooner or later you've got to deal with the real world. There's always a trade-off."

"How unromantic." With her cheek against Dare's chest, she listened to the sound of his heartbeat. He was hardly shivering now, and the earlier rapid rhythm had slowed to normal.

"Oh, I believe in romance," he said. "Moonlight, wine, roses—"

"Skip the roses."

He chuckled. "Quiet candlelit dinners, then. But I'm a realist, too, Andrea. Think about it. How would you feel if some man told you to choose between him and your career?"

There was a silence. "Yeah," she said quietly after a moment.

His hands began to move in slow, soothing circles on her back, and a kittenish purr escaped her.

"You're all tense," he said.

"It's the shoulder. I seem to be stiff all the time from trying to protect it. Mmm." His fingers were kneading gently, working the tension out.

"Andrea?"

"Sir?"

"I'm getting a nearly irresistible urge to kiss you again."

She surprised him with a low throaty chuckle. "I thought you'd never mention it."

It was crazy, it was insane, and he kissed her anyway. Outside, the wind howled and the snow whipped icily, but inside the blankets warmth began to grow.

It was a curiously sweet and tender episode. Between Andrea's shoulder, the confinement of the truck, and the deadly threat of the cold, their kisses could not evolve into passion. Instead they savored the warmth and closeness, the gentle, lin-

gering comfort of lips and tongues. It was enough to hold and
be held, to kiss and be kissed. They both began to realize what
they'd been missing.

Finally they simply leaned against one another, content and
comforted. There was a world of difference in Dare's mind between an embrace and a hug. He was hugging Andrea, and she
him. It occurred to him he couldn't have picked a worse person
to make the object of that kind of affection. Andrea was a career
woman, determined to pursue her goals. There was pain waiting
for him at the end of this road. Sighing, he drew her a little
closer. He was old enough to understand that all good things
had a price. You just had to decide whether something was
worth it.

"Penny?" said Andrea from where she was nestled against
his shoulder.

"I was just thinking how huggable you are."

"Mmm. I like the way that sounds. You're huggable, too."

"Am I?" He'd never thought of himself that way. It pleased
him.

"You are." She snuggled closer. In their warm cocoon, cut
off from the world, it was easy to forget everything, and Andrea
let herself do just that. She understood that eventually reality
would intrude, but for the moment she refused to care.

He raised his hand to cradle her cheek. "Was it rough being
Charlie Burke's daughter?" he asked.

The perception of the question amazed Andrea. People who
knew her father always assumed he was a great dad, that he'd
encouraged Andrea's independence and her Air Force career. In
fact, he'd seized every opportunity to try to grind her down and
turn her into a submissive, dependent female. There wasn't anything personal in it. It was just the way Charlie Burke thought
women ought to be. In fact, the only thing in the world tougher
than being Charlie Burke's daughter was being Charlie Burke's
son.

It was her brothers who had saved Andrea from her intended
fate by treating her as one of them, by expecting her to play
their games and take part in their escapades. Being kids, they
just didn't know how else to treat a sister, particularly one
whose competitive spirit was fierce. She never hesitated, so it
never occurred to them to balk.

"Sometimes it was rough," she admitted, intensely aware of Dare's thumb stroking her cheek. His gentleness continually amazed her. He looked hard, tough, competent, yet when he held her, he made her feel precious and safe. He managed to treat her as if she were fragile without in any way diminishing her strength and independence. It was a dangerously addicting sensation.

"You have so many contrasts, Andrea," Dare said suddenly. "That night I was in the accident, you were so easy and boyish. I distinctly remember deciding that you were going to be a handful. Then there's the prickly pear cactus who glares at me when I step on her toes. And there's the smartmouth who slips her zingers almost unnoticed into the conversation. There's the cool, capable officer with a steady gaze, and there's the tough cookie who can dress a trooper down with all the punch of Patton. And then there's *this* Andrea."

"What's this Andrea?" There was a smile in her voice.

"This Andrea is a soft, warm, wonderful woman who can put her arms around a man and make him feel like he's come home."

Andrea lifted her head. "Dare," she said uneasily.

"Leave it alone, Andrea," he said gently. "I'm old enough to know what I'm doing. You'll forget your damn career long before I do."

She was surprised to realize that she believed him. He would be the last one of them to forget all the obstacles in their path.

For Dare, the night was endless. He had wadded a blanket and slipped it between him and the door to provide insulation, then stretched out, his long legs on the passenger side floor, his back wedged against the blanket and seat. Andrea lay half over him, her face burrowed into his shoulder, one hand tucked into the warmth of his armpit. His own arms were wrapped snugly around her waist inside her parka. Every time he drew a breath, her warmth and sweetly feminine scent wafted into his nostrils. They kept each other warm, but it was more than Andrea's body heat that raised Dare's temperature.

Andrea slept, but Dare kept watch over her, so there was no escape from the tingling in his loins that kept trying to turn into a full throbbing. He'd never been a promiscuous man, had never indulged in casual relationships. Such things just didn't appeal to him. Consequently the span since his last relationship could be counted in years. Too many years, to judge by his present discomfort.

The fact that Andrea really wasn't his type made his attraction to her all the more serious. Like Andrea, he'd been raised in a large family of boys, but on a ranch in Montana, where life had been hard. His mother had died while he was still very young, so there had been no female influence in his life. It was the femininity of women that usually attracted him, their softness and gentleness, their ruffles and frills, their perfume and long hair. He was attracted to all the things that his life had always lacked.

Andrea enticed him with none of those things. In so many ways, his relationship with her was no different from his relationship with his male officers. He could easily see her becoming a poker buddy, or a drinking buddy, or even a hunting buddy. He could not, hard as he might try, imagine her in any typical female role. Yet on those rare occasions when they gave free rein to the man-woman urges between them, he found her incredibly feminine, irresistibly sexy. Why?

Why did she feel so right in his arms, even now, when it was sheer torment? Why did he take such delight at the spark of annoyance in her eyes, or the way she bedeviled him and zinged him? Why, when she was being cool, collected, competent Captain Burke, did she make him feel like he was a man in possession of a wonderful secret?

Sighing, he shifted just a little and then nearly groaned when the movement brought her hip into more intimate contact with him. If he weren't a gentleman, he would slip his hands up inside her uniform blouse and find out if her skin was as satiny as it looked. It probably was, damn it. And those better-than-standard-issue breasts were probably high and pink-tipped. And her fanny, which he'd eyeballed from time to time when she wore slacks, was gently rounded and ever so slightly fuller than average in a way that made him want to—

He muttered an oath and forced his mind from such thoughts. He might be going crazy, but there was no point in being masochistic about it. The woman had made it clear that she would do nothing to risk her career, so he'd better just focus his thoughts on something safe, like work.

* * *

Rescue arrived before dawn. The winds had quieted enough that the blowing snow snaked along at ground level, leaving visibility unlimited. A drift had grown against one side of the truck, nearly covering it, but Sergeant Nickerson was able to walk around and open the door on Andrea's side.

He found the two officers shivering and exhausted but otherwise all right. Andrea never wanted to see another candy bar.

"We'll send someone out for the truck later, sir, ma'am," Nickerson said. "Right now, let's just get you two to the hospital."

"Forget the hospital," Andrea snapped. "Just take me to the chow hall. I'm gonna drink a gallon of coffee."

Dare and Nickerson eyed one another over Andrea's head, sharing a look of masculine patience.

"Chow hall," said Dare after a moment.

Nickerson nodded. "Yes, sir." He reached up to help Andrea down, but she brushed his hand away, insisting that she could get out of the truck under her own steam.

She managed it, too, in spite of nearly tripping over the blanket, being able to steady herself with only one hand and discovering that hypothermia had affected her coordination. When she climbed into the crew cab of Nickerson's truck, the blast from the heater was painful to her cold skin.

The sun was just beginning its slow rise when they cleared the main gate and drove onto the base. This far north, it didn't have all that far to lift. It was going to be a clear, bright, cold day.

Nickerson pulled into the parking lot near the chow hall, and the three of them went inside to begin the day the way Andrea thought it should begin, with a gallon of coffee, bacon, and eggs. She was still shivering somewhat, but it didn't take long for the coffee to thaw her.

Gradually the world began to return to normal. The night had been an aberration, she told herself. It was the danger that had brought her and Dare together in a brief time of openness and gentleness. It was over, and time to forget it.

"How come you decided to go out to Romeo, ma'am?" Nickerson asked.

Andrea looked up from her plate, telling herself that it was her tiredness that made Nickerson's question seem out of line.

She lifted one brow and paused before answering. Nickerson had been working with her for two years, she reminded herself. Like a lot of high-ranking sergeants, he treated young officers in a somewhat fatherly fashion. Or maybe it just seemed out of line because she couldn't answer truthfully. Dare had made it clear that no one but he and Andrea was to know about the OSI investigation.

"Why do I ever go out to the sites, Sergeant?" she asked coolly.

Dare noticed that Nickerson didn't miss Andrea's zingers, either. The sergeant, who was accustomed to Andrea calling him Nick, retreated instantly.

"None of my business, ma'am," he said.

Andrea ate a piece of egg. "No, it's not," she agreed. "In point of fact, I hadn't been out to a couple of those sites in too long. My timing was atrocious, I guess." She was aware that that left the question of why Dare had gone with her. "Nick, have you heard anything about a crap game out at Romeo Four Two?"

Nickerson looked surprised. "No, ma'am," he said swiftly. "I can't believe—no, ma'am, I sure haven't. Wouldn't be much of a crap game with only a couple of guys."

"There are mobile units, too, Nick. It would be easy enough for them to get in on it."

Nickerson nodded slowly. "I'll sure keep my ear to the ground. But ma'am, I just don't think—"

"Unthinkable things happen, Nick."

Let him put that in his pipe and smoke it, Andrea thought. He probably figured she'd gone round the bend. That was fine. He would quit asking questions, and after a week or so he'd probably decide this had been a temporary aberration on her part.

She shoved back her chair. "I'm still starved," she announced and took her plate back to the chow line.

Dare saw the look on Nickerson's face and gave Andrea high marks for redirecting his attention.

Andrea returned with a heaping plateful of home fries and scrambled eggs. Dare's lips quirked in amusement, and he wondered how she stayed so lean if she ate like a football player.

"Do you always eat like this?" he asked her.

"Like what, sir?" She didn't even look up, occupied with peppering her potatoes.

"Never mind," Dare said. "Just finish so I can get you safely dumped off at the BOQ with orders to stay in bed today."

"That's really not necessary, sir," she said coolly. Of course, she couldn't see the purple rings under her eyes.

"I don't recall asking for your opinion on the subject, Captain." Dare's voice had suddenly taken on a note of command. It startled her; she'd never heard him use quite that tone before. He generally seemed to manage men with an easy style and didn't have to bring authority to bear.

"Sorry, sir," she said promptly.

Dare might have relented if Nickerson hadn't been there. As it was, he left the colonel and the captain once again firmly in their places. There was one advantage to being Andrea's CO, he thought ruefully. He could shut her up when he had a mind to.

The morning of Christmas Eve, Andrea arrived at her desk to find a summons from the CBPO, the personnel office. Her heart quickened at once. That kind of summons usually meant only one thing: a new assignment. She indulged a few moments of speculation, thinking that there could be worse Christmas presents. It would get her away from Dare, who continued to have the most devastating affect on her tranquillity in spite of the fact that they had kept strictly to business since the night they had gone off the road. In fact, they hadn't even discussed spending Christmas together, as he had once suggested, and she gathered he planned to spend the holiday in solitude, just as she did.

She was grateful to him for letting the matter drop. Grateful and annoyed. On the one hand, a relationship with him was impossible, given the circumstances, and she was honest enough to admit to herself that if he'd pushed the matter, she would have given in eventually. On the other hand, she wished he *had* pushed it. In all honesty, while she might have hated herself for it afterward, she would have loved to be swept off her feet, pushed past the decisions and problems, and brought to a fulfillment she still could only imagine. He had begun to invade her dreams, had Alisdair MacLendon, and she was getting tired of waking in the morning with an ache in her heart and soul that made her want to weep.

Dare. Even his name was a challenge, and she felt like a coward for not daring to meet it.

Sighing, she grabbed her parka and headed for personnel. With her luck, they'd probably be sending her to Alaska. She hadn't had a single warm assignment since joining this damn outfit.

It was an assignment. The sergeant she spoke with handed her a stack of rosters with a laconic, "Merry Christmas, Captain. You've won an all-expense paid trip to Minot, North Dakota."

Andrea looked down at the inch-thick stack of orders. "Somebody must love me."

The sergeant grinned. "If it's any consolation, ma'am, while the climate won't improve, you'll be in command of a larger squadron."

Andrea hardly knew whether to laugh or swear. She would be moving to the other end of the state to command the larger security squadron at Minot, but she'd have the same North Dakota winters to contend with, the same missile fields, the same problems. It hardly seemed worth the effort of moving her. Shrugging, she headed back to the Squadron HQ, telling herself that this was a big step up in her career. The climate didn't matter.

She walked back into the building and lifted the stack of papers as she passed the front desk. "I got orders," she said. The cops at the desk grinned.

"Where to, ma'am?" one of them asked.

"You'll never believe it."

"Hawaii?"

She shook her head. "Minot."

Their roars of laughter followed her all the way down the corridor.

Back in the privacy of her own office, however, she didn't feel like laughing, and a step up in her career suddenly seemed relatively unimportant. In five weeks she would be leaving. In five weeks Dare MacLendon would be gone from her life. She'd told herself that nothing could ever have come of it, but that didn't stop her from feeling cheated.

Resting her elbows on the desk and steepling her hands, she pressed her fingers against her lips and closed her eyes. She felt—and no amount of internal argument dispelled the feeling—that she was about to lose an opportunity that came only once in a lifetime. But what could she do? Orders were orders.

Twenty minutes later, Dare was on the phone. "You got orders?" he asked, hoping it wasn't true.

It never failed to amaze Andrea how fast gossip traveled. "Yes, sir. I'm leaving January thirtieth for Minot."

"Minot, huh." Dare forced a laugh into his voice. "Luck of the draw, Captain. Just one of the wonders of GI life. You could say you're so good at what you do that they just don't want to waste you."

"I could also say somebody doesn't like me."

"You could." He could say the same about her departure, but he figured she was in no mood to hear it. He doubted very much that Minot was on anyone's Dream Sheet of preferred assignments. He opted instead to tease her. "Next Christmas, I'll send you a set of red long johns. Just don't get caught in any ditches with any colonels."

A gleam came to Andrea's hazy green eyes. "I don't repeat my mistakes, Colonel."

The ensuing silence was so long that Andrea realized Dare hadn't liked her teasing remark. Good Lord, did he think she was saying *he* was a mistake? That the little bit of human warmth they'd shared was a mistake? Her mind began to scramble for a way to explain herself while a mocking little voice said, What's the matter, Burke? Isn't that what you've been saying all along? That it's one big mistake?

It was Dare, however, who broke the silence. "I've got this problem," he said. Quietly. Gravely.

Andrea's heart nearly stopped as she waited tensely. "Oh?"

"I've got a Christmas tree to decorate tonight. Funny how I haven't gotten around to it yet. And I have a bottle of B&B, but I hate to drink alone." He sighed. "That's the problem with giving twenty years of your life to your career. You wind up drinking alone." With that, he hung up.

And left Andrea to wonder if she had just been given an invitation.

She struggled with that possibility for the rest of the day and right through dinner. Along about seven o'clock, it occurred to her that her orders had just set her free from a whole boatload of problems. Some of the other bachelors stopped by to invite her to come along to the Officers' Club, but she turned them down, saying she had been invited to a friend's home for the evening.

Suddenly excited, she dug a seldom-worn royal blue jersey dress out of the closet, along with a pair of stiletto-heeled pumps. She even managed to find a little eyeshadow and mascara and a pale lipstick, left over from so long ago that she wasn't sure they were still safe to use. It was only when she stood at the door, parka in hand, that she questioned the wisdom of what she was about to do.

If she parked her car at Dare's place, the entire squadron would know it. The patrolling cops would recognize it. She might as well take an ad out in the base newspaper. And it was too cold to walk over there dressed like this, with nothing between her legs and frostbite but a layer of nylon mesh.

Sighing, she turned back, ready to relinquish the whole idea. And then she saw the telephone. Why not? said the daring voice that had carried her through the academy and into a career that was unusual for a woman. Why the heck not?

She dialed Dare's number and didn't begin to get nervous until she heard his voice.

"Hello?" he repeated when she didn't immediately answer.

She found her voice at last. "It's Andrea," she said.

"What's up?" His voice told her nothing; indeed he sounded businesslike, as if he thought she were calling about work.

"Uh, I wondered if you wanted any help with the tree."

"I'd love some." His voice grew warm, and it caused something inside her to quiver. "Come on over."

"Uh, my car—" She couldn't lie, but she couldn't explain her reasoning, either. It sounded so dumb.

"I'm on my way," he said briskly. "I'll pull up right out front."

Shrouded in her parka with the concealing snorkel hood pulled up, she darted through the empty hallway and down the back stairway to the parking lot. She might have been any of the thirty female officers in residence in the BOQ, and there was nothing about Dare's Bronco to set it apart from dozens of others on base. Five minutes later she was climbing into the warmth of his car, somehow feeling that she had just burned a bridge behind her.

Chapter 8

Dare's Christmas tree stood in front of the curtained patio doors. He had already strung the lights, and they were twinkling gaily. While Andrea admired the tree, Dare admired her.

A new side to his Captain Burke, he thought. She looked so soft and womanly in that clinging blue jersey that he didn't know how he was going to keep his hands off her. He had held her in his arms three times, yet he'd never really realized just how perfectly she was constructed. The full skirt and high heels accentuated a pair of legs that were long and exquisitely formed. All the boyishness she ordinarily presented had vanished.

Or maybe he was just besotted. He didn't care. Stirring himself, he poured a B&B and handed it to her.

"It's a lovely tree, Dare," she said shyly.

Dare? Pleasure swooped through him. This was promising indeed. He'd been feeling gloomy all day because she was leaving in a month. For the first time it occurred to him that those orders might be a blessing.

"I baked some cookies earlier," he said, feeling suddenly awkward. "I'll go get some."

"You baked cookies?" She looked surprised.

"Now who's being the chauvinist?" he asked wryly. "It hap-

pens I like Christmas cookies.'' He enjoyed the blush that suf-
fused her cheeks for a moment and then forced himself to go
get the cookies. Keep it cool, MacLendon, he warned himself,
or she'll turn into Captain Burke again and start yes-sirring and
no-sirring you to death.

While he was in the kitchen, Andrea set her brandy down and
went over to the couch to peer into the ornament box. She noticed he had a new painting on the wall over the couch, a scene
of the desert Southwest at twilight. Done in oils, it conveyed
the texture of the scene, as well as its wildness and beauty.
Forgetting the ornaments, she lost herself in the painting. One
of the many things lacking in her life, she realized suddenly,
was art. Good music, good painting, good books.

''Like it?'' Dare asked. He stood at her elbow, a plate of
cookies in his hand.

''I love it.'' She smiled at him, her shyness forgotten. ''It's
beautiful.''

''Have a cookie.'' His eyes were warm, making her feel
warm, too.

He put a record of Christmas carols on the stereo and then
handed her a box of ornaments. ''These are my favorite ones,''
he said. ''You do the honors.''

His taste in Christmas ornaments surprised her, too. Each was
unique; all were handmade of wood or fabric or stained glass.
There were sleighs and skiers, Santas and bells and trees. Some
were shapes she didn't recognize, and he told her they were
Indian good luck symbols. Before long she was as excited as a
child herself, each new ornament a surprise.

Finally it was all done. Dare turned out all the lights, and they
stood side by side in the dark, admiring the tree.

''It's so perfect,'' Andrea said in a hushed voice. ''I've never
seen such a beautiful tree.''

As if it were the most natural thing in the world, Dare slipped
his arm around her shoulders. And as if it were the most natural
thing in the world, Andrea leaned against him.

''Andrea?''

''Hmm?''

''Who are we tonight?'' He had to know. There was no way
he was going to stumble around blind tonight, perhaps offending
her, perhaps losing her. He had to know where he stood. He

heard the catch of her breath and tensed, waiting for her answer. After a moment, she turned slowly to face him. He looked down into her eyes, dark pools in the dim light.

She spoke steadily. "I left my uniform back at the BOQ, sir. Just for tonight, I'm nobody at all."

"You're not nobody, Andrea," he said huskily. "You're the most enchanting, bewitching woman in the world. Just for tonight," he added, seeing the sudden flicker of concern on her face. "Just for tonight."

She relaxed then, a small smile lifting the corners of her mouth. What a role reversal, Dare thought, with a brief sense of the wry humor of the situation. She was concerned that he might be hurt. She was the one who wanted no strings to interfere with her future, no obligations to bind her. Quite a man, his Captain Burke.

"I am so very glad," he said, spacing his words as his blue eyes fixed on her mouth, "that you left your uniform behind." It was such a soft, inviting mouth, he thought, and it had started to tremble ever so slightly at the corners. "You don't need to be afraid of me, Andrea."

"I'm not. At least, not exactly."

"Nervous?"

"A little."

Lightly, as if he were touching the wings of a butterfly, he brushed his thumb across her lower lip. "What are you nervous about?"

She blinked and gnawed the lip he'd just caressed. "Everything," she answered finally.

"Everything?" He moved a little closer. "That's an awful lot to be nervous about. Just how inexperienced *are* you?"

She blinked twice this time, rapidly, and had to clear her throat before she could speak. The low intimacy of his tone made strange things happen deep inside her, as did the feathery caress of his fingers on her cheek. "Very inexperienced," she croaked.

"Tell me, Andrea," he coaxed. "I have to know, for both our sakes."

Her courage failed her at last, and she closed her eyes tightly. "Never," she whispered, and wondered how long her rubbery knees would hold her. She wouldn't blame him if he backed off right now, but, oh, now that she'd finally come to this point, she didn't think she could survive the disappointment.

A virgin. He'd suspected as much. As if she were glass that might shatter at a careless touch, Dare wrapped his arms carefully around her and drew her head into the comforting hollow of his shoulder. Hearing her shaky sigh, he sought to soothe her with a gentle kiss to her temple.

"I'm going to try very hard to seduce you, Andrea."

"Yes, sir." Her voice was little more than a choked whisper.

"But," he said softly against her hair, "I have very strict rules about seduction. Would you like to hear them?"

"Mmm."

"First of all, I won't do anything you don't want me to. That's a promise, Andrea."

She made a small sound of acknowledgment.

"Secondly, you can tell me to stop at any point, and I won't get mad."

She nodded.

"Finally, you have to enjoy this and want this every bit as much as I do, or I'll stop. This is supposed to be a mutually wonderful experience. I'll do my best to make it that way for you, but I don't want you to feel pressured in any way."

Slowly Andrea's hazy green eyes opened, and she looked up at him. "I believe *I* called *you*, sir."

Dare smiled. "So you did. You're still allowed to change your mind. I don't take this lightly, so I don't expect you to. I want you to be very, very sure about this."

Lifting her right arm, she wrapped it around his neck, looking at once shy and brave.

"Colonel MacLendon?"

"Yes, Captain?"

"I believe I'm already seduced."

His heart slipped into high gear at that admission.

"Oh, no, Captain," he whispered huskily, zeroing in on her mouth. "I haven't yet begun to seduce you."

He stole her breath in a kiss that left her shaken. He knew her mouth now, knew just what to do to send electric shocks racing through her, knew just how to make her shiver and burn.

My God, thought Andrea, if he learns any more about me I'll be defenseless. But she wanted to learn those very things about herself as much as he wanted to discover them. Tightening her arm around his neck, she stood on tiptoes and murmured deep in her throat at the pleasurable feeling as her breasts were crushed against the hard wall of his chest.

Oh yes, thought Dare. Oh yes. It seemed as if he'd been aching all his life to hold this woman, and the thin jersey was little barrier to his hands as they stroked her back from neck to hip. Each time he held her, he was astonished anew at how small and delicate she felt. He'd seen the way she carried herself and talked with her troops and faced things straight on, and nobody in the whole world would think to call Andrea Burke either small or delicate.

Nobody except Alisdair MacLendon when he held her close and felt every delicate bit of her womanliness. That slender waist was almost small enough for him to span with both hands. Those shoulders disappeared in his grasp, and the curving line of her back and hips had all the grace of a swan. She was lovely, his Captain Burke, and he said so.

Looking down at her flushed face and dazed eyes, Dare swept his hands from her neck to her hips one more time. This time, however, he went farther, bending a little as he cupped that sweet, soft bottom that had been driving him crazy for months and pulled her snugly up against him. Andrea's breath caught in her throat as she felt his unashamed arousal hot against her abdomen.

"Dare..." she breathed in wonder. Her fingernails bit into his shoulder as slowly, slowly, he rocked his hips against her and groaned. Her breath stopped, and perhaps her heart, too, as the ache in her was at once answered and worsened.

Groaning again, Dare stilled himself, or tried to, but Andrea could still feel minute movements against her as if two forces were in opposition and one was just a little bit stronger. Why was he stopping? She didn't want him to stop. She wanted every bit of his hunger. The thought that she excited him so greatly thrilled her every bit as much as his kisses did.

"Dare?"

His face was hard with passion and self-control, but he heard the doubt and the edge of worry in her voice, and he responded with a crooked smile.

"It's okay, Andrea," he said huskily. "It's okay. I nearly blew it, that's all."

"Did you?" Slowly a very female smile dawned on her swollen lips.

A choked chuckle escaped him as he saw her satisfaction. "I *knew* you were going to be a handful."

"Yes, sir," she answered demurely, but her desire to tease him vanished as swiftly as it had been born. Green eyes wide, she looked up at him. "I never felt like this before."

He dropped another kiss on her cheek. "How do you feel?"

"Like—like every part of me aches so badly to be touched. I want—I want—" Words and courage both failed her.

"Me too," Dare said hoarsely, gathering her closer. "Me too. But I was close to forgetting my rules, and I don't want to do that. Not this first time."

"What rules?" she asked, dropping her forehead against his chest. "Did I ever tell you you smell good?" She nuzzled his shoulder and sighed.

"So do you. And you feel even better."

A laugh sparkled in her misty eyes as she craned her neck to look up at him. "Do I?"

Here she was again, he thought delightedly, his very favorite smartmouth captain who'd so pertly told him she had a pair of standard female issue breasts. He wanted this Andrea as much as he wanted the softer Andrea she so rarely allowed to show. He wanted *all* of her in his bed, not just bits and pieces of her.

"You know you feel good, you little minx," he retorted gruffly. Back firmly in control of his body, he was able to search out that sensitive place behind her ear and, with the tip of his tongue, send a shiver rippling through her.

"Dare?"

"Hmm?" He found an equally interesting spot where her neck met her shoulder.

"I think my knees are going to give out."

"Mmm. I like the sound of that." Lifting his head, he smiled. "Are you brave enough to let me carry you to my bed? Or are you still unsure?"

Clinging to his shoulders, she cocked her head. "Why are you so sure I don't know what I'm doing?"

"Because until tonight you've been dead set against this. Because you're inexperienced, and that gives you the right to have second thoughts.''

"I don't believe this," she said after a moment's thought.

"Believe what?"

"When I graduated from the Academy, my father had only one comment to make regarding my career. He warned me to look out for you pilots because you'd tumble anything that looked vaguely willing.''

"I *told* you I always thought he was an ass." Dare tunnelled his fingers into her short, reddish hair, enjoying its silkiness. "Just what are you saying?"

She stepped back a few inches so she could see him better. "I may be inexperienced and nervous, I may even get a little shy and embarrassed, but I've made up my mind. I wish you'd just quit worrying about it.''

"Sweet Andrea." Her jaw had that bulldog set he knew so well, and he had to smile. "Are your knees still rubbery?"

She shook her head slowly, looking him right in the eye. "No, sir.''

"We'll have to do something about that." He closed the small distance between them.

"Yes, sir." Her eyelids fluttered in anticipation of his kiss, but he astonished her by scooping her up in his arms as easily as if she weighed nothing.

"I always wanted to carry a woman off to my bed," he remarked humorously as he started down the hall.

"Thank God," she muttered against his throat.

"For what?"

"We both finally agree I'm a woman.''

He laughed. "And at the same time, no less.''

Dare was still chuckling when he carefully lowered her to her feet beside the king-size water bed. "Off with your shoes, Captain." He kicked off his own, as well.

For just a moment he held her by the shoulders and studied her face, as if verifying her resolve. "What are you wearing under your dress?"

Startled by the question, Andrea blinked. "Standard undergarments.''

"Good." His smile was crooked. "In the books and movies,

clothes just conveniently vanish. In real life there's no romantic, easy way to take care of them.''

Drawing her into his arms once again, he reached for the zipper on the back of her dress. ''Lean on me, Andrea.''

She couldn't have done anything else. The instant he tugged the zipper tab, her knees turned to water again. Instinctively, she wrapped her arms around his waist and clung.

''Why does it matter what I'm wearing?'' she asked shakily, trying to concentrate. Heavens, he was pulling that zipper slowly.

''Because you're not ready to be naked with me, but it's easier to deal with undergarments than a dress. Now, shut up, Andrea. Pay attention to what I'm doing to you.''

As if she could pay attention to anything else. All the while he eased that zipper down, his mouth insisted on pillaging her face and throat. His tongue streaked lightning along nerve endings she'd never been aware of before. And then...then his hands slipped inside her dress, warm against the smooth, sensitive skin of her back. Andrea gasped with pleasure, and Dare took advantage of it to kiss her long and deep.

When he raised his head again, her dress had somehow slipped off her shoulders, and she could feel it sliding down, down. His mouth followed, trailing hot little kisses across her shoulder to the swelling rise of one breast above her bra. Andrea froze, her heart hammering painfully as she waited for what was to come next. She guessed, half in fright and half in hope, that he would kiss her there where no one had ever....

With a cool caress, her dress puddled about her ankles, and she stood within the circle of his arms clad in nothing but her bra, half-slip, and panty hose.

''Shh,'' Dare whispered when she gave a small cry of surprise. ''Shh, sweetheart. It's all right. Everything's all right.''

Of course it was all right, she thought hazily, unable to raise eyelids that had somehow become weighted with lead. What was he talking about? It felt so good to feel the warm skin of his arms around her bare back, to feel the fabric of his shirt against her stomach.

Gently, Dare loosened her hold on him, and then, lifting her once again, he tucked her into his bed, beneath a comforter. Startled, Andrea opened her eyes, and in the dim light from the hallway she saw that he was discarding his own clothes. For an instant she felt a pang of fear. This was really happening, and she must be mad, insane. She'd sworn she would never do this, not ever, yet here she was, and it was far too late to back out. She'd insisted she wanted this, and she couldn't possibly change her mind when he was so—so—*ready*.

Suddenly he was in the bed beside her, beneath the coverlet, the warm, furry skin of his chest brushing her arm. The sensation electrified her, and her doubts no longer seemed as important.

"Andrea?" Propped on one elbow, he leaned over her, brushing her hair gently back as he studied her in the dim light. "Second thoughts? Don't be afraid to tell me." Disappointment might kill him, but he didn't want to harm a hair on her head.

Andrea's eyes opened again, and she looked up into his concerned face. That face, she realized uncomfortably, had become very dear to her in ways she was afraid to examine. Drawing a deep breath, she unconsciously squared her shoulders.

"You were right," she said on a breath. "Clothes are very awkward to deal with."

Slowly, he smiled. "Ah," he said with understanding. "Not second thoughts but cooling fires. We can remedy that."

Bravely lifting her arms, she twined them around his neck. Well, Burke, she told herself, you wanted this. You've been fantasizing about it for weeks. Now you're going to find out. Don't be a damn chicken.

Dare accepted her invitation, claiming her mouth in a soul-searing kiss that made everything else seem insignificant. There, beneath the comforter, in the sheltering shadows, he warmed her with his hands and lips, and when her bra vanished, her only thought was to press closer, to ease the ache in her breasts against the hardness of his chest. When she felt him shudder in response, she was further emboldened to rub against him.

"Andrea, Andrea," he muttered, "oh, *yes!*"

Arching his body away from her suddenly, he ducked his head beneath the comforter. A cry escaped Andrea as at last, at last, his mouth found the swollen peak of her breast, closing on it gently. Each suckling motion of his mouth and tongue sent a shaft of need spiraling to her core, feeding the ache there. She wanted him never to stop, but she wanted more, too.

His hands suddenly slipped beneath her slip, panty hose, and panties, cupping her round bottom and kneading in a rhythmic motion that made her sway in time to the pulsing fires inside her. In fact, her whole body throbbed in time to his hands and mouth.

When he suddenly took his mouth from her breasts, she cried out in disappointment, only to freeze in renewed excitement as he sat up and dispensed at last with her remaining garments. In one sweeping movement he stripped them down her legs and tossed them onto the floor before pulling up the comforter once more and returning to lie half over her.

"God, you feel so good to me," he grated near her ear, and Andrea realized he felt good to her, as well. One whole half of her body was pressed intimately to his, and she was acutely aware of the wondrous differences between a man and a woman. With an instinct as old as humanity, she accommodated herself to him, parting her legs so that one of his fell between them. She was instantly rewarded with a renewed throb of sensation that led her to turn toward him, to seek him with her hands.

"That's it, Andrea," he said huskily, controlling himself with difficulty. "Do whatever you want, whatever feels good to you."

"I want to make you feel good, too," she said thickly as she nibbled on the flat muscles across his chest.

"Oh, baby, you do. You do."

Finding a small, hard male nipple in the fur, she nipped at it experimentally and heard a groan rip from deep within him.

"If you do that too many times," he said roughly, "this'll be over before it's started."

Liking the way he reacted, she did it again and felt him jerk from head to foot. "You like that, too?" she asked breathlessly.

"God, yes."

So she did it again, and for her sake Dare rolled on top of her and kissed her into breathlessness. He'd been ready to go almost from the outset, but he wanted Andrea to be right at his side. With lips and tongue he suckled first one breast and then the other, while his hand foraged downward toward her silken secrets. His fingers didn't get much below her navel before she was writhing against him and sobbing something that sounded like a plea.

With each kiss his own control had grown weaker, and he knew he wasn't going to be able to keep his own promises about drawing this out, not this time.

"Andrea? Andrea, my timing is terrible, but this is important. You're not protected are you?"

Her hands were clutching at his head, holding him to her breast, and he felt them suddenly grow still.

"Andrea?"

"It's okay," she groaned. She took the pill to regulate her cycle, and never had she been so grateful for that little inconvenience.

"You're sure?"

"It's my career. Dare, please. *Please!*"

Slowly he slid over her, parting her legs gently with his hands, rising to his knees.

"Oh, baby," he sighed against her mouth. "Touch me, Andrea. Touch me."

With the instincts of the ages, she reached for his velvet hardness, felt him stiffen and groan with a pleasure equal to her own. The sound thrilled her, and she guided him closer, needing that hardness as if it were a lost part of her.

"Now, Dare," she begged. "Now. Now."

"Yes, honey. Yes."

He thrust slowly, hanging on to the dregs of his control, giving her time to accommodate him. She was so tight that he knew she must hurt, but when he felt the barrier and hesitated, she arched up suddenly and fully sheathed him in her welcoming softness. A cry escaped her, and Dare grew instantly still, lifting his head to look into her face. He knew there was no way to avoid the pain, but he felt suddenly helpless and ignorant. How long would it last? Was there anything he should do to help her? Her eyes were closed, and her mouth was open on a gasp that told him nothing.

"Andrea? Are you all right?"

Her eyelids fluttered, and her hands tightened on his waist. "I'm fine," she whispered. "I'm fine." The pain was passing off, leaving her aware of a wondrous, satisfying fullness.

"So good," she sighed. "You feel so good." She arched toward him.

He needed no more. Pulling back, he thrust again, and she

met him eagerly, long legs twining around his hips, hands gripping his shoulders. "Yes," she groaned. "Yes."

Higher and higher he took them, racing for a place she could only guess at. A hard, exquisite pressure grew in her, seeking his thrusts, until it filled her completely, and the universe focused in that small place where they joined together, meeting, retreating, seeking.

Suddenly Andrea shattered as she never had before, bursting into blazing fireworks of scattering sparks, convulsing just as Dare convulsed with a hard groan, his short sharp jerks answering the rippling contractions inside her. His head fell to her shoulder; her arms fell to the bed. Only slowly, however, did her legs release him, reluctant to give up the fullness of their sharing.

And only slowly did Andrea come back to herself. "If that isn't illegal," she said huskily, feeling dizzy and weak, "it ought to be."

Dare kissed her and rolled off her, drawing her carefully to his side so that her head was cradled on his shoulder. It was on the tip of his tongue to tell her that never had it been so good for him, but some instinct warned him not to. She could believe the wonder of it came from her inexperience, but she wouldn't be able to believe that about him. She wanted no strings, so he would give her none. But God, it wasn't easy. If he had wanted her before, he wanted her more now.

"Do you have any aspirin?" Andrea asked.

Dare, who was engaged in gently stroking her arm with his fingertips, paused. "Headache?"

"I think I overdid it with my shoulder."

"Bad?"

"Not really. Just a little too much to ignore is all."

He dropped a kiss on her temple. "I'll be right back."

Rising, he thoughtfully pulled the comforter to her chin before padding away on bare feet.

Andrea decided she liked water beds. This was her first experience of one, and she thought it felt like floating. No hardness to remind her of reality. Reality was that she was leaving in a month and would never see Dare again. Reality was knowing how much she was going to hurt.

Turning over, she pressed her face into the pillow. She tried to tell herself she felt this way because he had just set her free of a lot of misconceptions, had just showed her something so wonderful she was greedy for more. But she didn't believe her own rationalizations. It was more than the last couple of hours. It was the way his lips twitched and his eyes twinkled when she zinged him. It was the way he intuitively understood what it meant to be Charlie Burke's daughter. It was the way he was so firmly and squarely centered in himself that he wasn't threatened by her. It was the way he seemed to take pleasure in Andrea Burke just the way she was.

"Andrea?" His voice was quiet, his touch on her shoulder gentle.

She rolled over at once and tried to smile at him. Dare saw past the smile, however. In the smoky mists that swirled in her green eyes, he saw the shadow of longing and loss. He'd put that there. Suddenly he didn't feel so good about himself.

Andrea took the aspirin he offered, swallowing it with water. The scar on her left shoulder was an angry red, puckered. Dare touched it lightly with a fingertip and thought how incredibly brave she was. Not grandstand brave. Andrea wasn't a grandstander. Just quietly and continuously day-in-and-day-out brave. Bending forward, he kissed the scar.

She closed her arms around him, hugging him, fingers stroking the nape of his neck.

"Andrea?"

"Sir?"

He smiled against her shoulder. "When do you go back on duty?"

"What day is it?"

"It just turned into Christmas Day ten minutes ago."

"Then I go back on duty tomorrow. Lieutenant Dolan wanted an extra day at New Year's, so he's working today."

"Finally learning to delegate, I see."

"Yes, sir."

"Andrea?" She smelled so sweet.

"Yes?"

"Would I be imposing if I asked you to stay with me?"

She drew a deep breath. "No," she said softly. "You wouldn't be imposing at all."

He raised his head, looking into her hazy green eyes. "Do you want to stay with me, Andrea?"

"There's nothing I want more in the whole world, Dare."

He brushed the lightest of kisses on her lips. "Sweet Andrea. Tell me something."

"Yes, sir."

"Are you a Christmas morning person, or a Christmas Eve person?"

"How do you mean?"

"Do you like to open your presents in the morning or on Christmas Eve?"

"We always opened them in the morning at home. But I always thought Christmas Eve would be more romantic."

His fingers found their way into her short, silky hair. Before Andrea, he'd always preferred long hair on a woman. Somehow her strawberry blond boyish cut had become incredibly sexy to him. He liked the way it hid nothing of her face, her ears, her neck. He even liked her Huck Finn freckles.

"So you've thought about romance from time to time, Captain?"

"Once in a while it has crossed my mind."

"We missed Christmas Eve."

"I didn't notice."

"But it's still not morning. We can pretend it's still Christmas Eve."

She considered gravely. "I don't see any problem with that. I wouldn't find it difficult to pretend at all."

"Tell me what would be a romantic Christmas Eve for you, Andrea."

She smiled suddenly, a soft, melting smile. "I just had it."

His smile answered her. "But you didn't open your presents."

"But I did. The best present of all."

He couldn't help it; he had to kiss her, had to kiss her until her eyes glazed and she melted into softness in his arms.

"What if I told you," he asked huskily, "that there's a present under the tree right now for you."

"For me?"

"For you. I was going to risk your undying wrath and drop it by the BOQ this morning."

He gave her his robe to wear, a thick royal blue terry cloth robe that dwarfed her, but for once in her life Andrea didn't mind being made to feel small. Dare pulled on his jeans and a gray sweatshirt, and they returned to the living room hand in hand.

"Brandy?" he asked.

"I'd really like coffee, if it wouldn't be too much trouble."

"No trouble at all. But it might keep you awake."

The smile she gave him stirred the banked fires in his loins. It became a feat of willpower to walk the short distance into his kitchen and make the coffee.

Together they sat on the couch, Andrea with her legs tucked under her, sipping coffee and eating cookies.

"At my place in Montana," Dare said, "I have a fireplace. Two, actually. One in the living room and one in the master bedroom."

"You have a house there?"

"Yep. And right now we'd be sitting in front of a blazing fire. Outside, snow would be falling gently on the deck, and I'd have the floods on, so we could see it through the glass doors, behind the Christmas tree."

"Sounds nice." The words were a sigh.

"It is nice," he agreed. "I've had the house for five years now, and I spend my leave there. There's always enough snow for skiing. And the summers are super. I practically live outside when I'm there."

"Where are you from originally, Dare?"

"Montana." He kissed her, running his tongue along her lips. "You taste like chocolate chip cookies. Want your present?"

Her eyes looked dazed. It tickled him to death that his kiss could daze his cool Captain Burke.

"But, Dare, I don't have anything for you."

"Oh, yes, you do." He kissed her again, this time slipping his hand inside the terry robe to cup her breast. Andrea trembled, leaning into him. "You have plenty for me," he murmured against her hair, "and I plan to open my presents again and again."

He drew away reluctantly and went to the tree, picking up a

medium-sized box. "I figured this would make you furious enough to splutter at me. Maybe now it won't."

He stood over her uneasily while she tore away the red paper. She could tell he was nervous about it, so she drew the moment out, glancing up at him with that devilish gleam he knew so well.

"Captain Burke," he said finally, "do I need to remind you that it isn't wise to keep your CO in uncomfortable suspense?"

"Why are you in uncomfortable suspense, Colonel? What is it? A chastity belt?"

He gave a muffled laugh. "Worse. I saw it at the mall, and from the minute I saw it I was possessed. I had to give it to you, even if you threw it back in my face. Go on. Open it."

"Sounds to me like you were the one being unwise, sir," she said primly, and then gasped as she opened the box.

Inside was green silk, beautiful, brilliant green silk. Lifting it gently from the box, she tested its softness and admired its loveliness. It was a peignoir, she realized.

"Will you put it on?" he asked huskily.

She raised her face slowly, and he saw tears sparkling on her lashes.

"Andrea? Andrea, if it offends you, throw it away." He was suddenly panic-stricken. Her spluttering fury was one thing. Her tears were altogether something else.

"It doesn't offend me," she said, a catch in her voice. Rising, she took the box with her to the bedroom.

He had touched her, she realized as she slipped into the peignoir, her hands trembling almost too much to manage the bows. He had reached down inside her and found an Andrea that had never been allowed to exist. In there somewhere was an Andrea who wanted to be beautiful for a man, an Andrea who loved beautiful things, who craved the softness of silk and the heat of a man's need. Inside, buried in the tomboy, hidden in the officer, was a woman, and Dare had found her and touched her.

There was a full-length mirror on the back of the bedroom door, and Andrea stood before it, looking at herself in emerald silk. The peignoir concealed nothing, really. It was meant to be viewed only by a lover. She looked at herself and realized this was how Dare saw her, realized that he had guessed at something she'd never known about herself. To him, she was all the things she believed herself to be, but she was also more, much more.

He was right. Yesterday she would have thrown it in his face in fury. Tonight she hurried back down the hall to share her discovery with him.

Dare was pacing, scared to death he'd offended her beyond bearing. He called himself seven kinds of idiot for giving in to the compulsion to give her that gown.

"Dare?"

He turned swiftly. Andrea stood just inside the living room, wearing the peignoir. He sucked in his breath at the sight of her, her every curve outlined in clinging, soft silk. Her eyes were shining at him, as if he'd given her the most precious gift in the world.

"Is it...?" She hesitated. "Is it what you hoped?"

"You're everything I hoped for," he said huskily, deliberately changing the pronoun. "And more. Andrea, you're stunning."

She smiled then, and fresh tears filled her eyes. "I didn't know this was me, Dare," she said unsteadily, and then she flew into his arms.

He held her tenderly, kissing away the tears. "Andrea, sweetheart, you're not upset?"

"No, sir," she answered forthrightly. "Somehow I'm tickled to death."

"Quit calling me sir."

"Yes, sir."

He lifted his head, looking down into her gently smiling face. "If you call me sir when I'm making love to you, I'm going to be very upset."

"Yes, sir." Her lips twitched, and her damp eyes gleamed wickedly.

"Andrea, you drive me to the edge of madness."

"Sorry, sir."

There was only one way to deal with this insubordination, he decided. Scooping her up easily in his arms, he carried her back down the hall to bed. In a very short while she was no longer sir-ring him. She was saying his name in a very satisfactory way indeed.

This time he turned the bedside lamp on, a warm glow across

the silk of Andrea's peignoir. For the longest time Dare caressed her through the silk. It was little barrier to his hands, and the glide of its cool smoothness on her skin provided her with a newly erotic sensation.

"I bought this gown right after Thanksgiving," he told her softly as he shaped her breast with his hand and watched her nipple tighten against the silk. "I lost count of the nights I lay here in the dark and imagined you just like this."

She drew a soft, shaky breath. "Did you?" Her insides were turning liquid. It had never entered her head that she might be the subject of his fantasies. "I thought about you, too," she admitted unsteadily.

His blue eyes lifted to hers. "Did you?" With thumb and forefinger he teased an exquisitely sensitive nipple. "Did you imagine me touching you like this?"

Her eyelids fluttered heavily. "No."

His fingers paused in their caress. "Why not? Don't you like this?"

Her hand closed over his, holding it to her breast. "Don't stop," she sighed. "Dare..."

Lowering his head, he suckled her through the silk and groaned when he felt her twist eagerly toward him.

"How could I imagine this?" she asked breathlessly, hands grasping his head, hips rising toward him. "I had no idea."

"You still have no idea," he murmured, lifting his head to kiss her mouth. While his tongue stroked hers rhythmically, erotically, he slowly drew up the skirt of her gown. Only when his fingers gained unfettered access to her dewy core did he lift his head. Looking down at her, he smiled. "But I've got more than a few secrets to share with you, honey." Parting her moist petals, he stroked her deeply, gently, and listened to the catch of her breath. "Is that good?"

"Yes. Oh, yes." So good it almost hurt. Turning toward him, she flung her arms around his neck and pressed her face to his shoulder. "Dare, please..."

"Shh," he said soothingly. "Shh." He wanted this night to be as perfect as it was possible for him to make it. Eventually, though, he gave in to her pleas and his own needs. He rose above her and looked down at her as she lay in the pool of green silk that was bunched around her torso.

"It's better than I imagined," he said huskily. "*You're* better."

Before she could gather her wits enough to respond, his driving thrust carried them both away.

Chapter 9

It had begun to snow during the night, and Dare stood before the window of his kitchen looking out at North Dakota's all-too-common white whirlwind. Snow so dry and fine never had an opportunity to settle in the winds that never ceased. It was unlikely that they'd gotten more than an inch of fresh snowfall, but the wind had drifted it into a four-foot dune across his driveway and front yard. Snowed-in, he thought with pleasure. He couldn't even see the neighboring houses except as faint ghosts in the blowing snow. In all likelihood this meant no one would decide to pay a courtesy call on a lonely bachelor this Christmas day. He couldn't have planned it better.

The coffeepot made the loud gurgles that signaled it had finished brewing. Dare reached for it and filled two mugs, then put them on a tray beside two plates filled with coffee cake. Ordinarily he avoided sweets, but Christmas demanded things that were out of the ordinary or it would be just an ordinary day.

Strange things happened to him when he thought about the fact that Andrea was soundly asleep in his bed. His heart zipped into high speed, his loins ached, and his mouth grew dry. Reaching back through his memory as he poured two glasses of orange juice, he tried to remember the last time merely thinking about a woman in his bed had caused such a strong reaction. Adolescence?

He lit a cigarette and returned his attention to the white world outside. He was afraid to wake her, he realized. He was afraid she would regret last night and look at him with hurt or horror. It was very possible she might, because there was nothing as awkward as the bright light of morning after a passion-filled night.

Muttering a soft oath, Dare stubbed out his cigarette and picked up the tray. The best way to handle it, of course, was not to let her wake alone while he stewed out here in the kitchen.

Andrea woke the same way she'd fallen asleep in the wee hours of the morning, with a strong arm around her and fingers lightly caressing her bare arm.

"I brought you coffee," Dare murmured near her ear, his breath warm and tickling.

"Mmm." Stirring, she turned a little toward him. Her eyes remained closed, but he could see the beginning of a smile on her lips.

"And coffee cake," he added softly.

"Mmm." She sighed, and her smile grew a little wider.

"Orange juice."

"Coffee," she said on a mere breath. "Coffee and thee."

"Me?"

Her eyes opened sleepily, misty green pools. "Most especially thee."

Dare felt his own smile start to dawn. "In which order, Captain Burke?"

"That's the Colonel's decision, sir."

"The coffee will get cold."

"Too bad." Her arm slipped around his neck, causing her to wince slightly.

"Andrea? Your shoulder hurts."

"Just a little." Her eyes opened wider. "Don't let that keep you from waking me up."

He trailed a string of kisses along her smooth jaw. "Just how awake do you want to be?"

"As awake as it's possible to be."

Her hand found his cheek, tracing the strong bones and fine lines, as she watched the blue flames begin to burn in his eyes.

"The first time I saw you in uniform," she said, "that morning in my office, I knew I was a sham."

"Sham?" He ran his thumb lightly over her lower lip.

"Sham. I knew right then I was really a woman after all."

"And what a woman," he said roughly as her silken thigh rubbed against his.

Andrea's smile grew satisfied as she felt his building response to her light touches. "Yes, sir," she murmured. "There's something about the way you look in a uniform that makes me forget I'm wearing one, too."

Dare sucked in a sharp breath as she began to lightly pinch the kernel of his nipple. Inexperienced as she was, she was teaching him things he hadn't known about himself.

"Too much?"

"Not enough. What other tricks have you got?" His arm tightened convulsively around her.

"I don't know yet," she answered gravely. "Do you want me to experiment on you?"

He drew a ragged breath and looked down into her hazy, hot green eyes. "You go right ahead and try anything that occurs to you, honey. In the meantime, I'm going to try a few tricks of my own."

Bending his head, he kissed her deeply while his hand foraged along her length. When he was sufficiently pleased by the ragged, rapid way she breathed, and by the way her hips kept rolling gently toward him, he sat up, throwing the comforter aside.

Andrea made a protesting sound and her eyes fluttered open. "Dare..."

"Hush, baby. It's experiment time."

Gently he pressed her legs apart and knelt between them. Andrea was dazed enough to let him do as he wished while crazy half-thoughts ran through her head about how magnificent he looked, how big he was, how...

Dare sat back on his heels and drew Andrea's hips up onto his knees, pressing her legs yet farther apart. He knew the exact moment she realized how exposed she was to his eyes. Her breath locked in her throat, and her eyes flew open. He saw wild color flare in her cheeks and heard her murmured protest, but he also saw the unmistakable flare of excitement in her eyes.

And she *was* excited. No one had ever looked at her this way, and part of her wanted to hide, but another part of her was inflamed. Frozen, caught between conflicting impulses, she could only watch as he reached out with a forefinger and touched her. She jerked.

"Easy, Andrea," he whispered roughly. "Easy. It's okay. You're so lovely, so perfect. Don't hide from me."

She couldn't have hidden. His gently stroking, gently seeking fingers made a joke of her last inhibitions. Last night's hungers paled beside the desire he stoked in her now.

"Let go, Andrea," he crooned. "Do it for me, honey. Let it all go." He wanted it all, all of her, all of the wildly passionate woman she hadn't yet fully unleashed. Dare had always been a considerate lover, but never before had he wanted so badly to strip away the civilized veneer, to crack the last bonds of self-control in his partner. He wanted Andrea Burke, woman elemental, without a vestige of Captain Burke left to come between them. He wanted her complete and total surrender to the fires that raged between them. He wanted her partnership in this adventure.

And he got it. Suddenly, without warning, she sat up and straddled him, impaling herself on him, wrapping her arms tightly around his shoulders. Her short nails dug into his back, and her teeth closed on the soft flesh of his shoulder.

Grasping her soft rump, he almost shouted his pleasure as she groaned deeply. Lifting her, he let her settle slowly on him and watched as she threw her head back and gasped. His own needs were pounding at him, but he gritted his teeth, wanting to give her every possible bit of pleasure and sensation before he succumbed.

"Dare!" She sounded almost frightened.

"I'm here, Andrea. I'm here. I'll keep you safe. I'll catch you when you fall." He meant every word.

Her eyelids fluttered, and she arched backward. "Fall with me," she gasped.

"Baby, I fell a long time ago." But he let her pull him down, and as soon as he felt her beneath him he lost it, lost it all. With her legs wrapped around his waist, he fell into a hard, driving rhythm that pushed them to the brink and then over.

* * *

"I'm embarrassed."

The muffled words against his shoulder brought a smile to Dare's face. He lay on his side, holding her snugly against him, his leg thrown possessively over her hip. "Why should you be embarrassed?" he asked gently. "Nothing happened here that we didn't do together."

"Mmph."

He chuckled. "You were shameless, Captain."

She groaned and burrowed her face deeper into his shoulder. "I liked it a whole lot. It's what I wanted."

"Well, you're the CO. We aim to please."

He laughed then. "Andrea, Andrea, you're a marvel. You delight me. Everything about you delights me."

Slowly, blushing profusely, she tilted her head back and stole a look at him. "Really?" she asked shyly.

"Really and truly."

Yielding a sigh, she relaxed against him. "I like everything about you, too."

Bending, he kissed the tip of her nose. "Are you ready for your coffee? Shall I bring a fresh cup in here, or do you want to get up?"

"I think I'll get up. I've been decadent enough for one morning."

"I bet I could make you even more decadent."

Green eyes met blue. "No contest," she said after a moment, and grinned her elfish grin. Suddenly she threw her arms around him and hugged him tight. "Thank you, Dare," she whispered. "I'll never be able to thank you enough."

His throat tightened uncomfortably. When he spoke, his voice was rough. "Come on, Captain. Get your pretty little rump out of bed before you miss your coffee again."

Fresh from a shower and wrapped in one of his flannel shirts, Andrea joined Dare at the breakfast table in the kitchen. He'd used the time to rustle up eggs and bacon, having seen Andrea's morning appetite once before. She dug in like a trooper. Smoking a cigarette and drinking coffee, Dare watched her eat.

"How would you like to spend Christmas day, Andrea?"

She set her fork down and picked up her mug, taking a sip of coffee before replying. "I keep wishing there weren't so many complications, but there are." Her green eyes lifted to regard him steadily. "Reality won't go away, Colonel."

Sighing, he stubbed out his cigarette. "I know it won't. I don't live in a fool's paradise either, Captain."

"I never meant to imply that you did."

He arched a questioning brow at her. "Are you turning into Captain Burke again?"

She smiled faintly. "I never stopped being Captain Burke."

"Okay, I get it. I'll take you home."

"No!" She startled him by reaching out and grabbing his forearm. "That isn't what I meant, either! Will you just hear me out?"

Dare settled back in his chair and wondered why the devil he'd been so hell-bent on tangling himself up with a woman. He'd forgotten how confusing they could be. Lighting another cigarette, he sighed. "Burke, you're going to be the death of me. Get to the point, will you?"

"I will, but it's not easy. It's embarrassing."

"I thought we'd dealt with embarrassment."

"We did." Color rose to her cheeks again, and Dare was charmed. God, she delighted him!

"But," she continued bravely, "that doesn't make it easier."

"Just close your eyes and spit it out," he said kindly. "I promise I won't laugh."

"Well, actually," Andrea said hesitantly, "what I want to do today is—live in a fool's paradise."

It took him a moment to comprehend, but when he did, he smiled with such gentleness that Andrea blinked. "Consider it done," he told her.

"You don't mind?"

"Why would I mind? It's exactly the way I'd like to spend the day myself."

"Really?"

"Really." And, Charlie Burke, may you burn for what you did to your daughter, Dare thought grimly. Competent, capable Captain Burke had absolutely no confidence in herself when she shucked the uniform and the role that went with it. Was she such a disappointment, Charlie? Dare wondered. Were you so blind?

"Dare?"

Andrea was looking worriedly at him, and he realized she must have seen some of the anger he felt on his face. At once he stomped down on it and smiled at her. "Sorry, I just got to thinking about something else. Lack of sleep, I guess. What kind of fool's paradise do you have in mind?"

Again her color heightened. "Well, I'm not really sure. I've never lived in one before."

His smile deepened. "Come on, Andrea, you admitted last night that you occasionally indulged in a romantic fantasy or two. Everyone has. Share one of yours."

But her chin took on the stubborn set he recognized, and she shook her head.

"It's hardly fair," he pointed out, "if we only live out *my* romantic fantasies."

"I think yours will do just fine."

He considered arguing with her, then decided against it. "Well, you can't say you didn't ask for it."

That evening, by the light of the Christmas tree, they lay side by side against pillows on the floor. Andrea curled against Dare, her head on his shoulder, and listened contentedly to the slow, steady sound of his heartbeat. Well, she had asked for it, she thought, but never in a million years would she have envisioned a romantic day that involved making Christmas dinner and playing cards. It had been a homey day, the kind of day she'd missed all her life, it seemed. And, surprisingly, it had been very romantic.

Dare lifted her hand from his chest and brought it to his lips. "Tired?" he asked.

"Pleasantly so." Tilting her head, she looked up at him. "Do you have something in mind?"

"Like a starving man has food in mind."

A chuckle escaped Andrea. "You're not starving."

Dare turned a little, bringing Andrea closer. "Oh, yes, I am. I haven't made love to you in ten whole hours."

"Well, *you* were the one who wanted to play games."

"How about a game right now?"

"I might be persuaded," she said demurely.

"What kind of persuasion do you need?"

"Oh, a little of this and a little of that."

"A little of this?" he asked, his hand grazing her breast. "Or some of that?" He slipped his hand between her legs and pressed gently.

Andrea's eyes grew wide. "All of it," she answered, suddenly breathless. "All of it."

But all too soon it was time for Andrea to leave. They both needed their sleep, for tomorrow was a duty day, and neither of them argued against the inevitable. Still, they lingered over a last cup of coffee in the kitchen, watching the clock tick steadily toward midnight, knowing the fantasy was over.

"Andrea?" Dare spoke into a silence that had grown too long.

She lifted her head and gave him a questioning look.

"I just want you to know. Regardless of what your father told you about pilots, I've never gone in for one night stands or casual relationships."

"Oh." Her color heightened a shade.

"In fact," he continued, "this is the first time in my life I've gone into something like this knowing there was no future."

Her eyes shied away from the intensity of his stare, and she concentrated on her coffee cup. "Are you saying it shouldn't have happened?"

"No, I'm saying I don't give myself cheaply. I know you don't, either. So someday, down the road, when you think back over this, don't feel cheapened by it."

Slowly, very slowly, her eyes rose to meet his once again. "No," she whispered. "Oh, no, I wouldn't ever think that. But, Dare..."

He waved a dismissing hand. "Forget it, Andrea. I told you, I already know all the arguments and all the reasons. Your career comes first. Don't worry about it. Tomorrow, when we're captain and colonel again, I just want you to be sure that this is one of my treasured memories. Don't ever doubt it." Standing, he reached for her, pulling her to her feet.

"One last kiss, Andrea," he said. "One last kiss. And if you ever, ever again think you'd like to be with me, don't hesitate to call me. I mean it."

Before she could answer, he covered her mouth with his, drinking deeply of the sweetness he feared he might never know again. One last time he held her close, squeezing his eyes shut against the ache that had taken root in his heart. "This is a relationship, Andrea," he whispered. "Like it or not. We'll do it on your terms, but you can't escape the fact that it exists."

"All quiet on the Northern Front, skipper," Nickerson said to her the following morning as he entered her office. "Nothing happened, and Lieutenant Dolan managed nothing very well."

Halting before her desk, he peered down at her. "And *you* look like the morning after a heavy-duty night before. You get hit by a truck or something?"

"Or something." Andrea managed a travesty of a smile. "Just some trouble sleeping, Nick. Nothing exciting."

"I've seen Marines look better after a forty-eight-hour pass in Saigon."

Andrea chuckled. "I imagine they didn't feel much worse."

"Shoulder bothering you?"

"A little." Which was the truth, although not the truth of why she hadn't slept. No, she'd lain awake all night wishing she were in Dare's bed instead of her own, which was why she should never have broken her own rules by going over there in the first place. And Nick's eyes were too sharp and too wise for her comfort.

Nick poured himself a cup of coffee and sat in one of the straight-backed metal chairs that faced her desk. "You sure nothing's wrong?"

"What could be wrong? Honestly, I just didn't get enough sleep. A few more cups of coffee and I'll pass for normal. So we didn't have any more intruders?"

"Not a thing. Never fear, we'll make up for all the peace and quiet on New Year's Eve. You know, I was talking to Halliday about how somebody could slip past the electronic security system, and he says it can't be done."

Andrea rubbed her forehead. "That's Halliday. Those circuits of his are infallible. *Somebody* got past them."

"I told him that. I think I'm in his black books."

"That'll do it, all right."

"But I was thinking, what if Halliday's right?"

Alerted, Andrea dropped her hand from her forehead and looked at Nick. "What if?"

"*If* Halliday's right, then it's an inside job, right?"

"What's an inside job?"

"Scuttlebutt has it that it wasn't a goose that took out the nose of that B-52."

Andrea gripped the edge of her desk. "I'd be very interested in the source of this scuttlebutt."

Nickerson ran his index finger alongside his jaw. "You know what they say. You can't keep a secret from military wives, and once a military wife knows, it ain't no secret."

"Damn." Andrea slumped back in her chair. Unfortunately she'd experienced the truth of that sexist military aphorism more than once during her life. Like the time the Tactical Fighter Wing had been secretly sent to Cambodia. They were not to tell their wives a thing except that they were flying out for a few days. Before the first plane even took off, all twenty-five thousand people at the air base had known their departure time and destination. Too often GIs felt that keeping a secret didn't mean they couldn't tell their wives. And unfortunately the wives too often felt that rules about secrecy didn't apply to them, because they were civilians.

"I take it," Nickerson said, "that scuttlebutt is true. Which means we've got a king-size problem. What's being done about it?"

"I can't tell you that."

"Well, damn near everybody's talking about it, Captain. If that's a problem, maybe you'd better tell Colonel MacLendon."

Just then the phone on Andrea's desk rang, and she looked at it as if it were a rattlesnake. "Speak of the devil," she said to Nick. "How much do you want to bet?"

"I ain't a betting man, skipper, but I might take this one. Bet his First Shirt's just dumped the same story in his lap."

Groaning inwardly, Andrea lifted the receiver. "Captain Burke."

"Andrea, we have a problem," Dare's voice said into her ear. "I want you and Nickerson over here on the double."

"What's wrong?"

"The rumor mill's running at full speed, and we need to take steps to contain it."

"We're on our way." Replacing the receiver, Andrea looked at Nick. "You would have won this one. He wants us both over there five minutes ago." Rising, she grabbed her parka from the coat tree in the corner. "You know, Nick, I could resign."

"Been a long tour?" Nick asked, matching his pace to hers as they headed for the parking lot.

"No, just a long two months."

"That'll do it."

Already present at Dare's office were the Bomb Wing deputy commander, Major West, and the Wing's First Sergeant, Matt Hawley. Dare was nodding in response to something Hawley was saying, but his eyes followed Andrea as she entered and took a seat. Instantly he saw the weariness on her face and guessed she hadn't slept any better than he had. When her eyes lifted to his, she colored faintly and looked quickly down. Dare forced himself to look away, worried that one of them would give the game away, wishing that he could just go to her and take her into his arms.

God! Andrea thought, clasping her hands to still their trembling. One look at him and her heart started thundering like a stampeding horse. And how was it possible for him to look better this morning than she remembered him? How was she going to survive the next month if she felt this way every time she saw him?

"You've heard the rumors?" Dare asked Nickerson.

"Yes, sir. I was just telling Captain Burke about them when you called."

"Well, we can't have people buzzing about a terrorist attack on this base. First of all, we don't know it *was* a terrorist act. It might have been the act of someone who's mentally ill, or someone with a grudge. Secondly, if the rumor gets off the base, the locals will be upset, maybe panicked. Some of you remember the uproar a couple of years ago when a jet engine fell off a truck and word got around that it contained radioactive cesium. I don't need to tell you that the Department of the Air Force isn't going to be very happy with us if this hits the pages of the local newspaper. And if it makes headlines here, it'll undoubtedly make the national news. So put your heads to work and come up with a suitably innocent official explanation for what happened to that plane."

"Too bad a goose won't hack it," Hawley remarked. "None of the locals would believe that, though."

"Even if we had feathers?" Major West asked. "What if we showed them feathers and blood and claimed it was a sick goose that hadn't migrated."

"A brain-sick goose," suggested Nickerson. "Maybe the base vet could come up with some disease that could make a goose crazy."

"Something that doesn't kill," Andrea put in. "The geese migrated more than a month before the accident."

Dare nodded. "It would work if he can come up with something legitimate." His eyes lingered on Andrea just an instant too long. "Hawley, get Captain Emory up here, will you?" Emory was the base veterinarian. As he was largely involved in the care of the police dogs and, when time allowed, servicemen's pets, Dare doubted he would know much more than the rest of them about geese. Still, it was worth looking into.

Dare sat back in his chair, steepling his hands on his chest. "You know, the only people who knew this wasn't a goose were a couple of mechanics, Captain Burke, and myself. I guess one of the mechanics must have shot off his mouth. To his wife, probably."

Andrea and Nickerson exchanged amused glances.

Major West spoke. "I'm not sure any of the pilots really believed it was a goose, sir. Somebody could have speculated."

"I guess, but you're telling me that somebody was talking about explosives."

"When you've got a hole that size in the nose of an aircraft, explosives make sense in the absence of other causes."

"Well, the source of the rumor has to be someone in the Bomb Wing," Dare said. "West, you and Hawley see if you can track it down. I know it'll be damn near impossible, but try anyhow."

Dare swiveled his chair suddenly and looked at Andrea. "I know you've beefed up security, but damn it, I want something more than that. I want to get to the bottom of this, Burke."

"We all do, sir."

One corner of his mouth quirked. "Point taken. Sorry. I had trouble sleeping last night."

Andrea felt Nickerson glance at her, but she managed to keep her face impassive, although some perverse part of her took delight in the fact that Dare had been as miserable as she was last night. And what had Nickerson sensed that made him look at her like that? Was she wearing a sign on her forehead?

Availing himself of one of the privileges of rank, Dare lit a cigarette. He should have quit the damn things completely by now, but here he was, still smoking half a pack a day. More, if he got to thinking too much about Andrea. She didn't look as if she'd slept too well, either. He took some satisfaction in that, remembering how only a few short hours ago he'd been standing at his bedroom window wishing for sleep that wouldn't come. He'd been doing too much of that since Andrea popped into his life.

Captain Emory arrived only a few minutes later. "I suppose," he said when he'd been briefed, "there must be something I could come up with." He pushed his glasses up on the narrow bridge of his nose. "You understand, I'll need to research the problem, Colonel. I'm not exactly familiar with Canadian geese."

"But does it sound plausible?" Dare asked.

"Oh, yes, off the cuff, I'd say it's a possibility. Of course, we really don't understand all the mechanisms of migration. It's entirely possible such an event could occur and we'd never know why. As in the case of that whale in Alaska. We may never understand what happened there."

Dare rubbed his chin. "If worse comes to worse, I guess we'll just call it a freak accident, but I'd really rather have something more convincing than that, given the rumors. And goose feathers. I need some goose feathers."

Emory smiled. "Oh, I can provide those, Colonel. My wife makes artsy-craftsy things with them. She'll never miss a couple."

"Just make sure she doesn't know you've taken them. All I need is another wife in on what's going on. Okay, people, that's our story, then. A goose hit the plane. If Captain Emory can come up with a disease, so much the better. If not, we'll just go with the freak accident idea, unless somebody has a better one."

But nobody had a better explanation for a six-foot hole in the cockpit of a B-52.

"What are we going to do about it, ma'am?" Nickerson asked Andrea as they drove back to the security squadron headquarters.

"Do?"

"Well, somebody blew a hole in a plane with plastique. That's not something you overlook. We've got to find out who did it."

"People are looking into it, Nick. I can't tell you any more than that."

"Why aren't *we* looking into it?"

Andrea sighed. "I have it on good authority that we don't have the training or experience to handle this case."

Nick frowned. "Oh yeah? Maybe not the technical end of it, but we know people, Skipper. We need a list of possible suspects, and then we find a motive. Basic police work."

"The suspect list is pretty big. Just about any aircraft mechanic would have unsupervised access to those planes. If it wasn't a mechanic, it could be one of our cops, because it had to be somebody who could get through security. That's another couple of dozen people, even if we allow only a narrow time frame. It could be any one of the aircrews, too. So how long is the list now? A hundred? More?"

Nick scowled. "So we eliminate as many as we can."

"Sure. Who do we eliminate? People without any gripes? *Every* GI has a gripe. Besides, it's hands-off. I told you."

"That doesn't mean we can't *think* about it, ma'am."

"I guess not." Rubbing the back of her neck, Andrea sighed. "Sorry, Nick. Not enough sleep. You think about it. I'll think about it. But frankly, I just can't imagine anyone I know wanting to blow a hole in that aircraft."

"Isn't that always what the next door neighbor says after the ax murder? *He wouldn't hurt a fly.*"

Tired or not, Andrea laughed. It was true, of course. Nobody could ever imagine that somebody they knew would do such a thing. "You're right, Nick. That's what they always say."

Chapter 10

Several afternoons later, Andrea sat at her desk, studying the list of names her staff had compiled. Finding people with the opportunity to get to that aircraft had been easy. What with aircrews, mechanics, and cops, the list held thirty-three names. Discovering who might have a motive was a different matter altogether. OSI had probably compiled this same list of names weeks ago, and they'd gotten nowhere.

Absently rubbing her shoulder to ease the faint ache that still plagued her, Andrea leaned back in her chair and stared off into space. She would probably be long gone before they discovered the culprit, if they ever did. There just wasn't enough evidence to go on.

Why would anyone do such a thing? Greed and revenge were the commonest motivations among people. It was possible that some airman had been paid to set an explosive on that bomber, but that still left the question of the motivation of whoever had paid him. Greed couldn't be behind that, because it was against official policy for the Air Force to give in to extortion. That left revenge and terrorism, and she had trouble accepting the notion of terrorism, because nobody had called the local or national news. Where was the point in doing something like this if you didn't call the news and get your free publicity out of it? On the other hand, if somebody had a grudge against a member of that plane's crew, then there were easier and surer ways of achieving revenge.

So what did that leave? No motive at all?

Frustrated with the circles she seemed to be going in, tired from too many nights of not enough sleep and too much thinking about a certain Colonel who appeared to have forgotten her existence, Andrea decided to leave Dolan in charge for the night. She would have an early dinner at the O-Club, followed by a hot shower, and then she'd hit the sack.

It wasn't steak night, and it was too early for the evening crowd, so the dining room was fairly empty. A group of B-52 crew members on alert sat in one corner eating dinner and laughing together. Their flight suits indicated their alert status and gave them precedence, whether in being served dinner or in the checkout line at the exchange.

In another corner a young couple, looking as if they were barely old enough to be married, argued with quiet intensity. Andrea took a corner for herself and sat with her back to the wall as she nursed a beer and waited for her dinner.

The room was not brightly lit, and Andrea wasn't certain how long she had stared absently at the laughing pilots before she realized that one of them, glimpsed occasionally as another pilot leaned backward, was Dare MacLendon.

What was he doing with the alert pilots? she wondered blankly, and then looked quickly away, unwilling to let him catch her staring. She wouldn't give him the satisfaction, not when he'd ignored her since Christmas. But wasn't that what she wanted? No strings? No messy involvement? Her mind said yes, but her heart kept clamoring for more.

Which was why she should never have broken her own rules. And why she must be sure never to break them again.

"Good evening, Burke."

Well, damn, she thought even as her heart tripped into high gear. Of course he couldn't just leave without stopping to say something. She looked up, and up, and thought that nobody with the extraordinary build and looks of Dare MacLendon ought to be allowed to parade around in a flight suit. He was smiling down at her, a pleasant, friendly expression.

"Good evening, Colonel," she answered politely.

"Can you give me a minute?"

"Of course, sir."

"Good." He turned, looking over his shoulder to answer a remark from the departing pilots, and then pulled out a chair and straddled it. He rested his arms along its back and studied Andrea in silence as she leaned to one side to allow the waiter to serve her dinner.

"Just a coffee for me," Dare said in answer to the waiter's question.

Andrea felt pleased with the steadiness of her hands as she sliced into her chicken breast. She would *not* let him know how his proximity affected her. No way. Absolutely not.

"You look tired, Andrea," he said quietly in a tone so gentle that her throat tightened. When had anyone ever spoken to her with so much concern? If anyone ever had, she couldn't recall it.

She cleared her throat. "I've been busy, sir. Have you been flying?"

"I took up one of the bombers this afternoon on a low-level run. I hear you've started a little investigation of your own."

Her hands tightened on her knife and fork, and she looked across the table at him. "Who told you that?" And why did she have to remember so vividly just how soft his mouth could be?

"One of my people told me that one of your folks wanted to know who in the Wing could have had access to that damaged plane. I don't need somebody to lay it out like a map for me, Andrea."

Anger sparked in her green eyes. Now it would come, she thought. He would tell her to leave it alone and to mind her p's and q's. And if he did she'd—well, she didn't know what she'd do. "So?" she asked, and almost winced at the belligerence of her own tone.

Dare's eyes narrowed. His voice turned soft as silk, a dangerous sound. "You have a problem with the chain of command, Burke?"

"No, sir," she said swiftly, and then sighed. "I'm sorry. Not enough sleep. Right now I think I'm my own worst enemy."

He softened, recognizing her fatigue and admitting to himself that it had been easy for her to misconstrue the direction of this conversation. "I only wanted to know if you've come up with anything."

"Oh." After a moment she gave him a sheepish smile. "Actually," she admitted, "all I've done is chase my own tail so far. I decided there were three possible motives for the bombing—revenge, money, and terrorism—and then I came up with reasons why it couldn't be any of them." Briefly she outlined her reasoning.

He smiled, and the expression melted the last of the steel from his gaze. "Well, if it's any consolation, that's about all OSI has accomplished so far."

"You're kidding."

"Nope. All that muscle and brainpower, and they're still standing around scratching their heads. I'm not supposed to know that, of course, so don't tell anyone else."

"How did you find out?"

"I know a few people." God, how he wanted to reach out and touch her. Wrong time, wrong place. Besides, he'd told her to call him if she ever wanted to be with him again, and she hadn't called. Because of his position, he felt he had to let her set the boundaries on their relationship. He didn't want her ever to feel that he was using his rank to pressure her into anything.

"I can tell you one thing," he said, and fell silent while the waiter served his coffee. He didn't speak again until he was sure no one was near enough to overhear. "The plastic explosive is of U.S. manufacture. It's typical government stock."

"Not a homemade brew," Andrea remarked. "That's interesting."

"Yeah, but it evidently doesn't tell us much. OSI concludes from it that the incident wasn't staged by known terrorist groups, but evidently U.S. manufacturers sell a lot of the stuff to other countries the same way they sell countermeasures and weapons. Theoretically it only goes to friendlies, but who can say for sure?"

"There haven't been any calls to the press about it, either," Andrea said. "That's another mark against terrorism. Or have there been calls?"

Dare shook his head. "None. My source would have mentioned it. No, OSI is just about convinced we're dealing with an individual or a small group of individuals. The fact that there hasn't been another incident of any kind in nearly a month even has them speculating that the shooting scared the guy off. That and your beefed up security. They're still impressed with your squadron, by the way.''

Andrea smiled. It was nice to hear, especially when she was feeling low and useless. ''Well, if it's not terrorism, that leaves sabotage or murder for possible intent, and greed or revenge for the motive.''

''That's how it looks.'' Sipping his coffee, he studied her over the rim of the cup as she took another mouthful of her supper. He knew Andrea's appetite, and he was disturbed to see her peck at her food the way she was right now. ''Are you coming down with something?'' he asked abruptly.

Startled, she looked up. ''I don't think so.''

He shook his head and set his cup aside. ''You don't look very good,'' he remarked as he stood. ''Get to bed and get some sleep. And call me if you come up with anything new. Good night, Burke.''

She watched him stride away and thought once again that he shouldn't be allowed to wear a flight suit. On him it was positively lethal to her peace of mind. With a heavy sigh, she tried to convince herself that she really didn't mind the fact that he seemed to have no further interest in her. After all, she was leaving soon, so it really didn't make any difference.

As soon as she arrived at work in the morning, Andrea buzzed the front desk. ''See if you can round up Sergeant Halliday for me, Crocker. I'd like to see him in my office.''

''Yes, ma'am. I think he's over at Delta Zulu checking something out. It'll be a few minutes.''

''Thank you.'' What the hell had happened now? Andrea wondered as she replaced the receiver. What was Halliday doing over there?

Twenty minutes passed before Halliday showed up, and he arrived looking cold.

''Warm up with some coffee, Sarge,'' Andrea told him, pointing to the pot on the file cabinet. ''Did something happen over at Delta Zulu?''

"No, ma'am. Just checking on things. It's twenty-two below out there."

"I noticed." Andrea watched Halliday fill a cup and take a seat across from her.

"I worry about the systems," he told her. "Especially after what's been happening. The cold shouldn't affect them, but you never know."

Andrea nodded. "You're very conscientious." Most people didn't volunteer to go out in these temperatures. "Is everything okay?"

"Right as rain, Captain."

"Well, I asked you to come in here because I need your help with something. You know how I pull these little inspections."

Halliday smiled. "Everyone knows about them."

"I think I'm getting a little too predictable. I also think the troops are getting too dependent on the electronic systems. So, what if I wanted to give them a real surprise? How could I bypass the system?"

Halliday looked smug. "You can't."

Andrea shook her head slowly. "No system is infallible, Sergeant. There has to be a way. Think about it."

Halliday shrugged. "I don't have to think about it. I know the system like the back of my hand. Maybe better. Everything is redundant, especially around weapons storage. We've got backups on top of backups. To get around them you'd either have to knock out a whole section of the system at the control center, which isn't easy to do, or you'd have to know where each and every sensor is. If you want, though, I can disable part of the system for you so you can surprise the guys."

"You're absolutely convinced I can't do it any other way?"

Halliday's smile broadened into a grin. "I get the feeling you take that as a challenge, ma'am. You *could* memorize the layout. You might be able to do it then, but why go to so much trouble? It's easier just to have me shut it down."

"Who besides you knows the layout?"

"All the guys on my crew." Halliday frowned. "Look, if something's going on…"

Andrea shook her head. "No. It's just that I was asked about it at staff conference yesterday, and I realized I really don't know as much as I should about how things are done. And that was when somebody remarked that my inspections must be getting predictable if I always avoid the electronic systems."

"Well, ma'am, there's not all that much to it. I'm probably the only one who knows the entire system, because each of my technicians specializes in just one part of it. We're the only five people who have access to the classified plans and blueprints on a routine basis. We keep a copy of all that stuff in the safe in my office. If you want to look at it, I can get it for you, or you can look at the copy the document custodian keeps. Anybody with a need-to-know authorization can look at the stuff. I don't reckon there'd be too many folks other than me and my techs with a need to know, though."

"Certainly not me," Andrea said pleasantly. "Not that I could make much sense out of a lot of circuit diagrams."

Halliday smiled, his eyes pallid behind his glasses. "No, but you could read the map."

"And try to tiptoe past all that stuff?" Andrea laughed and shook her head. "Forget it, Sarge. It was a dumb idea."

Well, Andrea thought, now she could add even more names to the list, and she hadn't eliminated any yet. How many people might be able to gain access to the plans? The document custodians sprang to mind, and there were surely others who had a legitimate need to see them. Nope, she had to come at this from a different angle.

"But," she said, asking one last question, "if I *wanted* to learn the layout, I could get past the system?"

"Sure. It's too damn expensive to carpet all those areas with sensors, so they're scattered in a random fashion that makes it impossible to get by them all unless you know where they're at. Captain, I swear, it's a no-man's-land. It's more difficult to get through than a maze. You have to know what you're doing to stand a chance."

Late that night Andrea lay in bed, restless and strangely sad, and tried not to think about Alisdair MacLendon. Just a few short days had passed since Christmas, but they felt like years. All her nerves seemed hypersensitive. The brush of her nightgown against her breasts made her think of his hands. A tingling ache filled her. A nagging sense of incompletion gnawed at her, and some traitorous part of her mind kept demanding to know why she was in bed alone.

It was during the process of trying not to think about Dare that she had a realization so startling that it brought her upright in her bed: somebody wanted revenge, all right. They wanted revenge against Dare.

The evidence for that was slim, so slim that it seemed almost ridiculous. What did she have to substantiate it? The fact that the trouble had begun with his arrival. The fact that it seemed to be directed against the Bomb Wing. The fact that the charge set in the bomber hadn't killed anyone. And all those little pieces of so-called evidence could be argued against. The fact that the explosive in the bomber hadn't killed anyone, for example, could have been purely accidental.

Slender evidence indeed. Falling back against the pillows, Andrea considered. Her suspicion was so wild as to be embarrassing, but it *felt* right. She wouldn't dare tell anyone without more proof, but she could use the assumption as a starting point. It might make her alert to things she would otherwise miss. And it might also make her blind to other things. Troubled, she tossed and turned well into the night.

On the Saturday after New Year's, Andrea stood in her kitchenette yawning widely and thinking that maybe when she got to Minot she would rent an apartment rather than live in the BOQ. Waiting for the coffeepot to finish brewing, she looked around at her cramped efficiency quarters and decided that it was time she stopped living out of a mental suitcase. If she had more room and owned some furniture, maybe she would feel as if she had a home. It would mean a longer drive when she got a call in the middle of the night, but maybe she wouldn't feel so rootless. Maybe she wouldn't feel like a tumbleweed, rolling here and there and leaving no mark anywhere.

The tile floor was cold beneath her feet, causing her to shiver, and she rubbed her hands up and down the silk sleeves of the peignoir Dare had given her. It wasn't warm enough for the draughty rooms, and it wasn't practical by any stretch of the imagination, but she wore it often anyhow and then lay wide awake remembering Christmas. Remembering how it had felt to be a woman. Time and again she caught herself trying to think up excuses to go over to his house.

Like a teenager with a crush, she thought sourly as she headed for the bedroom. Hadn't she deliberately avoided this all these years? What was it about Alisdair MacLendon that made her forget all her common sense?

She was halfway across the small living area when someone knocked on her door. "Who is it?" she called.

"MacLendon."

Hurrying to the door, she released the lock and opened it a crack to see a very irate-looking Colonel MacLendon. Beneath his olive drab survival parka he wore his flight suit. He must have been flying again, Andrea thought. Rated pilots who'd been promoted to desk jobs were allowed to keep their ratings by flying a certain number of hours every month, and the Air Force provided planes for them, usually T-38 jets.

Raising her eyes to Dare's face, Andrea took an instinctive step backward. There was murder in Dare's face, Andrea took an instinctive step backward. There was murder in those icy blue eyes.

As she stepped back, Dare stepped in, easing through the opening and closing the door soundly behind him.

"Tell me, Burke," he growled down at her, "do your troops *sleep* on the job? Or are they doing dope?"

Andrea blinked rapidly and drew herself up to her full five foot six. "Sir! I can't let you say—"

"I'll say anything I damn well please!"

Andrea stood her ground, chin thrust forward, arms folded across her breasts.

"I almost *died* this morning," Dare said, advancing on her. "I almost augered in at Mach 1 because somebody fiddled with my hydraulics. That upsets me, Burke. That upsets the living hell out of me."

Andrea froze, horrified by the image evoked by his words: Dare's plane nosing into the ground at the speed of sound.

As he spoke, he cast his parka aside and took another step toward her.

"And all the time I was fighting the damn stick and pedals and trying to keep from being splattered all over the state of North Dakota, I could only think about one thing. This!"

Grabbing her with hands like steel, he hauled her up against him, forced her head back, and seized her mouth in a punishing, ruthless kiss.

Andrea fought him, twisting and turning like a wildcat, but he held her effortlessly. Moving with her struggles, he made her feel as if she were wrapped in an invisible net, never once hurting her, but giving her no escape from his ravaging mouth.

Suddenly Dare lifted his head and looked down at her with burning eyes. "What if I'd died?" he asked.

Andrea went utterly still, her swollen lips parted, her green eyes huge. What if he'd died? she asked herself.

Dare saw her lower lip quiver, and then she melted against him where she belonged, closing her arms around his waist in a fierce hug. She cared, he thought, shutting his eyes with relief. Whether she would admit it or not, she cared. At twenty thousand feet, when only brute strength had given him any control at all over his plane, in those interminable minutes when he'd been sure he was about to die, he'd wondered about that. He'd wondered if he would ever find out, and it had seemed incredibly important to know.

Wrapping his arms around her now, he held her as close as he could, as tightly as he could, without hurting her, and wished he could pull her right inside him. "Kiss me, Andrea," he said hoarsely. "Kiss me. Please."

She lifted her face and sought his mouth blindly, seeking the warmth, the passion, the essence, of this man. One of her hands crept upward to cradle his rough cheek, to slide into his hair and then hold on for dear life. Without reservation she gave him the kiss he wanted.

"I need you, Andrea," Dare said raggedly when he let her catch her breath. "We've got to talk. About this. About what happened. About everything." His blue eyes were intense as he tilted her head up. "We can't do any of that here."

With difficulty, Andrea concentrated on what he was saying. At the moment the only thing that seemed important was that a half-dozen steps would carry them to her bedroom. "No," she agreed, dimly aware that before long everybody in the BOQ would know Dare was here.

"Call Dolan," Dare said. "Tell him he's in charge for the rest of the weekend. Meet me at the Gasthaus in Devil's Lake."

Andrea blinked, coming to her senses. "I can't just—"

"You *can*," he interrupted her. "You can damn well do anything you please. When are you going to believe that?"

"But your hydraulics! We need to—"

"We'll talk about that later. Right now there's not a damn thing you can do about that."

Releasing her, Dare stepped back. "I'm going to Devil's Lake," he said. "I'll give you until one o'clock to meet me. It's up to you, Andrea. It always is. But I won't ask again."

Without another word, he left.

Nothing was up to her, thought Andrea miserably. Nothing had been up to her since Dare had crashed into her life. Closing her eyes, she clenched her hands into fists and tried to tell herself that she wouldn't do as he'd asked.

She didn't believe it herself. For an entire week now she'd been lying awake, full of yearnings no amount of argument could quash. In little less than a month she would be leaving for Minot, and in all likelihood she wouldn't see Dare again for years, if ever. Why not have a fling during these few weeks? Why not give in just this once in her life? Chances were she would never again have such an opportunity.

Chances were she would never again meet a man like Dare. Squeezing her eyelids tighter, she drew a breath that sounded like a sob. What was happening to her? Just a few short months ago, everything had been so simple and clear-cut. Now she didn't know where she was going, or why she was doing what she did. She didn't even feel like herself. Why was it when she closed her eyes all she could see was Dare? Where had this wrenching need for him come from, and why was she so helpless against it? Why, when she thought of how close he'd come to dying, did her heart stop?

And how the devil was she going to get on with her life and her career when all she wanted to do was punch out and go along for the ride with Dare?

Drawing another deep breath, Andrea stiffened her spine and opened her eyes. She couldn't let him do this to her. She couldn't let any man do this to her. She had a life and a career of her own, and she was going to keep it that way.

No, she wouldn't go to Devil's Lake. He would get the message then and leave her alone. And the longer she stayed away from him, the dimmer her unwanted feelings would grow.

She squared her shoulders. She would go over to Squadron HQ and see what she could find out about Dare's near miss. It looked like she'd been right about the motive behind what was happening, but it gave her no satisfaction.

The Gasthaus Restaurant in Devil's Lake was a large, Swiss-style chalet with a gleaming wood interior and numerous nooks and crannies for guests to disappear into. Dare had chosen it because it afforded privacy to dining couples but had no guest rooms to imply anything more intimate. He hoped Andrea would agree to stay overnight with him, but he didn't want her to think he expected it. He was discovering that dealing with an emancipated female could be every bit as touchy as dealing with the unliberated types of his youth.

As one o'clock crept closer, his state of tension grew almost intolerable. He hadn't handled his encounter with Andrea very well, he knew. Maybe he'd blown it completely. After his near miss, he'd been so full of adrenaline that he'd acted without thinking. No woman would like being grabbed and kissed the way he'd kissed Andrea, and certainly not on the tail end of such a ridiculous accusation. Worse, he'd practically ordered her to meet him here, which was guaranteed to rouse a woman's perversity. Andrea, he'd discovered, could be perverse with the best of them.

So he watched the minute hand on his watch crawl toward one with a steadily sinking heart. She wasn't coming. She could have been here over an hour ago if she'd really wanted to come. Yep, he'd blown it. The same experience that had made him realize just how much she meant to him had also driven him to ruin his chances. So it went. Only right now he was in no mood to feel philosophical about it. Staring into his beer stein, he decided to give her fifteen more minutes and then go home and get royally drunk.

"There's no future in this, sir."

Dare's breath locked in his suddenly tight throat. Slowly, hardly daring to believe his ears, he looked up and found Andrea standing by the booth. Her cheeks were pink from the cold, and her hair was ruffled from the wind. Her eyes—her eyes were hazy with both sorrow and yearning. Dare thought he'd never seen a more beautiful sight.

"I know. Sit down, Andrea."

But she didn't obey immediately. "I almost didn't come."

"I know." His heart beat in a slow, painful rhythm.

She blinked. "It'll hurt worse if we don't stop this right now."

"I'll risk it. What about you?"

Slowly, very slowly, she slid into the seat facing him. "I don't want either of us to be hurt, Colonel."

"I've got a feeling it's already too late to avoid it."

"It feels that way." Abruptly she reached out and covered both his large hands with her small ones. Dare immediately turned his hands over and clasped hers.

"I keep thinking," she said in a tense, un-Andrea-like voice, "of what almost happened to you this morning. I've seen it happen before, so it doesn't take a whole lot of imagination—" She looked to the side, blinking rapidly. "It'll be like that when I leave for Minot."

"Do you think if we pretend it doesn't exist that it won't hurt?"

Her green eyes came back to meet his. "No," she said steadily. "It hurts already. I've been lying to myself all along, I guess. I thought I could handle a fling. I kept telling myself that's all this is. That was a really stupid assumption from someone who's never had a fling before."

He squeezed her hands gently. "I told you this wasn't casual. This is no fling."

She drew a deep, unsteady breath. "No, it's not. And it'll hurt just as much when I leave whether we make love again or not. I'd rather have the memories than nothing at all."

"Would you like the menu now, sir?" The waitress's voice startled both of them.

"Yes," Dare answered without taking his eyes from Andrea. "And a couple of beers."

Releasing one of her hands, he pulled a pack of cigarettes from his breast pocket, shook one out, and lit it. "This morning wasn't my first close call, but it reminded me of something I've lost sight of over the past few years. Life doesn't give any guarantees, Andrea. Today is the only day we've got for sure. Tomorrow might never come."

"I know. I was thinking the same thing. I was thinking..." She shook her head as if she couldn't find the words. Dare waited patiently.

"I was thinking," she said presently, "that I've been so busy following this schedule I have in my head that I haven't had time for anything else. I guess I've been missing a lot."

"And so?"

"And so maybe I should accept these next few weeks as a gift and quit trying to fight it. I—I really don't want to miss it."

Dare squeezed her hand.

"But..." Her voice quavered and then steadied. "But I have to know exactly what it is you want from me."

"Exactly what you've offered me."

Andrea drew a deep breath. "I can only give you the next few weeks," she said straightly. "There's no future."

He nodded. "I understand that. Didn't I just tell you that there's no guarantee tomorrow will ever come? I want *now*, Andrea. The moment in our grasp."

She looked into his blue eyes, eyes so close to the color of the North Dakota sky, and it was like racing down a ski slope at eighty miles an hour, like the time she'd gone skydiving and she'd been falling, falling, only this time there was no rip cord.

Letting go of her, he leaned back, allowing the waitress to set two frosty steins of beer on the table along with two menus. "Give us ten or fifteen minutes before we order," he told the girl.

Food? Andrea thought. He wanted her to think about *food?* Wrapping her hands around her stein as if it were the last anchor in the universe, she stared down into the frothy beer and tried to find a rip cord. Any rip cord. Oh, God, she was so scared. She could only fail. She couldn't be what he wanted, even for a few weeks, any more than she'd ever been able to be what her father wanted. She wasn't that kind of woman. She was unnatural.

"Relax, Andrea."

Dare's deep voice beat back her panic a little, and she managed to look up.

"I told you," he said gently, "I don't want anything you can't give, so quit worrying about it."

"You don't know that."

"Yes, I do, and for the third time—Charlie Burke is a horse's ass. Just pick up your menu and think about lunch. Let me worry about everything else."

It was tempting to do exactly that, Andrea thought as she obediently picked up the menu. His shoulders looked broad enough to handle all his own worries and hers, as well.

"I'd like to get my hands on the son of a bitch who messed up my hydraulics," Dare remarked.

The words had a salutary effect. Andrea was immediately diverted, anger rising at the thought of anyone pulling a stunt like that. With her anger came her appetite. She hadn't eaten breakfast, because she'd been too upset by Dare's visit to her quarters. Suddenly everything on the menu looked good.

"I'm surprised you didn't punch out," she said. "Most pilots would have. You couldn't have had much control."

"Barely enough," he agreed. "But if I'd ejected, all the evidence would have been gone."

"And that was worth your life?" Andrea looked outraged.

"I didn't say that. I felt I could make it or I wouldn't have tried."

"Exactly what happened?"

"Slow leak. Slow enough so that I'd been in the air more than an hour before I lost enough fluid to make control extremely difficult. I wasn't doing any fancy flying, just straight, level stuff, so I didn't need much stick, but every time I used the pedals, I squeezed out a little more fluid. I thought I was getting a little mushy, but I couldn't be sure. And then I decided to try a stall and spin out of it."

Andrea's eyes were wide. "That's when you knew you were in trouble?"

Dare nodded. "I fell from forty thousand to twenty thousand feet before I could come out of the spin. By then I had more air than fluid in the system, and every time I hit those pedals I was leaking. Air's a lot harder to compress than hydraulic fluid, and it leaked out the holes a whole lot faster. Still, I had just enough control to make it."

"Thank God." She bit her lip, looking hesitant. "Has it—

has it occurred to you that somebody might have it in for you personally?"

He looked surprised. "What makes you think that?"

Andrea flushed. "It occurred to me last week that all this business started right at the time you arrived here."

Before he could reply, the waitress came to take their orders.

"Well," said Dare when they were again alone, "I imagine I have a few enemies, but I can't think of any who'd have that kind of grudge against me. But then, who can?"

"It's a horrifying thought," Andrea agreed. "Maybe it's just coincidence."

Dare lit another cigarette, saying a mental farewell to his attempts to quit. Maybe next year. "You know, Andrea, I fly that trainer every Saturday morning. You could say it has my name on it."

Andrea sucked a sharp breath. "Nobody else flies it?"

"Not on Saturday morning."

Andrea's hands knotted into fists. "Maybe we should go back to the base and—"

"And what?" he interrupted. "Damn it, Andrea, I called in the OSI to handle this, and if you think I like the OSI any better than any other Blue Suiter, you're wrong. I've got those guys tramping all over my bailiwick, poking their noses into every little nook and cranny—God knows what dirt they're digging up to look into another time—and I want you to let them handle this. This is *our* time."

He looked so irritated that she almost smiled. "Poking their noses everywhere, huh?"

"*Everywhere,*" he said emphatically. "Hell, you've been in the service long enough to know. I'll bet they've got a complete list of every glove that's disappeared from Supply in the last six months."

"Probably." At last her smile broke through. "Okay, Colonel, have it your way. I'll let OSI handle it until Monday. Then, whether you like it or not, I'm getting involved."

"Just what do you think you can do that they can't?"

Andrea shrugged. "My brothers always said I had a mind like Sherlock Holmes. We'll see. Just don't order me to back off, because I won't. My job is to investigate, and that's just what I'm going to do."

Her chin was set like a bulldog's, and Dare decided to let it ride. What would it hurt, anyway? By Monday everybody on the base would know what happened with his plane, and they weren't going to be able to cover this one with tales of sick geese.

"Fair enough," he said. "And if you ask me nicely enough, I might tell you everything I told OSI this morning."

Her eyes widened. "You mean there's more?"

"Actually," he said, letting a smile come through, "the only thing more is that they debriefed me for two solid hours this morning. I'd rather wrestle with a shot hydraulic system any day. It was like a bad scene out of a third-rate movie, the same questions over and over and over."

"Why? They couldn't possibly think you had anything to do with the damage to your plane!"

Dare shook his head. "No. They just wanted to be sure I wasn't overlooking anything. I got away from them by promising that if I thought of anything over the weekend I'd write it down and let them know Monday morning."

"You'll let *me* know if you think of anything, won't you?"

He smiled. "Of course I will. You can count on it."

Chapter 11

The temperature had reached its daytime high of seventeen below zero when Andrea and Dare were ready to leave the restaurant. Standing in the vestibule, they began to zip and button up.

"Where do we go from here, Andrea?"

She paused in the process of zipping her snorkel hood. "I thought you had it all planned."

"I had hopes, not plans."

"Oh." Smiling slightly, she finished zipping the snorkel and peered at him from a small, round opening that was edged in gray fur. "I packed an overnight bag."

She'd packed an overnight bag. Dare felt his face split into a wide grin, the first time he'd felt like grinning since Christmas. "Follow me, Captain."

"Yes, sir."

She drove behind him to a two-story, half-timbered motel on the frozen lake. At this time of year there were few people traveling this way who needed a place to stay, but one wing was open, and they were assured that the dining room served dinner until seven. If they wanted to risk frostbite, they could rent skates and go out on the lake, or they could go tobogganing

on a hill two miles up the road. Dare thanked the desk clerk for
the information and picked up his overnight bag and Andrea's.

"Do you feel like ice-skating, Captain?" he asked as he and
Andrea rode the elevator to the second floor.

"No, sir, not especially."

"Tobogganing?"

"No, sir. It's too damn cold."

The corners of his blue eyes creased as he smiled down at
her. "Indoor sports?"

She smiled back. "The best kind."

"Nooky?"

Andrea threw her head back and laughed. "Absolutely."

Dare had splurged on a two-room suite, and in the sitting
room there was a fireplace with gas logs. He bent to light it
while Andrea shucked her outer gear. When the flame was adjusted to his satisfaction, he straightened and turned to face her.

"Come here, woman," he said roughly, then grinned as she
laughed and flew into his arms. Lifting her from her feet, he
whirled her in circles. Whatever her reservations, she'd clearly
left them behind for now. He was grateful for that, very grateful.

Her nose was still cold from the outdoors when he bent his
head to kiss her, but her mouth was warm, so very warm and
moist, making him think of those secret places he longed to
explore. Later there would be time to take things slow, but right
now he felt like a man who'd been starving all his life.

Setting Andrea on her feet, he took one of her hands and
pressed it to his swollen manhood. Then, never taking his eyes
from hers, he reached for her sweater and began to pull it up.

"Do you know what I'm going to do to you, Andrea?"

Her eyelids fluttered, and a secret smile came to her lips as
she raised her arms over her head. "Tell me," she suggested.
"In detail."

A choked laugh escaped him as he tugged the sweater over
her head. As soon as Andrea freed her hands form the sleeves
of her sweater, she reached for him. Her fingers released the
snap of his jeans and tugged his zipper down. Bending to place
his mouth near her ear, he told her in titillating detail just what
he had in mind.

He heard her swiftly drawn breath, heard her smothered
moan, felt her tremble beneath his hands as he whispered his

intentions and unfastened her bra. The bra went the way of her sweater, somewhere across the room, and his hands went to the fastening of her jeans as he bent lower and took the tip of her breast into his mouth.

"Dare!" She gasped his name and hooked her fingers into the waistband of his pants, yanking downward. She was as impatient as he was now. Electric currents tingled along her nerves, and she felt herself melting, growing liquid and weak. She moaned with disappointment when he tore his mouth from her breast so that he could pull her jeans the rest of the way off. There was a horrible moment of delay while he dealt with her boots, and then she was free of all the restrictions of her clothes.

Before he could prevent it, she fell to her knees before him and reached for his pants to finish what she'd started. He went to work on the buttons of his shirt, but his fingers fumbled and then froze in utter amazement as Andrea pressed her face into his groin. Tremors like an earthquake shook him, and he tried to hold perfectly still for fear a single movement might cause her to pull back.

Andrea nuzzled him slowly, inhaling deeply of his male scent. His hair was so thick there, she thought, and so crisp against her cheek, a sharp contrast to skin as unexpectedly smooth as satin. Then slowly, daringly, she licked him delicately with the tip of her tongue.

That put paid to the last of Dare's self-control. Dropping to his own knees, he eased Andrea swiftly onto her back, and then he was on her and in her, taking her with a driving rhythm as primitive and basic as his hunger for this woman.

Andrea slept deeply and soundly, so deeply and soundly that she didn't wake when Dare lifted her from the sitting room carpet and carried her to the king-size bed in the next room. When he drew the blankets up over her, she sighed and turned onto her side, but her eyes never opened. Dare stood over her for a while, smiling faintly. Clearly she hadn't slept any better this week than he had.

He felt a little embarrassed by the rough, quick way he'd taken her. Hell, he'd come back to himself to discover that he still wore his shirt, and that his jeans were twisted around his ankles, caught on his boots. There was something indecent in that, especially for a man who'd always tried to be a considerate lover. Talk about jumping a woman's bones!

It was just after four, and beyond the windows, daylight was rapidly fading. Soon the northern night would blanket the world. Outside, the wind was kicking up again, and though the windows were double-paned, he could swear he felt a cold draft. Leaving Andrea, he went to close the insulated curtains in both rooms.

He wanted to lie down beside her, but mindful of the fact that the dining room would close at seven, he couldn't risk it. If he closed his eyes, he would be apt to sleep for hours. A long week of sleepless nights and this morning's events virtually guaranteed it. Knowing Andrea's appetite, he couldn't imagine her making it until tomorrow morning without a meal, especially not with the activities he had in mind for later.

A frown came to his brow as he thought about what had happened and the suspicions Andrea had shared with him at lunch. He'd managed to put her on hold, but in fact, the more he thought about it, the more he thought she might just be right about what was going on. But why would somebody be out to get him? He was no saint, but he couldn't remember ever having done anything to make anyone that angry. If somebody really did have that big a grudge against him, they must be a little unhinged.

The thing was, he didn't want to think that whoever had punctured his hydraulic lines had meant to kill him. Scare the devil out of him, yes, but kill him, no. Killing him would have involved no more effort—less, in fact—than making those small, careful holes. A person with access to plastique didn't have to make tiny punctures in hydraulic lines.

Or maybe, like most people, he was just unable to believe that someone had genuinely tried to kill him. Because, if he were to be honest with himself, he had survived only by the skin of his teeth. And when he thought about those endless minutes in the dive as he battled to gain control, it was almost possible to believe that someone had meant him to suffer that excruciating awareness of his impending fate. Whoever had made those little holes would probably be disappointed to know that during those interminable minutes, Dare had been too busy and too full of adrenaline to feel any fear.

Rubbing his eyes wearily, he decided he'd better call room service and have them send up something that would keep for a few hours. He had the feeling that he was going to sleep whether he wanted to or not, so he might as well do it comfortably, at Andrea's side, rather than in uncomfortable snatches sitting up on the couch and fighting it.

Forty minutes later, stripped to the buff, he crawled under the covers beside her. In her sleep she turned into his arms, resting her head on his chest, twining her legs with his. Contented, he let himself sleep at last.

Andrea awoke hours later to a dark room, but she knew instantly where she was. Only once before in her life had she wakened with arms around her, and with Dare's arms around her it didn't seem to matter where on the planet she was.

They were tucked together like spoons, one of his arms beneath her head, one resting heavily on her waist. She could hear his deep, steady breathing above her head, and against her back she could feel the springy hair of his chest and groin. It would be nice, she thought dreamily, if they could stay like this forever.

The memory of their earlier lovemaking was vivid in her mind, and she indulged herself in the luxury of a mental replay. She'd never thought herself the kind to inspire passion in any man, but there was little doubt that Dare had been impassioned. The rough and ready way he'd taken her had been testimony to that, and she hadn't imagined the shudders that had ripped through him. On the other hand, she couldn't be sure *she* had inspired that passion. She'd heard that a close brush with death could cause reactions like that. Maybe it wouldn't have made any difference to him who he'd been with.

He'd almost died. The thought slithered into her mind, poisoning her afterglow. At the age of six, out at Edwards Air Force Base, she'd seen a plane auger in, and no one had thought to keep the pilot's identity from her. Dave Wallace had been a buddy of her father's, and whenever he happened to come by the Burke home he always had a piece of candy for little Andrea, and a place on his lap. Andrea had been fascinated by his ribbons, and Wallace had made up outrageous stories about how

An Officer and a Gentleman   167

he'd gotten them. "I got this one for punching General LeMay in the nose," he would tell her. "And that's for beating Mike Metger at poker. And they gave me this one over here for the time I slammed my finger shut in the canopy." Even at six she hadn't believed him and had giggled until her sides ached.

Dave Wallace had augered in at better than Mach 2, riding a shrieking metal demon straight down out of the sky to end his life in an explosion that sent pillars of flame and black smoke nearly to the clouds. "God!" Charlie Burke had said hours later when telling his wife what he and his three children had seen. "Can you imagine it? He must have felt so alive in those last few seconds!" Andrea had had nightmares for months afterward.

She was having a nightmare right now. With the vivid memory of fountaining flames in her head, she squeezed her eyes shut. He hadn't died. He hadn't died. He was right here with her. The wind rattled the glass in the windows, a forlorn sound, a cold sound. Unconsciously she wiggled backward a little, trying to get as close to Dare as she could.

"Don't move, Andrea" said a sleepy, thick voice above her head.

"Dare?"

"Shh," he whispered soothingly. "Shh. Don't move. Not a muscle."

She held perfectly still.

"That's it," he whispered. His hand left her waist, sliding slowly, ever so slowly, upward, skimming over the skin of her stomach in feathery circles that left a tingling sensitivity in their wake. Andrea's breath caught and held as his fingers glided upward some more, reaching the underside of her breast. Helpless to stop herself, she twisted, trying to bring him more fully into contact with her.

"Uh-uh," Dare said huskily. "Don't move, darlin'. We've got all night, and I want to pleasure you."

His words, the huskiness of his voice, sent tingles arcing across her nerve endings, and she began to grow heavy.

"That's it," he whispered again. "Let me, Andrea. Just let me."

She might try to hurry him, but not even to save her life could she have stopped him. Her muscles were growing syrupy with the feelings he drizzled over her, and when his fingertip brushed her beaded nipple, she could only gasp. Movement was suddenly beyond her.

Dare cupped the weight of her full breast in his palm and kneaded gently, oh so gently, as he found the nape of her neck with his mouth and began to nibble softly. Shivers raced down Andrea's spine, adding to the weight growing at her center.

"Dare..." She sighed his name from the depths of her.

That was how he wanted her to say his name. Again and again. Forever.

"So lovely," he murmured. "So sweet." His hand slipped to her other breast, testing its heaviness, tormenting softly. "They're better than standard issue, Andrea."

A short, breathless laugh escaped her. "You like my breasts?"

It was his turn to laugh hoarsely. "I love your breasts. I especially love to see you in uniform, because nobody but me would ever know how perfect and lovely your body is."

It was true. It still amazed him that she was so perfect in every way. Full breasts, fuller than he'd ever expected, narrow waist, hips that flared just right and joined to legs that were long and slender. Thinking about those hips joining to those legs caused him to sweep his hand downward to the apex of her thighs. They both groaned as he touched her.

"Don't move, Andrea," he said again. "Don't move." He was far from finished with her, but his own control was getting more precarious by the second as he felt the heat blooming in her.

Slipping his hand between her thighs, he lifted her leg and pulled it back over his, leaving her opened to his seeking, stroking fingers.

"So hot," he murmured, a catch in his voice. "So wild and sweet..."

"Dare...Dare..." She began to chant his name on each quickening breath as he parted her with his fingers and stroked her deeper. Her hips began a gentle, helpless undulation against his hand, and this time he didn't try to still her. He couldn't. Each movement pressed that wonderful rump gently against his manhood, and with each touch he became more helpless against his own needs.

"Do you know what it did to me before when you licked me?" he asked her. His voice was rough, hoarse. He heard her catch her breath again at the memory. "I'm going to show you, Andrea."

Pressing her onto her back, he drew a couple of breaths to steady himself, and then he knelt between her legs, pressing her soft thighs apart. It was dark in the room, and she thought he was going to touch her as he had on Christmas, so it came as an utter shock when she realized that it was his tongue that now followed the path he'd blazed with his fingers.

"Dare?" She sounded almost frightened.

"It's okay," he said, raising his head. "It's okay, Andrea."

It was more than okay. It was too much. She was riding a shooting star at transluminal speeds, burning in the heat of the sun, melting, melting....

Dare felt the convulsions take her, and he slid swiftly up over her, filling her, giving her the last ounce of pleasure he could wring out of the moment for her. Holding her snugly within his strong arms, he sheltered her vulnerability and brought her safely back.

"And now," he whispered, when her breathing slowed and her shuddering eased, "now we go together, sweetheart."

She would have said it was impossible. It wasn't.

Champagne, club sandwiches and cherry cheesecake made their dinner before the gas fire. Andrea wore her green peignoir; Dare had pulled on his jeans. There was, Andrea thought, something incredibly sexy about a man wearing nothing but jeans, jeans with the snap suggestively undone. It gave her the freedom to drink her fill of his broad, muscular chest, and from time to time she couldn't resist reaching out to run her fingers through the whorls of dark, springy hair that patterned him. When she did, he invariably sighed and smiled.

Three weeks, Dare thought. In just three short weeks she would walk out of his life. Minot wasn't that far away, and he hoped to persuade her to see him from time to time. He could always fly out there for a weekend. But now wasn't the time to discuss it. She still hadn't really come to terms with their relationship, and he strongly suspected she had come this far only because there was a definite time limit. She felt safe giving in because she knew it would end on January thirtieth.

Charlie Burke had a lot to do with that, he suspected. Old Charlie had been—probably still was—a male chauvinist pig of the first order. While Dare didn't much care for the indiscriminate way a lot of feminists flung that term around, he had to admit there were some men who fit the bill perfectly. On the occasions when Dare had met Andrea's mother, he'd thought he'd never seen a woman so downtrodden. Clara Burke didn't have a thought or a wish of her own, and whenever Charlie said jump, she jumped. Clara might as well have been a dog and Charlie her master. Hell, Charlie probably would have treated a dog better.

Andrea had grown up seeing that. She'd grown up with her father trying to turn her into another Clara. Small wonder that she probably couldn't imagine other men not wanting the same. Dare could only hope that eventually Andrea would realize that a man who fell in love with Captain Burke was hardly looking for a Clara Burke clone.

Nor was now the time to tell Andrea just how much he admired the strength of will and determination that had allowed her to rise above that kind of upbringing. Now she was still too defensive, still too sure that she was somehow different, somehow *wrong*. She would misunderstand what he was trying to say. Later, when she was surer of him and his feelings, surer that he really didn't want to change a hair on her head, then he would tell her how much he admired her.

If she gave him enough time. Later, he told himself sternly. Think about tomorrow later. No sense coloring this weekend with the shadows of losses that might never happen.

Andrea's hands dipped into the hair on his chest again, and Dare smiled.

"I like it when you touch me," he told her, catching her hand and rubbing it over his pectorals. "Are you fascinated by my chest hair?"

Her cheeks colored faintly. "Yes, sir."

"Why?"

"Because I don't have any."

Dare laughed. "You've got something much better."

"That's all a matter of perspective, Colonel."

"I suppose it is." Seizing her about the waist, he lifted her onto his lap. "There. Now you can comb my hair to your heart's content, and I can enjoy your soft little tush." Her blush deepened, and his smile broadened. "Your tush drove me crazy for weeks, you know. If you had any idea how enticing it looks in your uniform slacks, you'd wear skirts forever."

She slanted a look at him from the corner of her eye. "Your tush drove me crazy, too."

"Mine?" He looked disbelieving.

"Yes, sir. Hard and flat. *Very* male. Every time you write on a chalkboard—"

"You little minx! I had no idea you were eyeballing me that way."

"You weren't supposed to. And I was trying very hard not to. The truth is—and I probably shouldn't admit this to my CO—I never heard a word you said when you wrote on the board."

"I love it. And all the time I thought you were utterly impervious."

"If I were impervious, I wouldn't have called you on Christmas Eve."

"No," he agreed, "I guess you wouldn't."

His blue eyes were smiling and warm, their corners crinkled in the way she loved.

"You're going to hate me for this, Andrea."

"For what?"

"I think you look cute in battle dress."

"Cute? In *fatigues?* Colonel MacLendon, sir, may I respectfully suggest that you've gone crazy? Nobody looks cute in fatigues."

"You do." He nuzzled her cheek and blew softly in her ear, enjoying the way she shivered. "And you look adorable in your Academy sweat suit. Promise me one thing, Andrea. Promise me you'll never stand at attention in that sweat suit again. I could hardly keep my mind on what I was saying because your breasts were—"

She clapped a hand over his mouth. "Don't say it! I'll die of embarrassment."

"It's humanly impossible to die of embarrassment."

She ducked her head. "No, it isn't," she said in a smothered voice. "God, I'll never be able to wear my sweats again."

"You can wear them for me," he suggested. "And stand at attention—"

"Don't." But the eyes she raised to his were laughing despite the painful color in her cheeks. "All the while, I thought that wooden expression on your face was because you were mad at me."

"Never. I was trying not to pounce on you."

"I'll bet. You were probably every bit as embarrassed as I am now."

"I don't embarrass. Believe me, embarrassment was the last thing I felt. Actually, I was annoyed with you when I first arrived. Your conduct was unprofessional, you know."

"I know," Andrea admitted. "I should never have called you cowboy. I don't know what possessed me."

"I do. It's that little imp that lives inside you. Every so often your imp gets out. Anyhow, I was annoyed, just a little. Nothing serious. And the whole time I was there talking to you, I was coming to like you more and more. By the time I left, I was laughing."

"You were not!"

"I was. I just didn't dare let you see it. I like your imp, Andrea." He ran a gentle fingertip along her hairline to her ear. "I like every damn thing about you just fine. I wouldn't change one hair, one eyelash, one thought in your head." Which was not strictly true. There was a thought or two he had every intention of changing.

Looking into his eyes, she almost believed him. Those blue eyes were warm, intense, determined. She wished she could believe him, but even so, she didn't see how their careers would sustain any kind of a relationship, and she wasn't about to sacrifice her life's goals for anything. Of course, he knew that. So when he said he wouldn't change one thought in her head, it could only mean that he was content with the way things were, that he accepted that it would all end when she left.

Well, hey, she told herself bluntly. The man's past forty, and he must have had numerous opportunities to remarry, if that was what he wanted. And to women whose career wouldn't be a problem.

Dare saw the sorrow slip across her face. "Did I say something wrong?"

She shook her head. "I was just remembering that tomorrow always comes."

"Tomorrow we're going to stay here," he said firmly. "We'll go back early on Monday morning."

"That isn't what I meant."

"I know. I'm just trying to tell you that you don't need to think about tomorrow. Don't waste today thinking about what hasn't happened yet, Andrea."

Nodding, she tucked her face into the curve between his neck and shoulder. "I'll try not to. But it always comes, Colonel. Sooner or later, tomorrow always comes."

And he couldn't have made it any plainer that he wanted no more than the moment from her. Well, that was what she wanted, too, she reminded herself. That being the case, why did she feel so sad?

Monday morning came all too quickly, the way dreaded tomorrows always do. Once again Andrea was in uniform, sitting behind the polished expanse of her large desk, sipping coffee and trying to relegate the weekend to memory, where it belonged. Images insisted on flashing before her mind's eyes, however, images of Dare stepping stark naked out of the shower and grabbing her, tickling her until she begged for mercy. Images of the way he threw back his head and laughed full-throatedly. Images of the way the hair on his chest arrowed down to the perpetually, suggestively, unfastened snap of his jeans.

Her body remembered things, too: the way his hands felt sliding over her skin, cupping her breasts, grazing their peaks until she ached. The way his buttocks bunched under her hands when he thrust into her.

"Damn it, Burke," she said aloud. *"Quit it!"* Two solid days of lovemaking and laughter, and she was greedy for more. Unbelievable.

It was with great relief that she heard Nickerson's familiar knock on her door. Now maybe she would get her mind on work, where it belonged.

Nick carried a large envelope with him, as well as his usual folder, and he handed the envelope to her.

"For you, ma'am. It arrived just a couple minutes ago."

Andrea recognized Dare's office code in the return address block. "What now?" she wondered, then shrugged, setting it aside. It could wait until after Nick brought her up to date. "What do you have for me, Nick?"

"The usual." He helped himself to coffee and took a seat. "Do you really want the litany?"

Andrea had to smile. "Photocopy it and give me a copy. What's on your mind?"

"Did you hear what almost happened to MacLendon Saturday morning?"

Andrea was surprised that Dare's visit to the BOQ wasn't all over the base by now. The military grapevine usually worked better than this. "I heard. Somebody punctured his hydraulic lines."

Nick nodded. "So he told you. I wondered if it was true."

"Yes."

"Begging your pardon, ma'am, but what the hell are we going to do about it?"

"I told him I was going to investigate whether he liked it or not."

Nickerson nodded. "I'm glad you did, skipper. I don't know who he called in to handle this mess, but I reckon it was OSI, and if you'll excuse me for saying so, they ain't accomplished diddly squat so far. I was going to ask for your permission to pursue an investigation on my own."

"I was going to ask you to join me in mine."

Nickerson smiled. "I'm with you all the way, Captain."

Andrea reached for the envelope and cut it open. Inside, as she had half expected, was an incident report on the events of Saturday morning. A hand-written note was attached.

You said you were going ahead whether I wanted you to or not, so I thought you should have all the available information. Unfortunately I don't have access to everything OSI may have learned, but everything we've been able to give them is here.

Andrea looked up. "It's all here, Nick, everything Mac-Lendon can put together about what happened. After I read it, I'll pass it on to you, but I don't want anyone else to see it or to know that you and I are investigating."

"Yes, ma'am." Nickerson looked satisfied as he rose. "I'll get you a copy of the weekend incident report."

Dare's mood was, to put it mildly, crummy. He and the entire Wing were grounded as a result of Saturday's events. No more flying until the culprit was found. The alert planes, the bombers that stood ready with nuclear weapons aboard, were surrounded by a tight cordon of security guards, some of whom were OSI. Dare had been angry enough on Saturday, but it was nothing compared to what he felt now at having his Wing's operations hampered. One entire SAC bomb wing, an essential link in the nation's defenses, had been brought to its knees by one or two crazies with a grudge. It was enough to make *him* crazy.

The higher-ups didn't like it, either. He had been in some uncomfortable positions in his life, but never before had one so closely resembled the Iroquois torture of roasting a man alive over hot coals. He was under pressure from all directions, yet there wasn't a damn thing he could personally do except ensure that SAC didn't get another black eye by losing a plane and crew. OSI was doing what it could, eliminating suspects one by one, but nothing was moving fast enough to please anyone.

Wednesday afternoon brought the only bright spot to his entire week. During the early afternoon, Andrea called him.

"Colonel, if you can see your way to coming over here, I'd highly recommend it."

Dare looked out his window at the blowing snow and frowned. "What is it?"

"I don't want to spoil the surprise, sir, but you could classify this as a sort of public relations matter. A pleasant one."

Well, he thought, it would give him an opportunity to see Andrea, even if only formally. Maybe he could even find a private minute with her to discuss the upcoming weekend.

"Give me twenty minutes, Captain." It would take him almost that long to get into his cold weather gear. With the temperature at twenty-seven below and the wind blowing at forty to forty-five miles an hour, it was no day for cutting corners, even for a short trip.

Andrea was waiting for him in the front office of Security Police Headquarters. With her stood a wizened man of about seventy with a ramrod posture that belied his years. Throwing back his hood and peeling off his gloves, Dare strode toward them.

"You wanted to see me, Captain?"

"Yes, sir. Thank you for coming. Colonel, this is Mr. Selfridge. He farms up toward the Canadian border. Mr. Selfridge, Colonel MacLendon, commander of the 447th Bombardment Wing."

Dare shook the old farmer's hand, saying, "It's a pleasure to meet you, Mr. Selfridge."

Selfridge eyed him keenly and then gave an approving nod. "Reckon you've seen combat."

"Vietnam."

"I was in the South Pacific from '41 on. Navy."

Dare smiled. "Then it's an *honor* to meet you. What can I do for you, Mr. Selfridge?"

"Not a thing," said Selfridge, surprising him with a laugh. "Not a thing. Just have something to return to you."

Perplexed, MacLendon looked at Andrea and saw the devil lights in her hazy green eyes. At once he felt the corner of his mouth lift in anticipation. Well, he could use a good joke.

"Mr. Selfridge," Andrea said, "came to return some government property."

"What's that?" Dare asked, totally at sea now.

Andrea pointed to a box at her feet. "This, sir. Mr. Selfridge collected three more boxes as well."

"They're out in my truck," Selfridge assured him.

Andrea's eyes sparkled with humor, and Dare decided to go along with her. Squatting, he opened the top of the box and stared. It was filled with hair-fine, aluminum-coated glass fibers.

"This is chaff," Dare said blankly.

"Yes, sir," Andrea said gravely, betrayed by a faint tremor in her voice. "Four whole boxes of chaff."

"Saw it fall off one of your planes," Selfridge said. "Damn stuff went everywhere. Had a hell of a time collecting it all, but I think I got most of it."

Dare froze in his squatting position and hastily covered his mouth with his hand, rubbing it as if lost in thought. He didn't dare look at Andrea for fear he would be unable to contain his laughter. These fine little fibers, called chaff, were dispensed by aircraft in order to confuse radar. Millions upon millions of these dipoles were often expended in a single evasive maneuver, and they had absolutely no further value once they were emptied from their tubes. Dare almost couldn't bear to think of Mr. Selfridge conscientiously collecting all these little hairs.

Dare cleared his throat. "Ah, Captain Burke?"

"Sir?"

"Why don't you get a photographer over here. I want to thank Mr. Selfridge properly, and I'd like him to have a photograph as a mark of our appreciation."

"Yes, sir." Pivoting, Andrea strode up the hallway.

Slowly rising to his feet, Dare glanced at the two desk cops. That wasn't a safe direction to look, either. From their wooden expressions, he gathered they were close to strangling on their suppressed laughter. The only place left to look was at Selfridge.

"I can't imagine," Dare said to the farmer, "how you ever found all these on the snow."

"Twasn't difficult to see them. They're gray against the snow. It was the devil to collect 'em. Thought they might be secret, though, and I couldn't see letting them blow all over where anyone might find them."

Dare managed a nod. "Why don't we go to Captain Burke's office and have some coffee while we wait for the photographer?"

"Let me get the other boxes of that stuff in here first."

"That won't be necessary. These two airmen will get them for you." The two desk cops no longer looked like laughing, Dare saw. Satisfied, he escorted Selfridge to Andrea's office. She was just hanging up the phone when the two men entered.

"The photographer's on his way over, sir."

"Good, good." Smiling broadly, Dare ushered Selfridge to a chair. "Pour Mr. Selfridge some coffee, Captain." He enjoyed the flash of irritation the order brought to her green eyes.

"What do you raise, Mr. Selfridge?" Dare asked while Andrea dealt with the coffee.

"Durum wheat. My boys do most of the work these days, but

it don't hardly seem fair to them. There ain't much money in it, for sure. Not like there used to be. Time was a farmer could expect to make a fair living from the soil, but the price of seed and fertilizer's shot to the moon.''

''It's rough,'' Dare agreed. ''My dad and brothers ranch in Montana, over toward Kalispell, and it's a struggle to make ends meet.''

Eventually—none too soon, in Dare's estimation—the photographer showed up and snapped a photo of Dare and Selfridge as they shook hands in front of the U.S. flag. The desk sergeant was summoned to escort Selfridge back to his truck.

''You know, Mr. Selfridge,'' Dare said as the farmer turned to leave, ''it's not often that I meet someone as honest and patriotic as you are. I don't think one man in ten million would have gone to so much trouble to return that chaff. I'm truly honored to have met you.''

Selfridge actually blushed. ''Just doing my duty, Colonel.''

When he and Andrea were alone, Dare turned to look at her, fully expecting to find her doubled over with laughter. He was astonished to find her regarding him with wide, dewy eyes.

''What's wrong?'' he asked. Damn, she looked as if she were about to weep, and he couldn't stand the thought of Andrea weeping.

''Nothing.''

''Then why are you crying?''

''I'm not crying, sir. I never cry. You saw it. I didn't know for sure if you would.''

''Saw what?''

''What an adorable, selfless, touching thing that man did. It was funny, of course, but only because we know how worthless that chaff is. What Selfridge did is beautiful. Can you imagine how many days he must have spent gathering that stuff?''

''My back aches at the thought.'' More than his back ached, right now. His heart ached at the way she was looking at him. He couldn't remember anybody ever having looked at him that way, as if he were the most wonderful man in the world. ''Andrea, I—''

''Thank you for coming over here, Colonel,'' she interrupted. ''I felt he deserved some kind of recognition.''

''No problem. Andrea—''

"I just couldn't send him all that way back without—"

Goaded by her evident determination to avoid personal conversation, Dare took matters into his own hands. Rounding her desk, he hauled her into his arms and kissed her into quivering submission. When she was finally clinging to him for support, he decided to risk trying to talk to her again.

"About this weekend, Andrea." He sounded a little breathless himself, but that was okay. He wanted her to know what she did to him. Damn all these clothes!

"Yes, sir?"

"We've got to make plans."

Her eyelids lifted a fraction, revealing just a glimpse of her green irises. "Plans?"

"Plans for the weekend," he repeated patiently. "Damn it, Andrea, you can't look at me like that and then tell me to get lost. I want to spend the weekend with you again."

"Oh." Blinking, she made an effort to gather her wits. Why not? she thought. She was already in so deep that one more weekend wouldn't make a bit of difference.

A knock on the door jolted them apart. Andrea turned away from him.

"Burke, damn it, look at me and answer me."

"That's Nickerson," she said breathlessly. "You make the plans and let me know."

Relieved, Dare yielded a sigh. "Okay," he said, just as Andrea called out, "Come on in, Nick."

Dare exited swiftly, leaving Andrea and Nickerson to their meeting.

Nick, who'd stared after MacLendon, turned to look at Andrea, and his face went suddenly and totally wooden. From his unusual and utter lack of expression, Andrea guessed he'd somehow picked up on something in the atmosphere. Hell!

"We've got work to do, Nick," she said abruptly.

"Yes, ma'am."

He glanced at her and then away, but not before she caught the twinkle in his eye. Damn all nosy NCO's, she thought irritably, and snatched up the report she wanted to discuss with him.

Chapter 12

In the early hours of Thursday morning, one of the alert planes caught fire. After recent events, no one doubted that the fire had been deliberately set, but the question no one could answer was *how*. Even under ordinary circumstances those planes were closely guarded, because their bomb bays were full of nuclear weapons. Lately, security around them had been so tight that Andrea would have said even a field mouse couldn't have slipped past unnoticed.

"I want the s.o.b. who did this," Andrea told Nick that morning as she sat bleary-eyed at her desk. "I've got one measly week left, and I want him before I leave."

Nick stood at her window, hands on his narrow hips, and looked out at the bleak morning. The Security Squadron had gone on full alert the instant the fire was reported, and it had been a long night for everyone. He sighed now and rotated his shoulders to ease the tension.

"The fire marshal promised to call me as soon as he knows what caused the fire," he said.

Andrea looked at his back. "But he said it was arson."

"*Thinks* it was," Nick said. "I expect he's right. Merle

knows what he's doing. But he won't commit himself till all the evidence is in.''

"Sensible," Andrea admitted, rubbing the back of her neck. "Did he tell you how long that should be?"

"He hopes to know by sometime tomorrow. He's in one hell of a hot seat, ma'am. Did you hear the news on the radio this morning?"

"You mean all the uproar in town because there were weapons on the plane? That's the kind of noise politicians get paid to make. And, of course, the locals are nervous about it. Most people don't understand how harmless an unarmed nuclear weapon is. As far as hot seats go, I think MacLendon's must be the hottest."

Nodding, Nickerson faced her. "I hear he's talking to the news people and the city council this morning."

"Probably. I really don't know." Sighing, Andrea stood and went to the file cabinet to pour another in an endless stream of cups of coffee. "I want the squadron to stay on full alert for the time being. And I'm going to activate the Pyramid tonight to make sure nobody's ignoring our status."

The Pyramid Alert System was an ingeniously simple system whereby each person on the pyramid telephoned the two persons below him to pass along information or to bring the squadron to full alert. In less than twenty minutes, Andrea's entire four hundred man squadron could be communicated with individually. In only slightly more time, the Bombardment Wing commander could bring the entire base to alert status through the same system.

"I guess that's it for now, Nick," she said after a moment, dismissing him. "When you go by Lieutenant Dolan's office, stick your head in and tell him I'd like a word with him."

"Yes, ma'am." He departed, shutting the door quietly after him.

Poor Dare, Andrea thought as she settled behind her desk again. Closing her eyes, she leaned her head back against the chair and sighed. Between SAC HQ, the press, and the local politicians, he must really have his hands full. Through it all, he would have to be courteous, concerned, understanding, and firm. Quite a recipe, especially for a man who'd had no more sleep than he had, thanks to last night's events.

With her eyes closed, his image rose vividly in her mind, and now that there was no one to betray herself to, she admitted just how much she'd missed him this week. She went to bed at night longing for him and woke in the morning feeling empty because he wasn't there. It was a ridiculous dependency, she told herself, especially since they'd only had three nights together. How could he have become a habit so fast? Why was it that after such a short time, such a brief acquaintance, a dozen times a day she wanted to turn to him to share some thought?

And only last night she'd awakened in the dark and mistaken the shape of a pillow for his shoulder. She didn't like to remember how her throat had ached and her eyes had burned when she'd realized it was just a pillow.

Well, she told herself firmly, it didn't matter. January thirtieth was fast approaching. Dare was clearly content to let the relationship end there, and after a time she would get over this ridiculous emotional reaction.

A knock on the door announced Lieutenant Dolan's arrival, and Andrea straightened. "Come in," she called in a brisk, businesslike voice, relieved to have the distraction of work.

"Still working, I see."

It was after ten that evening when Andrea looked up to see Dare standing in the doorway of her office. Her neck was stiff from hours of hunching over lists that refused to shed any light on the case, and her eyes were red and burning.

Dare had never looked so good to her as he did now, leaning against the doorjamb. His unbuttoned parka revealed a teal blue sweater, and his fingers were tucked into the front pockets of snug, worn blue jeans.

"Give it up, Andrea," he said roughly. "You're out of here in a little over a week. It won't be your problem anymore."

"It's my problem right now, sir."

"It's the OSI's problem."

"They don't seem to be getting very far with it."

He looked tired, too, she noticed. And angry and frustrated. The lines of his face seemed to have grown deeper just since yesterday. She resisted a totally feminine and totally ridiculous impulse to smooth them away. Or soothe them away.

"Got any coffee?"

"I just brewed a fresh pot." She watched him lever himself away from the door frame and stride to the coffeepot on top of her filing cabinet. She'd forgotten how big he was, just since yesterday. How tall and lean and hard he was. She always felt a clenching thrill when she saw him for the first time after an absence, however brief. Why was that?

Her eyes never left him as he filled a cup and settled into one of the chairs facing her desk. He crossed his legs loosely, one ankle on the opposite knee, and leaned back, rubbing his eyes wearily.

"The guy doesn't leave a trail," he said. "Not a hint or a sign of what he's up to. What's the point of all this if he doesn't get the satisfaction of telling somebody why?"

"Maybe he gets all the satisfaction he needs just from doing it. Or maybe he's saving up his explanations for some grand finale."

"That thought's cost me some sleep, I can tell you." He sipped the coffee and grimaced. "I've swallowed enough coffee today to float a battleship. At this rate I'll have an ulcer in a week."

Andrea opened her desk drawer and pulled out a bottle of antacids. She tossed them to him. "Help yourself."

"You, too, huh? Thanks."

"I keep thinking I'm missing something that's as plain as the nose on my face," Andrea remarked. "Like I've got all the puzzle pieces but I just can't see how to fit them together."

"Well, if you're right that I'm the target, he's doing a damn fine job. My career's getting more tenuous with every passing minute."

"But why, Dare? You've done everything you can to stop him."

He shrugged. "The buck stops here, as they say. They're starting to ask some tough questions at the top, like why the devil everything's gone to hell in a handbasket since I took command here."

Andrea ached for him. "Everything has *not* gone to hell since you took command. Everything is just fine, except for some loony, and you can't be responsible for loonies."

"That's not how it looks if you're sitting up at SAC head-

quarters and one of your bases is all but out of commission, and
the guy in charge out there isn't doing diddly about it."

"That's not fair!"

"Who said life was fair?"

"Who said it shouldn't be?"

A faint smile came to Dare's mouth, lifting the corners
slightly, as he took in the pugnacious set of Andrea's chin.

"I need a cigarette," was all he said, but he was thinking
how badly he needed her in his arms right now, needed to feel
her warmth and the gentleness she kept so well hidden.

Andrea pulled open yet another drawer and retrieved an ashtray, setting it down on the desk between them. "So smoke,"
she said.

"Prepared for all eventualities, I see," he remarked as he
pulled a pack of cigarettes from his parka pocket.

"Yes, sir. We try." She rose and refilled her own cup with
coffee, then started to pace around her office, unaware that Dare
spared a few moments to admire her bottom in the ugly blue
Air Force slacks.

"What have we got?" she asked rhetorically a few minutes
later. "I was shot by somebody who was evidently trying to get
through the perimeter fence. That doesn't fit with the rest of it."

"Why not?" Suddenly he looked over his shoulder at the
door to her office. "Andrea, maybe I'm paranoid, but if you
want to discuss this mess in any detail, maybe you should close
your office door."

"There's plenty of reason to be paranoid lately." She even
glanced into the hallway before closing her door and, after a
moment's hesitation, locking it.

"So what doesn't fit about you being shot?"

Andrea perched on the edge of the desk and set her mug down
so she could rub the back of her neck. "It's not just me being
shot that doesn't fit. It's that at this point I'm not sure our loony
is an intentional murderer."

"Why not? Want me to rub your neck for you?"

Andrea looked at him, her green eyes growing smoky.
"Maybe later," she said. "I don't think too clearly when you
touch me, and right now I want to think."

There was no way he could repress the grin that seemed to
rise from the tips of his toes and banish his fatigue. From Andrea

that was one hell of an admission. The lady admitted very little, he'd learned.

"I'm having trouble with the idea that this guy is a mad killer," she said, "because nobody has died. Anybody who's been around B-52s for a while knows how hard it is to knock one out of the sky. That charge didn't knock out anything essential to the aircraft's survival. That may have been deliberate."

"It could also have been an accident," Dare pointed out.

"But don't forget last night. Setting fire to a plane on the runway was hardly designed to kill. It seems to me that it was designed to give you a hard time. Tell me you haven't had a hellish day today, with more to come."

He smiled faintly. "I can't. It was awful, start to finish. What about my hydraulics? For a while I believed that hadn't been intended to kill me, but I've had a lot of time to think about it since Saturday, Andrea. Nobody messes around with an aircraft's hydraulic system if he *doesn't* want to kill."

"He could have intended for you to punch out, which any pilot in his right mind would have done, Dare. I still can't believe you didn't eject as soon as you knew you were in trouble. My God!"

"A pilot has to believe he's got no other option before he'll punch out, honey. I didn't believe it."

For a long moment she appeared to be incapable of speech. Dare watched the way her eyes sparked with outrage and darkened with remembered fright. God, he needed to hold this woman.

"Anyhow," Andrea continued when she had a grip on the surge of unwelcome emotion, "I was shot because I scared the guy. I can understand that. No, my problem is that it just doesn't fit with the rest of what's been going on. We've agreed that our man must be somebody who can get past security, who probably has a legitimate reason to be on the flight line. Halliday keeps telling me—"

"Halliday?"

"My electronic security expert. He keeps telling me the perimeter is a no-man's-land of sensors, that nobody who doesn't know the location of those sensors could get through without detection—unless the sensors are turned off. If we agree to that, and I don't see any reason why we shouldn't, then I can't understand why anyone was trying to get through the perimeter. And even if somebody could get through the perimeter, he'd have to get past all the security guards, which brings us right back to someone who has a legitimate reason to be out there—''

''And therefore has no need to cut the fence and dodge the sensors.''

''Exactly.''

Dare rubbed his chin and then took another swig of coffee, steeling himself for the fire when it hit his stomach. Life dealt rotten hands sometimes, and right now he was feeling that the most rotten hand was that he couldn't take Andrea home with him and fall asleep wrapped around her. Instead he forced himself to consider what she was saying.

''Maybe,'' he said presently, ''we ought to look at it another way. Say our man has a legitimate reason to be out there, but not one legitimate enough to cover multiple visits to the flight line. Say he doesn't want anyone to know he's been there if he can avoid it, but if he gets stopped his cover story is good, just once.''

''Just once?''

Dare shrugged. ''Well, not enough times to explain repeated visits, but good enough that he'd be overlooked once or maybe twice.''

Andrea nodded. ''He still has to get past all the sensors.''

''There must be people who can do that.''

''Not according to Halliday. According to him, only he and his technicians know anything about the layout of the sensors. He said each of them knows part of it, and only he knows all of it.''

''So maybe Halliday's wrong. Maybe he just likes to think he's the only one—''

Andrea shook her head. ''I looked into it. The plans are highly classified. There's one copy in Halliday's safe and one copy with central document control. Nobody on the base has checked out the copy from document control, and none of the document custodians has enough technical background to understand the stuff, so that rules them out. That leaves only—'' Andrea's head snapped up. ''Dare!''

He leaned forward. ''What?''

"Maybe he *is* the only one."

"Who? What? Run that by me again, Andrea."

"Maybe Halliday *is* the only one who can get by all the sensors. And he'd have a legitimate excuse to be on the flight line, but not too often."

"How so?"

"He could say he was checking out the security systems. My guys know who he is. They'd let him pass without a second thought. But if he was out there too often, they'd get suspicious."

"Well, I guess he's a possibility, then, but that doesn't prove anything, Andrea."

She sighed. "I guess not. I can't imagine why he'd do this, anyway."

"That's been a problem all along—no apparent motive. Look, maybe it wouldn't hurt to keep an eye on him."

"Damn straight," Andrea said briskly, standing. "I'll talk to Nickerson in the morning. Honestly, Dare, he sat right here and told me he was the only person who could bypass the electronic surveillance. I thought he was bragging, but it never occurred to me that he might be laughing at me."

"Maybe he wasn't." Dare stood, too. "Maybe we're too tired to think straight."

"Yeah." She gave a short laugh and rubbed her neck again.

Dare moved around behind her and put both his hands on her shoulders, rubbing deeply but gently. Andrea released a soft groan of satisfaction.

"Feel good?" Dare asked.

"Mmm."

"You know what I want more than anything, Andrea?"

"Hmm?"

Bending his head, he closed his teeth gently on her earlobe. "To take you home with me and go to sleep with your head tucked under my chin and your legs all tangled with mine."

He heard her softly indrawn breath and waited for the anticipated refusal.

"Okay," she said.

Stunned, Dare froze, his hands locked on her shoulders, his mouth near her ear. He had to clear his throat before he could find his voice.

"What did you say?"

"I said 'okay.'" Turning, she faced him.

Dare drank in her face, noting that her eyes were incredibly weary, but also incredibly soft. This Andrea was the one who'd reached in and plucked something from his heart that he'd thought himself incapable of giving. He was fond of all the Andreas, but this one, so rarely in evidence, held a special place in his soul.

"Are you sure?" he asked, daring to touch her hair, her cheek, with the gentleness she so easily evoked in him.

"I'm sure." She met his look squarely.

"You won't regret it?"

"I'll regret even more spending tonight alone," she said steadily. So little time. So very little time. It was suddenly important not to waste even a minute of it.

"I'll get you back before the world is up."

She nodded. "I know you will, Dare." The words conveyed her trust, surprising them both, for neither of them had realized just how much she trusted him.

"Give me ten minutes to warm up the Bronco, then come out," he told her. Not for anything would he have the cops at the front desk see them depart together. It wouldn't bother him, but it would bother Andrea.

A short while later, Andrea snuggled into Dare's embrace, her head tucked under his chin, her thigh caught between his, just the way he'd wanted her so badly.

"Now," she murmured, "I don't want to sleep."

"You should. You're pooped."

"So are you. Are you sleepy?"

"Only a little."

"I needed this," she sighed. "God, how I needed this."

"You only had to tell me."

"I know. That scares me."

He slipped his fingers into her short hair and stroked her scalp gently. "Why does that scare you, Andrea?"

She was silent for so long that he began to think sleep had claimed her, but then he heard her draw a deep breath.

"I've never had anyone want to please me before," she said finally.

"But why should that scare you?"

"Because it's so different. Because it changes the rules."

"How does it change the rules?" Patiently he caressed her, waiting for her to work her own way through her feelings.

"It's a responsibility," she said. "A big responsibility."

"How so?"

"I could hurt you."

He sighed heavily and hugged her tighter. "That's not your responsibility, Andrea."

"Maybe. Maybe not. I don't think I'm explaining myself very well."

"Take your time."

"It doesn't matter."

"Yes, it does," he said. "It's as important as hell because it bothers you. Are you afraid you'll disappoint me?"

"Yes!"

The way the word burst out of her told Dare more about Andrea's real fears than any number of words could have. So she wasn't terrified of being turned into another woman like her mother; she wasn't terrified of being devoured by him. She was terrified of disappointing him the way she'd disappointed her father.

Dare had a sudden painful image of Andrea the way he'd seen her at chapel when she was all of what—thirteen? fourteen?—in that ridiculous, frilly dress. Had she been trying to please the father who could never be pleased? Had she given up finally, burying the hurt deep inside, and gone her own way, thinking she couldn't please any man, that she was a failure as a woman?

He had no difficulty imagining Andrea even younger, five or six maybe, with her freckles and pert face, being hollered at because she was dirty, or because she'd been playing with the boys. Because she wasn't Charlie Burke's notion of a female.

"Andrea," her name came out hoarsely, torn from some place deep inside him, "you won't disappoint me."

"You don't know that, Dare."

"Sure I do." He tried to keep his tone light enough that she wouldn't pull away from the depth of the feelings she'd just drawn out of him. Rolling onto his back, he pulled her with him so that she lay on top of him and hugged her so tightly she squeaked a protest. "You can make me mad," he said, "and you can make me hurt, but you can't ever disappoint me."

Andrea told herself it was because she was so tired, but tears sprang to her eyes and dropped onto Dare's chest.

"Andrea, honey, don't cry. You're worrying me."

"I'm just tired," she said, sniffling forlornly. "It's one of those stupid female things I do sometimes."

What could he say to that? Not knowing what else to do, he kissed her soundly.

"Now sleep, darlin'," he said, once again tucking her securely into the curve of his large body. "I'll wake you in time to get you back."

Andrea woke at the first sound of Dare's alarm clock in the morning. Still tucked against his shoulder and side, she waited while he cursed softly and felt around his night table. The buzzing stopped, and he relaxed back into the bed with a sigh.

"Andrea?" His voice was hushed. "Time to get you back."

"What time is it?"

"Five."

She snuggled closer. "How about a quickie, cowboy?"

"I was going to feed you breakfast."

"I'll eat at the O'Club."

"A quickie, huh?"

"Very quick," she said, nuzzling his nipple. "I can't believe I climbed into bed with you last night and *slept.* Not when all I've been able to think about all week..."

With a growling laugh he rolled over onto her. Moments later he was sheathed in her moist warmth. "That quick enough for you?"

Andrea rolled her hips suggestively. "Not quite, cowboy. You forgot the rest of it."

"The rest of wha—" The words died in a groan as she tightened herself around him. "Now you've done it, woman," he growled. "Now I'm going to—" He whispered the rest of the words into her ear, very earthy words. Andrea might have giggled except that he was doing exactly what he'd threatened, and it felt so damned good....

"You can talk dirty to me any time you want, sir," Andrea told him breathlessly a few minutes later. "Just as long as you follow through."

Dare was still chuckling when he drove her back to the BOQ.

Nickerson knocked on her office door almost before she settled into the chair behind her desk.

"Oh hell, what now?" she asked on a sigh as she watched him close the door and come to stand in front of her.

"The fire marshal called me at three this morning, ma'am. I thought you'd want to know what he said."

Andrea was silent, thinking the only thing she really wanted to do was curl up in some cozy corner and enjoy the glow Dare had left her with. He always left her feeling good, she realized with a dawning sense of wonder. He always made her feel good about herself.

"Ma'am?"

Nickerson's voice called her back to the present with a thud.

"Sorry," she said. "I guess I'm not really awake yet." Looking up at Nick, it suddenly dawned on her that he had probably tried to raise her as soon as the fire marshal called him, but she'd left her radio on her desk because Dolan had taken the command, and she hadn't been in the BOQ to answer her phone. Her cheeks began to heat, and the oddly wooden expression on Nickerson's face didn't help.

"What did the fire marshal say?" she asked, hoping he wouldn't notice her rising color.

"The fire was definitely arson, Captain. Merle says it was started by a homemade electronic fire starter that was hidden behind the instrument panel in the cockpit. He also said that whoever built and hid the ignition device has a fairly sophisticated knowledge of electronics."

"You could say that about half the airmen on this base, Nick. This is the high tech Air Force, remember? Anything else?"

Nick shook his head. "That's the big development. Not real helpful."

"I'm beginning to think this is one case where we'll have to make our own breaks."

"Ma'am?"

Andrea waved her hand dismissively. "Just thinking aloud, Nick. Never mind."

When Nick had gone, she found her thoughts straying away from business again and back to Dare and the warm glow he'd left her with. Maybe she was in love with him.

The thought trickled into her mind almost casually, forming fully before it really registered. When it did, shock caused her heart to slam. Love? Why that, of all things? In all her planning and dreaming for her future, that was one contingency she'd never considered, one possibility she'd never reckoned on. She didn't want to be in love, for crying out loud! But the more the word turned in her mind, the more realistic it sounded.

If she was in love with Dare now, then she had certainly been in love with him even before Christmas. Maybe, she thought with a reluctant smile, ever since the moment he'd come marching up to her at gunpoint the night her cops had brought him in for loitering near the weapons depot. Maybe since the moment he'd told her that he would be grateful if she wouldn't go around addressing people as "cowboy." Certainly at least since he kissed her at Thanksgiving, because after that he'd begun to seriously preoccupy her thoughts.

And what difference did it make exactly when it had happened? There was a deep certainty in her that it *had*, happened and for the worst possible person at the worst possible time. Her departure for Minot had been looming unpleasantly for some time, but now it yawned before her like a step into a black pit. She didn't want to give up her career, and she wasn't certain any longer that she could give up Dare.

What now?

Dare spent the day in a considerably more optimistic frame of mind. SAC might be breathing down his neck for a resolution to the problem, OSI might be crawling into every nook and cranny on the base, but his night with Andrea had persuaded him that he was winning on that front. She had finally confided her fears to him, a sign of trust he valued fully. She'd wept in his arms, slept in his arms, and played this morning with a blossoming confidence in her womanhood. What more could he ask?

A commitment. The word nearly made him break into a cold sweat, and his confidence took a sharp dip. She'd certainly given him no indication that she no longer considered their relationship temporary. For all he knew, she was still planning to leave for Minot free as a bird and without a backward glance. How could he possibly persuade her that he was capable of giving her the freedom she needed for her career while nailing her down to permanence in a relationship?

Because he wanted that kind of permanence. All his life long he'd wanted it, except for a brief spell after his first marriage. He could have had it a half-dozen times over, too, except that he was particular about things like companionship and friendship. And love? If the day ever came when he was sitting in a rocker and leaning on a cane, he wanted to be with someone he liked, not someone he tolerated. And, by God, he *liked* Andrea. There wasn't a shadow of a doubt in his mind that she would still be zinging him when he was ninety.

It was too soon, he decided with a sigh, to press for a commitment from her. For now he'd better stick with persuading her to let him visit her out in Minot on weekends. Then, when she saw he was willing to commute any distance to be with her, maybe she would consider more. Maybe all she needed to know was that they could make it work whatever the difficulties.

With that thought, he felt a resurgence of optimism, and he was still feeling pretty good when he closed up his office and headed over to the Security Squadron. It was the weekend at last.

"Hi," Andrea said with a shy smile when Dare appeared in her doorway.

"Hi," he replied, stepping inside and closing the door. "It's Friday." Why did she look so shy? he wondered. What had happened?

"So it is," she agreed. "What are your plans?"

"Our plans," he corrected gently. "How about options, instead? There are a number of places we can go."

She bit her lower lip, lifting her eyes hesitantly to his.

"Would you—would you mind very much if we didn't go any-where?"

Dare wouldn't have believed he could plunge so far so fast. "What's wrong?" His tone was sharper than he intended, and he regretted it instantly when he saw her head snap up and her chin thrust out.

"Nothing's wrong, sir," she replied coolly.

Dare started backpedaling immediately. "I didn't mean to snap at you, Andrea. It's been a long week. Has something come up?"

Little by little her chin softened and the flare in her green eyes died. "I just don't want to be out of touch this weekend. I need to be accessible if something happens."

Well, he thought, here's your chance to prove you can let her career come first. It didn't thrill him. "All right. Maybe we can squeeze in a little time together."

Andrea gnawed her lip and darted a couple of uncertain looks at him.

"Andrea, is something wrong?"

Only that he hadn't even argued with her, she thought mis-erably. Her feelings were so new, so fragile and so frightening, that she needed the reassurance of knowing they were returned, at least a little.

"Actually," she said after a moment, then cleared her sud-denly dry throat, "actually, I thought maybe—if it wouldn't be too much trouble—that I could—that is—"

Dare couldn't stand it another minute. His hopes for the weekend were dashed, and now Andrea was acting like she was afraid of him. Damning the consequences, he rounded her desk, pulled her up from her chair, and kissed her soundly. When he lifted his head, her green eyes looked glazed.

"Spit it out, Andrea," he coaxed. "If *what* isn't too much trouble?"

"Can I stay with you this weekend?" The words came out in a breathless sigh.

He couldn't help it. He kissed her again, then tucked her head against his shoulder. "You can stay with me any weekend, every weekend, and every night in between if you want, honey. You don't even have to ask. But someone might find out. I thought that bothered you."

"Nobody will know." She lifted her head and looked up at him with eyes so soft that Dare felt his heart turn into instant mush. "I just have to be reachable by radio."

"Done." He brushed a stray tendril of strawberry blond hair back from her forehead. "Do you want to come with me now?"

"I need to pack an overnight bag first. I'll walk over later."

"Andrea, sweetheart, it's twenty-three below outside."

A smile rose from her lips to touch her eyes. "That's okay. I've got the gear for it. Besides, nobody will ever recognize me all bundled up like an Eskimo."

Dare shook his head. "Uh-uh. I'll pick you up in front of the base library at seven. You're not going to walk more than half a block in this."

She tilted her head. "If you're going to come out anyway, then you might as well pick me up in front of the BOQ."

"Aren't you worried there might be gossip?"

Andrea shrugged. "Let 'em talk. I'm leaving in just over a week."

A cold fist clenched Dare's heart. She sounded so damn cool that it hurt. "Yeah," was the only reply he could manage. "Yeah."

Chapter 13

Dare's romantic streak showed that evening. While a polar air mass moved in, sending the temperature ever lower and obscuring the world with blowing snow, he and Andrea ate by candlelight in his dining el. Afterward he put a tape on the stereo, and the sadly haunting strains of "The Tennessee Waltz" filled the room.

"Dance with me, Andrea."

"I can't dance," she protested, feeling shy again.

"It doesn't matter," he coaxed, his blue eyes as warm as the candle flames. "Just lean on me."

She ought to be wearing some beautiful gauzy creation, Andrea thought, not jeans and a sweater, but it ceased to matter the instant she stepped into his arms. She felt as if she were floating, and as she relaxed it became easier to follow Dare's slow movements. Before long they were waltzing slowly around the room.

With a deep sigh, Andrea rested her head on his chest and gave herself up to all the good feelings. Through the soft wool beneath her cheek she could hear the steady beat of his heart, and she was surrounded by the soapy, musky scent that was particularly his. He felt so strong and solid against her, made her feel so secure and cherished when he held her. It was going to hurt badly when she left next week. She sighed again.

"That sounded sad." Dare's voice rumbled deep in his chest.

"I guess it was, a little."

"Anything I can do to help?"

Tell me it won't be all over in twelve days, Andrea thought. "Not really," she said.

Bending, he pressed his face to the top of her head. "Just let it all go, Andrea," he murmured. "Don't think, don't worry. Just *be*."

It was a tempting invitation, and Andrea tilted her head back, seeking his mouth with hers. Finding it, she kissed him with every bit of longing in her heart, pressing closer to him, wrapping her arms tightly around his neck.

Dare felt her desperation and wondered at it. Her kiss, however, was evoking thunder in his blood, and he didn't feel like thinking right now. Reaching down, he cupped her delightful derriere and drew her snugly up against him. Slipping his leg between hers, he pressed against her and felt her thighs tighten around him.

Andrea leaned back a little and smiled hazily at him. "You always manage to teach me something new."

He flexed his thigh again and smiled when she drew a deep breath. "I like dancing with you, Captain."

"Is that what this is? Dancing?"

Dare tightened his grip on her, rocking her suggestively against his leg. "Maybe it's flying," he said. "It sure feels every bit as good."

Andrea buried her face against his sweater. "Maybe we should go fly in the bedroom, Colonel."

"Not yet." He drew his leg from between hers and began again to move in time to the music. "Right now, Captain, I just want to enjoy holding you and dancing with you. We've got all weekend."

"Yes, sir."

"I don't get to hold you enough, Andrea. I don't get to be with you enough."

He expected her to stiffen, to withdraw in that subtle way she had when she was uncomfortable. Instead she seemed to soften even more against him, and Dare began to really relax.

"I remember you at Mather," he told her. "I used to see you in chapel. You had a pink dress with flounces and ruffles all over it."

Andrea groaned. "I hated that dress. I hoped there wasn't a living soul who noticed me in it."

"Why'd you wear it?"

"My father made me. He told my mother to get me something feminine to wear to chapel so I wouldn't embarrass him. My mother had terrible taste."

"Maybe she just knew what your father considered feminine."

"That's entirely possible. It used to drive me crazy, the way she always buckled under and let him dictate everything."

"You're certainly not the type to let anyone do that."

She looked up at him, a teasing glint in her eye. "And here I thought I was the model of an obedient subordinate officer."

"You've never been insubordinate, Captain. You have other methods."

She dropped one of her hands from his neck and slipped it up under his sweater, finding the soft mat of hair on his chest. There was no way, she realized, that she would ever get her fill of touching him.

"Are you into my chest hair again, Captain Burke?"

"Yes, sir." She curled her fingers, giving it a playful tug. "I don't suppose I can persuade the Colonel to ditch his sweater?"

"What's wrong with my sweater?"

"It's in my way."

So he ditched it, and while he was at it, he ditched hers, as well. And he discovered that Andrea could still blush when he looked at her.

"Save the blushes for when I remove your bra, Captain."

She looked at him from beneath lowered lashes. "And when are you going to get around to that, sir?"

"Soon, Captain. Very soon."

But he continued to dance with her, holding her close and stroking her back from neck to hip. Andrea pressed her cheek to his chest and closed her eyes.

"Tell me about where you grew up," she said.

"My dad has a ranch near Kalispell, Montana. A few years

back I bought some acreage farther west, closer to the mountains. When I retire, I hope I can spend more time there.''

"You want to ranch?"

"No." He kissed her temple and cuddled her ever closer. "I just want to spend a little more time enjoying life. I see it more as a vacation place."

"What'll you do with the rest of your time?"

That'll depend on you, he thought. "There's always a market for retired generals," he said. "I'll see what develops."

Andrea looked up at him, the devil light in her eyes. "You're pretty sure of that promotion."

"I'm positive about it."

"Nothing like a pilot's ego, I always say. Has something to do with the 'right stuff,' I guess. Maybe it adds lift to the plane."

Chuckling, he stole a kiss. "Actually," he said, when she was suitably breathless, "I got the word this morning. I pin on my stars April first."

"Dare! That's wonderful!" Her green eyes shone as she looked up at him.

"I guess that means I'll outrank you for at least a couple more years."

But Andrea was in no mood to joke about it. Her joy for him seemed to swell until she felt she could barely contain it.

"I'm so pleased for you," she said softly.

That softness got him every time. Forgetting his determination to drag out every moment of this evening, he scooped Andrea up into his arms and carried her to his bedroom.

"Celebrate with me, Andrea," he said as he lowered her to his bed.

"I've never made love with a general before," she whispered, drawing him down with her.

"Big deal. You'd never made love with a colonel before, either."

The soft smile lingered on her lips and in her eyes as he hovered over her.

"I'd never made *love* before," she answered.

"Me either," he murmured as he released the clasp of her bra.

Before she could wonder at his meaning, he closed his lips

and teeth over her swollen nipple and sent shock waves of pleasure radiating outward to join with the ache that had been building all evening.

He had one intention and one intention only: to love Andrea so well, so perfectly, that if she never again allowed him to give her anything, he would already have given her the best he had in him. In seemingly no time at all, she reached a fever pitch, but he refused to give in to her pleas and tugs. Instead he trailed his mouth in lazy, tormenting spirals lower, across the sensitive skin of her stomach. Millimeter by millimeter, he drew down the zipper of her jeans, teasing her with hesitations. And finally he sent his hand foraging where she wanted his mouth, then his mouth where she wanted him.

All he wanted, all he needed, all he sought, was her pleasure. Only when he at last could please her no other way did he join himself to her and give her the gift of his own pleasure.

Sunday afternoon came all too swiftly. Andrea sat between Dare's legs on the floor of the living room, her back resting against his chest. They'd been sitting in companionable silence for some time, and she found herself thinking how nice it was to be able to share a comfortable silence with someone else.

She also found herself thinking about the swift passage of time. She was racing against it neck-and-neck now. One more weekend. Nine more days. The more she dreaded her departure, the faster it bore down on her.

Looking back over the past two years, she had the uneasy realization that time had been racing past her all along but she had been too busy to notice it. Hadn't she promised herself when she arrived here that she would make the terrible climate tolerable by taking the time to go cross-country skiing? Not once in two years had she taken her skis out of the closet. Instead she'd put her nose to the grindstone, determined to make her squadron the best in SAC.

And what had that gotten her? A slightly bigger squadron in the same execrable climate. Two years had passed in the blink of an eye, and the next two years would probably pass even faster, and maybe she would garner a somewhat bigger command with all its attendant extra headaches. By then she would surely have made major, and she would immediately set her sights on light colonel.

Some morning, inevitably, she would wake to discover that twenty years had flown by in the blink of an eye. Would she look back at those twenty years and think that the only time she'd ever really lived was during her last few weeks here, on these too-short weekends with Dare?

As for Dare, Andrea was no fool. She knew very well that men like him didn't grow on trees. He was strong enough to be gentle and secure enough not to be threatened by her. In her experience, that was a very rare combination.

"Something wrong?" he asked when she stirred restlessly against him.

"Time," she said obscurely, but he understood.

"Little enough of it in a lifetime, let alone a week."

Slowly, she tilted her head and looked up at him, wondering not for the first time if he could read her mind. "Yes," she said on a soft sigh.

No time like the present, Dare thought, to take that forward step and see if his foot landed on solid ground. "I'll visit you on weekends, Andrea. If you want me to."

"Will you?"

Her misty green eyes held a flare of hope, and he smiled as much from relief as pleasure. "Yes."

Andrea turned over, still lying between his legs and against his chest, and kissed him. "Thank you," she said.

He wrapped his arms around her, holding her snugly. "My pleasure. You won't be that far away. I'll just avail myself of one of the prerogatives of my position and fly out there. Things can almost always be managed if you want to badly enough."

"You won't mind?" she asked him.

"Are you kidding?" Tilting her chin up a little more, he looked into her eyes. It still shocked him to realize that his calmly confident Captain Burke was truly confident only in her job and her uniform. If he'd had a magic wand, he would have used it to give her all the personal self-confidence she lacked. But there was no magic wand, and all he could do was hope she would eventually get the message.

"Andrea, darlin'," he said gently, "the only thing I'd mind is never seeing you again."

Her eyelids fluttered closed, and he was horrified to see a silvery tear squeeze out from beneath one lid.

"Andrea? Andrea, what's wrong?"

"Nothing," she said shakily, and managed an unsteady smile. "Damn, every time I turn around, you're making me cry. I *hate* to cry."

"Then don't."

"I can't help it. You say the damnedest things sometimes. Nobody's ever said so many nice things to me."

He gave her a bruising hug. "I'm just being truthful, sweetheart." And only partially truthful, at that.

For a long time they sat like that, her head on his shoulder, arms wrapped around one another, but finally Dare's stomach started rumbling. Reluctant as he was to disturb the cocoon of closeness they shared, he was going to have to do something about dinner.

"Give me a few minutes to get dinner started, Andrea."

"Can I help?"

"Nope." He kissed the tip of her nose. "When I come to visit you, you can do the honors."

"Every time?"

He caught the wicked sparkle in her eye. "Well, maybe just sometimes."

She let him go reluctantly and stretched out on the floor, unwilling to disturb the warm glow she was feeling. He was going to fly out to see her. She hugged the thought to her, more relieved than she could say. Even though he wanted nothing but an affair, at least he wasn't casual in his feelings about her. He cared, or he certainly wouldn't be willing to visit her in Minot.

Now, if she could just catch their homegrown saboteur. Why couldn't there be some way to smoke him out, right into a trap?

Toying with the idea, she wandered out to the kitchen and helped herself to one of the carrot sticks Dare had set out on the counter.

"I can almost smell smoke," Dare remarked as he lifted a steak off the electric grill. "What's got your brain on overdrive?"

Andrea shrugged. "Just wondering if there isn't some way to lay a trap for our saboteur."

"To lay a trap you need some kind of enticement to draw

your quarry out. We don't know enough about him to come up with the right bait."

"That's what has me stymied. But maybe we *do* know enough and just can't see it."

"You keep saying that. Pull the milk out of the fridge, will you?"

Andrea complied. "I keep saying that because I can't shake the feeling that the answer's staring me in the face. It just keeps nagging at me."

"Maybe you ought to let it rest awhile."

"I've let it rest all weekend." Walking up behind him, she wrapped her arms around his waist from behind and leaned against him. "You smell so good."

"Better than steak?"

"Always." Sighing, she nuzzled his spine. "I keep wondering, if the culprit really is Halliday, why he'd be doing this. I always thought he seemed pretty happy with his niche. You haven't served with him before, have you?"

"Not to my knowledge. We might have been posted to the same base at some time or another, but we've never been in the same unit." He flipped the second steak off the grill. "Come on, let's eat. You still think I'm the target?"

"Well, you're the only person being consistently harmed by all this. It makes more sense than the entire Bomb Wing being the target, or SAC."

"I guess." Dare held out her chair for her and snagged a quick kiss as she sat. He rounded the table and took his own seat, then unfolded his napkin. After a moment he shook his head.

"Nope, I can't remember ever knowing a Halliday. Now back in Nam there was this kid named Holi—" He broke off abruptly, his eyes growing distant with recollection.

"What is it, Dare?" Andrea asked impatiently. "What kid?"

"Holiday. I thought his name was Holiday, but maybe it wasn't."

"What kid?" Andrea demanded.

For a long moment he didn't answer. "Just a kid, an airman. He was in my ground crew. He got hit in a firefight one night at Tan Son Nhut, and I tried to get to him, but I couldn't. I wrote to his family afterward, but there wasn't much to say.

He'd been out there exactly one week, he was eighteen years old, and he was dead because he was on mission for me when the firefight broke out.''

Andrea set her fork down, aching for him, for the shadow of old sorrow she read on his face. "It was war, Dare," she said after a moment. "You can't hold yourself responsible."

His blue eyes focused on her. "I don't. Oh, maybe that was my first reaction when it happened. You're bound to think *if only* when something like that happens, but nobody is responsible for the accidents of war. No, I was just wondering if his name was Halliday, not Holiday. It's possible, I guess. It's been a long time. My memory could be playing tricks." He shrugged. "And where does it get us if his name *was* Halliday?"

Andrea pushed a piece of steak round and round on her plate. "Well," she said presently, "maybe a younger brother grew up thinking you were responsible for his older brother's death because you sent him on an errand."

"That's sick."

"So's poking holes in your hydraulic lines and blowing a hole in the nose of a flying B-52. We're clearly not dealing with a normal mind here. And it would fit with this feeling I can't shake that you're the real target."

"Then why didn't he kill me?"

"Damn it, Dare, he almost did! If you weren't as physically strong as you are, you would probably never have come out of that nosedive. I know you don't want to believe it. I sure as hell don't want to believe that somebody is trying to kill you. But I think we're both going to have to accept it. This creep wanted to kill you, and he wanted to be sure you were aware every agonizing moment of your approaching death."

Dare shoved his plate to one side. "I just lost my appetite. Andrea, we're really reaching with this."

"You mean *I* am." She'd lost her appetite, too. And then slowly she raised her head, looking at him. "I've got it."

"Got what?"

"An idea for a trap." Suddenly she was excited. "Say this guy wants to ruin you."

"I thought he wanted to kill me?"

"Say he does, but say he wants to get you into hot water before he does you in. Look, he put a hole in one bomber cockpit and set fire to another. Neither one of those incidents was physically dangerous to you, but both of them have made your life miserable."

Dare sighed and looked truly dubious. "All right, I'll agree with that for the sake of argument." He pulled out his cigarettes and lit one.

"Well, if he wants to ruin you, I bet he couldn't resist a chance to do it spectacularly."

Dare exhaled smoke. "How spectacularly? Why do I get the feeling I'm not going to like this?"

"You'll like it. Listen, let's use the grapevine. I swear it works better than the base paper. Schedule a generation for Wednesday or Thursday."

"I can't do that. We're grounded until—"

"You can always cancel it right beforehand," Andrea interrupted. "Say you schedule a generation, and then we put it on the grapevine that some important congressman or other is going to be on base—unofficially, of course—and that the generation's being held for his benefit. We can even increase security under the guise of protecting this congressmen."

"And then?"

"And then we put somebody on each and every one of the bombers from now until then. If our man can't resist the opportunity to give you a black eye in front of the world, he won't be able to resist this. And we'll catch him."

"We haven't caught him so far," Dare pointed out. "Despite stepped-up security."

"Dogs," Andrea said. "Let's use the K-9's. Put one on every plane with a handler."

Dare gave a grudging nod. "I can almost believe dogs might work. But Halliday, if it is Halliday, is bound to hear about it."

Andrea shook her head. "Nick can handle it. He can order the dogs out on some kind of maneuver, keep the entire unit out of contact with the rest of the squadron. Once it's dark they can move around the airstrip without anybody being the wiser. There's not even a moon this week."

"Somebody will hear about it."

"So I'll slap a classification on the whole damn thing. Nick can pick guards who he trusts to keep their mouths shut. The group of people who'll know what's really going on will be small enough that they'll know I can court-martial every one of them if word gets out."

Rubbing his chin, Dare thought about it. The plan was a rough sketch, of course, and a lot of details needed to be worked out, but it was a hell of a lot better than no plan at all.

"Okay," he said. "First thing tomorrow, I'll schedule a generation for Wednesday."

Andrea grinned. "Thanks."

"Thank me when it works." And it just might. At least they would be *doing* something, which agreed with him a hell of a lot more than sitting on his hands waiting for events to unfold. In fact, it gave him back his appetite.

"Eat up," he said after a moment. "And tell me how you're going to manage the security on this trap."

Dare ate and listened, thinking that Andrea had a tactician's mind. Steadily, piece by piece, she outlined a covert operation in which handpicked troops would move in and occupy all the bombers without tipping off the other guards. She'd learned well at the Academy, he thought, and displayed a natural talent for applying the things she'd learned. If she were a man...

The thought brought Dare up short. *If she were a man.* How many times must Andrea have thought the same thing and been forced to face the fact that she had to work harder and perform better and yet would never have the same opportunities? If she were a man, she wouldn't have set her sights on making colonel. No, she would be aiming for brigadier, at the very least, and he would have put his money on her to make it.

It was no wonder she was so fiercely independent, so determined to let nothing affect her career, so reluctant to let her femininity come forward. She worked under a major disadvantage and had to struggle continuously to overcome it.

He hadn't really thought about it like that before, but then, he'd never really been burdened by notions of what women should and shouldn't do. If an officer was capable, Dare didn't particularly care if the officer was male, female, black, or white or green with purple polka dots. Finding women in positions of command responsibility was a relatively new experience, a facet of the changing Air Force, and one that still caught him unawares at times, but he never held gender to be a mark against someone. Unfortunately he doubted that all his fellow officers felt the same.

When all was said and done, he decided, it was pretty remarkable that Andrea had let go as much as she had with him. And the fact that she *had* must mean that she felt something for him, something strong, because Andrea obviously wasn't the type to be led astray by mere hormones, not levelheaded, sensible, virgin Andrea Burke.

When Andrea at last fell silent, it was nearly nine. Dare was already thinking of taking her to bed for some long, lazy lovemaking that would still leave time for a good night's sleep before he took her back to the BOQ. She, however, was clearly revved up, thinking over her plans for the trap. He watched her for a while, but his patience began to wear thin as the minutes ticked by.

"Captain Burke."

She looked up from the pad she was making notes on. "Sir?"

"It's getting late. Are you planning to make notes all night?"

Andrea blinked, obviously coming out of her preoccupation with difficulty, but then a smile appeared, warming her hazy green eyes. "Do you have a better idea of what I should be making tonight, sir?"

"A much better idea. Can I interest you?"

Andrea crossed the living room and slid onto his lap. With a smile, she wrapped her arms around his neck. "I might have a few ideas of my own."

The ache that never entirely left him when he was within sight of her began to deepen. "Have I told you just how special you are?" he asked, capturing her face so she couldn't look away.

A faint blush stole into her cheeks, and her eyelids fluttered. "I'm not special," she protested in a smothered voice.

"Oh, yes, you are," he said gently, never taking his eyes from hers.

Unable to bear the intensity of emotion she was feeling, Andrea ducked her head, wiggling until she was able to tuck it into his shoulder. "No more, please," she begged in a small voice.

"All right, darlin'. No more. Just know that I think you're pretty damn special."

He felt her arms tighten convulsively around his neck, and he smiled against her ear. She was so small, so soft, so sweet, his lovely Captain Burke. And she would probably kill him for even thinking such a thing.

"Let's go to bed, sweetheart," he said. "I need to get as close to you as I can."

Much, much later Andrea said, "You never told me about your childhood."

They lay snuggled together under a down comforter, basking in the afterglow while the wind keened noisily around the corner of the house and rattled the windowpanes.

"There's not much to tell. I grew up with three brothers, working hard and playing harder. It was a good life for a kid. Plenty of fresh air and open space, horses to ride and a creek to fish in. My brothers are still on the ranch, and their kids are playing in the creek now."

"How come you didn't stay on the ranch?"

"I just always wanted to fly. To hear my father tell it, I was plane crazy from the age of two. I can't remember ever wanting to do anything else."

"Did it ever wear off?"

"A lot of things wore off, especially in Nam, but I still love being all alone at forty thousand feet in a clear sky." Turning onto his side, he wrapped his other arm around her.

"What about you, Andrea? When did you make up your mind to go to the Academy?"

"As soon as they announced they were going to take women as cadets. Before that I'd planned to go ROTC in college."

"But why?"

"Oh, I don't know. Maybe I wanted my father to have to salute me."

There was a laugh in her voice, and Dare smiled. "But you could have done so many things. Why this?"

"I just never seriously thought about doing anything else. I don't know why. Maybe it was because I grew up with the Air Force. I just wanted to do it, and do it well."

"You certainly do it well. Why didn't you want me to notify your family when you were shot?" As he spoke, he stroked the puckered scar on her shoulder with a gentle finger.

Andrea sighed. "Because my dad would have gotten on my

case again about resigning, settling down and having a family. Because he would have said I wouldn't have been shot if I'd been doing my job right.''

"You don't believe that, do you?''

"No. I know better. That's just my father.''

Dare kissed her. "Do you want a family someday?'' He nearly held his breath.

"I never thought about it.''

"Never?''

"Never. Why? Do you?''

"I think about it.'' Though she didn't move a muscle, Dare could feel her withdrawal. "You *could* have a family, you know,'' he said quickly. "Lots of career Air Force women do these days.''

"Child care would be a pain,'' Andrea said distantly. "Base day-care isn't open in the middle of the night.''

"Are you planning to do this without a husband?''

"I'm not planning anything at all!''

She was rigid in his arms now, and he could tell she felt cornered, but he couldn't understand why.

"Easy, honey. This is just a theoretical discussion.'' With one hand he kneaded her shoulders, willing her to relax.

"It may be theoretical,'' she said stiffly, "but I'm a realist. You can't expect me to believe any man would tolerate being a baby-sitter while his wife went running out in the middle of the night.''

Dare held his peace, stroking her soothingly.

"Well,'' she said after a moment, "it doesn't matter. It's all academic.''

He wanted to shake her then, shake her until her teeth rattled. *It doesn't matter? It's all academic?* Never had mere words cut him so deeply or hit him so hard. Take it easy, MacLendon, he warned himself. Take it easy or you'll drive her away.

Andrea bit her lip, sensing that she'd angered him, stunned to realize that she wanted him to argue with her, to tell her it wasn't academic. To say he wanted her to have his children.

But he hadn't said it. He'd been the one to say the discussion was theoretical, and he hadn't argued with her. All of a sudden she was terrified in a way she'd never been terrified before. Everything was out of whack, as if she'd become a person she hardly recognized. All those things she'd never thought she would want had suddenly become paramount. She wanted to talk about them, argue about them, hammer them out until she'd built a modified version of her future that included Alisdair MacLendon.

"You're mad at me, Dare."

"No, I'm not mad." Just frustrated all to hell. He forced himself to relax and resume caressing her back.

Presently he remarked casually, "You know, I learned a long time ago that if a person feels they're sacrificing too much they become bitter. I had a bitter wife."

"That wasn't your fault."

"I could have given up the Air Force. I didn't. I wouldn't. And I wouldn't ask anybody else to do what I won't do."

"But some compromises have to be made."

"Sure, but the compromises can't be all on one side."

Unsettled, Andrea moved even closer, seeking comfort. Dare turned a little to accommodate her. What compromises would she be prepared to make, she wondered, if she could have Dare? Could she set her sights a little lower and not work quite so hard? Well, of course, if she had a home to come back to each night she might be a little more eager to knock off at the end of the day. And a little less eager to go to work on weekends. But that couldn't possibly be enough, could it?

"Take it easy, Andrea," Dare said. "I was just talking generally, not trying to upset you."

"Weren't you?" The challenge was out before she could stop it, and they both froze. Dare spoke first, his tone dangerously silky.

"Do you want a confrontation, Captain?"

Andrea pulled out of his arms and sat up. "Yes!" And then, swiftly, before he could respond, "No! No, I don't."

Dare sat up, facing her, and saw the minute quiver to her lips and chin. God, she *was* upset! He really hadn't meant to upset her. "Andrea—"

"I'm sorry," she said unsteadily. "I don't know what's wrong with me."

Her distress tugged at his heart, creating an ache deeper than any he'd ever felt before. Reaching out, he lifted her onto his lap and cradled her close.

"Don't worry about anything, Andrea," he said gently. "Just let me love you. Everything will be all right."

Before she could register his words, he bent his head and captured her mouth in a deep, soul-searing kiss. His tongue teased hers, incited hers, until hers followed his blindly into the consuming, hungry warmth of his mouth. She became his willing prisoner, surrounded by arms that were powerful yet gentle, held by hands that were strong yet caring. When he lifted her so that he could capture her breast with his lips and teeth, she groaned and threw her head back in utter surrender.

"Dare," she begged. "Dare…"

Carefully he lowered her to the bed, his every muscle trembling with the strain of his restraint. Her hand blindly sought and found the rigid proof of his hunger for her. He groaned, nearly losing his grip on his massive self-control.

"Not yet, honey," he whispered hoarsely, and gently removed her stroking hand. "Not yet."

Surprising her, he captured her small feet in his large hands and kissed each of them gently on the arch and instep. Then his mouth found her delicate ankles, his tongue her shapely calves.

"I'm going to kiss you from head to foot," he said in a passion-rough voice. Turning her, he found the backs of her knees and the sensitive undersides of her thighs.

"You're beautiful, woman," he said roughly. "God, you're beautiful!"

She writhed and whimpered, everything forgotten in the tidal waves of yearning his caresses caused in her. Her hands gripped wildly at the bedsheets, at the headboard, and finally at him. When at last Dare covered her, she was so open, so receptive, so defenseless, that it was as if there was no skin to separate them. His pleasure was hers, and hers was his. They sighed as one, and cried as one, and found completion as one.

Chapter 14

Dare's parting kiss was still warm on Andrea's lips when she settled behind her desk on Monday morning of her last week. *Her last week.* Those simple words held all the threat of a death sentence. She didn't know how she would bear the separation, let alone the inevitable end of the relationship. For it would end. How long would he continue to fly out to Minot to visit her when, right here, there were any number of warm and willing women? Women who were more feminine, who could provide all the things that men seemed to want from women.

Andrea couldn't begin to imagine what it was that had drawn Dare to her in the first place, and being unable to imagine that, she couldn't imagine that he wouldn't swiftly tire of her. She must simply be a novelty to him, she thought. He was caring and kind, but that was because he was a decent human being. He treated her with the same consideration he would show anyone. Their relationship wasn't casual, because he wasn't a casual person, but that didn't mean he cared about her the way she cared about him.

And so she would leave, and time and distance would slowly sunder them. How was she ever going to bear it? Yet how could she not? She couldn't sacrifice everything she'd worked for, everything she believed about herself, every need of her own.

"Morning, skipper," Nickerson greeted her as he entered her office. "We had a surprisingly quiet weekend, all things considered." He set his list on the desk in front of her and poured coffee.

"Nick, skip the weekend incident report. I want to discuss something with you."

Last night, Andrea thought, it had all been so clear and certain. Now she was uneasily aware that she might be making a gigantic mistake, one that could conceivably stain her career. Her conviction that Halliday was involved in these incidents was a guess supported only by the slenderest thread of evidence. The entire premise behind her idea of setting a trap was equally shaky. There was certainly no sort of discernible logic behind the sequence of events.

For a long moment she hesitated, uncertain whether to go ahead with this. She would be leaving in a week, after all. No one would condemn her for letting events unfold in their normal course. No one would condemn her for failing to risk everything on a last-ditch attempt to solve the mystery before she departed.

But she would condemn herself, Andrea realized. Looking at Nickerson, she plunged ahead.

"Nick, we're going to set a trap for the saboteur."

Nickerson nodded approvingly. "Who's in on it?"

"You, me and MacLendon. I don't want anybody else to know what's really going on. We're going to use the dogs, because it's a hell of a lot harder to slip past a dog than a tired human. And I'm going to need you to handpick me a group of the most trustworthy cops in the squadron."

Nickerson chuckled unexpectedly. "Now ain't that ironic, skipper?"

Andrea looked blankly at him. "What's ironic?"

"Oh, it's just that Halliday and his crew have really ticked off the dog handlers a few times. Halliday's always insisting that the dogs are a waste of government money, that his electronic gizmos can do the job a hundred times better. I finally shut him up by asking if he had a gizmo that could sniff drugs or explosives half as good as a dog."

"So why is that ironic?" Andrea asked, wondering if Nick also suspected Halliday.

"Because," Nick said, "when push finally came to shove around here, his electronic gizmos failed and we're turning to the dogs. He's not gonna like it."

"He damn well better not know about it," Andrea said sharply.

Nickerson lifted a brow. "No, ma'am. Not until it's over. You made that clear."

Asking for input, Andrea laid out her plan to Nick: the dogs on each plane to prevent any more sabotage to them; the phony news of a congressman's impending visit; the staged generation. Nick was concerned that the magnitude of the security preparations alone would tip the perpetrator to the trap. Andrea had already considered that.

"He's got to pick up on something or this whole thing will fall through. Look, Nick, if a congressman were really coming on Wednesday and a generation were planned, we'd be up to our eyeballs in security preparations after what's happened around here. I suggest you just start arranging additional security and fit the real briefing to the dog handlers somewhere in the middle so it doesn't stick out. Once our man thinks he knows what's going on, he'll buy whatever cover story you give our operatives."

Nick nodded. "I figure I'll order the dogs out on night patrol in the family housing area. Then, during shift change tonight, we can move 'em onto the planes. It'll sound okay that we're putting the dogs in the housing area, because we'll be calling in every available man for added security."

"What about patrols in the housing area? We can't leave every family on this base without police protection. I realize almost nothing ever happens out there, but if we leave them unprotected, you can bet your boots something will happen."

"I thought of that. I plan to peel off a couple of regular patrols to replace them. The problem is explaining why we're mobilizing all the dogs, and a patrol in family housing is the best I can come up with that doesn't sound suspicious."

"Okay. You get started on preparations, Nick. I have to go to staff conference."

The weather, which had turned thoroughly inhospitable on

Friday night, remained so. Dry crystals of snow blew in a hazy, hissing cloud that resembled a light fog. The drift at the end of the building had reached ten feet in height, but the walk in front of the building was dry, with the snow snaking across it in undulating lines. Andrea unplugged her truck's engine block heater from the pole in front of her parking slot and ran the engine until the cab was warm enough that she could pull off her snorkel hood. While she waited, her breath formed a mist of ice on the driver-side window, and she had to scrape it off.

Boy, did Florida sound good right now, Andrea thought as she wheeled out of the parking lot. Instead she got Minot.

Twenty minutes later, Dare dropped his bomb at the staff conference.

"Well, people, on Wednesday we're receiving an unofficial visit from Bill Thomas. In case some of you don't know, he's the senior member of the House Armed Services Committee. He'll be on base for approximately two hours, and for his benefit I'm scheduling a generation."

The reactions were immediate and negative, but Dare waved them aside.

"Look, folks, this one's on my head. SAC left it to my discretion, but I think you realize the higher-ups aren't going to be very happy if Thomas discovered that an entire bomb wing is out of operation thanks to what seems to be a solo saboteur."

"The rock and the hard place," remarked his deputy commander. "Damned if you do and damned if you don't."

"Essentially," Dare agreed. "Anyhow, this visit is not to be officially announced. The fewer people who know, the better. Maybe we can keep our troublemaker from finding out. Burke?"

"Sir?"

"I expect you to step up security accordingly. Even if we can't catch this guy, I want things tight enough that we'll get wind of anything unusual. If there's a whisper of anything out of line, I'll cancel the generation."

"Yes, sir."

"Maybe we'll luck out and have a blizzard," Captain Bradley remarked.

Dare snorted. "That would be lucky only if it kept Thomas

from getting here. Those planes are supposed to be able to take off under all conditions, Bradley.'' He looked down at the pad on the table before him. "I think that covers everything I've got. Anything else, people?''

No one had anything else to bring up.

"Dismissed, then,'' Dare said. "Burke, I want you in my office to discuss security.''

"Yes, sir.''

Dare's office was larger and more impressive than Andrea's, complete with wood paneling, and his desk dwarfed hers. Perks of rank, she thought as she closed the door behind them.

As soon as the latch clicked, Dare turned and tugged her into his embrace.

"God, woman,'' he said gruffly, "it drives me crazy to be in the same room with you and have to stay cool.''

Resting her hands on his upper arms, she smiled up at him. "Me, too.'' It did indeed, and it thrilled her to know he felt the same.

"I want like hell to kiss you, but I can't have you walking out of here looking thoroughly kissed.''

"Just a little one, then,'' Andrea said, rising on tiptoe to brush her lips lightly against his. She felt the tension in him, the control, and everything inside her clenched with the pleasure of knowing she was desired.

Dare sighed and released her. "Okay, back to business.'' He rounded his desk and took his chair, then motioned her to do the same. "I've cleared this little operation of yours with SAC HQ. We've got the go-ahead for just about anything short of actually launching a generation.''

"Good.'' Andrea nodded her pleasure, but suddenly had one of those schizophrenic moments when she saw everything from a different perspective. She was busting her behind to try to reach Dare's position, yet he was sitting here and telling her that he'd had to clear everything with *his* superiors. She'd cleared it with him, he'd cleared it with them, and maybe they'd cleared it with somebody even higher. In other words, no matter how high you got, there was always somebody higher to appease. Was it worth the effort? Unsettled, she shook herself.

"Are you with me, Andrea?''

Blinking, she looked at him. "Yes, sir.''

"This is the part you'll like. SAC HQ notified OSI that this is your baby. They can cooperate at your request, but they're not to interfere in any way."

Andrea *did* like that. She grinned. "Yes, sir." Dare must have had a great deal to do with this, she realized. After all, what would SAC HQ know about her except what Dare told them? Her heart swelled.

"Andrea, you do realize that your neck is on the block now?" His expression was disturbed. "I made it clear that there are no guarantees this operation will work, but you know how that goes. They want a resolution, and if they don't get it, they'll be looking to lay the blame somewhere. When I called OSI in, I took you off the firing line, but now you're right back in the way of all the flack that'll fly if this falls through."

Andrea's stomach did an unpleasant little flip, but she nodded serenely. "It goes with the territory."

"Yes, it does. We can still call it off."

She shook her head. "No, sir. This is how I earn my keep. Risks go with the job."

Damn, but he admired this woman! "I wish all my officers were like you, Andrea," he said gruffly. "I'm speaking as your commanding officer when I say that."

Rising, he came around the desk and bent over her. "Speaking as a man, I want another quick kiss before you go. But just a quick one, or I'll forget you can't walk out of here with swollen lips, mussed hair, and a rumpled uniform."

But oh, how she wished she could, she thought as his lips nestled against hers, caressing gently.

"I guess you'll be too busy to stay with me until this is over," he murmured regretfully. "Thursday night?"

Andrea nodded. "Thursday night."

He smiled and straightened. "Go get him, Captain."

Andrea had a few doubts before the day was over, the worst of them having to do with the number of assumptions they'd been making. She was flying on instinct, and she knew it. Assuming Halliday was the culprit was the least problematic of all her assumptions, because they could just as easily catch someone else with this trap as Halliday. A shakier assumption was the notion that their man would move at night, based solely on the fact that she'd been shot at night. What if the incidents were unrelated? What if the guy wasn't interested in ruining anyone at all? What if he was just a crazy who was striking out in random, pointless ways? What if this bait didn't tempt him? What if it scared him off?

Doubts notwithstanding, she sat on the edge of the flight line in her truck at eleven that night while Nickerson positioned the dogs and their handlers. Shivering as much from tension as cold, she waited impatiently and tried not to envision the dozens of things that could go wrong. She had to try equally hard not to think of how she could be lying in Dare's arms right now if only she weren't so pigheadedly determined to catch this guy before she left. There just wasn't enough time!

At twenty minutes after eleven the passenger door opened, and Nickerson climbed into the cab of the truck with her.

"Done," he said, pulling back his hood and blowing a cloud of frozen breath. "You know what really bugs me?"

"Tell me." Leaning forward, Andrea turned over the ignition.

"I just moved fifteen men and dogs past supposedly tight security, and not one damn sentry challenged us."

"Well, they can't sit under the planes, Nick. It's too cold. You had the advantage of knowing when the patrols would be passing."

"True, but it still bugs me. You still planning to come back later tonight?"

"About 4:00 a.m.," Andrea confirmed. "Just when everybody's at their lowest ebb."

"Might be the time our guy pulls his pranks. If I was doing something like that, that's the time I'd pick for it. Do you want me to come get you at MacLendon's?"

Andrea paused in the process of shifting into reverse and looked at Nick. How had he known? It was a question she didn't dare ask. His half smile was evident even in the dim glow of the dash lights.

"Go for it, skipper," he said.

Ten minutes later she stood in front of Dare's house, watching Nick drive off down the street. The sound of the truck's engine faded, leaving only the hiss of the blowing snow, loud on the dark, deserted street. Drawing a deep breath of frigid air, Andrea looked up at the starless sky and then turned to face the house.

Her stomach fluttered nervously as she took in the dark windows and drew another deep breath. What if he was annoyed at her for waking him up? Well, she'd burned her bridge behind her when she sent Nickerson on his way. It was either ring Dare's bell or take a long, cold walk to the BOQ. Gulping yet another breath, she squared her shoulders and marched up the sidewalk to the front door. Her hand trembled only a little bit when she punched the doorbell.

Two minutes later Dare, wrapped in his terry robe, opened his front door and peered through the storm door at a not-very-large figure in anonymous survival garb. Andrea? he wondered.

"Andrea!" Flinging open the storm door, he grabbed her unceremoniously by the arm and tugged her inside as he swiftly closed both doors behind her. "What's wrong?"

Pulling back her hood, she smiled uncertainly up at him. "I got lonely," she admitted in a small voice.

God, he looked good, she thought. Had it only been twelve hours since she'd left him in his office? His short dark hair was tousled, and there was a crease in his stubbled cheek from his pillow. His eyes were wide awake and alert, however, those wonderful blue eyes that seemed to see right into her heart.

"I was too lonely to sleep," he told her, a smile deepening the creases at the corners of his eyes. Reaching out, he began to unfasten her parka, buttons first and then the zipper. "That damn bed feels so big and empty without you. I keep wanting to roll over and put my arms around you. Are you here for the night?"

"Nick's coming back for me at a quarter to four." She pulled off her mittens so he could tug the parka down her arms.

Dare hung her parka carefully on the coat tree, but then he turned and gathered her into his arms, lifting her from her feet and burying his face in the curve of her neck.

"My boots," Andrea protested weakly as he carried her down the hall to his bedroom.

"I'll get to them," he laughed, raising his head and looking down into her eyes. "I intend to get to every damn thing you're wearing, one piece at a time."

"You don't mind that I just dropped in like this?"

"Mind? How can you even think that?" Still smiling, he lowered her to the bed, leaving her feet dangling over the edge. He paused to drop a kiss on her lips before turning his attention to the laces of her boots. "Come and go as you like, sweetheart." He pulled her boots off and dropped them beside the bed. Next he went to work on her snow pants.

Andrea's response was little more than a whisper. "I don't want to go."

Slowly his eyes rose to meet hers.

"I've never felt like this before, all confused about what I want to do and where I'm going. Everything seems all mixed up."

"Maybe you're just making things too complicated." Grabbing the cuffs of the snow pants, he pulled them off and then sat beside her, reaching for the button of her slacks. "It's really not all that complicated, Andrea, unless you get bogged down in the details. You just have to look at the big picture."

"What's the big picture for you?"

He paused in the act of removing her slacks. "Enjoying what we have together whenever we're able to be together."

"You make it sound so simple." *And so terminal,* she thought miserably. Whatever they had for however long they had it. Until next week was all they had.

"That's because it is, when you get down to what really matters." He stripped away her slacks and reached for the fastenings on her blouse. "Like this. Once you get past all the games, all the worries and doubts, all the false starts and hesitations, it's really quite simple—two people wanting and needing each other. Me needing to feel your arms around me, your skin against mine. Me needing to hear your sighs and needing to please you as much as you please me. What could be simpler, Andrea? Yet how much did you agonize over this?"

A whole lot, she thought as he cast aside his robe and stretched out beside her, gathering her into his warmth.

"Make love to me, Dare," she begged. "Just make love to me, please."

So he did just that, loving her with his lips, his hands and finally his whole body. Andrea felt the silken threads of his caring tighten about her, but that was all right, for now. His caring made her feel safe, and then it drove all the worries from her mind until the only reality was the gentle one he created for her.

"Reveille, Andrea," said a deep, husky voice in her ear. "It's 0300. The coffee's brewing, and the eggs'll be ready by the time you dress."

Andrea was lying facedown. With a groan, she rolled over onto her side and pried one eye open. As many times as she'd been rousted out of bed in the middle of the night, she'd never gotten used to it. Invariably her stomach and eyes burned, and there was a sense of unreality to everything.

"Did you say coffee?" she mumbled.

"Hot and black."

"Nobody ever woke me up with coffee before." She yawned and pushed herself up onto one elbow. "God, I hate getting up in the middle of the night."

"We all do. Are you really awake?"

"I won't go back to sleep, if that's what you mean." She shoved herself up into a sitting position and rubbed her eyes, unleashing another groan.

Dare thought she made a fetching sight as she sat there, blinking herself awake, completely unaware that the sheet had fallen to her waist, exposing the tempting white globes of her breasts. He damned Halliday for making it impossible for him to succumb to the temptation. No way would he ever get enough of this woman.

"I'll go start the eggs," he said, wrenching his eyes from her and standing up. "Ten minutes, Captain."

Stifling another yawn, Andrea looked over at him as he walked out of the bedroom and realized he was wearing battle dress. "How come you're dressed?"

"I'm going with you," he said over his shoulder.

"Oh." It was nice, she thought as she tossed back the blankets and climbed out of bed, to wake up in the middle of the night to find breakfast and coffee waiting. He had the damnedest way of making her feel cherished.

He was going with her?

"You're not going with me," she said ten minutes later, facing Dare over a generous breakfast. She refused to touch it until this was settled, but her stomach gave a betraying growl.

Dare grinned. "Eat up, Andrea. I know your appetite."

"I said you're not going."

"I heard you."

She regarded him suspiciously. "And?"

"And I'm still going."

"You'll get in the way."

"No, I won't." He spread marmalade on a piece of toast. "Save your breath, kiddo. My mind is made up."

"Nickerson and I know what to do," Andrea argued. "We'll split up and check things out. You'll just make it more likely that somebody will spot us."

"Did I ever tell you about the time I evaded the Vietcong for six weeks?"

Andrea ground her teeth. "There isn't a jungle out there to provide cover."

"The same principles still apply. Eat, Andrea. I promise I won't mess anything up."

"But—".

He looked at her, and all the gentleness was gone from his face. There was a steely, implacable look to him now, a glimpse of the man who'd made general. "Don't make me pull rank, Andrea," he said quietly.

"But *why?*" She had to know that, at least.

Dare shoved his plate aside and lit a cigarette. "The last time you went after this guy you got shot. He was armed, and he used that weapon on you rather than be caught. He tried to kill me. In the expert opinion of some people who examined my hydraulic system after it was tampered with, the holes were a very cunning way of leaving no trace, because if I'd augered in from forty thousand feet, it would have been impossible to tell what caused them."

"When did you hear that?"

"The report came in this afternoon. The investigators concluded that it *was* an attempt to kill me and I was damn lucky to have survived it. He's no sick little mind trying to ruin my career, Andrea. This guy *means* to kill, and he's not particular about who. You get in his way, you get killed. You accused me of not being able to accept the fact that somebody wants to kill me, but you've been treating this the same way, babe. You haven't really believed it, either. Not really.''

Sickened, shaken, Andrea looked down at her untouched plate. Here he'd gone to all the trouble to make sure she had breakfast and she wasn't even eating it. "If he's trying to kill you, you should stay away as far as possible.''

"Absolutely not. I'm not letting you go out there alone to face a killer.''

"If you weren't involved with me—''

"Damn it all to hell, woman. That makes absolutely no difference in what I'm doing! Do you think I'd let *anyone* go out to face a bullet that's meant for me?''

Looking into the icy blue chips his eyes had become, Andrea knew she'd said exactly the wrong thing, made exactly the wrong assumption. As well as she felt she knew him, she knew him not at all. She kept making assumptions about him and what he was doing based on something that wasn't Alisdair MacLendon at all. The realization shook her.

"We need to clear the air on something, Andrea,'' he said sternly. "I may care about you, but that has absolutely no bearing on my judgment. I didn't clear this operation of yours with the brass hats because I'm fond of you. I did it because, in my judgment, it's a good plan and stands as much chance of success as we could hope for. I would have done the same if you were Captain Joe Blow. I'm going out with you tonight because, whether you like it or not, I'm your CO and I've got oversight on this operation, and because I never send anybody else where I won't go. This is my usual mode of operation, and I'm not changing it for you or anyone else.''

"I'm sorry,'' Andrea said. "I didn't mean to insult you.''

He puffed on his cigarette, still frowning. "You're too damn defensive. You've got to stop filtering everything I do through your idea of how men treat women. I trust you to do your job right. Give me the same respect. Trust me to do mine.''

He stubbed out his cigarette. "Now eat, damn it. It's cold out there, and you need the energy.''

Instead she reached across the table and covered his larger hand with hers. "I'm a pain in the neck.''

A faint smile banished his frown. "Sometimes, but that was one of the first things I liked about you.'' Turning his hand over, he squeezed her fingers briefly and then released them. "Now are you going to eat, or do I get to be a pain in your neck?"

Nickerson arrived promptly at three forty-five, and Andrea sandwiched herself between the two men in the cab of the truck. If Nick was surprised to see Dare, he betrayed no sign of it, merely greeting him with a laconic, "Morning, sir."

Nick had barely pulled away from the curb when the radio crackled to life. "Bravo Bravo One, this is Tango Four Two, do you read?"

"Roger, Tango Four Two, this is Bravo Bravo One. What's wrong? You guys got frostbitten toes? Over."

"Ah, Bravo One, we've got a breach at Zulu Delta three-oh-one. Request backup and suggest you alert the duty officer."

Andrea yanked her brick off her belt and broke into the conversation. "Bravo One, this is Alpha Tango Niner. Tell those yokels to get on a secure frequency and then patch me through. Over."

"Roger, Alpha Tango Niner. Tango Four Two, do you copy?"

"This is Tango Four Two. I copy. Changing frequency, now."

Andrea punched in the new frequency on her radio in time to hear, "Alpha Tango Niner, this is Bravo One. We've got you patched. Go ahead, ma'am. Over."

"Tango Four Two, this is Alpha Tango Niner. Tell me what you've got."

"The perimeter fence has been breached about four hundred yards from the guard shack at the west end of the strip, ma'am. There's a boot print in the snow on the other side, but after that the ground's frozen and there's no more snow. We're waiting for backup, but if we go in there, we'll trigger all the alarms."

"Are you mobile or on foot?"

"On foot, ma'am. It was only going to be a short walk. Man, it's cold."

"We'll get a truck out to you, Tango Four Two, but you stay put in case the intruder tries to exit the same way."

"Yes, ma'am."

"Bravo One?"

"Bravo One, I read you, ma'am. Mobile backup is on the way to Tango Four Two. Anything else?"

"Notify all units to go to secure frequency and be alert. I'm on my way to the strip to check things out."

"Damn," said Nick. "Maybe this is it."

Andrea wondered the same thing as tension coiled in the pit of her stomach. "Still not a betting man, Nick?"

"Maybe this time, skipper. Maybe this time."

Yes, maybe this time. Andrea glanced up at Dare and found him looking steadily at her. He seemed to be waiting for her next decision, and nothing could have impressed upon her more clearly that he considered this to be her show. It was as if blinders fell from her eyes and she finally saw him unshadowed by memories of other men. Dare MacLendon looked at her as an equal.

"Where to, ma'am?" Nickerson asked as he neared the flight line.

"The guard shack near the alert planes," Andrea responded. "If the intruder's on the flight line, he'll be less alarmed to see a truck pulling up there."

When she stepped out of the truck, a gust of wind blew up the snorkel of her parka and stung her eyes to tearing.

"Damn, it's cold," Nickerson muttered as he caught her arm to steady her. He reached back into the truck and pulled out two M-16s, then handed her one.

Andrea felt the familiar heaviness of the rifle in her arms but looked at it as if she'd never seen it before. Was this really necessary? Looking up, she felt as if Dare were staring intently at her, but his snorkel shadowed his eyes completely, and she couldn't be sure. For a long moment she stood utterly still, and then she squared her shoulders, hefting the rifle more securely.

"Let's find out if the sentries have seen anything," she said briskly.

The guard shack was heated, allowing them to dispense with their hoods. In the dim red night lighting, Andrea could see that her troops were sleepy looking but alert.

"No, ma'am, we haven't seen anything," the senior airman answered her question. "After we heard the fence was breached, me and Lewis went out to look around, but we didn't see anything unusual. Sergeant Nickerson said we weren't to go close to the planes, though."

"That's right." With a dog and its handler on each plane, the bombers should be secure. Even if the handler fell asleep on the job, the dog would be guard enough, alerted by the faintest of noises.

"Has there been any trouble with the electronic systems?" she asked.

"No, ma'am. Not since we came on duty. Maybe earlier, though. Want me to check the logs?"

"Please."

While she waited for the sergeant to scan the logs by the illumination of a penlight, Andrea turned to look out at the B-52s as she had the night Halliday claimed to have found the fault in the system that had caused the intruder alert. The night Alisdair MacLendon had arrived on base. No way could she have guessed then just how much he would shake up her life. Apart from small whirlwinds of blowing snow, everything looked just as it had that night four months ago, yet Andrea felt the woman she'd been then was a complete stranger. What had she thought as she stood here that night so long ago? What had been uppermost on her mind then, except the loss of sleep?

"Ma'am?" said the sergeant from behind her. "Sergeant Halliday was out here at nineteen-thirty hours. The log shows he did some work on the system. There was an intermittent circuit failure."

"Where have I heard that before?" Andrea mused aloud, remembering that Halliday had used those same words four months ago. "Nick—" She broke off and leaned forward. "Nick, something's moving out there."

"Douse that light, Kavitch," Nickerson said sharply to the sentry. "Where, Captain?"

"Three planes down and to the right. I could swear I saw something."

It was gone, though, and after thirty seconds of staring intently into the night, Andrea gave up.

"Let's go, Nick. Kavitch, get on the radio and tell everyone to look alive. Our man is out there, and he's going to be trying to get away very shortly."

"Yes, ma'am."

"Andrea."

Dare's voice drew her up short just as she was about to go

out the door. Wheeling, she glared at him as she struggled to zip her snorkel with one hand.

"Damn it, Colonel, stay here," she said shortly. "Don't get in my way." She heard Nickerson draw a sharp breath, but she was past caring. The intruder was out there, and every moment's delay increased the chance he would escape.

Dare's voice reached her, deceptively mild. "I was just going to say that I saw a shadow moving under the fourth plane down. Take it easy, Captain."

"Damn fool thing to say, skipper," Nickerson remarked near her ear as they stepped out of the guard shack.

"I'll apologize later. Stow it, Nick. Let's split up and move in on the third and fourth planes from opposite sides." She kept her voice low even though they were downwind from the planes and their voices shouldn't carry.

"I'll take the left side," Nick said. "Likely he'll try to make a break toward the perimeter, and I'm bound to be at least as big as he is."

And I'm not, Andrea admitted silently, bowing to reality. "Okay. Let's move out."

Just then the door of the guard shack opened and closed quickly. Turning, Andrea recognized Dare's large shape. In his gloved right hand was his pistol.

"Not a word, Burke," he said flatly. "I'm pulling rank."

She should have known, Andrea thought. Right from the start he'd been the kind of CO to stick his nose everywhere and get involved where he wasn't wanted. She should have known. She wanted to get angry, but she couldn't, because part of her warmed to the fact that somebody in the world wanted to stand shoulder-to-shoulder with her. "How do you want to proceed, sir?" she asked stiffly.

"It's your show," he said levelly. "Just get it through your head that it includes me."

She could live with that, Andrea thought. "Okay. Nick, you go ahead to the left. The Colonel and I will come up along on the right. Let's move out."

Chapter 15

Andrea crouched, keeping low, and moved swiftly across the tarmac to the right of the parked planes. She hadn't gone a dozen steps before a sense of déjà vu assailed her, reminding her of the night she'd been shot. Her neck and scalp prickled with unexpected fear, and her step faltered, but only for an instant. Nickerson was out there, depending on her to do her share, and he could be in serious danger without backup. There was no choice but to go on, and no point in thinking about what might happen.

Suddenly and unexpectedly, she was extremely grateful for Dare's presence at her side. He moved stealthily, reminding her of a jungle cat, but when she inexplicably reached out for him, he paused and caught her hand in his.

What the hell am I doing in this business? The thought came out of nowhere, stunning her with its ferocity. She'd lied when she told Dare she'd never considered anything else, lied to him and to herself. Somewhere along the way all those other ideas had gotten lost in a burning desire to prove herself as an Air Force officer, but not even then had she imagined herself in this situation. Law Enforcement had never been her goal; it had been thrust on her, and she'd been making the best of it ever since.

Now here she was in the dead of night, stalking a killer with an M-16 in her hands. If she had an ounce of sense, she would be back in the guard shack directing this operation, the way a commander should. No, she had to get into it up to her neck. She always had and wondered if she always would.

"Andrea?" Dare's whisper was barely audible, although he'd turned so that his mouth was only several inches from her ear. "Something wrong?"

Andrea drew a deep breath and managed to shake her head. An instant later she released his hand a crept forward again. A faint rustle told her that he was following her.

Approaching the third plane, she slowed up and crouched lower. With her teeth, she pulled the mitten off her right hand and let it fall to the tarmac. The liner glove wasn't nearly as warm, but she had to be able to wrap her finger around the trigger. As quietly as she could, she released the safety and crept forward. The dog wouldn't be able to smell anyone under the planes, not when the wind was blowing at a stinging thirty-five miles an hour, and the same wind would carry away any reasonably quiet sounds. Andrea didn't want to chance it, though, for fear of scaring away their quarry. Those dogs were squirreled away on the sealed-up planes, but she had no idea whether their barking might be audible to someone on the tarmac below.

Seeing nothing around the undercarriage of the third plane, she edged forward to the fourth. Her heart was beating wildly now, and adrenaline soured and dried her mouth. Pausing, she pushed back her snorkel to widen her field of view. Now only a knit stocking cap covered her head, and the cold made her scalp ache.

A sudden groan and clatter to her left brought her swinging sharply around, and she peered intently into the shadow of the bomber. Lord, it was dark under there. Turning, she sought Dare.

"Did you hear it?" she barely whispered.

He nodded. "Nick."

That was what she thought, too. Dare gestured with his hands, indicating that if she moved to the left, toward the sound, he would swing around from the right and try to come up from the rear. Andrea nodded her agreement.

Licking her cold lips, she changed direction, creeping toward the bomber's rear wheels. Those tires were big, big enough to hide a crouched man easily. And she was exposed, mercilessly exposed. Cautiously, she eased into the protection of the big plane's shadow. Maybe the dog in the fuselage above her had heard the clatter, too. Maybe he was even now alerting his handler, who was under orders to immediately radio for backup. Straining her ears, she couldn't hear a thing except the ceaseless wind and her own ragged breathing.

She approached the bomber's right rear tires from the outside, then edged around them and nearly tripped over Nickerson's crumpled form. Dropping immediately to one knee, rifle cradled in her left arm, she shook him.

"Nick?" she whispered, and was relieved when she heard a faint moan. Reaching under his head, she made sure his cheek wasn't touching the frozen pavement. He needed help, but he would have to wait a few minutes.

Her eyes zeroed in on the other set of rear tires. There was only one place the intruder could be now, otherwise she would have seen his shadow as he ran in one direction or another. But between her and the concealment of the other tires, there was only open space. No way could she simply cross it.

She would have to brazen it out.

"I know you're over there, Halliday. Come on out. You won't get out of here."

There was no response.

"The perimeter's been sealed, Halliday. We know what you're up to. You can't run far enough."

A shot cracked on the wind, and chips of tarmac flew up at Andrea's face.

"Damn it!" she swore, and threw herself protectively across Nickerson.

Dare's voice suddenly cut through the night. "She's not alone, Halliday. Put your hands up and come out."

Dear God, don't let him be exposed, Andrea prayed as she huddled over Nickerson. Lifting her head, she looked in the direction Dare's voice had come from and saw his bulky shape striding slowly, almost casually, across the tarmac and into the plane's shadow. "Oh, my God," she whispered. "Oh, my God." He couldn't have made a better target of himself, his shape clearly silhouetted against the background light of the vapor lamps.

Another shot rang out, and this time the bullet smacked the pavement in front of Dare. His step never faltered.

"I'm the one you want, Halliday," he called out. "Come on out and fight like a man. I'm not even armed."

Halliday was going to kill him! The certainty settled in Andrea's stomach like a cold lump of lead. Grabbing her rifle, she waited for Dare to speak again.

"Come on," he said. "This is what you really want. You really want to slug it out with me, not with the whole Air Force. Well, I'm here, Halliday. Here's your chance."

There was no way Halliday could watch both herself and Dare and keep himself concealed from them both at the same time, she figured. Those tires were just too big. Resting her rifle on her forearms, she began to crawl forward on her stomach.

"Don't move another step, MacLendon!"

It was Halliday, all right. Andrea recognized his frightened voice.

"Why not?" Dare asked almost pleasantly. "You want to have it out with me. Well, you can't do it from behind those tires. Come out and face me. We can talk about what's bugging you."

"You killed my brother!"

So that *was* it. Andrea's stomach lurched sickeningly, and she crawled faster. From the sound of Halliday's voice, he was wired on fear and anger. There was no telling what he would do. Damn Dare for sticking his nose into this.

"Tell me about your brother, Halliday," Dare suggested, halting and standing with his hands in plain sight. "I don't remember your brother."

He was buying time, Andrea realized. He was buying time for her to reach Halliday. Ignoring the frozen ache of her ears and nose, ignoring the way her muscles ached from her unaccustomed crawl, she hurried toward those tires.

"He was in Nam with you. He was just a kid."

"I don't remember him," Dare insisted. "I never knew a Halliday."

"Sure you did," Halliday said on a sobbing laugh. "I figured you'd forget him. No reason the big pilot should remember a kid in his ground crew.''

Oh, God, Andrea thought sickly. Six more feet. Just six more feet and she could come around behind Halliday.

"Tell me what happened," Dare said gently. "Tell me about it. There's no point in killing me until I know what I'm dying for, right?''

"You sent him out into a firefight at Tan Son Nhut. You sent him out to carry some stupid message.''

"Oh. I remember him," Dare replied slowly. "Only you got it wrong, Halliday. The firefight broke out *after* I sent him with the messages. He got caught in the first salvo.''

"You're lying!''

Andrea reached the base of the tires and eased up cautiously to her feet.

"I'm not lying," Dare said calmly. "I remember very distinctly that I sent him before the fight broke out. There was no rush. He could have waited until morning for all I cared, but he was young and eager to please. Thirty seconds after he walked out the door, the bombardment started. I didn't send him into it.''

Andrea whipped around the tires and shoved the barrel of her rifle into Halliday's back.

"Drop it, Halliday," she said coldly. "Slowly, very slowly, put your hands on your head.''

But he turned and pointed his pistol straight at Andrea. Even in the dark she could see the wildness in his eyes. He'd cracked. He'd cracked badly.

"You don't have the guts to shoot me," he said flatly.

He was right, Andrea realized with a sick sense of horror. She couldn't shoot him. But she couldn't let him know that.

"It sure would be messy," she said harshly. "Pieces of you would scatter all over the place. And you'd better not pull that trigger, because my finger's on *this* trigger and the rifle's on automatic. Have you ever seen what an M-16 can do to a man?''

"Stand-off, Captain?" Halliday asked, and laughed wildly.

But it wasn't, not quite. Beneath her layers of winter clothing, Andrea's muscles tensed, and she eased her finger from the trigger. Suddenly, without any warning at all, she swept the barrel of the rifle around and knocked the pistol from Halliday's hand.

A yelp of surprise barely escaped his lips before a dark shape hurtled out of the night and knocked Halliday to the ground.

"Got any cuffs, Andrea?" Dare asked with a grunt as he wrestled Halliday onto his face and pulled his arms up behind his back.

"Yes, sir! Somewhere under all these clothes."

"Use mine, skipper," said Nickerson.

Whirling, Andrea let out a happy cry as she saw Nickerson sagging against a tire but on his own feet. "Nick! Are you okay?"

"One hell of a headache, ma'am, but I've had worse after a night—"

"In Saigon," Andrea completed. "I know. I know."

"Damn it, Andrea," Dare said breathlessly. "The cuffs! Give me the damn cuffs. This guy won't quit."

"I was gonna say after a night of shore leave, ma'am," Nick said as he handed Andrea the cuffs that dangled from his hand.

Yanking off her other mitten, Andrea knelt beside Dare and the writhing Halliday. Together they managed to get the handcuffs on him, and then Halliday grew instantly, surprisingly still. The fight was gone from him.

Andrea's earlobes ached so sharply that she rubbed them and almost groaned from the pain. Tugging up her hood with one hand, she pulled the radio from her belt with the other and called for backup.

"I feel like such a jerk," Nick said. "I can't believe I let him get to me like that. I should have known he'd be hiding there."

"Things happen," Dare remarked, rotating the shoulder he'd bruised in his flying tackle of Halliday. "Worse things could have happened." Permanently engraved on his mind was a stark snapshot of Halliday's pistol aimed right at Andrea's stomach. Adrenaline-induced nausea churned in him. "Burke, if you ever go off half-cocked like this again, I'm going to hang your hide out to dry."

"Half-cocked!" Andrea leapt to her feet, still super-charged on her own adrenaline. "I did *not* go off half-cocked!"

"You sure as hell did!" His stomach kept sinking at the thought of what might have happened to her, and adrenaline was making him act like a damn fool, but he didn't care. This woman had scared the wits out of him. "Do you think you're supersoldier? You and Nickerson should never have come out here alone to deal with an intruder who was probably armed and dangerous. You should have waited for backup.''

"If I'd waited for backup, he might have gotten away! There was no time—''

"There were two guys in the guard shack you could have taken with you.''

"So write me up!'' Andrea said hotly, glaring at him. How dare he!

"I just may. You scared me out of ten years of life! I don't know whether to shake you or—''

Nickerson cleared his throat noisily. "Beggin' your pardon, sir, ma'am, but there are two trucks headed this way and more comin'. These fellows might not understand your, uh, disagreement the way I do.''

Andrea clamped her teeth together, but she couldn't resist snapping, "And I told you not to get in my way, but *you* had to pull rank. You could have been killed.'' That thought scared her half to death.

"So could you,'' Dare growled back, keeping his voice low. "It's a damn good thing I came with you. And who's the ranking officer here, anyway?''

"I told you,'' Andrea murmured too sweetly, "that I couldn't kiss you at night and act like it never happened the next day. If you think I'm going to kiss your—''

"Skipper,'' Nick interrupted quickly, "someone might hear.''

This time Andrea sealed her teeth with an audible click, and she took satisfaction in hearing Dare grind his. They were both acting like irrational idiots, some objective corner of her mind noted. It was the adrenaline, of course, but she was too incensed to care.

In midafternoon, when the first rush of details and paperwork had been cleared out of the way, Andrea returned to the BOQ to clean herself up before her meeting with Dare. She was sure he'd been handling his end of things just fine all day, since he knew everything anyway, but a phone call at noon had informed her that "The Colonel expects Captain Burke in his office at 1530 to deliver her report.''

Standing under the needle spray of the shower, Andrea battled bone-numbing fatigue and promised herself that just as soon as this meeting was over, she was coming back here to sleep straight through until tomorrow morning. Dolan could have the command and all the joys that went with it.

Time for another haircut, she thought as she dried her hair in front of the bathroom mirror. And suddenly, from out of nowhere, came a memory of the long, long hair her father had never allowed her to cut. It had fallen below her hips, and she had always caught it back in an impatient ponytail to keep it out of her way. How fiercely glad she'd been when she arrived at the Academy and had it all cut off. Now she wondered, actually wondered, if she should let it grow out.

"You're crazy from lack of sleep, Burke," she told her reflection sourly. She didn't have time to mess with her hair.

Dressed in a pressed, creased and impeccable uniform, she presented herself in Dare's office promptly at three-thirty. Her weary eyes devoured every detail of his appearance, from the lock of hair that tumbled onto his forehead to the broad shoulders that stretched his uniform shirt. No two ways about it, the man looked good enough to eat.

Placing the typed report on his desk, Andrea sank into the chair he indicated.

"I've talked to SAC HQ," he said without preamble. "You're the hero of the day, Andrea."

"Me?" She kept remembering how her goose would probably have been royally cooked if Dare hadn't followed her out onto the tarmac.

"You. I know I sounded off this morning, but I'm convinced you would have handled matters even if I hadn't involved myself."

Andrea blinked. "That's very generous of you, sir."

"Just the truth." She looked exhausted, he thought, and troubled. What was troubling her? "I wanted to warn you that they're sending out a reporter from the *Air Force Times* to do a feature story on you. He'll be here tomorrow."

"Oh, no." She was horrified. "Do I have to?"

"I'm afraid so, Andrea." He smiled faintly. "They just can't pass up the opportunity to show you off. Female Academy graduate turns hero. If you ask me, they'll want a picture of you in battle dress and toting your rifle."

"That's ridiculous!"

"Why? The Department of the Air Force just dropped its enlistment quotas. Now everything's based on ability. Truly an equal opportunity environment. Do you really think they're going to pass up a chance to justify their decision by showing that women can do the job just as well?"

"But I can't do it just as well," she burst out.

Astonished, Dare sat back in his chair and studied her intently. "You *can*, Andrea. What makes you think you can't?"

"I'm a sham," she said tensely, and leapt up from her chair. "The only question is what I'm going to do about it."

Dare watched her pace, a frown on his face. "Tell me about it."

"Last night Halliday pointed a loaded gun at me and told me I didn't have the guts to shoot him. And he was right. I didn't."

Dare rubbed his chin, never taking his eyes from her. "I don't think," he said carefully, "that it takes guts to shoot somebody."

"Whatever it takes, I haven't got it."

"You did once before, not that I'm saying that's a good thing."

"And that's why I can't do it again. If I'd done more than graze him that first time, I don't know if I could live with myself. That's been hard enough to deal with. All I know is that I can't do it again. What kind of soldier does that make me?"

A wounded one, Dare thought, watching her. Nor did he feel he should be arguing in favor of shooting anyone. "You don't think the circumstances had something to do with it?" he asked after a few moments. "After all, you were face-to-face with the guy, and he's somebody you've known for a couple of years. I don't think most of us would have been able to pull the trigger under those circumstances."

"Maybe. Maybe not." Coming to a halt, Andrea wrapped her arms around her waist and bowed her head. "I'm not sure I want to be able to pull the trigger. I told you that once before. I guess I've been ignoring the question, but I think it's time to face it. I've got to decide whether I have what it takes to be a soldier, or even if I want to have what it takes. It's not a game anymore, Dare. Twice, now, it's been real.''

"I don't think any of us want to have what it takes, or to like it, Andrea. We just do what we have to when we have to. That's the bottom line.''

"Well, I'm not sure I can do what I have to." She raised bleak eyes to look at him. "Some cop.''

"I don't know about that. You handled yourself admirably last night, and you managed to do it without bloodshed. That's something to be proud of. And I don't know if you should be worrying because you couldn't shoot a man who's been a friend of sorts for the last couple of years. I don't think we want soldiers who are capable of shooting people they know. I know I don't want any in *my* command."

He rose and came around his desk, then folded her into his arms, holding her snugly against his chest. "Don't beat yourself with this, Andrea. Honest to God, I don't think I could have pulled the trigger, either."

The green eyes she lifted to his were bright with unshed tears, and the sight sent an aching shaft through his heart.

"Come home with me right now, Andrea," he said. "The duty day's over in fifteen minutes anyway, and after the night we put in, we're entitled to take off. Come home and let me take care of you."

Home. The word made her throat ache with yearning. Unable to speak, she simply nodded.

They walked together out of the building, neither of them caring any longer who saw them and what they might speculate. Dare's only concession was that he didn't put his arm around Andrea until they were in his Bronco.

"Let me fix you something to eat," he said when they entered his house.

"I'm not hungry," Andrea replied listlessly. "Really. I just need to sleep." And I need to be held. Desperately.

He seemed to know. He helped her out of her clothes and into bed, and moments later he joined her, tucking her into the sheltering strength of his large body, stroking her hair and back with gentle hands.

"Sleep, sweetheart," he murmured. "Sleep."

Her hands were clenched into cold fists against his chest, and every muscle in her body was drawn tight with tension, but gradually fatigue battered down the last of her resistance. Dare felt her relax against him finally, growing soft and yielding as sleep claimed her. He brushed a light kiss against her forehead and closed his own eyes, welcoming the end of a day that had been too long and too difficult.

Andrea woke with a start in the dark, her heart racing.

"Easy, babe," said a drowsy voice near her ear, and powerful arms surrounded her, hugging her. "It's over."

She turned toward him, burrowing into his warmth and strength, afraid that she was coming to depend on him too much, afraid that she wouldn't be able to stand being alone when the time came. The person she'd thought she was didn't seem to exist anymore. The last thing on earth she wanted to be was a dependent, clinging female, yet here she was clinging like mad and grateful she had Dare to cling to. "I'm scared," she admitted in a whisper. "I'm so scared."

"You've had a rough couple of months," he rumbled reassuringly. "Anybody would be having a crisis of confidence."

As always, he went right to the root of things. She could have sworn he was able to read her mind.

"You know," he continued, "we all go through life running on automatic most of the time. Every so often, though, something comes up. Maybe it's something that happens, or something someone says, but it shakes us up and makes us look at things differently for a while. I guess it's good for us in the long run, but it sure isn't fun."

"It sure isn't," she agreed, nuzzling his shoulder and filling herself with his scent. It felt so good to be held this way, to feel his skin against hers. Why was she so afraid of what felt so right?

"Are you getting hungry?" he asked. "I am. Why don't I go make some soup and sandwiches? I'll even let you pick the soup."

She was so long joining him in the kitchen, however, that he went back to the bedroom to find out what was wrong. She was sitting on the edge of the bed, wrapped in his terry robe, a pair of his black wool socks flopping on her feet.

"Andrea?"

She looked up slowly and gave him a sad smile. "You know what I'm going to say, don't you."

A fist clenched around his heart, and for a moment there didn't seem to be any air in the universe. "I guess so," he said finally. He couldn't even make himself move. "Come on and have something to eat, and then you can tell me. And I'll argue, anyway."

Not until they were seated at the table in front of steaming bowls of soup did Andrea speak. Dare took what consolation he could from the fact that it clearly wasn't any easier for her to say what was on her mind than it was going to be for him to listen to it.

"I need to stop seeing you for a while," she said through a throat that had become painfully tight.

"I know." Yep, he'd known. Damn it, he'd known.

"I've got to find myself, Dare. I've lost me somewhere." The smile she gave him was pathetic. "I don't know myself anymore."

He lit a cigarette and managed a short nod. "I don't quite see how I'd prevent you from finding yourself."

"Because you're so strong that you're easy to lean on. Too easy. And you'd let me lean, just the way you did earlier."

"Everybody needs to lean sometimes, Andrea. It doesn't mean we're weak when we do."

She hadn't touched her soup, and now she pushed the bowl aside, a sure indicator of how lousy she was feeling. Even as he tried to manage the pain of his own impending loss, he felt sympathy for her.

"You've got to understand the dimensions of the problem," she said presently. "You're part of it. I've come to need you. I've never needed anybody in my life before, and suddenly I need you the way I need air to breathe. That's scary enough, but that's what makes leaning on you come close to dependency. I don't want to become a limpet, and I don't think you want one clinging to you."

He wanted to argue, but she was making sense. He didn't want to see her damaged and gutted, not even if it meant losing her entirely.

"So, okay," he said, and took a steadying breath. "What's the plan?"

"I won't see you again until I figure out who I am and what kind of future I really want."

"And just how long might that take?"

She sighed heavily. "I don't now. The first thing I have to do is figure out what kind of future I have with the Air Force. Or even *if* I have one. I'll go to Minot and take it one step at a time. That's all I can do."

"Will you at least write?"

Suddenly tears were running down her cheeks, huge, silent and heartbreaking. "I'll write," she said brokenly. "Will you?"

Dare stood, knocking his chair over with a crash, and scooped her up into his arms. Jaw working, he carried her to his bedroom and lowered her gently to the mattress.

"You remember this, Andrea," he said as he flung his clothes around the room and then stretched out beside her. Catching her chin in his hand, he turned her face toward him and looked deep into her wet eyes. "I...I care about you, woman. Body and soul. And I'm going to miss you like hell."

She threw her arms around him and clung tightly, pierced by his unexpected declaration, but she didn't answer it. Both of them were aware of her silence. It hung in the room around them as Dare made love to her, adding desperation to his desire and sorrow to hers.

Never had Andrea hated getting dressed the way she did that morning. Each item of clothing she donned removed her that much farther from Dare and brought the moment of separation that much closer. During the night, moments had become infinitely precious, each one to be treasured and drawn out. Andrea clutched every one of them to her heart against the long, lonely days ahead.

Maybe she really had lost her marbles. Trouble was, she kept remembering her mother and how she had depended on Charlie Burke. Andrea had grown up feeling scornful of her mother's utter dependency, and while adulthood had made her more sympathetic to her mother's weakness, she was terrified of becoming a similar shadow. It was a wonder that Clara Burke had managed to get dressed in the morning without Charlie's direction. She had depended on him for everything else, every decision, every opinion, every action beyond the woman's work of household chores.

It wasn't that Dare would want or even try to turn her into that kind of person. Andrea honestly believed he would never knowingly do such a thing. No, she was afraid of the weakness in herself, the desire to curl up in Dare's sheltering arms and let him face the world for them both. In that weakness she felt like her mother, and once and for all she had to prove she could stand on her own.

"Almost ready?"

Andrea looked up from smoothing her slacks over her hips and caught her breath. God, he was magnificent! He stood tall and straight in the doorway, turning the ordinary cut and color of his uniform into something far more. In every inch, he was a soldier, right down to his firm jaw. That jaw was set, containing all the arguments he hadn't voiced, all the emotions he hadn't unleashed.

"Dare..." She spoke his name faintly, uncertainly.

"No talk," he said flatly. "Except for one or two notable occasions, I've never pushed you in any way, and I don't want to start now. You've stated your position. I accept it. End of discussion."

His withdrawal was a tangible thing, leaving her feeling colder and more abandoned then she'd ever dreamed was possible. If he cared about her, how could he let her go like this, so coldly?

He broke the silence between them only when he pulled up in front of the BOQ. Setting the car in neutral, he turned to face her one last time.

"Goodbye, Andrea," he said in that same flat, emotionless tone.

Standing in the dry snow, with the icy predawn wind whipping around her, she watched him drive away. Now she knew what it meant to be truly alone.

Chapter 16

I care about you, woman. Body and soul.

Andrea jerked bolt upright in bed, surfacing from a restless sleep with her heart pounding and her breath coming in ragged gasps. Dare's words rang in her ears as if he'd just spoken them. When she realized she was alone once again in her bed, she flopped back onto her pillow with a groan.

Call him.

No. No. If he really cared about her—if he loved her—he wouldn't have let her go so easily.

But you love him, and you were the one who walked away.

She'd had to. It was a matter of self-preservation.

Oh sure...

Rolling onto her side, she hugged her pillow tightly and fought back the tears that had been close to the surface for the last several days. He could have called, but he hadn't. He'd made no effort to get in touch with her at all.

Except for one or two notable occasions, I've never pressured you. I'm not going to start now.

Andrea drew a shuddery breath. He didn't really want her. Not if he could let her go so easily.

But had he? Had he really let her go easily?

I care about you, woman. Body and soul.

What did he want from her? She'd never understood that. He'd never told her, never explained what it was he needed from her. She'd made assumptions, but...

Once again she sat bolt upright, this time to throw aside the covers, to rise and pace her small quarters. When she passed by the open door of the bathroom, her reflection in the mirror caught her eye. Andrea Burke in green silk. Andrea Burke looking like the woman who Dare MacLendon had seen in her.

Halting, she faced her reflection and tried to see herself as he must have seen her. A man who gave such a gown to a woman was saying something. Well, of course, she'd already recognized that he'd seen the woman inside, the woman who hid behind the officer. That had been evident to her the first time she'd looked at herself in this gown, just a few short weeks ago at Christmas. He'd seen a woman who wanted to be beautiful for a man, and he'd made her feel beautiful.

Staring at herself, Andrea suddenly drew a sharp breath and held it. He hadn't given her this to make her feel beautiful or because he knew she wanted to feel like a woman. He had given her this because she *was* a woman, because to him she *was* beautiful.

Turning swiftly, she hunted up her jeans and sweater. No more guessing. No more assuming. Damn it, she was going to find out what it was he really wanted from her. An affair? A long-term relationship? Or nothing at all.

The latter possibility terrified her, but she would face it. She would face the truth of this relationship at long last. No more hiding, no more running, no more avoiding.

The frigid predawn air was unnaturally still when Andrea climbed out of her car in front of Dare's house. It was so cold that by the time she crossed the short walk to his front door, the moisture of her own perspiration had frozen into a thin sheen of frost on the legs of her jeans, stiffening them.

Afraid to hold still lest she grow hypothermic, she hopped from one foot to the other as she rang the bell and waited. Several minutes passed, and by then she was certain something must be frostbitten.

On her third ring, the door abruptly flew open and Dare stood there, eyes widening as he recognized her through the storm door.

"Andrea!" Throwing open the storm door, he seized her hand and tugged her indoors. "God, woman, you feel like ice," he said as he closed both doors behind them. "What's wrong? Why are you here?"

For a long time she said nothing. Instead she stood there silently, shivering from head to foot and drinking him in with her eyes as if she could fill her soul. He was rumpled from sleep, stubbled with a day's beard growth, wrapped in the frayed blue terry robe he'd once let her wear. He was, simply, the most beautiful sight she'd ever seen.

Dare stared back at her, noting the tremors that shook her, recognizing that she was cold but at a loss as to what to do about it. Once he would have touched her, warmed her with his body. Now he simply didn't know if he was any longer entitled to such intimacy.

What had brought her out in the middle of such a cold night? he wondered. What couldn't wait until morning?

"Andrea," he said gently, "what's wrong? Has something happened?"

Shivering, she stepped toward him. "Hold me," she whispered. "Please hold me."

He was more than willing to oblige. Closing the last bit of distance between them, he unbuttoned her parka with swift fingers and flung it aside. He started to bend so he could lift her, then suddenly paused. Taking her trembling shoulders in his hands, he looked down at her, forcing her to meet his gaze.

"No more games, Andrea," he said gruffly. "I'm in no mood for another scene like Wednesday morning. If you're planning to kiss me off again—"

"No..." she said hoarsely. "Oh, no. Dare, please..."

He obliged, sweeping her trembling body up into his arms. She coiled her arms around his neck, clinging with a fierceness he'd never felt in her before as shivers continued to rack her.

"Damn it," he said roughly as he laid her on his bed, "why didn't you call me before you came? How long did you stand out there?"

She didn't answer, watching him with hazy green eyes as, by

the light of the small bedside lamp, he tugged her boots and then her jeans from her frozen body. His scent rose around her from the very sheets, warming the coldest place of all: her heart.

"Come on, honey," he said, lifting her. "Let's get this sweater off so I can warm you."

Finally, at long last, her naked, shivering body was wrapped in the heat of his, swaddled in his arms, in his blankets, in his bed. He stroked her hair and shoulder, tucked her head under his chin, covered her legs with his.

"What happened, darlin'?" he asked gently. "Tell me what happened."

The endearments, the tender caresses, his concern, thawed her as much as his heat. She'd feared he might have come to hate her for the way she'd left him, but he didn't hate her. Of that much she was sure. Now she had to face whatever it was he really felt, and she had no right to ask that of him until she'd given him her own honesty.

"I'm sorry," she said in a small voice, her breath stirring the soft hair on his chest.

"Sorry for what?" he asked, his soothing hands never hesitating in their caresses.

"Leaving you."

Now his hands did hesitate. Noticeably. "You did what you felt you had to," he said gruffly, and resumed stroking her shoulder.

"I was afraid," she admitted. "I was terrified."

"Of me?" He was stunned by the notion.

"No, not of you. Of me. Leaving you was the hardest thing I've ever done, but I was afraid to stay."

Something in him started to unknot, just a little, and made it possible for him to drop a kiss on her forehead. "I kind of got that feeling," he said in what he hoped was an encouraging voice.

"I was afraid of myself," she admitted in a voice that was barely above a whisper. Her heart had climbed into her throat, and she knew that this time there was truly no rip cord. Closing her eyes tightly, she stepped out into space. "I was afraid of how much I love you."

Dare was electrified by her words. He had practically given up hope of ever hearing them. He closed his eyes and hugged her nearer. "Just how much do you love me?" he heard himself ask huskily.

Andrea's voice quavered. "I love you so much that I don't want to imagine life without you."

"I love you, too," he managed to say gruffly through a tightening throat. "For the last couple of days my future had been looking about as barren as the prairie in January."

"But what do you want from me?"

The cry pierced his heart. Bending his head, he sought her mouth with his and kissed her with aching tenderness. "Sweetheart, what I want from you is you. Just the way you are. I never hoped I'd find a woman who can give me as much as you do. You're a friend, a colleague and a lover. I couldn't ask for more."

There was more she needed to ask, but for the moment she was overwhelmed by the need to show him her love. Pushing him gently backward, she rose above him beneath the tent of the blankets. On hands and knees she straddled him, then lowered her head to take hungry possession of his mouth.

At first Dare was content to let her lead, but before long the hunger she always evoked in him began to pulse through him, and he reached for her, wanting her closer, much closer.

Andrea caught his hands, lacing her fingers with his. "No," she whispered huskily, smiling almost drowsily down at him. "Let me. This time, let *me*."

This was the first time he had ever taken the passive role in lovemaking, and he found the experience at once gratifying and torturous. In relinquishing control, he began to learn the awesome dimensions of the need this woman could arouse in him.

Because Dare had always taken charge of their lovemaking, Andrea knew very little of what he liked for himself. Aware of her lack of experience, she moved slowly, listening attentively to his breathing, heeding the responsive movements of his muscles. She found a sensitive spot behind his jaw, a cord in his neck where a nip could make him groan. She already knew that his nipples were as sensitive as hers, but when she found one hard little button in the soft fur, she set about discovering just what pleased him best.

"Oh! Andrea..."

She wriggled away from his hands and sought lower, as excited by his responses as she had ever been excited by his touches and kisses. She loved everything about this man, she realized. Everything. His rough-soft contrasts, his hardness and smoothness. The hair on his chest and legs, and in his groin. The way his muscles bunched beneath her hands, the way his hands grasped her and held her and guided her...

The way he groaned and caught her hips, this time refusing to let her escape. The way he showed her how to lower herself onto him, the way he reached out and touched her most secret place, depriving her of any will at all except the will to be his.

The way he made her his woman. The way he completed her and filled her and let her know she was all this man would ever need.

The way he held her to his chest with trembling arms afterward. The way he kissed her and stroked her hair back from her damp face, the way he pulled the comforter over them but wouldn't let her move away. The way he fell asleep with her, their bodies still joined, his arms snug around her, her weight a reassurance on his chest.

"Wake up, darlin'," a husky male voice growled in her ear. "It's noon, and I've run out of patience."

Andrea was smiling even before she pried open her eyelids. A gentle kiss on the lips broadened the smile even more.

"Tell me I didn't dream last night," she murmured, fully opening her sleepy eyes.

"I was going to ask you to tell me the same thing, sweetheart." His face just inches from hers, he ran a finger along her cheek and smiled into her eyes. "Did you really say you love me?"

"I love you." She said it positively, in a soft, sleepy voice. "With my whole heart."

"Enough to discuss marriage?"

Her breath caught, and the sleepiness vanished from her eyes. When she didn't say anything immediately, tension began to grow in Dare. He honestly didn't know if he had the patience to wait her out again.

"Okay," he said. "Too heavy before coffee."

He rolled out of bed, and Andrea saw that he was wearing

jeans and a white T-shirt. He grabbed his blue terry robe from the back of the closet door and tossed it to her.

"The coffee's ready. I'll make some eggs for you."

"Dare—"

But he'd already left the room, closing the door behind him.

"Damn!" Andrea said in frustration. "Double damn!" He'd caught her by surprise, and now she'd hurt him. Disappointed him.

By the time he heard Andrea come into the kitchen behind him, Dare was feeling pretty annoyed with himself. Just because proposing to her had him all uptight was no reason to be short with her. He *knew* how hard all of this was for her.

"I'm sorry," he said, turning as soon as he heard her step. "I shouldn't have—"

She covered his mouth with her fingertips. "Shh," she said softly. "Shh. You just took me by surprise." For a long moment she stood and simply looked up at him, her expression growing softer.

"I wanted to tell you something about my career goals," she said finally, running her index finger back and forth across his lower lip in a way that made it difficult for him to concentrate on her words.

"You keep touching me like this," he said huskily, "and we're going to wind up in bed pursuing a few physical goals."

A breathless laugh escaped her, and she dropped her hand. "Sorry."

"Never apologize for that, honey." Catching her hand, he astonished her by pressing a kiss into her palm. "What's this about your career goals?"

"Well..." She looked down and to the side, and then stole a look at him from the corner of her eye, as if worrying what his reaction would be.

"Go on," he prompted.

"Well, I decided that I don't really want to be Colonel Andrea Burke after all."

He thought his heart was going to stop right there. She couldn't give up her career. He wouldn't let her. Choosing his words carefully, he asked, "What do you want to be, then?"

The corners of her mouth twitched upward. "How does Colonel Andrea MacLendon sound?"

Understanding crashed through him, overwhelming him. "Are you proposing to me?" he asked, hardly daring to believe it.

Andrea bit her lower lip and looked up at him, shaking her head slowly. "No, sir. I thought about it, but then I decided you should propose to me."

He was beginning to believe. "Why?"

A smile quirked the corners of her mouth. "I imagine I'll never again have a chance to bring a general to his knees."

A snort of laughter escaped him. "I'm not a general yet," he reminded her, struggling to restrain the urge to crush her to him.

"Close enough," she argued with apparent satisfaction. "Well?"

"On my knees?"

She nodded. There was a wicked sparkle in her eyes that quickly gave way to something much softer, much warmer, when, without the least hesitation, he dropped to one knee and took her hands in his.

Tilting back his head, Dare looked up at her, and now there was a teasing glint in his blue eyes. "I always wondered what would happen if I double-dared you."

Andrea smiled. "Try me."

"Captain Burke, I love you with my whole heart and soul. Will you marry me?"

She blinked rapidly as tears welled unexpectedly to her eyes. "Yes, sir, I will," she said and dropped to her own knees to throw her arms around his neck and hold him close. "I love you, Dare," she whispered fiercely. "I love you more than I can possibly say."

He kissed her thirstily, then lifted his head to look down at her. "It doesn't scare you anymore?"

"No." She shook her head. "I was afraid that I'd wind up being like my mother, totally dependent. And then I realized that I had the strength to walk away from you when I needed you most. I'm not weak. I'll never be like my mother."

"I can guarantee that, love," he said, cradling her cheek in his palm. "And what about the rest of it?"

"My problems with being a cop and a soldier, you mean?"

Dare nodded, his gaze skimming her features as if he didn't want to miss a single nuance of her expression.

"I figure I'll always have a problem with that," Andrea said frankly. "There would be something wrong with me if I *didn't* have a problem with guns. It hasn't kept me from doing my job yet, and I don't see any reason why it should. You were right about why I didn't shoot Halliday, and since I didn't have to shoot to protect someone, that's not something I should have to apologize for."

"Thank God!" he sighed with heartfelt relief.

Much later, in the intimacy of his big water bed, Dare tilted her face up to his. "Have you ever refused a dare?"

Andrea shook her head. "Never. You said you were going to double-dare me. You forgot."

"Uh-uh, I didn't forget. I saved it up."

Andrea's eyes sparkled. "Well then? I'm waiting."

Under the blanket, he crossed his fingers. "What would you say if I double-dared you to start a family?"

Andrea stared at him solemnly for a long time, so long that he began to think he'd really blown it bad. Finally she spoke.

"I'd better warn you that twins run in my family."

He started breathing again.

"Do you still want to dare me?" she asked.

He never answered. He just held her so close and so tight that she got the definite impression she'd made him a happy man.

"I love you," he said a long time later. "I'll love you with my dying breath."

Andrea had no doubt that she would love him just as long.

* * * * *

Rachel Lee's Conard County *series is filled with romance, adventure, suspense and passion. Look for the next original title in Intimate Moments late in 1999. And if you want to catch up on the wonderful stories,* A CONARD COUNTY HOMECOMING *will be available from Silhouette Books in August 1999, and it features the much-beloved* MISS EMMALINE AND THE ARCHANGEL *and* IRONHEART.

Dear Reader,

Christmas! It's candles burning in red luminaria along the front walk, and letters from old friends. It's Christmas carols on every radio station, and food drives in the local school. It's trying to put the tree up in spite of the cats' help, and sometimes for the cat has watching here if Christmas dishes, and Christmas kisses believe that in the show.

Every family has its own traditions and they seem to evolve into new ones over time, yet the very basic best of the holidays seems not to have changed for us: love and joy and giving and sharing.

Away from all the hype and glitter and TV specials, Christmas is a chance to reaffirm who we are and who we want to be. It's a time to share ourselves with those we love and those we care about and with our community.

We hope to find spirit the magic of believing that anything is possible.

Dear Reader,

Christmas! It's candles burning in red luminarias along the front walk, and letters from old friends. It's Christmas carols on every radio station, and food drives in the local schools. It's trying to put the tree up in spite of the cats' help, and suet cakes for the cardinals wintering here. It's Christmas dishes, and Christmas baskets delivered in the snow.

Every family has its own traditions and they seem to evolve into new ones over time, yet the very basic heart of the holiday seems not to have changed for ages. Love and peace and sharing.

Away from all the hype and glitter and TV specials, Christmas is a chance to reaffirm who we are and who we want to be. It's a time to share ourselves with those we love and those we care about, and with our community.

It's a time to find again the magic of believing that anything is possible.

Andrea Edwards

THE MAGIC OF CHRISTMAS

Andrea Edwards

THE MAGIC OF CHRISTMAS

Andrea Edwards

Chapter One

The room was empty, just as every other room had been. No furniture, no light, no laughter. Peter crossed over to the other room, the sounds of his steps echoing in mockery. He reached out to turn the knob, his heart filling with hope as it had so many times before. But there was no Kelly, no Sean, no life here....

A phone began to ring somewhere, and the empty room faded into nothing.

The ringing continued, and Peter opened his eyes to the night. He looked through the shadows toward the other side of the bed. It was empty. It had been empty since Kelly had died over a year ago. He snatched up the phone.

"MacAllister," he barked.

"Huh?"

"MacAllister," he repeated.

This time he was greeted by silence. What the hell was this, some stupid kid prank? His eyes went to the digital clock on his nightstand. Just past five-thirty. No kid would be up this early.

"This is Peter MacAllister," he said. "What do you want?"

"Daddy?" a tiny voice asked.

"Sean?"

"Of course, it's Sean." Peter's mother's voice came briskly over the telephone lines to scold him. "Who else would be calling you Daddy?"

"Is something wrong?" Peter asked.

"There has to be something wrong for a son to call his father? Honey." The softening of her voice made it clear she was no longer talking to Peter, but to Sean. "Go ahead now."

"I don't wanna," Sean said. "He's mad at me."

"He's not mad at you, dear."

"Of course I'm not mad at you, Sean." Peter sighed and tried to regain his senses. "What're you doing up this early?"

"We wanted to get you the very first thing this morning."

"The very first thing in the morning is too early for a five-year-old," Peter said.

"Indiana's an hour ahead of you folks in Chicago," his mother replied. "And if you spent more time with your son, you'd realize that the younger they are, the earlier they like to get up."

"Mom." He didn't need another lecture. He would spend more time with Sean if they weren't a hundred-fifty miles apart. And they wouldn't be so far apart if he and his mother hadn't both agreed that Sean was too young to bounce around between day-care and an assortment of nannies.

"So, Sean." Peter forced joviality into his voice. "What can I do for you?"

His son screamed out his silence.

"Go ahead, dear," Peter's mother said.

"Happy birthday," Sean mumbled.

Oh, God. So it was.

Peter pushed aside his own sinking awareness and concentrated on his son. "Thank you, Sean," Peter said. And thank you, Mom. He'd been doing his best to suppress all his little anniversaries. There seemed to be a zillion of them, full of memorable moments. Like the fact that Kelly always used to serve him breakfast in bed on his birthday.

"And what else were you going to do, honey?" his mother gently prodded Sean. "You were going to sing your daddy a birthday song, remember?"

His son stayed silent. Peter knew that between the two of them, he and his son couldn't carry a tune in a bucket. "That's okay, Mom. There's no need to—"

"Yes, there is. You two are family and rituals help keep a family together, especially when the members are apart from each other. Go ahead, Sean."

"Happy birthday to you. Happy birthday to you. Happy birthday, dear Daddy. Happy birthday to you." The words were spoken rapidly and totally without melody.

"Thank you, Sean," Peter said. "That was great."

"Can I have my pancakes now?" Sean asked.

"Of course, sweetie," Peter's mother replied. "Go wash your hands."

There was a pause, then the sound of a receiver slammed into its cradle. Peter's mother sighed heavily. "He should have said goodbye."

"That's okay, Mom," Peter replied. "Don't worry about it. He's just a little kid."

"He gets nervous around you," his mother said. "You only see him a few times a month, and he's just not sure how to please you."

"He doesn't have to do anything to please me."

"You and I know that, but he's just a little boy."

Peter leaned back against the headboard and closed his eyes. His mother with an agenda was like a Sherman tank, undeterred by any logic or facts that might fall in her way.

She felt he should spend more time with Sean, but his job was here in Chicago and his son was in Mentone. And that was best for the kid. Sean needed to be around happy people, not a widower still subject to fits of depression.

"You want me to bring you anything from Chicago?" he asked, trying to divert the conversation to lighter channels.

"Just yourself."

"That's easy enough."

"When will you be in?"

"Sometime this evening. I've got a presentation this afternoon, but I should be able to get out by three. Nobody wants to work late the day before Thanksgiving."

"You shouldn't be working today at all. You should have

come down yesterday and spent your whole birthday here with your family.''

"Mom, I'll be home for two weeks over Christmas and New Year's. We'll have plenty of time to visit then.''

"I guess.'' There was a long pause. "There are a lot of people moving back home these days.''

"Oh?''

"Yes,'' his mother said. "Denise Wharton just moved back, along with her two children. You remember her. She used to be Denise Nance. She was a few grades behind you.''

"When did she become Denise Wharton? I thought she'd married some guy named Gustafson.''

His mother cleared her throat. "Things didn't work out and now she's single again. Used to live around Washington, D.C. someplace. Just got plumb tired of the big city and all those crowds. Now she's back home in Indiana.''

Peter rubbed his forehead, feeling a dull ache building. He knew where she was headed. "Mom.''

"I'm glad that we cleared up when you're coming in. Maybe I'll have some people over for cake and coffee this evening.''

Her ploy was transparent as glass. "Mom, don't go counting on me. Something could happen and I could get tied up.''

"That hasn't happened yet, in all the times you've made the trip.''

"That doesn't make my arrival time a given. As an actuary and a statistician, I can tell you with absolute certainty that what happened in the past does not guarantee the future.'' In fact, he would make sure of it.

"You've been working too much, Peter. You should try spending some time with people who talk plain, ordinary English.''

A huge ice ball formed in his stomach causing him to break into the shivers. His mother and her agendas. Damn. He wasn't up to any more disasters. He knew that it was over a year since Kelly died, but just barely. The thought of dating or even man-woman small talk made his blood run cold.

"Mom, don't fix me up with somebody again.'' How was that for plain English?

"Oh, my goodness. Sean is ready for his pancakes. Blueberry ones. Remember how you used to love them?''

She'd made up her mind and was charging full steam ahead. There had to be a way to derail her. "Mom, I mean it. Don't start shopping around for a girlfriend for me."

"For goodness sakes, Peter. I'm not doing anything of the kind."

"Then there won't be any guests?"

"How would I know? People are always dropping by. That's what friends and neighbors do. Especially over the holidays."

His hand tightened on the phone as he remembered the previous casual "meetings" his mother had arranged. "Mom, don't. It could embarrass everyone."

"Embarrass?" She sounded puzzled, then laughed suddenly. "Oh, you mean you're bringing somebody with you for the holidays? Why, Peter, that's wonderful."

It wasn't wonderful. It wasn't anything close to what he'd meant. "No, I—"

"What's she like?"

He stopped and consciously closed his mouth on the explanation he wanted to make. What would be more effective in keeping his mother from matchmaking than convincing her it wasn't necessary?

"Just a friend," he said and felt the ensuing silence weighing on him. "Actually, a pretty good friend, but still just a friend." He cleared his throat, trying to force his brain to think fast. "I met her after work and...and we sort of got to be friends."

"That's such good news. What's her name?"

"Uh..." He should have known his mother would give him the third degree. "Mom, I really can't talk now. I have an early morning meeting and I haven't even taken my shower yet."

"A name is one word, Peter. If you have time to make that speech, you have time to say one word."

"We'll talk when I get down there."

"Skip goodbye and say her name."

"I really gotta go, Mom."

"Peter." She took an audible deep breath. "Fine, so don't tell me. I'll just call her Miss Mystery when I meet her tonight. See you." And then she hung up.

Peter listened to the dial tone in stunned paralysis for a long moment. Tonight? When had he ever said he was bringing someone tonight? He slowly hung up the phone. His mother was in for some disappointment when she found out he was coming alone, but she should learn not to jump to conclusions like that.

But then his mother was good at jumping to things. Like jumping in to take care of Sean when Kelly died.

Suddenly warring with his pain and absolute revulsion of relationships was his realization of all his mother had done for him in the past year. She'd buried her own hurt, put aside her own life to take care of Sean. Any pestering she did was only because she loved him and Sean and wanted them to live like a real family again.

Peter got out of bed and walked to the glass wall of windows, pulling back the drapes. A sweeping view of Lake Michigan lay before him. He stared down from his perch on the twenty-third floor, letting his vision blur out to where the lake met the sky. It was a humongous expanse of space. Like standing on the edge of a rolling Indiana cornfield, except the corn varied in shades of green, where the lake varied from blue green to gray. And in the early morning stages of awakening today, the lake was gray, preparing for the gloom of winter.

Peter watched the choppy waters below him, whitecaps high and rolling over the cement walkways lining the shore, and suddenly felt himself shivering. The apartment was cool, but his body wasn't reacting to that. The surface of the lake twisted and turned as if fighting off the oppressive weight of an even grayer sky. The scene before him awakened the seeds of his own dark mood.

It was more than a year now since Kelly had plunged off the road in that thunderstorm up in McHenry County. She'd been scouting out country homes for them, looking for a place full of trees, fresh air, horses and all the other things her city-girl fantasies had told her were part of the good life. Fortunately, Sean had had the sniffles and had been with a sitter that day.

More than a year, and the world decided it was now time for the widower to move on with his life. And for a widower with a child that meant getting into another relationship, one that his mother would define as a serious relationship.

His mother meant well, but...

Peter rubbed his face and eyes. First, she'd found him a divorcée with a four year old daughter. They'd been introduced

during his Fourth of July visit at Cousin Bob's lake cottage.
Sean and the girl hated each other at first sight and it had taken
an effort by both of them for Peter and the woman to part on
civil terms.

The next catastrophe occurred over Labor Day weekend. His
mother's bridge partner had had her unmarried niece visiting.
Peter had taken her to the Lakeview in Warsaw for dinner where
she'd smoked continuously. They spoke no more than ten words
the entire evening.

Shaking his head, Peter pushed himself away from the windows. He couldn't take another arranged meeting. He couldn't
make small talk with a woman, he couldn't smile and laugh
with her, and he couldn't possibly be part of a couple again, not
even for an evening. He would do whatever he had to to keep
his mother from fixing him up again.

He stalked into the bathroom and jerked back the shower
curtain. It ripped off the rod. Damn. He wanted to scream, but
he just closed his eyes and leaned his forehead on the cool tile.

What a day. He had two reports to finish up. He had to pack.
And then he had a three-hour auto trip to Mentone. And on top
of it all, he had to find a make-believe girlfriend to bring home.

"Merry, aren't you out of the shower yet?"

Merry Roberts paused in drying her hair to glare at the door.
What was this nonsense? She thought that her roommates were
sleeping in today. Sandi was flying to Tucson with her boyfriend
and ZeeZee was going to Minneapolis with her sister's family
to visit relatives, but neither was leaving until this afternoon.

"I'm drying," Merry called out.

"You don't have to do that in the bathroom," ZeeZee
shouted.

True. Merry didn't have to, but she wanted to. Then, gri-
macing, she admitted to herself that for a girl who'd never seen
a flush toilet until she was six, she was getting mighty fussy in
her old age. In another five years, she'd hit the big three-O. At
the rate she was going, she'd really be cranky by then.

"Dry yourself in your room," ZeeZee said. "I need to get
in there."

In her room? Right, Merry thought to herself, but only if she stood on her bed. If she faced the window, she wouldn't be able to stretch out her arms. Her room wasn't quite six feet wide and the width of the single bed took up a good bit of that.

But that was nothing to complain about, she realized as the album of her childhood she always carried in the back of her mind pushed forward a snapshot. Growing up, the only way she could take a shower in Four Corners, Tennessee was if it was raining. And since she slept in the living room with her five brothers and sisters, the only way she could get any privacy was to go into the woods. Her present room might be small, but it had a window and she had it all to herself. Life could be a lot worse.

"Just a minute," Merry said. She wrapped the towel around her body and gathered up her toothbrush and toothpaste. "It's all yours," she said as she stepped through the doorway.

"Oh," ZeeZee said, touching Merry's hair as she walked by. "I'd kill for red hair like yours. Why can't they put color like that in a bottle?"

"My momma said an angel has to come down and paint your hair for it to be this red."

"Aw, that's sweet."

"Yeah." Merry opened the door to her room. "She had her moments."

"Oh, hey, Merry." ZeeZee dashed up to Merry's open door. "JoJo's got this really big van."

Merry just looked at ZeeZee.

"I mean, she wouldn't mind if you came along. I know you don't like kids, but hers are really great. I mean, they aren't brats or anything."

Merry winced and tried to sound not quite so crotchety. "It's not that I don't like kids," she said. "I'm allergic to them."

"But you're going to be here all alone and on Thanksgiving."

"That's the best part. I can spread my papers out as much as I like, stay up all night reading and get lots done."

"It's no trouble. Really."

"ZeeZee, I don't want to go anyplace. I have a sociology paper due in two weeks and I need to work on it. Being here by myself is the best way to get it written."

ZeeZee nodded her head rapidly. "I dig it." Then she gave a quick wave and was gone.

Merry closed her door, threw her towel over the chair and slipped into a robe before plopping down onto the bed. There were a lot of things her roommates didn't understand. The main one being that not everyone was comfortable around kids. She didn't dislike them—no, just the opposite. But she also feared them, feared their power to awaken memories best left hidden. It was safest for her to just stay far away from kids.

The other thing her roommates didn't understand was that the holidays meant different things to different people. Merry didn't have any Kodak moments of the family gathering around the turkey. The closest she'd come to a real Thanksgiving meal as a kid had been when some do-gooders brought turkey and the trimmings to church, but being somebody's charity case tended to suck the flavor out of the food.

No, to Merry, Thanksgiving was just an annoyance. The restaurant would be closed two extra days because of it and that meant losing two days' wages. It was hard enough to scrape together tuition money without having the holidays screw up everything. Oh, well. Wouldn't be the first time she had to stretch a nickel.

Merry plugged in her hair dryer and settled on the corner of her bed with the dryer in one hand and her brush in the other; then she propped a book up in front of her. It was about this weird guy who turned into a bug, but it had made Number 26 on the list of Harvard's All-Time Classics that *USA Today* had published, so she figured it had to be good.

This education business was a lot of work, but then if it were easy, everybody would be smart, and being able to discuss Kafka wouldn't impress anybody.

She glanced almost without choice toward a faded newspaper clipping tucked into the edge of her mirror. It would all be worth it, though, when she finally was somebody. Jason Byron O'Connell was one smart cookie, and she was determined to be worthy of him.

Peter walked the length of the restaurant to his usual booth in back and dropped his body into the seat with a sigh. He put his face down in his hands and rubbed at his eyes. What a crappy day this had been so far.

He'd gotten to the office even earlier than usual and had accomplished absolutely nothing. After talking with Sean, being reminded of his birthday and the victim of his mother's maneuvering, he'd been tense before the day had even started.

What was he going to do about this girlfriend thing? If he showed up alone, with only a lame excuse in tow, his mother would start arranging dates again. And now that his allotted year of mourning was over, there was no way to avoid future potential disasters. He had to find somebody to play his girlfriend. But how?

An employment bureau had hung up on him and a talent agency had just laughed. The two dating services he'd called had given him long spiels about filling out forms and providing references before being allowed to check through the notebooks of available women.

Peter raised his head from his hands and looked around for someone to take his order. If he didn't get a sandwich, and fast, he'd eat the tablecloth.

He signaled to a waitress sitting at the bar as she glanced his way. She smiled and nodded before turning her back to him. From the movements of her body, Peter guessed the woman was slipping her shoes back on.

A sigh eased from his lips as his mind danced back to his lazy days of youthful summer. He was down by the creek, his bare feet dangling in the water as tension flowed out of him. He could almost feel the warm sun caressing his body.

It was a time when everything was so simple, and so possible. No goal was too great, no achievement unattainable. It was...

"What can I get you?" the waitress interrupted his thought.

Peter looked up. The overhead lights hit the waitress's head just right, bringing out the dark cherry color in her hair. Her blue eyes were sparkling and her wide, generous mouth was ready to overflow with joy. She was medium tall, with a curvy body and words that came wrapped in a soft twang.

"Would you like to order?"

She was the nice one. The young one. The fast, efficient one with the wisecracking mouth. She was one of the few who Peter remembered by name. Merry.

"Sir. What would you like?"

Peter sighed and rubbed the back of his neck, his mind suddenly filled with fuzz. *What would he like?*

"A woman. I really need a woman."

God, no. He hadn't really said that, had he?

He had been working hard the past several weeks and the dreams were haunting him again, but he'd never, ever talked so stupidly. Never in his whole life.

"Sorry," the waitress said, the laughter in her voice tickling his ears. "All we've got is burgers, BLTs and stuff like that."

"I—" His cheeks were hot, but his tongue was frozen. Peter tried to force some words out. Words of apology, explanation, anything.

"Now if you still want something hot—" her grin spread wide across her face, forcing a dimple into each cheek "—there's our regular chili. Large bowl or small. With or without mac."

The flame in his cheeks flared into a white-hot heat. His tongue tied itself into a double step-over slipknot. She was laughing at him just like Kelly used to when he got too technical answering Sean's questions.

"But if a lady's what you gotta have, then that's what you gotta have." Merry put her hands on her hips, a saucy grin on her lips. "Now I don't know this for a fact, since I've never been in the need myself, but I've heard that the Pink Pussycat is the place. Folks say a body can find most anything they want there."

He could feel the tension in his neck slowly ease up. He started to shake his head.

"It's over on Clark Street," she said. "About three blocks north of the river."

"It came out wrong. That's not what I meant." Peter wasn't really sure she was buying it. "I'm just hungry. I haven't eaten all day."

"Oh. Poor baby."

There might have been a flicker of sympathy in her eyes, but Peter didn't feel up to a close examination. He hurried on. "I've been working hard for more than a month. Lots of overtime, that kind of thing. And then my—" He stopped and changed direction slightly. "I got this call at five this morning. Denise Nance is divorced again."

"Not again? Poor, old Denise." The waitress shook her head in pretend sadness as she pulled out her notepad. "You want your regular?"

"Regular?"

"Turkey sandwich, chips, coleslaw and soup of the day," the waitress said. "You have it all the time."

He did? Peter had a momentary glimpse of a gray-haired old man gumming his sandwich and slurping his soup, but he sent that image packing in a hurry. So he'd fallen into some ruts since Kelly had died, it was just that other parts of his life were more important than lunch, requiring all his energy and attention.

"That's fine," he said briskly. "And—"

"Hot tea to drink," she finished for him.

Peter just nodded as the waitress hurried off to place his order. Would he have to find another place to eat now? He really didn't want to, but if this waitress started to talk...

Nah, she wouldn't do that. Servers in a place like this made good money. And he was usually quite generous. A momentary cloud of concern passed before his eyes as he hoped that the waitress shared his definition of generous.

"There you go."

She set his cup of soup before him along with his pot of tea. "Your sandwich'll be right up. Need anything else?"

"Not right now," he murmured. "Thank you."

"Give me a holler if you do," she said with a wink and then went back to her seat at the bar.

The wink bothered him momentarily, but then Peter decided that it was a signal that everything that had been said before was their little joke. This waitress was always joking around with the patrons. Young and lively as she was, she probably got all kinds of propositions. And a few could even be weird. Given the way things were today, they had to be.

His soup was hot and he slowly stirred it, staring out the window at the city scene passing before him. It looked like it was starting to snow. He hoped that bad weather wasn't on the way.

The thought of his trip took the taste out of his food. He looked at his watch. Great. He had only two hours left to find a girlfriend, and he sure as hell wasn't going to the Pink Pussy-cat.

"Here you go."

He looked up as Merry put his sandwich down in front of him. Her smile seemed to comfort, to say that she could handle anything.

"Need any mustard?"

Peter shook his head. "No, this is fine, thank you." He bit into his sandwich as she walked away.

This was Chicago, a big city. All kinds of services were available to meet members of the opposite sex. A professional escort service might be the thing. Those women were probably more up to handling the unusual. It would probably be an easy gig for most of them.

Except that he'd seen a number of those women, especially in more expensive restaurants with older men. They were good-looking women. But they looked so...so professional. Yeah, that was the word. Professional.

That type of woman would fit in at Mentone about as well as some exotic animal from the jungles of Asia. He needed someone more down to earth.

"How's it going?"

His eyes looked into a broad smile, bright enough to drive the gray back out over the lake. "Fine," he replied.

"Little slow eating there," she said as she poured more hot water into his tea.

Peter shrugged. "I got a lot to think about."

"Denise Nance?" She shook her head. "My momma always said it's best to run with your fuel gauge on full."

He smiled, an idea taking shape, and pushed his dish back. "Things are probably going to be a little slow around here for a few days."

"Yeah," she agreed. "Most of the offices around here are closed Thursday and Friday for Thanksgiving. We're closing at three today and won't open until Monday."

"Going anyplace over the holidays?"

"Yeah," she said with a laugh. "But I haven't decided where yet. It's a toss-up between laying on the beach at Cancun or skiing in the Alps."

He smiled himself. A working girl who couldn't afford to go to either.

"Maybe I'll just go to both."

Everyone had a right to their fantasies. "Gonna be tiring, hopping back and forth."

"Yeah, but what's a vacation for if not to get worn out?" She broadened her smile. "Actually. I've got a lot of work to do."

"Oh? I thought you said the restaurant would be closed."

"I go to school," she replied. "Columbia College. I'm studying acting."

Peter nodded. "They have a good program."

She looked down at his plate. "Can I get you anything else?"

He slowly shook his head. She was good-looking, with a pleasant personality. Obviously intelligent. And she was cool. Handled that stupid remark of his just as if it were an everyday kind of request. A country girl like this would fit right in with the folks in Mentone, his mother, the whole nine yards.

"Actually, I would like something else," he said.

"Apple, custard and pumpkin pie, chocolate cake or vanilla, chocolate and strawberry ice cream."

"I need someone to go to Indiana with me," he blurted out.

"You mean a bodyguard to protect you from Denise?"

He gritted his teeth. What he had was a business proposition. If she'd stop being a smart aleck for a minute, he could lay it out.

"Look," he said, trying to be patient. "What I need is a woman to go with me and visit my mother in Indiana."

Merry didn't reply. Instead, she turned her attention to the check and totaled up the tab. Then she placed it face down on the table and patted him on the shoulder. "I really think you should try the Pink Pussycat. And if that don't work, try a bell captain at any of those big hotels along Michigan Avenue."

"Damn it!" Peter sent his fist crashing down on the tabletop. "If I don't produce my own girlfriend, I'm going to get fixed up with Denise, and I don't want to be."

Merry stepped back, but continued looking at him full in the face. "Ever hear of the word no?"

"It's not that easy," he said and took a deep breath. "Look,

I'm willing to pay for your time. How about a hundred dollars? Two hundred?"

She edged away slightly. "I've already got plans."

"How about five hundred?"

She stopped edging.

Chapter Two

Dumb. Dumb. Dumb! This was the absolute dumbest thing she'd ever done. And she'd done some real dumb things before this.

"Pretty soon we'll be in the real Indiana."

Merry stared and glanced quickly at Peter, then back out the window. They had just left Interstate and the area around the interchange was ordinary white-bread suburban America. Strip malls, office buildings, motels and fast-food joints as far as the eye could see, all surrounded by a hundred zillion acres of gray asphalt.

"Great. This fake stuff is really depressing." Merry said.

Peter just laughed. "The real Indiana is small towns," he said. "With grain elevators and flat, open farmland stretching from one end of the earth to the other."

"Oh."

Great response. Bet he was really impressed with that. He was probably thinking the same thing she was—that this was the dumbest idea ever.

She was actually surprised that he was making small talk with her. He was obviously much better educated than she was. He probably had a master's degree from some high-class Ivy League University.

"And train tracks," Peter added. "Most of the grain used to be transported by train. Now they use trucks."

"Things are always changing," she murmured while staring out her window.

Silence returned to their midst, taking up the space between the two of them, pushing them farther apart into their respective corners. Merry scrunched down in her seat and let her peripheral vision take in Peter as he drove the car. He was a tallish kind of guy. Husky, with strong hands. Sort of rugged looking, but it was obvious that he hadn't come up in the world chopping cotton. And once he started talking, the upper-class background and education came spilling out.

She forced her eyes forward and concentrated on the road before them. Peter was the type of man that girls like her got into trouble with. Of course, she had let that happen once in her life, but that little mistake had been a whamdoozer.

Merry sat up straight and clenched her jaw. She was a big girl now. Been around the county a few times and was taking care of herself. Like her granny used to say, first time a mistake, second time stupid.

This little deal had potential for disaster, no matter what way she looked at it. Peter could be a tremendous actor, hiding a heart full of evil behind a cool, gentle facade. Then all she'd have to look forward to was a fight and a hike back to civilization. But it wouldn't be the first time. Growing up in Four Corners, fighting came natural to a kid. And she was wearing a good, solid pair of hiking boots, so she was well prepared.

More likely, Peter was exactly what he looked to be—an upper-class kind of a guy with a good job and a family full of upstanding citizens in some small town hidden away in the cornfields of Indiana. Then what she had to fear was somebody breaking through her pretense and finding out what she really was—a dumb, illegitimate girl from the backwoods of Tennessee.

But it was too late to back out now. She was just going to have to concentrate and play her part. Then, when the curtain came down, she would run like the devil was after her.

"I went to school there," Peter said, nodding toward a cluster of red-brick buildings interspersed among the trees. "That's Valparaiso University. It's a small liberal-arts college, although they do have a law school and some graduate departments."

She would have guessed that he was an Ivy Leaguer. "What did you study?"

"Math."

"You look more like a Harvard M.B.A. type."

A smile split Peter's face. "A real snob type, huh?"

"No." Merry felt her cheeks starting to glow. "No. I didn't mean that at all. I meant..." She shrugged helplessly.

"Actually, I do have an M.B.A.," he said. "But I got it from the University of Chicago."

"They're sort of the same thing, aren't they?"

"Yeah," he agreed. "Graduates from either school think rather highly of themselves."

They were out in the country now, flat, open fields filled with nothing but empty. Houses were few and far between. Mostly just filling stations and restaurants at the major crossroads.

"I did go to Harvard." Peter cleared his throat. "But it was to get a Ph.D. in statistics. I had very little to do with the business school there."

Jeez. Merry's stomach sank. She'd thought he was educated, but three college degrees had been beyond even her wildest guess.

"And I have a master's in actuarial science from the University of Michigan."

Oh, damnation. No wonder he talked the way he did. He didn't have a reason or need to talk like regular folk.

"You sure spent a lot of time in school," Merry said.

"It was either go to school or go to work. And I'm on the lazy side."

The words were backed by that smile again. Broad like the Indiana landscape. Right, as if he were just a simple country boy. Uh-huh. Merry turned to stare out the window again.

They passed a sign for Hanna, Indiana. The towns had nice, cozy names, almost like down home, but the land wasn't anything like Tennessee. It was flat. There were none of the hills and hollers that made up the coal country, dips in the land where a body could hide.

There'd be no place for her to hide in Mentone. Merry knew

that for an absolute fact. She'd be onstage tonight, Thursday, Friday, Saturday and part of Sunday. Almost four days, counting them off on her fingers. She prayed that she would make it. It was going to be tough.

"We probably ought to cover some background for each other."

She turned to look at him. His gaze was shy, almost sheepish. The man's smile had more variations than the Chicago weather.

"Want to go first?"

Merry swallowed hard. "Not much to tell." She'd used this same story for years now, but for some reason her tongue seemed frozen stiff. She took a deep breath. "I'm just your average kind of gal. I grew up in the suburbs, went to public schools and moved around a little bit."

"Where did you grow up?" he asked.

"Near Atlanta," Merry fibbed. "Just north of the city."

"That's surprising," he said. "I thought you were more of a country girl."

A moment's panic washed over her, but she fought it back. How did he know? "Nope, not me."

He let it pass. "Any brothers or sisters?"

"Nope."

"What did your father do?"

"He was in business. Worked for a restaurant-equipment company." For all she knew, that could be true.

"Your mother?"

"She stayed home when I was little. Then she worked as a secretary." That sounded so nice, so maternal, so "Ozzie and Harriet."

They were heading east into the dusk that had fallen on the Indiana countryside. The flat fields were clothed in the drab colors of the Midwest's late autumn garb. Black to dark brown earth, interspersed with yellow stubble, mostly corn or soybeans. Merry knew that she should talk more about herself or Peter would think that she was holding back, but her fabrication only went so deep. She'd learned the first rule of lying long ago; don't include too many facts, it makes it easier to keep things straight.

"So, what's your story?" she asked him.

He frowned into the growing shadows. "Well, you know

about my educational background. Otherwise, I grew up in Mentone. I was a good student, top of my class and good at baseball and basketball. The expectations were the hardest thing about growing up.''

Merry nodded, pretending she understood. Nobody had expected anything of her when she was a kid, and she didn't know which was worse.

"I was close to my grandparents, and they really helped me keep things in perspective. Grandma always had a plate full of cookies. And Gramps always had a fence to fix, a barn to paint or just a stick that needed whittling.''

Merry wondered for a moment whether she should lay out some sweet, little memory for herself, but she quickly discarded that thought. "I didn't really know what to do when high school ended,'' she said. "So I just moved around a bit, taking up odd jobs like waitressing wherever I went.''

"That must have been a bit of a challenge,'' he said. "I mean, suburban life is usually fairly protected.''

Merry shrugged. "I guess. So what did you do after college?''

"Got my job as an actuary and got married.''

Whoa. This was a new wrinkle to the scheme. She opened her mouth to ask for an explanation, but then closed it again when she saw how tightly his hands were gripping the steering wheel.

"Kelly died last year,'' he said slowly. "It was an automobile accident.''

"I'm sorry.'' The words seemed so inadequate when faced with his obvious pain. She didn't know how to deal with the thick silence that descended upon them.

He did, though. "Where do your parents live now?''

"My parents?'' She was startled, and her mind rolled about in confusion. "Uh, they're dead. They died a while ago.'' At least, that was true. Her mother had died when Merry was twenty. And her father—well, since she had no idea who he was, he'd always been dead to her.

"I'm sorry,'' Peter murmured.

"You've only mentioned your mother,'' she said. "Does your father live in Mentone?''

"No,'' Peter said. "He died—'' he paused a moment "—fifteen years ago. He was the town doctor.''

"So your mother lives alone?"

Peter did not reply, and as she waited Merry could feel the silence grow heavier. She turned to look at him. Maybe it was her imagination, but in the dim lights of the oncoming cars he looked grimmer.

"Not exactly. There's a lot of family around." He nodded toward a green-and-white highway sign that announced it was only one mile to Etna Green. "Almost there."

Damn. That was pure cowardice. She was going to find out about Sean soon, anyway, so why was he playing stupid games? It was just that he'd seen how women changed when they found out about Sean, turning all sympathetic and motherly in the blink of an eye. And he didn't want this to be anything but a business relationship.

"How do you pronounce that?" Merry asked, pointing to the sign announcing that they had left Marshall and were entering Kosciusko County.

"Most folks around here pronounce it Ka-zee-osco," Peter replied. "Although I went to school with a guy from South Bend whose grandparents came from Poland, and he said that was wrong. But I could never make my tongue say it the way he did."

"Was the county settled by Polish immigrants?"

The turn for Etna Green came up and he slowed down, making a right onto State Road 19. Another eight or ten minutes and they'd be in Mentone.

"I'm not much into any kind of history," Peter replied. "Ask my mother. That's her thing."

Ask my mother anything you want, he wanted to say. Ask her a million questions. Keep her busy. If you don't, she'll start prying into your life. And his mother had a way of getting people to spill their guts. Must be a skill they worked on at teacher's colleges back in the old days when his mother was a college student.

They were through Etna Green in a flicker of an eyelash, and open country stretched before them. There was no turning back now. Sean was probably watching television, but his mother would be on the window seat in the library, staring out into the night.

He couldn't even fake a flat tire. As was his practice, Peter had called from the gas station, just past Bourbon. His mother always said it made her feel better to know that he was close to home. If he turned back now and called again from that station, his mother would just send one of the neighbors out after him. He could run, but he couldn't hide.

Peter took his left hand off the steering wheel and wiped his palm on his pant leg. Then he did the same for his right. As he did so, he fervently prayed this harmless little scam wouldn't blow up in his face.

If it did? Well, that was just the way it was going to have to be. He couldn't face up to his mother's matchmaking. He was well aware that widowers, especially those with small children, were supposed to mourn for a year, then jump right back into the thick of things. But he didn't give a damn what custom dictated. He wasn't ready yet. He might never be ready.

Bringing Merry along was actually doing everyone a favor. His mother wouldn't feel pressured to push women at him. They could all relax, including Sean. Besides, Merry would do just fine. Hell, if she could handle that crowd at the restaurant, she should be able to handle anybody in Mentone.

"It's just like you said."

"What?" Peter snapped the question out. He'd been in his own little world there. "What's just like I said?"

"There's the railroad track," Merry said, pointing up ahead of them. "And right alongside are the grain elevators."

Peter glared down the street. Damn. He'd been daydreaming. He turned the car around. "Yeah, and here's Main Street."

They drove slowly down the quiet, almost deserted street. Now what? Did he point out the hardware store as the place Sean got his new sled last winter? Or Teel's Restaurant as the boy's favorite place to eat?

Peter made a left and drove north through the old residential district. Some folks had moved into new houses on the edge of town, but his mother wasn't about to leave the old homestead.

"My parents moved in here soon after they married," he told Merry. "Dad used to walk the two blocks downtown to his office. When he worked, which was almost all the time, Mom would make soup and sandwiches. Then we would go down and eat lunch with Dad.''

"That's nice," Merry said, and the softness in her voice made it obvious she meant it.

"There it is." Peter pulled into the driveway and around to the back by the garage. "This is where I grew up."

Merry looked at the house. The light from the back porch softened her features, giving a glow to her face. "I like old houses."

"Then you should love this one," Peter said. "It's very old."

His mother was already out on the porch as they stepped out of the car. She and Belle, their old springer spaniel, waited at the top of the stairs. "Mom," he said. "You're going to catch a cold standing out here with no coat on."

"Nonsense, Peter," his mother snapped. "Coddling just weakens a body."

If standing out in the chilly night air was so great, then where was Sean? No doubt sitting inside the warm house where his grandmother would have told him to stay.

Their old dog gave a couple of woofs, as if to second his mother's opinions. Both of them, Belle and his mother, were super ornery.

"Mom," Peter said as they came up the steps. "This is Merry Roberts. Merry, this is my mother."

"Hello, Mrs. MacAllister," Merry said putting out her hand. "I'm pleased to meet you."

His mother took Merry's hand, a wary look in her eye. Merry had a broad, easy smile on her face, but it always took his mother a while to warm up to somebody new.

"How do you do, Miss Roberts?"

"Just call me Merry. No one calls me Miss Roberts, and I might forget you're talking to me."

"Very well, Merry," his mother replied with a short nod. "Welcome to Mentone. I hope our quiet little town doesn't bore you to death."

"It'll be a nice change from Chicago," Merry replied. "I'm glad to be here."

Peter could see a softening in his mother's posture and relaxed.

"And that's Annabelle Lee," he said. Merry was already on

her knees, eliciting grunts of pleasure from the dog as she
scratched behind its ears. "We call her Belle for short."

"Hello, Belle," Merry said, kissing the dog on the nose and
getting her face slobbered in turn.

"Peter, get the luggage, please. Belle, mind your manners."
His mother took Merry by the arm and led her toward the door.
"Let's get on in the house, Merry. It's getting a touch bitter out
here."

Merry and his mother were starting up the stairs to the second
floor when Peter entered the house with the suitcases. He paused
to peek into the living room and the den. Sean wasn't in either
room. Could he be in the kitchen having a snack? That was
doubtful. His mother wouldn't let the kid eat this close to dinner.

"Quit lollygagging, boy," his mother said from the top of
the stairs. "We need to get Merry settled in. Supper's waiting."

Sean was probably upstairs, playing in his room. Maybe they
could get Merry settled in first. Then he could introduce her to
his son. Peter made his way up the stairs. Belle, panting encouragement, waited for him at the top.

The difference this time was that Merry was there to flash
him a sympathetic smile. He noticed the bags seemed lighter
than usual, even with the addition of Merry's stuff. Those thrice-
weekly workouts at the gym were starting to do the job.

"I'm putting you in this room, Merry," his mother said.

Peter stepped through the door after them and stared about
the room, his face wrinkled in thought. Something wasn't right.
"This has always been your sewing room," he finally blurted
out.

"Land sakes, Peter," his mother snapped. "The world
doesn't stand still and wait for nobody. A body's got to change,
improve themselves."

Blinking, Peter looked around the room again and wondered
what he'd done to bring on that little sermon.

"This is your bathroom," his mother was saying to Merry as
she turned on the lights. "Your towels are peach."

"Thank you," Merry murmured.

"You'll have to share the bathroom with Peter," his mother
said. "His bedroom is on the other side through that door."

"That's no problem," Merry replied.

"I figured as much," his mother said with a snort. "From

what I hear, young folks these days no sooner get their how-de-do's out of the way and they're sharing a lot more than a bathroom.''

"Mother—" But his protest went no further as his mother ignored him and continued talking to Merry.

"You can lock this door from inside your room," his mother said, pointing at the old-fashioned flip latch.

"Oh, good," Merry said.

Peter was about to give Merry a supercharged glare, one that would knock her back into a respectful type of silence, but his mother turned just as he was ready to fire up.

"Peter, put Merry's bag on the bed. No reason for her to be all bent over just to unpack."

Storing his controlling force for later, he put the bag on the bed, where he was greeted by a complaining meow/growl.

"Oh, good heavens." For one of the few times in his life, Peter saw his mother flustered. "Zachary, I told you your new room is over in the back corner."

She looked at Peter. "He doesn't adapt well to change."

"Hi, Zachary," Merry said. She reached out to scratch the Burmese cat under the chin, who gave her a purr of regal acceptance. "My goodness, look at all that gray. You're an old feller, aren't you?"

"He's twenty years old," his mother said. "And he's blind now."

"Poor guy," Merry crooned, kissing the cat lightly on the top of the head.

Zachary just grumbled, and Peter frowned. He bet there were a lot of guys in Chicago that would like Merry to treat them like that. The cat should appreciate what he was getting.

"That's why he doesn't like change," his mother said. "Here, let me take him."

"That's okay," Merry said. "He can stay."

"No, no," Peter's mother insisted. "He should be in his own room."

"I think as far as he's concerned, this is his room," Merry replied. "I'm only going to be here a few days. I've got no right to push him out."

His mother looked thoughtful and seemed about to say something when a shout from downstairs seized their attention.

"I'm home!"

His mother poked her head out into the hallway. "We're upstairs, dear."

Small footsteps stomped up the stairs, sounding as if they carried the weight of an elephant. Peter felt his heart beat to the tune of the rapidly advancing noise. He sure missed the little guy.

Sean stepped into the room, giving them all the open, wide-eyed stare of a five-year-old. "Hi, Daddy," he said.

"Hi, Sean," Peter said softly, squatting down. God, it was so good to see him. And so painful, too. Kelly's eyes looked back at him from Sean's face, and he had to swallow away the hurt. "How are you?"

His son shrugged. "Okay."

They stared at each other a long moment, stared until his mother broke the silence.

"Sean, give your father a hug."

Peter held his arms open. Sean paused a moment to examine Merry, then came forward and gave the required greeting. Freeing himself after a quick moment, the boy turned to face his grandmother.

"I thought you said Zachary was gonna sleep in your new sewing room."

Peter glanced at Merry. She was just sitting there, staring at Sean as if he were a creature from a faraway planet.

"Zachary needs a little more time," his mother was telling Sean. "But Merry said he could stay here. Isn't that nice of her?"

Merry wasn't even blinking. Her face was pale and her eyes were wide. She looked as if she had stepped into hell.

"Finding out you had a son kind of threw me for a minute," Merry said with a laugh.

Peter thought she had seemed a little more than just "thrown," but he said nothing. By the time they'd sat down to dinner, she'd seemed almost normal, though she hadn't said much to Sean. And after the boy had gone to bed and Peter suggested taking an evening stroll down toward Main Street, she had been herself, laughingly warning him not to show her too much excitement the first evening.

"I worked for a few years at the Abracadabra Café on the north side," she said. "We had to do magic tricks for the kids, and I guess I just got kind of overdosed on them."

Her laugh seemed shakier this time and, though he wasn't sure why, he took her hand in his. "I should have told you about Sean. It's just..." His reasons seemed lame and silly now.

"That there wasn't a chance," she finished for him. "It's not like we had time to cover our whole lives in that three-hour drive down here."

The existence of a son could be covered in a few seconds, Peter thought, but allowed Merry to believe her excuses. At least she hadn't turned into a motherly, simpering female, ready to take over his life.

They turned onto Main Street. The buildings filled the shadows while empty circles of light dotted the sidewalks. No one else was in sight.

"We'd best not stay out too long," Merry said. "I don't think my heart can take all this excitement."

He let her turn him from his thoughts. "It looks like we're the only two people left on earth."

"Well, that ain't all bad," Merry said as she squeezed his hand. "Don't need but two folks to have a little fun."

"Depends on the folks involved," Peter agreed. "Some two-somes seem to have a whole lot of fun."

Merry laughed, and Peter felt his ears warm. He couldn't believe what he'd said. Was it this woman who inspired some hidden persona to come to life or was it the clear night air?

"So when is Denise going to jump out of the bushes at you?" Merry asked.

"What?"

"You know, the one I'm supposed to be protecting you from."

"Oh, that Denise." He relaxed as they strolled down toward the post office, their steps sounding softly in the night. The breeze held a slight chill, but it felt good, invigorating.

"I think I'm probably safe from her," he said. "But you'd be surprised at the reactions a widower inspires in women. They all assume that I'm looking for an immediate, serious commitment because of Sean. So either they run away like a scared rabbit or they jump on me. I get the feeling some of them view my ready-made family in the same vein as buying a mature dog instead of a puppy."

"So, in other words, you've got all the women coming or going."

He laughed, and the sound seemed to echo around them. "I guess. Trouble is my mother encourages the 'coming' ones."

"So that's where I come in. I get to pounce on any woman who comes too close. God, I can see it now—bodies flying all over the Indiana countryside."

"Uh, I don't think you'll be quite that busy."

"Don't be too sure. I'm taking this job seriously. We go to the grocery and some little old lady pushes her cart too close to you, and she's history."

"Jeez, I've created a monster."

"I'm just making sure you're getting your money's worth."

"So I'm getting a bargain?"

"You'd better believe it."

Peter chuckled. He'd been right to hire her. She had a great sense of humor.

"Are you going to show me the grain elevators?" she asked.

"Nah," he replied as they crossed the street and went back in the direction they'd come. "Don't want to show you everything in one night. Then what will we do the rest of the weekend?"

They walked in silence for a block or two, letting the darkness lay like a cloak around them. The stillness felt good, comforting. He relaxed, letting the tension slip from his shoulders like rain off a windshield.

"I take it that you haven't started dating again," Merry said softly.

"Oh, I've made a few forays into that alien territory," he admitted. "I tried a single's bar a few times about six months after Kelly's accident."

"Rough place to start."

"You aren't kidding. I thought I could handle dating again, but learned pretty fast I was wrong." He wasn't sure why he was telling her all this, but it felt right. Maybe it was the night that seemed to offer anonymity, or maybe it was the open way she listened. He felt he could tell her anything.

"Single's bars aren't dating, they're a meat market."

"So I found out." He agreed. "Then friends fixed me up a few times."

"With the widows and divorcées?"

He nodded. "My mother's favorites."

"I guess I'm lucky I don't have any family around. Nobody but my roommates to bug me about dating."

"They think you ought to, or they don't like your current flame?"

She laughed, the sound rippling comfortably around them. "They think I'm too serious."

"You?"

"Not jokewise, but lifewise. They say I do nothing but go to work and school."

"Do you?"

"Once in a while," she admitted. "But it's not easy to attend college piecemeal. It doesn't leave you much free time. Besides, my plans don't leave room for worrying about somebody else."

"Oh, no?" He wondered just what her plans were, but it felt like it would be prying to ask.

"Goodness," Merry exclaimed and screeched to a halt. "That certainly is a big rock."

He looked ahead of them at the six-foot shape hulking at the edge of the parking lot and smiled. "That's not a rock. That's an egg."

"An egg?" she repeated, doubt hanging heavy in her tone. "You mean like the kind laid by a chicken?"

"Yup."

"Well, I hope she was a big, old bird. Otherwise, she probably had a serious case of hemorrhoids."

Peter found himself laughing out loud, something he hadn't done for ages, as he took her arm to lead her forward. He'd have to get together with Merry once they got back to Chicago. Take her out to some nice restaurant and maybe a show.

Then it hit him, like the proverbial bolt of lightning. He was a single parent and he was going to stay a single parent, but that didn't mean he had to be a monk. He could date and do all the other things a normal single man did. The key was to limit himself to the proper kind of women. Women who were intelligent and had a sense of humor but no desire for any major commitments. A woman like Merry.

They stopped in front of the stone egg, and Merry bent close. "It says here that Mentone is Egg Basket of the Midwest."

"I'm sure I told you that," Peter said. "And I never lie."

"Never?" She straightened up to look at him, and suddenly her eyes weren't laughing anymore.

A warmth moved and stirred inside him. It was a slow, lumbering sensation, like something waking up stiffly from a long sleep. It felt good, welcome even, but at the same time worrisome. He didn't want to feel anything; he liked the numbness he'd been living in.

"We better get back," Peter said and took her arm again. "Mom will think we got lost."

"Did your mother worry about you when you were a kid?" she asked.

"Nah. Not in a place like this."

"Yeah," she agreed. "This isn't like Chicago."

"I walked all over this town when I was a little kid. To school, to the library, to the store, everywhere. And I didn't have a baby-sitter, a nanny, or some other adult constantly dogging my steps."

"Sounds good."

"It was great. Oh, I know now that a whole bunch of adults were keeping an eye on me. But as far as I was concerned, I was a big shot, off on my own, exploring the big world around me."

He paused. "And that's how I want my son to grow up," Peter said. "Free, with a strong sense of self and independence. He couldn't do that in Chicago or its suburbs. I'd have to hire some adult to act like a bodyguard for him."

"I'm sure he likes it here," Merry said.

"I miss him," Peter said. "But I have to think of what's best for him."

They walked the last block in silence, Merry's body brushing up against his own. That sensation came back, stronger this time and less alien seeming. Being attracted to Merry wouldn't hurt him. She was one he could be attracted to and stay safe. He was definitely going to ask her out once they returned to Chicago.

The front-porch light was on when they got back to the house. Peter paused at the bottom of the steps and turned to face Merry. "I really appreciate you helping me out," he said. "Especially on such a short notice."

"Hey," Merry replied. "I've never been to the Egg Basket to the Midwest before. I couldn't let the opportunity pass."

Peter laughed and put his hands on her shoulders. "Seriously. Thank you." He held her for a long moment. She felt warm and soft beneath his touch and hungers grew suddenly within him. "Maybe we can do something together once we get back to Chicago."

"Maybe," she replied.

Her lips drew him closer and closer, mesmerizing him until he had no will of his own. He leaned forward and kissed her lightly. Her lips were softer than he expected and radiated passion that filled him to overflowing. A lightness seized his heart; a smile wanted to take over his lips. He let her go with a strange reluctance in his heart and led her up the stairs.

The blind, old cat gave a low, growling meow, and Merry put him in front of his water dish. "There you go, old feller. Have yourself a tall one before we get in bed." She leaned against the doorway to the bathroom and listened to the *lap-lap* of the cat's tiny tongue.

"He never told me he had a kid."

The old cat continued drinking.

"Not that it mattered," Merry said. "Sean seems really nice. I just wasn't expecting it." She shrugged. "I don't like being around kids."

The cat quit drinking and turned away from the water dish. Merry picked up Zachary and carried him to the bed. She placed him near the foot where he'd been sleeping when she'd come into the room.

"Oh, who am I fooling?" she said. "I'd like being around one certain kid very much, and since I can't, it hurts too much to be around any."

The cat grunted and settled down into the covers. Merry lay back next to him, staring up at the ceiling. There was a pattern in the plaster, almost like waves, one following the other, end-lessly on toward the wall. She rolled over onto her side.

"Promise not to tell if I show you my secret?" She reached for her purse and took the tattered newspaper picture of the Calhoun County spelling-bee finalists from her wallet, spreading it out on the bed. "There he is, the fourth kid from the right in the back row. My son."

She squinted at the photo as she had a million times since the newspaper had come in the mail, but she couldn't really get an idea of what Jason looked like. She couldn't get even the slightest hint of what kind of a person he was. Was he wearing a sports team T-shirt? Was he a shirt-and-tie guy? Did he wear braces?

"What do you think?" she asked Zachary. "Does he look like a neat kid? He must be smart, right? I mean, he made it to the spelling-bee finals, which is something I couldn't have done in a million years."

She gently rubbed the top of the cat's head as she continued to stare at the photo. "One of these days I'm going to meet him, though," she said. "When I've got my degree and I'm a famous actress, I'm going to march right down there to Calhoun County and introduce myself. He's going to be so excited, so proud that his mother's really somebody special, that he's going to take me around to meet all his friends."

The cat just yawned.

"Okay, okay. I get the hint. That point's years away and you're tired." She folded the picture back up and put it into her wallet. "You know, I was just thinking. Maybe I should practice being around kids when I'm with Sean. Instead of thinking that I'm not with Jason, I could pretend that I was. Think it would work?"

Zachary just grumbled slightly and curled up, his tail flicking over his face.

Merry reached for the light, but before she could turn the switch, there was a light rap on the door. "Yes?"

The door opened slightly and Peter's mother looked in. "I'm sorry to bother you, but Zachary usually needs a little help to get settled for the night."

Merry searched Mrs. MacAllister's eyes as fear clutched at her stomach. Had she heard any of Merry's conversation with the old cat? Merry relaxed when she saw that the woman's smile seemed open. She thought she was safe and turned to the cat.

"He had himself a long drink of water just a few minutes ago."

"Oh." Mrs. MacAllister stepped into the room. "That's very kind of you to take care of him. Are you sure he won't be a bother?"

"No," Merry replied, shaking her head. "I just hope he won't be bothered by my big feet and all the space they'll take up."

"He'll enjoy something warm to lean against."

Merry smiled and scratched the cat on the top of his head. He grunted quietly. Mrs. MacAllister seemed ready to leave but didn't. She probably had something to say. Merry's stomach twisted slightly.

"I'm glad you could find time to visit us," Mrs. MacAllister said.

"It's kind of you to have me. Like I said, I enjoy a little vacation away from the big city."

There was another long pause as Peter's mother gathered up her robe around her neck. "Peter doesn't exactly share things of a personal nature with others."

Merry blinked, wondering what was coming.

"So I've had to learn to read him," Mrs. MacAllister said. "You know, check the nonverbal signals he gives off."

Merry nodded as the woman looked down and studied the floor for a long moment. "You're the first woman he's brought home since Kelly," she said, looking up at Merry.

"Oh?"

"I'm very glad my son has found you. I can tell you're going to make him and Sean very happy."

She was gone before Merry could say a word.

Chapter Three

Peter checked the back door and made sure it was locked. Growing up here, no one had to lock their doors, day or night. He doubted that crime had become a real problem in Mentone in the last few years, but he wasn't all that trusting anymore.

After turning off the kitchen light, he paused in the hall and gazed into the dining room. He'd always think of it as their holiday room. The big country kitchen had more than enough room for the three of them to eat regular meals when he was a boy, but the dining room was for holidays.

There'd been times when they'd had as many as fifty people over for a holiday meal. Peter had loved those times, sitting back, quiet as a mouse, and listening to the stories the adults told about the youthful escapades of the elders.

As a boy, Peter had been pleased to find out that his father didn't spring to life as Dr. Charles MacAllister. That stern, disciplined, hardworking town doctor had had another life as Chuckie MacAllister.

Chuckie MacAllister had been smack dab in the middle of Pete and Bertha MacAllister's brood of five children. He'd been an ordinary kid, who was kept after school often, got into mischief and spent a lot of time trying to ditch Sunday school. His academics improved once he reached high school but, according to the stories, his mischievous ways stayed with him well into adulthood.

Peter had always been in awe of his father. As a young child, he'd always gone to his mother with his problems, but when he reached puberty, there were things that he thought a boy just couldn't discuss with his mother.

It was then that the memories of dining room stories of a boy named Chuckie turned the stern man into a regular guy. One who'd torn his brand-new Sunday pants on Mr. Yoder's fence as he tried to escape with a "borrowed" watermelon. A boy who'd been caught kissing his girlfriend behind her garage and had to run for his life as her mother chased him with a broom. The type of person who would understand a teenage boy's fears and concerns.

The stories had not lied. Peter had spent many a late night talking things over with his dad, finding wisdom and guidance as well as friendship.

A twinge of pain pulled at Peter's heart as he wondered what Sean thought of him. Did he even think of him at all? Peter's father had worked a lot, but he'd still been a part of Peter's daily life. He didn't live and work in a distant city, keeping in touch by telephone and periodic visits.

Clenching his teeth, Peter punched the light switch. This was the best place in the world for Sean Charles MacAllister to grow into a man. And it wasn't as if Peter didn't spend any time with his son. And he planned to spend a lot more with him as the boy grew older.

Peter went quietly up the stairs, stepping carefully, trying to find the quiet spot on one tread before he advanced to the next. The house was as still as an empty church until he reached the top of the stairs, where he was greeted by a rather substantial woof.

"Quiet, Belle," he whispered.

The old dog woofed again, although a bit quieter.

"Damn it," he whispered. "It's me."

She growled.

That wasn't the reaction he wanted. Peter glared at her a

moment. "Go to bed," he whispered hoarsely. "Go on. Go to Sean."

Belle glared back at him.

"Get moving," he said, waving his hand toward his son's room. "Go on now. Get in there."

Grumbling, the dog slowly made her way down the hall. Peter waited until she had slipped in through the partially open door. Then, shaking his head slightly, he made his way carefully toward his room.

"Ssst."

Peter paused, his hand on the doorknob, and looked toward the sound. Merry was peeking around the edge of her door, beckoning to him. He looked quizzically at her as he slowly approached her door.

"What's wrong?" he whispered, stopping a couple lengths outside Merry's door.

She beckoned again, more vigorously this time.

As he took a step, Merry opened her door wider. She was wearing a short robe that barely threw a shadow over her knees. The sight of her two very shapely legs caused him to pause and smile.

Suddenly his mouth opened wide as he gasped in pain. Merry had stepped out into the hall, grabbed him by the shirt front, along with a few chest hairs, and yanked him into her bedroom. In simultaneous motions, she shut the door while slamming Peter up against the wall.

"What did you tell your mother?" she demanded.

Peter stared at Merry, the bewilderment in his mind feuding with the excitement growing in his body. What in the world was she talking about? He had never seen Merry in anything except street clothes or her waitress uniform, and there was a certain feminine muscularity to her frame that, along with her boldness, he found very arousing.

"I asked you a question," she pointed out.

"Ouch," Peter yelped. She was pulling his chest hairs again. "About what?"

"About us."

"Us?"

"Your mother was in here just a minute ago," Merry said.

"She left me with the distinct impression that she thought we were on the verge of getting engaged."

"Engaged?" Peter tried to move Merry's hand. He needed space to think, but she held on tight.

"Yes," Merry hissed through her teeth. "You know, as in engaged to be married."

"Oh."

"Yeah, oh," she snapped. "That's an interesting place for us to be, considering that we barely know each other. I'd be hard put to call us acquaintances."

"Could you let go of me?"

Merry blinked once, then looked down at her hand. "I guess," she replied.

"I'd really appreciate it."

"Shucks," she said with a grin. "I was just starting to enjoy myself."

Peter swallowed hard to still the excitement that wanted to dance in his loins. So was he, but he pushed that thought away. "What did my mother say?"

"I don't remember exactly," Merry said. "But she did say that I was the first woman you'd brought here since Kelly."

He stepped away and rubbed his hand down over his face. His physical excitement had almost completely died. "Well, you are."

"And that I was going to make you and Sean very happy."

Peter had to fight to keep his eyes from dancing along the sweet curve of her legs. "She's got a lot of things mixed up," Peter said. "I'll talk to her tomorrow."

"I think it would be best if you did."

Peter nodded. "Good night," he murmured before he opened the door.

"Good night," she whispered.

He shut Merry's door quietly behind him and was about to walk to his own room when he heard another door, further down the hall, shut quietly.

Oh, great. His mother was awake, no doubt jumping to her own conclusions. He briefly considered talking to her then, but decided against it. Eleven at night was not a good time to get into a discussion with Mom. The morning would be better. Probably not much better, but every little bit would help.

He hurried into his room and softly closed his own door behind him. He'd been bothered by dreams for the past few months now. But he had a feeling that tonight's dream would be different. It would star a barefoot, red-haired beauty.

Merry bounced down the stairs and followed the trail of delicious smells pulling her toward the back of the house Thanksgiving morning. The turkey was already in the oven.

"Good morning, Mrs. MacAllister," she said as she stopped at the kitchen door. Pie tins were scattered about the countertop, and Peter's mother was rolling out a circle of dough. It sure enough looked like the woman was going to bake a mess of pies.

"Good morning, Merry," Mrs. MacAllister said. "How did you sleep?"

"Just fine."

It didn't look as if Peter or Sean were anywhere about. Merry wondered if Peter had had that little chat with his mother yet.

"You don't have to call me Mrs. MacAllister, dear."

The tone of voice indicated that Peter hadn't. At least not about the true nature of their relationship, or even the semitrue nature.

"I just wouldn't feel right about calling you by your first name, ma'am."

The smile stayed in place, but Merry couldn't really read the gleam in the old woman's eyes. "I see," Mrs. MacAllister finally said after a long moment. Then she turned her attention back to rolling the dough.

"Can I help you?" Merry asked.

"Only after you've had breakfast. The boys had blueberry waffles this morning and there's some batter and berries left."

Merry moved quickly to the waffle iron. "Where are Peter and Sean?"

"Peter took Sean to the playground."

Merry nodded as she turned the hot plate on.

"It's good for them to do things together." Mrs. MacAllister slapped the dough for emphasis. "They should do more of it."

"It's hard with Sean living here and Peter working in Chicago."

His mother snorted. "It doesn't have to be that way. Sean could live with him in Chicago."

"Peter knows that." Merry opened the hot plate and poured the batter over it. "But he'd like his son to grow up in a small town, just like he did."

"Then Pete can stay here," his mother said. "I heard him talking to his cousin Gene once. Peter said that with what he does and with computers being what they are, he could live most anyplace in the world, and it would be just as if he were in his office in downtown Chicago. So he could spend a lot more time in Mentone."

Merry nodded as she watched the signal light on the waffle iron. Her granny said that the truth always stayed out of family arguments, so Merry preferred not to take sides. Her waffle was cooked and a great deal of it eaten in the silence that followed. Mrs. MacAllister left her pie crust and went to pour a cup of coffee for each of them.

"What he really needs," Mrs. MacAllister said, as she brought the cups over and sat down, "is a wife."

Swallowing the last piece of waffle, Merry grabbed the coffee cup. It was a good-size cup—big enough to hold a lot of coffee and big enough to hide behind.

"Folks say a maid is cheaper, even at today's prices."

Oh, boy. The pinched look Mrs. MacAllister gave her had the friendly all squeezed out of it. If Merry concentrated real hard, she might be able to drink her coffee around the foot in her mouth.

"Kelly's been dead and buried more than a year now. It's time for Peter to be getting on with his life."

Merry forced a smile. Maybe she should suggest getting on with the pies.

"I'm a widow myself," Mrs. MacAllister said. "I know all that a body has to go through. Saying goodbye takes time, usually about a year." The woman gulped at her own coffee. "You have to shed your tears and bid your farewells a step at a time. There's so many anniversaries to go through."

A silence descended on the kitchen as his mother took time to stare at the gray scene outside the kitchen windows. "It isn't just the major ones like birthdays. There's things like your first snowfall together, the first time you got caught in the rain, the first time you both woke up at four and watched the new day creep up over the horizon. In a lot of ways, it's worse if you had a good marriage. Then you usually had something special every day of the year.''

Her eyes turned inward, but they didn't seem to be seeing anything. Merry wondered if Mrs. MacAllister had finished saying goodbye to Peter's father. If she was still doing it after fifteen years, why should Peter be done after only one?

''Some folks need more time than others,'' Merry said softly.

Mrs. MacAllister snorted and shook her head. ''Men do. They're such fragile, romantic creatures. You sometimes wonder if they live in the real world.''

Merry went back to her coffee.

The older woman just sighed. ''But it's hard to say goodbye when you're carrying a heart full of hurt,'' she said. ''Things weren't going well for Peter and Kelly before she died. Neither of them said anything about it, but I knew.''

Merry looked around the kitchen. She had a strong feeling that it was time to get to those pies. There were already more secrets spilled than she had a need to know.

''Kelly had a really difficult time when Sean was born and couldn't have more children,'' Mrs. MacAllister went on. ''It didn't bother Peter too much, he was just glad that Kelly and Sean were all right. Kelly was really devastated, though. She didn't want Sean to grow up an only child, but wouldn't consider adoption.''

''I'm not sure you ought to be telling me all this,'' Merry said, trying to get her to change the subject.

''Peter needs somebody who understands,'' the other woman said. ''You need to know who he is.''

''I'm sure he'll tell me when he feels I should know.''

''Kelly seemed to grow more frantic the older Sean got, though she learned to hide it from Peter,'' Mrs. MacAllister went on as if Merry hadn't spoken. ''She just kept searching for something to fill the void she felt was in her life. Finally she decided a big house in the country was what they needed. Peter had no real interest in moving. All he knew was that with the commute, he'd have even less time with her and Sean.''

Merry clutched her cup. She didn't need to know all this, didn't *want* to know all this. But how could she tell Mrs.

MacAllister that without explaining that her and Peter's relationship was just a farce? The woman hurt so much for her son. It wasn't fair to let her think Peter was farther along the road of healing than he really was. But telling her the truth would subject Peter to his mother's matchmaking, and he didn't need that in his fragile emotional state right now.

"The morning Kelly died, they had a terrible fight," Mrs. MacAllister said. "They were all supposed to go look at houses, but it was a miserable rainy day and Peter thought they should postpone it. She didn't want to, but he went to work, thinking she had agreed. Except once he'd gone, she left Sean with a sitter and went alone. Peter blamed himself for the accident. I think he still does."

"If they had all gone, they all might have died."

"If he'd been driving, they might not have had the accident."

There were no answers; they both knew that and sat in shared silence as the pain of love weighed down around them.

"Poor Peter," Merry said finally as she stared into the remains of her coffee. "Guilt always makes for a heavy load."

Mrs. MacAllister nodded with a grim smile and pushed herself upright. "We'd better be getting to those pies before we need that oven for the sweet potatoes. You're just too nice, letting an old woman rattle on so. Next time you just reach over and give me a shake. You don't, and I'll just talk your ear off."

"Catch me, Daddy!" Sean squealed as he slid down the slide into Peter's arms.

Peter barely had time to hold him before the boy had freed himself and was running back around to climb the ladder again. The playground seemed to have shrunk since Peter had played there as a child. The slide that had seemed so sleek and so high looked scratched and tame now.

"Here I come, Daddy!" Sean shouted and flew down the slide again. He hit the bottom about the same time as the first few drops of rain spattered about on the gravel around them.

"Uh-oh," Peter said as he steadied the boy. "Looks like we're going to have to hit the trail. It's starting to rain."

"Do we have to?" Sean's cry was a pleading whine, but he

slipped his hand into Peter's and walked along with him away from the playground equipment.

Sean's hand felt so small and defenseless as Peter held it. He tightened his hold automatically. Was he really doing what was best for the boy, letting him grow up here? Peter'd lost Kelly and given up Sean. Was his self-imposed isolation making life better or worse for the boy?

"I wish you lived here," Sean said suddenly.

"Me, too."

"Grandma says I'm too little to go on that slide," he volunteered.

Peter smiled at him. "Don't go on it by yourself."

"I don't." Sean kicked at the stones, shuffling his feet as they walked. "Is Merry going to be my new mommy?"

Peter's feet stopped moving, surprise stunning him. "Your new mother?" he repeated, then shook his head. "No. Where did you get that idea?"

Sean just shrugged. "Grandma said I might get a new mommy someday."

The raindrops were coming down a little faster, and Peter started walking again. Good, old Mom. "No, Merry's just a friend of mine," he said. The image of her in her robe last night flashed into his heart, making it race, but he kept his voice steady. "She didn't have anyplace to go for Thanksgiving, so I invited her here."

"Oh."

"That okay with you?"

"Sure."

They reached the house a few minutes later and hurried up the stairs. The warm aromas of apple pie and turkey welcomed them.

"'Bout time you two got back." Peter's mother came to the kitchen door to greet them.

Merry was just behind her, the young woman's cheek decorated with a smear of flour that Peter suddenly had a desperate urge to wipe off. He squatted down, concentrating on taking Sean's jacket off.

"Did you need our help?" Peter asked.

"The boards need putting in the big table, and the card tables need to be set up in the living room."

"Think we can handle that, champ?" he asked Sean.

"If you carry the stuff."

Peter mussed Sean's hair as he stood up to find Merry smiling at him. He remembered the taste of her lips, could feel their softness beneath his once more.

"You guys get wet?" she asked.

"Nah," Sean said, scrambling for the basement door. "Come on, Daddy. The stuff's down here."

Peter just smiled at Merry. "I gotta get the stuff," he said.

And he had to talk to his mother, he reminded himself. Get her straight on the relationship. Then Merry wouldn't have to smile at him that way, wouldn't have to pretend that they had some torrid affair going. The cool air of the basement only partially cooled his thoughts.

Between setting up the tables, finding chairs and starting a fire in the fireplace, there wasn't a moment to spare for his talk. If he had a minute to breathe, his mother was rushing around. When she had a free moment, she took Sean off to get dressed, then changed clothes herself. By that time, family had started arriving and there was no chance to really talk to anybody.

What was he actually supposed to say to her anyway? Peter asked himself as they sat down to Thanksgiving dinner. *We're just friends, Mom.* He'd already said that on the phone, but he supposed he could repeat it.

Peter looked across the table at Merry, who was seated next to his mother. Working in the kitchen had brought a flush to Merry's cheeks and a sparkle to her eye that hinted at a fire smoldering deep inside. Would his mother believe that any man could just be friends with someone as beautiful as Merry?

"And, man, he came down like a rock." Cheryl slapped her hands together, one on top of the other. "*Splat!* Actually, it was more like a wet dishrag. A wet dishrag that was as heavy as a rock."

Peter awoke from his thoughts to find his cousin Cheryl telling the story of a ten-year-old Peter who, using a blanket for his Superman cape, had jumped off the highest point of the garage. The whole room joined in laughter, especially Sean.

"I tell you," Cheryl went on, "Aunt Claire about killed us all."

Tears were flowing down Peter's mother's cheeks as she

laughed. Merry, sitting next to her, seemed even more alive as her laughter wrapped around them all. He felt drawn to her smile, to the warmth in her eyes.

"She kept saying, 'You're older, you should know better,'" Cheryl went on.

Merry briefly glanced Peter's way, then bent down to murmur to his mother, who just shook her head and kept on laughing. Peter felt a strange sensation of being left out. He wanted those lips to laugh for him, to whisper words for him to hear.

"And all I could say was, 'But Auntie Claire, how was I to know your boy was so stupid?'" Cheryl concluded her story to a roar of laughter, which subsided into a gentle hum of chuckles as people returned to their meal.

Merry turned to his mother, and the two of them chatted as they ate. He was too far away to hear the words, but he could see the genuine friendship building between them. He felt a shadow fall across his heart. He didn't like deceiving his mother this way. Maybe when they had their little talk, he should tell her the truth.

"I'm so glad to see you're dating again," Aunt Martha said, leaning across Uncle Paul to tell Peter. "It's about time."

"Told you the boy'd start when he was ready to," Paul grumbled.

Peter went back to his turkey. He guessed his mother wasn't the only one watching him and his social life.

"And she's such a nice girl," Martha went on. "Where did you meet her?"

"Where do you think you meet such a pretty girl?" Paul said. "In your dreams. You ask the boy too many questions."

Suddenly everyone's happiness for Peter seemed too much. "Looks like we're low on potatoes." He grabbed the bowl and hurried into the kitchen.

The silence was welcome and wonderful. He put the bowl down on the counter and walked to the back window. The yard looked dreary in the steady drizzle. Fallen leaves that had escaped the rake were a weary brown, the grass was lifeless. The garden held only occasional brown stalks.

Peter felt a nudge at his leg and looked down to see Belle. He patted the old dog on the head. Her eyes were tired, but filled with love.

"I know, old girl," he said softly. "Spring'll come again and everything will be filled with life once more."

But would it? Spring wouldn't bring youth to the dog's old body or sunshine to his own heart.

"My goodness, there you are."

He looked up to see his mother had come into the room. She took the bowl and began to put in more potatoes. "Thought you got lost."

"No, just visiting with Belle." He rose to his feet and took the now empty potato pot from her. Putting it into the sink, he let it fill with water. "Sure is dreary outside."

"Good reason not to look there then," his mother said.

As if it were that easy.

"You know, Peter—" she slipped her arm into his and leaned against his body "—I really like your Merry."

"She's not my Merry," he said. "We're just friends."

His mother patted his hand as she pulled away, much the same as he had patted Belle. "I've seen the way you look at her," she said with a laugh. "You can't fool me."

"Look, Mom, I'm not ready for a relationship. Merry and I are just friends." He remembered back to his walk with Sean. "She didn't have anyplace to spend Thanksgiving, so I invited her along."

"Sure."

"I mean it."

She shook her head as she picked up the potato bowl. "For a very smart man, you are very slow," she said.

"What's that supposed to mean?"

"Your eyes and your heart tell you when you're ready to risk love again, not your head. Listen to your head, and you'll always be alone." She backed into the swinging door, pushing it open and stepping through. Belle hurried after her.

Peter stayed in the kitchen a moment, watching the door swing shut and the stillness return. No, not quite. He could hear chatter from the other side and laughter. Merry's laughter.

Suddenly he felt very left out.

"You just tell me where things go, and I'll put them away."

"No, no." Mrs. MacAllister grabbed Merry's arm and led

her toward the living room. "You just sit down and relax. Peter will be down in a minute."

Merry looked for a long moment into the eyes shining up at her. She wondered what Peter had told his mother about them. Judging from the twinkle in the old woman's eyes, Merry would guess nothing. Looked like she was going to have to talk to that man again. And this time she would pull more than a few chest hairs.

"I don't mind helping," Merry insisted.

"You've done more than three people put together," Mrs. MacAllister said.

"Well, I ate enough for five people."

"Nonsense," the old woman replied as she pulled at Merry again. "Just sit down and relax. I'll put the dishes away in the morning. Does them good to air dry overnight."

There was no doubt in Merry's mind that Mrs. MacAllister had been a strong woman in her younger days. The spirit was still there, but physically the old woman was growing frail. It wouldn't take anything to set her down on her butt, march into the kitchen and put the dishes away. But it wasn't what the woman wanted, and it was her house. Merry smiled and let herself be set down in a large, comfortable old sofa.

"Peter's reading a story to Sean. He'll be down momentarily. It's just a short story."

The words had no sooner escaped Mrs. MacAllister's lips when there was a soft creak on the stairs, followed by Peter himself stepping into the living room. He smiled and nodded at them both.

"Your turn, Mom."

He was a nice-looking guy. Tall, with a soft smile and lively eyes. He'd replaced his shirt with a sweatshirt and now had moccasins on his feet instead of dress shoes.

"What story did you read?" his mother asked.

His brow wrinkled. "Something really depressing about a baby elephant. Sean loved it."

Peter seemed nicer and more relaxed here than he'd been back in Chicago. Must be the atmosphere. He was home among family and friends. No back-stabbing competitors here. He didn't have to wear his armor.

His mother nodded. "Babar. I'll read him something else."

Mrs. MacAllister walked toward the door and was about to step out of the room, when she stopped. A soft grin covered her face. "I've had a hard day. I'm going to bed myself right after I read Sean his story. You children behave yourselves."

Merry sighed as Mrs. MacAllister disappeared into the foyer. There had definitely been no talk. The slow advance of creaks indicated Mrs. MacAllister was going upstairs.

"Have a nice chat with your mother?" Merry asked.

Peter sat down next to her, a look of surprise on his face. "I tried, I really did, but she just wouldn't listen."

Merry glared at him, but it did no good. Peter just went right on looking alone and vulnerable. Merry hated that combination. It was guaranteed to do her in if she let it.

He leaned against the sofa back, closing his eyes with a sigh. He seemed tired, and she fought the urge to rub his shoulders. This whole situation couldn't be easy on him. These were people he cared about, people it probably hurt to fool.

He opened his eyes to look at her. "Care for a nightcap? Mom has some very good sherry."

His gaze was soft, vulnerable. She could see a lost little boy in those eyes, someone needing help, needing a hand to hold.

"No, thank you," she replied, picking up a magazine and flipping through it. Too many things were getting to her. This old house. Peter's family. Not to mention Peter himself. It was all too much. The last thing she needed was a nip of sherry.

Guys like Peter, with money, background and education, had always been the downfall of girls like her. Joe O'Connell had made her feel special, too, being her boss and all at the hardware store, and look how long that lasted. Just until she got pregnant; then she found out what he really thought of her.

She suddenly sprang to her feet. "It's been a long day all around," she said. "I'm going upstairs."

"You can relax here," Peter said, patting the sofa by his side.

"What I really want to do is get these shoes off," Merry said. "My toes want to be free and my feet want to breathe."

"Take off anything you like," Peter replied. "Whatever makes you comfortable."

A sweet, boyish smile came to his face. He looked so soft, his stiffness seemed to have melted away. Her heart twisted. It had been so long since someone had held her, since someone had made her feel special. And it would have to be even longer, since she wasn't giving in and jeopardizing her goals this time.

With a sigh, she bent down and kissed him lightly on the lips. A tiny flame inside her begged to be allowed to come to life, but she refused. "Good night, Peter."

He took her hand before she could escape. "The night's still young."

"But I'm not," she replied as she fled up the stairs.

Chapter Four

Peter sipped his coffee as he glared out at the gloomy overcast pressing down on the backyard. Winter had followed them in from Chicago, and only the warmth of the lake had turned the flurries into a cold, drizzly kind of a rain.

Now what were he and Sean going to do? They certainly couldn't play outside, and he didn't really like the kind of board games a five-year-old kid could play. While he was pondering their day, Sean was slurping the last drop of chocolate milk from his glass.

"Good morning, all."

Peter's gloom suddenly dissipated. "Good morning."

"Good morning, dear," his mother said.

Sean continued sucking on his straw.

"Sean," Peter's mother said gently.

"Hi," Sean said.

"Would you like to borrow some slippers, dear?"

His mother's question caused Peter to look at Merry's feet, clad in thick white socks.

"No, ma'am," Merry replied. "These socks are just fine. Besides I doubt you've got slippers that would fit me."

"Land sakes, child. Your feet aren't that big."

Merry just shook her head, a soft smile looking into the past. "My granny always said that I was supposed to be twins, but by the time the Lord finished making my feet, there wasn't enough material left over for another body."

Peter's mother laughed. "You're stuffed fuller than a Christmas turkey."

"You're truly right."

She had a lovely accent, Peter thought, soft with fingers that soothed the frazzled endings of his nerves. He could listen to her voice for hours.

"What's her name?"

All eyes turned toward Sean. Outside of the forced greetings Wednesday night and this morning, this was the first time he'd spoken directly to Merry.

"Your twin sister," Sean said. "What's her name?"

"Oh," Merry replied. "You mean the one that wasn't born?" Sean nodded.

Merry paused for just the slightest moment, enough time for a shadow to fall across her sparkling eyes. Peter felt his breathing grow a bit strained.

"Louise."

"Do you talk to her?" Sean asked.

"Sometimes."

Peter was uncomfortable, although he couldn't say why.

"Especially when I have something secret to talk about," Merry said. "Then I always tell Louise first, because I know she won't tell anybody else."

Sean slowly nodded his head in solemn agreement, pumping tension into the silence that hung over them.

"I have a twin brother," he said.

Peter felt his stomach tighten as the memories of Kelly's longing for another child swept over him. *Sean can't grow up an only child. He's alone too much. He needs a brother or sister.* Had Sean heard Kelly's worries and taken them as his own?

"His name's Barney," Sean said. "And no one else can see him or talk to him but me."

Everyone stared at Sean. From the corner of his eye Peter saw Merry's lips smile, a smile tinged by the gray of the overcast day outside. He'd been hoping that Sean and Merry would warm up to each other, but he hadn't wanted this unique affinity for the melancholy.

"Well, what should we do today, sport?" Peter put an extra measure of hearty into his voice.

Sean shrugged.

"It looks pretty yucky out there," Peter said. "I don't really want to play outside, do you?"

Sean shrugged.

"Want to play a game?"

He shrugged again.

"Want me to run out and get a movie?"

He shrugged still again, and Peter felt his nerves approaching the edge. Damn it, why did the kid have to be so difficult?

"Why don't you all go out to the Bell Museum?" his mother suggested. "He just loves that place. Don't you, Sean?"

Sean nodded. It was a slow, reluctant response, but at least it wasn't a shrug.

"Great, great!" Peter exclaimed. "We'll have ourselves a look-see. Then we can skip out to Warsaw and grab a burger and fries. How about it, big guy?"

His son had returned to shrugging, sending Peter back to gritting his teeth.

"Would you like to come along?" Sean asked Merry.

"Why, sure."

"We gotta wear shoes," Sean said, raising one stockinged foot up to the table.

Merry made a face. "Oh, well. If we gotta, we gotta."

"Is Louise coming?" Sean asked.

That discomfort washed over Peter again and he searched for a way to change the subject.

"She sure is," Merry replied. "She goes everyplace with me."

Sean nodded, his face so solemn that it almost hurt Peter to look at him. "Barney's coming, too."

"Good," Merry said. "I'll go with you and Louise will go with Barney. It'll be a double date."

"I never been on a date before."

"That's okay. I've been on a lot of them. You just watch what I do. Hey, what's this?" Merry stopped and reached over by Sean's ear. "It's a quarter!"

Sean, mouth open in astonishment, took it from her. "Wow!" he breathed and slipped his other hand into hers as he continued to stare at the quarter. "How'd you do that?"

Peter watched them until they were out in the hall, and then the creaking sounds told him they were upstairs. It was amazing how completely Merry had turned things around. One day she looked to be scared to death of the kid, and the next they're old pals going on a date.

"Where'd she ever learn magic tricks?" his mother asked.

"At some café she used to work at." He was unable to get Sean's words out of his mind. "How long has Sean had this imaginary pal?"

"All children have imaginary friends," she assured him, getting up to rinse out her coffee cup. "Especially only children."

He stared at her.

"For heaven's sake, don't look so solemn. You had a number of them yourself."

He let his eyes drift toward the window. The mood of the weather was unchanged. Gloomy and wet. "Sean has quite an imagination," Peter said.

"He's a normal, intelligent little boy. You'd have cause to worry if he didn't have one."

But a longing for someone who didn't exist? Or was the real longing for someone who had existed but was gone? Maybe a five-year-old couldn't express his grief and acted it out in other ways.

Sean's laughter came into the room just ahead of him as he raced away from Merry. His face was more alight and childlike than Peter had seen for ages.

"Help! Help!" Sean darted behind Peter.

"He's not gonna be able to save you." Merry laughed as she grabbed at the squealing boy.

Peter wanted to be part of their laughter. He wanted to feel that glow of pure happiness on his face, too. "Hey," he cried. "Grandma doesn't like people fooling around in her kitchen."

They paused in their roughhousing and stared at him. Sean's look was filled with disgust.

"Well, I got her to stop," Peter told his son. "I saved you. Just like you asked."

Sean was not impressed by his father's creativity and didn't let him into his sunshine. "Let's go get our coats," Sean told Merry, taking her by the hand.

Peter trailed along after them, feeling as awkward and gawky as a twelve-year-old.

That feeling went away somewhat as the weekend progressed. Merry was aptly named, as her cheerful, sunny attitude warmed all of them. Peter couldn't remember a time in the past year when laughter had rung out as much as it had in the past few days.

By the time Saturday evening came around, Peter was congratulating himself on his wisdom in bringing Merry home with him. She was even willing to go to his cousin's high school basketball game.

"This is a little beyond the call of duty," Peter said as he pulled into the Tippecanoe Valley High School parking lot. "I may have to give you a hardship bonus."

"I like high school basketball."

Peter found a spot and parked his car. "I'm not fooling. The noise in that gym is going to be deafening."

"No problem. My eardrums can use the exercise."

They got out of the car, and Peter hurried around to take Merry's hand. She was dressed in what she'd called her city slushing outfit—hiking boots, jeans and a down jacket. She fit in as if she'd been born and raised right here.

"A daughter of one of my dad's brother's kids—I guess that makes her a second cousin—plays for Valley and she's starting tonight. Mom said I had to go as a representative of our branch of the family."

"Good," Merry replied. "I wasn't in the mood for chamber music."

"I wouldn't have done anything that dull."

"I never said chamber music was dull. I just said I wasn't in the mood for it tonight."

Peter gave her a quick frowning look, but Merry's expression was as innocent as an angel's. He decided not to press his luck. Merry seemed to be able to more than hold her own in verbal sparring matches. Though they did hold a certain appeal, he chose to keep the conversation on the upcoming game.

"These events can get a little rowdy at times," he warned.

"That's okay," Merry said, patting his arm. "Don't you worry yourself none. I'm here to protect you."

"Thank you," Peter said. "I feel so safe now."

"You should."

Peter growled deep in his throat. It was obvious that this was a woman who always had the last word. He took her arm again and led her into the high school gym. She felt good at his side. He liked the feeling of being part of a pair again. It would definitely be a good idea to date her when he got back to Chicago. Then his attitude would stay on the corner of Bright Avenue and Chipper Street.

The old gym was filling rapidly, and the low murmur of the crowd was making the rafters hum. Once the game started, the roof would be set to flapping. Valley was playing Rochester. They were bitter rivals back when he went to school and it looked as if they would forever remain such.

Peter bent close to Merry's ear. "Where would you like to sit?"

"Right smack dab in the center of things."

"That's where a lot of the students and young folks sit," he warned her.

She gave him an ornery grin. "Don't you fret none. I told you I'd take care of you."

"Right," he said. "I keep forgetting you're my bodyguard."

Peter hesitated as he looked over the gym. *Ladies first* wasn't a good concept when it came to plowing through this crowd. Before he could take a first step, though, Merry was already well ahead of him. She gave him a wink over her shoulder and started up the bleachers.

She didn't exactly shove or push anybody, but the crowd parted before them like the Red Sea. He followed her, trying not to stare at the shapely legs just ahead of him, but it was impossible not to. She moved with such strength and grace. She could be a figure skater or ballerina. Or maybe a diver. Lord, but he'd love to see her in a swimsuit, getting ready to do a double flip.

"How is this?" Merry asked.

He cleared his throat and his thoughts. "Very good."

"I told you I'd take care of you," she replied.

"Yeah, I can see that now." They both sat down. "You take care of me like I was a rock star or something."

"No problem."

Pretending to look elsewhere, Peter watched Merry from the corner of his eye. Her eyes were sparkling and a broad smile lit her face as she watched the girls in their green-and-gold uniforms warming up on the court below.

A brief question bubbled in the back of his mind. Merry had said that she'd grown up in the suburbs, yet she didn't quite fit the image he had of middle-class suburban women. He turned his full attention back to the playing floor. She seemed more like...

Country. That was the only word that came to mind. The type of girl who could milk the cows, put a splint on a broken arm and drive the tractor as well as any man. Sighing, Peter forced himself to concentrate on the girls going through their pregame rituals.

"Hey, Pete." A heavy hand slapped him on the back. A tall man with black hair, brown eyes and a long jaw stood at Peter's side. "How the hell are you?"

Peter stood up and took the man's hand as he began scanning his memory bank, searching for a name. "Just fine. And yourself?"

"Not bad. Get three squares a day, the roof don't leak and my wife lets me sleep with her."

The man's name was on the tip of Peter's consciousness, but it wouldn't step out to the forefront. He wanted to take another few seconds and see what his memory came up with, but the man was standing there, grinning at Merry.

"This is a friend of mine," Peter said, taking Merry by her hand as she stood up.

The man's grin grew broader. "Yeah, I heard about that." He thrust his hand out toward her. "Hi, Merry. Welcome to Indiana. I'm Matt Browder."

Browder. Relief and irritation met head on. Peter remembered Matt now. The man had been a senior in high school when Peter had been a freshman.

The irritation came as he wondered how the hell Matt knew Merry's name, but then they'd been here two days now. A small town like Mentone didn't need much time. Most folks probably knew her shoe size and color of underwear by now. He had a uneasy flash of curiosity as to just what color she did wear, but he pushed it aside.

"Matt was three years ahead of me," Peter said. "We were on the baseball team together. I was his backup. We both played second base."

"I got out while the gettin' was good," Matt said with a hearty laugh. "If I'd stayed around any longer, I would have been riding the bench backing this guy up. Old Pete here was a helluva player."

"I get better as the years go by," Peter told Merry.

"Hey, he made all-state in his junior and senior years."

Peter shrugged. "That was all ages ago. So, what are you doing here? I didn't know you cared about basketball."

"Baseball is still my first love, but my oldest daughter lives for basketball."

"So you brought her to the game?"

Matt laughed. "She's on the team." He pointed down toward the Lady Vikings. "She's the tall, thin blonde underneath the basket. Made varsity even though she's just a freshman."

"That's very good," Merry said, as Peter just stared at Matt.

Matt noticed Peter's stunned silence and just laughed more. "Time moves on, old buddy. We're all getting older."

"You have a daughter in high school?"

"Ain't no mystery to that. All you gotta do is get married right after you finish college." Matt paused a moment to broaden his already wide smile. "Janie is our first one. Got five more at home."

"Must keep you busy," Peter said.

"Keeps me out of bars and from chasing wild women," Matt said before he turned to Merry. "Where're you from? You're not from these parts, are you?"

"Atlanta," Merry replied.

"Oh, yeah?" Matt said. "My wife's got a cousin in Atlanta."

"I actually lived in the suburbs of Atlanta."

"So does her cousin. He lives in Stone Mountain."

Merry nodded. "I've heard of it." She turned to Peter. "You want any popcorn or a candy bar?"

"I don't," Peter replied. "Which do you want? I'll get it for you."

"Don't you fuss," she said with a laugh. "I need to go to the little girls' room anyway."

"You're going to leave me all alone?" Peter asked.

"I'll hurry back, sugar." She kissed him on the cheek. "Besides, Matt will look after you, won't you?"

"Sure thing, ma'am. And I'll see that no wild women come by and snatch him away."

Merry left them with a quick wave and a smile before being swallowed up in the crowd. Peter watched her cap of dark red hair bob and weave through the people in the stands. It was absurd, but he missed her. He felt alone and lost.

"That's a mighty fine young lady you got there, old buddy."

Peter had been savoring the warm spot on his cheek where Merry had kissed him. "Yeah," he said, finding it almost hard to speak. "She is nice."

A whistle sounded on the floor and the two teams collected their balls and gathered around their respective coaches.

"Folks are all glad to see that things are working out for you again. Man wasn't made to live alone, Pete. Especially when you have kids."

His old teammate's obvious joy and concern brought such pain to his heart that Peter had to look away.

"Well, I gotta run, old buddy." Matt reached out and seized Peter's hand, shaking it vigorously. "I'm sure you've got enough to do this weekend, but if you find yourself with some time and nothing to do, drop in on us. We're always home."

Peter nodded.

"Dad's retired and I run the old family place now. Grow corn and raise pigs. Regular pigs for hams, and then I raise some of them Vietnamese pot-bellied critters. Folks buy 'em for pets. Can you beat that?"

Peter shook his head.

"Well, don't be no stranger," Matt said. "And bring your boy with you when you come visit. He'll have a ball."

Then, with a last slap on the back, Matt was gone to join his family, leaving Peter alone to stare at everything and nothing before him. He sank down into his seat, letting the crowd and its noise fade away into the oblivion on the edge of his consciousness.

What a joke he was. What an absolute fraud. Merry was right.

She was his bodyguard. He'd thought it was a joke, but now he knew how true it was. He, Peter Blair MacAllister had hired a pretty, bright-smiling, redheaded woman to protect him from the real world.

"Boy, are you looking solemn!" Merry laughed as she fell into her seat next to him. "Somebody steal your scooter?"

His world was suddenly light and happy. Her thigh pressed against his and it became more than happy; it held the promise of all sorts of joys. "And where was my bodyguard when it was happening?" he teased.

She leaned over to brush his lips with hers. "Poor baby. Want to share my popcorn?"

"Maybe."

She offered him the box, and he reached in for a handful. God, her eyes were so bright. It was as if she were so full of sunshine and cheer that it had to spill out her gaze and her grin. Could her life have held only good things? Whatever, he wanted to stay close to her, stay where that sunshine would spill out over him.

Merry snuggled up close all of a sudden, slipping her arm through his. "I hear we're playing our arch rival," she whispered, her words tickling his ear. "Does this mean we get to be rowdy?"

He looked at her. She was so close, so alluring, her lips were just too tempting. Heaven danced between them, pulling them together. He leaned in just a bit and found her lips meeting his.

She tasted slightly like popcorn and somehow it seemed right. She was Saturday night at the movies and curling up before a roaring fire. She was football games and parties. Warmth and joy and laughter all tumbled into his heart. He felt young and alive, ready to do battle, ready to slay dragons.

Cheering erupted around them, and the teams parted. The starting lineups were about to be introduced. A silly reason for their kiss to be interrupted. Maybe Merry felt the same, for she snuggled up close, taking his hand in hers. He was sorry all of a sudden that they were going back to Chicago tomorrow.

"Well, Zach, it's just about over," Merry told the old cat as she folded her robe and put it into her suitcase. "Peter's picking up his mother's prescription at the pharmacy, and once he gets back we're on our way. I'd say it went really well, wouldn't you?"

The old cat just sat up and stretched.

"I must be a reasonable actress. No one doubted a thing." Merry took a last look around the room, then closed her suitcase. "Best of all, I earned some pretty easy money toward next semester's tuition."

Zachary yawned.

Merry put her suitcase on the floor and bent over to brush the top of the cat's head with her lips. "Thanks for sharing your room, pal."

Zachary made no stirring farewell speeches. In fact, he just turned around and began to wash his face. Merry took her case downstairs where Mrs. MacAllister was cleaning up the lunch dishes.

"You sure you don't want me to help you clean up?" Merry asked her.

"Don't be silly. You're our guest."

"But—"

"No buts, young lady." The older woman turned from the sink and gave Merry a quick smile over her shoulder. "You aren't a hired girl, you know."

Merry felt as if she'd taken a punch to her stomach. All right, so that aspect of the weekend hadn't been easy. Once she'd gotten to know Mrs. MacAllister, it had been downright hard to deceive her, but it was Peter's business to tell his mother the truth, not hers.

Still, it would be good to get back to Chicago. Back to the big city and back to her own life.

"I just don't feel right doing nothing," Merry said.

Before Mrs. MacAllister could reply, Sean walked into the kitchen, swinging over to the counter to pick up an oatmeal-raisin cookie.

"Sean, would you please take Merry and keep her busy until she and your father are ready to leave?"

The boy looked at Merry solemnly as he completely chewed the cookie he had in his mouth. "Wanna go outside?"

"Sure," Merry replied. "I don't want to get any of us in trouble."

Sean blinked at her; then he reached for another handful of cookies. "Want some?" he asked, turning to look at her over his shoulder.

"No, thank you," Merry answered.

They moved toward the back door, Merry holding his cookies while Sean slipped into his jacket. After returning his goodies, Merry put on her own coat. They stepped out into the backyard and stood there until Sean finished the last of his snack.

"What do you wanna do now?" he asked, his eyes solemn as they stared at her.

"Why don't you show me around town?" Merry suggested.

Sean shrugged. "It's just a bunch of houses and stuff like that."

"Show me where your friends live."

He looked at her doubtfully, but then, shrugging again, he said, "Okay," and led her out to the street.

They walked quickly and purposefully down the narrow streets just north of Mentone's small business section. Sean pointed out where his best friend, Roger, lived, and his good friends, Ronny and Susie, as well as where Meg, Johnny and Rachel resided. Although the latter were not really good friends, he played with all of them. After the tour, they found themselves standing across the street from the egg.

"I got other friends," he said. "But we gotta have a car if you want to see their houses. Can you drive?"

"Yes, but I don't have a car."

"We can ask Grandma for hers," he replied.

"That's okay," Merry said. "Let's save something for next time."

"You coming back?"

His solemn child's eyes stared at her, and Merry found herself growing uncomfortable. All right, so this part of the weekend wasn't a snap, either. It wasn't as if she and Sean had become such great buddies that he was going to miss her.

Merry glanced across the street at the egg. "I think this is the only town in the world with a giant egg on Main Street."

"It ain't really an egg," Sean replied. "It's just a big rock that they painted."

The boy stood there and stared, almost glared, at the rock masquerading as an egg. He was such a solemn little guy.

"Well, I think it really is an egg," Merry said. "And I think one of these days the giant chicken that laid it will come back. And when it does, it's going to bring so much magic back to town that nobody'll ever be unhappy here."

Sean just stared at her, skepticism and hope warring on his earnest little face. He wanted to believe her, she could see that, but giant chickens probably seemed a bit much for even a five-year-old.

"Want to go back home?" Sean asked.

"Okay," she replied.

They walked quietly back to the big yellow house on First Street. Merry would have held the boy's hand, but there really wasn't a chance to. Not even at the crosswalks. There wasn't any traffic in this town.

Sean stopped at the driveway of his grandmother's house. "Wanna see the backyard?"

"Sure thing, sport," she said heartily.

Her voice sounded false even to herself, but Sean seemed not to notice. He led her up the driveway, past Peter's car and around to the back of the house. There was a broad expanse of backyard lined with evergreens and a big, old oak in the center.

"Daddy says when I get bigger, he's gonna build me a tree house in that tree there," he said, pointing at the oak.

"That'll be fun."

He shrugged.

"Hey, you can have your friends sleep over in it."

Sean blinked but, from the momentary brightness in his face, it was obvious that he hadn't thought of that.

"We got a lot of grass. And Grandma's got a whole bunch of flowers, but they're all dead now."

"Not all of them are dead," Merry said. "Some of them are just dormant. That means they're asleep until spring."

He made a face.

Merry looked around the yard. She wanted to find a perennial so she could scratch the bark and show Sean the living green skin underneath. Her eyes fell on a plant by the back door still clinging to its summer mantle of green.

"That one's still alive. And it isn't even dormant yet."

"That's a dumb plant," Sean replied.

"How do you know it's dumb? Did you give it a test?"

Sean ignored her attempt at humor. "Grandma said it sometimes blooms on Christmas."

Merry looked closer at the formation of the leaves. "Oh, it's a Christmas rose."

"I never seen it bloom."

His young eyes were hard, as they had been when they looked at the rock that adults called an egg.

"Maybe the winters have been too cold," Merry said. "Maybe the magic's not here yet."

"I bet it don't never bloom."

A wind whipped around the corner of the garage, and Sean's small shoulders shivered in their jacket. Merry felt a prickling at her eyes, but blinked it away. These weren't her kin; these weren't her problems. She had her own woes awaiting her, practically more than she could handle. She didn't need any more.

"We'd best get in the house," Merry said. "Your daddy will be wanting to leave soon."

Without a word, he turned and made his way up to the back porch, with Merry following. She forced herself to think of the homework waiting for her, of all the time lost to finish her research for her sociology paper.

"Did Sean show you my Christmas rose?" Mrs. MacAllister asked as they stepped into the kitchen.

Peter was sitting at the table with a cup of coffee. He put his arms around his son as the boy came near him. Sean didn't pull away, but he didn't fold into his father's grasp, either. It hurt to look at them, but Merry couldn't take her eyes away.

"I do believe that rose is going to bloom this year," Mrs. MacAllister said. "I just have this feeling."

Merry forced a smile. "I hope it does." Neither Sean nor Peter seemed even slightly moved by her cheerfulness. Each hurting, and each locked away in himself. Damnation, not one thing about this weekend had been easy.

"And I hope you'll be here to see it," Mrs. MacAllister said.

"I surely will, ma'am."

Judging from Peter's expression, he was shocked at the words that had come out of her mouth. Well, the hell with him. He'd paid her a lot of money and the job wasn't done yet.

Chapter Five

"You don't have to come back over Christmas," Peter said once they were on Route 30 heading west.

"It's okay."

"No, it's not okay." His voice sounded snappish even to him and he tried to force the annoyance away. It was just that a part of him wouldn't mind her coming back. Not at all. "I didn't expect Mom to put you on the spot like that."

"It's still three weeks away," she said as she stared out the window. "Why don't we wait and see?"

Wait for what? He thought of how his mother had warmed to her and how Sean's face had been so alive when Merry had been chasing him. How the kid had clung to her hand as they wandered through the tiny Bell Museum, telling her all about native Mentonian Lawrence Bell and the jet-propelled airplane he designed, the first plane to fly faster than the speed of sound. How even Zachary had gravitated to her warmth.

Hell, why not be honest? He had been no exception. Every touch, no matter how slight, had driven all rational thought from his mind. He felt as if he were waking up after a long sleep, feeling alive again. But those same feelings also brought along a measure of fear. And fear made him want to drive her away.

"I only agreed to pay you for Thanksgiving," he said suddenly.

She turned at that, her eyes burning. "That was a cruddy thing to say. I don't remember asking you for money. For all I care, you can keep what you already offered."

He bit at his lip, staring at the road ahead of him. The heavy gray sky was unforgiving. The wind whipping across the empty fields was brutal. The angry beast inside him deflated.

"I'm sorry," he said. There was so much more he ought to say, but no words would come out. He couldn't explain his fears, not even to himself.

She glanced his way. Though she said nothing, he sensed he'd been forgiven. He'd make it up to her, he promised himself. He'd show her that he wasn't the churl he acted.

They drove on in silence for some time, until they were nearing the Indiana-Illinois border. A restaurant sign popped over the far edge of the land, and Peter considered stopping. A cup of coffee and maybe a piece of pie would be nice. Give the two of them a chance to talk.

"Care to stop for a bite to eat or some coffee?" Peter asked.

"I'm not hungry," Merry replied. "But if you want to, that's fine with me."

"You're easy to get along with."

A soft smile lit on her lips, like a small bird on a tree branch. "Sometimes," she said softly. "I can guarantee, though, with hundred percent certainty, that that's not an absolutely permanent condition."

He laughed, chasing the last of his dark mood away. "All right," he said. "What're the Christmas holidays going to cost me?"

She looked at him for a long moment, and Peter began feeling uneasy. Maybe she hadn't forgiven him.

But the storm in her eyes seemed to pass just as quickly as it came on. She turned to look out the window. "I didn't hardly earn my fee," she said. "Figure you already paid for Christmas and New Year's."

"No, fair's fair. Name your price."

She stared at him as he drove, her eyes narrow and thoughtful.

When she finally turned away, he felt relieved. "Tell your mother the truth," she said. "I'll come over Christmas if you tell her we're just friends."

"I did tell her that," he said. "She didn't believe me."

He wasn't going to repeat everything else his mother had said, her implications that he was more interested in Merry than he knew or that if he'd stop thinking, his heart would tell him where to go.

He was interested in Merry, just not in the way his mother thought. She'd be a fun companion, but he wasn't looking at her as a substitute wife or mother. He wasn't looking at anyone that way.

"Don't you miss him?"

Peter felt grabbed by the back of the neck and yanked back into the real world. "Huh?"

"Sean," Merry said. "I just wondered if you missed him."

He blinked at the overcast sky that was darkening before them. A storm was blowing in from the west, coming in over Iowa and southern Minnesota and bringing cold, wet misery for all.

"I mean, you don't see him all that often, do you?"

"Two, three times a month." Peter shrugged. "Sometimes just two when I've gotten tied up at work."

His cheeks grew warm and Peter felt angry all of a sudden. Angry at Merry, angry at the situation, but most of all angry at himself. He didn't have to submit to this third degree. Hell, he was doing the best he could. He knew that some men living in the same house with their kids saw them less.

"You miss so much when you're not there every day." Dark clouds inhabited her voice, and she was back to staring out the window. "You're not there to welcome them home from school. You don't hear their latest news firsthand. Yours isn't the first smile they see every morning. You're not there to tuck them in at night."

The pain in her voice opened up the scars in his own heart. Peter concentrated on the steering wheel, on the road, on his driving.

"Someone else raises them for you," Merry said softly. "You don't do any of the work, but you don't get to share any of the joy."

Merry's cloud of gloom spread and reached out to wrap itself around Peter like a suffocating mantle of despair. He felt himself getting angrier.

Here she was, twenty-five, single, with no one dependent on her. Where did she get off with this crap about not being there for the important parts of his son's life? He was doing the best he could for Sean. Sean was growing up in a house full of love and stability, just as Peter had.

Maybe Merry was watching too many soap operas. Or more than likely, she was planning to audition for one.

"Hey, Captain," Merry suddenly shouted. "Restaurant up ahead."

He flicked her a glare.

"Well, this land is so flat that it feels like we're sailing the ocean."

Peter glared hard at the horizon. Now she was cheerful and happy. And all he had to do was fall in.

"You said we could stop for coffee, didn't you? Well, I decided I want to."

Still silent, Peter slowed down and pulled into the parking lot. He turned off the ignition, set the hand brake, undid his seat belt, stepped out of the car and walked around to open the door for Merry.

But she was already scrambling out the door by the time he got there. It was obvious that she didn't know how to act around a gentleman. Maybe he shouldn't even bother. He turned on his heel and stalked toward the restaurant.

"Hey, wait up." Merry ran up, putting her arm through his. "You're mad at me, aren't you?"

"Of course not."

"You don't look like a happy camper."

"I didn't know we were camping."

She didn't reply, and they continued walking toward the restaurant. His body leaned into hers without any thought on his part. It was a nice, compact body. Soft where it was supposed to be soft and hard where it was supposed to be hard. Every muscle and bone was in the right place, honed to the right tension.

A smile pushed itself through his anger. Peter MacAllister,

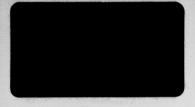

WELCOME TO THE
CASINO!
Try your luck at the Roulette Wheel ...
Play a hand of Twenty-One!

How to play:

1. Play the Roulette and Twenty-One scratch-off games, as instructed on the

opposite page, to see that you are eligible for FREE BOOKS and a FREE GIFT!

2. Send back the card and you'll receive TWO brand-new Harlequin Romance® novels. These books have a cover price of $3.50 each, but they are yours to keep absolutely free.

3. There's no catch. You're under no obligation to buy anything. We charge nothing — ZERO — for your first shipment. And you don't have to make any minimum number of purchases — not even one!

4. The fact is, thousands of readers enjoy receiving books by mail from the Harlequin Reader Service® before they're available in stores. They like the convenience of home delivery, and they love our discount prices!

5. We hope that after receiving your free books you'll want to remain a subscriber. But the choice is yours — to continue or cancel, any time at all! So why not take us up on our invitation, with no risk of any kind. You'll be glad you did!

Play Twenty-One For This Exquisite Free Gift!

THIS SURPRISE MYSTERY GIFT COULD BE YOURS FREE WHEN YOU PLAY
TWENTY-ONE

It's fun, and we're giving away **FREE GIFTS** to all players!

PLAY **ROULETTE!**

Scratch the silver to see where the ball has landed—7 RED or 11 BLACK makes you eligible for TWO FREE romance novels!

PLAY **TWENTY-ONE!**

Scratch the silver to reveal a winning hand! Congratulations, you have Twenty-One. Return this card promptly and you'll receive a fabulous free mystery gift, along with your free books!

YES!

Please send me all the free Harlequin Romance® books and the gift for which I qualify! I understand that I am under no obligation to purchase any books, as explained on the back of this card.

Name (please print clearly)

Address

Apt.#

City

State

Zip

The Harlequin Reader Service® — Here's how it works:

Accepting free books places you under no obligation to buy anything. You may keep the books and gift and return the shipping statement marked "cancel." If you do not cancel, about a month later we'll send you 6 additional novels and bill you just $2.90 each, plus 25¢ delivery per book and applicable sales tax, if any.* That's the complete price — and compared to cover prices of $3.50 each — quite a bargain! You may cancel at any time, but if you choose to continue, every month we'll send you 6 more books, which you may either purchase at the discount price...or return to us and cancel your subscription.

*Terms and prices subject to change without notice. Sales tax applicable in N.Y.

If offer card is missing write to: Harlequin Reader Service, 3010 Walden Ave., P.O. Box 1867, Buffalo, NY 14240-9952

BUSINESS REPLY MAIL
FIRST-CLASS MAIL   PERMIT NO 717   BUFFALO NY

POSTAGE WILL BE PAID BY ADDRESSEE

HARLEQUIN READER SERVICE
3010 WALDEN AVE
PO BOX 1867
BUFFALO NY 14240-9952

NO POSTAGE
NECESSARY
IF MAILED
IN THE
UNITED STATES

he told himself, you're just plain horny. It was time he stopped being a monk.

She let him open the door for her and once they were seated, she put her hand over his. "I'm sorry."

"Don't worry about it."

"No," she said. "It's none of my business. And everybody is doing the best they can for Sean."

He nodded.

"His grandma loves him dearly."

"We should do more things together," Peter said.

Suddenly her smile faded; her eyes turned serious. "It doesn't matter any if you do things together," she said, her voice almost hoarse. "All that matters is how much love you carry in your heart for him."

She had a rare understanding of things. He turned his hand under hers so that he had hold of her. He wasn't sure he wanted to let go.

"No, really, this is fine," Merry said. "This is closer than any parking place."

"But your bag—"

She just laughed as she hopped out of the car. "I've carried heavier. Pop open the trunk, will you?"

They were double-parked just outside her apartment. Peter'd wanted to park and carry her bag up to her apartment for her, but Merry knew from experience that the nearest parking spot could be blocks away, and that the sooner she said goodbye to him, the better. Too much had happened over the past few days, and she needed some time alone to sort it out.

Rather than use the trunk control inside the car, Peter got out and opened the trunk for her. She grabbed her bag out and slammed the lid down before facing him.

"Thanks for everything," she said, ignoring the annoyed look on his face. She was forcing him to violate every rule in his Gentleman's Handbook. "I imagine I'll see you at the restaurant."

He started to say something, but a truck was waiting behind and loudly protesting the wait. He glared its way, then took a step closer.

"Thank you for everything," he said.

Before she could escape, she was in his arms. He must have thrown away his Gentleman's Handbook for his touch was anything but soft and polite. His lips were hungry and as impatient as the truck driver honking behind them. She felt equal hungers awakening in her soul, fires that wanted to flare up and consume.

The trucker honked again, punctuating his impatience with a few choice words. Merry pulled away. She felt shaky and uncertain.

"Guess I'd better let you go," she said and hurried up to the sidewalk. From that position of safety, she waved as Peter got into his car and with a look of extreme annoyance at the truck driver finally pulled away.

"So long, buddy boy," Merry whispered and took a deep breath that ended in a shiver. A cold, damp wind was blowing off the lake, suggesting the need for a blazing fire and a body to cuddle up to. Well, she didn't have to have either, not with a good, thick blanket on her bed and an extra pair of socks in her drawer.

She went into the tiny lobby between the drugstore and the dry cleaner's. Their mailbox was fair to middling full, which meant she was the first one back. Just as well, that meant no explanations needed to be made.

Tucking the mail under one arm, she climbed the flight of stairs to the apartment and unlocked the door. The apartment seemed drearier than usual, so she turned on all the lights before she took her suitcase into her room. After about two minutes spent unpacking, she went back into the kitchen to make herself a cup of tea while she sorted through the mail. A few bills for Sandi, a few letters for ZeeZee and a newspaper for her. The tea was forgotten as she opened up the previous week's edition of the *Calhoun County Courier*.

The front page held the usual news—a holdup at the gas station, a tax referendum that was voted down and the annual Thanksgiving dinner for the poor and elderly at the social center. Some of the names were familiar, bringing to mind a few friendly memories and a few not so friendly ones, but she'd learned to deal with those emotions ages ago.

She waded through church news and school-luncheon menus before she hit pay dirt. There it was on page eight, right below the accident report, the schedule for the local schools' Christmas pageants.

Washington Elementary's "Home for the Holidays" would be performed two weeks from Tuesday.

She closed her eyes and saw herself there. Dressed to kill, surrounded by friends as she watched Jason sing Christmas carols with his class. Afterward, he'd rush over to her side where she'd hug and hug and hug him as if she'd never let him go.

"Hello there," Sandi called from the living room. The bumping and thumping of luggage being dropped to the floor accompanied her call.

Merry got to her feet and went into the other room. "Hi, have a good trip?"

"Great. Just the best." Sandi shoved one suitcase into the living room with her foot and shut the door. "I love getting away."

Merry just smiled and suddenly awoke to the whistling of the teakettle. "I've got some hot water on, if you'd like some tea."

"Sounds divine. I feel halfway to warm at just the mention of it."

While Sandi took her bags to her room, Merry went back to the kitchen and poured the boiling water over tea bags. As she waited for the tea to steep, she glanced out the window. An icy rain had started to fall, coating the glass and distorting the world outside. The neighbor's porch across the way became a tree house, the stop light at the corner her very own star.

Halfway to warm. She could be halfway to meeting Jason. She could go to his show. She couldn't meet him yet; she wasn't ready. But that was all right. She didn't have to meet him, didn't have to talk to anybody. There'd be a big crowd there, enough to lose herself in. And she could actually see him, maybe even hear his voice.

Dare she try? Dare she go back, after all the threats Joe had made? Hell, she wasn't a scared kid anymore, with no one to turn to. She was an adult and knew that all those things he'd said were just to keep her quiet and to convince her to give Jason up.

She'd held all the trump cards back then, if only she'd known how to play them. Joe'd been her boss at the hardware store and had begun wooing her as soon as she'd started working there. She'd been so stupidly flattered. He was older, wiser, had money and a pinky ring. What could he see in little, old her, she often wondered, but she loved the rush of fire his looks brought to her face and the little trinkets he used to surprise her with. A set of fluorescent bangle bracelets. A little book of poems. The red satin bikini underwear that should have shouted a warning to her. But no one'd ever made her feel so special before. She could still remember racing to her part-time job after the school day was finally over.

Living as he did way over in Highland, she had no idea he had a wife. She didn't find that out until she got pregnant and he wanted the child. His wife had been barren through the seven years they'd been married, and Joe would have done anything to keep his child. With a little luck and someone to turn to, Merry could have fought him and won.

The rain came down harder, blurring the magic outside into a swarm of colors, muted and miserable. No, she wouldn't have won, not really. No matter why Joe had said the things he did, he had been right. She was a nobody. She had nothing to offer their child, just a life of poverty and hopelessness like she'd had. Would she want him working in the mines, assuming they were still open by the time he was old enough? Or would she want him to run a chain of hardware stores across the county? Did she want him to be respected and educated, or in trouble with the law for underage drinking and vandalism like her younger brother?

The only thing she'd been able to give him was away.

Her eyes watered and she blinked at the wetness. Things were different now. She could go back and see him. She could get a camera and have a real picture to carry in her wallet, not an old newspaper photo.

Excitement grew in her heart until it was fit to burst. She wanted to tell someone, wanted someone to tell her that it was possible, that she should do it. She closed her eyes, and the first one who came to mind was Peter. She wanted to talk it over with him.

She opened her eyes. And how could she do that? How could she explain that this middle-class girl from the Atlanta suburbs had had a child out of wedlock while a teenager in Tennessee?

Nope, she was still alone and she'd better not let her heart forget it. She went into the bedroom and got her copy of *The Brothers Karamazov*. Number 27 on the list. Only twenty-three more classics to go.

Peter stepped into the restaurant, shivered from the chill wind and let his eyes search the room for Merry. It was two days since they'd gotten back, but this was the first time he'd made it to the restaurant. Not that he was avoiding her. No, he'd just been really busy. He had customers in yesterday, and they'd wanted to go to the Blackhawk for lunch. Then today, he'd had so much work that he had planned to eat at his desk, but his computer crashed just after noon and the system didn't want to come back up. He had no excuses to stay away.

He found himself holding his breath as his eyes swept the room, then holding it even more when Merry didn't seem to be anywhere about. Damn. Was Tuesday her day off?

No, most of these lunch places closed on Saturday and Sunday, so Merry would have the weekend off. She just had to be here. His regular table in back was empty, so he started walking toward it.

"Hey, stranger."

The air seemed lighter and a smile popped in place even before he saw her. "Hi," he said.

"I was afraid you didn't like us anymore." She came toward him with bright eyes and an easy smile.

"I got all tied up yesterday," Peter said.

"Whoo." She raised her eyebrows. "Was it fun?"

He tried to frown at her but failed miserably. "It was all business."

"Don't mean it can't be fun."

Peter gave his smile free rein. He grew more relaxed as he felt its glow fill his face. "Are you going to let me eat or are you planning on starving me to death?"

"I heard there were better ways to kill a man," she replied. "Ways that are more fun for all involved."

"Is that so?"

"Must be," she said with a shrug. "I read it in a book."

His heart wanted him to throw his head back and laugh, but

his mind would only let him chuckle. There was no controlling the joy that spread through his being, though.

"Your table is available," Merry said, looking toward the back of the dining room.

"I don't own a table here, so I can sit anywhere I want." He looked around the restaurant, somehow feeling the need to prove that he wasn't stodgy and bound by tradition. "I'll sit here," he said, pointing to a small table near the window.

"Okay." Merry followed him to the table. "Our soup of the day is chicken noodle."

"I'll have the chef's salad." She was already writing in her order pad even before he spoke, so he hurried on with the rest of his order. "With blue-cheese dressing on the side and—" he hesitated for just a moment "—coffee to drink."

She stared at him for a long time, but Peter wouldn't let his returning gaze waver.

"Boy," she said, looking down to finish writing on her order pad. "You're just a wild, crazy kind of guy."

"Just call me unpredictable. You know, like hard to pigeonhole."

Merry didn't say anything as she turned to go to the kitchen with his order, but she did leave the golden glow of her smile behind.

He glanced out the window, surprised to see that the sun was shining through the clouds overhead. Probably all caused by Merry's smile. He should tell her to go easy on spreading all that joy around. Another few days and she'd melt the polar ice cap and they'd lose California.

"There you go."

A bowl of salad dropped gently before him, pulling Peter back to the present. She placed the salad dressing by the bowl along with a cup of coffee.

"Are you busy?" he asked.

"Not really," she said, shaking her head. "Most of the lunch crowd has come and gone by now."

"Would you mind sitting down a minute?" he asked, indicating the seat across from him.

"Who do I have to protect you from now?"

Peter forced a frown onto his face. "You know why donkeys don't go to college?"

Her grin spread wider as she sat down. "Because nobody likes a smart ass."

"Where did you learn all your punch lines?"

"Here and there."

Peter thought he saw a momentary flicker to her smile. Just like a light bulb when the power would fade for an instant. He pushed aside the hard-boiled egg and tomatoes and spread dressing over the rest.

"Don't you like eggs?" she asked.

"Nor tomatoes," he replied. "Would you like them?"

"Sure."

He speared the hard-boiled egg and stretched toward her generous mouth.

"I'll get you another fork," she said.

"Don't worry about it. I like to live dangerously." After giving her the other egg, Peter started on the tomatoes. "You haven't had lunch yet, have you?"

She shook her head.

"Hope I'm not spoiling your appetite."

Merry laughed. "It would take a lot to do that. I eat like a horse."

"You don't look like a horse."

"I walk a lot," she replied. "Walk and climb stairs."

Peter openly admired her form. "Seems to be working. You ought to bottle it."

"Ain't no secret to hard work."

He started nibbling at his salad. Ask her, stupid, he berated himself. If you don't ask her, she'll think you just want to hire her as a bodyguard, or what she called a bodyguard.

"Let's go out to dinner," he blurted out.

Merry didn't reply immediately, so Peter plunged on.

"I mean, if you want to." He sighed. "Would you like to go out to dinner with me tonight?"

"I'm sorry, I can't. I have class tonight."

"Tomorrow?"

She shook her head. "I have this big research paper I have to do, and the only time the computers at school are free is around dinnertime."

"We can go afterward."

Merry didn't say anything, but her face looked as though she wished he'd stop asking her.

"We need to get to know each other better," he said.

Merry frowned.

"I mean, we did okay for a few days, but if we don't sound like we go out on a regular basis, my mother is going to get suspicious."

"We'll do okay."

"No," Peter insisted. "Mothers know about these things. It's like radar."

She laughed, but didn't say she would go out with him.

"I have a computer at home. You can use it any time you want."

"You have word-processing software?" Merry asked.

"But of course." She just needed a nudge, a little one. "There are no lines at my computer."

She blinked once.

"You can use it as long as you like. Come early, stay late."

She looked off in the distance before turning to him again. "I really do have a lot of work. I can't afford to take time off to go out to dinner."

"We can order in."

"I pay," she said.

"Sure," he replied. Anything to get her to agree.

"We could have taken the stairs," Peter said as he pushed the button in the elevator.

Merry just nodded. And miss this? The elevator wasn't very large, but it was about a hundred times ritzier than anything she'd ever seen. The whole back wall was mirrors and they reflected the polished wood and gold trim of the other walls. Even the carpeting on the floor was special—it was about a foot thick, so that a body sank into it.

The elevator glided to a stop, and the doors parted silently. Peter led her into a hallway that seemed an extension of the elevator—mirrors and ritzy trim. There were also tables here and there, and not cheap pressed-wood ones, either. Dark carved wood with gold lines painted on them and marble tops that held

flowers. She felt lucky when her hallway didn't have somebody's garbage dumped in it.

They came to a door marked 23 A and not saying anything,
Peter unlocked it. Then he stood back, waving her in.

Merry stepped into an entry foyer with white walls and a
highly polished parquet floor. Brightly colored modern paintings
covered the walls and a small metal sculpture that didn't look
like anything in particular stood in one corner.

It all looked rather simple, but Merry had been in the big city
long enough to know that simplicity meant really expensive.
Geez, was she out of her league. How had anybody in Mentone
believed that Peter was dating her? She considered turning tail
and running, but a body could never go back, just forward.

"Nice place," she said, trying hard for nonchalant.

"Can I take your bag?" he asked.

"No, that's okay." She slung her backpack down off her
shoulder. "Just show me where I can work."

"Right down here."

Peter started down a hallway and Merry followed, trying not
to stare at his broad shoulders. His smile could make this place
seem like home. His laughter could take all the scariness out of
it all. They crossed the living room, and her eyes wandered
away from Peter. Her feet stopped moving altogether.

The other side of the room was all windows and they looked
out over the lake, dark and brooding in the lingering light of
the late afternoon. Nothing but sky and water unless, Merry
suspected, one tiptoed right over to the edge and looked down
at the street. She inched forward slightly. But even that looked
magical as the streetlights wove a glittering chain into the distance.

Back home in Tennessee, Old Baldy had been the highest
point in the whole county. A body could see all the way over
to White Pigeon. Merry didn't know whether Old Baldy was
higher or lower than Peter's twenty-three stories, but the view
out his wall of windows was enough to take a person's breath
clean away.

"It's a beautiful sight," she whispered to Peter, who had
stopped to wait for her.

He nodded as if the beauty failed to move him anymore.
"Come on, I'll give you a quick tour."

She watched him go down the hall. How could this beauty not move him? she wondered. Was it just natural grief over his wife's death or, as his mother thought, lingering guilt? She wanted to rush after him and drag him back to the living room. She wanted to make him see the magic and beauty. She wanted him to feel the potency of nature as she had felt it. But he was too far away, and not just in feet.

He opened the double doors at the end of the hallway. "This is the master bedroom," he said.

She hurried to catch up. The bedroom was large with a king-size bed in the middle. The furniture was big and heavy, a white rug covered the floor, and like the living room, there was a wonderful wall of windows all along one side. She had a moment's vision of the sun waking her up as she slept in Peter's arms, but pushed that thought quickly out of her mind. The last time she'd let thoughts like that take control of her body, she'd landed in a heap of trouble.

"I imagine your wife loved this view," Merry said.

"She was looking for a place in the suburbs."

There was an undertone to Peter's voice. It sounded like anger, but Merry wasn't sure. She was sure that the message was, let's not talk about my wife. Maybe he still pined for her. For some reason, the idea hurt.

Peter went on and opened another door. "This is Sean's room."

She looked through the door into a little boy's room. The bed was a race car, and posters of Chicago Bulls and Chicago Bears players decorated the wall.

"Nice," Merry said.

"It's for when he visits me."

Merry nodded as Peter went on to the last door.

"And this is my home office," he said.

This was the smallest room she'd seen in the apartment so far, but it was still bigger than the living room of her apartment. The stainless-steel-and-leather furniture was very male and somehow almost like being in Peter's arms. She forced herself to stare at the pure white area rug on the floor.

"I'd better take my shoes off," she said.

"You don't have to."

"I couldn't work with my shoes on. I'd be scared to death that I was spreading dirt all over that beautiful white rug."

He shrugged. "Make yourself comfortable."

Comfort, now there was an interesting concept. There were all sorts of ways she could be comfortable. In Peter's arms, leaning against his shoulder, lying at his side. She shut down those thoughts and walked over to the computer.

"This it?"

"Yeah," he said as he came over to turn it on. "Need any help?"

"Nope." She shook her head and took off her coat. "Everything looks like it should." She took her diskette out and sat down at the desk. "If I run into any problems, I'll holler."

"We're here to help."

Merry smiled at him and felt a little ripple run down her spine. This place was intoxicating all by itself. Throw in Peter with those sad eyes and lost-little-boy air, and she'd be beyond recall. She forced herself to concentrate on the computer.

"You need any technical assistance, a tall, cool drink, a back rub, anything. All you have to do is call."

She doubted her need for any technical assistance, but those other two things were sure tempting. Squinting her eyes up, she stared hard at the screen. "Goodbye, Peter."

"You sure you don't need anything?"

Her body was getting downright needful, but she had to finish her paper and, even more important, she needed to stay out of trouble. "Out," she growled.

"Boy," he muttered.

His footsteps were muted by the thick rug, and Merry held her breath until the door closed behind her. Then she breathed a deep sigh of relief. She didn't know if there was a lock on the door, but knew that keeping Peter out wasn't the problem. What she needed was a bolt on the other side to keep herself in. Sighing, she sorted through her notes, hoping that her mind would follow.

Her mind did follow, although it took Merry a while to accustom herself to the quiet of Peter's office. The library at school was quiet, but it was different. It was muffled coughs, shuffling footsteps and whispers generated by crowds of people.

Here she had only herself, and out beyond the closed door, Peter.

She forced her fingers to move across the keyboard. Between work and school, she'd met her share of men and had had her share of come-ons. She'd had no trouble turning them down, one and all, and staying focused on her goal of a degree and success. Yet there was something much more appealing about Peter, and much more dangerous. He was drowning and didn't seem to know it. Locked within himself, he was going down for the third time, and she seemed to be the only one around to pull him back.

That was crazy, she told herself. He had a family, friends, people he worked with. He didn't need her, except as a temporary pretend girlfriend, not as a real-life savior.

Her scoldings lost steam about the same time her stomach became active. Luckily, she'd actually gotten a fair amount done on her paper, too. She leaned back and wiggled her toes in the thick rug, letting her mind savor the pizza that Peter was going to order in. Had he ordered it yet or was he waiting for her to finish?

She got up and walked to the door, savoring every soft tickle on the soles of her feet. Merry frowned. She'd better be careful or she'd go completely soft. She had a long way to go before she could relax.

As she was about to open the door, there was a light tap on the other side. She opened the door.

"Ready to eat?"

Peter had changed into a beige sweater, dark slacks and moccasins, and his face had lost some of the tightness he'd brought home with him. He looked as if he might actually enjoy the evening.

"Sure am," she replied.

"Then," he said, stepping aside, "dinner is served."

"Okay." She stepped back into the room to rummage in her backpack. "How much do I owe you?"

He blinked.

"Come on now. We agreed I was paying for the pizza."

"I didn't exactly get pizza."

She started to glare at him, but he reached out and took her hand. It was either wrestle him or follow him. Merry chose to follow. For now. "What did you get?"

"I had some old fish lying around," he said offhandedly. "So I took that and threw some odds and ends together."

Some old fish and odds and ends? He made it sound like something he found while jogging along the lake that he just tossed together with some old socks and an empty pop can, but she wasn't fooled. The smells from the kitchen were heavenly. There were spices, many of which she couldn't identify, cheeses and fish. Peter led her to the dining room and pulled out a chair for her.

"I don't need anybody waiting on me," Merry said, trying not to be awed by the wall of windows in front of her.

"Let me do it," Peter insisted. "I want to make sure that I haven't lost my touch. There haven't been guests here for a long time."

There was a poignancy in his voice. A sad-little-boy tone of a lad who'd been denied the pleasures of life. Who was she to deny a man simple pleasures? She sat down and let Peter serve the meal.

He filled her plate with fish, potatoes and vegetables. Then he took warm bread out of the oven, pouring each of them a glass of white wine before he sat down. They touched glasses, sipped and began eating.

The food was as wonderful as the scents had promised. The view was magnificent. But the company...

Well, she couldn't get Peter to maintain a conversation to save her life.

"Food's great," she began.

"Thanks." Silence again.

She nodded toward the windows. "Guess you must not be bothered by heights."

"Nope."

After some French vanilla ice cream covered with sinfully delicious cherry sauce and a glass of Japanese plum wine, Merry leaned back and gazed at her host.

He looked so alone, with the vast night beyond him. That bleakness that had been in the clouds over the lake seemed reflected in his eyes, making her want to lead him away from the dark storms. She could help him back into the warmth of sunshine, if he would let her. She would make him feel he wasn't alone.

The room swam before her eyes as ideas and desires danced in her mind. She ought to go home before she got into trouble. But there was a world of difference between being a kid and being an adult. As a kid, trouble could be overwhelming. As an adult, trouble could even be fun.

"What do I owe you?" she asked.

Peter's brow wrinkled.

"I'm supposed to be paying for the meal. So what do I owe you?" She could feel a lazy smile slowly roll across her face. "In cash money, that is."

He looked down at his now empty wineglass for a moment. "That's hard to say." He looked up. "I don't remember what the fish cost. And the stuff like the potatoes, spices and cheeses, I only used a part of what I already had on hand. I don't think I can come up with a dollar amount."

"Well, there are other ways of repaying a debt."

For just the smallest moment Merry was shocked at the words that fell from her mouth. But what the hell? The food was good, the wine was great, Peter was so handsome. And there were times when a girl just couldn't take any more lonely. A pleasant warmth radiated through her body.

He got up and began to clear the table. She followed him into the kitchen with the wineglasses.

She came in closer, taking her time but moving with purpose as she took the dishes from his hands and placed them on the counter. Then she went into his arms ever so smoothly. They closed around her surely and possessively as if she were coming home.

Her lips came up to meet his and they touched softly at first, like the gentle drizzle of rain on the petals of a rose. Their dance was hesitant and restrained, but then something happened. Like a storm suddenly bursting into life, the gentleness fled. He was the thunder; she was the lightning. He was the wind; she was the rain. Their hunger, their needs grew more intense.

His arms tightened around her, pulling her into his heart, and she strained to be even closer. The sweet tenderness of the first touch was gone as his lips devoured hers, taking her raging hungers and blending them into a tempest of passion. The room spun, disappearing into a misty haze of unimportance. They clung together, then suddenly they were apart. He had let go.

Peter just stood there, barely a foot away, but miles distant from her in some way. His gaze was on some far-off place or time. The cold from the floor seeped into her bare feet and doused the flame within her body. Didn't he want her?

"Maybe you can return the favor," he said, looking at her then. "Dinner can be on you one night."

Wasn't he attracted to her or was he just a decent man? "Okay," she said simply.

"You got much more to do on your paper?"

Merry cleared her throat. "I'm about as far as I can get today. I need to be getting on home."

"You can use my computer any time you want."

"Thanks."

"I'll take you home," he said.

"That's okay." She walked back into the dining room for the rest of the dishes. "I only live a few blocks from here."

"I don't care if you live a few doors from here," Peter said. "I'm not letting you walk the streets alone at this time of the night."

Merry smiled. He was a decent man, just not particularly attracted to her, she thought.

Chapter Six

"There you go, sport," Merry said, handing the man some bills. "Keep the change."

The cabdriver's sharp features and dark visage were merged into a scowl as he looked at the money in his hand. Merry just nodded to Peter as they got out of the cab.

Peter suspected that Merry's unhappiness with the man's driving had been reflected in her tip, but the guy had been driving like a demented ambulance chaser racing to an accident scene, weaving in and out of traffic, driving into the oncoming flow to pass and totally ignoring traffic signals.

"Sure was a cheerful little feller," Merry said. "Especially for a man with suicidal tendencies."

Peter laughed and put an arm around her shoulder, brushing her hair with his lips. "Don't worry about it. You're safe now." He liked the feel of her. Not just the way her softness brushed against him as they walked, awakening a slow heat in his blood, but also the way she made him feel deep down in his soul. As if he mattered, as if he were needed.

Not that he was always sure what he wanted to do about those feelings. Like the other night when she'd been at his apartment.

She would have stayed if he'd asked her, but as much as his body longed for hers, just the thought of holding—loving— someone made all the shadows come rushing back. Even now, they hovered not too far in the distance.

"I don't know how long that cabdriver's been in this country," Merry said. "But he sure doesn't have the hang of traffic lights. Green was go, yellow was speed up and red was go like the devil was after you."

Her smile warmed him. "I offered to drive, you know."

She shrugged. "I didn't want your car to get ripped off. This isn't the greatest of neighborhoods."

Peter looked around at the dim city streets. The small businesses were now dark, windows protected by steel grates. Litter filled all the stray corners and gathered along the curb, while old beaters lined both sides of the street. The neighborhood didn't have the boarded-up despair of a slum, but it was hanging on to respectability by its fingernails.

"I doubt if there would have been a problem," he said. "All the professional car thieves are working the expensive neighborhoods. They like a wider selection of new cars."

"Well, it doesn't matter," she said. "This is my treat."

He let his hand slip off her shoulder and took her hand, letting her lead them down the street. Funny how he didn't want to let go of her. They'd only really known each other a couple of weeks, but she had become important to him, to his sense of peace.

"It's not much farther," she said. "It's a little Mexican place back here. The food is great."

She stopped them in front of a narrow store. The sign in the window, if Peter remembered his college Spanish correctly, advertised the Little Rooster. A menu, all in Spanish, was taped to the inside of the door.

"Smells good," Peter said, as he opened the door for Merry.

"It better be." Her voice was grim, but there was a twinkle in her eye. "Or José's gonna be singing soprano in the church choir."

The door nudged him in the back and Peter stepped in to let it close. The dining room was long and narrow. Rough-hewn booths lined one side of the wall. The lights were dim and a narrow path led to a brightly lit kitchen in back.

"Hey, José," Merry shouted, and a tall, thin man turned toward them. A bright smile split his face as he saw Merry.

"Merry, so good to see you." He bowed slightly and kissed both her hands before he turned toward the kitchen. "Mama," he called. "Tía."

Peter frowned. José still had hold of Merry's hands, as if he was renting them for the evening. A knot formed in the pit of Peter's stomach.

"José's in some of my classes," Merry said over her shoulder to Peter as two older women, gray streaking their black hair, hurried toward them. "He shared some enchiladas with me one day. I thought I'd died and gone to heaven."

Peter just grunted an acknowledgment and tried not to glare. She hadn't raved this much about his food.

José spoke in Spanish to the women, who then hugged and kissed Merry, forcing José to let go of her hands.

"I told my mother and my aunt that your name means happy," José said. "My mother said that your smile says that more beautifully than any words."

"Tell her she's too kind," Merry replied.

Her smile brought sunshine to all the dark corners of the room, but its warmth wasn't aimed at Peter, and his heart kept a slight chill. He could have told her that about her smile, but he hadn't thought he should be so personal.

José's mother pulled at his sleeve and murmured something to him. "My mother wishes to make the acquaintance of your friend," he said.

"Oh, sorry." It was hard to tell in the dim light, but it looked as though Merry was blushing. "This is Peter MacAllister."

Peter shook hands with José and bowed his head to the women, before putting his arm around Merry's shoulders. He wasn't sure why he did it, it just felt right. Felt necessary.

"A special friend?" José asked, arching one eyebrow.

Merry's face was still flushed, and the women stood smiling at them. "Sort of," Merry replied.

José shot a few words of Spanish toward his mother and aunt. Their smiles broadened. Peter found himself smiling back. They were special friends. There was something exceptional in their relationship.

"Actually, he's more like an employer."

Peter's smile fell slightly. Didn't she feel it, too?

"He hires me as a bodyguard when he goes to Indiana."

Peter frowned as José translated that. The smiles dimmed for both women, his mother spoke to José.

"My mother says that parts of Indiana can be very dangerous. We have cousins that live in Gary. She says she wishes we had a bodyguard when we go visit them."

Peter frowned even more at Merry, but her grin stayed in place. "The really dangerous place is Mentone," she said.

"Mentone?" José said.

"Oh, yeah," Merry replied. "They got this egg in the center of town that's bigger than I am. The chicken that laid it has gotta weigh at least three hundred pounds."

José blinked once, then turned to speak to his mother and aunt. The women laughed, hugged Merry and shook Peter's hand before hurrying off to the kitchen in back.

"I told them that you two were very hungry," José said. "Maybe later, when there is more time, I will tell them about those three-hundred-pound killer chickens."

He led them to a booth in the center of the dining room, much to Peter's relief. He didn't like sharing Merry, he realized. He was never sure of where he stood with her when others were around. Her laughter seemed more mocking, like quicksilver, and he couldn't get ahold of what it meant.

José started to hand them menus, but Merry stopped him. "I want you to take care of everything, José. You know, from *A* to *Z*, soup to nuts. Everything."

José smiled and bowed, before going back to the kitchen. Peter watched him go, then turned back to Merry. Now that he had her alone, he wasn't sure just what to say to her.

"I hope the Mentone chamber of commerce never hears about you," he said. "They wouldn't take too kindly to your rumors about three-hundred-pound killer chickens."

She giggled. "Hey, that might bring in the tourists in droves. You could give giant chicken roasts, organize killer-chicken hunts, all kinds of exciting stuff."

José returned with a bottle of wine in an ice bucket and glasses, as well as a basket of tortilla chips and salsa. "I have spoken with my mother and aunt," he said. "We will start with a chicken soup. Then we will prepare a combination plate. Enchiladas, tostadas, tortillas."

"Sounds great to me, José," Merry said.

Once José returned to the kitchen, Peter picked up his glass. *Here's to your beautiful blue eyes. Here's to the way your laughter sets me afire.* "Here's to three-hundred-pound killer chickens," he said.

Merry lifted her glass and touched his. "And giant eggs."

"And giant eggs," he agreed.

He sipped his wine. It was a smooth, pleasant California blend and went down easily. He took another sip. It might be the wine or maybe the lights, but Merry's eyes seemed to have a special glow to them. Their cool blue depths had always been inviting, but tonight they seemed to hold something more. He reached over and took her hand in his.

"This is a great place," he said. It was quiet and dimly lit. The high walls of their booth created a cocoon around them and held them safe.

"Yeah, it is nice." She squeezed his hand and her smile grew. "The city is full of neat little places like this. I love trying to find them."

She would. She was the type who would love trying something new and different, and he would love tagging along, being her bodyguard and companion. Suddenly his life seemed so tame and ordinary.

Just as suddenly, guilt churned his stomach into a seething cauldron. Just because Kelly would never have come to a place like this didn't mean that their life together hadn't been good. So she'd never been one for unknown, ethnic little places like this. She had been filled with love. Maybe too much love, since her inability to have more kids seemed to have eaten away at her. A melancholy Spanish love song was playing in the restaurant, and his depression grew.

"A dime for your thoughts." Merry's smiling face tried to lure him from his thoughts.

It was a hard job, but he shook some of his moodiness free. "A dime?"

"Yeah, a dime." She sipped a bit of her wine. "I didn't think a penny would do. There's inflation, and then you have so many degrees to you that I figured your thoughts ought to cost more than most.''

With the help of those eyes, he managed to find a smile somewhere inside of him and put it on. ''Not really.''

''Still worried about those three-hundred-pound killer chickens?''

He shook his head and reached for her hands again. Maybe her touch could keep his thoughts at bay. Maybe her sunshine could chase away the storm clouds, if not for good then at least for the evening.

''Excuse me.'' José put hot, steaming bowls of soup in front of them.

''Boy, I'm glad you finally got here, José,'' Merry said. ''I was almost ready to start chewing on the table.''

José laughed. ''How about you, *Señor?* Were you also going to attack the table?''

''Yeah,'' he agreed with a halfhearted laugh. Merry frowned at him, as if sensing his deeper mood, but he just smiled at her. It was easier this time, not nearly so hard to find or force to his lips. There was something in her presence, just knowing she was there, that gave him strength.

Sandi and ZeeZee were both there when Merry got home from school the next night. Sitting in the living room, they looked up at her entrance with such anticipation that Merry felt uneasy.

''Boy.'' She laughed as she hung up her coat. ''You guys are a pair to draw to.''

''We want to have a party this weekend,'' Sandi said. ''You know, like before all the rest of the Christmas parties start.''

''Fine by me.'' They all pitched in with the apartment, so Merry had no problem with her roommates having a party. She'd just go to the library or a movie. Maybe both.

''We want you to help us,'' ZeeZee said.

''Sure,'' Merry said. ''I'll help clean Saturday morn—''

Sandi butted in. ''We want you to come to the party.''

Merry shook her head. ''Nah.''

''Come on, you're always working. If it's not your job, it's school. You gotta take some time off for fun.''

"We can find you a date."

"Yeah, Brad knows this real cool guy."

"And he's just been dying to meet you."

Oh, Lordy. They were on their Let's-fix-Merry-up-with-a-date kick. "Look, roomies, I—"

They were staring at her, determination in their eyes. Suddenly she was tired of being the odd man out. "I have to check with...with my gentleman friend and see what he has going."

Surprise filled their faces, but only for a moment. "What's his name?"

"What does he do?"

"Where did you meet him?"

"How long have you guys been going together?"

"Hey, hey." Merry dropped her book and raised her arms in a protective gesture. "Back off, will ya?"

They did, but their eyes still burned with fervent eagerness, like that of a scientist about to discover the cure for frizzy hair. Merry took a deep breath. Their excitement was contagious, but still she didn't want to say too much.

"His name is Peter," Merry said slowly. "And he works downtown. We met at the restaurant."

"Was it like sparks across the room?" Sandi asked. "Have you known him long?"

Merry shook her head. "We met just before Thanksgiving."

"Ah-ha," ZeeZee said. "That's why you didn't want to go with me to Minneapolis."

"What did you guys do over the holidays?" Sandi asked.

"We went to Indiana," Merry said. "To Mentone."

"Huh?"

"It's the Egg Basket to the Midwest."

That little bit of information was obviously overwhelming, as neither of her roommates could reply.

"It's a three-hour drive," Merry said. "We went down Wednesday afternoon, right after I got off work, and spent the long weekend with his mother and son."

"Oh."

The word was said knowingly, and though she had no reason to, Merry blushed. "Look, we just took a little trip. Had plenty of home cooking, fresh air, quiet and friendly folks. It was real nice."

"I imagine it was," Sandi said.

"Was that it?" ZeeZee asked.

Merry shrugged. "He had me over to his place a few days later."

Their grins returned.

"I had to work on my sociology paper," Merry said hotly. "And I was having trouble finding computer time. He has a computer at home."

"What does he do?" ZeeZee asked.

"He's got a bunch of degrees," Merry replied. "He does statistical and actuarial stuff for a bunch of big companies."

"Whew," Sandi said. "He's big-bucks kind of people."

Merry frowned at her. She guessed he must be, considering his apartment, but she hadn't really thought about it. Why would a "big bucks" person want to be friends with her?

"Seriously," her roommate assured her. "My dad uses people like that. I mean, we're talking six-figure income. Easy."

Six figures? Lordy, was she that good an actress that she could fool someone with a million degrees and more money than she could ever imagine?

"Actually, we're just friends," she said slowly.

"A good place to start," ZeeZee said.

"Yeah," Sandi said. "Some of your better relationships start that way."

"We don't have a relationship. We're just friends."

"But isn't friendship a—" Sandi stopped and waved her hand. "Ah, forget it. Just call him. This Saturday. Have him come early, maybe he can help."

Merry just nodded and wandered down to her room. How could she have been so blind? Everything about his life here in Chicago said money, yet she was treating him like one of her fellow students.

What was she going to do about the party? She couldn't really go calling on him again. It was his turn to decide things. If she called now, he would think she was chasing him.

Hell, this whole thing was all his fault. If he had ordered a pizza like she'd asked him to, she would have paid for it. Then they would have been even and there would have been no need to take him out to dinner last night.

Sighing, Merry stood staring out her window at the night. Damn, damn, damn! Suddenly she was afraid to ask him.

Why?

The sinking sensation in the pit of her stomach told her why. Because he might say no. Because he might be tired of her.

Hell. She closed her eyes and leaned her forehead against the cool glass of the window. She was tired of this modern-woman stuff. She was ready to go back to when the guys did all the asking.

"Mrs. Hanson took my turkey down today," Sean said.

His son's voice seemed especially faint this evening. It was probably just a bad connection, but Peter felt it was symbolic. His son was drifting farther and farther away from him.

"She probably took everyone's turkey down," Peter said, trying to stay upbeat.

"Uh-huh."

"I'm sorry I didn't get to see it."

"That's okay," Sean replied.

Peter restrained his urge to sigh. His mother had been right. He should have gone down earlier. Then he would have had time to go to Sean's school and see all the decorations his son's kindergarten class had put up on the walls. Hell. This remote parenting was turning out to be a flop. Although it was probably single parenting that was the culprit.

"You brought your turkey home, didn't you?"

"Yeah."

"That's good. I'll get to see it the next time I'm home. Or maybe you can bring it up when you come in next weekend."

"Grandma says I can't come. I got a cold."

Peter felt like a balloon whose air had swooshed all out. Damn! He'd had all these plans. Shopping at Water Tower Place, a trip to the Sears Tower and then lunch at that place in Lincolnwood where the waitresses were all on skates.

"Grandma's saving all my school stuff," Sean said.

"That's good," he replied, fighting a valiant but losing battle to keep the cheer in his voice. "Then I can get to see it all."

"Yeah."

He was indeed lucky that his mother was helping. Peter

wasn't sure that he'd keep up with things, saving all Sean's drawings and schoolwork the way his mother was. He'd read someplace that women were the keepers of the bonds, the connectors of the generations. Now he knew what that meant.

"I gotta go," Sean said, interrupting his thoughts.

"Oh. Okay."

"He's going to feed Zachary." His mother was on the phone now. "He does it every night. He enjoys taking care of that blind old cat."

Obviously he enjoys it more than talking to his father, Peter thought.

"Actually, he's very good at taking care of anybody who needs it. He might be a doctor someday, like his grandfather."

His mother paused, and Peter rubbed his eyes. He should go take a walk or something. His depression was building. It looked like dump-city time again.

"I think he'd be a good doctor, don't you?"

"I have no idea," he said. "I hardly know him."

"Of course you do. You're just feeling sorry for yourself again."

He wasn't feeling sorry for himself. He was just being realistic. "He hardly talks to me. He tells one thing that happened that day, gives me thirty seconds of monosyllabic responses and he's gone."

"Very few five-year-olds have acquired the fine art of sipping sherry and carrying on long conversations." His mother was in one of her sarcastic moods. "Five-year-old boys are like little bumblebees. They spend their days zipping about and nibbling on a wide variety of life's experiences."

Peter grunted.

"You call almost every day. That's good. It gives Sean a chance to tell you something that's important at the moment. It gives him a chance to stay in touch. Two minutes every day is better for him than two hours once a week."

"I guess."

"There's no 'I guess' to it. I know what I'm talking about." She sighed. "Well, that's enough trying to cheer you up. You're too old to be needing my help anymore. At my age, you should be cheering me up. Tell me something happy about yourself. How are things with Merry?"

"Okay," he replied. She was like a bright star in his sky. She brought cheer and warmth to his heart, but he couldn't let himself get too close.

"Just okay? Is something wrong?"

"No, Mom. Nothing's wrong. Things are fine. Just like I told you."

"You're spending too much time with numbers, Peter. Words are much better. They give richer and better explanations." Suddenly there was a murmur in the background. Then his mother was back on the phone. "Sean's ready for bed. We have to go."

"Okay, Mom. See you. Take care." He waited, holding the phone to his ear.

"Good night, Daddy," Sean said.

"Good night, Sean. Sleep tight."

"Yeah. And I won't let the bedbugs bite."

The phone went dead, the dial tone replacing the string of childish giggles. Peter set the receiver down and walked over to the wall of windows.

It was night. An overcast, dark night, so that the only thing he could see was a large black abyss. He felt as if he were staring at his life.

He should call Merry. Ask her out, even if it was just for a walk along the lake. The dismal emptiness of his life was getting to him.

Before he could gather the strength to lift up the phone, though, it rang. It was Merry. Some mischievous god must have been eavesdropping on his thoughts.

"Hey, me and my roommates are having a party Saturday night," she said. "Want to come?"

"A party?"

"Yeah. You know, food, drinks, fun and games." She paused. "It's okay if you can't, though. I'll understand."

She sounded ready to to sign him off, to leave him to that black abyss. Fear dried his mouth and he had to swallow fast. "No, I'll come. I'd like to." He was suddenly afraid of being alone.

"Great. Eight, okay?"

"Sure. Fine."

"See ya." She was gone, and without her smile in the air, the shadows came rushing back.

He hadn't gone to a party for eons, not as Peter MacAllister, anyway. His most recent forays into partying had been as half of the unit known as Mr. and Mrs. MacAllister. He didn't have that identity anymore.

What would he say to a roomful of strangers? He wasn't up on the latest movies or singers or sports news. Managing his work and staying in touch with Sean had seemed all he could handle. Now it seemed he was woefully out of it. There was no way that he could become a social being in two days. It was like having to cram for a final when you haven't attended class all semester.

He should call Merry back. Give her an excuse. Make up an illness. Anything. Just get out of it. He knew it was going to be a disaster.

It started off badly. He arrived promptly at eight with a box of Godiva chocolates—hazelnut rum balls to be exact.

"Ooh, groovy," ZeeZee purred. "Merry hates hazelnuts. That means we get to eat them all."

"Great choice," Sandi echoed.

"It's the thought that counts," Merry assured him, kissing him for his thoughtfulness, but not nearly long enough or hard enough to make him forget he'd goofed. He made do with a drink while Merry and her roommates did their last-minute prepping.

The evening moved into catastrophe mode when the guests started arriving. He was the only one wearing a suit.

"I think you look handsome," Merry told him, but he knew he looked stiff and foolish. Taking the jacket off and loosening his tie only made him look worse, pretending to be casual. Another drink made him feel less stiff, no matter how he looked.

Merry went off to greet some of her friends from school and that's when the evening went cataclysmic. Left to his own devices, he wandered about the living room, sipping at still another drink and trying not to look lost.

He hated being on his own at these things. He needed somebody to laugh with, somebody to remind him who everybody was when he forgot. He needed somebody to talk to, because he was no good at ten-way conversations. All he saw were happy groups of people with no need for another participant, certainly not one who was a stranger in a suit. He should have stayed home.

Peter glanced around the room, seeking refuge. The Christmas tree in the corner had an odd appearance, and he sauntered over. He frowned. It looked as though someone had tossed garbage into it. Crushed beer cans were stuck on branches, the plastic rings from the top of a six-pack was tangled into a knot and tossed onto the top. He reached in for one of the beer cans.

"Hey, buddy, don't mess with the ornaments," Merry said with mock brusqueness.

Peter jumped and let the can in his hand fall to the floor. "Sorry," he said. Ornament? He hung the can back up on the tree. "I was just fixing it...."

Merry took his hand and led him away from the tree. "ZeeZee's our resident artist. The Christmas tree is her baby. She feels it makes a environmental statement."

"Oh. Sorry." Just went to show how bad he was at partying. Everybody else looked at the other guests, he looked at trees. He started to smile, but then noticed the drink in his hand. He gulped at that instead.

"Merry," someone called from over near the door. "Paging Miss Merry."

Merry glanced toward the voice, then back at Peter. "There's a group about to play a game of Trivial Pursuit. Why don't you join them?"

He made a face. "I'm not very good at games."

"Merry," the call was repeated. She glanced up, then back at Peter. "Come on, you'd probably be good at it. Put all those degrees to work."

He wasn't enthused, but followed along behind her. Why was she always mentioning his degrees? Did she think he was some super-educated nerd who knew nothing about life? He wished he had never come. He stopped to refill his drink, then caught up with her in the dining room.

"Hey, guys," Merry said. "Got room for Peter on one of your teams?"

"Sure. He can be on our team," Sandi said. She scooted her chair over to make room for his. "Merry says you're one smart cookie."

He just smiled and tried not to feel panic as Merry wove toward the door. He'd been stupid to think she'd be spending her whole evening with him. A hostess had responsibilities.

"Get ready, Peter," Sandi said. She nudged him as she rolled the die. "Here we go. Oh, great. Science."

A member of the other team pulled a card from the box. "Who first measured the distance from the earth to the sun?"

Sandi groaned. "You know?" she whispered to her boyfriend, Bill.

He just frowned. "Galileo?"

Peter shook his head. "Foucault."

"What's your answer?" the question reader asked.

Sandi looked from Bill to Peter. "Foucault," she said.

"Right."

Sandi cheered while Bill just rolled the dice again and moved their token. "History," he said, his voice a bit surly.

"What canal opened in 1869 that enabled sailors to bypass an entire continent and speed up world trade?"

"Panama," Bill said.

"Suez," Peter said.

"Panama," Bill repeated, just little louder.

Sandi swallowed hard, then with an apologetic smile at Peter, said, "Panama."

"Wrong. Suez." The other team was gleeful and went about taking their turn.

"Looks like you know everything," Bill muttered.

"Not by a long shot," Peter said. "I'm really lousy at stuff like literature." He gazed anxiously toward the door, but Merry was nowhere in sight. He finished the rest of his drink as it became their turn again.

"Literature," Sandi said after moving their token.

Bill sneered, or at least Peter could have sworn he did. Peter ignored it, pretending to listen carefully to the question. It wouldn't do to get into a fight with Sandi's boyfriend.

"What's the name of the baby elephant made popular in a series of children's books?"

"Dumbo," Bill decreed.

Sandi turned to look at Peter when he said nothing.

"Babar."

Sandi bit her lip in indecision, so Bill jumped in to answer. "Dumbo."

"Wrong. Babar." The other team roared with laughter.

Bill flung himself back in his chair, his face red and his angry gaze on Peter. "I thought you didn't know literature," he snapped.

"So I got lucky." Peter didn't need this. He got to his feet. "I think I'll go find Merry."

"Guess we're not smart enough for you, huh?"

Bill was rapidly becoming a jerk, but Peter did his best to ignore him. "If you'll all excuse me..." he said to the group as a whole, as he skirted around the table.

"I won't, fella."

"Bill." Sandi sounded like she was trying to calm him down. Everyone else in the room seemed to have gone mute.

"You can't come here and make a fool of me, then just waltz off."

Bill's voice echoed around him, and Peter had had enough. "I don't think you need anyone to make of fool of you," he said smoothly. "You're doing that quite well on your own."

"Hey," Sandi cried. The mother hen in her rose up in protection of her own, but Peter managed to escape into the crowd in the living room. It swallowed him up, and like the sun coming out from behind a cloud, the murmur of conversation came slowly back.

"What's going on?" Merry was suddenly at his side.

A frown rested between her eyes, and he had a real longing to kiss it away. And while he was there, kiss a number of other things, too. Those deep blue eyes that promised peace and rest. That nose that curled up so intriguingly when she laughed. Those ears that were almost hidden behind the curtain of dusky red hair. And that hair—how he'd love to bury his face in it, to lose himself in its softness.

"What's Sandi so upset about?"

Peter shook his daydreams from his mind and forced it back to more trivial matters. He shrugged. "I guess she just found out that her boyfriend is a jerk."

Merry glanced back into the dining room, then frowned up at Peter. "Did something happen?"

Her scent was intoxicating. It set his blood to boiling. "Not yet, but if we left this dumb party, something probably could."

She scowled at him. "How much have you had to drink?"

"Not enough," he said, peering into his empty glass. "I'm not having any fun yet."

She gave him a look that he knew wasn't good, then grabbed hold of his arm, dragging him out of the apartment and down the stairs to the front stoop. He stood there a long moment, staring at the street and its passing stream of traffic. What in the world were they doing out here? He'd much rather they retired to the privacy of his place.

"It's cold out here," he said, moving a little closer to her.

"It looks like you still have some normal feelings left."

Showed how little she knew. "I've got nothing but normal feelings left." He wrapped his arms around her. "Want to see?"

The look in her eyes didn't match the fire in his body. "You're going to be suffering feelings of extreme pain if you don't let go of me."

He didn't have the slightest idea why she was so upset, but he let go of her. The steel in her voice told him to.

"Want to go back in?" she asked.

For more torture? Reality poked its ugly head up through the fog of all those drinks he'd had. He hadn't belonged here earlier and he sure didn't belong here now. He shook his head. "I should be getting home." He looked down the street. "It's not far from here. And a walk would do me good."

"The walk might be good for you," she said. "But I don't think a mugging would help any."

Peter glared at her.

"Hey," she said. "You're a first-class kind of pigeon. Had a little too much to drink and are obviously wealthy."

"I can take care of myself." Hadn't he been having to do that for the past year? He didn't need or want her help.

"Here comes a cab," she said and dashed to the curb to flag it down. Once it stopped, she helped him into the backseat. "Thirty-four hundred Lake Shore Drive."

The driver pulled away in a squeal of tires. Well, all evening he'd been longing to go home. Why didn't he feel excited now that the wish was becoming reality?

Chapter Seven

Peter dragged himself down to the restaurant. Saturday night replayed itself in his mind like a greasy meal sending up bubbles of heartburn. Both left him with a bad taste in his mouth, feeling sick and disgusted with himself.

He knew that Merry could never forgive him for being such a jerk, but he couldn't part on that kind of a note. Certainly, she'd never want to see him again, and she shouldn't have to. But he just had to let her know that although he was an adult and responsible for his actions, what he'd done could only be explained by stupidity.

"Good afternoon, Mr. MacAllister." The hostess's greeting was friendly, her lips were smiling, and her gaze was open and pleasant. "Would you like your usual table? Or would you like to sit up closer to the front?"

Peter looked at the booth, far in the back. It was private even when the restaurant was at its most crowded. Now it was almost like an island in the middle of the ocean.

"I'll take my usual."

"Very good, sir." The hostess led him toward the back. "I'll send a server right over," she said, as she seated him and handed him a menu.

"Ah." Peter swallowed hard. "Is Merry around?"

"Yes, she's back in the kitchen. I'll tell her you're here."

Suddenly he was alone, awaiting his doom. He tried to read the menu, but the letters swam before his eyes. Merry could do two things. She could refuse to wait on him or she could grab a cleaver and storm into the dining room after him. Either way things weren't going to turn out well.

"What can I get you, sir?"

His eyes slowly left the menu and climbed up Merry's soft curves. Unlike the words outlining his meal choices, reading Merry's body language was no trouble at all. Her smile was still broad, but it had a newfound rigidity to it and her eyes had no sparkle.

"Could you sit down?"

"We always stand when we take customer orders, sir. That way we can get to the kitchen quicker and you'll get your food that much sooner."

"I'm not really hungry."

"Would you just like something to drink, sir?"

Peter looked outside for a moment. The sunshine was gone and snow was falling. Coming down sideways, the flakes were pushed along by a cold, biting, chill-you-down-to-the-bone northwest wind that he could feel even inside.

"Actually, all I want is a piece of pie."

"Apple, custard, banana cream—"

"Humble," he said. "And make it an extra large piece."

Her smile sagged and she blinked, obviously confused.

"I want to apologize for being an utter, absolute, total ass."

Merry took a deep breath. She dropped her order pad into her pocket, crossed her arms and jacked up her smile a couple of feet. "That's okay," she said. "I shouldn't have asked you to come."

His mouth just dropped open and hung there. "You shouldn't have asked me? Why? Is something the matter with me?"

"Oh, no," she hastened to explain. "It's just that—" she looked away a long moment, appearing to gather her thoughts "—you're who you are and my friends are who they are."

Peter flashed back to the party. There were many things he

didn't remember, but the people were easy to recall. They were an eclectic mixture of rich and poor, multiethnic, multicultural. Interesting and exciting in their attitudes and ideas. His feelings of self-worth fell even further.

"I'd also like to apologize for acting like a snob," he said. "I haven't been out socially like that for a long time, and I screwed up royally."

Merry looked away and time stood still. He'd been a jerk, he knew that, and he didn't deserve to be forgiven, but if only she would...

She slowly turned back to face him, reaching into her pocket for her order pad. "Can I get you anything?" she asked softly.

"Get us both some coffee and sit down and talk with me."

"Peter, I—"

"If you don't, I will throw a tantrum."

Her look was disbelieving.

"I mean it," Peter said. "I'll roll around on the floor, kicking and screaming."

She hesitated, and he pressed his advantage.

"Look, just sit across from me and pretend you're listening. I'll say my piece, then I'll get out of your life."

She kept her silence.

"Please. If the hostess says anything about it, I'll pay for fifty meals, a hundred. I just want to try to explain things."

Merry turned on her heels and went into the kitchen. There was a chance that she wasn't coming back, but he was sure that she would. She didn't look like the type who ran away from anything.

He rubbed his face with both hands. And he didn't want her to. Oh, Lord, how he didn't want her to.

Within moments, Merry burst through the double doors out of the kitchen and strode toward him, carrying two large, steaming mugs. She set them on the table and sat down across from him. He clutched his cup, sucking its warmth, hoping to drive away the cold fear that filled his heart.

"I don't know where to start," he said. "Except to apologize again."

"Peter—"

He held up his hand. "I was in poor shape when I arrived at your place."

Her brow wrinkled. "You seemed fine to me."

"Physically, I was fine. But I was a wreck inside. I know I'm single again, but I'm not used to partying alone. When I had too much to drink, the controls just gave way."

"I see," she said, looking into her cup.

He knew that she didn't really, so he hastened to explain. "I was absolutely terrified of going to your party."

For the first time since he'd stepped in today, her smile stretched out to near its natural limits. "There wasn't any reason for you to worry," she said. "I'm your bodyguard. I protected you in Mentone and I'd have protected you in Chicago."

The laugh they shared felt so good, like ice-cold lemonade after a day of tasseling corn in the hot July sun. He wanted to reach out and touch her, but he was afraid that, like a nervous young doe, she would just take off and run.

"I appreciate that." He took a moment to get control of his hungry hands. After taking a big swallow of hot coffee, he went on. "I've been a widower for a little over a year. I should have the hang of it by now. But I'm obviously not coping as well as I should be."

"I thought you were doing fine," she said.

"I'm getting through the day-to-day things. And, according to my mother, I'm even doing okay by Sean."

"That's the most important thing."

He paused and nodded. "Anyway, I was scared to death about going to your party. I almost turned and ran a million times."

"But why?" Merry asked. "My friends are a little different, but they aren't all that bad."

"It has nothing to do with your friends and everything to do with me. Since Kelly passed away, I've had nothing but social disasters. Women are pushed at me, I push myself at women. If I didn't have Sean, I'd go become a hermit."

"Then it's a good thing you have Sean. Not everyone is so lucky."

Peter paused for a moment. He thought there was a catch to her voice, but she said nothing else. "Anyway, I wanted you to know that I'm very sorry."

Merry said nothing as she stared out the window. Suddenly,

as if she'd just noticed he'd quit talking, she started. "Don't worry about it," she said. "We all do dumb things at times."

Peter felt it was safe to take her hands. "Am I forgiven?"

"Sure." The smile was still there, but it seemed somewhat subdued. "But it's more important that you forgive yourself."

He nodded. "I just want to make it up to you."

She laughed and pulled her hands away. "Let's not do a party for a while."

"Can I take you out to dinner?"

She shrugged.

"Please."

She nodded. "When we're both ready again."

"When will that be?" he asked.

"I would guess soon." She stood up from the table, collecting both mugs. "After all, we have to keep practicing for our return visit to Mentone."

Turning on her heels, she walked quickly toward the back of the restaurant. Peter had never ordered lunch, but he didn't really feel hungry. Damn. He'd hurt Merry and now he'd have to give her time to heal.

Peter stamped his feet on the sidewalk and pulled his coat collar up closer. The bitter wind just seemed to blow right through him, but he wasn't budging. According to Sandi, Merry'd be getting off this train on her way to school.

He looked at his watch. She'd have to come by here. Unless she took a bus or a cab. Peter clenched his teeth. This was stupid. So what that he had been out of town for a few days; he should have just waited until lunchtime tomorrow.

The screech of metal wheels on metal rails told him that an elevated train had arrived at the station above. He looked at his watch again. Merry would have to be on this train or she would be late for class.

Within moments, the aging structure rumbled and rattled as the train left. He scanned the faces streaming down the steps and onto the streets. There seemed to be either young students coming to their night classes or middle-aged women who cleaned offices at night.

Suddenly he saw Merry's face, smiling like the sun breaking

through a bank of dark clouds. He took a step forward. Then, just as suddenly, Peter stopped. Merry was walking with a small group of men. Young men. Handsome men, in a sloppy, studentish sort of way.

But why shouldn't she be walking with men? They certainly weren't going to run away from her. Not to mention that it wasn't a good idea to wander around alone here at night.

How would she greet him, if she even did? Maybe she didn't want to see him here. Sure, she'd forgiven him, but she didn't appear all that enthusiastic about going out with him again. That little crack about their need to keep up appearances for his mother hadn't exactly been encouraging.

"Peter?" She stopped. "What are you doing here?"

"Waiting for you."

Merry turned to her companions. "Why don't you guys go ahead? I'll catch up with you."

The young men voiced their agreement and nodded at Peter before they went on ahead. Peter waited a moment, savoring the warmth in her eyes and the safety of her smile.

"I tried to call you," he said finally.

"I got your messages on the answering machine, but I couldn't get ahold of you. I called your office, but all they'd say was that you were out of town."

"I could have told them to give you a number to reach me, but I didn't want you to be making any long-distance calls. Besides, I was hard to reach."

"That's okay. It's cool."

Her smile seemed to echo her words, and he began to believe that maybe she wasn't still angry at him. They began to walk toward the college. Slowly, though, as if to treasure every second.

"I was hoping that it was soon enough to take you to dinner," he said.

"Tonight?"

Something in her voice made his heart sink. "Got a date?"

"Yep. A date with Professor Crawford. I've got a big sociology test."

Relief swept over him. "Maybe you'll be hungry afterward."

"It'll be late."

"That's okay. This is the night I get to stay up late."

"The test period is two hours long, and I'm going to need every minute of the time."

Two hours. Hell, that was nothing, not with the prospect of seeing Merry's smile at the end of it.

"I have a lot of reading with me." He held up his slender briefcase. "Why don't I wait in the library for you?"

By the time they stepped out of the college a few hours later, the few clouds had dissipated. The night was clear and the stars so bright that Peter almost felt he could reach up and touch them. Suddenly he felt so very much alive.

A cab came into view, and Peter started to raise his hand, but Merry caught it. "Let's walk."

"Walk where?"

"I don't know," she replied. "Let's just walk north."

"It's late."

"Don't worry," she said. "I'm a fully certified bodyguard and I'll take care of you."

Would she? He was more than willing to let her. He didn't feel he needed protection especially, but he could use some taking care of. Someone to chase away the nightmares, to bring the sun back into his life. She had done all that to some extent already. Would she do more? He took her hand in his, and they started walking north up Michigan Avenue.

Lights illuminated the tops of the Prudential Building, the Standard Oil Tower and the other skyscrapers on the lake side of the Loop. Down closer to the ground, there were lights playing on the two stone lions guarding the entrance to the Art Institute.

There was a sense of magic in the air that he hadn't felt before. He squeezed her hand and smiled down at her. The cold air was invigorating, stimulating, not a reason to run away and hide.

"So am I finally forgiven?" he asked.

"I guess."

Her voice sounded thoughtful and for a moment his heart stopped.

"Let's go this way." She tugged at him, turning him first

onto a side street, then back north onto the State Street mall. "Now, this is the real Christmas."

Lights were strung from every tree. Giant candy canes protruded from light poles. Store after store had carols blasting forth from loud speakers.

"This is the real Christmas?" he repeated, wondering how she could be impressed by any of it. "It's all commercial."

"Nah, it's lights and sounds and magic." She pointed toward a vendor along the mall. "Roasted chestnuts. Want some?"

"Do I have to sing the carol?"

She just hurried him over to the cart and ordered a small bag of them. He was surprised as he munched on his first. There was something special about the warm, crunchy nut and the cold starry night. Best of all was the sparkling laughter of the woman with him.

"Okay. I agree these are good."

She cuddled up close to his side, hugging his arm to her. "It's all good, if you just let it be."

"Hmm."

With her looking at him that way, he could almost believe she was right. That the world could hold happiness and the stars held a magic that could make him smile.

She stopped at a store window. A mammoth animated display of an Alpine town lay before them. A train ran continuously on a serpentine track while villagers came in and out of houses.

"You see that little guy over there?" Merry said, pointing to an old man far off in one corner, sweeping his front step. "That's you."

He frowned. "I'm short, pudgy and wear a red hat?"

She punched him playfully. "You're all by yourself."

"I am not," he protested. "I'm with you."

He'd meant for her to laugh. He wanted to see her smile light her eyes, but she just shook her head.

"It may be your turn to get mad," she said. "But there are some things I think you should hear."

He didn't like the sound of that and concentrated on the train weaving its way through the village, on Santa in his sleigh up amid the clouds.

"You have to stop comparing the way you do things now to the way you used to do them."

"I don't."

She ignored him. "You have to believe that even if things are different, they can still be good."

"I do." His eyes were somehow on the little old man in the red hat. No matter what happened around him, he just kept on sweeping.

"You have to let yourself have a good time without asking if you deserve to."

He didn't bother to answer her. Just as the man in the red hat didn't bother to look up when the carolers came by. Sweep, sweep, sweep, that's all the man did. A heaviness seemed to come over Peter, weighing him down suddenly.

Merry pulled at his arm and started walking again. People and sounds surrounded them. The Alpine scene was lost, except in memory.

"We all lose loved ones," she said softly. "And if we all shut down, it would be a pretty miserable place. We'd be sad and grumpy and never want to be anyplace but by ourselves."

"I'm not grumpy."

She laughed, and the sound of magic seemed to echo around them. The stars shone brighter, the carols were sweeter. A bell ringer was up ahead, and Merry stopped to dig in her pockets.

"I've got it," he said and pulled out his wallet.

She still pulled a wad of change and bills from her pocket and stuffed it into the bucket.

"Bless you," the woman said, never losing the rhythm of her bell.

Peter put his own money in, then frowned down at Merry. "Why didn't you let me put in something for both of us?" he asked. "I can afford it a lot more than you can."

Merry just shook her head. "Because the giving says I'm doing great compared to some others, and my recognition of that makes me alive. It puts all my little problems in perspective."

"Some problems are harder to put aside," he pointed out.

"And those are the ones that just have to be accepted. Look, you can't bring Kelly back, no matter what you do or don't do."

"I know that." He was starting to lose patience. He had been looking for some lighthearted fun this evening, not a lecture.

"Suppose you had died in the accident, not her. Would you want her moping around, being only half alive?"

"For god's sake, I just screwed up one party."

"Would you want her moping around?"

He sighed. "No, of course not."

"So why are you? Are you saying you're a better person than she was, that you loved her more than she loved you?"

He suddenly stuck his hands into his jacket pockets. "Love is such a huge commitment. It's opening yourself up totally to someone else. It's letting them see everything about you, the good parts and the bad parts. Letting them see the polish on your shoes as well as the holes in your underwear. I will never let myself get that close again." He paused. "It would have to snow in Death Valley. Pigs would have to fly. And the three-hundred-pound chickens would have to come back to Mentone."

She shook her head. "Love is seeing the holes in someone else's underwear and not caring about those holes. But I wasn't talking about loving again. I was talking about living. Oh, look," she exclaimed as she pulled him to a sudden stop before a window filled with stuffed toys. "Isn't that great?"

Peter stared at the collection. It was like Noah's ark, with every animal imaginable crammed into the window.

"Look at the snake," Merry said, pointing to a huge stuffed snake, curled like a cobra. "Sean would love that!"

It would be fifteen feet long when stretched out. "He would?"

"Little boys love snakes. They sit in them, sleep in them, wrap them around themselves and pretend they're being squeezed to death. Stuffed snakes are very versatile."

"I was thinking of getting him a computer for Christmas."

Merry just looked at him. "He's five years old!"

"That's not too young."

She just shook her head and pulled Peter along. "Buy him both. There are just some things the soul needs that can't be explained."

He felt her hand tighten on his and she was suddenly his lifeline, his link with the rest of the world. He knew exactly what she meant. He couldn't explain it, but he needed her with him.

"Since you're such an expert on parties, want to come to one with me on Saturday?" Peter asked. "You can make sure I behave and have a good time."

Merry stepped out of Peter's car. The houses here were huge, mansions even. Bigger than the school in Four Corners. Bigger than the mayor's house in White Pigeon. And the Christmas decorations—well, they were like something out of a movie. Tiny white lights all over the trees, houses and the street-side mailboxes. Even the snow here was fresher and prettier than in the city.

Merry's heart sank into her stomach. What was she doing here? These people would have about as much to say to her as a bird did to a worm.

Peter took her hand and smiled at her, making her almost believe certain things were possible. With her hand in his, she felt strong. And when he smiled at her that way, she was sure that nothing bad could touch her.

She glanced up at the sky and its canopy of stars as they walked up the long, curving drive lined with luminaries. They were the same stars she used to wish upon back home. She bet if she were sitting on one of those stars, everyplace down here would look the same.

She tightened her hold on Peter's arm. "I like the city and all," she said, "but I like it out here where you can see the stars."

He looked up at the sky, but said nothing.

She continued to stare upward, knowing he didn't find the peace and strength in the stars that she did. She wished she could open his eyes to the joy around him. Not just the stars, but friendships and Sean, too. But the stars were a place to start.

"Sometimes stars are the only thing you can share with somebody you love," she said. Her eyes closed and she saw the shadowy figure of Jason.

She felt Peter stir and opened her eyes to find his gaze on her. "Sean could be looking at these same stars right now."

He looked back at the sky a moment, as if searching for something he couldn't see. "It's late. He said he was going to bed right after I talked to him."

Merry shook her head. "There you go again, refusing to believe. Come on, you've got to let a little magic in sometimes."

He just laughed softly. "Someday I will, I promise."

"Sure."

They walked the rest of the way up the driveway, the night's stillness closing in on them. In the safety of the flickering darkness, all sorts of warring emotions were colliding within her. She was so thrilled about her trip to see Jason; she didn't know how not to share her excitement. But she was also scared. Not really of Joe's threats, but of the whole idea of going back. Afraid somehow that the poverty and despair would capture her.

"Nice neighborhood, isn't it?" Peter said.

"Very." She shook off her preoccupations and forced her mind back to the task at hand. She knew all about this place. Although the architecture was different from the Pill Hill area back home, Winnetka smelled the same. The scent of power and money hung heavy in the air, telling the world that folks here didn't have to play by the same rules as regular folks. They could make their own rules as they went along. Nobody or nothing was gonna stop them. Merry shivered in spite of her resolve.

"I told you that you should have worn boots," Peter scolded.

"Wasn't worth it." She nodded at the brushing of snow barely covering the driveway. "I could walk barefoot in this."

"Sure."

That would have made some impression on his managing partner, she thought, even more so than Peter had made on her friends. She had a strong feeling, though, that her friends were more tolerant than his.

Tonight she was going to have to be careful. More than careful. She was going to have to do the acting job of her life.

"Why do you always have to sound so tough?" he asked. "Maybe you should pamper yourself the way others would like to pamper you."

His words surprised her, as did the sudden softness of his voice. She turned to look at him and he reached out, brushing a stray curl away with a gentle touch.

"It'll never stay put," she warned. "My hair's got a mind of it's own."

"And why do you always have to joke?"

His voice came on a breath, like the stirring of angel wings, as his lips came down to hers. The night was so silent and still that the touch seemed almost like a blessing. Her wishes would be granted, favors bestowed, all from the magic of his kiss.

Her heart churned, wanting to fire up with hungers and needs. But it wasn't the time for that. Her spirit found peace and certainty in the touch of Peter's lips. Strength flowed from his mouth, his soul, and she knew that the stars were smiling on her.

"We're kind of late," Peter said as he slowly pulled away and rang the doorbell. "Most of the people are going to be well on their way to loose."

Merry smiled, reveling in the lingering scent of his embrace.

The door flew open, and a young woman stood there. "Peter," she squealed and gave him a big hug while holding firmly onto her drink glass.

"Hi, Liz," he replied, rolling his eyes at Merry. It was obvious that Liz was past her first glass. Peter freed himself and stepped back, taking Merry's arm. "This is a friend of mine, Merry Roberts. Merry, this is Liz Terrell."

They exchanged greetings. Liz's smile stayed in place but uncertainty flickered in her eyes. She was probably wondering where she'd seen Merry before.

"Merry is a drama student at Columbia College," Peter said.

The uncertainty in Liz's eyes dimmed, and Merry smiled. That was good. Liz would probably think she'd seen Merry on a TV ad. A lot of kids at school took background jobs.

"Come on in," Liz said, stepping back. "Bart will probably tell us that he has no intention of heating the whole outdoors."

Both Merry and Peter laughed as they walked through the door. Liz indicated they should put their coats in the den, then disappeared in the crowd.

"Care for anything to drink?" Peter asked as he helped Merry with her coat.

"I'm not much of a drinker," Merry said.

"I'll get you a glass that you can carry around then," Peter said. "That way no one will bother you."

Peter went over to the bar, leaving Merry to smile at those around her, acting as if she couldn't be more relaxed. ZeeZee had lent her this black velvet dress with assurances that it would be perfect for the occasion, but Merry wasn't so sure. It didn't have any of the glitter and sparkle of those around her. She should have made some wishes on those stars she was admiring outside. She should have made Peter stay with her.

"Oh, what a lovely dress," an older woman said, pausing at Merry's side to finger the dress's full skirt. "Armani's?"

Merry shook her head. "ZeeZee's."

The woman's eyes widened slightly. "A new designer? Oh, don't you just adore finding these new people before the crowd does?"

"Definitely."

Peter arrived just as the woman left. He handed Merry a glass of ginger ale. "You don't waste time, do you?"

"What?"

He nodded at the woman who was almost lost in the crowd. "Mrs. Kripner. Bart's wife. A notorious snob, and she was smiling at you."

"Was she?" Merry sipped at her ginger ale, a smile of satisfaction deep in her heart. She gazed into his eyes and relaxed. Suddenly this whole evening was unimportant. She could get through it in a snap because the only one she had to please was Peter, and she could see by the look in his eyes that she was already succeeding.

The only stars she needed to wish on were the ones Peter made spin around her.

Chapter Eight

Peter watched Merry wolf down the salad they'd picked up
after she'd finished her research at the library. The impatient
honk from behind pointed out that the light was green. He turned
his attention back to driving.

"You're going to give yourself an ulcer," he warned. "The
way you stuff that junk down your gullet."

"What do you mean 'junk?' This is healthy stuff here," she
said, nodding at the plastic container sitting on her lap. "It's all
rabbit food and low-cal dressing."

His eyes weren't really interested in the container of salad,
though. No, they preferred to wander over her jeans, which
showed off her waist-down curves and a short jacket that emphasized her waist-up curves. That impish smile on her face was
enough to drive a sane man over the edge. And those riotous
curls, they had to reflect the fire in her heart. In fact, everything
about her shouted passionate energy.

Peter shook his head, forcing himself to watch the traffic before him. Next time he gave her a ride home, she'd have to ride
in the trunk. Otherwise his own dam of restraint would break.

Then what would control him? They'd probably get arrested for blocking traffic or something.

"I'm not talking about what you're eating," he pointed out. "I'm talking about how fast you eat."

"When my body says it's hungry, I feed it."

He glanced at her face, shining in the light of the streetlights, then quickly looked away as he swallowed hard. God, she was so beautiful, so alive.

"I don't believe in teasing it."

"Does that apply to everything?" he asked.

"You betcha."

The window before him appeared to be steaming up. Peter wiped it with the back of his glove, then gripped the steering wheel hard and rolled his head to relax his neck muscles. Given the way his body was reacting to Merry, you'd think he'd had a bucket of oysters for lunch, instead of an egg-salad sandwich and soup. The sound of paper rustling told him that Merry had completed her dinner.

"I'm thirsty," she announced.

"I told you to get something to drink when you bought the salad."

"I didn't want anything then. Besides, I have some fresh squeezed orange juice at home. Want some?"

"Sure."

As they neared Merry's building, a minivan pulled out, leaving a parking space free in the same block as her apartment. "The gods are smiling on me tonight," he said, maneuvering his car. "I've never found a space this close to your door before."

"Actually, it's me they like."

Peter finished parking, killed the ignition and took a moment to look at Merry. Her mouth, generous like everything about her, was stretched in a coast-to-coast grin. He wanted to wrap her in his arms and turn that grin into a soft smile of ecstasy. God, how he wanted her.

"I can't argue with you there," he said gruffly before getting out of the car.

She was already out and waiting for him by the time he'd come around the car.

"You're supposed to let the gentleman help you out of the car," he said.

"What for? I'm no cripple."

"It gives a young gentleman something to do," he replied. "Makes him feel useful."

"You'd best be able to do more than just open a car door if you want to feel useful." She turned and gave him a full blast of her impish smile. "I mean, if you're really all that young."

Unable to resist her any longer, Peter reached out and crushed her to his chest. His lips met hers in a blinding rush of passion. Soft and moist, her mouth opened like a flower beneath his touch, and he could barely contain his hunger for her.

It was like holding fire in his arms. She filled his embrace so completely, her softness threatening to consume him. He knew to go deeper, to hold her tighter was to risk being burned, but his heart was about to explode with needs and longings. He pressed her closer, his hands denying that they would ever part while his mouth took strength from her. The city night sounds suddenly intruded, and he let her go.

"What was that for?" she asked, her voice more than just a little breathless.

"That's for nothing." His voice was husky, as if speech were a new skill. "So you better watch your step."

Merry said nothing as they walked to her apartment. "Hi, guys," she said to her roommates, who were lounging in the living room.

"Hi, yourself," they replied, staring at the two of them. Their voices sounded just a bit tentative. They were probably worried about what he was going to do.

"I brought Peter in for a drink," Merry said.

"Just orange juice," he explained before they spooked and called the police.

Merry took her coat off and threw it onto the chair; then she kicked her boots off into a corner. She was wearing a Bulls sweatshirt that did nothing to hide her curves.

"We were just going to our room," Sandi said, standing up.

"Yeah," ZeeZee echoed. "We were going to watch that National Wildlife special on tigers in Africa."

"I thought tigers lived in Asia," Peter said.

"Most of them do," ZeeZee replied. "That's why these are so special."

Sandi just nodded as the women quickly left.

"I guess that could have been an interesting conversation," Peter said. "But I wasn't sure that I wanted to get involved."

Merry laughed. "Just sit down. I'll be right back."

He watched her walk into the kitchen with mixed emotions. He was glad to get a moment to pull himself back together, yet he didn't want her out of his sight.

Calm down, boy, he told himself as he leaned his head against the back of the sofa, closing his eyes. Merry was so vibrant, so full of passion and life that it was only natural for him to be attracted to her. But it was best to go slow. Think things through.

"Here you go."

He opened his eyes as she sat down next to him, holding out his glass of orange juice. She'd also removed her socks.

"That's the one bad thing about winter," she said, putting her feet up on the low table in front of the sofa. "My feet come near to dying, being cooped up all day."

"How about the rest of your body?" Peter asked. Lord, what a question. Slow and easy, that's what he had decided just moments ago.

Merry looked at him with her sparkling blue eyes. They were so cool and inviting, like a pristine pond in the wilderness on a hot summer's day.

How he wanted to dive into those eyes. He wanted their coolness to soothe the fevered heat of his body. He wanted to wrap his arms around her curves, wanted those strong legs to wrap themselves around him.

He set his glass down, and Merry did the same. An unseen hand reached down, pushing them together. Peter could feel his heart stop and his mouth go dry. She was in his arms again, his hunger feeding off hers. His lips dying for a taste of her sweetness.

"Excuse me."

They both jumped back, like children found with their hands in the cookie jar.

"I gotta go to the bathroom," Sandi said, a lopsided grin on her face. "Sorry."

They sat back. Peter didn't know about Merry, but it took an effort on his part to resume normal breathing. They'd have to wait for Sandi to come out. Then what if ZeeZee needed to use the bathroom?

This was insane. He was insane. Just the slightest, merest touch and his body was on fire. There was no way he could sit here on her couch, necking like a pair of teenagers. He'd better get out of here before her roommates had real reason to call the police.

"I have to get going." He stood up. "I have to call Sean, then I have to pack. I'm leaving for a couple of days in Omaha tomorrow morning."

Merry also stood up. "Take care of yourself."

Her voice sounded almost normal, while his seemed thready and weak. Wasn't she affected by his touch?

He grabbed up his coat, fighting the need to grab her back into his arms instead. "You, too. I'll call you."

"Okay."

"Oh." He stopped at the door. "I have a couple of clients and their wives coming in Friday. I promised to take them to dinner at Ambrosia. Could you go with me?"

"Will I have to protect you from them?"

"No," he said frowning. "Why do you ask?"

"Just wanted to know whether I should charge my regular bodyguard rate or what."

"You'll just be a dinner companion."

"Well." She moved up close, put her hand behind his head and pulled him down to her lips. "Then I guess you'll get the regular dinner-companion rate."

"You planning on putting your brand on this little girl, Pete?"

Merry almost laughed out loud at the expression of shock and disbelief that sat for the briefest of moments on Peter's face. Old Mr. Wright had called him Pete, called Merry a little girl and talked about Peter owning her all in one sentence. In a few short words, the old feller got himself an *F-* in political correctness.

Peter seized his glass of water, obviously taking the time to compose himself. "No, Mr. Wright," Peter replied. "Merry and I are just friends."

"I sure don't understand being just friends with such a beautiful woman," the old man snorted.

Mr. Wright was in his early sixties, the CEO of a large computer company in Minneapolis and about to retire. Tall, with longish white hair and a face like old shoe leather, he was an old-fashioned Texan with a native shrewdness behind his bluff, hearty manner and country ways.

"Aren't you friends with your wife?" Merry asked.

"Hell's fire, young lady," he replied with a laugh. "At my age, there ain't nothin' else we can be but friends."

"Yeah," Mrs. Wright, a short, pleasingly plump grandmother type, said. "He's fading fast. I'm looking around for a replacement. A young fella that's still got a lot of juice left in his battery."

They all laughed, then settled into a long moment of silence. The dinner had been delicious and everyone was sitting back, relaxed.

"I'm certainly glad you could come with us," Mr. Roegiers said.

Peter had filled her in on both men before dinner. Mr. Roegiers had been recently appointed to succeed Mr. Wright as CEO upon the latter's retirement. Although completely different personalities—Mr. Roegiers was a sophisticated man who'd graduated from Harvard—the two men and their wives got along quite well.

"I'm glad you could join us also," Mrs. Roegiers said softly. "I've always been fascinated with the theater. Although, what I really appreciated was your wine selection for dinner. The chardonnay was out of this world."

"Thank you," Merry murmured.

She settled back to bask in an aura of satisfaction. She hated to brag but, like the folks said, she had done quite well. The food and drink recommendations she'd made were good, and she had no trouble at all in holding up her end of the conversation.

The Roegiers were interested in her theater classes and experience, while the Wrights enjoyed her waitress stories. Merry smiled. She'd learned way back that as long as a woman labeled herself an actress, she could work at anything from waitress to call girl and be quite acceptable.

"Would the ladies and gentlemen like anything else? Some chocolate mints perhaps?"

Their waiter had returned to check on them. Merry noticed that his French accent had been getting a little heavy as the evening had progressed. Peter scanned the group as everyone indicated they'd had enough. Good. She'd enjoyed herself, but the evening had been long and it was time for Cinderella to head back to her hearth, kick off her shoes and flop down in bed. Although as long as she was in bed, there was one other little thing she wouldn't mind doing.

Merry could feel her cheeks warm slightly. Like Peter said, they were just friends. But the vibes she'd gotten the other night said that he'd be interested in being *really* good friends. And her body was screaming out its own agreement.

"That'll be all, Charles," Peter said. "Just the check, please."

The waiter bowed slightly and walked away.

Mr. Wright stood up. "I'm going to visit the little boys' room before we leave."

"I want to freshen up myself," Mrs. Wright said.

The Roegiers got up and followed the Wrights, leaving Merry and Peter alone at the table.

"Thanks for helping me out," he said softly.

"No problem," Merry replied. "Hope they'll still be your customers after tonight."

"Are you kidding?"

He smiled at her, a broad smile that spread its heat from the top of her her head down to the tips of her toes. She could live in that smile, take it to the bank as collateral for a million-dollar loan. Or use it to heat the house in the dead of winter and still have enough left over to steam up her soul.

Peter took her hand, his touch sending shivers up and down her spine. "I think they're going to demand that I bring you along whenever I go to Minneapolis on business."

"I hear Minneapolis is a nice town," she said, trying to sound cool and unaffected.

"I have a feeling that any town would be nice with you in it."

"Better be careful." She tried to sound stern, but her voice came out all soft and wavery. "Flattery is liable to get you everything."

The silence surrounded them and filled their ears. Peter had those big brown eyes, the kind that could go from puppy soft to rock hard in a split second. Right now they seemed to burn with a hidden fire that invited her to come closer.

"Here's your check, sir. I'll take it whenever you're ready."

The spell was broken and they parted. Peter's eyes flicked up to the waiter, then he did a double take as the lack of French accent dawned on him. Merry and the waiter began to laugh.

"Sorry, Merry," the waiter said. "It's been a long day."

Peter was sitting back, faint question lines furrowing his brow. "You two know each other?"

"Yep," Merry replied. "This is Bobby Wisnewski. He's a student at Columbia. Works here nights as a waiter. Bobby, this is my friend, Peter MacAllister."

The two men shook hands, then Peter pulled a credit card from his wallet and gave it to Bobby Wisnewski, aka Charles, the French waiter.

"I guess it's all show biz," Peter said once Bobby had left.

Merry nodded. "Sure is. Didn't old Willie Shakespeare say something about life being nothing but a stage?"

"Something like that."

Voices floated over from the front of the dining room, announcing the return of the Wrights and the Roegierses. Peter put on his pleasant business face, and Merry turned up her smile a notch.

Just because it was show biz didn't mean it was easy. Sure, this little restaurant gig had turned out well for her, but it hadn't just happened. She'd spent almost an hour here after work, talking to the waiters and chefs. Seeing what was going to be served that evening and getting wine recommendations. Checking ingredients so she could talk knowledgeably about the food. She also talked to the piano player and found out which tunes he could do best.

Peter had been depending on her, and she wasn't about to let him down.

* * *

"Yahoo!" Merry shouted as she stepped into Peter's living room.

He was lying back in his recliner, watching television. He rolled his head toward her. "What are you yahooing about?"

"I finished my paper. I'm done! *Finis*."

She walked over to the back of the recliner and glanced at the TV set. The Bulls were playing the New York Knicks and they were only ahead by one point. She bent down and hugged Peter around his neck.

"Hey, down in front." He squirmed around to keep his eye on the screen. "This is a good game."

Merry dropped down in his lap. "I know another good game."

"Oh?"

She let her hands roam over his shoulders until her arms encircled him; then she leaned forward to ever so gently brush his lips with hers. He leaned into her, but she backed away, climbing back off his lap.

"Oops, I forgot. You want to watch the game."

"Get back here," he said with laugh and pulled her back into his lap.

"Are you sure?" she asked. Her fingers ran through his hair. She felt so good. She wanted to celebrate.

He picked up the TV's remote control, aimed it at the set and turned it off. "Positive." He tossed the remote onto the table as he slipped his arms around her.

"Now, about this game of yours. What's it called?"

She just laughed and snuggled into his arms. "It's called Your-Sociology-Paper's-Done Celebration."

"I see. Is it a hard game to learn?"

"Not really." She ran a finger along his jaw. It was so strong, so rigid. It seemed to say he was unbending, but she had seen softer, gentler sides to him.

He grabbed her hand suddenly and brought it to his lips. The look in his eyes said her teasing caress had been too much. He held it, held her as if he'd never let her go. Which was absolutely just fine with her.

"So what are the rules to this game?" he asked.

"Well, first of all you have to choose a topic," she said as she leaned over to touch his lips with her tongue. She felt the shiver go down his spine, felt the fire leap up in him. And felt the answering hunger in her soul.

"You know," she said. "Some area you'd like to explore."

"I see."

His hands slipped under her sweatshirt. They felt cool against her suddenly feverish skin, cool and delicious as they roamed over her back. There were so many needs that came rushing forward, clamoring to be met. She closed her eyes and let her body call to his.

His lips pressed against hers, a questioning, examining kiss that asked things of her heart. Things that her mind couldn't answer, that her ears couldn't hear. That only the very depth of her understood and responded to. Then he gently pulled away his mouth, and she lay against him, her heart racing and her breath hard to catch.

"So," she said after a few moments. "Did you see an area you'd like to explore?"

"Several."

His voice was as thready and weak as hers. Maybe together they could find strength. She covered his mouth with hers, a union of their souls, a blending of their voices. They moved and danced against each other until time stood still. It was wonder, it was magic.

There was no yesterday, no tomorrow. There was only now and here. Only this moment in Peter's arms and the deepening desire to find fulfillment in his embrace. Dark shadows of the past held no terror, for they were forgotten.

"So what is this now?" Peter whispered into her hair. "Are we doing research?"

"Definitely," she said. She kissed the corner of his mouth, then blazed a tiny trail down to his neck. "The more we do, the better the end result."

"We could be at this a while," he said.

"I hope so."

His hands were under her sweatshirt again, loosening her bra so her breasts were free. He touched them, cupped them, ran his fingers over their surface. Her breath came faster, her hunger for more of his touch came on stronger.

"Might be very late when we're done," he warned.

"That's okay. This is my night to stay up."

His hands stopped their caress, and she felt lonely, abandoned. She frowned at him. What was wrong? Had she done something? Not done something?

"What do you say we adjourn to someplace with a little more room?" he said.

She had dreamed of that bedroom, of lying there beneath a blanket of stars, but she couldn't. Not yet. That was Kelly's room. Kelly's bed. She looked into Peter's eyes. He wasn't Kelly's husband anymore, at least not tonight, not with that hunger for her in his eyes.

She looked at the floor. "Looks like lots of room right here."

He frowned at her, confusion and concern colliding in his eyes. "Why? Are you worried that I—"

She covered his mouth with the tips of her fingers. "Because I love this room," she said. "There's only one thing I'd change."

He just stared at her, so she got up and turned off the light by his chair, then the light in the entryway. In the semi darkness of the night, she found her way back across the living room and pulled open the drapes. The night spilled into the room. Stars danced across the sky and into her heart.

"Now it's perfect," she whispered and, taking him by the hand, she pulled him to the floor.

Under the blessing of the stars, she slowly pulled off her sweatshirt, then her bra. Peter lay her back onto the thick white rug and kissed her. First her lips until she couldn't breath, then her neck, creating a necklace of feather-light kisses until she thought her heart would stop. Then his lips caressed her breasts, tugging, holding, teasing her nipples until she felt the stars rising up to meet her.

"You're so beautiful," he whispered.

She couldn't speak, her voice was lost amid the night somewhere. She'd never felt so cherished, so wanted. Her hands tugged at the buttons on his shirt, then pushed it off his shoulders. She wanted to run her fingers over his chest, to feel his heart beating beneath her touch. She wanted to belong, to be possessed.

Suddenly Peter's touch was fevered. An urgency had crept into the darkness and swallowed them. Their needs took over, their hearts cried out for fulfillment. Hands stroked heatedly, with purpose and insistence.

It was suddenly so right and necessary. It was what life was all about. They came together in the darkness. She took his passion inside her and together they exploded into wonder and joy and contentment. The stars came down to meet them and carried them up to the heavens. Then ever so slowly, wrapped in each other's arms, they floated back to earth.

Peter stopped at the closed bedroom door, his hand on the knob. Sure, Merry was in there and he didn't know if she was dressed yet, but why should that matter? It wasn't as if they didn't know each other. After all, people who make love, sleep together and then make love again in the morning can hardly classify themselves as strangers.

"Oh, hell," he muttered, knocking lightly on the door. "I'm about to put the omelets on. Are you almost ready?"

"Ready when you are, Freddy."

Suddenly the door opened and he started back. Merry leaned against the doorjamb, dressed only in his black Bulls championship T-shirt. The sight caused everything to tighten up on him. With her white skin and red hair, she looked like no other woman he'd ever seen.

"Hello, sailor. Looking for anything special?"

Peter cleared his throat. "Cheese-and-bacon omelet okay?"

"Sure."

A tightness appeared around Merry's mouth. Maybe she'd wanted him to say something else, but he didn't know what. He wasn't sure how to act or what to think. This was all new territory for him, and he definitely didn't feel at ease.

"I could run out and get a green pepper if you want," he said.

She shook her head. "Whatever you have is fine. I'm flexible."

She certainly was, but then she was many things. As well as flexible, Merry was strong, Merry was...

Merry was hungry. His face warmed. Merry was hungry for an omelet and so was he. Peter turned on his heel and hurried toward the kitchen. Soft footsteps behind him told him that Merry was following.

"Need any help?"

"No."

"Are you sure?"

"Quite sure," he snapped. "I normally live alone, you know."

She looked uncertain for a moment, then sat down at the small table in the kitchenette. He went about making the omelets and pouring the orange juice and coffee.

All right, so he hadn't meant to snap at her. It was just that he didn't know how he was supposed to handle all this. Did it change things between them? Would she think it did?

Neither spoke as they ate breakfast. Merry didn't seem as hungry as usual. Maybe she wasn't a morning person or maybe he wasn't reacting right. Sighing internally, he sipped at his coffee. Damn.

"This is cold," he said. "Want a warm-up?"

She shook her head.

Boy, he certainly was handling this smoothly. What did she want from him? Maybe more importantly, how did *he* feel about things now? He peered deep into his soul. Damn! He didn't know.

"You still want me go to your mother's with you?"

"Huh?" That was an intelligent response. It wasn't that he hadn't heard her. His mind was just out of sync with his senses.

"I said, do you—"

"Yeah, yeah. Of course. Why not?" He forced a laugh out of his throat. "I still need a bodyguard."

She nodded and stared into her cup. "Good."

"Is it still okay with you?" he asked. "I mean, if you have something else planned...."

"I don't."

"That's good."

"I just didn't know if you'd want to change your mind."

"No," he protested. "Why would I?"

She shrugged. "You know, sometimes you do things with a guy and..." she hesitated, wagging her head from side to side "...and things change."

"Change?" Who was thinking up this dialogue for him? Wasn't change just what he was worried about?

"Yeah," she replied.

They stared at each other a long moment. He tried to read her eyes, but failed miserably. Was she saying last night had changed things for her? Did she want them to change or not want them to? He took a chance.

"It would be dumb if it did," he said.

"Yeah," she agreed.

"I mean, if we're friends, we're friends."

"Right."

"If we're not, we're not."

"Right."

So which were they? They shared another well of silence that brought him no answers.

"Want another omelet?"

"No," she said, standing up. "I'm full to overflowing. Gonna have to walk some extra miles the way it is."

He stood up and started clearing the table. "I've heard that ice-skating is even better," Peter said. "It burns more energy."

"It does?" She began rinsing the dishes in the sink.

"Yeah." He took the dishes from Merry and put them into the dishwasher. "They've opened up the ice rink downtown. Wanna go one of these days?"

"Yeah," she said shrugging. "I guess. You want to?"

He shrugged. "It might be fun."

"Stuff like that is always more fun when you do it with friends."

"Oh, absolutely."

They stood in the center of his kitchen, looking everywhere but at each other. He wanted to take her into his arms again and relive the magic they'd found last night, but he couldn't. Passion had burned away at his senses, but the fires were under control now. The bright light of reality was shining down on him, and he felt blinded by all the possible directions that lay before them. Rather than take a misstep, he didn't move at all.

"I'd better get going," she said. "I have to clean my room."

"I should do some shopping for Sean."

They nodded in unison.

"See you," he said.

"Right."

Chapter Nine

"Maybe Prince Charming is off on a business trip."

Merry spun away from the window, turning her wrath on the gray-haired bartender. "If you want to be wearing that smile on the back of your head, Willy, then keep putting your nose where it doesn't belong."

"Hey, ease up," Willy said, raising his hands in surrender. "I'm sorry."

She continued glaring at him, but the fire of her anger was already fizzling out. It was too damn bad that Willy was such a nice, old guy. Merry was just aching to mix it up with someone.

"That's all right," Merry said. "Sorry I took a bite out of you."

"No problem," he replied with a soft smile. "That's what us old guys are for."

She turned back to stare out the window. It had warmed up a bit today. That meant instead of a bitter-cold wind there were gray clouds hanging overhead, threatening to dump rain on them at any minute.

"I'm probably right," Willy said. "You know how it is with

these big-business hotshots. There ain't a minute they can call their own. They got phone calls, meetings, trips out of town, what have you."

"Yeah," she agreed.

Except that she wasn't watching out the window, fretting because Peter hadn't come to lunch yet. No, she was worrying that he would. She just wasn't ready to face him yet. What had she been thinking of Saturday night? Actually, thinking hadn't entered the picture at all.

Hell, she'd practically jumped on his bones. A pleasurable warmth returned to the far points of her body, but she refused to let it sway her. She had goals to reach, goals that were still years away. She couldn't afford to have someone distracting her from them.

Yet here she was, staring out the window for a glimpse of him like some love-struck teenager. Afraid he wasn't coming and afraid that he was.

It was obvious that they couldn't be friends anymore. She should have known better than to hook up with a smooth-talking moneybag. He'd wined and dined and romanced her, whispered sweet nothings in her ear and put her under his spell better than any hypnotist.

Well, she was going to have to send out some signals, strong and clear. Bye, bye. Adios. Farewell. Goodbye.

There'd be no skating date. No nothing date anymore. If she had to go to Mentone with him, she would, for Sean's sake. But it would be all business. She'd let her feelings for a man run her life once and was still trying to recover from it. It definitely was not going to happen again.

Suddenly her trip to White Pigeon tomorrow morning loomed importantly. It would refocus her, set her feet on the right path again. Jason was the center of her life, not Peter.

"Guess he was just running late today."

Willy's voice cleared enough of the fog from her eyes to see Peter standing outside the restaurant talking to someone. Her heart quivered at the sight of him; her resolution wobbled. She wanted to smile and dance, to run over and greet him, to bask in his smile forever.

She had to go. She couldn't stay here and see him. It was obvious that her heart wasn't strong enough, not yet.

"Willy, I'm gonna duck out a little early. Remind Denise that I won't be in for two days, will you?"

"You gotta go now?"

"I surely do," she replied.

"What about your gentleman friend?"

"I'm not the only waitress in this place," she said. "Someone else can wait on him."

She had to get out while she could. Maybe she was being a coward, but there were some things that were more important than childish name-calling. Like her sanity.

"Merry!"

Damn. She'd been too slow.

She turned, pasting a bright smile on her lips. "Hi, Peter. How you doing?"

"Starving to death."

His eyes were laughing, inviting her to join in. Oh, how she wanted to! She would have liked nothing better than to dive into his arms and let him hold her until forever was over. She had an overwhelming need to belong, to put an end to the parade of lonely nights.

But that was just being weak. The very reason she'd wanted to leave before he'd seen her. Whatever silliness her heart wanted to indulge in, her mind knew better.

"Want your regular table?" she asked.

"Any'll do." He nodded toward the nearest one. "This is your station?"

Her heart wavered. Those brown eyes could make her smile, make her feel alive. Why was she being so silly? What harm would it do to serve him lunch? They were friends, after all.

They'd been lovers, her mind contradicted. And now she was acting like a lovesick schoolgirl.

"Actually, it doesn't matter," she said before she lost her nerve. "I was just on my way out."

"You were?" His voice echoed his disappointment, his eyes were shadowed with regret. He looked like a little kid who'd come too late to see Santa.

Merry stiffened her resolve. "I was taking off a little early today."

Those eyes were on her, bringing back memories of passion and tenderness, of longing and fulfillment. For a few minutes the other night, he had been everything to her, but those moments had passed. She had to cling to her own life, her own path. She would make no explanations.

Merry smiled at him. "I'll get Lona to take care of you. She won't let you starve." She glanced around and spotted the waitress coming out of the kitchen. "Lona, can you take care of this customer?"

"Sure thing, Merry. Be right there." She sent a smile their way as she went to deliver a bowl of soup.

"The chicken noodle was great today," Merry told Peter. "But I'd stay away from the patty melt. I had a number of complaints."

"Can't you—"

"Oops, look at the time," Merry cried, glancing toward the clock before she grinned at Peter. "Gotta run. See ya."

This time she did escape and didn't falter a step, even though she felt his eyes on her back and his hurt in the air. There were times when a girl had to take care of herself.

"Oh, Lordy," Merry gasped as she fought the steering wheel and attempted to bring the rental car under control. "You'd better pay attention to business, gal. Else you're going to roll this heap and let the whole three-county area know that Lu-Ellen's little girl is back."

Those dark clouds that had been hanging over the mountaintops when she'd landed in Charleston were fulfilling their promise now that evening had fallen. Huge snowflakes, just dripping with water, were covering the ground and making the roads slick and treacherous. The snow plus the mountains made for a devilish combination, and she breathed a sigh of relief as she eased the car back into the flow of traffic.

The palms of her hands were covered with sweat, and Merry wiped first the right, then the left on her jeans. She was rapidly becoming a basket case.

This was foolhardy. Absolutely crazy. She might be an adult now and not so vulnerable to Joe's threats, but there were just so many ways this whole thing could backfire. The paper could have gotten the date of the pageant wrong. Jason might have transferred schools and no longer be at Washington. Joe might recognize her and publicly humiliate her.

Worse, Jason could be miserable or ill or a spoiled brat, and there'd be nothing she could do about it. Or what if somehow the whole story came out and Jason rejected her? What if he treated her like dirt, the way his father had ten years ago?

If only she'd been able to talk this over with Peter. But then that had been a whole other something that had backfired.

She took a deep breath. She should have known better than to get involved in Peter's life in the first place. What made her think she could dictate her emotions? She'd gotten this far because she'd been so careful to avoid involvement. Now she had to back up, reassess things and find her path again. And stay on it, no matter what.

A sign appeared on the side of the road, warning that the speed limit would drop ahead. She was almost there.

Nothing would go wrong, she reassured herself. She had a long coat to hide her body, a dark wig to hide her red hair and wraparound sunglasses to mask her face. No one would recognize her. And if the paper was wrong, or Jason wasn't at that school anymore, it would be disappointing, but not the end of the world.

She rounded a bend and was suddenly in White Pigeon. It felt so much the same, she was scared. About two streets over was where Momma had moved with the kids about a year after Merry'd left, and somewhere around here was the jail her younger brother Billy had ended up in many a night. He had died in an alley fight about six years ago, just before Cassie'd run off. Momma died not too long after, and Merry lost track of the rest of her kin. She knew Robbie'd joined the army and Beth Ann had married some boy from school, but Merry thought they'd moved out west someplace. Jackson, the baby of the family, had been following in Billy's footsteps the last she'd heard.

She turned a corner and there was the drugstore where she used to get a soda after work on Saturdays. On the next block was Minnie's, the dress store where everybody bought their prom dresses. Well, not everybody. She'd never made it to that magic time. That blue satin with the tiny rosebuds had made someone else feel like a princess.

Swallowing hard, Merry drove on. The past didn't matter, just tonight. Tonight this town would hold nothing but happiness for her. She paused at a flickering yellow warning light, then proceeded through the intersection. The school was just down the street.

She drove past the parking lot. People were still heading toward the entrance, so she took another turn around the block. Best not to join the crowd going in. Strangers stuck out like sore thumbs around here. She'd go in when she could go in alone. If the performance had started, the lights would be dimmed and everyone's attention would be focused on stage.

The parking lot was deserted when she came back around, so she pulled in, putting the car into a slot over in a far corner. For a long moment, she just sat there, still gripping the steering wheel. Now that the moment was here, she was terrified. She longed for Peter's reassurance, for that look in his eye that made her feel anything was possible.

Finally, after gritting her teeth until her jaw muscles ached, Merry undid her seat belt and got out of the car. She didn't need Peter to tell her she was competent. She wasn't some weak, simpering little miss who couldn't do a thing without a man to protect her. She moved across the deserted parking lot like a rabbit crossing a road, ready to dart at any shadow.

She had timed it well. The performance had already started, and no one was standing in the halls as she approached the auditorium. Even the collecting table was empty, so Merry just left a five-dollar bill. She picked up a program, her stomach tying itself in knots as her eyes scanned the list of students.

There he was! Jason Byron O'Connell, her son. Merry's knees felt weak, her eyes stupidly watery. Geez, it was just his name, she scolded herself. Taking a deep breath, she went into the auditorium.

The munchkins up on stage were all dressed as Christmas trees, looking absolutely adorable as they sang their hearts out. They must be kindergartners. She slumped against the back wall as the tears returned.

Jason had once been that age, probably wearing the same mixture of solemnity and terror as most of those kids. But she hadn't been there to watch his fledgling steps.

Her eyes closed and she saw another little boy, one just at

this age now. Did Peter know how special all these little moments in Sean's life were? Did he realize how they'd never
come again? If only she could make him see all he was missing,
realize how precious every second was. But to do that she'd
have to knock down that wall he'd built around his heart and
she suspected that even Sean couldn't do that.

She put her hands in her coat pockets, the fingers of her right
hand wrapping themselves around the small throwaway camera
she'd bought.

The little critters were being herded offstage and the whole
scene began swimming before Merry. She took a deep breath
and gripped her lower lip with her teeth. Her plan was to be
inconspicuous. Bursting into tears would sure put the kibosh to
that. Just concentrate on the show and don't think, she admon-
ished herself.

Fortunately, the first-, second-and third-grade performances
went by quickly. When the principal came on to announce the
fourth grade, Merry had only a slight tremor in her hands. She
held the camera tightly, staring hard at the stage. The kids
marched out, dressed in their Sunday best.

Her throat tightened up, her breath seemed gone as she
searched each boy's face as he came onto the stage. What if she
didn't recognize him? She had been so sure....

He was there. One of the last to come onto the stage, but it
had to be him, with Joe's height and her red hair. He settled in
his place on the riser and smiled slightly. She bit her lip. He
had her brother Robbie's smile. The scene blurred before her,
and she swiped impatiently at her eyes.

The class started their performance with ''The Twelve Days
of Christmas,'' but Merry barely heard the words. Her eyes
scoured Jason's face, trying to read his childhood in a few moments. Was that a scar on his chin? How'd he get it? He seemed
to be squinting slightly. Was it just the lights or did he need
glasses?

She slid forward along the side wall, needing to be closer.
The boy next to him must be a friend because they kept nudging
each other. Their little grins told of unspoken conspiracies, and
she felt incredibly left out. She didn't even know his friend's
name.

Jason was so tall, getting close to her height, and so grown up that he barely seemed a child anymore. She had missed his whole childhood. He would be a teenager soon, and she hadn't seen any of the pieces that had made him who he was.

Tears began to flow, but they were silent tears, and Merry didn't even try to stop them. Granny had always said there was no sense crying over spilled milk, and she was right. But sometimes the tears just had to come out. Sometimes a body was so sad that there was no way to stop them.

The little boy she'd carried for nine months under her heart, the one who squirmed and kicked like he was too alive to be cooped up inside her, the tiny, squawling child she'd held for such a few precious moments, was suddenly tall and confident.

And a stranger.

She'd let him go because she'd had nothing to offer him, and he hadn't missed her in the slightest. It was how it should be. It was how she wanted it to be. But, oh, Lordy, how it hurt!

The tears started to come down even harder, and Merry fought to blink them away. She couldn't fall apart now, not yet.

But then the kids were marching off the stage. Her moment with Jason was almost over. She pulled out her camera, trying to find Jason through the viewfinder and failing miserably. She dropped it slightly, her eyes searching frantically, but he was already gone. His row of the risers was empty.

Stupid, stupid, stupid! Joe had been right. She was just a stupid nobody who couldn't do anything right. This was her one chance to have something to hold and cherish and she blew it.

She turned and ran out of the auditorium, tripping over numerous unseen feet along the way. Hot tears poured down her face, but she didn't care. Soon she was outside and running for the car.

Damn Joe O'Connell. Damn him and all the rich guys of the world.

She managed to get into the car just as she started to sob, but she started the motor, anyway, and pulled out of the parking lot. The car somehow found the route back to Charleston.

Damn their rotten deal.

Joe's deal was that he would take the baby and give him advantages that she couldn't even dream of. All she had to do was stay away from Jason the rest of his life. No big deal, at least not in Joe's mind.

The snow was coming down harder now, and Merry turned the windshield wipers up to their top speed. She shouldn't have come. She should have kept up her end of the agreement. Occasionally missing a shadowy figure would have been a snap compared to missing the tall, red-haired boy with the wide grin. With her grin.

Suddenly the tears were flowing as if a dam had burst and along with them came painful, gut-racking sobs that shook her whole self. She finally had to pull over to the side of the road; there was no way she could continue.

She didn't know whether it was two minutes or two hours, but she cried and cried and cried until there were no more tears, then she cried some more. She cried because her son'd never get to know how much she loved him. She cried because she'd never gotten to hug him when he'd hit a home run or hold him when he scraped his knee. And she cried because Peter didn't understand what a precious thing he was letting slip through his fingers.

Eventually she was too exhausted. There were no more tears, no more pain. Just a growing anger seeking a focus.

It was too late to walk her son to school his first day, to take him trick-or-treating or to see his first baseball game, but it wasn't too late for Peter. How could he turn his back on what she'd give half her life to have?

"I called you," Peter said. "No one would tell me where you were."

He'd had a lousy couple of days—battling a cold, up to his neck in projects at work and trying to buy Christmas presents even though he didn't know what anybody wanted or the size they wore. He'd needed her smile, her teasing, her laughter, but she seemed to have fallen off the face of the earth.

Merry didn't reply, concentrating instead on lacing up her skates. When she was finished, she stood up to stretch her legs. They were very nice legs, but Peter wasn't up to admiring them.

"I wondered what happened to you." He could hear the growing tension in his voice but didn't try to control it. He didn't like needing her, and certainly didn't like admitting to himself that he did. "After all, we did have a date."

"Not really," she said as she started to skate in small circles near him. Her voice was as cold as the ice she stood on. "We said we'd go skating sometime."

"I assumed 'sometime' meant sometime soon. Like in the next day or so." He finished lacing up his own skates and got to his feet. The world felt wobbly and uncertain beneath him, not a feeling he liked. It made his voice snappish. "You were damn rude going off without saying anything."

"I didn't think I had to report in to you," she said, slowing to a stop.

"You don't. But you've never taken off like that before." He sounded angry and impatient even to himself, but he didn't care. He'd thought they'd been friends, that she was someone who understood his pain, but obviously he'd been wrong.

"I didn't just take off," she said. "I had to go out of town for a couple of days, that's all. You go off all the time. Aren't I allowed to do the same?"

What was with her? Two days ago at the restaurant she'd been rushed but fine. He'd been worrying that somehow that night of love would change their comfortable relationship, but she had seemed just fine. So what had happened in the meantime?

"Of course you're allowed to go out of town," he said. "But I would have thought you owed me the courtesy of letting me know. I always tell you."

Her eyes were chips of ice. "That sounds an awful lot like a relationship," she said. "I didn't think you wanted to be that close to anybody. Not even to Sean."

He felt like the floor had been knocked from beneath him. Anger was the nearest thing to cling to. "What the hell is that supposed to mean?"

"Exactly what I said. You've locked yourself in an ivory tower and seem to be quite proud of the way you've shut everybody else out."

"You make it sound like some choice I've made."

"Haven't you?"

"No, I haven't." Who was she to question his love for his son? She was a drifter by her own admission, someone who'd probably never made a minute's commitment to someone else. "And I happen to love Sean very much."

"I don't think you know the meaning of the word love."

Suddenly his anger made it all crystal clear and it wasn't a pleasant revelation. "Oh, I get it now," he said. "This all goes back to the other night, doesn't it? I was supposed to say some magic words and I didn't, so you punished me by refusing my calls. Was I supposed to just declare my love and propose marriage, too?"

Even as her eyes blazed, her hand swung out and slapped him on the cheek. It was a hard, stinging blow that almost knocked him off his feet. His hand automatically went up to rub his cheek, but their eyes stayed locked. Anger, betrayal, regret all mingled in their gazes.

Christmas carols blared out over the loudspeakers, but they couldn't drown out the angry words. They hung there like dark storm clouds hanging over an Indiana cornfield.

In that long moment, he saw that he'd been wrong. Whatever the reason why he hadn't been able to reach her, it had nothing to do with her expectations of him. Fear of this strangely argumentative Merry had made him act stupidly. He took a deep breath and looked away.

He knew only one thing for certain—that they were through now. His stupidity had made sure of that. Well, it was probably for the best. They'd been seeing too much of each other and that would just lead to problems that neither of them wanted, anyway.

"You don't have to come to Mentone with me over the holidays," he said.

She shrugged, her anger seemed to have dissipated also. "I don't mind going, but I won't if you don't want me."

If he didn't want her? Want didn't begin to describe the feelings raging in his heart, but he couldn't actually put a title to them. All he knew was that the intensity of his emotions scared him. They were stronger than they had any right to be, than he wanted them to be.

What happened to his isolated existence? He'd been happy alone, concentrating on existing, on staying a safe distance from smiles that warmed the chill in his soul and eyes that set fire to his heart.

Peter looked into Merry's blue eyes. Just a second ago they had been filled with the fires of anger. Now they mirrored only

the clouds of despair. He wanted nothing more than to take her
in his arms, but he couldn't.

"I don't want to impose on you," he said softly.

"I told your mother I'd be there."

"She'll understand."

"I told Sean I'd see him."

He felt his shoulders slump in defeat. What the heck could
he tell a five-year-old kid? Daddy made an ass of himself and
now Merry hated him for it?

Chapter Ten

"There's a lot more snow here than in Chicago," Peter said.

From the corner of his eye, he saw Merry look out the passenger-side window. She stared at the snow-covered expanse stretching from one end of the horizon to the other. The stubble-filled sea of brown that they'd sailed through on their last trip to Mentone was now winter white.

"That's lake-effect snow," he added.

"I see," she replied without looking at him.

"The cold air moves across Canada from west to east," he explained. "In the winter a portion of that air mass called the Alberta Clipper dips down into the Midwest. It picks up moisture as it passes over Lake Michigan, which is still relatively warm, and turns it into snow. Which, in keeping with the holiday spirit, then dumps it on Indiana and Michigan."

"Interesting," Merry said.

"That's why the average temperature is colder on the west side of the lake, while the average precipitation is greater on the east side."

"Very interesting."

"Well, at least I'm trying to keep up a conversation."

"Peter, I'm not asking you to keep up anything."

Her words had such a tone of sorrow to them. He looked her full in the face for a moment. Merry's eyes matched the sadness she carried in her voice.

"Merry, I'm sorry I said that the other day."

"I know." Her voice carried more weariness than anger. "This whole thing has been a mistake from the beginning. Nothing has gone right."

Nothing? There had been moments when he'd thought things had been pretty great.

"I think I'll take a nap," she said. "I've been up late studying for exams."

Before she barely finished her sentence, she had let her seat back down slightly and faced away from him. Peter swallowed the soft words on his tongue. Years of marriage had trained him well in reading a woman's stiff back. It clearly said that she didn't want to talk anymore. He turned his full attention to driving.

"Peter." Her voice was soft and tentative.

"Yes?" His was careful and cautious.

"If you get tired of driving, I'll be glad to take my turn."

"That's okay."

"Just let me know."

"Sure."

Peter slumped back in his seat. It was going to be a long trip to Mentone, no matter who drove. He didn't think Santa Claus himself could bring any joy to this trip.

Maybe it would have been better if they'd just called it quits a few days ago. Yet he hadn't been able to do that, not so abruptly. Once they were back in Chicago for good, they would no doubt drift apart, but there'd been too many people expecting her this time. He hadn't wanted to disappoint them all.

He stopped at Bourbon where he made his usual almost-home call. "Hi, Mom. I'm at Bourbon and everything's going along fine." Merry wasn't talking to him and he was down in the dumps, but otherwise things were just ginger peachy-keen.

"That's good," she replied. "And how is Merry?"

"Fine." As far as he could tell. "How is Sean? Is he over his cold?"

"Oh, my, yes. He's all excited about Christmas and eating cookies by the ton."

"That's good," Peter replied.

"Well, there's no need keeping you. Everybody is anxious to visit with you and Merry again. So the sooner I let you go, the sooner you'll be home."

"We'll be there in about a half hour."

Merry didn't stir as he got back into the car. Though he would have liked to get some things more settled between them, he was glad she was able to get some rest. Working from about ten o'clock to four or five each day, then having classes each evening would wear out anybody. He was surprised that she hadn't worn herself out earlier.

As he made the turn for Etna Green, Peter cleared his throat. Merry stirred and rolled over slightly. She looked so soft, so vulnerable as she awoke from sleep. Normally she was strong and tough, needing nobody, but just for a moment he could believe she needed protection and sheltering. He had either been incredibly stupid or naive in believing that they could be just friends.

"We're almost there," he said and paused a moment. "We should try and act at least semifriendly."

"I know that." She put her seat back in an upright position. "I have no intention of ruining your mother and Sean's holiday."

How about my holiday? How about your holiday? he wanted to ask, but he knew that no answers would be forthcoming. At least no answers that would bring happiness back into their relationship.

Merry spent the rest of the trip checking out her hair and face in a small mirror. Peter could have told her that everything was perfect, but he knew that she wasn't really looking at herself. She was an actress psyching herself up to play a tough role. He wished he had the training that would get him through the next two weeks.

He turned onto the street and saw his mother and Sean standing on the front porch along with Belle. By the time he parked the car, they were down the steps, waving and otherwise acting disgustingly happy.

"Merry Christmas," Sean shouted, jumping up and down and clapping his hands.

"Merry Christmas." Merry's face was bathed in what looked like genuine excitement as she hugged Sean and then Peter's mother.

Peter said his hellos and then got the bags.

"Santa's coming soon," Sean told them all. Belle barked, probably adding her orders for Santa in canine.

Peter shut the trunk and, picking up the bags, turned toward the porch. His mother intercepted him.

"Welcome home, Peter." She gave him a vigorous hug. "Smile. This won't hurt."

Oh, great, he thought. She was really in a good mood. How the hell was he going to keep up pretenses for two weeks? Maybe he'd be lucky and get hit by a truck before the day was out.

"Come in. Come in," his mother said, shooing them into the house. "Come in before you catch your death of cold."

Belle helped with the herding and they were quickly in the house, stamping snow off their shoes. His mother went around collecting coats.

"We got cookies," Sean told Merry. "Lots of 'em."

"Can I have some?" she asked.

A crafty look came over his son's face as he pondered that question for a moment. "Three," Sean replied, holding up that number of fingers.

"Sean," his grandmother protested. "That's not nice."

"But she's big," Sean said. "She'll eat 'em all."

"I surely would, ma'am," Merry assured Peter's mother. "I surely would."

The three of them laughed, but the best Peter could do was a smile. He watched as they reveled in their holiday cheer, passing it back and forth like a beach ball that they weren't going to let him play with.

"Peter, let's quit this lollygagging," his mother said briskly. "Get the bags upstairs. You two have the same rooms as before." Then she turned toward Merry and said. "Zachary was quite anxious for your return."

"Yeah," Sean agreed. "He wanted someone warm to sleep with."

"We all do, honey," his grandmother replied with a wink at Peter. "We all do."

Peter thought that he'd been carrying a heavy load of depression when he came into the house, but his load just picked up a partner. He could hardly lift their bags.

Get ahold of yourself, he scolded silently. At least pretend you're having a good time.

Peter walked toward them from the little shed on the edge of the parking lot. He carried an ax and saw in his hands and a smile on his lips.

"Okay, guys," he said. "Let's do it."

"Right," Sean agreed. "Let's do it."

They were at a cut-it-yourself Christmas-tree farm, ready to harvest their yule tree. Sean was sparkling like a Christmas star and even Peter was bright and cheerful, apparently having left his mopies behind. Although she tried to control it, Merry felt a childlike excitement growing within her own heart.

"I'm ready," Merry said.

"Daddy, can I ride on your back?"

"Aren't you getting a little big for that?"

"Nope," Sean replied, shaking his head vigorously.

"I'll carry the tools," Merry said.

She took the tools from Peter as he bent down for Sean to jump onto his back. Bundled up in a snowsuit with boots and thick mittens covering his extremities, "jumping" wasn't quite possible, but with Merry's help, he was soon aboard. Peter stood up and Sean grinned at Merry, sending a quivering warmth all through her.

"The best trees are over this way," Peter said as he hitched Sean into a more comfortable position. "On the west side of the property."

Merry nodded, and they marched up the snow-crusted path with Peter slightly to the front of her. She was doing all right. It was hard keeping her emotions in check around Peter, but she was managing. Slowly but surely, her anger over what he was missing in Sean's life was dying out and she was able to just relax.

"This has become a tradition for us," Peter told her.

"Yeah," Sean added. "And we do it every Christmas."

"That's the way to do it, sport," Merry said.

It was good to see the little guy smile. He was usually so solemn that she often wondered if Sean had the heart of a little, old man. But then his young life had taken more hits than normal.

"How about that one?" Peter asked, pointing at a tree ahead of them. It was lightly dusted with snow and looked just beautiful.

"Nope," Sean said. "Too short."

"Hey, it's taller than I am."

"Grandma says you're always getting trees that are too short. She said they look like little midgets when you bring them into the house."

"What does Grandma know?" Peter asked.

"She knows everything."

"Oh, yeah?"

"Yeah."

Merry smiled at the byplay between father and son, but refused to let it touch her. Peter was an adult; he could run his life the way he wanted. She didn't have any right to agree or disagree. And it wasn't as if Sean were being mistreated.

She looked around her at the acres of evergreen trees covering the gently rolling hills and inhaled the wonderful scent of pine needles. The air was brisk and sharp; there was the promise of more snow in the wings. She should treasure this time as an interlude of peace.

"What do you say?" Peter asked her. "Is this tree too small or not?"

She suddenly found both sets of eyes on her and turned back to the tree. If she agreed it was a good choice, the time out here would soon be over. "Let's look at a few more."

Peter made a low growling sound.

She patted his arm. It was the first time she chanced a playful gesture since they had argued, and she felt a comforting rush of familiarity. "Your mother said the tree goes in the living room," she said. "And you've got a nine-or ten-foot ceiling there."

"Ha, ha, Daddy." Sean obviously took it as his victory.

"You want to get dumped on your head?"

The boy squealed in mock fear as he squeezed his arms tighter around Peter's neck. Merry laughed as they walked along, the joy of Christmas swallowing her up. She was right to have pulled back, to have recognized that her heart was becoming just a little too attached to Peter, but she was wrong to have let her hurt over losing Jason spill out into anger.

"How about this one?" Peter asked.

"Too skinny," Sean cried, making a face.

"That one?"

"Too crooked," Merry said.

She'd never put much thought into a tree before. Back home, the boys would go out and get one a few days before Christmas; then they'd all decorate it with colored paper and pictures cut out of magazines. But now, for this Christmas, the perfect tree seemed of real importance. As if it would somehow heal all their hurts and make them whole again.

Suddenly Merry saw it. "This one. Let's take this one."

"Yeah," Sean shouted in agreement.

"You guys sure?" Peter asked. "I mean, it's shorter than the pyramids."

She and Sean just exchanged glances and secret smiles.

"Okay, okay." Peter let Sean slide to the ground. "I was just asking." He took the tools from Merry and prepared to notch the tree trunk.

"Dad, no," Sean cried. "We got to talk to it first."

Suddenly Peter's holiday joy vanished like a rabbit in the brush. Darkness seemed to hover over him. "That's okay, Sean," he said softly. "We don't have to always do everything the same."

"Yeah, we do. What if it's not ready? Then it'll be sad all Christmas."

"Sean, please."

The boy turned toward Merry, his eyes were watery, his smile gone. "My mother always talked to the tree before we cut it down. She told it all about Christmas. And she told it how it would make everyone happy by coming into our house. She said only a happy tree was a good Christmas tree."

Merry didn't know what to say. It was obvious that Sean's holiday joy rested on a very fragile foundation.

"Come on, Sean," Peter said softly. "Things change."

"My Mommy died," Sean said, still talking to Merry.

"Yes, I know," Merry murmured. She stooped down to be at his eye level. "Your dad told me."

"I bet she's already talked to this tree," Peter said.

Sean turned to him, a flicker of hope just barely visible in his eye. "How do you know? Did she tell you she did?"

Peter hesitated, obviously not comfortable with the little white lie.

"She doesn't talk to me, either," Sean said, the flicker of hope gone. His voice was lifeless as he turned toward Merry again. "Grandma says that Mommy lives on a star."

Merry just nodded and took his little hand in hers.

"She says that I can talk to her. And she says that Mommy'll talk back to me." He looked down at the ground and shivered. "She says I gotta listen real hard."

"Come on, Sean." Peter's voice was almost a whisper, pain spilling out over them all. "Let me cut the tree and we'll get on home. Grandma has cookies and hot chocolate waiting for us."

"I listen hard." Sean was either ignoring Peter or not hearing him. "Real hard but—"

"I'll talk to the tree," Merry said.

The words just burst out of her mouth, but there was no way she was going to pull them back. If talking to a tree was going to ease this pain just a tiny bit, it was an easy price to pay.

"But are you a mommy?" Sean stared at her. His eyes were two sparkling bubbles of hope floating in a sea of doubt. "Only mommies can talk to trees."

There was no other way around the task at hand. "Yeah, sport," she said softly. "I'm a mommy."

His smile was like the sun popping through a break in the clouds. Merry closed her own eyes for a moment.

"Okay, guys," she said, stepping up to the tree. "Here goes nothing."

"You don't have to talk too long," Sean warned her.

"Right, sport," Merry replied. "We don't want the cookies and hot chocolate spoiling. Do we?"

Sean just grinned, looking suddenly like a regular little boy. Maybe there was such a thing as magic. She turned to the tree, staring hard at it, but couldn't think of what to say.

"Well, Mr. Tree, the holidays are upon us and the Mac-Allisters here are in need of a Christmas tree. Are you willing?"

The three of them stared at the tree and waited. No answer was forthcoming.

"The cookies are all baked and most of the presents are wrapped, along with some presents for poorer folks. There's gonna be a whole passel of folks over the next week or so and we'd be mighty honored to have you visit us for a spell." Merry looked down at Sean.

He nodded. "I think the tree wants to come to our house now, Daddy."

With just a slight nod of his head, Peter notched the tree, then they each took a turn at the saw. Once the tree was down, they carried it to the car and tied it to the roof.

Nobody talked much on the way home. Sean dozed, leaning against Merry while she sat with her arm around him, staring ahead. After stopping the car at a stoplight, Peter just turned to smile at her. There was so much in his glance—gratitude, joy and even a little sadness. She reached for his hand and squeezed it. It had been a special time.

He leaned over then, kissing her with the briefest of touches. So many emotions raced through her that she couldn't begin to sort out her feelings. An exquisite kind of joy tried to drown out the confusion and pain, the loneliness and wondering. For the moment, she let her soul be wreathed in sunshine.

"This is Rudolph," Sean said, holding aloft a reindeer ornament made out of clothespins. "I made him in school."

"Hey, he's pretty super," Merry said. "Where should he go?"

"Near Santa."

Sean tried to hang the ornament's loop over a branch, but his little fingers had trouble and Merry had to help him. His eyes were so solemn, his mouth so determined that she just wanted to hug him to pieces.

"Don't put too many ornaments on yet," Peter warned. "Let me get the lights up right first."

"But Merry can't wait, Daddy," Sean said. "You gotta hurry."

"Merry can't wait?"

Peter's eyes met hers in laughter, and a wonderful, warm sensation coursed through her. All the more special because of its rarity as of late. There had been so much anger, so much misunderstanding between them; it was nice to share a smile.

She wished she could sort through the mess and find the friendship they'd had. Why couldn't things be simple? Why couldn't life be simple?

"Are they done yet?" Sean pestered.

Peter started, as if suddenly awoken, and quickly went back to stringing the lights. Merry grinned. Trust a little kid to keep things moving. She suddenly saw Jason at that age, saw his impatience and his eagerness as Joe would have put the lights on their tree. But someone else helped his little fingers with the hanging loops, not her.

She closed her eyes in sudden pain. She had a real face to put into her dreams now, and it brought a real pain along with it. Her imaginings were more substantial, and so was the hurt.

"All right. Flick the switch."

Sean raced to the corner, climbing into the chair, and turned the lights on. The room was bathed with a magical glow.

"Aw, right," the little boy said on a sigh. "It's boo-ti-ful."

There was so much wonder and awe in his eyes. What was it like to be so young and so full of dreams? To believe that anything and everything was possible? Yet he'd been touched by tragedy in his young life. Maybe you had to be young to be able to escape its shadow.

"I think we've got some ornament hanging to do," Merry said. She lifted him off the chair. "And I bet it's gonna look even more boo-ti-ful then."

"Yeah." Sean raced over to the boxes spread out on the coffee table and carefully lifted out a snowman.

"My goodness, you've all been working really hard." Mrs. MacAllister came into the room with a plate of cookies. "I brought a snack in case you were hungry, and me in case you needed some more help."

"I'm going to put Frosty on," Sean announced, holding up his ornament.

"Well, I should hope so. Can't be Christmas without him up

there.'' The older woman joined Sean at the tree, helping him decide just where the snowman should go. "How about here?"

"I want him way, way up high."

"Oh, do you?" Peter said with a laugh. "Good thing we've got a tall tree then.'' He took the boy in his arms and helped him hang the ornament near the top.

Merry watched the three of them, not more than ten feet from her, but feeling a lifetime away. There was so much love here, it hurt. She could walk over to Peter's other side and he'd put his arm around her, partly out of pretense, partly out of friendship. She could pretend to be a part of their love for a time, if she wanted. She could close her memory to the deal she and Peter had struck and have a real Christmas. But her feet wouldn't take her in that direction.

Instead, she went silently over to the sofa and sat looking at the ornaments, pretending that the colored balls and smiling elves were fascinating. In truth, she barely saw them. She was a fool to have come with Peter over Thanksgiving; she was a double fool to have come back over Christmas.

All this was was a reminder of what she had lost and what she would never have. It was so tempting to pretend to be part of it, but she wasn't and never would be. The longer she pretended, the greater the risk that she'd forget it was all pretense. The greater the risk that it would stop being pretense for her.

Jason was her goal, her life. Peter was a job.

"I really appreciate what you did earlier."

She looked up, finding Peter at her side. There was a seriousness in his eyes that bothered her. She felt vulnerable at the moment, weakened by the emotions set in play by the day, and chose to misunderstand rather than let him venture into forbidden ground.

"That's okay," she joked. "Sitting at a desk all week probably causes you to lose muscle tone real quick."

"I didn't mean your help in cutting down the tree," he said. "I meant how you helped with Sean."

Her gaze skittered away, avoiding his, but she said nothing.

"Besides, I exercise three times a week at the health club in my building."

"Glad to hear that, sport." She flicked the words out like dimes to a beggar, not even looking at him. You said your piece, now go, she silently told him. Leave me alone to repair the chinks in my wall.

"He really settled down after you talked to him," Peter said.

She glanced at him briefly. Don't say anything else, she pleaded. Just drop the whole thing.

"Especially when you told him you were a mommy so you could talk to the tree. He's too young to realize the incongruity of it all."

What? Her heart stopped. What was incongruous about her being a mother? She looked away, sudden secret tears burning in the back of her eyes. She would have been a good mother, in terms of love and caring, even if she'd had no money for bikes or fancy clothes. The suggestion she wouldn't have been a good one stung, and she wanted to strike back.

"It seemed the right direction for the script to take," she said, her voice distant and unemotional. "I hadn't planned for the role to be involved, but there's nothing I won't do to make my character more convincing."

He seemed stunned by her sudden harshness. "I'm sorry," he said. "If I'd realized the role would demand so much of you, I would have paid you more. As a matter of fact, we could still renegotiate the contract."

She'd had all she could take of his trampling all over her pain, however well-meaning it might be. "Stuff it," she said and turned on her heels, stalking off to the kitchen.

Chapter Eleven

Peter slumped against the frame of the wide double doors leading into the living room. Traditions ruled his mother's life, but the holidays were especially intense in that regard. The day before Christmas Eve she always invited the neighbors over for cookies and nonalcoholic punch.

His arm was tired from carrying a half glass of punch around all evening, but if he didn't do that, someone would be shoving food and drink in his face.

"Sure is a purty little filly," said their neighbor from across the street. Herb Janisek had gone to grade school with Peter's father, and speaking his mind was the one thing he did best these days. "Got that big smile, pert as a new puppy and sharp as a whip."

Peter didn't ask who Herb was talking about. Merry had charmed the whole county. Charmed him, too, to a certain extent, even though he knew this was all a game.

"Too many fillies today, they ain't nothin' but skin and bones. Got no grit or bottom to them. Can't carry their share of the load."

Merry sure carried her share, maybe more than her share.

When she decided to settle down, some guy would be damned lucky. The thought ate at him for some reason.

"Daddy." Sean was tugging at Peter's sweater. "Daddy, can I have another cookie?"

"Sure."

Herb patted Sean on the head. "You're getting to be quite the young man," he said. "We're all gonna miss you when you go back to live with your dad."

"Oh, Sean loves it here. I don't expect him to be going for quite a while." Peter smiled at his son. "Just one cookie, kiddo. It's almost your bedtime."

Sean left as Herb's daughter came over to take his arm. "We should be getting on home, Pop."

"Here's the warden," Mr. Janisek growled. "She don't want me chasing no wild women."

"I had a chat with Merry," the woman told Peter. "She's a real nice person. And so funny. She must know a million jokes."

Funny? It seemed to him lately that Merry was having a hard time living up to her name. His eyes strayed over to the far corner and found her. A new set of neighbors surrounded her, and her smile was still stretched from coast to coast, but even at this distance Peter could sense a sadness in her eyes.

What had happened that afternoon? All he'd done was try to thank her for going above and beyond the call of duty to make Sean happy. He had replayed his words over and over in his mind and couldn't figure out what he'd said to offend her. But offend her he had, and most royally so. She'd barely said two words to him since then.

Some older woman had moved on to Merry, and Peter's conscience nipped at him. She had been alone long enough. It was time for him to go over to her side and lend a helping hand, pretend that they were a couple. As Herb and his daughter left, Peter walked across the room.

"Hi," he said as he came on Merry. "How you holding up?"

"Just fine, sport. Just fine."

"What's with the 'sport' bit? Forget my name again?" His words were a gentle teasing, but she didn't respond.

At least, she didn't send him on his way. That could be because she was surrounded by their guests, though, not because of any warmer feelings on her part. He decided not to quibble over reasons, but to accept the gifts when the gods chose to bestow them. He sat on the arm of her chair, putting his arm around her shoulders.

"Can I get you anything? More punch? Some cookies?"

"No, I'm fine, but I think your mom might need some help. She told me she didn't, but you know how she is."

So much for not sending him on his way. He got to his feet. "I'll check on her."

Merry went right back to the conversation she'd been in the middle of, apparently not about to miss him in the slightest. But that's how it should be, he reminded himself as he went to the kitchen.

"Hi, Mom. Need any help?"

His mother didn't look up, but went on arranging some cookies on a plate. "You two been arguing? Merry was in here no more than two minutes ago, all by herself, looking to be helpful."

"We're just very helpful people," Peter said.

She made a face and looked at him sharply. "What are you two arguing about?"

"We're not arguing, Mom. Honest." How could they argue when they were barely talking to each other?

"You're a lucky man, Peter."

"Yeah, I suppose I am." He started putting sugar-coated crescents on another plate.

"Suppose nothing," his mother snapped. "You got your health, a beautiful little boy and now you have a fine lady."

"Sorry about the phrasing, Mom." He reached across her for the can of cherry-topped butter cookies. "I was just trying to be cool."

"You be careful you stay cool and don't cross over into cold."

Peter fought desperately to hold on to his smile. The only crossover problem he could see was in this conversation. It was moving into an area filled with mines. Even stepping carefully might not be enough to keep him safe.

"Sometimes people who've spent a good bit of their time swimming in a river of pain forget that." His mother's face hardened a bit. "Of course, talking to machines all day doesn't help any."

"Mom," he protested softly. "I don't talk to machines. I use computers in my work. There's a big difference, you know."

"She's been good for you, Peter."

Good for him? Why wasn't he sleeping, then? Why was he mad and irritable all the time? All he needed to top off his life at the moment was the plague. He opened the can of jam puffs.

"You've changed," his mother said. "You're gentler, more personable, more approachable. Your lady's worked her magic on you."

"Yep, that certainly describes her. Merry the Magician."

His mother took the can from his hands. "Go out and find your lady. Kiss and make up," his mother said. "That's the fun part of an argument."

"We're not arguing, Mom."

"So what? Is there a law that says you have to be mad at each other before you can kiss and make up?"

His mother grabbed him by the arm and dragged him to the door leading into the dining room. She looked over the holiday crowd filling their living and dining rooms with the air of Christmas cheer.

"Ahh, there she is," his mother exclaimed.

He saw Merry at the same time his mother did. She had moved and was now talking to one of the younger couples from the neighborhood.

"You'd better get out there and keep her entertained," his mother warned. "You don't and someone'll come along and snatch her on up. Then you'll be left with nothing."

Maybe he was happy with his nothing. "Have a heart, Mom. I spent a good part of the day tramping around the hills and cutting down a tree. All that fresh air and exercise is making me sleepy. I'm not up to entertaining. I need some shut-eye."

"Sounds to me like you need a little more excitement in your life. Get over there and give Merry a hug," his mother said. "That should set your blood to racing."

"Mom."

"That's if you don't let all those numbers get in the way of your normal male emotions."

"Thanks, Mom."

"Peter."

"I'm going," he snapped. "I'm going."

Peter moved slowly across the room toward Merry. His feet felt like lead and he was extra polite in moving around people. If he played his cards right, he shouldn't reach Merry until late tomorrow. That would keep away the pain of interacting with her. But not the pain of being away from her.

Damned if he did and damned if he didn't. Between a rock and a hard place. Right smack dab in the middle of cliché heaven.

As he got closer, Peter could see Merry was still wearing her mismatched combo of a broad smile and sad eyes. Her speech and hands appeared animated, but there were tiny lines of fatigue around her eyes and mouth.

What in the world was wrong with her tonight? She had seemed fine when they'd gotten the tree, and she'd been lively and funny as they'd decorated it. Her mood swings were totally baffling to him.

"How you doing?" Peter asked softly when he finally reached her side.

"Hey, sport." Her voice was loud and full of seasonal joviality. She threw an arm around his shoulders. "Where you been?"

Now what? Obviously, she was adding a new dimension to the part she was playing. "I've been around," he said.

"Didn't notice you." She turned, laughing to the couple in front of her. "He's such a quiet little feller," she said. "I swear, I'm going to put a string of those little bells on him. That way I'll always know where he's at."

The young couple—he thought their name was Barton—stood and grinned at him. He wondered if their smiles would stay in place if he banged their heads together.

"Yeah, that's me. Quiet Peter."

It didn't have much of a ring to it, but it was the best he could do on short notice. He wondered if Merry was a tad tipsy. His mother's punch was nonalcoholic, but he knew that some of the neighbors brought their own liquid pepper to spice up their drinks.

"Hey, Peter," Merry said. "The Bartons here and some of

their friends are going to the VFW hall in Warsaw after this. Let's go with.''

''Mom will need help cleaning up.''

''I know that.''

A slight frown creased Merry's forehead, and he wasn't sure what her eyes were saying. What he was sure of was the message her body was sending. Young, alive, vibrant.

''But we're all going to pitch in. Then us young'uns will head for Warsaw and the old folks will head for home.''

That glint in her eyes was a challenge. They were asking which group he placed himself in. He thought briefly of dragging her upstairs to her room and giving her a personal demonstration. He turned his smile up a notch or two.

''We can stay here and have a private party.''

Merry didn't even blink. ''I want to stomp and holler,'' she said. ''That wouldn't be fair to your Momma or Sean. There's no reason for them to stay up unless they want to.''

''All right,'' he said. ''I'll go with you. But only after the house is all cleaned up.''

''Hot dog!'' Merry kissed him hard on the mouth, sending shivers of excitement down his spine. ''And I'll promise your momma that I'll look after you, like a good little bodyguard.''

Peter was all set to kiss her back, just as hard, just as rough, to try to stir up some response in her, but he remembered the Bartons. Glancing from the corner of his eye, he saw that they were still there, big grins on their faces. He settled for a squeeze of her waist.

''I can take care of myself,'' he murmured.

Merry stared at him, deep blue eyes showing just the hint of mystery. He had no idea what was in her mind, but it didn't seem to matter, compared to the raging hunger for her that swept over him.

She was so beautiful, so vibrant. He ached with the desire to hold her. Yet even as he felt ready to drown in that hunger, other needs pushed themselves forward. The need for tenderness, for softness, for humor. The whole range of human emotions, all of which had been satisfied at one time or another by Merry.

Damn. He was in too deep. No matter how deep the abyss, he knew he'd better run.

* * *

Merry gazed around the VFW hall with a frown. Like homes all over Mentone, the hall was fully saturated with the holiday atmosphere, but there sure were differences from the Mac-Allister house.

Both places had had Christmas carols playing in the background and groups of happy people. But the music at Peter's mother's house had been traditional; the conversation, soft. Here the carols were definitely modern and mocking and warred with loud laughter and chatter for dominance.

Trouble was, none of it was loud enough to drown out her thoughts.

This whole thing was a mess. She couldn't cope with any of it anymore—not with Peter's touch, not with Sean's eyes, not with Jason's grin. She grimaced at the empty glass in her hand. How many of these would she have to drink before it brought strength? Obviously more than she'd had already.

"Merry, I think we should talk," Peter said.

Why? Her life was filled with talk. She suddenly wanted action. She wanted to be held and cherished, to feel as if she belonged to someone, even if only for a few minutes. "I want to dance."

"We can dance later, after we talk."

Merry shook her head. "Uh-uh."

"Why not?"

"We'll just get into an argument."

"There's no reason for us to argue."

"Good." She threw her arms around his neck and leaned heavily against him. Why wouldn't he dance with her? Didn't he find her attractive? He had once, but maybe he was regretting that.

"Let's dance," she repeated.

"Merry." He pulled her arms down but kept his arm around her shoulders. "We had some problems and—"

"Not with everything," she said, laughing low and husky in her throat.

"I'd like us to get to know each other better," he said.

What for? Neither of them was looking for a commitment. All she wanted was some tenderness for an evening. She drew back out of his arms and stuck her hand out. "Hi, I'm Merry Roberts."

"I know that," he said evenly.

"Well," she said. "There you go. Aren't you glad we got that taken care of?"

"Merry."

"If you're not willing to dance with me, I'm going to throw you on the floor and stomp you until you are."

He got slowly to his feet. "Hard to refuse an offer like that."

"Momma always told me that a body could catch more flies with honey than vinegar." She got up also, running her fingertips along his cheek. "Although, I don't know what a body would want with a bunch of flies. They're such dirty things."

"'Lead on, Macduff,'" he said, taking her hand and nodding toward the open lane to the dance floor that lay beyond her.

She didn't move, though. "What's that mean?" she asked. "My name's not Macduff."

"It's a quote from *Macbeth*," he said. Moving beyond her, he led her through the tables to the dance floor.

"Oh." She felt really stupid all of sudden for not knowing. The gap between her and Peter loomed large and uncrossable.

He turned to take her in his arms once he reached the dance floor. It should have felt great. It was what she'd been waiting for all evening, for days, actually, but now it felt lousy.

They swayed slowly to the sensuous beat of a wailing Christmas love song, but she felt as out of place as a worn sneaker at Cinderella's ball. Peter's arms were so strong and safe, but they weren't holding the real her. They were holding the pretend her, the fake Merry that she'd made up. Not the one who'd grown up dirt-poor, who'd had herself a baby before she had a high-school diploma and who'd scrambled for years to find a new person to be.

The pretend Merry would know who Shakespeare was. The real Merry only knew milk shakes, how to shake a stick and how to shake, rattle and roll. A sour taste rose from her stomach. She missed a step and landed on Peter's foot.

"Sorry," she said. "Maybe dancing wasn't a great idea. Too many people out here."

"It's not that crowded," he said, pulling her a little closer.

His embrace should have melted the resistance in her, made her heart soar, but it only made the pain grow. She was a fraud. She had no right to be here. This wasn't part of their bargain.

She'd been lonely and morose and looking for something she had no business wanting. Funny, how fate put you back in your place when you stepped out of line.

"Why'd you get so upset this afternoon when I tried to thank you for helping Sean?" he asked.

"I wasn't upset," she lied. "I guess I was self-conscious."

"Come on, I can't believe you've been self-conscious for one second in your life."

"Shows how much you know."

"Then tell me," he said. "Tell me who the real Merry Roberts is."

"What you see is what you get," she said with a grin that was meant to disarm him.

He didn't seem to notice. "Why won't you confide in me?"

She bumped into another couple and stopped dancing. "Hey, this isn't working. Why don't we try the bar instead? I could use another drink."

"Why don't we go on home?" he suggested. "I'm tired of crowds."

Without a crowd, what would she hide behind when his questions came too close to dangerous ground? "Are you kidding? This is the most fun I've had since I came to this little burg. If you're going to force me to stay out here in the sticks for another two weeks, at least let me have tonight."

He looked as if she'd walloped him a good one. His hands dropped from her, leaving her prey for the cold winds of loneliness to find. His eyes made the wintry winds outside seem downright tropical.

"I certainly wouldn't want to stand in the way of you having a good time," he said stiffly.

She had no idea why she'd said what she had, but she wasn't surprised that it had made her feel no better. Sometimes she just had a perverse way of knowing best how to kill any chance of joy rising in her heart.

Sometimes it was for the best, though, and this was one of those times.

Merry sat up in bed, looking about. She thought she'd heard an animal cry. Was it a dream or was it real?

Blinking, she slowly returned from the land of the living dead and saw that she was in a bedroom. Ah, she thought, as individual brain cells exploded in slow motion. The room that had been Mrs. MacAllister's sewing room. The one that shared the bathroom with Peter. Again, the animal sound rippled through the room. This time recognition replaced fear.

"Sorry, Zach."

The old cat, apparently disoriented, was wandering about the room, softly bumping into furniture. Once he heard her voice, Zachary turned his head in her direction and scolded her again.

"All right," Merry said, swinging her feet to the floor. "All right."

She'd meant to to get right up, but her body wasn't up to the good intentions of her spirit. The room spun and it took some doing to get her feet firmly planted.

"Oh, Zachary," she moaned. "I've got me a whamdoozer of a headache."

The old cat just muttered, probably expressing how little he cared.

"I know it's my fault, and I'm not looking for sympathy. I'm just explaining the situation to you."

Her head's mild protest turned into violent objections as she bent down to pick up the old cat. He grumbled about her clumsy efforts.

"Don't complain," she growled as she hauled him to the bathroom. "If you don't like how I do things, then go ahead and fire me."

Merry watched Zachary as he got carefully out of his litter box, shaking each foot in turn before bumping his way to his water dish. The edges around the skinny old cat blurred as she stared at him, the tiny lapping of his tongue in the water echoing in the empty caverns of her mind.

Actually, there was no need for him to fire her. She was going to be gone soon, anyway. Wasn't anything Old Zach had to do about it. Her usefulness was coming to an end.

He growled that he was done, and Merry picked the old cat up and carried him to the bed. After placing him at the foot, Merry got into bed herself, leaning against the backboard, legs stretched out in front of her. Zachary indulged in some grumbling and spinning around before settling down against her feet.

"I don't know that I was all that useful, anyway, Zach."

Her mind's eye went back to the previous night and her emotions dipped even lower. She'd been into playing a party girl, hoping to get a rise out of Peter. Instead, she'd picked a fight with him. Well, not really a fight, since no angry words were exchanged, just hurt looks and then a real cold kind of distance came between them.

Fortunately, his mother and Sean had been asleep by the time they'd returned home. By then she'd drifted down to the depths of gloom and they'd quietly crept up to their rooms. Peter bade her a good-night, but he hadn't done anything else. Hadn't even given her a good-night peck on the cheek.

"Don't know why I'm moping, old fella. I wanted to be rid of him. And now I am, so why am I unhappy?"

Zachary flicked one of his scarred old ears.

Yeah, she thought, he didn't want to hear about it, either. The whole thing was just too dumb. Why in the world had she ever agreed to be Peter's pretend girlfriend? Should have told him to not let other folks run his life.

A bitter smile twisted her face as the pain twisted in her heart. Good advice. Why didn't she follow it herself? Why didn't she just admit to who she was, instead of playing a thousand different roles, all depending on who she was with.

Like that little gig with Peter's customers from Minneapolis. Sure, she'd fooled them, but what did that buy her? Nothing.

The pain in her heart became so severe that it almost brought tears to her eyes. It was bad enough fooling some strangers, but that was just fibbing. What was really bad was that she'd been fooling Peter all this time. That had been behind her weird behavior last night, a real discomfort at knowing she'd been lying to him all along.

It had been all right in the beginning. After all, he'd hired her to fool his momma. But somewhere along the line all her fibs had become lies. When? She wished she knew.

This time the tears did come. A single river from each eye, winding their way down her cheek like streams down the mountainsides.

She knew exactly when fibs became lies—when you started caring for a person.

"Damn, Zachary!" she exclaimed. "When am I ever going

to learn? A body would think that even a poor, dumb girl from the hills would know better than to make the exact same mistake twice.''

The old cat sat up and howled.

"What's the matter, old fella? My feet aren't cold, are they?" Merry looked at the clock by the bedside. It was past nine o'clock. "Are you hungry, old buddy?"

Zachary yowled again. Slipping her robe on over her flannel nightgown, Merry carried the cat downstairs and padded into the kitchen.

"Hello, dear," Mrs. MacAllister said. "Did Zachary wake you up?"

"No, ma'am. We just decided it was time for breakfast."

While Mrs. MacAllister opened a can of cat food, Merry poured herself a cup of coffee.

Once the older woman had the cat eating, she turned to Merry. "What can I fix you, dear?"

The idea of food was enough to start the world spinning again. "This is just fine for now," Merry said. "Where are the boys?"

"Peter went to the hardware store. Sean's someplace around. In the living room maybe."

The phone rang as she was speaking and she went to answer. It was obviously either an old friend or relative she hadn't seen recently, and rather than seem to be eavesdropping Merry took her coffee cup and wandered into the living room. Sean was sitting on the floor, staring at the Christmas tree. His whole being sang out dejection.

"Hey, sport, whatcha doing?" Merry sat down next to him, curling her bare feet up under her nightgown.

He turned to look at her, but only briefly. He turned back to the tree with a sigh. "Nothing."

"Doesn't seem like a happy nothing," she said, flicking a brass bell ornament. It had a high-pitched tinkly sound that hurt her head. Didn't do anything for Sean, either, so she didn't ask it for an encore.

"So what did you ask Santa to bring you?" Merry asked.

He shrugged. "Nothing."

She sipped at her coffee. "Nothing? Boy, Santa must like

you. You must be the only kid in the world who isn't bugging him for something.''

He didn't even crack a smile. ''There's no such thing as Santa, anyway.''

''You're saying there's no such thing as Santa on Christmas Eve?'' She was pretty inexperienced in this area, but she thought he was awfully young to have abandoned Santa. ''Who told you that?''

''Nobody,'' he said. ''I just know.''

His voice was so low and spiritless that Merry pulled him over into her lap. ''Okay,'' she said. ''Spill the beans, sport.''

The little boy leaned against her, seeking her strength. She closed her eyes against the hot tears that wanted to flow.

''It's 'cause of Daddy,'' he said slowly. ''What he said last night.''

''And what was that?''

He was silent a long moment, reaching down to play with her fingers, touching the red polish on her nails. ''I wrote this letter to Santa,'' he said. ''All I wanted was to go live with Daddy again like I used to.''

''It can't ever be like it was,'' she pointed out gently.

''I know Mommy's not coming back,'' he said, his voice cracking. ''But it could be kinda like it was. 'Cept Daddy told Mr. Janisek that I wasn't ever gonna live with him again. That I was staying here with Grandma forever.''

''I see.''

''So it didn't matter what I wrote to Santa. Daddy said I wasn't going home.''

Merry wrapped her arms around him, pulling him close while she rested her chin on his forehead. She could feel his little body quiver as he fought back tears. Jeez, what was she supposed to say? How did you tell a little kid that his father was hurting, too, and didn't know that it would hurt less if they were together?

You couldn't tell the kid anything. You had to tell the father. Which she had tried, a number of times.

''You know what I think, sport?'' She wiped away some of his tears with the end of her robe's belt. ''I think you've got a basic misunderstanding here.''

"Huh?" He was confused enough to stop crying and look up at her.

"What your dad says has nothing to do with what Santa does. You know, dads are just grown-up kids. They've got no idea what Santa's got planned for anybody."

"They don't?"

"Course not. How could they? Think Santa tells all his secrets? Not on your life."

"I thought daddies knew everything."

"Everything but Santa's plans." She smiled down at him. "And the other thing is, sometimes you ask for something really, really hard and it takes Santa a little longer to get it done."

"Is this really hard?"

"Not as hard as some things," she said. "But kinda hard. See, new sleds and bikes and stuff are a lot easier. He just tells the elves to make them and then he brings them. Something like going back to live with your dad is a lot trickier. He's got to have a special kind of magic to make it happen."

His depression came back to weigh him down. "There's no such thing as magic. Not really."

"No magic?" She pretended to be shocked and turned him around slightly to frown at him. "Hey, kiddo. Watch it. Magic's powerful stuff. You just got to know how to see it. If you look real close tomorrow on Christmas, I bet you'll see a sign from Santa telling you that the magic's coming and just to be patient."

His eyes reflected mostly skepticism, with just a tiny trace of hope. "Really?"

"Really." She'd make sure of it. No kid should think his dreams couldn't come true. And as for his wish, she'd do her damnedest to make that happen, too.

Sean turned even more, getting to his knees to face her. He put his arms around her neck and hugged her close. "I'm glad you came," he said. "I like you. You wanta come sledding with me and Daddy?"

"Sure, sport." She hugged him back as she tried to hide the sudden rush of tears. "I love sledding."

He sat back on his heels for a moment and regarded her. His face was solemn. "Is it a little girl or a boy?"

"Who?"

"Your kid."

She stared at him. Her heart sinking suddenly. What was she supposed to say? She'd never told anybody about Jason before, except her mother. Yet if she denied having a child, in Sean's eyes she would have lied. Her need for secrecy warred with Sean's need to trust.

"It's a boy," she said.

"How come he's not here? Does he live with his grandma like me?"

She swallowed hard. "He lives with his daddy and a different mommy."

"Oh." He thought for a long moment. "Don't you miss him?"

"Yes. Terribly."

His eyes were sad, sharing her hurt. "Did you ask Santa to let him live with you?"

If only it were that simple. "He's got a mommy and daddy who love him very much. I think he's happy where he is."

Sean didn't look convinced. "I still think you should ask Santa. Maybe there'll be enough magic for you."

She thought she should concentrate on the possible, not dream about the impossible.

Chapter Twelve

"Sure are a lot of folks here," Merry said.

Peter turned from the vista of rolling semiwooded hills to look at her. Eyes glowing, cheeks a rosy red, Merry radiated robust vitality and good health. She didn't appear to be suffering from the strange mood that had inhabited her yesterday or the effects of the alcohol she'd had.

Either would have been preferable. She was too dangerous as she was, brimming with life and good spirits. She made a person want to laugh and dance and sing out the joy of life. She made a man want to hold her, to feel her softness and know her warmth.

He frowned, instead, at the people around them. "Yeah," he grumbled. "The day before Christmas they ought be out doing their last-minute shopping."

They were at St. Patrick's, a county park up near the Indiana-Michigan border, and the three of them were standing in line, waiting for their turn to go down the tubing hill.

"Boy, you're a cheerful little feller," Merry said.

"Aren't you having fun, Dad?"

Peter looked down at his son's earnest face and pulled the

kid's stocking cap down over his eyes. "I'm having a ball, champ. Glad you brought me along."

"I can bring you along lotsa times," Sean replied, as he pushed his hat back up.

"That's good." Peter patted his son lightly on the back.

"He really means that," Merry pointed out, a sharp tone in her voice.

Peter glanced at her, slightly bewildered.

"Like every day," Merry said. "He'd like to take you places every day."

"But I'm not with him every day."

"You could be."

He sighed. "We've had this conversation before, haven't we?"

Merry just grinned at him. "No, not this exact one."

"The way it is is the best way," Peter said. He knew his voice sounded a bit impatient, but he didn't try to hide it.

"Best for who?"

"For everybody."

"Statistically speaking, I doubt that's possible," she said.

He would have laughed if he hadn't been on the verge of being annoyed.

"I mean, what are the chances that the best possible course of action for three people in a given situation would be exactly the same? I can see where it might be good for one, and okay for the others. Or even good for two and lousy for the other. But best for all three? How can what's best for you be what's best for Sean?"

"Give it a rest, will you?" he snapped, then conscious that Sean's eyes were on him, he smiled. "Almost our turn."

Thankfully Merry did drop it. "Who do you want to go down with this time, big guy?" she asked.

"I want to go with my dad," Sean replied. "But you two got to hold hands. Okay?"

"You got it," Merry answered.

They sat down in the huge inner tubes and Peter took Merry's hand. With a slight push from those behind them, they went zipping down the long, iced slope to the bottom of the hill. Sean squealed in excitement. Merry's face shone with a pure childlike joy. The bottom of the hill came up sooner than Peter wanted, and they coasted to a stop.

"Watch to see if anyone is coming behind us," Peter warned as Sean wiggled out of his lap.

"Nobody, Dad."

Peter stood up and helped Merry out of her tube. She lost her balance slightly while getting to her feet and fell against him. It was pure heaven for a moment, her body pressed against his. He wanted to hold her, to keep her with him always, but instead he just steadied her until she could stand.

He was suddenly struck by how life was like a day at the old tubing hill. There were moments of exhilaration, squeezed in between long periods of trudging to get to the top of the hill. Then there were times, like with Kelly, when you couldn't hold on anymore and your partner drifted off to where you couldn't follow her. Then everything changed.

Was Merry right? How could what was best for him also be best for Sean and his mother?

"Are you getting tired, Daddy?"

"He's not tired, honey," Merry said. "He's just getting old."

Peter didn't much care for the snicker in her voice, but she didn't look the least bit sheepish. Instead, she had on that mile-wide smile and her baby blues looked as inviting as a country pond on a hot day in July.

"Dad."

"Huh?" He looked down at Sean pulling at his hand.

"Whatcha doing, Dad?"

"I'm thinking." And he damn well wasn't going to say what he was thinking about.

Peter tried to keep his face inscrutable, but he could feel a frown building. Not wanting his son to think he was mad at him, Peter looked up toward the top of the hill. Figures snaked up the hill, looking like a movie rendition of laborers building the pyramids.

"I think those lines are getting kind of long," Peter said.

Sean looked solemn while Merry's grin just grew even brighter. Peter stared at her broad expanse of joy and told himself that he found it aggravating. For a moment, he considered what he might have done to those smiling lips if he and Merry had been alone. Smash them into submission with his own or rain kisses on them until they drowned.

"We've been here more than two hours, big guy," Merry said.

Sean put a hangdog expression on his face and nodded slowly. The kid was good. Obviously inspiring guilt feelings within your parents was a natural facility. Peter sure as heck hadn't taught him that.

"We can grab a bite to eat," Peter said.

"I get to pick?" his son asked.

Suppressing a smile, Peter nodded.

"I'll show you where it is," Sean said. "It's on the way home."

They turned in their tubes, then slogged their way to the car. Sean bounced ahead, while Peter and Merry walked hand in hand. Even with thick gloves on both their hands, he could feel the warmth of her radiating through. He could feel her heart beating, he was almost certain, and he could feel her energy.

Slow down, boy, he told himself. She had just come because she'd promised his mother and Sean. He shouldn't read things into her natural joy. He unlocked the car, and they all climbed in.

"We're not that far from Mentone, are we?" Merry asked. "They have a lot more snow here."

"Hope it doesn't get warm in the next twenty-four hours," Peter agreed as they drove from the park. "If it does, we won't have a white Christmas."

"Then Santa Claus will have to put wheels on his sled," Merry said.

"Ricky says there's no such thing as Santa," Sean said.

"And you let him get away with that?" Merry said, turning to grin wickedly at his son. "The last person who told me there was no Santa Claus is still in the hospital."

"He's been in the hospital a whole year?" Sean tried to make his voice tough, but there was too much uncertainty hanging onto his words.

"That's right," Merry replied.

From the image in the rearview mirror, Peter could see that his son wasn't fully accepting Merry's words, but he wasn't disputing them, either. He slouched back and stared out his side window.

Peter knew just how he felt, except the dilemma of Santa's existence wasn't what filled his thoughts. No, Merry was doing that quite nicely. He glanced her way, catching her gaze on him and feeling the warmth of her smile as potently as if she'd touched him. He turned back to the road.

What the hell was happening to him?

One minute he was ready to ship Merry packing back to Chicago for interfering. The next minute he could think of nothing but her smile. With just a joking word, she dissolved Sean's worries, knowing just what to say to erase the shadows that a five-year-old feared most.

What about his worries? He wasn't five, but thirty-five. Would she know what fears haunted him? Did he want her to?

"There it is."

Sean's sudden shout caused Peter to jump, but he chose not to say anything as he turned into the fast-food restaurant's parking lot. He was just hungry, that was all. An empty stomach always made his mind drift into strange areas.

"All right," Merry said as Peter took the box from the closet. "How do we do this?"

"You mean you've never put together a computer on Christmas Eve before? I thought I was getting experienced help."

"Watch it, buddy, or you'll need a bodyguard to protect you from your bodyguard."

He just laughed and laid the box in the middle of the living room floor. Merry pushed the furniture out of the way. There was such a rush of excitement coursing through her. She tried to tell herself it was because tomorrow was Christmas, but she knew it was something much more elemental than that. It was a hunger to be held, a need coursing through everyone to be needed.

"We just have to plug all this in and load the programs," Peter said, plugging the keyboard in. "Want to open that package of disks?"

"Wait a minute," she protested. "What do the directions say?"

"Directions?" He sat back on his heels. "Who reads directions?"

She just laughed and paged through the documentation. "I think I'd better. I didn't know I was dealing with someone who didn't know what went where."

Even as she said the words, Merry felt a delicious fire spread through her. She wasn't surprised when Peter was there at her side, pulling the direction sheet from her hands.

"So I don't know what goes where?" he said, his voice quiet and deadly.

A tension gripped the pit of her stomach, a wonderful tightening of her nerves that spread warmth over her soul. She looked up into his eyes, and that tension grew into hunger. Needs and longings all raced together to throw caution out the window.

"I don't know," she teased. "Do you?"

"Care for a demonstration?"

"Sure, I'm always willing to be proven wrong."

Peter'd been ready for her challenge and ready to meet her fire head on, for without any dancing about, she was in his arms. His touch was blazing, consuming everything. His lips devoured hers, his hands found every pulsating spot that awoke even deeper hungers in her.

It felt so good, so right. She didn't care about tomorrow or any of the silly things they'd said yesterday. She just wanted to be in his arms, to feel his longing match hers. The night was so silent. Her hungers so strong.

"Oh, Peter," she sighed, lying in his arms and longing for the night to never end. "I've never felt like this. Never knew it could be like this."

"It gets better," he vowed and smothered her lips with his.

There was no time for breathing, for thinking or dreaming. There was only now, only their hungers and the silent, empty night. His hands awoke a scorching need in her. Without words, they slipped out of their clothes and met again. Hunger to hunger. Need to need. Fire to fire.

They clung together—lips, then hands, then hearts. They were one with the stars and the night, soaring into the peaks, then floating down to earth, the voice of ecstasy still echoing in their ears.

* * *

The blind old cat stood up and growled at her.

"I'm sorry, Zachary," Merry said. "I'm just not up to sleeping."

He muttered something under his breath, and Merry felt her cheeks grow warm. Her body remembered Peter's warmth, but so did her mind.

"I know I should be all relaxed, but I'm not."

Still muttering, he turned in circles, trying to find a comfortable spot. Merry knew that she wasn't going to sleep for a while, so she sat up in bed.

"Here," she said, putting the old cat up by her pillow. "I got a spot all warmed up for you. I'll be back before it cools."

Zachary's words weren't very accepting, but Merry decided that that was the best she could do for the moment. She pulled the covers up over his skinny old body. All the poor old guy wanted was warmth.

After taking care of her feline roommate, Merry walked over to the window and looked out. It had started to flurry early that evening and now the flakes were getting larger. The weatherman had forecast a white Christmas for Mentone. She was happy to see that the promise was going to ring true.

A blurred image of Sean's solemn face floated up in the frosted edges of the window. Poor little guy. He was too young to have so many disappointments.

The picture outside her window blurred somewhat as she flipped through her scrapbook of Christmases past. There was never much, but she remembered how the excitement would build in the days before Christmas.

Bittersweet memories brought a lump to Merry's throat. There were times when she had just plain hated her momma. The woman couldn't keep her kids' daddies straight. But then there were other times when love would fill Merry's heart. Momma had always made sure every kid had something special on their birthday and Christmas. It wouldn't be anything expensive and was usually handmade, but it would be unique and individual.

In the end, the only measure of worth was how well a person did with what they had. The more years that passed, the higher the grade Merry found herself giving Momma.

She wasn't quite ready to lay aside the resentment she felt toward her mother, but Merry found she was getting closer.

Maybe it was because she was more and more conscious of her own inadequacies.

And the more she thought of them, the more inadequacies she discovered in herself.

Merry closed her eyes and leaned forward against the window, savoring the cool glass against her forehead. She was a triple-A, number-one fool. She had pretended to be so motivated, so focused, and what had she gone and done?

She had fallen in love with Peter.

It was such a mind-boggling example of her stupidity that she couldn't sit still. The room suddenly seemed confining, the walls closing in on her, suffocating her with the warmth and acceptance of the whole family. She had to get where she could breathe.

She pulled on a pair of sweatpants and a sweatshirt, then opened her door slowly. There were no sounds in the hallway. She tiptoed out. Belle came to the door of Sean's room and watched her.

Merry pressed her finger to her lips, as if the dog could understand her desire for silence, and crept down the stairs. Belle followed. By the backdoor, Merry slipped into her boots and coat, pulling her stocking cap over her hair before letting herself out. Belle whined softly.

"All right," Merry whispered. "But no barking, you hear?"

Belle raced out into the snowy night, frolicking like a puppy across the yard. Once Merry headed toward the front of the house, though, she raced along after her. The streets were all deserted. The night was all silence, the magic of the softly falling snow weaving a spell over the darkness.

"I'd never do this in Chicago," Merry told Belle. "Course, you'd never find a time when the streets were as empty as this."

Belle looked up, wagging her tail as if she agreed that Mentone was in every way superior to Chicago. Merry just stared ahead. Right now, she'd have to agree that Mentone was superior. In a few weeks, though, when Peter was back in Chicago, her opinion was quite likely to change.

Merry sighed as they headed toward the downtown area. "What the hell am I doing?" she asked the dog. "It doesn't matter where Peter is, since we are not going to be seeing each other by that time."

Belle didn't seem to have any answers and just raced across a lawn, nose down, plowing a path through the snow. Merry stopped to watch her, fighting back a smile at the dog's antics. Belle stopped, and catching Merry's gaze on her, wagged her tail.

"That's the goofiest thing I ever saw," Merry scolded. "All you do is end up with snow in your nose."

Merry sighed. "I know. I'm not one to talk. Snow on your nose melts. A crack in your heart takes a lot longer to heal." If it ever did.

They crossed the street and came to the giant egg. Its top was covered with a blanket of snow, but there was no denying it was a giant egg.

"An egg is an egg is an egg," she told the dog. After brushing the snow off the edge of a nearby planter, she sat down. "Do you know that even if you change into a bug, you're still the same person inside?"

Belle was more interested in sniffing around the base of the egg than discussing Kafka.

"So I guess that means that even if I'm in love with Peter, I'm still the same person I've always been. A liar."

There was no way her relationship with Peter could progress. No way at all. A relationship that wasn't based on mutual honesty was based on nothing.

"How do you think he'd feel about me if he knew everything?" she asked Belle. "Think he'd mind that I'd been lying all along?"

She got to her feet and brushed the snow from her butt. "What a stupid question, huh? Like asking a body if they minded being swindled."

They started back toward the house. The snow was already filling in their footprints. In another hour, no one would know they'd been out.

In a short time, Peter would forget she'd been in his life.

Chapter Thirteen

"I think you ought to get changed," Peter told Sean. "We should be leaving for Aunt Emma's soon."

"Aw, Dad," Sean moaned, but trudged toward the stairs, dragging his giant snake behind him.

Peter watched him with a smile, then put his arms around Merry. "You were right about little boys and snakes. He really loves that thing."

Merry smiled, or tried to smile. Her expression hung heavy with fatigue and there wasn't any sparkle in her eyes. "I'm glad."

"You all right?" he asked. She'd been quiet all morning, showing some enthusiasm when she opened the crystal egg he'd given her and the snowman sweatshirt from Sean. She even laughed aloud when she saw the furry chicken slippers his mother had given her, but somehow he'd known her heart wasn't in it.

"I'm just a little under the weather," Merry said.

"Can I get anything for you?"

Merry shook her head.

"You sure?"

"If there was anything you could do," she said, "you can be sure I'd tell you." Merry smiled up at him, a strangely mysterious smile, then pulled away.

He let her go, watching as she walked over to the sofa and sat down. His arms felt so empty and useless, but his heart felt even worse. There was something in the air that made him worried, frightened almost.

He watched her staring at the snow-draped Currier and Ives scene outside, a feeling of melancholy surrounding her. Maybe it was his silly imagination, but he could almost feel her drifting away from him. If she didn't look at him soon, she'd be too far away to ever get back.

"Is it something I've done?" he asked.

Merry turned slightly and gazed at him. Her eyes held such sadness. "It's nothing you did or didn't do, Peter." She went back to staring outside.

Peter sighed quietly. It wasn't anything he did or did not do. Hell. That didn't leave any room for maneuvering. In fact, it pretty much left him sitting out in the cold.

"Is there anything I can do to help?"

"Nope." She didn't even bother turning around to look at him.

Peter dropped his lanky frame into a chair. Hell's fire and damnation. Merry was a woman of many moods, but this one really scared the hell out of him. What was wrong?

Things had been wonderful last night. And not just for him. He would have sworn on a stack of Bibles that she'd felt that way, too. So what happened in between?

A good night's sleep, opening some presents and then breakfast.

"Peter." Merry had turned from the window and was facing him. "If you don't mind, I think I'll stay here today."

Panic suddenly clutched at his stomach. He didn't know what to say. He just knew that something was terribly wrong.

"I really don't feel all that good."

"Is it something you ate?" He asked, though he seriously doubted it.

"I don't know. I just have this terrible headache."

"Want me to stay with you?" Christmas dinners and family

parties had paled to insignificance compared to the fear consuming him.

"Heavens no," Merry said.

"Aren't you two ready yet?" His mother had stepped into the room.

"Merry's not going," Peter said.

"Oh?"

"I really don't feel well, ma'am."

"Oh, dear," his mother murmured. "Maybe one of us should stay here with you."

"Oh, no. You can't." For the briefest of moments, panic seemed to take its turn on her face. "I mean, Christmas is for families. Dinners and stuff like that. I'd feel just awful if you missed that because of me."

His mother looked hard at her.

"And there's so much food in the house," Merry went on to explain. "I'll be just fine."

His mother's face softened. "The Millers down the street will be staying home today," she said. "I'll tell them to keep an eye on you."

"Oh, don't do that," Merry said. "I'm a big girl. I can take care of myself."

"Don't be so proud," his mother said. "A person can always use the help of another."

Merry looked down at the floor. Peter tried to steady his panicking heart. They needed to talk, to open up and be honest with each other. Whatever was so wrong, they would work it out. But how would he get her to believe that?

"Daddy," Sean called down the stairs. "I can't get my shirt right."

Peter sighed and glanced back at Merry, afraid if he took his eyes off of her she'd disappear.

"Can't Grandma help you?" he called up to Sean.

"Grandma's a girl," Sean said. "I've got a guy's shirt."

Peter bit off his irritation, or tried to. "I don't know what's with that kid lately," he grumbled. "I've got to do everything for him. He suddenly thinks his grandmother is totally incompetent."

"Oh, for heaven's sakes, Peter," Merry snapped. The anger

in her tone was obvious and heavy. "What's the big deal? You're hardly ever around for him, anyway."

Peter just stared at her—angry, hurt and more than a little confused. Where had all that come from? He wanted to demand she explain, demand that she stop shutting him out. But Merry looked more than ready for a fight. And his mother just looked hurt.

The hell with it, he decided. Then he turned and stomped up the stairs. It wasn't as though this was some kind of lasting relationship anyway.

Merry stood at the window a long time after Peter, his mother, Sean and even Belle had left for Aunt Emma's. The house was deathly silent. There was no more need for pretending happiness, and tears suddenly welled up, flowing down her cheeks. Sobs quickly followed.

There was so much pain and agony bottled up inside her. So many hopes that had been smothered. So many dreams that would never see the light of day. Peter, Jason, Sean. They were all part of some distant star that she could never reach. That she was stupid to have even been looking toward.

There was so much misery in her soul that Merry couldn't stop the crying even if she wanted to. And she didn't want to.

It wouldn't cleanse her, but maybe it would give her a moment of relief. Just a moment to be free of guilt and fear. Just a moment to not be haunted by memories. Images from the past that pulled and tore at her.

She should never have started any of this. It was like the Christmas Eve she and Cassie had peeked in the window of the mayor's house to see all the lights and ornaments and presents spread out. All it had done was made them dissatisfied with what they had at home. Showed them what life could hold, but never would. Momma'd told them they'd been stupid, that looking at what others had was like looking into the sun and would make you blind.

She'd been right.

Eons later the tears finally ended. Merry was drained, exhausted, sucked completely dry of all feeling. No good feelings, no bad feelings, just numb.

Although she knew it wouldn't last, she savored the moment of no pain. She looked out the window. The day was still cloudy and the snow covering the small, quiet street didn't look any fresher. Realistically, she knew that she'd been crying only a few minutes, but she felt as if she'd returned from another world and another time.

She turned and saw Sean's snake, curled up where he'd carefully left it under the tree once Peter had told him it was too big to take to Aunt Emma's. But instead of the plaid skin of the snake, she saw the hurt look in Sean's eyes when she'd said she wasn't going with them to dinner. It was for their own good, his and Peter's, that she was doing what she was doing, but that didn't make it any easier to bear.

Maybe she ought to stop moping about, then, and get it done.

She went to get the bag of silk roses and floral tape that she'd brought. Then, after putting on her coat and boots, she went outside.

The Christmas rosebush stood straight and tall just outside the kitchen door. Squatting down, she fastened her silk roses onto the bare branches. Her fingers got pricked by occasional thorns, but she almost relished the pain. Maybe if she used up enough, there wouldn't be any left in the air for Peter and Sean.

Once all the roses were attached to the bush, she sat back on her heels to look at the result. Not bad. Six red roses in full bloom amid the snow. Granny said that a body should always let things follow their own course, unless they weren't working out the way you wanted them to. The magic here just needed a little help.

Merry collected her things and went inside, up to her room. As usual, Zachary was sound asleep on the bed they had shared. His heart-shaped face, liberally covered with gray, rested in peaceful repose. Whatever dreams the old cat had, came from pleasant memories.

She bent down and kissed him on the head. "You take care of yourself, old feller."

Zachary's reply was a short grunt.

He grunted again when she put her suitcase on the bed, but that couldn't be helped. She had herself a train to catch and had to pack. Tears bubbled behind her eyes but Merry held them back, saving them. The trip to Chicago was a long one, and she'd need something to fill her time. Crying would do as well as anything.

"Peter," Aunt Emma said. "It's your neighbor, Joni Miller."

"Oh." There was a sinking feeling in his stomach. He knew that it was about Merry. It had to be.

"Joni said she'd talk to you or your mother."

"Sure, Emma." Peter struggled to put a smile on his lips. It felt as if he had an anvil hanging off each corner. "I'll take it."

He followed his aunt to the little den off the front door. The phone was on top of an old rolltop desk. Taking a deep breath, he picked up the receiver.

"Peter MacAllister."

"Peter? This is Joni Miller." Her voice was filled with concern. "Your Merry hired our Luke to drive her to the train in South Bend. They just left."

The heaviness in his heart told him it was what he had expected. "Yeah," he said slowly. "She has some things she has to take care of in Chicago. Family business."

"I didn't know she had family. Isn't she an only child and aren't her parents deceased?"

Lord, they couldn't have done better if they'd published Merry's bio in the *Akron-Mentone News*. Peter considered asking Joni if she knew Merry's shoe size, but he stayed polite like always.

"It's a distant cousin," he said. "An emergency came up."

"Oh, that's too bad. Your mother said Merry wasn't feeling well. So we were just keeping an eye on her."

"Thanks, Joni," Peter said. "Thanks a lot for your help."

They exchanged farewells, then Peter hung up. He stood there for a long moment, the murmur of voices steeped in holiday cheer hung around him like the rotting stench of a dead carcass. Turning quickly on his heel, Peter strode for the back door. He needed air.

There was no one out on the back porch, thankfully. He leaned his hands on the railing, staring out at the snow-covered backyard that sloped down into a cornfield. He could see for miles. Acre after acre of barren land, covered with a frozen blanket of snow. No life, no promise of warmth or sweet sunshine. Just like his tomorrows.

Damn Merry and her smile. Damn her laughing eyes and teasing voice that made him care.

He blinked away an unwanted wetness in his eyes and stood up. She bounced into his life with all sorts of promises, then when he started feeling alive again, she disappeared.

Damn her and the sunshine she'd brought.

Peter breathed a sigh of relief once they turned off Aunt Emma's property and onto the county road. It had taken them forever to get out the door what with all the kisses, wishes of happiness for the remainder of the holiday and the God-willing-see-you-next-years. If any more happiness touched him, he'd have barfed all over those damned happy relatives.

They rode in silence, his mother in the front with him, Sean dozing in back with Belle. When they came up on the south edge of town, over by the trailer park, Peter knew that he couldn't wait any longer. It wouldn't be right for them to go into an empty house when his mother and son were expecting otherwise. He cleared his throat.

"Merry left," he said softly.

He'd just wanted to tell his mother, hoping that Sean wouldn't hear. But his mother remained silent.

"Where did she go?" Sean asked. "How come she left?"

"She had to go back to Chicago."

"How come?"

Peter concentrated on crossing the railroad tracks. He'd lied once, he might as well do it again. "She had some family problems."

"I thought she said her mommy and daddy were dead."

Peter sighed quietly.

"Maybe she went to see her little boy," Sean said.

"Her little boy?" Peter's mother turned around to stare at Sean. "What little boy?"

"She doesn't have a son," Peter said.

"Don't you remember, Daddy? She said she could talk to the tree because she was a mommy."

Peter exchanged glances with his mother and shrugged.

"Kelly always talked to the tree before we cut it. We needed a mommy to do it this year."

His mother nodded and patted his hand. Peter had the feeling that Merry's leaving didn't come as a surprise to her, either. She must have had her suspicions when Merry announced herself ill. He should have let his mother fix him up with Daphne or Denise or whoever.

They were all quiet as he pulled the car into the garage. No one said a word as they got out of the car. Sean was leading the way to the house when he suddenly stopped. His mother gasped, and Peter pushed ahead, wondering what was wrong now.

"Oh, my goodness," his mother said. "That bush is blooming."

Peter's feet froze. There, up ahead in the soft glow from the outside door light, the Christmas rosebush was covered with flowers.

Sean walked slowly to the plant and gently touched a flower. "It's blooming!" he said, his voice filled with wonder. "It's magic, just like Merry said."

Peter found the ability to move had returned. "Merry couldn't make the roses bloom," he said impatiently and went over to the bush. He pulled at a flower. It came off, along with a piece of green tape. "It's not real."

Sean just ran over and grabbed the flower from his hand. "It is too real," he cried and tried to put the bloom back on the plant. "Merry made it real."

With a definite glare at Peter, his mother joined Sean at the bush, stooping down to put an arm around his thin shoulders. "Sometimes the real magic is finding somebody who loves you so much that they'll put silk flowers on an old rosebush," she told the boy.

Peter had heard enough. He unlocked the back door and went storming inside. She walked out on them, abandoned them all without a thought for their feelings, and yet she was some wonderful person who supposedly loved them all. Right.

Peter stomped through the house and up to his room. What about all they'd said last night? Had it all been a lie? Or just part of the pretense? Maybe he should find her and offer her a bonus for acting like she cared about him so convincingly. He slammed his door shut, noticing an envelope on his dresser as he did.

His heart fell into the pit of his stomach as he walked over to get it. His name was written on it in Merry's big, bold handwriting. He stared at it for the longest time, desperate to know what it said, but terrified to find out.

Finally he ripped open the back and took out the single sheet. Her words barely filled one side, not nearly enough to answer all the questions in his heart.

Dear Peter,

I'm sorry to be leaving without a word like this, but I thought it best. Things were getting out of hand, something neither of us wanted. We started out with the best of intentions, so I think it's best we return to them. Thanks for all the fun you showed me. Give your mom and Sean a big hug from me.

Love,
Merry

P.S. Sean is really hurting. He lost his mother and feels rejected by you. Find some way to keep him with you. Kelly died trying to find the perfect life for you two. Honor her memory by making your lives as perfect as you can. Together.
P.P.S. Give Belle and Zachary a big hug, too.

Peter read the letter, then read it again. What the hell did any of this mean? Just that she was tired of them all and had left. He crumpled the letter in his hand and threw it across the room.

He went over to the window to stare down at the backyard. Just below him he could see the stupid roses taped to a frozen rosebush. He wanted to close his eyes, to shut out the sight, but for some reason he couldn't.

Thank God, he hadn't fallen in love. All this escapade had done was prove to him that he was right to keep his heart protected. Right to stay as far from love as possible.

Chapter Fourteen

"Why do we have to go see Aunt Rosa anyway?" Sean's tone was pouty and he was hanging back, shuffling his feet as they they made their way to the car.

"Because she hurt her knee," Peter's mother said. "And she hasn't been able to get out much. And it's our Christian duty to visit the infirm."

"What's infirm?" Sean asked.

"Sick," Peter replied. "Those who are so sick or hurt that they can't do a lot of things for themselves."

His son glared at him, then took his grandmother's hand. He'd been that way, ignoring Peter whenever possible, since yesterday. Since Merry had left.

When they reached the car, he opened the back door for Sean. He was about to open the front for his mother when Sean paused and turned toward them.

"Can you sit back here with me, Grandma?"

"Certainly, dear."

Peter tried to hide his grimace as he watched his mother get into the back seat next to Sean. Great. Now his son was relegating him to the position of chauffeur. Peter didn't think it was a promotion, but the job sounded easier and the benefits appeared to be the same. He slammed the door shut on them, then walked around to the driver's side and got in himself.

"There was no need to slam the door like that," his mother said.

"Sorry," Peter murmured as he fastened his seat belt.

He really wasn't sorry. In fact, he was getting darn sick and tired of being the bad guy. Maybe he wasn't really the bad guy, but he certainly was the sandwich filling. Caught in between his elderly mother and his young son. It was a lose-lose situation no matter which of them he argued with.

Hell with it. He'd be back in Chicago soon. Alone, but at least no one would be bugging him, blaming him for everything bad that happened. Clenching his jaw, Peter put the car in reverse and began backing out of the driveway.

"What if Merry comes while we're gone?" Sean asked.

"She won't," Peter snapped. He spun out into the street, stopped, put the car in first and made his way down toward Main Street.

"How do you know?" Sean's voice was just as sharp as his own.

Surprisingly, Peter's mother made no move to correct the boy. When Peter looked up into the rearview mirror, he saw that she was looking at him, her blue eyes hard like cut glass.

"She has some family problems," Peter said. "Those kind of things aren't solved in a few minutes."

Now two sets of eyes stared at him. Hard eyes, almost disbelieving.

"She explained it all to me."

"Did she call?" Sean asked. "How come you didn't let me talk to her?"

"She didn't call," Peter said tiredly. "She left me a letter."

Neither of his back seat passengers replied, but Peter was happy to see that he made them blink. He turned his attention to the road before him.

The way to Aunt Rosa's farm was down a series of county blacktops, stretching out over the flat Indiana landscape like interconnected straight lines. None of the lines contained even the hint of a curve. They didn't require much attention and his passengers, sitting and staring out their respective windows, called for even less. His mind drifted. Drifted to Merry, her letter, Sean and the whole sorry state of Peter's existence.

What was he supposed to do about Sean? Did Sean want him to live in Mentone? Or did he want to come to Chicago to live with Peter? If his son agreed to come to Chicago, was he really able to understand what that meant? Even if Peter explained it to him, could his son conceive what it would be like living with a single parent?

The big question would be who would take care of Sean while Peter worked. Fortunately, his salary didn't make money a problem, but that still didn't help all that much. Should he hire a live-in nanny? Or would day care be better? But if he chose day care, what would happen when he had to travel?

Hell! He almost missed his turn and took a sharp left. Apparently, he took it a little too fast.

"I know I said Aunt Rosa wasn't well," his mother protested. "But I don't think she's at death's door."

"Sorry," Peter murmured.

"Even if she is, I don't know as we could do anything about it."

"I said I was sorry."

Cold icicles of anger filled the car. They each retreated to their own corner.

Maybe he should move back to Mentone. That way he could spend more time with Sean and his mother could still help care for the kid. His son wouldn't have to leave his friends and would still have the freedom he was used to.

Sean would lose a great deal if he moved in with Peter on Lake Shore Drive. Of course, they could move to the suburbs, but that wasn't all that much better. Peter's commuting time would go out of sight; he'd spend even less time with Sean. Plus, the suburbs were built around the automobile so Sean would still lose his freedom.

Hell's fire! Peter didn't see any kind of viable solution to the problem. And, although he didn't like to put Sean second, Peter didn't see a solution. The one that presently colored his whole world gray. That was loneliness.

He hated to admit it to himself, but even though he'd managed to avoid the snares of commitment, Merry and her mile-wide smile still haunted him.

Little things snuck into his thoughts at the strangest times. Her smile, her laughter, her eyes. He looked up and saw Tippecanoe Valley High School. The time he and Merry had gone to his cousin's basketball game.

Worst of all was the emptiness he felt. As if the very core of him were hollow and barren. His heart was gone, as was his soul. All that was left was just pain and desolation, rattling around inside. He tried to put aside his melancholy thoughts and read the announcement sign in front of the high school complex. Boys' basketball was in full swing.

"That's where Daddy went to school," his mother murmured in the back seat.

Sean's response was a grunt. The kid probably couldn't care less what Daddy did.

"He played baseball and basketball."

"Didn't he play football?"

"A little bit," his mother replied.

The snow-covered football field came up next. Peter'd always made the team and earned his share of bruises, but football had never been his game. Along with the bruises, most of which came during practice, Peter earned his share of splinters from riding the bench.

"Death Valley's all covered with snow," Sean said.

"What?" Peter screamed. His foot went out and hit the brakes. They began fishtailing all over the slippery road.

"Peter," his mother shouted. "What in the world are you doing?"

Trying to keep the car on the road, he wanted to shout back, but he didn't say anything. Because, first of all, the skidding was his fault. And secondly, it took all his skill and attention to keep them from sliding into a snowbank. He was finally able to ease the car to a stop. After putting it in neutral and locking the emergency brake, Peter turned around.

"Don't ever say something like that again," he said, glaring at his son.

Sean stared at him, bewildered.

"Peter," his mother said. "Have you lost whatever sense you were born with?"

"Death Valley isn't covered in snow," he said, speaking

slowly and carefully. "It never snows in Death Valley. It's usually the hottest spot in the whole United States."

Shaking his head, Sean turned to look out the window. "It's all covered with snow," he said, pointing at the football field.

Peter stared at the field.

"Land sakes," his mother said. "Everyone calls that field Death Valley. They have for the last ten years, at least."

"Yeah," Sean said. "'Cause our football teams play real good there."

"I didn't know that." Peter could feel a weakness waiting to fill his body. He gripped the steering wheel hard, trying to hold back all his unnameable fears. His words about love were not coming back to haunt him. "But, anyway, that's not the real Death Valley."

"Is that true, Grandma?"

"I don't know what your father means. Folks around here call it Death Valley, so Death Valley it is."

"But it's not the real one," Peter insisted.

"Just about every town in America has a Main Street," his mother said. "Does that mean only one of them is real and all the others are fake?"

"Mom, you just don't understand."

"You're absolutely right, Peter. I don't understand you."

He shook his head. She really didn't understand. It didn't snow in Death Valley. It couldn't snow in Death Valley. Death Valley was a hot, barren desert.

He had to get ahold of himself and get going. He slowly eased the car into gear. She just wouldn't understand. But it didn't matter. No matter what the folks around here called it, the Tippecanoe Valley High School football field wasn't the real Death Valley. It could be Death Valley to the high school's opponents but it didn't count anywhere else.

It didn't count where Fate was concerned. Or Love.

"Are you and Mr. Browder friends, Daddy?"

"Yeah, sort of." Peter quickly checked the total for their breakfast, then left three dollars for a tip. "We went to school together. But he's older, so we weren't in the same grade."

They walked over to the front of the pancake house, where a

short teenager with a long black ponytail and a big smile waited behind the register.

"Hi, Sean," she sang out loudly. "Is this your daddy?"

"Yeah."

"Hi, Mr. MacAllister," she said. "How was everything?"

"Just fine—" he paused to look at her name tag "—Wendy."

Peter paid his bill, then Wendy returned his change with a thank-you and an even brighter smile. Sean was already waiting at the door, so Peter nodded and turned away.

"Goodbye, Sean," Wendy said.

His son just hung his head and gave an offhanded wave over his shoulder.

"Do you know her?" Peter asked Sean as they walked to the car.

"Yeah. She's Robbie Hatfield's big sister." His son's tone definitely wasn't congenial. "She's always saying hi to me and stuff."

"She's just being friendly."

"I think she's got the hots for me."

Peter stared at his son for a moment, who was now shuffling along, kicking at ice chunks. He didn't know whether to laugh or be worried. Sean was growing up, though, that was for certain, and at a much faster rate than Peter had. If he weren't careful, he'd have no place at all in his son's life.

"I think she should chase older guys, don't you, Dad?"

"Ah, yeah. Definitely."

"Do you think you could talk to her?" Sean stood looking up at him, his hands on the door handle.

"Sure."

"Thanks, Dad."

Peter opened the door and held it while Sean hopped in. Then he fastened his son's seat belt before going around to the driver's side. Maybe it was time Sean and he lived together again. Maybe Merry was right.

Merry. Just thinking the name hurt. Though the hurt was there whether he thought it or not. It would just take practice putting it farther into the background of his thoughts.

Just as it took a little work to calm down after his shock about Death Valley yesterday. It was such a silly coincidence. How was he supposed to know the nickname of the high school's football field? It was laughable really. Peter headed toward the Browder's farm south of Mentone.

"Did you ever live on a farm, Dad?"

"No." Peter fastened his own seat belt. "I've always lived in the same house you do."

"Except now."

"Right, except now I live in Chicago." He turned on the motor and pulled out of the parking lot onto Route 30. A couple of wide-open miles passed before Sean spoke again.

"Farms are fun," he said. "But I like living in town better."

"They both have pluses and minuses."

"I like being able to walk to my friends' houses."

"You wouldn't be able to do that if you came to live with me."

Sean thought for a minute. "Are there kids where you live, Dad?"

"Some," Peter replied.

"Do they ever go outside and play?"

If an adult takes them. "Sometimes."

"Do they have subways in Chicago?"

"Sure." Peter glanced at his son and saw he was staring out the window. "You rode on one when you came to visit in the summer. Remember. We went on one to see the dinosaurs."

"Oh, yeah."

Oh, yeah. The words and tone sounded so easy. Was that really how Sean felt? Peter wished he could say the same about himself.

"Grandma will like it in Chicago."

"Grandma?"

"Yeah," Sean replied. "She'll like riding the subways. She doesn't like driving anymore."

"She doesn't?"

"Nope. She likes it when other people drive her."

Peter slumped down in the seat. Should he bring both of them to Chicago to live with him? Was his mother the one who needed care now? Even more than Sean? Should he hire someone to live with his mother?

Sean was staring out at the brown-and-white patterns of snow and dirt covering the fields on either side of them. "You know what I'd like best about Chicago?"

Peter shook his head. "What, champ?"

"I'd get to see Merry a whole lot."

"Merry? How—"

"Doesn't she live close to where you live?" Sean asked, his brow wrinkled in question. "She said she did."

Peter felt tired, so very tired. "Yeah, she does." So close, yet so far away. How did he explain that to his kid when he couldn't even explain it to himself? How, even though he lived a short walk from Merry, he couldn't even speak to her?

"There's Mr. Browder's farm," Sean shouted.

They turned up a narrow lane and pulled to a stop by a rambling farmhouse, as large dogs came charging out to greet them. Their barking brought Matt and a girl, probably one of his daughters, who looked a little older than Sean.

"Oh, oh," Sean said.

"What's the matter, champ?"

"That's Missy Browder. She's really mean."

"She is?"

"Yeah," Sean replied. "She'll kick you if you spit on her. I mean, really hard."

"Well, I guess I won't spit on her, then."

The words just spilled out and Peter wished he could retrieve them. No, he wished Merry had been here to hear the whole conversation. She would have thought it so funny. It was frightening just how much he missed her. But it would pass. Love might not, but attractions like he'd felt for her would. As long as it wasn't love, he would recover.

Sean was already out of the car and bouncing up the drive, shouting greetings at Missy as she shouted them back. Relieved that no one kicked or spit at the other, Peter released his seat belt and eased himself out.

"Hey, old buddy," Matt said heartily. "How ya been?"

"Fine," Peter answered, trying to match Matt in joviality. "Yourself?"

"Fit as an old boar hog."

"One of our pigs is going to California," Missy said, jumping up and down.

"He is not," Sean said.

"Is so," Missy replied.

"How's he gonna get there?" Sean asked.

"He's gonna fly, nerdface."

Fear exploded in the pit of Peter's stomach, but he told himself he was just being silly. Overly sensitive. The mention of pigs flying the day after the snow in Death Valley was just a coincidence. Another thing he'd laugh about some day.

"Pigs can't fly," Sean said.

That's right. You tell 'em, Peter thought.

Matt leaned down, putting his arm around Sean's shoulders. "Sure they can, little buddy," he said. "They can fly just as good as you and I."

Sean stared at him. So did Peter, his stomach lurching in sudden disagreement.

"They fly in an airplane, dummy," Missy said. "But that's still a pig flying."

Peter could taste his apple pancake souring in his stomach. No, it didn't mean anything. Not one damn thing.

"Missy," Matt said. "Why don't you take Sean and show him our little traveler?"

The two kids went racing off down to the pig sheds while Peter just stood there by the car.

"Peter?" Matt was staring at him. "You don't look too good, old buddy. What you been doing? Hitting all the joints since your little lady isn't here to keep an eye on you?"

Peter shook his head slowly. Snow in Death Valley and pigs flying. But it didn't mean this ache in his heart was love. It didn't mean anything of the sort. It just meant that the gods had a sense of humor. He just needed more time and he'd get over Merry.

"You staying up tonight to ring in the New Year?" Jim Rogers asked Sean as they paid for their light bulbs. "Got yourself a hot party to go to?"

Sean looked hopefully at his father, but Peter just shook his head. "You need your sleep."

Actually, Peter was the one who needed his sleep. This past week had been awful. He hadn't thought he was doing all that much, but he was exhausted most of the time. Then at night, when he should have collapsed, he tossed and turned, unable to get comfortable. He took their bag from the clerk with a nod and he and Sean walked with Jim toward the door.

"Better watch it," Jim said. "What you do on New Year's, you do all year long!"

"Golly, Daddy," Sean said, his eyes still on their neighbor as he left the store. "Are we going be at the hardware store all next year?"

Peter shook his head as he bent down to help Sean with his mittens. "No, Mr. Rogers meant what you're feeling at midnight, when the new year starts, you'll feel all year. If you're happy on New Year's Eve, you're happy all year long."

"Oh." Sean pulled his hat over his ears. "So I'm going to miss Merry all next year?"

"Of course not."

"Is she gonna be sad all next year?"

Peter just shoved the door open and led Sean out. That old saying was nonsense. No one was going to miss anyone for the whole next year. Still, when Sean immediately turned to his right, Peter stopped him.

"Hey, champ," he called. "Let's go this way."

Sean stopped and asked, "How come?"

Peter stared for a long moment at the giant egg sitting in the parking lot up the street.

"Because," he murmured.

"Because why?" his son persisted.

Because he'd already had snow in Death Valley and learned that pigs could fly. He was not going anywhere near that damn egg. He didn't want to see a giant chicken in any shape or form whatsoever.

"We always walk home that way," Peter replied. "I want to go a different way."

"Okay," Sean said. He shrugged and came back, skipping past Peter and going west on Main. "You're kinda weird, Dad."

"Thank you."

Sean turned around and walked backward.

"Be careful you don't fall on your head," Peter said.

"I never do."

Sean tried hopping backward but soon gave up on that and fell in by Peter's side, reaching up to take his father's hand.

Peter sighed. They were buddies again. It eased part of the ache in his heart, but not all of it.

"But you're not as weird as Mickey Frame's dad."

"Oh, no?"

"Nah. Mickey says he gets all dressed up before he eats breakfast."

"I think Mr. Frame works in an office in Warsaw," Peter said. "He's just getting dressed for work."

"He does other weird things," Sean assured him. "When do you think Merry'll be back?"

"She won't be."

"Yes, she will."

Peter just let the subject drop and looked around them. The street was empty and quiet. It wouldn't be bad to move back home to Mentone. It would be good for his mother and Sean. And it would work out nicely for him, too. He could turn one of the spare bedrooms into an office and put in some extra phone lines so he could connect his computer into the office network. If he needed to, he could go back to Chicago every couple of weeks.

He doubted his managers would see any problems. Most of his work was solitary. With the computer and communications technology available now, working in Mentone would be no different than working a couple floors down from where his office was now. And if his managers didn't agree, then he'd look into options of his own. Do a little consulting. Maybe set up a newsletter. There were a lot of things he could do.

"Hi, Peter." A woman stood in their way. "And how are you, young man?" she asked Sean.

"Fine, Mrs. Warren," Sean replied.

"Hear from that young lady of yours, Peter?"

His jaw clenched momentarily. Oh, the joys of living in a small town where everyone knew everyone else's business. "No, I haven't," Peter replied. "I imagine she has a lot on her mind."

"Yes," the woman said. "I understand one of her cousins is sick."

Peter moved his head slightly, noncommittally.

"You going to spend New Year's with her?" she asked. "Wouldn't want the two of you to spend the whole next year being apart. Well, give her my best when you see her. And say hello to your mother for me."

"We will," Sean said. "Bye, Mrs. Warren."

Peter just nodded, and they continued on their way home.

Damn. The whole town thought Merry was coming back. If he moved back here, would he spend the rest of his life answering questions about her?

"Daddy," Sean said, plodding along thoughtfully at his side. "'Member how we visited Aunt Rosa 'cause she was firm?"

"Infirm," Peter said.

"And Grandma said we were supposed to."

"Right. It was our Christian duty." What was Sean getting at?

The boy sloshed through a puddle. "Well, I think you gotta go see Merry."

"Sean." Peter bit back his impatience.

"'Cause I think she's maybe firm, too." His words raced along as if he feared his father would stop him. "You know, she's so sad that she can't do anything for herself. And if you don't make her smile at midnight, she's gonna be sad all year long."

"Sean, it's not that easy." Peter scrambled for wisdom, but none appeared. He couldn't tell Sean the real reason Merry left, because he had no idea what it was.

"But she talked to the tree for us. We gotta do something for her."

"Maybe we could write her a letter," Peter suggested. "You know—"

"Daddy, look!" Sean screamed. "There's a giant chicken!"

Peter's heart wanted to stop. Fear clutched at his stomach, but he followed Sean's eyes and found what his son was screaming about. There, over across the street from King's Memorial Home, stood a concrete statue of a rooster on a pedestal.

"That's not a chicken, Sean." Peter forced his heart to start beating again. "It's a rooster."

"Roosters are chickens."

This whole thing was so silly. "No, they're not. Chickens lay eggs and roosters can't."

"Dad!" Sean was taking this all seriously. The boy sounded

practically in tears. "Hens lay eggs, but they're both chickens. The giant chickens are back!"

"Sean, it's just a statue."

"You don't understand." Sean was almost screaming, his face frantic. "The magic's here. Daddy, you got to go get Merry."

"Get Merry? Why?"

"Because the magic's here." Sean was grabbing at Peter's hand, tugging at it as if it would make him see the urgency. "She said the rose would bloom and the chickens would come back and then the magic would be here and it would let me live with you. You got to get her so that the magic can give her her little boy back."

Peter stooped down, taking Sean's hands in his own. He didn't understand everything Sean was saying. Okay, the rose sort of bloomed and he was seriously trying to figure out how to have Sean live with him, but what was all this about Merry and a little boy? There was no doubt, though, that Sean really believed some sort of magic was here. How did Peter convince him that there was no magic, just...

Snow in Death Valley.

Pigs that flew.

And giant chickens back in Mentone.

Chapter Fifteen

"**C**ome on, Merry," ZeeZee pleaded. "It's New Year's Eve. Come with us to Georgie's party."

"Yeah," Sandi added. "It'll be a lot of fun."

"There'll be a lot of stray studs."

Merry had tried ignoring her roommates, sitting in bed and staring at the book in her lap. She'd been reading *The Brothers Karamazov* for a month now and getting nowhere. Maybe she wasn't meant to be smart and successful. She'd never be anybody somebody could be proud of.

"Leave me alone," she said with a sigh. "Can't you see I have a lot of work?"

"You're between semesters," Sandi said quietly.

"Well, I'm tired from working at the restaurant," Merry said. "And I want to get a head start on the next semester."

"Jeez, Merry, you're no fun lately," ZeeZee said. She and Sandi left the room, closing the door behind them.

Merry stopped pretending to read and threw the book onto the floor. She lay back on the bed and covered her eyes with her arm. Why, oh, why, did she have to be so stupid? She was always getting involved with these guys who were out of her class. Then she'd make up these big lies about who she was. Why couldn't she just get involved with someone from her own station? Like a guy who went to school with her.

Better yet, why did she have to get involved at all? The single life wasn't bad for her. A lot of women did it. There was no reason why she couldn't take care of herself. She might get a little lonely once in a while, but that would pass.

"Merry. Phone call for you."

"I'm not here. I told you that before."

"It's Mona, from the restaurant."

"Tell her—" Aw, heck. Mona was one of her close friends at work. She might as well see what she wanted. Merry got up from bed and pushed past Sandi to the phone. "Yeah, Mona. What do you want?"

"Nice to see you're still your cheery old self."

"Mona, please."

"Okay, okay." Mona shifted her ever present gum to the other side of her mouth. "How about working with me tonight? It's a New Year's Eve party at that retirement home on Wilson. It's good money."

"No, I—"

"You ain't doin' nothin'," Mona snapped. "Except maybe slitting your wrists."

"I got some reading I need to do."

"Hey," Mona said. "Work with me tonight. You'll still be down, but at least your wallet will be a little fatter. Besides, they're nice folks. I worked there last year."

Merry sighed. She'd avoided taking a New Year's Eve gig because she was afraid that the sight of happy young couples in each other's arms would send her off the edge and she would wind up beating the bejeebers out of all of them. But this would be different. It would be elderly folks, most of them probably women.

"Okay, okay," Merry said. "What time?"

"Great, kid. Great. I'll pick you up at seven."

"Isn't that early?"

"Merry, these are old folks. Two minutes after midnight and they'll be in dreamland. They gotta get their partying in early."

"All right, see you then."

She hung up the phone and went back into her room, shutting

the door firmly behind her. She really couldn't just sit around and mope. That wasn't healthy. What she needed was a full slate. Fill her time with work, work and more work. Eventually Mr. Peter MacAllister would fade away into a distant past. He had to. One dark memory was load enough for her.

Peter found a parking place just two blocks from Merry's, a record for him, and hurried along to her apartment. It was a little after seven-thirty, Chicago time. Eight-thirty, Mentone time.

Something really weird was happening back in Mentone. Sean said it was the magic. Peter wasn't sure, but he wasn't taking any chances. Sean was right when he said Merry'd been unhappy, and if happiness was in the air in Mentone at midnight, Peter wanted her there to get her share. And he had just enough time to do so.

The lobby door was open so he raced up the stairs, but no one answered his knocking at Merry's door. Damn! He looked at his watch again. Even if they had a big evening planned, they should still be home dressing.

He knocked at the next door. Maybe they were at a neighbor's or told someone where they were going. No answer.

He tried the next apartment.

"Yeah?" a surly voice called out.

"I'm looking for the residents in 2 B," he said. "I really need to find Merry or ZeeZee or Sandi."

"They ain't here."

"But do you know where they are? I really need to find them."

"Get lost 'fore I call the cops."

Great. No one answered at the next two doors, and Peter was getting really frustrated when the manager came home. Peter hurried to her door.

"I really need to find Merry or ZeeZee or Sandi."

She glared at him as she slipped through her door. "It ain't my business to keep an eye on three adults who aren't bothering anybody."

He stuck his foot in the doorway so she couldn't close the door. "But I really need to—"

She kicked his foot out of the way. "Beat it before I call my boyfriend." She slammed the door.

Damn. He sank onto the top step. What was he supposed to do, just sit here on the stairs until Merry came home? If he didn't find her soon, they'd never get to Mentone even close to midnight.

He supposed he could fight with the neighbors until they called the cops. It would make for some excitement, but he didn't want to spend New Year's Eve in jail, especially if the old saying was true. The thought of a year in Cook County Jail didn't thrill him.

"You got the door?"

"Oops, catch that will you?"

Peter stood up and stared down the stairs. He couldn't believe it. ZeeZee and Sandi had just come in.

"Uh-oh." ZeeZee stopped midway up the flight of stairs. "Trouble ahead."

Sandi peered around her roommate and frowned. "What do you want?"

"I'm looking for Merry."

"Well, tough. She's not looking for you." ZeeZee brushed past him and unlocked the apartment door.

"I just want to talk to her," he pleaded to Sandi.

She pushed past him also. "She's not here."

"I know that. Just tell me where she is." He followed them up to the apartment door.

"Why? So you can wreck another party for her?" Sandi asked. She went past ZeeZee into the apartment.

"I need to see her."

ZeeZee went into the apartment, too, but her eyes seemed uncertain. "If she wanted you to know where she was, she'd have told you."

"She didn't know I was coming. I drove in from Mentone because—"

"You drove in tonight just to see her?" ZeeZee asked and glanced over at Sandi. "It is New Year's. Maybe..."

Sandi sighed. "She's working a party with Mona over at the Wilson Towers."

Peter fought the urge to hug them both. No use tempting fate.

"Thanks. I really appreciate it." With a grin, he turned to race down the stairs.

"If she's mad at us for telling you, we'll find you and make you sorry," ZeeZee called after him.

He just waved his hand in acknowledgment. If he failed in his mission, they wouldn't be the only ones after him. Sean, his mother, Zachary. Hell, the whole town would make him suffer.

He jumped into his car and sped to Wilson Towers. There were no parking places immediately visible, and he didn't waste time cruising the neighborhood for one. He just double-parked in the curved drive, then bolted toward the doorway. A uniformed doorman gave him a hard stare over a newspaper but let him in.

The Wilson Avenue Retirement Home was a refurbished hotel, and Peter easily found the high-ceilinged old ballroom in the back. Tonight, it was gaily decorated with streamers and balloons, with music coming from records manipulated by a deejay. Residents, most of them women, milled about the large room so that Peter couldn't see more than a few feet ahead of him.

He came farther into the room. Damn it. Where was she?

Some party guests encircled him, smiling.

"Hi, honey."

"You come to our party?"

He smiled but edged along, trying to see where the serving tables were.

"Wanna dance, sugar?"

"Actually I'm looking for somebody," he said. "One of the servers."

"What's her name?"

"Merry, Merry Roberts."

"Merry," one of the old women called out. "Where are you?"

"Merry, Merry Roberts!" another one shouted.

Peter grinned at them and put his hands to his mouth. "Merry. Are you here?"

"Merry?" someone else asked. "Who's Merry?"

But in moments, it seemed that most of the room was calling her name. Magically, a few seconds later, a red-faced Merry was pushed forward. She stopped moving when she spotted him.

"Peter." She frowned. "What are you doing here?"

The crowd got deathly quiet.

"I'm not sure," he said, and looked around them. They were encircled by the elderly party goers, all with rapt expressions on their faces as they watched.

He turned back to Merry. "There's snow in Death Valley."

"Oh," someone sighed.

"Ah," another said knowingly.

"What'd he say?" someone from the edges cried out.

"There's snow in Death Valley," someone else repeated.

Merry bit at her lip. "Peter, please—"

He saw no anger in her eyes so he took a step closer. "And pigs can fly."

"No, they can't," a watcher argued.

"That's not possible."

"What'd he say?"

"They can fly in an airplane," Peter told her. "Just like you and me. But they can fly."

"I guess."

"He's got a point there."

Merry just shook her head. "Peter."

"And the three-hundred-pound chickens have returned to Mentone."

"Three-hundred-pound chickens?"

"They've come back to Mentone?"

"Where's that?"

"What'd he say?"

Merry looked away from him briefly, as if gathering strength. She folded her arms over her chest and faced him once more. "Peter, this is all nonsense."

"A three-hundred-pound chicken don't sound like nonsense to me," someone shouted.

Merry closed her eyes briefly. She was weakening, he could tell.

Peter turned to the crowd. "We have an egg in the center of town," he said. "It's about six feet tall."

"It would take a three-hundred-pound chicken to lay that kind of egg," someone agreed.

Merry opened her eyes. Her look bordered on a glare.

"All right." Peter grinned at her. "It's just one rooster, but there's got to be more coming."

"Oh, sure."

"You find one chicken, you got a flock."

"They don't like to be alone."

Merry stared hard at him. She should be smiling by now, or trying to fight back a smile. All he saw was sadness in her eyes. He took a giant step forward and grabbed her hands.

"Sean told me what this means," Peter said. "He says the magic has arrived."

She remained silent and staring.

"He said you said it would come and it has. The rose bloomed, the snow came to Death Valley, pigs are flying to California, the chickens are back and he's going to live with me. We all got our share of the magic. Now you have to come back so it can work its spell on you."

A collective, satisfied sigh erupted from the crowd. Merry's face quivered, then tears started from her eyes. "I don't deserve it," she said.

"Every woman deserves a warm bed," someone called out.

Merry's hold on Peter's hands tightened. "I lied to you," she said.

"What else do you do with a man?"

"They can't handle the truth at all."

"They're too fragile."

"They're like poets."

The hurt in her eyes was just too deep. He wanted to hold her, to kiss away the pain and shelter her from it forever. "I don't care," he said.

She shook her head. "I didn't grow up in Atlanta. I grew up in a little town in the hills of Tennessee."

"So?"

"So?" someone in the crowd echoed.

"I have a bunch of brothers and sisters," Merry rushed her words out.

"You didn't seem selfish like an only child."

"Listen to him, honey."

"My mother worked as a waitress in a bar on the only paved road in town." Merry's voice was growing more defiant, as if daring him to not be shocked and turn away.

But he wasn't, he didn't. "It isn't opportunities that make a person, it's what the person does with their opportunities."

"I never knew who my father was. My mother had a hard time placing him."

"That's not under your control."

She took a deep breath and looked him straight in the eye. "I've got a son."

Peter just nodded. "Sean told me."

"He's gonna be ten, come next April." All that strength in her voice was suddenly gone. She bit at her lip as if it could stop the flood of tears that was threatening.

"Who's taking care of him?" Peter asked gently.

"His father," Merry replied. "And his mother."

"He was adopted?"

Merry nodded, all her walls suddenly tumbling down. Peter gathered her into his arms. He felt her resist at first, a token challenge, but then she just let go and clung to him.

Peter buried his face in her hair and breathed in the wondrous scent of her. "I didn't believe Sean the first time he told me," he said softly. "But I began to wonder with all this magic stuff. He obviously knew more about everything than me."

Merry pushed herself away slightly. Her eyes were teary, her face flushed. "Oh, Peter, you can see why—"

But the magic had given him powers, too, and he wouldn't let her finish. Not when it was going to be such a silly statement. "All I can see is that you're badly in need of some magic, and I know just the place where it's at its strongest tonight."

She stared up at him. "But I've just told you everything. You can't still—"

He brought her hand up to his lips. Suddenly everything was very clear to him. The real meaning behind all the magic. "A very wise woman once told me that love was seeing the holes in someone else's underwear and loving her anyway."

"Oh, Peter."

"We can work anything out," he told her. "Just as long as we love each other."

"But—"

"He's right, Merry," someone called out.

Peter pulled her back into his arms, afraid that the return of the crowd's voice would spook her. "As long as we're together, we can fix anything," he told her. "And I want us together. I'm tired of being alone."

"Are you asking her to marry you?"

"Yes." Peter smiled down into Merry's eyes.

"Should get down on one knee," someone advised.

"They don't do that anymore," someone else argued.

"I think they should."

"All right." Peter let go of her and got down on his right knee. "Merry Roberts, I love you with my whole heart and soul. Will you please marry me?"

New tears were flowing down her cheeks, but Peter had a feeling that they were happy tears. He waited. But the crowd wasn't as patient.

"Go ahead, dear. He's a nice-looking fella."

"Does he have a job?"

"He looks like a professional. Probably a doctor or something like that."

Peter was waiting. "Merry, please."

Either unable or unwilling, she didn't reply.

He prodded her. "I want to spend New Year's Eve in the Egg Basket of the Midwest."

"He wants to live in a basket?"

"I thought you said he looked like a professional."

"Come on, Merry," Peter urged. "I want to get to Mentone by midnight."

Merry frowned in thought. "Do you think there's enough time?"

For the first time in weeks, Peter felt his heart dance. "If not, I'm sure we can make Bourbon."

"What did he say?"

"He wants to make Bourbon."

"What for? Why doesn't he make love instead?"

"Merry?"

She pulled him up and slipped into his arms. "Yes."

"Yes, what?" Peter asked.

"All of the above."

Epilogue

Dear Santa:

Grandma's writing this for me. She says you don't have to write thank-you notes to Santa, just to people like Aunt Rosa and Cousin Cheryl, but I wanted to thank you, anyway.

Everything came out just right. Both Merry and I are going to live with Daddy, and she's going to be my new mommy. For now, we're going to live part-time in Chicago and part-time in Mentone, and that's great 'cause I like both places.

And guess what? I'm getting a new cousin! His name is Jason and he's really Merry's little boy, but that's a secret. Daddy got Mr. Anderson to help him 'cause Mr. Anderson's a lawyer, and they got Jason's mommy and daddy to let Merry be his aunt. I don't know how a mommy can be an aunt, but Merry cried and cried when Daddy told her. I could tell it was 'cause she was so happy. Jason's going to come visit us on his spring break from school. I'm going to show him the egg.

I don't think any more giant chickens are coming to

Mentone. Grandma said the only reason the big rooster is here is 'cause people kept backing their cars into the pedestal in that parking lot. They couldn't get the pedestal out, so they saw this big rooster on sale someplace and bought it to sit on top of the pedestal so people can see it. Merry says that's still magic, but I think she's just kind of weird lately. She and Daddy are talking about painting Zachary's room either pink or blue, and I keep telling them Zachary's blind so he doesn't care what color the room is.

Ricky still says there's no such thing as Santa, but me and Missy made a deal, and he doesn't say it too loud any more.

Anyway, thank you for all the trouble you went to this year, and I promise next year I'll ask for something easy like a bike or sled.

Your pal,
Sean

* * * * *

Look for Andrea Edwards's newest series—
The Yellow Brick Road Brides—*coming in May, August
and November in the Silhouette Special Edition line.
The first title will be* **IF I ONLY HAD A...HUSBAND,**
*and all stories will feature the warmth of love and
friendship this author is known for!*

Dear Reader,

The holiday season marks the collision of Mars and Venus in *The Pendragon Virus*, my third book for Silhouette. I'm happy to have the opportunity to share Sam and Dallas with you again, especially during the Christmas season.

At my house, Christmas is a family time. We have a real tree, cook, make gifts, visit and always take a family ride to view the town's decorations and lights. It is a season for family and friends and for sharing with others. I believe in Santa Claus and am delighted on Christmas morning to find my stocking on the mantel stuffed with special things, just for me. Years ago, my daughters were eager to rise, to find what Santa had brought them, and I wanted a bit more sleep. Now, I'm nudging them awake! My personal holiday tradition involves calling those who are in my life, but perhaps not regularly. You might try that—it's keeping those who have touched your life near, and difficult to do in today's busy world. At Christmas, it's worth the special effort. I also polish furniture, preparing it for the New Year. In my private/relaxation time, I enjoy lots of good Silhouette books.

You, Silhouette readers, have been wonderful to me, and I treasure you. When I write a story, I think of it as a gift to you, the readers. Have a wonderful Christmas season, and enjoy the warmth of family, traditions and friends.

Merry Christmas,

Cait London

THE PENDRAGON VIRUS

Cait London

For the Ozark Romance Authors,
my RWA group, of Springfield, Missouri.
They teach love and inspire with a kindness
that reaches into the lives they touch.
For them, and you, my friends, Merry Christmas.

One

Sam Loring had one basic rule: locate the problem and get to the bottom of it—quick. Easing his six-foot-four frame on the folding metal chair, he crossed his arms over his chest. He surveyed the conference room with the air of a fighter who had come to study his opponent.

Rain tapped at the windows, the sound seeming gentler than the chatter surrounding him. The cold bite of the rain was typical of Seattle weather in early December and suited Sam's mood. Skimming the thirty faces of the class members, he spotted the one on the advertising brochure. Focusing on her, Sam took a deep breath. Dallas Pendragon needed to be taken out of the game—his game.

Youthful male executives peppered the predominantly female class. The fact that Sam was the only older man in a room of excited women didn't bother him at all. His staff at Brice Cleansers Company was coming down with a contagious business virus, and he intended to stop it. Christmas season or not.

He ran his palm across his flat stomach, easing the threatening ache. Remembering his morning business call, he scowled. A

competitor had almost ripped a contract out from under his nose,
and Sam had spent the better part of his morning angling to
undercut the low bid. Wooing the buyer had cost him a precious
morning hour.

Sam rotated his tense shoulders slowly. His sales team captain
had been too eager to get the contract for commercial washroom
soap. Johnson had missed presenting an important feature of the
dispenser to the buyer. The mistake wouldn't be repeated, Sam
thought grimly. He'd called Johnson on the carpet at seven this
morning.

Sliding an antacid tablet from his suit pocket, Sam ground it
between his teeth. At forty-six, he'd survived a nasty divorce
and a few corporate battles. Along the way, he'd buried an Ap-
palachian Southern drawl and rebuilt a sagging company.

He tugged at his collar, loosening it slightly around the tense
cords of his neck. He could survive the Pendragon virus.

Pendragon, the inventive owner and lecturer of a business-
stress school, had damn near incited a mutiny in his staff of two
hundred workers. The best portion of his staff at Brice were
loyal, trained professionals. But somehow Pendragon had
whipped his smooth waters into a tidal wave. She was a fire-
brand oozing karma, he decided darkly, watching the tall, lithe
woman step up to the stage.

Pendragon had just enough age—late thirties—on her to be
dangerous, he decided. The crusading age.

Tracing the strong clean line of her jaw, Sam shifted in his
chair uncomfortably. Pendragon had *professional woman* written all over her; it was a species he meticulously avoided.

He could almost feel her electricity from his seat in midclass.
With a traveling microphone attached to her pin-striped navy
blazer, she dominated the room. Sam could feel it—the Pendragon virus—crackle, lashing at him.

Her hair just touched her shoulders, swaying as she walked
across the portable stage, preparing for her lecture. The strands
shifted as she turned, a sleek sensuous movement of silk on silk.
With hair the color of burnished copper, she probably had a
temper to match.

Quickly stacking a variety of pamphlets and tapes across a

table, Pendragon paused to check her wristwatch, then continued her preparations. Sam shifted his weight uneasily, noting her professional conduct.

Pendragon was a long-legged witch, her skirt tightening as she strode across the stage to adjust the microphone stand. She had the loose stride of an athlete rather than a woman who kept her bottom plopped in a desk chair.

Sam watched as she took a moment to scan Seattle's downtown business area from the conference-room window. He studied that pale profile intently as Pendragon's slim, ringless finger gently rubbed the bridge of her nose. He recognized that trick— preparing for a presentation. Do your best to prepare, take a minute before showtime to center in on yourself, then give 'em your best shot.

He also recognized his own flash of admiration for her; Pendragon was a pro.

She lifted her head slightly, and a thick strand of hair slid to frame her face. The wave caressed her smooth cheek, then arched to expose the tiny diamond stud nestled in her ear. For some reason, Sam found that twinkling stone entirely too intriguing; his gaze was fastened upon it. The muscles of his neck tightened in an instinctive, self-protective gesture.

The small stone was too feminine, the curve of her lobe too vulnerable. Sam rapped a pencil against his palm impatiently.

Her face lighting, Pendragon spoke to a woman who had approached the stage. The lecturer listened intently, her mouth curving with a smile. Watching her, a chill ran up the nape of Sam's neck. Her full lips had the look of ripe strawberries, and he could almost feel them opening— Damn, he thought, forcing his gaze through the window to Seattle's famous waterfront street, bordered by shops and eateries.

If ever there was a woman he didn't want to experience sensually, it was the steel-in-silk type. Career women could cut a man in two, then walk over the pieces.

Sam slipped another antacid tablet into his mouth. When he wanted a woman, he liked lace and a lot of soft, comforting curves. But lately he hadn't found anything that had even tempted his tastes.

At promptly nine o'clock, Pendragon turned center stage and flashed a thousand-watt smile at the class. Thirty women stopped chattering and sat at attention, gripping their training manuals. In contrast, the young male executives looked wary.

Sam traced the manual's bold letters of the Pendragon Method of Handling Business Stress with his pen. He underlined the topic for handling difficult bosses, feeling the muscles in his jaw contract. He wanted—demanded—an efficient work force. But after his staff had attended Pendragon's one-day course, they had him under a microscope. His employees' curious glances and closed expressions had sent Sam's primed senses tingling.

For the past week, he'd waded through problems created by Pendragon's business-slash-stress school. Personnel had sent him a cute little notice: "Abnormal amount of requests for To-Whom-It-May-Concern job recommendations. Also requests for job record updates... Anything Personnel needs to know?"

If an employee suddenly wanted his personnel file updated, it usually meant he or she was job shopping, and that spelled trouble. An efficiency survey had revealed that it took a minimum of three years to train a good employee. If any one of the cogs were displaced—

The pencil Sam had been holding snapped between his fingers. Sam scowled at the usurper. Troublemakers came in all sorts of shapes and sizes, and there was always a way to put them out of commission.

For the past week, he'd been waiting for the employee virus to run its course. Emily Franzini, his personal secretary, hadn't had his morning coffee waiting for the first time in eleven years. Nor had she waited, quiet and with pen in hand, while he examined his morning mail. Then, as he had rummaged for a fitting business threat to close a letter, Emily had politely suggested he try a dictation recorder to save them both time.

Feeling confined, Sam rolled his broad shoulders against the back of the conference chair. He liked his morning coffee on his desk when he arrived and he didn't like dictating to a machine. Emily had quoted a high percentage of managers who possessed the marvelous ability, then had looked down her nose at him. "I'm merely suggesting an alternative. Ms. Pendragon says that offering helpful suggestions is a way to relieve stress. It gives one such a good, warm feeling to be helpful... Ah, did you know you've been dictating for an hour straight?" she had asked, flexing her fingers.

Sam leveled a dark stare at Pendragon, the proponent of taking regular breaks to alleviate stress. So he'd gotten wrapped up in his dictation; so he didn't catch Emily shifting restlessly in her chair after an hour. He liked Emily, but once he got started on a marketing analysis, his ideas were fresh and he wanted them written down. So he forgot sometimes.

Sam winced quietly, feeling guilty. He worked hard, pounding at problems until he'd tenderized the gristle. It was just that sometimes he forgot that Emily's fingers might ache. If he'd realized— Sam shifted on his chair, feeling guiltier.

In the middle of his dictation, Emily had glanced longingly at his private coffeepot, and Sam realized he had worked through her break. To compensate for his thoughtlessness, Sam had foolishly asked if Emily had any ideas about improving his relations with the staff. She had quietly suggested that he not greet his personal clerical staff each morning with "Hi, girls." Then she'd added, "They are trained professionals, Mr. Loring. Businesspersons, according to the Pendragon theory."

His staff was the blood of his business, Sam thought darkly, and he didn't need any interference from Pendragon.

Morrison Bradley, a friend and an executive from Delite's Pet Food Company, had called on Tuesday, raving. "No rush jobs, my staff says, Sam. I've got a memo in my hand from the employee representative who runs the suggestion program in the loading and delivery departments. We're out to sell cat and dog food here. How do the employees expect us to get the products on the top shelf without rush jobs? Scheduling cuts employee stress, they say. We do the same thing every year and they want routine projects scheduled by the month. Damn, in the old days workers did what you threw at 'em. When you threw it at 'em!"

Over lunch on Wednesday, Mort Radney was grim. "My secretaries either treat me like a child or they're too damned busy to talk. Nelson, my chief, had the nerve to say that they react

that way when I'm moody.... Moody," he repeated indignantly.
"He says they have feelings, too. 'They're people, for Pete's
sake,' he said."

On the stage, Pendragon adjusted the microphone attached to
her lapel. "Can you all hear me? Raise your hands if you
can't."

Noting her slight Western twang, Sam concentrated on the
husky undertone.

"Good. Everything is working fine then. Good morning, I'm
Dallas Pendragon," she began, walking across the stage and
displaying a neat length of leg beneath the slim skirt.

Dallas Pendragon, troublemaker, Sam thought. She had just
the right combination to stir his clerical workers into a potential
mutiny—she was bright and in total control of herself. The ul-
timate businessperson, Sam thought darkly, scanning the way
the slim skirt fitted her neat backside.

"Make sure you're wearing your name tag," she instructed
with another wide smile. "By the end of the day, we're all going
to know each other well."

Introducing herself as a divorced working mother who knew
about coping with stress and business, Dallas slid right into the
office workers' hearts. Sam got the feeling that the woman was
a bully. She liked having things her way.

He liked having things *his* way: without the clutter of day-
care centers and job-sharing positions. Career women were
fine—at a distance. But once they started mothering children on
company time....

Sam's gaze strolled down her slender body appraisingly. He
had to take her out of the game without too many bruises, he
decided—only because it wouldn't look good for someone with
his size to shove her into a corner.

When she instructed the class to turn to their booklets, Sam
leveled a hard scowl at her. He paid his people well, tagging on
bonuses, vacations and maternity leave. If Ms. Pendragon wasn't
stopped soon, every business in Seattle would be footing the bill
for day-care center accommodations and fitness gyms.

By the midmorning break, Sam knew he was right to experience Ms. Pendragon first hand. If she hadn't been his oppo-

nent, he would have admired her quick wit, which reached straight into the hearts of working women.

As a man who appreciated women, Sam couldn't help comparing her to his past collection of females. Pendragon dressed like sheer business and she probably wore practical cotton panties.

He edged his way through the crowd gathering at the coffeepot, just catching hints of "She's right. There's absolutely no reason not to have some kind of day-care center arrangement at work." And "I agree. A fit, healthy person does make a good worker. Diet is important. The company should provide a microwave oven."

One comment snagged and chafed. "I just can't wait to get back to work and get started on these new ideas. According to the Pendragon theory, it's important to analyze your boss. Study his needs and yours. Then go for a compromise... Or as a last resort, think about moving into another workplace that better suits you."

Sam scowled at the coffee urn. When he was twelve years old, he was working as a man to survive. Because he'd known genuine gnawing hunger, he paid top wages for good workers. As an employer, he didn't want to be compromised. Or feel like a lump of clay to be pushed and prodded into the employee's idea of a manager. And he didn't want his workers looking around for other jobs.

Hell, he liked his workers. Most of them had been with the company for years and had been perfectly happy until *The Virus* had gotten to them.

A blond woman with long, carefully mussed hair and heavily kohled eyes tracked him as he moved through the crowd. Accustomed to the knowing look, he nodded just as a short woman accidentally brushed his sleeve with her large bosom.

Edging past a sea of conflicting scents and chattering women, Sam finally reached his seat. Buffeted by the excitement racing around the room, he gripped the back of the chair like an anchor.

His stomach felt like hell.

"I liked the part about some companies having a sabbatical program after a five-year employment. A longer vacation would really be nice, like a present from the company," he heard as he slid back into his chair, coffee in hand.

A plump woman seated next to him leaned over and smiled knowingly. "Isn't the Pendragon concept great? I really liked the part about maybe not being in the right job...a square peg in a round hole. I mean if the company is going to treat workers like yesterday's newspaper, why not look around?"

Yesterday's newspaper. Sam repeated the phrase in a quiet snarl. He packed in a good, long work day and never asked as much of his people as of himself. His staff had the best of equipment to help manage their work loads, and he'd instituted top training programs. He wanted to keep his expert people, not have them shopping for other jobs. If Pendragon kept up at this rate, the entire Seattle clerical workforce would be in constant rotation.

When Pendragon stepped up to the stage, the cords running down Sam's neck went taut. He adjusted his black-rimmed glasses meticulously. He'd worked damned hard to establish a management-and-labor committee. Brice provided insurance, counseling for alcoholics and an hour-long Christmas party.

He'd written a manual for Brice employees defining goals, procedures and personal conduct. His managers had an open-door policy for employee problems and the latitude to handle them.

A thin woman leaned across him to speak to the lady on his other side. "Wouldn't it be great if management provided free counseling? I've got a teenage son who really resents his stepfather—"

"Okay, let's hit it!" Pendragon exclaimed enthusiastically, raising her arm. To Sam her wrist looked as though he could wrap his fingers around the pale column, and he felt a warning, cold trickle run up his neck. For just a moment, Sam allowed himself a glimpse of her soft curves beneath the business suit. He narrowed his eyes, settling back for another dose of the Pendragon virus.

A hotshot dynamo concealed in skirts and pantyhose, he thought. Ready to take the whole business world on to prove her theories. The next segment dealt with analyzing your boss, stroking his needs and getting what you want. While the class studiously checked off the personality type of their bosses and themselves, Sam studied Pendragon.

She would have made a great coach for major-league football, a female Gipper. An exciting speaker, Pendragon could toss off a quick joke at the same time she eased a shy woman into talking.

Unused to sitting for any length of time, Sam stirred in his chair. Pendragon scouted the crowd, then her eyes snagged on him. "Now that gentleman has the right idea."

Walking to him, Pendragon smiled. Just a mere lifting of one corner of her full lips. Sam had a glimpse of dark green eyes framed by sweeping lashes. He didn't trust the sparkling, gold flecked depths. They were witch's eyes.

"Time to stir up the oxygen level in the blood, people," she announced, reading his name tag. "Sam is going to show us how to exercise. Okay, Sam? Stand up," she ordered briskly.

Sam breathed heavily just once. He didn't like being hauled around like a schoolboy. Apparently Pendragon expected her orders to be followed because she tapped him lightly on one broad shoulder. A fine dark eyebrow arced high. "Coming, Sam?"

Rising slowly, Sam stood to his full height, noting that Pendragon in her practical pumps reached his chin. He also noted a delicate scent of flowers that reminded him of Georgia's Appalachia hills blooming in May. Or maybe it was his mother's sweet peas by the shack's back door.

Pendragon strode around him like a general studying an imposing fort before she addressed the class. "Okay. Here you have a sizeable man. You should all be able to see him well enough. Roll your head around like this, Sam. Loosens the shoulder and neck muscles."

Lifting her hands, she placed them just behind Sam's ears and rotated his head gently. "Think you can handle that, Sam?" she asked in a teasing tone.

Sam ground his teeth together.

The position of her body near his was a trespass. When he wanted a woman touching him, *he* reached out and snagged her.

She rubbed the taut cords in his neck soothingly, watching him for just that slice of an instant. "You really should relax, Sam," she offered gently.

Relax? How the hell did a man do that when a woman's soft hands were strolling all over him? In Sam's book of man-woman rules, the intimacy wasn't performed in front of a crew of women!

The soft curve of her breasts brushed his midsection as she guided his head, and Sam stiffened. "Relax, Sam. Close your eyes," she whispered, continuing the motion. "Easy...easy..."

"I can manage now," he returned a little gruffly. He was all too aware of her sweet-pea, down-home fragrance and the soft curves almost touching his body. Suddenly, he realized the impact of her hands. He hadn't been touched by a woman for some time, and now he was bordering a sensual discussion with the needs of his body!

"Okay, then do it by yourself." Her hands slid from him, and Sam felt just a twinge of regret.

But how much regret could he spend on a danger to his company? he wondered.

After Sam obeyed stiffly, Pendragon ran him through a series of stretching exercises, then called, "Minnie, would you bring a stool for Sam so he can relax for our next exercise?"

Noting the long wave of hair that coursed down her cheek, he had the urge to sweep it back from her face. She had one of those everlasting faces—the dark lifted eyebrows and high cheekbones and a short pert nose.

A nose dusted with freckles.

He glanced uneasily at her throat. He could almost wrap his hand around it. The pad of his thumb would just fit in the hollow at the base of her throat.

Pendragon leisurely appraised his navy suit and light blue shirt. "From the looks of him, this guy requires exercise. He's probably used to movement and works out somehow. So we know he's in pretty good shape...." Her eyes drifted to Sam's lean midsection. "Basically."

A small flick of pique raced through him. If she wanted to

find a soft gut, she could look somewhere else. His backside wasn't flabby, either.

She tugged the tall stool closer. "Sit down, Sam. You're our guinea pig for biofeedback. That's it," she said as he settled on the stool, "get really comfortable, then hold absolutely still so the feedback device won't pick up the sound of your clothing."

The softness of her breast brushed his sleeve, and Sam scowled, edging away from her.

Patting his shoulder, she flashed a grin up at him. "You're a good guy, Sam." Tilting the microphone away from her mouth, Pendragon whispered, "Since you're the only older man in class, I really appreciate your help. The younger guys probably don't have the sedentary job you may have, so they're not as good as examples. You know, less chance of heart problems, circulatory and so forth. I think it's important for women to see that older...middle-age men experience real stress, too. Thanks."

When she turned to the class, Sam shot a grim look down her backside. It was all there—the curves and the strength. Too bad it was wasted on a female shark. He hadn't volunteered; he'd been drafted. And he didn't like being patronized, either. Or called old. Or put on the spot to be dissected by twenty women and a few men.

She placed her hand on his sleeve. The slim pale fingers that squeezed his forearm had practical short nails. "We all have stress of some kind or another. Sometimes we recognize it immediately and other times we have to work at it. That's what this is for—" She held up a small wand. "This is a biofeedback monitor. Listen to the tone when I place it in Sam's hand."

When he took the monitor from her, his fingers slid along hers deliberately, testing her skin. Immediately Pendragon sliced a quick appraisal at him.

Instantly the amplifiers from her microphone picked up a high whine that seemed to hover like a raindrop clinging to the tip of a leaf.

She smiled briefly, clinically pleased by the demonstration. "Hear that, class? Sam's excited. Now listen to the tone as we talk. In areas that might be stressful to Sam, the pitch will rise."

Whipping around, she placed her hand on her hip studying him closely. "Sam's here to learn, so he's going to appreciate finding out for free about his private stress areas. This is helpful in the office place. If you can afford to buy the machine, take it to work. You'll find that things you didn't know bothered you are really stressful. And then you can deal with them."

Sam closed his eyes. The tone rose to a high whine as he thought of each of his employees holding one of the damned devices. The class giggled, but Pendragon only nodded.

"Okay, there's something causing Sam stress. Are you nervous?"

Sam wanted to crush the deceiving little device in his hand. Instead he pushed his lips back from his teeth to form a smile. "A little."

"It's only natural," she responded gently, patting his upper arm. "Don't worry. If things get too bad, I'll let you off the hook."

Her tone caused him to grip the device tighter. It cried out loudly. He wanted to toss it out the window. "I can manage," he stated between his teeth.

Patting him on the shoulder, Pendragon purred, "That's great." When she continued looking straight into him, a high whine penetrated the room. Sam breathed deeply, willing the damned thing to fail. He could feel her ticking off his emotional problems.

Okay, he admitted almost guiltily to himself. He was basically a private person. He didn't like grave diggers prowling around in his psyche.

"Settle down," Pendragon whispered, covering her microphone. "You're off the charts. Now let's just chat so the class can hear the different tones... Nothing too intimate, I promise." She smiled briefly and Sam caught the gleam of even white teeth.

The sound settled down to a steady hum as Pendragon swished around him, addressing the class. "These devices are really great. Hold them while you watch television. To deal with stress, you must first recognize it. Doing okay, Sam?"

"Great," he responded, pleased that the tone had settled somewhat.

She nodded. "You look like a man who knows himself pretty well," she began, her gaze following his broken nose and thrusting jaw.

"Pretty well," he agreed, realizing his palm had just begun to sweat as it cradled the humming device.

"Do you have a family, Sam?"

"No."

"Potential family? As in fianceé, stepchildren?"

Sam heard the threatening hum raise slightly. Pendragon caught the sound and smiled knowingly. "We're all friends here, Sam...trying to learn about ourselves. Do you want to explain?" she asked almost gently.

Damn it! No, he didn't want to explain—the tone raised and quivered throughout the room. His work was both his child and his mistress. He gripped the tattletale monitor tightly.

Okay, so he had an occasional long night. In fact, he dreaded the upcoming holidays when his friends and staff would be celebrating with their families. He just never seemed to fit in and hated the awkward feeling. "No one," he admitted through the line of his teeth as the humming increased.

"Ah, you see how well the device works, class? Sam, for some reason, is upset. You see, this is a typical stress point. Families can create as well as ease stress for a business person. It's all in how that individual manages problems. Sharing problems with a loved one is one of the best ways to ease tension. They're on your team, wanting to help. And that's good for us. Let's hope Sam gets that break one day."

Dallas placed her hand on Sam's arm deliberately. The man was literally grinding his teeth. A classic workaholic, she decided, noting the strong muscles shifting beneath her touch.

Sam Loring was the size of a mountain. He had a hard look, with searing gray eyes and ferocious thick brows. His neatly clipped hair just touched with silver, did little to soften his image.

If ever there was a man who needed lessons in dealing with

stress, it was Sam. His biofeedback sound was abnormally high. No wonder, she thought, unconsciously squeezing his forearm. No family and all alone during the holidays.

When she'd moved his head in the rotation exercise, she could feel his basic resistance to guidance. As a "touching" person, Dallas could almost read personalities through her fingertips. Sam was of the unbending variety, driven and badly needing softening.

In the exercise, she had caught his soapy scent. Sam wouldn't be too bad with his rough edges trimmed, she decided. Dallas rather liked the battered-old-tom image she sensed beneath his stiff exterior.

And she had liked touching him, feeling the rough masculine muscles beneath her fingertips. His dark brown hair was nice, sliding easily through her fingers. The course, defiant texture was no doubt representative of the man.

Dallas left her hand on Sam's arm as she ran him through a simple series of questions that seemed to upset him unreasonably. He had a raspy, deep voice that for some unknown reason could lift the hair at the back of her neck. A scar ran into the dark hair at his temple, which made him look all the more tough and serious. Dallas wondered if he knew how to laugh.

She smiled at him, willing him to know he had a friend in the world; for the moment she could spare Sam a little warmth. As she chatted with him, Dallas noted the high whine of the monitor. For some reason, Sam Loring was unjustifiably emotional!

Sympathetic to his loneliness during the impending holiday season, Dallas ended the session quickly and ordered the afternoon break. Taking the monitor from Sam's big hand, she noted the scars across his knuckles. Dallas smiled up at him as he stood. "Thank you so much, Sam. I hope you're enjoying the training session."

His lips moved, pressing together before he leaned down slightly. The lines between his eyebrows and framing his mouth deepened. "I want to talk with you privately, Ms. Pendragon."

She stepped back from him. Sam's gray eyes slashed at her.

"I have counselors available, Sam. Call the office for an appointment—"

"Not them. *You* Pendragon," he demanded in a tone that reminded her of her dog's low, menacing growl.

That slight touch of arrogance erased her sympathy for Sam's loneliness. His do-it-or-else tone also reminded her of her ex-husband when he was shoving his weight around.

T. J. McCall had been totally unsympathetic to her pressures. An overgrown boy, T.J. was frequently out of work. He had no understanding about her budding career and did nothing to contribute to their home and children.

Dallas *really* disliked that tone.

She wrapped the cord of the monitor neatly around the device and returned it to the box. She turned slowly, facing him. "Exactly what do you want, Sam?"

He glanced around at the curious women as though surveying enemy territory. "I'd like to talk with you. As soon as possible."

"Talk now," she stated, glancing at her wristwatch. She'd had enough of one man demanding and setting the restraints on her time. "We've got ten minutes left of the break."

Sam shot an angry look down at her—a man nettled by obeying someone else's rules. He rubbed his jaw with the flat of his hand. "What I've got in mind will take more time."

Dallas was in no mood to delicately handle a come-on from a man who looked hard as nails. She'd had a rough work week, made worse by her children coming down with flu. Besides, her mother had renewed her attack on Dallas's no-man status. According to Lisa Pendragon, every woman needed a good man now and then to keep her in fighting shape for the next one. Or she suggested, Dallas might try harder to capture one of the basic, dull variety.

It was Lisa who had gently but firmly informed Dallas that T.J. wasn't what she called "a real man." When Dallas stopped running long enough to take a slow, thorough look at their relationship, she found T.J. to be a spoiled child, more demanding than Nikki and Billy.

Dallas glanced up at Sam's tough jawline, taking in the heavy shadow of his beard. Somehow she suspected he wasn't dull. He had that elemental look that would please her mother, but just didn't suit herself. "Give me a rough idea, Sam."

He didn't like anyone setting conditions but himself, she noted as the muscle running the length of his cheek contracted. "I run Brice Cleansers, Ms. Pendragon. Some of my people took a class from you. The suggestion was from my personnel office, and I agreed to the company footing the bill for your contract. I now regret that decision."

"Exactly what is your complaint?"

"You've got my work force in an uproar," he stated flatly, leaning down toward her. "If you'll admit to them that all this stress analysis is malarkey, we can get back in running shape for the new year."

Dallas lifted her chin, remembering instantly the comments from Sam's employees. Though he paid well, Sam expected his people to work every bit as hard as himself. It wasn't unusual for him to call an employee or an entire work group back on Saturday morning to iron out production problems. Sam's problem wasn't in providing an overtime paycheck; it was in considering an employee's private commitments.

Under Sam's management, all employees were full-time workers with benefits provided such as insurance and paid major holidays. There were designated vacation periods determined by the company. This arrangement sometimes caused workers married to "outsiders" to have conflicting schedules.

Several Brice comment sheets stated that the employees were considering leaving the company because of the no part-timer policy. With babies and small children, the women really wanted to work half days until they could return full time. Other companies were looking into job sharing, but Brice remained rigid.

One middle-aged woman with slight medical problems wished that Brice would offer an exercise room available during her lunch hour.

Five years ago, Dallas had learned, Sam had decided that the Brice offices needed updating and had contracted a professional decorator. Given a variety of designs, Sam had selected a sterile, masculine one with ultramodern furniture and huge artificial plants. He'd promptly issued a memo that he didn't want the sleek offices "garbaged up by cutesy personal mementoes or made into a living-plant jungle." Two Brice workers had commented on the "cold" working environment, wanting living plants and pictures of their families.

While Brice provided training, the managers, backed by Sam, rarely listened to what the employees had learned from the sessions.

She also remembered the women's evaluation sheets for their boss. On paper, their composite opinions formed a hard-driving man who spent little time and attention on matters concerning other people's emotions. Loring ran the company by the book—his personal manual for profit. He spent no time considering anything but productivity. Loring did not take time to chat nor to take subtle hints.

One worker, while stating that Brice offered an excellent program for advancement, bonuses, grievances and harassments, gifted Sam with the tag, "a human machine."

"Your people were very excited about my ideas, Sam. I remember their comments specifically. Several of them were already discussing presenting ideas for day-care accommodation. They were relieved to know that I thought care centers would help their job performance."

"Uh-huh." He looked down his broken nose at her, the picture of male arrogance. "I run a profitable multimillion-dollar business, Pendragon. Complete with stockholders and board meetings. We have quality products and quality workers—"

"Why are they unhappy then, Sam?" she interrupted, feeling her anger rise. She remembered one specific complaint from a Brice worker: *I've been rated down on a messy desk at the company. Yet I'm the most creative, productive employee in our branch. At the end of the day, I place my files neatly in a stack. I know where everything is, too.*

Apparently, Brice wanted its workers to be neat, thoughtless robots, Dallas decided. And the man standing before her was the cause.

He narrowed his eyes, shifting his weight over his spread legs in a typical fighter's stance. "So far as I know, they aren't unhappy."

She arced an eyebrow, confident that she had her own fighting skills. "Have you been listening?"

He didn't like that shot. The muscles in his neck tightened as they ran into his expensive dress shirt. "Of course, I listen," he snapped, hooking a finger inside his collar to unbutton it. He tugged loose his tie. "I'm not the only employer experiencing problems over your classes. Suddenly good employees are beginning to question perfectly good, standard management practices. We're drowning in silly suggestions about this stress nonsense."

Dallas tilted her head to one side, studying Sam's dark face. "So you decided to check out the problem and attend my class in the flesh. I had hoped you were attending to learn something—"

"Lady, you are pushing. If you keep preaching this stress garbage—"

"Ah, you think your realm is threatened and you're not open to new ideas. In the first place, I'm not trying to start trouble. But stress management concerns most people and I'm merely trying to help people find ways to deal with it. Your stress level is so high, you nearly throttled the biofeedback monitor. Yet you won't concede that this is something that effects a workplace. I'd call that closed thinking," she volleyed back. Dallas normally didn't spend time fighting lost causes. But she deeply resented that she had been feeling sympathetic toward him earlier.

"I run my company how I see fit," he said between his teeth.

"So did Attila the Hun. Class will resume soon. I suggest you take your seat and learn a few things about opening your mind. For your own well being and for your employees."

When his eyes darkened and he leaned down toward her as though readying another attack, she lifted her head. "You have my number, call me when you're in a better mood. But for now, I'm in control of this class and you will either leave or take your seat. Though you probably won't chose the latter. You might not have the guts for it."

Two

"**Y**ou've just finished your second piece of chocolate pie, Dallas dear. Shouldn't you let that settle before you eat the popcorn you're planning?" Dallas's mother asked that evening. Lisa frequently used the guest bedroom, especially when she sensed her daughter was on edge. Tonight, Dallas appreciated the gesture, valuing Lisa as a parent and as a friend. An encounter with Sam Loring would upset anyone.

Curled up on the other end of the couch and dressed in scarlet satin pajamas, Lisa studied Dallas's worn, tight jeans and sweatshirt. "Of course you burn off the calories faster than they can lodge on your bones. Especially when you're in the crusading mood. Oh, don't look at me like that—I recognize the look."

Nikki looked up from her coloring book, spread before the television set. Only six years old, she could almost read her mother's moods. "Grandma, Mommy looks just like the time the store took too much candy money from me."

Billy stopped studying the Christmas tree's twinkling lights. He snuggled next to Dallas, wrapping his arms around her tightly. "Mommy," he muttered sleepily. "Hold me."

Kissing the top of his head, Dallas drew the sturdy four-year-old to her lap. She nuzzled Billy's hair, kissing his cheek. Nikki and Billy were the best and only things T.J. had given her.

She'd been twenty-nine and was just beginning her career as a management-employee consultant when she married T.J. At the time, T.J. was the most dazzling man she'd ever met, sweeping her out of years of serious studies and dull, exhausting office routines. Maybe she'd been subconsciously looking for an escape, and a tall, virile athletic office manager was just the white knight she'd been seeking. Though he protested her keeping her maiden name, T.J. was an elegant groom in a fairy-tale wedding.

She hadn't spent time delving into sexuality prior to her marriage, and T.J. offered a tempting, blinding initiation. Part of T.J.'s appeal was that he needed her...to help him meet deadlines, to balance his staff's budget and to care for him. T.J. liked being taken care of so well that he retired from the working world within one year of their marriage.

With the passing of time, Dallas realized that her love for T.J. wasn't deep or lasting.

While Dallas struggled to keep a dying marriage afloat in a reality of exhaustion, arguments and unpaid bills, she became pregnant with Nikki. The unborn baby nestling within her gave Dallas what she had been seeking—the peace of motherhood.

T.J. was aghast and outraged. While Dallas struggled with a demanding career, an apartment, a baby and a childish husband, she accidentally became pregnant with Billy. Now she realized that her last attempts at pleasing T.J. were made to ease her feeling of failure. Then T.J. walked out, signing away his parental rights with a sigh of relief— "Sorry, babe. I'm not spending my life wrapped up in kids. You're making enough money, and you know what the judge said about me taking a hike if I didn't pay support. That's fine with me: I won't be back."

Nikki was hers alone then, and her life was, too. With a fierce dedication, and in early months of pregnancy, Dallas began restructuring her life.

She had wanted a home for her children. Five years ago, she'd haunted the Seattle suburbs to find the snug two-story house. With a tiny garden and a gnarled old apple tree, the house had charm from its shutters to its wooden shingles. Built at the turn of the century with cedar timber, the house had its ailments. But Dallas enjoyed puttering and painting when she could and playing in the rose garden. She had just settled in when Billy was born.

Now, draped with holiday wreaths, the house sported a mistletoe ball over the couch—an area designated by the children for "easy kissing." The scents of holiday baking blended with the tangy essence of a simmering potpourri pot.

Lisa's still-beautiful face warmed as Nikki stopped coloring and came to sit against her. The older woman put the glamour magazine aside to place her arm around the little girl. "Your mother has that fighting gleam in her eyes, honey. She was like that at your age—when she beat up Freddie Linsey for tormenting a kitten. He was twice her size, but she was outraged. If she could just decide to fight for a man as hard as she does for her causes, we might get you a daddy."

"Mother, don't give Nikki any ideas. Just because you think a man is the solution to every problem...." Dallas protested lovingly. At sixty plus, her mother was widowed and socially active. A petite blonde, she danced until dawn and thrived on romance. Lisa appreciated and frequently sampled a promising male confection; she saw no reason why Dallas couldn't do the same.

Lisa's eyes sparkled. "Since when have men become obsolete? Dear, there are just some things you can't do alone.... Why, just the other day, I saw this marvelous peignoir set and I thought if you would just let go a little—"

"Mother, would you please wait until the children are in bed?"

From her end of the couch, Lisa grinned impishly. "You'll tell me all about it then, of course?"

"Mommy," Billy murmured. "Pauly's daddy fights the bears out of his room."

Dallas rocked his warm little body against her, kissing his drooping eyelids. "Why, honey, I do that. Every night. Your room is bear-proofed."

She kissed his soft cheek. Billy burrowed closer and she

tucked the blanket around him. He yawned, lifting a chubby hand to lazily toy with her hair. His other hand rubbed a tattered satin blanket. ''But Pauly's daddy shaves every morning. And carries him around on his shoulders.... I want a daddy for Christmas.'' With another yawn, the little boy drifted off into sleep in her arms.

''He's such a baby,'' Nikki whispered with a lofty tone as she disappeared into the kitchen.

Grinning at Dallas, Lisa asked. ''A work problem, perhaps? It surely couldn't be a man,'' she teased. ''I may have to buy that snazzy peignoir myself.''

''Mother, as it happens, the problem is both work related and a man. A very big man, with a bigger problem.''

''Mmm, my, that sounds promising. I'm glad I decided to spend the night here instead of my apartment,'' Lisa cooed. ''I'm waiting to hear what he looks like. Anything I'd be interested in? Or maybe you'd like to join me in my belly-dancing class just to shape up those unused muscles.''

Dallas went still, remembering every moment of her confrontation with Sam Loring. ''He's big and tough right to his bones. Absolutely blind to the problems of a worker's stress. He has no conception of how to manage a home and a family. Or what the company could do to cut absenteeism.''

Lisa raised her eyebrows. ''Mmm. Repeat the big-and-tough part. I like it. Come on, give. I'll bet he's one of those yummy macho men with muscles and a nice, tight tush. How old? Is he married?''

''He's not married or anything close,'' Dallas muttered, remembering the biofeedback experiment. How could she have felt so sorry for that unbending piece of chauvinistic male? ''There's not much market these days for a dictator.''

''And looks? Was he macho or just one of those wimps that you seem to attract?''

Dallas straightened her shoulders. ''There was absolutely nothing wrong with Douglas.''

''Well, he certainly wasn't bedroom material. The man was a cold fish if ever I saw one,'' Lisa returned adamantly. ''I don't believe any man has really lit your fire, not even T.J. Now, your father was the big, tough type. Real exciting... Know what I mean?"

"Dad was a softy, and you know it. Men like Loring went out with the stone age, Mother," Dallas returned. "I just feel sorry for his poor people. I wish I could do something for them."

"Ah!" Lisa exclaimed as though she'd just found a gold mine. "Maybe you can. Spend some time with this—"

"Sam person," Dallas provided without enthusiasm. Somehow she just couldn't see herself trying to open Loring's closed mind.

"Sam," Lisa repeated in a long, wistful breath. "Now that's a real man's name. I like the sound of it."

"I wouldn't spend time with that bully if he were the last man on earth—"

Lisa raised a finger and tilted her head. "Now, honey. Remember the down-trodden masses that need you. Think of it as a sacrifice for the good of mankind. We can work on the man part later."

"Mother, he thinks stress is just so much...hot air."

"Well, then. Give him a little taste. Make him see things your way. Open those rusty hinges."

"Just what are you suggesting, Mother?"

On Friday after working hours, Sam gritted his teeth and jabbed his punching bag in a quick one-two. He danced back, glad for the miniature gym next to his office. He shadow punched the bag with his taped fists, shaking sweat from his hair.

When he needed to trim real frustration, he worked out. Pendragon had been gnawing on him all week. When she hadn't returned Emily's calls, he'd taken the task upon himself. "Ms. Pendragon cannot take your call now, sir," he muttered, slamming into the swinging bag.

A trickle of sweat ran down his bare neck into his damp T-shirt. Somebody had to stop that crusading Joan of Arc before she turned profit into losses.

Sam glowered at the punching bag, lowering his head to

throw a series of quick punches at it. In his time, he'd worked with some high-powered women, recognizing their potential. But Pendragon was a damned usurper. Since taking over the company, he'd built a policy that turned profits. He didn't want anyone messing with his baby. Dancing around the bag, Sam battered it with powerful blows.

There was something else about Pendragon that gnawed at him too, he admitted reluctantly. It was the soft hands and sweet-pea-fragrance part.

He'd stayed through the entire class because of her challenge. "If I had the guts for it," he repeated, shaking a drop of sweat from his hair. "I can take anything that broad can dish out."

The speaker in the gym buzzed. Emily's even tone announced, "Ms. Pendragon is here to see you. And it's five o'clock."

"What the hell—" Sam exploded, grabbing the swinging bag. He pressed his lips together. He'd been calling her for the past two days to set up an appointment, and now she waltzed in to catch him unprepared. Throwing a towel around his neck, Sam shouldered through the swinging door. Pressing his thumb down on the intercom's button, he said, "Emily, show her in. Then you can go."

"Thank you, sir," Emily returned a little too sweetly. Sam wiped his brow with the back of his arm. He knew his secretary's tone—it usually meant she had something up her sleeve.

Sam patted his damp face with the towel and leaned his hips back against the desk. He decided to keep the tape on his hands—he might need to take out more frustration after Pendragon swooped out of his offices. She could have had him in a clean business suit, but if she preferred to enter his turf, she'd have to take pot luck. Either way, he intended to take Pendragon out of the game.

"This way, Ms. Pendragon," Emily instructed as she opened the door for the younger woman. She leaned down to whisper just loud enough for Sam to hear, "We haven't fed him for hours. Be careful."

Emily smiled blithely when Sam glowered at her. "Ms. Pendragon says you've left a few messages for her and she thought she'd drop by. See you on Monday, Sam.''

Dallas Pendragon, Sam mused, the perfect name for a crusader. Dressed in a maroon bulky-knit sweater and loose slacks, his antagonist slid the strap of her briefcase from her shoulder. The wind had caught her hair, Sam noted, tossing it in a softly feminine arrangement around her pink cheeks. The other thing Sam noted instantly was her soft rosy mouth. Like cool strawberries....

He was angry then. Because she'd dropped business protocol and hadn't arranged a meeting. Because he obviously couldn't stop noticing everything about her. Like the endless length of her legs.

She smiled slightly, just a fraction of a turn of her lips that caused something inside Sam's stomach to knot. Her gaze flicked down his T-shirt and sweat pants to the gym shoes. ''Hello, Sam. I thought it best to deal with you face-to-face. I hope this isn't too inconvenient.''

Wiping another drop of sweat from his jaw, Sam realized how few people had ever seen him like this. He'd had a taste of Pendragon's toughness and decided to cut the cream-and-sugar act. Pendragon was a pro; she could take it.

Sam paused a moment, savoring the moment. He was meeting her on equal ground. Pendragon wasn't the crying type. ''Your timing is great. I was just punching the hell out of my equipment. If you'd like another round, let's set an appointment for Monday.''

She flicked a thread from her sleeve leisurely, then glanced around his paneled office. ''It's the holiday season, Sam. I like to clear out any problems as soon as I can...for peace and goodwill.''

''Why didn't you return my calls?'' he asked bluntly, studying the interesting curve of her backside as she turned to sit in a large chair facing him. Wiping sweat from his jaw, Sam scowled at her. Pendragon definitely did more for the chair than Emily's raw-boned figure.

Dallas tilted her head, the sleek hair sliding to expose a small earlobe with a diamond stud. Sam found he hadn't lost his fascination for the twinkling stone as she looked at him evenly. "Because I felt that the tone of the messages was rather brusque. Like a king summoning a servant."

"In other words, you decided to let me stew in my own juices," Sam supplied, realizing that in her place, he would have done the same thing.

She shrugged, accepting his accusation. Sam got the feeling that this woman could take anything he could dish out. And serve it back to him on a platter. "Something like that. What did you want?" she asked.

"I want to know how to get you off my back," he stated bluntly. Dallas had an air of cool disdain that set him off, challenging him. He hadn't been held at arm's length since he was a green recruit in the business world.

"Really? Have I been on your back?" Dallas returned, watching him intently.

Oh, God, Sam thought, he'd forgotten how penetrating those green eyes were...witch's eyes. "You know you're causing a hell of a problem, Dallas. Not only in my company, but in others. I lost a good worker today because of your spouting off that stress nonsense. And I'd be a fool to propose an employee job-sharing plan to the board. They'd laugh me out of the company."

"Maybe we should discuss our different ideas then," she offered as another trickle of sweat slid into Sam's damp T-shirt. "Are you uncomfortable with me, Sam? Or is it just that you're not dressed in your normal protective armor?"

Rising from the chair, Dallas caught the end of the towel that lay upon his chest. She blotted the sweat at his temples. "I've taken some time out of a busy schedule to deal with this matter, Sam," she offered gently. "But if you're uncomfortable dressed like this, I can wait. I really do want to get this thing settled tonight."

Because she had him off balance, Sam stilled beneath the soft patting motion of the towel. Then he jerked his head away. He began tugging the tape loose with his teeth.

Taking the task from him, Dallas unrolled the wide strips. Her fingers were slender and pale, tipped with short, neat nails.

Against the broad strength of his own, they appeared very feminine and soft.

Standing close to her, Sam felt something he'd protected for years shift unsteadily.

He couldn't explain it. He just felt raw and very much in need of her attention.

He studied the soft turn of her cheeks, then again caught the fragrance that reminded him of his mother's backyard sweet peas. Taken aback, Sam stilled. Her hands completed the task efficiently, and he regretted the loss of her skin brushing his.

Dallas looked up at him unexpectedly, and Sam felt the jolt down to his gym shoes. "I want you to come home with me, Sam. For dinner." Her tone was equal to that of inviting him to a board meeting.

"I have plans," he returned roughly, moving away from her. She made him nervous, and he didn't know why. Near her, he felt as if he'd jogged fifteen miles and couldn't catch his breath.

"I know you don't have a family," Dallas added, watching him. "And that you usually work long hours. Of course, if you're afraid to accept my dinner invitation..."

Pendragon knew how to issue challenges, he decided darkly. He'd checked her out—she was a single mother. But he had to ask anyway, probing. "Does your husband know you're inviting me?"

She lifted a dark eyebrow. "If I had one, I don't think he'd mind." The air in Sam's lungs stilled. He'd damn well mind if he were her husband. "You could be taking a risk. Where I come from, men do the running," he added to cover his edgy reaction to her.

"Don't get any ideas, Sam. This is business. Think of it as a power dinner. And don't worry, there will be several other people there to protect you."

Sam didn't like the feeling that she fielded his remark too easily, as if she'd had much experience. He turned, running his fingers through his damp hair. "What's the point?"

Dallas glanced outside at the scant light and the drizzle hitting his office windows. "I want to take you into the working woman's point of view. See what it's like on the other side.

Unless you're afraid you can't handle it. Your employees see you as inflexible anyway.''

He didn't like being placed on the defensive, and Pendragon had a way of snagging his nerves. "I know what it's like to work and maintain a family—''

Crossing her arms over her chest, Dallas lifted a speculative eyebrow. "Uh-huh. You do it on a routine basis, of course.''

She shifted on her long legs and took a verbal dive at him. "Let me tell you what I think your life is like, Sam. I see you have your own fitness program, yet you haven't extended one to your employees. You've kept it in your private realm. Underlings need fitness, too, you know. You probably have a streamlined life free from household duties, childrearing, home upkeep and so forth.''

Sam shifted uneasily. He'd chosen his penthouse suite and employed a housekeeper because he didn't have the time nor the desire for a real home. In fact, he'd never had anything but cheap apartments early in his career and suites later. He'd chosen his present suite to accommodate occasional business parties; it was near his office, and Bertha had her own private, locked room in the basement garage. Battered and oil-sucking, the aged pickup was the one love of Sam's life. "My life-style isn't the problem.''

"Isn't it?'' Taking a deep breath, Dallas leveled the bottom line of her opinion straight at him. "The working class has to manage repairing their own houses and preparing their own food, right down to getting the groceries themselves. And that's all after work and picking up the kids from the babysitter. That's stress, Sam. The stuff heart attacks are made of.''

"Everyone has to eat, Dallas. How or when they do it isn't a company problem.''

Dallas's left eyebrow rose, her head tilting to one side in a gesture of skepticism. "So, of course, not having children and having your own private gym...and the ability to take extended vacations when you want them, completing your personal affairs with the help of a full-time secretary—you see no point in providing your employees with any of those benefits. Is that the bottom line, Sam?''

The muscles crossing his shoulders and running up his neck tightened. "You'd make a good kamikaze fighter, Pendragon," he admitted reluctantly. "But you don't know what you're talking about. I manage a full load here. I've got just as much stress as the next guy."

"Really?" Her appraising stare slid slowly down his body, then rose slowly upward to meet his eyes. "What I see is a man with one viewpoint. Are you afraid to experience the real working world, Sam?"

"Hell, I've worked since I can remember," he said too sharply, between his teeth. "I've done laundry and shopped for my food."

Dallas straightened her shoulders, and Sam forced himself not to glance at her breasts. "Of course, you're angry and defensive when confronted with the facts, Sam. Perhaps you're already too set in your ways to listen to new ideas...but I'm asking you to try. You seem very brittle in business circumstances. I'd like to give you an inside view of another side of life...and, of course, I'm willing to listen to yours. Think of it as a summit meeting."

The thick wave of hair slid along her jaw as she lifted her head, and Sam's fingers curled with the need to touch. "No, I'm not worried about the dangers of bringing home a stranger, Sam," she said quietly, as though sensing his next shot. "Despite the fact that you can be obstinate and overbearing, you're not a bad guy. You'll back an employee with a reasonable grievance, and last year you personally paid overdue medical expenses for an employee's child. And you never pick on anyone half your size. I checked."

She was tossing challenges at him again, Sam decided after a moment of grinding his teeth. She had tossed one too many. "My car or yours?"

"Actually, I took the bus to work today. I was hoping you'd give me a ride. Oh, and I'll have to pick up a few groceries along the way." She glanced at his sweaty workout clothes. "I can wait if you want to shower. No doubt along with your private gym, you have an executive washroom?"

Sam paused just a moment before looking down at her from

his superior height. "If," he began firmly, "we want to accomplish anything tonight, Pendragon, I suggest you give me a little space. There are limits."

"Your limits, of course," she returned, unruffled. "Your game rules."

"I play a fair game. I'll be out in a few moments." Walking to his washroom, Sam couldn't resist throwing out one more taunt. "By the way, this should be entertaining."

Sam slid his Lincoln Continental through Seattle's rain-slick streets. Along the way to Dallas's home, he had somehow acquired sacks of groceries and had retrieved two small children from a babysitter. He learned that Nikki was a first grader, staying after school at the sitter's.

Seated on the front seat between Dallas and himself, Nikki and Billy openly stared at him. "Big man, Mommy," Billy stated finally.

Dallas laughed, tucking the little boy against her side. Sam listened to the sound of her laughter, the humor genuine. The black-haired child nestled to her. "Sam is nice, Billy, for all his size. That's why I brought him home. Just so he could meet you."

Sam liked the low, rich sound of her voice; it was like her touch. He glanced at Nikki, seated beside him. Lifting an eyebrow, he asked, "These are the other people you mentioned, I presume."

Over Billy's head, Dallas's eyes twinkled. "Precious, aren't they?"

Nikki turned to her mother. "Mommy, did you go daddy-shopping today like Grandma said you should? Is he Billy's present?"

For just a moment, Sam experienced the definite delight of seeing Pendragon squirm. He liked that.

"Now, honey, we talked about Sam coming to dinner. He's just going to visit with us. We have some business to straighten out, okay?"

"He's awful big," Billy said, his eyes studying Sam from head to toe. "Can you carry me, Mr. Sam?"

Warmed by the little boy, Sam answered, "As long as you like."

Nikki's hand reached up to stroke Sam's cheek, and he realized he hadn't taken time to shave for the evening. He caught the scent of chocolate and fabric softener as the small hand explored his jaw then slid away.

Suddenly, he realized he hadn't been touched by a child for years. The thought nagged at him, making him aware of the family he'd wanted as a young man. But in building his career, he'd forgotten.

"You're frowning.... Children are by nature curious, Sam," Dallas explained quietly, watching his scowl with those quiet, contemplative eyes. "But if it bothers you, we can have our meeting another time without them. This isn't painful for you in any way, is it?"

"Do you have kids, Mr. Sam?" Billy interrupted as Sam slid into the designated driveway. He parked behind a dark red compact car, which reminded him of Dallas. The car was sleek and a high performer.

"Maybe he doesn't like kids," Nikki said slowly, watching him warily as her mother left the car and helped Billy out. "My friend Kathy says some grownups don't."

"I like kids, honey. I just wasn't lucky enough to have any," Sam returned, suddenly startled by what he had just said. His ex-wife hadn't wanted children, and somehow the matter of a family hadn't occurred for years. Sam felt his body tense, and he shoveled the thought back into oblivion. He'd never toyed with regrets and didn't intend to now.

Nikki eased across the seat to slide out the door. "I like Christmas."

"Sam, would you mind bringing the groceries in?" Dallas asked, probing her purse for her keys with one hand. Billy held tight to her free one, watching Sam with big, round eyes.

In the bare light, Sam could make out a small, well-kept yard with a white board fence enclosing the back. Going up the steps to the wide front porch, Sam felt the muscles running across his stomach tighten. The homey atmosphere began with the holly wreath on the front door and spread before him. He shifted the two sacks uneasily as Dallas changed into a busy dynamo, urging him into the kitchen. At the same time, she directed the children to take off their coats and put them away.

Holding the grocery sacks, Sam caught the scents of potpourri and love warming the house. He caught a drift of something long forgotten, something too painful to remember. Of forgotten wishes, rustling in his memories like dead leaves.

"Just put the sacks on the counter, Sam," she ordered, breezing by him to a bathroom just off the kitchen. "We're having stew and French bread tonight," he heard her say over the sound of running water. "On busy days, and especially on a really hectic Friday, I like to plan a slow-cooker meal."

She reentered the kitchen, tugging up her sleeves at the elbows. "Please make yourself at home, Sam."

When he hesitated, she shot him a knowing smile. "You look so stiff—take off your jacket and tie, if you want. Kick off your shoes. If you're not comfortable, my solution will never work."

Sam just caught her sweet-pea scent as she breezed by him, turning on lamps. He had the impression of a hummingbird, darting from flower to flower. "Come on, kids. I've got your bath water running," she called. "You first, Nikki!"

In the soft light of lamps and candles, Dallas's home presented a pretty picture right down to the twinkling lights on the Christmas tree and the gaily wrapped presents. Four patchwork stockings hung from a white-enameled mantle, and Sam studied them as he stripped off his coat. A mother and two children didn't add up to four Christmas stockings. He didn't like the implication of that fourth stocking. Pendragon wasn't married, but she hadn't said anything about a boyfriend. Sam found himself scowling at the patchwork stocking.

Dallas whizzed by him, her sweatsuit creating a streak of yellow. She grinned up at him as she began unpacking the groceries with quick efficiency. "It's like this every night. A steady run until almost bedtime...I think Nikki is almost ready. Would you mind helping Billy finish bathing? That would leave more time for us to talk."

When Sam shifted uncomfortably, she winked. "Working men and women go through this routine every night and survive.

But if you don't think you can handle a six and a four-year-old, supper will just be a little late.''

Sam frowned. She'd made him feel incapable of the simple task. Rolling up his shirt sleeves, he studied her closely. Dallas caught the inquiring look and returned it evenly. "Does something about me or tonight bother you, Sam? I really don't want you to be uncomfortable.''

"Everything is fine," he answered too roughly. Dallas's tone made him uneasy. Sam wasn't used to anyone genuinely being concerned about him to see to his comfort. When she used that tone, Sam had the feeling of a soft, loving hand caressing his worries away. Long ago, he'd given up any dreams about anyone caring for him. Her quiet stare was too unguarded, too patient, and it made Sam nervous as hell. She had a way of seeing too deep, down into the murky depths of his emotions. "You're tall," he said suddenly, startled by the words that seemed to just skim out of him.

Personal comments weren't his style, but neither was the Pendragon household. She had him off balance, like a masculine Alice in Wonderland. Or maybe the potpourri scent was going to his head. Whatever it was, Sam kept studying Dallas and wondering just what was going on inside himself. "You're tall, and you move fast," he said slowly.

Great, he thought, looking down into Dallas's green witch's eyes. Since when did he care about a woman's height or the way she moved?

When she licked her lips and looked away nervously, he wanted to know then just what type of man would slow her down, long enough to taste those soft, strawberry lips. The thought curled around him warmly, startling him with an image of Pendragon's white hands fluttering on his darker skin.

"I have to move fast. There is never enough time when you have a family," she returned without missing a beat. She opened the slow cooker to stir the bubbly contents with a wooden spoon. Leaning against the counter, Dallas studied the stew intently, probing it. "It's ready."

The motion brought the sweat pants tighter around her hips, and Sam felt a sensual tightening in his midsection. He rotated his suddenly taut neck muscles. If Sam ever wanted to place his hands on a woman's soft buttocks, it was now. His palms burned with the ache to cup— He rubbed his hands together briskly, knowing that he badly needed the support of a good stiff drink.

He turned to the bathroom, already hearing the children giggle and splash.

And then Dallas reached upward, opening a cabinet. The angle of her body caught Sam broadside. Her breasts were fuller than he had thought, her stomach just gently rounded to sweep into long slender legs...Dallas Pendragon was one neatly turned piece of woman....

She smiled over her shoulder. "Is something wrong, Sam?"

"Nothing." He swallowed to cover the tightening in his throat. Hell, he'd just been without sex for so long, he rationalized. Any woman would hit him the same way.

He had to watch Pendragon, he decided moodily. She moved inside people and turned them around. Like a virus.

Hunching his shoulders, Sam entered the steamy bathroom to find an assortment of toys and two laughing children. Nikki had already had her bath and was dressed in a flannel nightgown. Apparently she'd been handing Billy his favorite toys.

Seating himself on the closed lid of the commode, Sam grabbed the bottle of bubble bath just as Billy began pouring it liberally into the water. "Don't you think that's enough, Billy?"

The small boy looked at him seriously. "Mommy says you have to use soap to get clean," he answered piously. "Are we going to adopt you like we did our kitty? Baghdad won't come in the house even when we invite him. But you could stay in my room."

Sam reached over to drain the water from the tub. "I don't think so. Your mother and I have some business to finish tonight."

Nikki placed her hand on Sam's shoulder and he shifted uncomfortably under the light touch. Since when did kids start touching him? Since when did he like it? Sam swallowed uneasily when Nikki stroked his cheek. "Mommy always wraps Billy in a nice warm towel, then dresses him in jammies."

The boy climbed out of the tub and stared expectantly up at

him. "You could carry both of us, I bet, Mr. Sam. You're real big."

Sam's heart had stopped, then began beating slowly, heavily within his ribs. The two kids were getting to him, he admitted warily, as he wrapped Billy in a towel and helped him dress in pajamas. When the task was finished, his shirt was damp and the children were bounding off to their mother.

Sitting still for a moment, Sam struggled to regain his balance. Absently opening his shirt, he rubbed the hair-covered osurface thoughtfully. "Must be the Christmas season, old man," he muttered, running his fingers through his hair as he emerged from the towel-scattered bathroom.

Dallas turned from ladling stew into soup bowls just as Sam entered the large kitchen. Rumpled and distracted, Sam looked utterly...attractive, she decided after mulling the thought. "I've fed Baghdad—our cat. You can meet him later," she said, reminding herself that Sam was a business experiment, not a man—in the sensual sense. Actually Baghdad, a stray gray tom who kept returning to her home, reminded her of Sam—wary of any kindness.

Sam's hair was mussed slightly, and his frown, brooding. She ran a quick appraising look down Sam's fit body from broad shoulders to narrow hips. Maybe it was just that she wasn't used to seeing a man's chest. Dark and hairy, exposed by the damp, gaping shirt, the intriguing surface caught her gaze and held it.

Or maybe she was especially vulnerable at Christmastime, she rationalized, adjusting Billy's chair closer to hers. Pushing the thought from her mind, Dallas invited Sam to sit down. "It's not filet mignon or Baked Alaska. But it's a nourishing, easy meal for a working mother," she offered, smiling.

What was he thinking? she wondered as he continued to stare at his filled bowl. Then slowly he spoke, "I haven't had home-made stew for some time."

Nikki reached up to pat his cheek, consolingly. "Mr. Sam, you have to eat everything on your plate or Mommy won't let you have chocolate cake. It's awful good, too. She puts cherries on top. With stems, so you can eat 'em like this!" She mimed popping cherries into her mouth and jerking off the stems, grinning up at him.

"I guess I'd better eat my stew then, huh?" Sam returned the grin and Dallas noted the lines on his face shifting as though he didn't smile often. Yes, he needed help, and if her plan worked, his employees would benefit as well. He was a good sport when he wanted to be, she thought as he helped with dinner cleanup.

While Dallas tossed in a load of laundry, Sam settled down with Nikki on his lap. The little girl petted Sam's jaw and though he seemed mildly uncomfortable, he allowed the affectionate gesture. Both Billy and Nikki had instigated a study of him that Dallas considered normal; they weren't often exposed to a man within their home.

Except Douglas. She flicked a glance at Sam's long legs, the neat crease of his slacks smooth over a muscular thigh. He turned slightly, and she caught a glimpse of his chest when the shirt fell away. Douglas was absolutely hairless, she'd discovered one day at the beach. In comparison to Sam, the smaller man was...well, more academic looking, she decided loyally. To shield her thoughtful expression, Dallas reached to check the candle beneath the simmering potpourri pot.

"We're ready to go to bed now, Mr. Sam. You can help Mommy fight the bears away and tuck us in good-night." Nikki took the story book from Sam and kissed him.

Dallas almost melted as Sam's dark eyebrows jammed together fiercely, as though he'd just experienced a sudden shock. He touched the area of Nikki's kiss lightly. Oh, Dallas thought sadly as he awkwardly patted Nikki's pajama clad bottom. The poor man just wasn't used to any sort of affection. No wonder his poor employees thought of him as inflexible and uncaring. And at Christmas season, too.

Her fingers tightened on her mug of eggnog. She'd wanted Sam to experience the hustle of a working woman returning to her home, the physical and emotional demands. She couldn't possibly allow herself to soften now.

Billy hugged her neck as she carried him to bed. He whispered in her ear. "He's got no mommy and no kids. So he's ours by rights, huh? Finders keepers? Like Baghdad?"

"We'll talk about it when he's gone, okay?" she whispered back, feeling uneasy as Sam stood at the doorway, the light in the hallway outlining his tall body.

He did remind her of an orphan, his face in shadows and his hands in his pockets as he stood outside the children's bedroom. She forced the thought from her; Sam was the corporate head of a company, and a strict manager of his employees. From what she'd seen he was hard as steel inside and out. Rubbing her hands together, Dallas decided it was time to present her business package to Sam. He'd either buy it or she'd wasted her effort on him. And three helpings of stew, plus two sizeable pieces of chocolate cake.

"Did you kill all the grizzlies, Pendragon?" he asked easily, settling down on her couch. For an odd moment, Dallas contrasted the cabbage-rose upholstery pattern to Sam's stark masculinity.

Startled by the thought of Sam as a man instead of a project, she straightened her shoulders. She admitted that Sam nettled her. He seemed like such an immovable personality.

"Okay, you've been working up to presenting your plan all evening," he stated in an ominous low voice that brought the hairs on the back of her neck standing upright. His voice was deep, gravelly, with just a drop of soft Southern drawl she hadn't noticed before. She looked at him warily from beneath her lashes.

Normally his voice was clipped and demanding like a drill sergeant's. But now the tones seemed almost...sensual, riveting her stocking-covered feet to the hardwood floor as he said, "You've been explaining the plight of the working woman to me since I arrived. Get to the point, Dallas. Why did you invite me here tonight?"

Three

For the first time since she'd conceived the details of Lisa's sketchy plan, Dallas began to feel twinges of uncertainty. Looking too powerful, Sam occupied the major portion of her couch. With his arm resting along the back of her furniture, he looked mussed and well...delectable, she admitted reluctantly.

Reaching out from her past, a curl of bitterness lodged in her stomach. At twenty-nine, she'd been easy prey for T.J.'s practiced sensuality. Looking back, her romance with T.J. was more hormonal than the grand love she had thought. Now, at thirty-nine, she had decided that passion of the red-hot variety probably would not come her way. She'd settled for a good career, a warm home and had wrapped her children around her.

Dallas found her body inclining toward Sam's weight and straightened in a jerky movement. The hard-nosed businessman weighing down his end of *her* couch shouldn't have appeal. She didn't want to think about his delighted boyish expression when he ate chocolate cake. And she didn't want to think about how she had catered to T.J., falling for that same winsome masculine expression.

Uncomfortable with the direction of her thoughts, she needed something warm and comforting in her hand. "I always have a cup of tea just after putting the kids to bed. Would you like some?"

"Anything. I'm anxious to hear your proposal, Dallas. It should top off the evening perfectly. Do you want me to help?"

The idea of Sam's large body in her kitchen flattened the breath from Dallas. She'd needed some space to recover from the evening. She hadn't expected a sensual reaction to Sam when she invited him. Suddenly, Sam stretched leisurely, his hard thigh brushing hers, and something within her started clawing its way out. Her throat dried suddenly, and a funny aching tingle raced across the tips of her breasts. Dallas tramped down the urge to slide her hand across the rippling planes of that hard thigh. *Good Lord, what was wrong with her?*

A cold chill raced over her too-tight flesh. Sam was definitely not her kind of potential romantic material. In fact—she slid a sideways glance at him—concrete was not any woman's potential romantic stuff. The man lived to work—profits and gain were in his blood, not poems and flowers.

Almost leaping to her feet, Dallas walked quickly to the kitchen. "I can manage. Just make yourself comfortable." Squaring her shoulders, Dallas had the oddest feeling that Sam had touched her, a broad sweep of warm hands flowing down her backside.

Her hands shook when she prepared the tray for tea. She frowned, studying the orchid pattern of the delicate china. Nothing more than a business wall to be scaled, Sam's physical attributes shouldn't be upsetting her. People could benefit from her project. *And all she could think about was sex.*

Her past experience had not been monumental. Dallas spared a moment to look out of the window into the night, giving herself needed space. Accidentally, she caught a movement from the Deon's window next door. The newlyweds were tangled in a passionate embrace, kissing each other as though they needed the contact more than air.

Pressing her eyelids firmly closed, Dallas forced herself to breathe quietly for a moment. Rubbing her temple, she admitted

reluctantly that the sight of Sam—sweaty from his workout—
had first started her lapse. She'd patted his perspiration away
with the towel, when she really wanted to— Okay. Something
haywire within her wanted to tear off her sweater and press her
body against his hard one.

Her head throbbed. The whole idiotic notion was one for *The
Guiness Book of World Records.* Dallas Pendragon represented
the contemporary business woman, not Sheena of the Jungle
responding to sensual jungle drums. She willed the momentary
weakness to pass and dedicated herself to organizing her presentation. The daydreams of her approaching middle age could
wait.

Shaking her head, Dallas ran her thumb and forefinger up and
down the bridge of her nose. Loring presented an immense personal challenge to her. And lodged somewhere in her brain, her
mother's propaganda about peignoirs and nestling in bed with
an overheated male had gotten tangled.

She wasn't a primitive person; she never had been...or so T.J.
had said. To her, Loring shouldn't represent the male species;
he was an experiment—one of the toughest businessmen in Seattle. In her research, she'd found that he led the rat pack of
high-powered businessmen. Winning him over could institute
new practices that could benefit thousands of stressed workers....

Later, seated on the opposite end of the couch from Sam,
Dallas wished she would have purchased a chair in lieu of her
large floor pillows and the children's bean bags.

She sipped her tea, enjoying the English blend from the china
cup. The small ritual mattered and eased the tension distracting
her. Sam placed his empty cup and saucer on the coffee table,
then leaned back to watch her.

His hand shifted on the back of the couch, and Dallas sensed,
rather then saw, the powerful muscles of his forearm. She
glimpsed an expensive flat wristwatch. The short black hairs
covering his dark skin glistened in the candlelight.

Dallas swallowed, realizing the intimacy of the scene. She
placed her cup aside, then reached to turn on a lamp.

Sam's expression seemed to shift, tempering with humor. "It

is romantic, isn't it?" he asked, his deep voice laced with humor.

The oddest edge of guilt touched her; she could feel herself preparing to blush. To recover her control, Dallas gripped the arm of the couch, crushing the cabbage-rose chintz.

"That isn't what I had in mind at all, Sam. And you should know it. It's strictly business." Dallas instantly regretted not tossing off his remark. She leaned back against the opposite end of the couch and waited for her temper to settle. If he'd just stop watching her as if he were inspecting her ulterior motives.

His hard mouth lifted just slightly, mockingly. "Isn't this cozy? The kids are in bed—they want to adopt me, by the way—and finally, thee and me—"

She took a deep breath. If there was one person in whom she hadn't expected to find a humorous streak—and deep, beguiling dimples—it was Sam Loring. "What I propose may be a little difficult to comprehend at first, but just bear with me."

"I am listening, Dallas. You haven't had any problems expressing yourself up to this point. Why don't you just spell it out?"

Moistening her dry lips, Dallas was surprised to catch Sam following the motion. She swallowed, shifting back into the security of the throw pillows. She wanted to dive under them; Loring had slashing, gray, predator eyes that could spot momentary weakness instantly.

Dallas allowed herself a frown; she wasn't into trading sensual games for career gain. "I would like to place a wager with you, Sam. One that puts my reputation on the line, and I'm very serious about it. Your end of the wager isn't that difficult, just a matter of changing a life-style for a month. I'd stand to lose far more."

Taking a deep breath and watching Sam's intent features, Dallas fleetingly noted another quality about him missing from T.J.: *Sam listened.* While he didn't like her theories, he respected her right to express them.

Uneasily dismissing her continuing comparison between Sam and T.J., Dallas forced herself to proceed, "If I lose the wager, I will personally contact your employees and explain that my theories on stress were total nonsense. That's what you want me to do, isn't it? I really believe you'll see things differently after this experiment, Sam."

His forefinger traced the cabbage-rose design near her shoulder. "And I have an important part in this, no doubt. What's the part about changing a life-style for a month?"

Dallas leaned forward to explain her wager. "You'll lose the wager if you cannot—repeat, cannot—follow a working woman's routine for the most hectic work month of the year—December."

Bending to retrieve her briefcase from the floor, Dallas snapped open the latches. "I've prepared a list, and we can go over it together. So you can better understand a working woman's routine. Of course, you don't have the necessary children, so you'll have an easier time of it."

"What's the catch? My end of the deal is a snap," he said in clipped tones.

"We'll see," Dallas returned mildly, thinking of how she had stayed up all night with Billy and his flu. The next day she had worked twelve hours on classes. "But just for fun, let's say you couldn't manage running a home and working. Let's say you stepped into the life of a working woman and found it to be very uncomfortable."

Ignoring his slight snort of disbelief, Dallas prepared to slide into home base. Either he'd laugh and walk out now, or she had him interested. "Not everyone is up to the challenge of taking care of themselves and budgeting, Sam," she added in a I-dare-you tone that caused Sam's eyes to flicker dangerously.

He nodded curtly, lifting a thick eyebrow at her. "Go right on ahead, Pendragon. You're wading through too much bull to stop now. I've been taking care of myself for a long time, but for my own amusement, I'd like to know exactly what my end of the wager would be."

Warmed by the small victory of getting him hooked, Dallas set herself the task of reeling him in. She sensed him assessing her strengths and vulnerabilities. Whatever he was, Sam had turned his entire attention to her proposal. She had the impression that before he threw any ideas in the hogwash bucket, he'd inspect its uses first.

"My theory is that you, as a manager, just have not experienced the real working world," she said quietly, noting with satisfaction that his expression had changed to that of a bulldog determined to chew through anything in his fenced yard.

Dallas delicately threw him a bone. She shrugged and smiled with bland innocence. "If you lost—by some impossibility—I'd like to work on proposals and present them to your board—"

"Everybody wants something. But you've stepped into the wrong ball game this time, Dallas. Show me the damn list," he said in a flat tone that sounded like Billy's when his toys were endangered. "You don't know anything about me or what I can handle. I can breeze through anything you can shovel out, including a "working woman's world," he repeated the phrase with a confident sneer.

Dallas didn't want to lay out her proposal to an angry man. She wanted him receptive and in good humor. "I know you like chocolate cake, Sam," she teased lightly, foraging into his bristling manner.

"Okay, so I'm a pushover for cake," he snapped, his features hardening as though he regretted giving her a fraction of himself. "And you don't think I've got the stamina to maintain a working woman's life-style. What is it, anyway? They've got dishwashers and clothes driers, blow driers and curling irons. It's convenience all the way, right down to slower cookers and prepared foods."

"You think so? Let's look at the list and then you can either wager or—" Dallas edged closer to present the list and found her shoulder inches away from his side. At odds with Sam's masculine scent, the scent of Nikki's bubble bath crept up from his shirt sleeve.

Her heartbeat accelerated to double time and she hesitated, scouting out the scents and focusing on an uneasiness within her. Biting her lip, Dallas reluctantly chalked up one for Sam. She'd always hated the heavy scents men sometimes wore. They seemed dishonest somehow.

Like T.J.... Why did Sam cause T.J. to come strolling out of the sordid past?

"... Or I'll have you inciting riots all over Seattle, right? This whole thing is beginning to look like blackmail." Sam scowled, leaning down to read the list. He squinted, then shook his head. "I can't read anything without my glasses," he explained, reaching to extract a pair of black-rimmed glasses from his coat pocket. He slid them on, taking the list from her to study it.

Dallas found herself staring at the angle of his nose beneath the no-nonsense frames. She wondered how he had broken his nose.

Why should she care how he had broken his nose? Or why he had scars on his knuckles?

Running the palm of her hand stealthily across her rumbling stomach, Dallas decided the stew had been too spicy.

Studying Sam as he read the detailed tasks, Dallas could see that he was as receptive as hardened concrete. She shoved aside the image of his dimples; they must have been a mirage. Sam slapped the paper into her hand and sat back to stare at her. "There's not a thing there that would cause me the least bit of difficulty. You might as well start contacting those employees now."

She didn't like the high-handed way he'd thrown the wager back on her side of the court. Perhaps he needed help to realize the depth of the tasks. "Well, let's go down the items one by one and perhaps you'll see things differently—"

He sighed as though thoroughly bored. "Trust me. You are wasting our time."

Dallas felt her muscles tighten and her chin lift fractionally. She smiled, just once and without warmth. "Perhaps you really are inflexible. I understand your *Manual of Brice Employee Rules* has never been altered. That makes a pretty strong statement to me when the workplace is constantly changing and new techniques are being found every day."

She had the satisfaction of almost—but not quite—seeing Sam Loring wince. His gray eyes slashed down at her. "I wrote it. I stand by it."

"Not one change in ten years, Sam. Yet there has been research on the hazards of and ways to prevent stress," Dallas could feel him sliding, uncomfortable with her challenge. His head seemed to lower into the protective bulk of his shoulders, like a fighter on the defensive.

His fingers straightened slowly, then tightened on his thigh. "Go over the damn list, then. Lady, I'm going to take you up on your offer. Maybe it will teach you about taking risks with people who know their business."

Sam's smile wasn't nice, and Dallas found herself returning it in kind.

"Mmm. I admire your confidence. But we'll see what happens after the month is out." She opened the list, pointing to it. "Number one. Thou shalt do all your own private business—"

"Who the hell do you think does it?" he demanded between his teeth.

"Your secretary?" Dallas offered blithely. His scowl seemed to shift from anger to caution as he looked again at the list. Sam really had no idea about the life-style she proposed. But he would...in detail. "No secretaries doing your personal running, Sam. Or delivering your car to the mechanic's. Somehow during your day at work and at home, you have to find time to pick up your laundry at the cleaners. Ah, and that's another thing— nothing but dry cleaning is allowed at the cleaners. You have to do your everyday laundry yourself. That includes towels, sheets, rugs, etcet-era."

He muttered a disgruntled seaman's oath. The salty terms caused her to lift her eyebrows just once. Then pushing on, Dallas saw no reason to spare him any breathing room. "Of course, you must do your own cleaning—tub, floors, making beds, disposing of trash...."

Holding up a finger, Dallas continued while Sam began to carefully study the list. "Piece of cake," he muttered beneath his breath.

"Try number four, Sam. No use of private workout facilities. You're going to have to make time to exercise away from the company. Now that is not to say you can't use home equipment. Providing you can buy it on the average working salary. I'll tabulate that after scanning your employee wages. You must stay on that budget, Sam. That will include lunches and groceries. Oh, by the way, you have to do your own shopping and cooking and driving.''

Sam sat back in the couch and stared at her blankly as she rapped off more rules: "In the office, Sam, I suggest you use your breaks to conduct your personal business, like balancing checkbooks and so forth. And remember, under no condition is your secretary to help you. She can't even straighten your desk. Nor do your Christmas shopping.''

Pausing, she turned to him. Sam leveled a you-must-be-crazy look at her. Poor thing, he was just beginning to get the picture.

Because Dallas was basically sympathetic to his plight, she smiled. Then without a thought of the consequences, she reached to touch the back of his hand. "It's not a lot to ask, Sam...remember, I'm betting my reputation. For a professional to retract ideas is more dangerous than rearranging a life-style for a month.''

Sam felt the soft brush of her fingers on his skin. Wading through the reality of her proposal, he realized one thing at the moment: he ached for her touch, hating the moment when her hand left him.

Taking his glasses off to place them on the coffee table, Sam settled back into the upholstery to consider the entire picture. An expert at taking problems apart, Sam weighed the advantages against the minuses. Confident about winning the wager, he itemized the other pluses of playing along.

Studying Dallas's eyes, he wondered about their shade after lovemaking. Studying the turn of her mouth, he considered its taste.

His gaze slid down the slight curve of her breasts to her legs. Sam realized he had been challenged on another level. He'd always liked an intelligent woman and he missed the sensual excitement stirring him now. Unless he was mistaken, Dallas could be a passionate woman—one to linger over, like a fine wine. He smiled slowly, savoring the moment, his excitement growing as he considered the possibilities.

Pendragon needed to pay for her troublemaking, he decided

absently. But more than that, he wanted to feel the soft, lithe movement of her body beneath his.

Dallas Pendragon would share his bed—if only for a time. They were both adults; they could handle the situation when it ended. He slipped his hand lower, finding the firm curve of her shoulder. Sam liked the sleek ripple of muscle beneath his palm, like a cat being petted.

Pendragon—the woman—challenged him, made him want to hear her purr.

"I'd like to take you up on your offer, Pendragon, but I want to up the ante," he said, noting how she shifted slightly from him. He liked that—she wasn't using her femininity to add leverage to the deal. Skimming the light spray of freckles across her nose, he surveyed the corner of her mouth. It looked quite tasty. Like sweet Southern pecan pie.

The tip of Dallas's tongue flicked across her bottom lip. Sam felt his adrenaline level rise. She might be successful in business, but somehow he sensed that as a woman, Pendragon was very guarded in her relationships.

There was just something old-fashioned and very feminine about her, an element he would explore when he slipped aside her business suit and practical pumps. He allowed himself a genuine smile and added, "We're playing for big stakes here, Pendragon. It's a matter of business ethics. I don't want you to think I'm easy."

She rubbed the palm of her hand up and down her thigh briskly. For a time, Sam contented himself by studying the nervous movement. Unless he missed his bet, Pendragon had thighs like silk.

Watching her, Sam grinned at a thought skimming through him. As a boy in Georgia, he'd frolicked in a patch of sweet peas, warmed by the sun and caressed by the breeze. He had the feeling that Dallas could make him feel the same way. For a time. In his experience, good things never lasted.

Dallas faced him warily. "What do you have in mind?"

Funny, she thought, as his grin widened and the dimples crept out to full power. She hadn't thought Sam Loring would play games. But just now, he had the look of a Cheshire cat—with a mouse between his paws.

She didn't trust him. His look said he knew all about something she hadn't yet glimpsed.

His hand had somehow found her nape, his thumb caressing the length of her neck. She shivered instinctively; Sam's gray eyes darkened.

Something had shifted between them, and Dallas felt herself skidding along like a cat on ice. "Just what did you have in mind?"

He chuckled, and the sound went skittering through her—a low, sensual, barroom, know-it-all, male tone. Lifting her chin away from his stroking thumb, Dallas questioned the wisdom of inviting him to her house.

Glancing around the warmth of her home, he looked back at her. "Nice home, Dallas. Comes complete with Christmas spirit...kids and everything. I live in a penthouse with a housekeeper provided in the lease. I couldn't possibly manage its upkeep on a worker's salary."

"Uh-huh." She nodded slowly, watching his dimples creep into his cheeks. She felt as if she were walking on a circus tight rope, and her safety net below had huge holes in it.

Tilting his head to one side, Sam eased his left eyebrow upward. It was a scarred eyebrow; a gray hair refused to follow the line. Dallas wanted to trace her fingertip across it, smoothing it gently. But instead, she prodded, "Go ahead. I'm listening."

He sighed, stretching back against the upholstery. Lifting his arms behind his head, Sam yawned hugely. His legs stretched out endlessly and he crossed them at the ankle. "I'm going to have to work out the details."

Running his finger between his eyebrows, Sam studied the shine on his expensive dress shoes. "It's just a rough idea...but it goes something like this—I'm not one to overlook an opportunity to better production by new employee practices."

Frowning, he looked at her. "In the month while I'm paying my working-woman dues, I want you to make a list of the basic changes you think will benefit Brice employees. Then you and only you work up feasibility studies—costs, personnel, practices—whatever. If you can lay out a workable program—working with me—and I lose the wager, Brice will go for it. I'll back you before the board.''

He shot her a perceptive glance beneath his eyebrows. "I can influence other businesses, Dallas...so it would be to your benefit to indulge my small adjustments to your ideas. For the sake of a better wager.''

Reeling from the force of his offer, Dallas met his stare evenly. In her experience, the things that were too good to be true usually had big problems. Loring had a reputation for being a shrewd businessman. He wouldn't make that sizeable offer without catches. "And?" she probed slowly.

Rotating his shoulder against the cushions, Sam yawned again. He kicked off his shoes and studied the four Christmas stockings on the mantle. She waited as his gaze strolled across the gaily decorated tree. She had the sinking feeling Sam's big deal had a bigger catch. "Sam?"

"Uh-huh?" He turned lazily to her, the long lashes throwing spiky shadows down his lean cheeks.

Why stop now? Dallas wondered. Brice Cleansers would be a prize trophy—if only she didn't have this sinking feeling.... "Sam, I realize you're just creating ideas on the spur of the moment and I know it's rough to catch all the fine points. But let's have the major details. Now.''

Sam's seemingly drowsy eyes lingered on her legs, then swept slowly upward to her face. "Well, there is just one little thing—*me*. To really give your experiment its full potential, I'd need to feel every element of stress in the average worker's life. Like children. And I couldn't possibly get the real feeling of home life at my place. Too big. I couldn't possibly support the electricity bills on an average pay. And I don't want to fire my once-a-week cook. She's elderly and knows how to make bagels.''

"You're hedging, Sam. I think we've gone far enough into the discussion to lay all the cards on the table.''

Nodding almost absently, Sam studied her mouth as though he found it tempting.

Dallas shifted uncomfortably, feeling her insides flutter. Sam was up to the proverbial no-good.

"Well," he said, leaning his head back against the cushions and looking at her with drowsy eyes, "if I were to live in an average house—say something like this..."

He glanced around her home, then settled back into the cushion as though it were a snugly bed pillow.

Closing his eyes, Sam sighed. "I'd really like to spend my month of hardships here, Dallas. With you. You can keep an eye on me that way...see that I don't cheat."

Dallas dropped through the imaginary tight rope's safety net. For a moment she couldn't breathe. Living with a man was an experience she did not want to repeat. T.J. had watched television while she had struggled frantically with laundry, cleaning and managing insufficient-funds notices.

Sam couldn't possibly manage two children—

As she did frequently when upset, Dallas thought she could devour two boxes of cherry-covered chocolates. "Sam, you're tired. We'll have lunch tomorrow and discuss a more reasonable plan, okay?"

"Afraid?" The soft Southern drawl had returned, his eyes opening slowly to flicker over her face.

"Not on your life, Loring," she managed unsteadily after a moment.

"I'm housebroken. I'll make my bed and work out expenses with you. I'll do all the laundry and baby-sit like a live-in nanny anytime you want. What's more, I can experience the entire picture." He shrugged slowly. "Of course, it's up to you."

"No way..." Dallas said slowly in a low voice. "Look, Sam. Admit it. You can't cut it and you're looking for ways out—"

Suddenly, the drowsy eyes were replaced by a sharp, predatory gleam. "Oh, can't I? Lady, I can handle anything you can dish out."

While Dallas dealt with the new angles on her wager, Sam pulled out his dimples. "Come on, Pendragon. I'll be disappointed if you back out now...just because *you* couldn't cut it."

His thumb warmed a path down the side of her neck. Dallas forced herself to hold still as she took his wrist between her thumb and forefinger. Beneath her light grasp, his pulse was pounding as rapidly as hers. The thought that Sam was responding to her—excited by her—sent a series of shockwaves through her.

She swallowed the dry wad that seemed to be lodged in her throat. Sam, sitting with his shirt agape, his chest textured with a dark covering of hair, was too...stimulating. "No, Sam," she whispered unevenly. "How would I explain...?"

"You'll think of something," he answered quietly, soothingly. "I trust you."

Could she trust herself?

"No, Sam," she whispered weakly. She was either hearing her own heartbeat...or those damned jungle tom-toms.

"It's for the good of everyone," he insisted in that musical Southern drawl. But Dallas found she couldn't look away from that dark, hairy wedge exposed by his shirt. On her thigh, her fingertips flexed, wanting to stroke the rough hair on his chest. She swallowed, suddenly realizing how very much she wanted to nuzzle—

Forcing herself to look upward, Dallas found Sam watching her quietly. The hard gray eyes had darkened, the shadows of the room flickering about him. Taking her hand, Sam placed it upon his chest, holding it gently with his own. The rough hair shifted and tickled her palm, and Dallas's eyes involuntarily drifted down to their hands.

His heart beat slowly, heavily beneath her touch. Like a sleeping beast waiting to be awakened. The feelings she had about him during the biorhythm experiment came rushing back: his loneliness reached out to her. And she responded.

His fingers slid down to her wrist, raising it to his mouth. For a moment, his breath hovered against skin. Then holding her gaze, Sam put his lips in the center of her palm. Watching her, he waited, the hard lips warming her flesh without asking. Poor Sam, she thought, bemused by the sensations washing over her. He's so alone. He's aching—

Then his lips moved against her flesh, nibbling the sensitive pads. Dallas shivered, feeling a wave of heat beat against her.

Placing her hand along his jaw, Sam began to breathe unevenly. Then he trembled, making her aware of his vulnerability. Taking his time, Sam traced the shape of her mouth with his finger. "Don't be afraid," he whispered huskily.

Dallas couldn't move, savoring the warm path of his hand across her face. She saw him closing out the room, leaning toward her.

And then his mouth touched hers. The sweet, delicate brush of lips tasting, moving—

"Oh, Sam," she heard herself sigh as the touch went on, wooing, teasing, tormenting. Closing her eyelids, Dallas allowed herself to fall beneath his gentleness.

She hadn't expected that—the gentle, caring touch—she realized distantly. Somehow she hadn't thought about Sam that way at all. He cherished, she decided as she allowed his mouth to trace a path to her ear.

Resting against her cheek, he breathed slowly, the warmth swirling around her. "Come here, sweet pea," he whispered, gently drawing her into his arms.

Four

At eight o'clock on Saturday morning, Dallas lay dozing and tangled in her rosebud-patterned sheets. She tried to ignore the hushed, happy noises coming from her living room. She needed her rest to cope with Sam's new twist on her wager.

Turning over to her stomach, she covered her head with a pillow, muffling the children's excited tones. Sam's sweet kiss had destroyed a good night's sleep, filling her with doubts she didn't want explored.

For a woman who had decided romance had passed her over, Dallas recognized the disturbing signals created by the kiss. If Loring kissed her as though she was soft, feminine and much more delicate than her five foot, nine inches, it was because he was planning an ambush. Frowning and stretching her legs, Dallas groaned.

Sam wasn't anything but trouble. According to his employees, workaholic Sam Loring did not possess a smattering of sensitivity.

Groaning again, Dallas knew she should keep Loring at a distance. His style could only be compared with a Sherman tank.

A man his size was easy to see coming. She remembered how devastatingly male he had appeared in his workout suit. When she had touched him in the stress class, sensing him through her fingertips, she could feel the raw power simmering beneath his taut muscles.

She turned onto her side, holding the pillow over her ears and watching the stormy skies over Seattle through her lacy curtains. She closed her eyes and wondered why that single, tender kiss had devastated her.

She barely remembered T.J.'s kisses, and Douglas's pecks had reminded her of Billy's. But Sam's reached straight into the aching heart of her.

Scowling, Dallas labeled Sam as an ambusher with his sights set on invading her privacy just for sheer orneriness.

Dallas groaned aloud, kicking free of her tangled sheets. She unbuttoned her nightgown's high, frilly eyelet collar and pressed her fingers to her throat, thinking how her pulse had throbbed quietly after the kiss.

What nonsense, she groused, flopping onto her back. Here she was, a divorcée, sliding out of youth's idealistic bloom with two children in tow. Just last night—before the wager and the kiss—she had been headed for a comfortable middle-age and building a satisfying, profitable career. She didn't need Loring messing up her household or her life. True, he was a sizeable stumbling block, but she could cut him down to size.

Beat Sam Loring? she asked, thinking of his furious expression during the class and in his office. Savagery ran just beneath his expensive, well-groomed exterior. He handled his business affairs like a shark scenting blood, and she wanted to keep him out of her personal waters.

Dallas bit her lip, pushing down an uneasy premonition that Sam believed in an eye for an eye—she had invaded his territory, therefore he had squatter's rights on her home.

She frowned, scowling again at the gray skies. Loring was deceptive. He moved too fast for a big man and pulled out dimples and a Southern drawl on a whim. And last night, he even had the nerve to invite himself over for morning coffee.

If she hadn't been so dazed by that insidious, hateful, sweet kiss, she would have thrown him out on his ear.

In the living room, Billy let out a delighted shriek, and Dallas sighed. She caught the scent of coffee and jumped to her feet. The last time Nikki attempted to make coffee, the kitchen took an hour to clean. "I'm awake now," she teased in a loud, ominous tone as she walked toward the living room in a swirl of ankle-length, rosebud-flecked nightgown.

The sight of Sam Loring sprawled on his stomach over her carpeting, dressed in a navy-blue sweatshirt and worn jeans, stopped her in the doorway. Spread before Sam was the beginnings of a doll house, and Nikki was holding the directions up for him to read. Dressed in his pajamas, Billy lay down the length of Sam's broad back, examining the handiwork from over Sam's broad shoulder. Clutched in Billy's small hand was a shining new dump truck.

Baghdad, who had apparently felt safe entering the house with another grown male nearby, rubbed against Dallas's legs.

Nikki looked up at her mother and glowed, looking picture-adorable in her ruffly flannel nightgown. "He gave me a doll house, and then maybe this afternoon—or when you say it's okay—we're going shopping for furniture. He knows the Sunbird Girls' Group smile song. And he'll buy all the Sunbird Sunny Sugar Cookies I can carry at one time. Billy got a truck, and Sam's going to make him a sandpile to play in—if you say it's okay," she qualified with a grin.

"Oh no," Sam heard Dallas whisper as he turned his head to follow Nikki's wide grin.

Standing in the muted light of the hallway, Dallas closed her eyes as though willing him away into heavy Seattle traffic. Her fists pressed against the folds of her gown, and Sam found himself mentally stripping it from her to find the warm, soft welcoming flesh beneath.

Sam had spent an uneasy night sorting out the kiss he had given Dallas and the sweet, shy way she had responded. Resting pliantly in his arms later, Dallas's changing expressions had fascinated Sam. She had been surprised to find her fingers prowling through the hair on his chest, looking at her hand as though it were a disconnected probe. Dallas Pendragon, despite her career-woman exterior, was unjaded, untasted and highly desirable. That kiss had cost Sam two cold showers during the night. While Dallas wanted to undermine his kingdom, keeping business cold and above the heat of passion, Sam's inclinations ran more to seducing her.

The light behind her outlined long legs and gently curving hips beneath her gown. With a high neck and puffy sleeves that ended at her wrists, the modest gown was the sexiest thing Sam had experienced in years. It gave him the feeling of waiting for his Christmas package to be unwrapped layer by layer. The women in his past wore lace negligees and teddies designed to promote the response that Dallas's prim gown was so thoroughly doing.

Sam shifted uncomfortably. If ever he had wanted to carry a woman back to bed and linger throughout a lazy weekend, it was now. He'd ignored a potential virus before, but suddenly her ability to raise his temperature was appealing.

The thought startled him. In his lifetime, Sam had never lingered overlong with any bedmate. "I'm still here," Sam stated quietly, watching her.

He remembered the warm, silky feel of her hair sliding through his fingers. Now the sleek strands swirled about her face as she shook her head as if to clear it. "What are you doing here this early?"

With the morning light outlining her body, and her mouth tight with displeasure, Dallas was beautiful. Grinning and thoroughly enjoying the moment, Sam wanted to sweep her into his lap and kiss her awake. "I get up early," he said, watching her scowl at the nearly-completed dollhouse and the truck Billy clutched tightly to him.

"And I like privacy on Saturday mornings," she stated bluntly, running her fingers through her hair with the distracted air of one who has just crossed time warps.

"I'll remember that." Not taking his gaze from her, Sam shifted to a sitting position, pulling Billy, blanket and truck into his lap at the same time. Nikki knelt beside him, draping her arm around his neck.

Surrounded by the scent and warmth of the children, the colorful trappings of Christmas and a grumpy, displaced Dallas, Sam was totally happy.

The thought was disquieting. He hadn't relaxed for so long that it made him uneasy, but he pushed the feeling aside to watch Dallas's determined struggle for control.

Dallas swallowed, frowned and ordered quietly, "Nikki, Billy...go...feed the cat."

Nikki whispered loudly in Sam's ear, "See? She's not happy on Saturday mornings if we wake her up. Come on, Billy. Mommy's got *the look*."

Billy cast a wistful glance over his shoulder, but allowed himself to be drawn after Nikki into the kitchen. Immediately after the children left the room, Dallas hissed, "Go away, Sam. Shoo. Don't call me. I'll call you."

Rising carefully to avoid the scattered pieces of the doll house, Sam found himself walking toward Dallas. Looking confused and flushed and warm from her bed, she needed tormenting. Any woman who had caused him time and effort wondering how to take her out gently—dispensing with her meddling in his business—*and* explore her sensually was trouble. He was vaguely angry at himself for being tempted, and so he leered down at her. "I haven't been shooed away in years, sweet pea."

"Scat!" she added venomously as she took a step back, flicking her hand at him as though he were a worrisome puppy. When Sam stopped in front of her, she glared up at him sulkily and crossed her arms over her chest. "I'm not up to you this morning."

"Have your coffee. You'll feel better," he offered solicitously, feeling the soft heat of her cheek as he brushed aside a silky strand of her hair. He wondered suddenly what other men had seen her dressed so cuddly and sexy and felt himself go raw. When he had her in his bed, he'd wipe out any other players.

She jerked away from his light touch, breathing unevenly. Sam liked watching her flounder through waking up to his presence; he had a quick flash of what it would be to wake up beside her, to nuzzle that sweet spot just below the ear. Dallas, he sensed, was virtually untutored in waking up to a lover's demands. Now she threw up her hands. "You're too big, take up too much space, and I don't want you here. Scat," she repeated darkly.

"I could move in this afternoon and we can be practically right on schedule with the wager by Monday," he offered softly, watching her soft mouth part in surprise. A sudden gush of elation soared unaccountably to Sam's head, and if he were truthful, his body was reacting sensually to her nearness. When he gave in to an impulse and touched the rapidly pulsing vein in her throat, she swatted at him, and Sam caught her hand. Dallas obviously wasn't accustomed to being touched or kissed by a man. The angry color rose in her cheeks as he said, "You can tell the kids you're adopting me for a month—"

A key turned in the lock and the door swung open to reveal a small, sixtyish blond woman dressed in a pearl-studded gray sweater and matching pants. Her surprised expression changed when she scanned Dallas's nightgown and blush. Lazily, the woman's gaze drifted down Sam's fit backside, her mouth curving slowly, knowingly into a smile. "Well, well," she stated in a tone that said she had assessed the situation and had come to her own conclusions.

"He's not mine," Dallas stated flatly, jerking her hand away from Sam. "He's just getting ready to leave."

"Whose is he?" asked the woman, crossing over to him. "My dear, I didn't know you would actually take my advice and bring home a real live man—"

"Mother," Dallas said between her teeth, rubbing her wrist as though to rid herself of his touch. "This is Sam Loring. Sam...my mother, Lisa."

"Charmed," Lisa returned, her speculative gaze drifting between her daughter and Sam. "Married, are you, Sam?"

He liked Lisa immediately, recognizing her as a player. Sam lifted her hand to kiss it. "I'm available," he answered, grinning.

"Children?" Lisa cooed, flicking an oh-my-you'd-better-catch-this-one expression at Dallas.

Sam recognized the look and glanced down at Dallas, who was glaring at them both. "I'm hoping your daughter will loan me hers," he answered softly. "I'm going to be staying here, you know. We're setting up housekeeping and we'll be working together. A pilot project—"

"A pilot project at work—not here," Dallas interrupted.

"*Here* would be a first for me," Sam responded silkily.

"Don't hand me that—you're old enough to have lived through several situations just like this one," Dallas shot back hotly.

"Never...quite like this," Sam emphasized, his eyes sparkling.

Lisa's eyes widened, then the woman gave her daughter a brilliant, pleased smile. "Oh, my," she said in an ecstatic sigh.

"Oh...rats," Dallas hissed before throwing up her hands and stomping off to her room.

Lisa patted Sam's shoulder, tested the heavy muscles in a series of light probes, then slowly walked around him, eyeing him up and down. "My, you are a big one...." Lisa waved a dismissing hand in her daughter's direction, lowering her voice. "She hasn't had her coffee. Don't say anything until she has had at least two cups.... You have definite potential, you know. She usually picks wimps."

Sam grinned, recognizing a would-be partner in crime. "Ma'am, I'd be proud if you'd have coffee with the family and me. I brought fresh-baked bagels," he offered in his deepest Southern drawl.

"My, my, I do declare," Lisa exclaimed softly as Sam began to prepare the children's favorite cereal and poured her coffee. Without missing a beat, he stopped a threatening skirmish between the children by picking each one up, tossing them lightly in the air and catching them in a hug until they giggled and settled down to eating.

"Mother? Could I see you...*now*?" Dallas called ominously from her bedroom.

"I'm being summoned," Lisa whispered in the tone of a conspirator, then poured a cup of coffee for her daughter. "You won't go away until we can chat more, will you, Sam?"

Sam found a carafe and filled it with coffee, then placed it on a tray with Dallas's and Lisa's filled cups. Studying the effect, he toasted a bagel, buttered it and added it to the tray. "Tell her she can come out when she's feeling better, will you? I intend to spend the day with her and the kids...."

"It's nice here, isn't it, Sam?" Lisa asked knowingly, slanting a look up at him.

He nodded curtly, realizing suddenly how excited he had been throughout the long night, just waiting for morning. Dallas's rumpled, disgruntled ornery self hadn't disappointed him. While he intended to enjoy her, his game plan called for getting the controlling hand.

He met Lisa's assessing gaze unflinchingly, and the look held. "This should be quite interesting," she murmured quietly.

"Quite," he repeated smiling.

"Be gentle, dear...it's my duty as a mother to say that. But Dallas can be such a beast if you cross her. I'll send you flowers if you recover," Lisa advised, picking up the breakfast tray. She carried it into the beast's lair.

In her bedroom, Dallas was busily stripping off her nightgown and jerking on jeans and a sweatshirt. She glared at Lisa when the woman entered the feminine room and placed the tray on an antique oak dresser. Lisa's expression was too innocent. "Don't get any big ideas, Mother."

"Who, me?"

"He's business. He's the manager I was telling you about—the workaholic who needs to experience the working woman's world?"

"He's lovely. Has a raw sexual magnetism, dimples and a lovely Southern drawl—and all that genuine masculine charm. Of course, I don't have any big ideas," Lisa stated, handing Dallas her coffee. "He's just your typical run-of-the-mill wimp," she concluded airily, sipping from her cup.

"He wants to live here and experience *your* plan in my home, with my children," Dallas stated darkly, eyeing her mother as she sat on the four-poster bed's pink-and-mauve patchwork quilt. Lisa fussed with the assortment of throw pillows and studied the rosebuds, and Dallas didn't trust her a bit. "Don't encourage him."

"Oh, I wouldn't ever do that, dear," Lisa responded wryly. "Now, just what is the scam?"

Dallas glanced at the closed door, then lowered her voice in hushed tones. "It's your fault. When I proposed *your* plan to him, he started throwing in conditions. He wants to live here—with us. The whole thing is impossible. He just appeared in my living room this morning. He's bribed Nikki and Billy and he's *out there in my kitchen.*"

Dallas could feel the panic in her voice streaking through her. *Sweet pea* he had said, placing his mouth ever so carefully over hers. Somehow she had found herself sinking into that gentle kiss, warming to the security it offered. The thought was ridiculous, considering Sam Loring was out to get her. "He's just too big, too aggressive," she said firmly. "I don't like him."

"I think he's sweet. Why don't you try the bagel he buttered for you?"

Dallas stared at the bagel as though it were a live, venomous snake.

"He's quite domestic, Dallas dear—"

"You don't have any idea what sort of man he is," Dallas stated carefully. "Live with us," she repeated, thinking through exactly what that could mean. She had pampered T.J. until she was exhausted, and she never wanted to repeat the experience again. For his size, Loring would eat twice as much, be twice as sloppy, use more hot water when he showered...Dallas forced her negative projections to stop. She didn't want to think of Sam sleeping and taking showers under her roof.

"You took in Baghdad, didn't you?" Lisa shrugged, lifting her expressive eyebrows. "How bad do you want it?"

Caught unaware with the image of Sam's water-beaded body behind her eyelids, Dallas reddened instantly and turned angrily on her mother. "Want what?"

"Why, the miraculous cure for the working women you're fighting so hard for, dear," Lisa returned innocently. "What else could you possibly want?"

"He can't make it," Dallas stated firmly.

"Make what?"

"Mother! Sam Loring is not an average suburbanite. He's a business czar delegating his needs to others."

"Well, then. He's bound to lose the bet, isn't he?" Lisa interrupted smoothly. "He couldn't possibly do all the mundane things working women have to do, could he? Why are you so worried?"

"Why am I worried?" Dallas repeated warily as she entered her small kitchen to see Sam sprawled over a chair, reading the morning paper and drinking his coffee. She glared at his expensive, comfortable joggers which occupied two large linoleum squares. He was encroaching on her life and her precious Saturday morning, and she wanted him gone.

"What have you done with my children?" she demanded, discarding the way she had planned to tactfully remove him from her home.

He rattled the sports page, his head sinking lower into the paper. "They're getting dressed. The Seahawks are in great shape, aren't they?" he asked, referring to Seattle's football team.

When she didn't answer, he glanced up at her. "Something wrong?"

"Why are you here?" Inwardly, Dallas promised to pay her mother back for suggesting this insane idea.

"We have to make plans to move me in this weekend—"

"I'm leaving," Lisa called from the living room. "Nice meeting you, Sam."

"Come back soon," he returned as though he already were a resident in good standing. Uncoiling himself from the chair, Sam cleared the breakfast dishes, rinsed and placed them in the dishwasher, then sponged off the vinyl tablecloth. "The kids will be ready to go just as soon as you are. Nikki needs some furniture for her dollhouse, and we could use the outing to introduce the idea of me moving in."

"Moving in?" Dallas repeated dully, a quiver of fear beginning low in her stomach. She hadn't shared any part of her daily routine with a man since T.J. Her life was perfectly well ordered and liveable, and suited her totally.

He trailed a finger down the side of her throat. "I can't see any reason not to start as soon as possible. I'll leave it up to you what to tell the kids. But I suggest the adoption method as long as they know it's just for the holiday season. They already feel sorry for me because no one's hung a stocking for me...they think I'm deprived."

"Kind of you to offer suggestions." Dallas stepped away from that warm finger. "I haven't decided to accept your conditions yet. You just may have to stay in your pitiful penthouse and manage the best you can."

"It's lonely," he said quietly behind her.

Double Drat! Dallas thought warily as she remembered her sympathetic reaction to his loneliness in class. Ambushers typically pulled out unexpected weapons, and she could feel her heartstrings twang unaccountably. She couldn't afford to spend any sympathy on Loring, he'd use it against her. She could feel his warmth seeping through her clothes.

"Don't you want me to experience real stress? Kids? Upkeep? You're not frightened of me, are you, Dallas?"

The soft Southern taunt inflamed her. She turned slowly, looking up at his quiet, pensive expression. "Not on your best day, Loring. You haven't got anything that could possibly make me back down."

"Oh, haven't I?" he asked, his dimples appearing as he grinned. She noted the places and lines shifting within his dark skin. When he smiled, oozing charm, he could be dangerous.

"No," she answered huskily, then wondered if he really did have something that could make her—

Distracted momentarily, her thoughts went back to yesterday afternoon when she'd surprised him in his boxing workout. Looking sweaty, virile and totally sexy, Sam definitely possessed the right equipment.... But for some other woman, one without a mission.

"I can move in tonight, if the children are agreeable. That will give us all day tomorrow to work on budgets and routines. What are you telling the children?"

"We go to church on Sundays," she said, gloating that she had foiled his plans for encroaching.

He shrugged, grinning. "Fine. We can spend this afternoon plotting."

Forcing herself to breathe quietly despite her rising anger, Dallas eyed him menacingly. It was difficult to menace when a six-foot-four, very fit man with dimples was grinning down at her. Only the thought of how she could make him squirm at the office kept her from throwing him out into the gray Christmas-season day. "I'll work on it," she said between her teeth. "Okay, the deal is on. You can move in. But if you step out of line just once, you're out of here, Loring."

"I love it when you get tough, Pendragon. Where are you putting me?"

Dallas knew where she'd like to put him. But in lieu of cramming him into a mailing carton, she settled for a necessary conversation with her children. Sam discreetly vanished into the kitchen while the children and Dallas sat down for a couch conference. Nikki quickly understood that Sam would visit for a month, then return to his own home, rather like her friends did after her slumber parties. But Billy wanted to adopt Sam. "He's ours," the little boy argued.

Dallas took a deep breath and replied just as firmly that Sam could be borrowed, but had to be returned after a month, just like Billy's favorite library books.

When both children completely understood and agreed to the situation, Dallas took another deep breath. She turned to find Sam grinning at her from the kitchen. "Okay," she said without explanation, then watched his I'm-in grin widen.

By that evening, Sam had installed his larger bed in Dallas's guest bedroom. They had gone shopping for doll furniture and a smaller truck for Billy, although Sam had mentioned rather wistfully that he had always wanted a toy train set. Sam could be beguiling, Dallas noted reluctantly. She'd have to watch the way he appealed to her soft spots, because she intended to give him hell for wrecking her Saturday morning.

Dallas had reluctantly allowed Sam's longer, wider bed.

"Don't get the idea you can move in anything without my permission," Dallas had sniffed when he finished stowing her four-poster guest bed in the basement. "The neighbors are going to talk as it is. Your 'junkyard pickup isn't helping the picture."

Sam had really taken offense at that remark—Bertha had seen better days. A vintage Ford, she'd crossed the United States with him. He loved her, and where he went, Bertha would be parked.

"I'll make friends with the neighbors," he had stated too quietly. "If the Lincoln was parked in your driveway instead of Bertha, they might think I'm keeping you," he added smugly, watching her absorb the taunt.

Dallas had settled for slamming pots and pans around in the kitchen, and when he had asked if he could help her, she had glared at him. Sam retreated into the living room to watch cartoons with the children, who immediately dived on top of him for a brief tussle.

After dinner, Sam began clearing away the table. He worked with Dallas, who continued to shoot dark, threatening glances his way. "Something wrong?" he asked innocently as the dishwasher began first to hum, then changed to thumping noises.

She kicked it, pumped hand cream into her palms and rubbed them together briskly. "I don't have time to deal with you tonight, Loring. I've got a date, and Mother will be coming over to babysit. Just stay out of everyone's way until we can hash this out, will you?"

Something dark and ugly moved within Sam, something he hadn't felt for years, back when he made extra money by performing bare-knuckle fights in back alleys. "A date? With who?" he asked darkly, before he realized he had spoken. It hadn't occurred to him that Dallas would have a boyfriend or fiancé; her kiss had been too untutored.

She nodded, smiling sweetly. "Mmm. I have dates, you know. Just try not to make yourself too obvious until we work this whole thing out. You will have to keep your...women away from my home. And that's a ground rule. Don't tie up my phone with them, either," she added after a moment's thought.

"As you wish, my dear," he murmured, watching her wary expression. He'd moved corporations aside neatly in business, he wasn't about to let a wimp—as Lisa described Dallas's romantic interests—push him around. "I'll have to satisfy elsewhere," he drawled.

"I hope they aren't costly," she returned sweetly. "You'll be on a budget, you know." With that, she sauntered off to prepare for her date.

When Dallas entered the livingroom, she found Sam sitting at one end of the cabbage-rose couch, with Nikki and Billy seated on his lap. Beau Michaelson occupied the other end uneasily as the trio examined him as though he were about to commit a crime. Disney cartoons played happily across the television set as Sam asked quietly, "So, what do you do for a living, Beau?"

Spying Dallas, Beau rose to his feet, obviously relieved.

"Your mother can't babysit. She has a hot date," Sam seemed to growl. He took in the special care she had taken preparing for her date. His long, assessing look started its way at the top of her freshly shampooed and curled ringlets to the slight brush of cosmetics on her flushed skin.

The look lingered and held as it slid down the neat, basic-black sheath fitting her body closely. Just because she was in a rebellious mood, Dallas had added her favorite nylons—black silk with seams and embossed bows at the back of her ankles—and Sam slowly, inch by inch, took in every curve down her high, stylish heels. "Well, well," he said slowly, his eyes gleaming behind the glasses as they met hers. "Naughty, but nice."

"We'd better go," Beau muttered, stepping around Sam gingerly to place Dallas's coat on her shoulders.

"We'll be at this number, Sam." Dallas jotted down the theater's number and placed it by the phone. In doing so, she caught Sam's expression. His grey eyes were stormy, his tall muscular body tensed as though he wanted to beat someone. She had never seen such raw fury in a man's face, and the look bound her for a fraction of time...until Sam smiled nastily. He had the look of a junkyard dog baring his teeth quietly and waiting for one vulnerable moment. "Have fun, kids."

"Who is he?" Beau asked in a hiss as they walked to his

car. Glancing back at the gaily Christmas-trimmed house, Dallas spotted Sam standing in her doorway and looking as though he'd been wedged into it for the duration.

He waved and called again, "Have fun."

Beau glanced uneasily at Dallas. "Who is he?" he insisted, helping her into his car.

The matter was too complicated, and Dallas closed her eyes, resting her head against the support. "One of mother's friends, down on his luck," she lied, unable to tell the truth. "I'm just helping out."

"He looks tough," Beau commented anxiously. "Are you sure he's the right kind of house guest?"

"I can handle him," Dallas answered firmly, and meant it.

After her date, Sam cheerfully greeted them on the porch. Dallas *had* intended to compare Beau's kiss to Sam's and had wasted an entire evening encouraging the shy man.

"How about a beer, Beau? Dallas always has a nice cup of tea when things settle down for the night, don't you?" he asked warmly as his gaze thoroughly inventoried Dallas's dress and unkissed mouth. His tone implied that Dallas required tea and *him* to relax her.

Beau mumbled something about rechecking statistics and almost fell down the steps, then disappeared. While Dallas glared at Sam, he raised an eyebrow. "Did I interrupt?" he asked innocently as she marched past him into the sanctity of her bedroom.

At midnight, Dallas worked to up the ante, making lists of chores for Sam to share. She arranged a daily schedule, taking extreme care with the morning bathroom roster and the evening settling-down routine. Sitting cross-legged on her bed in the midst of her notes, legal pads and pens, Dallas tried not to notice the muffled noises in the bedroom next to hers. She viciously punched her hand calculator, averaging the Brice clerical workers' salaries, then smiled grimly. In a very short time, Sam would understand the stressful realities of a Brice worker.

Finally at three o'clock in the morning, she replaced her copious lists in her briefcase and crawled under her rosebud sheets.

She sighed, listened to the quiet house and snuggled down with the air of one who had performed a task well. Poised on the brink of sleep, she thought she heard Sam say softly, "Nite-nite."

Five

"**T**he Seahawks can wait," Dallas stated the next afternoon when they all had returned from church. Sam was sprawled before the television set, and the children were napping. "We have some sorting out to take care of, if you'll remember," she added nastily, still vexed about his "Nite-nite."

Ordinarily on a Sunday afternoon, Dallas would snuggle down on the couch, doze beneath her afghan and spend a leisurely evening with the children. But she thought of the workers depending upon her, the wager and Sam's tyrannical move into her home. She wondered briefly if it were possible to send a grown man to his room indefinitely—Sam wasn't the type to be shipped off anywhere without his consent. He was in her home to cause trouble, and she could see it coming in big, black spades.

The man was manipulative, insensitive. She glanced uneasily at his hard mouth. If Beau had just kissed her before Sam had appeared, then she could have had a comparison to that damn, nagging, sweet kiss.

She was too old to be called "sweet pea." Too seasoned to

believe in the promises of a man's raspy, sexy tone. After all, T.J. had taught her a hard lesson, and she should know better.

Why had she sunk into Sam's kiss with all the resistance of a kid to candy?

Sam was going to pay for that memorable kiss.

"Sure thing. If you want to talk, we'll turn off the Seahawks," Sam agreed, snapping off the television. In a blue cotton sweater, jeans and joggers, Sam was too appealing. The loose neckline had slipped aside, allowing Dallas a glimpse of dark hair on his chest, which unaccountably unsettled her. His hair was mussed and behind his lenses, Sam's gray eyes were saying things to her about ways to spend a lazy Sunday afternoon.

Waking up to his hushed voice quieting the children as they ate breakfast, entering the bathroom scented with his after-shave and seeing the array of masculine items on her shelf had already darkened Dallas's Sunday.

She had studied the razor and shaving cream for a moment, the expensive after-shave near her toiletries. Gripping the edge of the vanity, Dallas had closed her eyes. She just didn't want to remember how she had suffered at T.J.'s hands—the denigrating residue of a woman who had been used as a provider, a mother and a bed partner.

A bed partner, she had repeated. Classified by Lisa as a "lazy, egotistical jock," T.J.'s lovemaking left Dallas's expectations at the oh-well level.

She had been a fool, trusting a man who frequently indulged in other loves. Douglas, whom she'd dated casually, was an experiment, and she had regretted coaxing him into semipassion.

Well, passion for him, she admitted. With damp, limp lips and groping hands, he had interpreted her revulsion as an innocent's shyness. After explaining to him that she simply couldn't come up to his skilled standards, Dallas ended the relationship. Relieved that he had magnanimously accepted her explanation, Dallas gifted herself with a whole box of chocolate-covered cherries. It had taken her years to draw her shell and her family safely about her, and she didn't trust Sam's sexy look this afternoon at all.

The part of her that had been so repulsed at working up a passion for Douglas wanted to simply throw herself upon Sam's fit body. Drawing her nails down the couch's cabbage roses, Dallas expected that she wouldn't have to maneuver Sam into passion; he'd already be there, hot and waiting. She also expected that with the hunger roaming unsatisfied within her, she'd be equal to the challenge. And not at all repulsed by his hard hands exploring her body.

Dallas glanced at his backside and rephrased the matter of the hands on body. Was it her soft hands exploring *his* body?

She forced her eyelids closed and concentrated on the task at hand. Sam Loring had agreed to be stuffed into the mold of a working woman. Of course, he wouldn't be able to handle it, and that single thought warmed her. She decided to reward herself with two boxes of chocolates and a pecan pie for winning the wager.

Lying still on the floor, Sam propped his head on his hand and just looked at her. "Whatever you're mulling over isn't pleasant. The sooner we settle into a routine, the better it will be for the kids, don't you think?"

Dallas eased herself down on the sofa, taking care to place as much room between her and the squatter as possible. Sam had entered her children's lives. They were hers and she didn't intend for them to become attached to her temporary resident. He wouldn't be so glib once she read her extensive lists, she thought, anticipating his outrage, his anger, his bowing out of the wager like a whipped—

Sam barely scanned the lists she thrust at him. He shrugged, his gaze strolling over her rust-colored sweatsuit. "Fine."

He glanced again at the salary she had pinpointed for his use. When a small muscle in his cheek tensed, Dallas pursed her lips to keep from smiling.

"When was the last time you lived with a man?" he asked flatly, tossing the papers to her open briefcase on the floor.

Her body tightened, responding to Sam's intense stare. "You're supposed to be thorough. You've probably already had me checked out...you should know."

He nodded, his hard mouth lifting in a grim smile. "Okay, I know," he said softly.

When she looked at him closely, wondering what he actually knew, Sam picked up her pad and pen and began scrawling a list. "Groceries—no lima beans," he murmured absently. "You're almost out of everything...."

"Sam," she said, scanning the growing list, "remember, we share costs, although I'll take the bigger share because of the children—"

"You're not paying my way, lady. I take more food than the three of you." Sam pinned her with a deadly gray stare. "Nobody pays my way but me. Got it?"

That evening, Lisa baby-sat while Sam, Dallas and Bertha trekked off to a supermarket, leaving the pickup's oil spots on Dallas's driveway. Sam entered the market with the air of a hunter on safari, checking nutritional values, cost comparing prices with his calculator and eyeing the butcher's thumb suspiciously. "Yuk," he muttered when Dallas deliberately chose a package of lima beans, dropping them into the cart.

"Supermarket Sam Loring" was an encounter that Dallas did not want to repeat. After three laborious hours, she finally pried him away from a maze of household gadgets that intrigued him like a child in a toy department. Looking disgruntled, he whipped out his wallet when the checker totalled the figure.

"Halves," Dallas reminded him, writing a check for her amount.

Sam flipped open his wallet, then paused. Dallas had trimmed his carrying cash and his credit cards were safely tucked away. "We'll calculate later, honey," he said through his teeth, selecting the entire amount needed. "Cute, isn't she?" he asked the checker.

Drained by pulling him away from "really good buys," Dallas wasn't in the mood for chauvinism and wrote her check anyway. She hoped Bertha could be coaxed into returning to her favorite oil spot on the driveway.

The next day, Sam rubbed the back of his neck. At nine o'clock in the morning, he was looking forward to the afternoon when Dallas would begin dissecting his employee-relationship policy.

Sam tapped his pen on his desk. He'd had no idea his employees were unhappy. The thought nagged. He'd always expected more out of himself than others and wasn't aware of any dissatisfaction.

Dallas was good at bringing out dissatisfaction, he noted. A regular virus that ensnared and tormented. If he got any more worked up about cotton flannel nightgowns and rosebuds, he'd break out in a rash.

He was also slightly exhausted, he admitted, glancing ruefully at the paperwork already stacked on his desk. He hadn't had time to work out a schedule for himself, nor a budget. The groceries had swept away a large portion of his weekly allowance, and baby-sitting fees were due Friday. When his host had insisted on repaying him when the wager was finished, Sam's pride had been riffled. He wanted to take care of her, enter her tight little world and fix her thumping dishwasher.

The thought was novel, and Sam turned it over with as much distrust as he would salmon aspic on a bed of watercress. Saturday night, Beau had barely escaped a fist in his lovelorn-puppy face. Clearly, the little wimp had intended to put his lips on Dallas's strawberry ones. Sam scowled at his scarred knuckles, thinking about sinking one short jab in Beau's soft midsection. Dallas's mouth was destined to be his, and so were her other parts. He'd never liked poachers.

Sam had never wanted to place the stamp of his possession on another woman, not even his ex-wife. But Dallas was another matter, and the thought was disquieting. Maybe it was the Christmas season and the enfolding warmth of her home. Or the lack of morning coffee nagging at him. But Dallas's sweet-pea fragrance didn't help, nor did the way she'd looked at him in the bathroom. When he lay before the Seahawk's Sunday game, Sam sensed that Dallas momentarily wanted to slide into his arms. She would, eventually, and the conflicting emotions racing beneath her freckles gave him a shot of pure encouragement.

He wanted to treat her carefully, he decided, rummaging further into his disturbing emotions. It was obvious Dallas had carved out a business and a life-style that worked for her, and he respected that. Flitting happily through her safe, structured life, Dallas had all the markings of the wary.

Sidestepping a variety of entangling situations, Sam recognized those markings. The women in his background were quite happy to go sailing through his bankroll, but Dallas had been clearly offended when he'd offered to pay for the groceries. Dallas had calculated his share of the utility bills, and he had noticed her happy little smirk as he jotted the figure down on a small pad.

Drawing that pad from his pocket, he noted his weekly sum and quietly swallowed. The amount wouldn't cover drinks with a shareholder. Then there was Bertha. Sam flipped to a clean page and scribbled "Oil."

Replacing the pad in his pocket, he patted it. This morning, dressing and delivering the children went smoothly. Winning the wager was a piece of cake.

Sam flipped through the stack of Christmas cards from business associates. Addressed and sent by secretaries, they represented a courtesy rather than a genuine warmth shared on the holiday. In contrast, Dallas's home was warm, filled with scents and children anticipating Santa Claus.

He smiled softly, running his thumb over an embossed Rudolf the Reindeer. He'd have Emily pick up something—

Entering his office, Emily looked down her nose at him and smirked. "As I understand your intentions for the next month, I am not to make nor serve your coffee. Shall we include you in the coffee pool?"

"I'll provide my own. Did you have any other questions about Ms. Pendragon or the situation?"

Emily smiled, for once showing her teeth. Out of necessity, Sam had spread the bare bones of the situation before his secretary and had watched her openly gloat. Her memo to the remainder of the Brice employees included none of the particulars.

"I've informed everyone that they are to cooperate to the fullest with Ms. Pendragon." Her tone inferred that Pendragon would succeed, clearly spelling out his secretary's position in the matter. Sam had the uncomfortable feeling that Emily had coached each employee on the best way to present themselves for the Pendragon research. Franzini was never above stacking the cards to suit herself.

This morning he'd been careful to greet his staff in a method outlined in the Pendragon method. Surely a nod and a curt "Good morning," would earn him a few points on Pendragon's poll.

Beneath her raw-boned appearance, Emily seemed as pleased as a cat with a bowl of cream. "Just a hint, Mr. Loring. Find any coffee station and look for a donation cup. You'll get by for today. Any calls concerning the Pendragon family—Billy and Nikki Pendragon—are to be put immediately through to you," she continued, her teeth glistening.

When he nodded, Emily sniffed, "Children, a home and responsibilities of all the previously mentioned...this should be interesting. By the way, parking-lot maintenance called. Your...truck is gushing oil."

By noon, Sam was tired, splattered with oil from repairing Bertha, and he was starved. He'd spent more than his allotment for lunch on oil. In another hour, Pendragon would appear on his doorstep, digging away at his policies. And he hadn't even planned supper yet.

Thinking of Pendragon somehow eased his empty stomach as he slashed through letters prepared for his signature. This morning, he'd completely erased Dallas's rude manners and defamatory comments about Bertha. Freshly showered and shaving over the bathroom sink, Sam had left the door open. He'd wanted to catch the children before they woke Dallas. She'd looked strained the night before and he thought she could use the extra fifteen minutes rest.

Barely awake and dressed in her prim gown, Dallas had wandered into the bathroom. She yawned, groaned and began to fill the tub. Sam watched amused as she ran her fingers through her hair and bent to touch her toes. Pausing in midbend, Dallas had straightened slowly, as though afraid what she might see when she awoke fully.

In the steamy mirror, Dallas's gaze widened as it strolled down his bare back to his loose sweat pants, then back up to his lather-covered cheeks. She blinked as though trying to dislodge him from her small, feminine bathroom. As if he were a genie she could blink back into a bottle.

For an instant, Sam had the feeling of soft, shy fingers daintily exploring his backside. Because he wanted the feeling to last, he placed the razor next to her bath powder and turned to face her. Dallas blinked again, stared at his chest intently, then ran her tongue across her soft, parted lips.

Without thinking, Sam reached out, captured her hand and placed it on the damp hairs that seemed to entice her. "You can touch," he offered gallantly before bending to brush her parted lips with his.

Tousled and swathed by yards of violet-kissed flannel, Dallas seemed incredibly sweet and feminine. Sam noted with distraction that he wanted to take care of her, shelter her from her heavy burdens. His momentary notions were old-fashioned, but she did manage to stir him at some level he had long ago buried.

Tasting like strawberries, her lips had barely lifted to his when she stepped back. "Cut it out, Loring," she had snapped between her teeth, her color rising. "I don't come with the wager."

He'd felt a sliver of rage go stabbing through him. For some reason, Dallas deeply resented him.

In the quiet of her office, Dallas paused over rearranging her schedule and idly toyed with the biofeedback hand monitor as she thought of Sam. She had to spend a whole month sidestepping his sizeable body in her house.

The monitor fitted neatly in her palm as she remembered his sexy smile in the bathroom as he invited her palm to his chest. Listening to the monitor's rising whine, Dallas shook her head. Living next door to the Deons was dangerous; their newlywed hormonal imbalance seeping over to her home had taken its toil.

Rawly masculine, Sam wasn't anything like Douglas or Beau; he was more like T.J. She'd learned her lesson well and didn't intend to repeat it.

Except Sam had taken exquisite care to kiss her gently, brushing her lips softly, wooing a response from her.

Wooing, she repeated darkly, and rubbed her aching temple. Loring crashed through homes decorated with Christmastide. He'd obviously lured her mother into a leering, plotting relationship.

Dallas squeezed the monitor, oblivious to its rising protest. When he wanted to, Sam pulled out the enticing Southern male act, complete with dimples and lazy drawl.

Come here, sweet pea, he had murmured in a soft, Southern-night tone that could melt any woman's resistance.

She didn't want to respond to anything concerning him, not even the wistful comment about always wanting a toy train.

Sam was a player; she'd have to remember that when he pulled out the dimples or exposed his broad, hair-covered chest in her bathroom. He'd use the sentimentality of Christmas or any means at hand to disarm her, including a weakness for oversized men who loved chocolate cake.

Who else had discovered Sam's appetites? she wondered in a brief whimsy that she forced down.

The whole problem stemmed from the holiday season and the newlywed sexual seepage from the Deons. For some reason, when she came near Sam, she started breathing deeply. She'd badly wanted to rummage through those damp, intriguing whorls matting his chest. She'd wanted to place her lips against his skin. If he hadn't leaned toward her, startling her at that confusing moment, she might have obeyed her impulses.

Her head ached, probably from too many impulses. In her hand, the monitor throbbed loudly and Dallas tossed it to her desk. Sam had a lot to learn about playing with her, because she intended to win. If he thought he could manipulate her with sex, he was wrong—she'd already had that unexciting, frustrating education. Shuffling through the poll sheets prepared for Brice workers, Dallas smiled grimly...it was her game all the way. While Sam was studying Laundry 101 and Pot Roast Lab and dealing with baby-sitters, sniffles and bears, she would tear his theories about the uselessness of stress-management policies to itsy-bitsy shreds.

That afternoon, as she interviewed Brice employees, Dallas ignored the glowering look Sam cast in her direction when he passed frequently. Rather like an eagle waiting for an adventuresome mouse to cross his territory. She smiled sweetly, nodding and acknowledging his presence before turning back to her task.

As she interviewed Virginia, a secretary with three children and no husband, Dallas sensed a bristling presence behind her. When she turned, Sam loomed over her. His collar was open, his usually neat tie awry. Three new shaving nicks occupied his taut jaw, and his scowl was genuinely, magnificently unhappy. Spattered with oil, his shirt sleeves rolled back, he looked thunderous. "Everything going okay?" he asked gruffly, in true bear manner.

His eyes slashed at her neat white blouse and paisley puff tie, cutting away at the sensible gray business jacket and skirt to her black pumps.

"We're getting along nicely. Peachy," she added, relishing his hell-of-a-day look. He wouldn't last the month—two weeks at the most. The employees were excited, and the Brice experiment was in the palm of her hand.

This morning when he'd carried the sleepy, protesting children out to the car, Sam had been given a grace period: Billy didn't need another bathroom visit and Nikki had remembered her favorite doll.

Sam glanced at the office wall clock, then ran his big hand through his already mussed hair. "I have a conference at two," he muttered absently, glancing down at the oil stains on his slacks. "I'll have someone bring these pants to the cleaners or send someone home to get my others— What are you grinning at, Pendragon?"

"Ah-ah," she said lightly. "You handle your own personal items, remember?"

Sam shot her a look of pure deadly frustration. "This is business, Dallas. A matter of big bucks. Understand?"

Enjoying watching him squirm, Dallas braced her hip against Virginia's desk and folded her arms. "Tough," she said after a long, tense moment when the worker stared, fascinated with the exchange shooting over her desk like hot lead.

"In my office." Sam spaced the words out in deadly precison as his neck seemed to lower into his broad shoulders.

"When I'm finished. Virginia and I are calculating if she'd have enough time to work out and shower during lunch hour," Dallas returned evenly, watching him. Sam in a snit was quite capable of making a scene and she wanted to delve into the problem of the employees with little disturbance. Knowing their boss was unhappy, the staff might not respond openly.

But the matter of Sam's growling and menacing her was another matter. One that chafed. Thumping her fingers lightly against her arms, Dallas allowed herself a tiny, grim smile. Sam might push his employees around, but he couldn't get used to the idea that she was her own—

"Umph!" Dallas gasped as Sam grabbed her hand and yanked her into his office. He kicked the door shut, locked it, picked her up and plopped her bottom down on his desk.

Dallas's hand went flashing through the air before she considered the consequences. The blow to his face caused her palm to burn. "How dare you?"

"You really get to me, Pendragon. This time you just asked for it," he muttered tightly before reaching for her.

Dallas caught a quick image of thick, black eyebrows and stormy gray eyes as his arms went around her, lifting her up. Sam's mouth settled heavily upon hers, his hand cradling the back of her head as he positioned her for a long, deep kiss. Surrounded by the warmth and strength of him, she barely felt her shoes drop to the floor.

She tried to protest.

She tried to ignore how much her body loved the encroaching warmth of his, how it fitted neatly into the hard planes.

His fingers moved on her scalp, soothing her as his breath stroked her cheek unevenly; his other hand slid to cup her buttocks, lifting her to him.

Sam's mouth moved over hers hungrily…as though he needed her desperately. Dallas felt herself moving into his demand, needing to ease the loneliness she felt within him. Sam ached with a cold void, carried it within him, and hid it successfully from the world.

But she knew now how much he needed her warmth. Dallas absorbed his pain, taking it into her and soothing it. Sam needed gentle care and she knew instinctively how to provide it.

Dallas eased her fingers through his hair, framing his face. Gently she lifted and fitted her parted lips to his.

Sam's kiss was pure possession, a man staking his rights on his woman.

Something went happily skipping through Dallas when? he groaned deep in his throat, a hungry sound as he urged her body to come closer.

That was the last sweet sensible thought she remembered as his tongue gently probed her lips, asking entry. Sam, for all his threatening savagery, was asking for her response. He was exposing his soul to her and asking for little in return.

Dallas locked her arms around his neck and proceeded to care for Sam. She gave him little, nibbling kisses. She caressed the back of his taut neck and smoothed the crisp dark hair growing there.

Intent upon her task, she didn't notice the stillness in him nor the gentle answering pressure of his mouth responding to hers. She barely noticed his arms gathering her closer as he leaned back against the desk, fitting her between his thighs.

Sam rubbed her cheek with his, easing toward her throat, and Dallas sighed, surrounded by the heat seeping into her. His mouth caressed her skin, and she gave him access by snuggling to his wide shoulder. Sam just seemed so safe.

His teeth tugged on her earlobe and a stirring warmth went soaring through her. She moved closer to the heat, parting her lips as his tongue again gently probed them.

When her tongue shyly met his, Sam slanted his lips against hers, his tongue entering her mouth. The moist, gentle flicking tasted her, teased her, and Dallas responded to the sweetness of the temptation. His hands moved over her, light, caressing and smoothing down the front of her blouse. She was too warm, she realized distantly, relieved when he removed her suit jacket.

Somehow her fingers had nudged aside Sam's tie, unbuttoned and removed his shirt, then slid to his chest. It seemed only fair that the large hands shaping her waist and tugging at her blouse should explore her.

He breathed unevenly as his calloused palms moved leisurely, comfortingly against her back, stroking the long line gently, firmly. Dallas had the image of being petted and cherished and enjoyed. Of being tasted. She sank deeper into the feeling, trembling a little as Sam's hands eased upward to cover her breasts.

His fingers smoothed the sensible cotton, easing it gently aside as his kiss deepened and lured her on. With a desperate need to accept his offer, Dallas drew him closer, fitting her mouth to the sweet enticement.

Sam did have an enticing body, she realized as she stroked the hair-covered, hard surface of his chest. As she snuggled more closely against his hands, his fingers found the tips of her taut breasts and tantalized them lightly. Dallas sighed, allowing him to slide her free from her confining blouse and bra.

Lifting and turning her slightly, Sam nibbled a trail downward, warming her shoulders, her chest. Dallas loved the soothing, the gentle warming of her skin as she stroked his bare back. He rippled when she touched him, she discovered, following the hard muscles flowing beneath his hot skin.

When Sam's mouth gently found her softness, exploring it, Dallas gasped. The exquisite feeling he caused when he gently suckled the hardened tip loosed a savage, hungry heat.

"Oh, Sam," she found herself sighing against his hair, giving herself more fully to him. Her wandering hands had found his taut stomach, and the tense muscles quivered beneath her light stroking.

"Sweet pea," he rasped deeply against her hot skin, kissing his way back up to her mouth. Placing her arms around him, Sam eased his warm chest against her sensitized breasts, then slowly lowered his lips to hers.

He sighed lightly, as though the softness resting against his brought him sheer pleasure.

The sound brought her hunger leaping to the surface. Her nails drew lines down his back, urging him closer as Sam's hands swept lower to smooth her hips and thighs.

Sliding upward beneath her skirt, Sam's hands were warm

and secure, gentle and caressing. Taking his time, he flipped open the snap to her hose. Pressing warmly against her inner thighs, Sam's fingertips trembled. They moved too slowly for the hunger careening through her as he removed her garter belt.

Slipping a finger under the elastic of her cotton briefs, Sam traced the sensitive area.

"Ohh," she sighed helplessly as he softly tantalized her warmth. Then she was desperate for his touch to fill the void within her. Sliding her breasts against his chest until he sighed that deep, raspy hungry sigh that so surprised her, Dallas found herself moving against the delicate brush of his fingers.

Her lungs ached with the air she had been holding as those enticing fingers moved, exploring her. She bit his shoulder then, desperate for the tantalizing intimacy, and he inhaled sharply as her teeth nibbled a trail across the taut line. Dallas's tongue flicked the warm, slightly salted surface, and she realized distantly that she loved his taste.

Barely aware of being lowered to the lush carpeting behind Sam's desk, Dallas curled to his warmth, nuzzling the pelt covering his chest. She tasted the flat male nipple, delighted with his response. She gently nipped at the nub, scouting it intently.

When he groaned, a raw sigh of pleasure and delight, Dallas smiled against his chest. Sam's arms around her were rigid, his fingers trembling. Fitting herself over him, Dallas had a distant memory of being forcefully pinned beneath a sweaty male body. And the taunts, reminding her of a woman's place. The memory flitted quietly away as Sam's fingers found her intimately. Again her teeth nipped his hard shoulder as a hot surge of pleasure went ricocheting through her.

"Dallas," she heard him groan helplessly before the heat swept over her in waves. She held him closely, an anchor in her first voyage in sensual seas.

Dallas rose to the heat, sought it, drew it into her exquisitely. She sought his mouth, exploring it as a wave of unexpected pleasure crashed over her. Running her palms down his body, she delighted in the hardness of his thighs covered by his slacks, the restless surging of his hips as the second wave caught her broadside, causing her to tense, hoarding the full throbbing head within.

Beneath her, he trembled, breathing unevenly, his face hot against hers as she fell delicately, softly from the crest of a wave. When Sam eased her down beside him, Dallas wondered helplessly if her flesh was feverish over her seemingly limp bones. She needed every ounce of her willpower to lift her hand and stroke his lean, rough cheek. Dazed by her own emotions, Dallas knew that Sam needed her soft touch. She stroked his damp brow, his mussed hair and taut cords standing out in relief on his shoulders.

Sam needed petting. Poor Sam.

His hands were gentle now as he turned her to him. He watched her as though he was turning over his thoughts carefully...examining each one with methodical precision. Tenderly, he eased a damp strand of hair away from her flushed cheek, and drew her palm up to kiss it. Over their hands, his smoky eyes held hers, promising things she couldn't dissect. Private things. Intimate things with dark, heated passages that excited her, leaving her breathless.

After a lingering survey of her face, Sam's gaze swept to her breasts. When she moved to cover herself, he tugged his shirt across her protectively. Sam eased her closer to his taut body, giving her shelter against the cold. The movement reminded her of gallantry and possession.

He rocked her slightly, and Dallas allowed her cheek to rest upon his chest. She liked being folded to him and listened to his heart beating loudly beneath her. Sliding downward, his palm flattened against her spine until her upper thighs pocketed his bold shape.

He thrust against her, watching her reaction.

"Oh, my," she whispered shakily between lips that were sensitive and swollen. "Oh, my," she repeated, realizing the carpeting waited at her back and the hard look Sam continued to rake over her. "Oh, my," she repeated a third time, scrambling out of his arms and clutching his shirt to her as she stood.

"Yes. Oh, my. Surprise isn't the word, is it?" Sam's tone mocked with grin lines as he rose slowly to his feet. When he

took one menacing step toward her, Dallas's eyes flowed downward involuntarily and widened.

"If you say, 'Oh, my,' one more time, sweet pea..." Sam
murmured as she pivoted from him and the blatant evidence of
her maiden flight into passion.

While Seattle sprawled beyond the corporate building
swathed in cold winter drizzle, Dallas shook with the knowledge
that she had bitten Sam savagely, attacking him on the floor
with obvious sexual intent.

She shivered, tugging his shirt closer and catching the scent
of his body. The shirt reminded her of how she had—She
pressed her lids closed, trying to erase the image of Sam's bare,
damp chest and the tiny red marks on his broad shoulders from
her teeth and nails. And the sensual, well-kissed fullness of his
hard mouth.

"Oh!" she gasped quietly, fighting the realization that she
had never allowed herself to— "Oh," she groaned, frustrated.
If ever she wanted to taste passion, it wasn't at this time of her
life. Just when everything had settled down nicely. And she
definitely didn't want to experience anything intimate with Sam.

His body heat warmed her back, seeping into her skin as she
had wanted to seep into his. "Those are lots of little *Oh*s," Sam
murmured quietly behind her. "Here, get into this," he ordered,
easing her into her bra and blouse.

Though she was grateful, Dallas shivered and avoided looking
at him. She resented the certainly of his hands, deftly fitting her
into her clothing. She resented his experienced lovemaking and
her naive response to his skills. She resented trembling so hard
she couldn't button her blouse and the easy way his hands performed the task.

She resented the shirt he had drawn on, covering the chest
that condemned her from beneath the fine cotton. She looked
away from his throat, which bore a shaving nick—and the reddened imprint of her teeth.

"Well," she began airily, hoping he wouldn't notice the
husky, emotional tone underlying her bravado. "That
was...pleasant. But now that we've dispensed with that—"

"It isn't the end of the world," he said quietly as he finished buttoning her blouse. Avoiding his eyes, Dallas allowed herself a glimpse of those large, dark hands as they completed the task.

The backs were scarred and lightly covered with dark hair. They weren't a lover's gentle hands, yet Sam had touched her lightly, reverently, allowing her to set the pace. His fingers trembled slightly, and she savored the knowledge that he was affected. By her. Because of her.

He hadn't touched her as though she were a body to be used.

Sam had touched her as though she were made of sheer silk and spiderweb lace and he was frightened of hurting her.

"We'll both live, Dallas. Don't make too much of it," he whispered gently as his fingers misplaced a button. Clumsily, he corrected the error.

His gentleness caused the tear that had been waiting beneath her eyelids to come oozing out, spilling down her cheek. Horrified, she watched it dampen the hair on his shaking hand, and then Sam took her slowly, safely into his arms. "Come on, sweet pea," he whispered raggedly against her cheek, rocking her almost awkwardly, as though he seldom offered comfort. Or had been offered comfort.

"I'll get you for this," she promised shakily, unable to move away from his warmth. She doubted her legs would support her in one retreating step.

Sam's hand stopped stroking the taut line of her back. "Me? I think you've misplaced the guilt. You're like some damned fever virus—"

Taking a deep, steadying breath, Dallas stepped away from him, not shielding the frustration rocking her. She'd been safe, tucked away in her structured world, and then Sam came plunging merrily through the protective layers. "You'll pay for this," she threatened again.

"You think I'm not?" he asked wryly, glancing downward.

She refused to follow his gaze, focusing instead on his dark, rigid features. Her hand shook traitorously, wanting to trace the bold lines of his face. "Don't try anything like this again," she stated from between her teeth. "I've got you pegged."

Those smoky gray eyes lit and slashed at her. "If you think I planned—"

"Didn't you?" she asked quietly, thrusting a shaking hand through her hair as T.J.'s remarks came slithering back to haunt her. "Oh, didn't you? Isn't it a fact that chauvinists prefer women on their backs—"

He frowned, leaning toward her. "Let's check that position again, Pendragon. You were *on me*," he clarified. "Don't say another word, Dallas. If you're smart, you'll straighten up in the washroom and walk out of here. Now. Otherwise—" He glanced meaningfully at the desktop.

When Dallas's eyes widened, he thrust her jacket and tie into her hands as though they were criminal evidence marked "Exhibit A."

Glancing at Sam's dark scowl, Dallas took the wiser option and walked toward the washroom with as much dignity as she could muster. With her hand on the safety of the doorknob, she turned slightly. "Sneaky," she said, and meant it.

"The hell I am!" he snapped belligerently.

"Are too."

"Am not!" he snapped loudly as the lock clicked behind her.

Six

An hour later, Sam cheated on the wager and didn't care. Punching the bag in his private gym, he jabbed and sweated. Then he continued, the physical exhaustion trimming the raw edge off his desire for Dallas Pendragon. "Pendragon *is* a virus. She's getting to me," he said through gritted teeth as he dug deeper into his reserves, fighting her and himself as he pounded away at the bag.

Okay, he'd been around long enough to know better.

Dallas Pendragon wasn't aware of her latent sensuality. She didn't know what soft hands and softer surprised cries did to a man who'd kept his emotions in tight rein.

She needed protecting from men who might take advantage of her.

Damn. He intended to be one of those men.

Men? As in plural? He battered the bag, dancing around it.

"So why am I worrying about her? She's an adult with the right equipment...." Sam threw a series of hard one-two punches at the bag, feeling angry, frustrated and sexually deprived. He ached from his scalp downward and wondered if his basic body inventory would ever be the same. The first chance he got after this mess, he was taking a solid week off to accept Delilah Philburn's invitation into her bed. He felt he'd been set up by his body, betrayed by sexual abstinence. Evidently he wasn't as over-the-hill as he thought.

He'd avoided sweet little innocent things with a stubborn dedication, knowing that they were really lace-trimmed landmines of destruction.

He began cursing viciously, timing the phrases to the hard punches. He'd tasted her silky soft skin, had been caught in the scents of sweet peas and Appalachia mountain air. When she'd sighed, the sound filled him with a taste of all he ever wanted.

Sam jabbed at the bag, classifying himself as, "Damned lump of two-hundred-pound putty."

He could still feel her body ripple, contracting and heating against him. Sam wanted to fill her with himself, let her make him a part of her world. Let that heat make him warm for the first time in his entire life. She'd been stunned by the passion, and he had wanted to comfort her. To fold her in his arms and tell her it was all right.

Well, it wasn't. None of it.

Angry with her and frustrated by the hectic morning, Sam hadn't meant for the scene behind his desk to occur. Dallas just seemed to—respond, damn it!

Ignite was a better word.

Breathing hard, Sam stepped back from the bag. Dallas could reach right inside him and tear him apart if he weren't careful. There was something inside him long forgotten and it was too vulnerable to be exposed to her dangerous virus. Why was she getting to him anyway?

Lowering his head, Sam punched the bag as though it were his worst demon.

Beneath her obvious business savvy, Dallas was sweet. Feeling guilty for glimpsing something she didn't know herself, feeling guilty for having caused it, Sam knew he'd have to watch himself. Because there would be hell to pay when Dallas knew exactly how potent she was.

His fist slammed into the bag as though it were Beau's face.

Once the business community discovered the experiment, as Sam knew they would a là Franzini, he'd have his hands full of protecting her. Or them.

How the hell was he supposed to know that the clerical staff was under stress?

At five-thirty that afternoon, Dallas spread her hands over the Brice polls covering her office desk. Without a doubt, they demonstrated the necessity of job-sharing, a child-care center, a business day—a paid day off so that employees could conduct personal business—a fitness program and lastly, a sabbatical after five years on the job. She clicked on her computer and started working on outlines for each project.

Her mother had promised to check on Sam's progress tonight. That left the evening free for her to scrape away at Sam's corporate management-employee plans. She had three weeks to prove her theories were right—that stress-relieved employees meant less absenteeism and more productivity, keeping the turnover to a minimum.

Fifteen percent of Brice's clerical staff would qualify for her job-sharing program. They had volunteered to act in a pilot program, which Dallas worked out easily. It was simply a matter of scheduling and fitting workers together into a single, effective niche. The business day off was also a matter of scheduling; but the child-care center and physical-fitness programs demanded cost estimates. She needed architectural guidance for the proper remodeling; the child-care center would require proper staffing and furniture.

She tapped a worker's comment with her finger. "Mr. Loring wants a well-oiled organization and honestly, the pay is good. It's just that we're not all twenty-four-hour workaholics like him. We have families and other commitments, while Brice is his whole life."

How sad, Dallas mused for a moment. As a temporarily adopted father, Sam fitted into Nikki and Billy's lives perfectly.

As a pseudo house husband, Sam showed definite, endearing moments of confusion mixed with a determination to succeed.

As a man, he was too experienced. Sam Loring was the original type who preferred classy, worldly blondes.

Then why had he kissed her? She traced the shape of her mouth, thinking of his firm one. He had tasted just right.

She couldn't afford to get mixed up with his preferences.

Sam's kisses had big, fat motives written all over them. But now that she knew exactly how underhanded he could be when losing, she'd watch him closer.

If he just didn't have that scruffy I've-never-been-hugged look.

Dallas winced at that thought and began typing. According to Seattle business gossip, Sam's business practices made rawhide look soft. "It must be the season," she muttered. "After this is over, I'm treating myself to a whole box of chocolate-covered cherries."

Added to the challenge of integrating the Brice master plan, she tucked in a neat little stress education package for management. Tentatively titled The Whammy Plan, it needed more work and would be more difficult.

She began entering another poll into the computer, one that dealt with scheduled work loads and management courtesy to employees.

At eight-thirty, she rubbed the nape of her neck, leaned back in her chair and tried not to think about Sam.

While she tried not to think of the way his mouth warmed hers, cherishing, she fought the restlessness in her body. Dallas picked up a note, crushed it and tossed it into the trash. The most shameless thing about the entire scene was the way she could have actually ripped off his clothes.

He'd planned the whole disgusting thing, of course. Sam wouldn't wait for her to fail at the project—he'd be pushing, trying to get her back against the wall.

When the phone rang at ten o'clock, Dallas had just turned off her computer. She answered it absently, her eyes feeling gritty and her body heavy with fatigue.

"Dallas?" Sam's deep tone slid over the lines. "Are you all right?"

Nettled that he had invaded her domain, Dallas snapped, "Why wouldn't I be?"

On the other end of the line, he breathed once, deeply as though trying to control himself. "Get home," he ordered curtly before disconnecting the line.

"Look you oversized...I'm not on a curfew—"

Then Dallas stilled, mentally rapping off the things that could make Sam call her. When she'd called earlier, Nikki and Billy were excited, shrieking with delight as Sam fought the bubbles flowing out of the washer. They'd be asleep now—unless Sam didn't fare well on his bear hunt.

Tearing out of her office, Dallas crossed Seattle traffic in record time and came to a screeching, skidding stop just inches from Bertha's rusty back bumper. She ignored the Deons making out beneath their doorway mistletoe ball and concentrated on the waiting disaster...children's cuts, fevers, accidents....

The Christmas lights sparkled on her tree and the house was just as welcoming as ever—except Sam lurked in the open doorway. Baghdad seemed to grin, hanging from Sam's large hand and twitching his tail.

Hurrying up the steps, Dallas listened for crying and looked for the distraught children. "What's wrong?" she asked, rushing past Sam's imposing bulk into the house.

Peeling off her coat and kicking off her heels, Dallas rushed into the children's room to find them sleeping peacefully, undisturbed by bears. She padded over to them, looked for dried tear trails and found none. Kissing each warm cheek, Dallas eased out of the room.

Standing in the center of her living room, hands on hips, Sam glowered at her. In socks, jeans and a T-shirt, his hair mussed and a beard threatening his hard jaw, Sam was both fierce and—

Ignoring the patch of faded red on his cotton shirt, Dallas didn't want to think about the "and" part. She'd experienced enough of the "and" part on the floor behind his desk. "Why did you call me?"

Sam glared at her for a full minute, then stalked into the kitchen, leaving her to follow. A burned odor clung to the potpourri scents in his wake. His open briefcase sat on the table, papers scattered around it and a collection of recipe books stacked to one side. She noted the tabs marking the cookbooks and his glasses tossed carelessly aside. Working at the kitchen counter, Sam's large body was tense beneath the cotton T-shirt. His muscles rippled as he filled a plate and placed it in the microwave oven. She looked away from the marks her teeth had caused on his neck.

"Dinner is cold," he muttered ominously, setting the timer. "I expected you home before six."

The odd tone of frustration and anger surprised Dallas. She'd heard it before—from Lisa. She tossed that disquieting thought aside. Sam was just interested in making her play jumping frog. "I had work to do. Is anything wrong with Nikki or Billy?" she asked again, suspecting Sam's motives.

"Not a damn thing," he muttered in the tone of a person whose nose was definitely out of joint. "I spent the better part of an hour on supper. The kids appreciated my hamburger specialty anyway."

Sam's stare accused her of an unspecified crime. "You'd better not have eaten," he stated in that junkyard dog growl of his.

"You called me away from work for that?" Dallas glanced at the set of his shoulders and took a deep breath. She'd just left a string of potential accidents in her wake across Seattle for an executive who had cooked a hamburger. She'd been dangled at the end of one man's string and she hadn't forgotten the feeling. "We'll talk about this after I change," she said more quietly than she felt.

"You have one minute."

Sam began setting a place for her, and the odd sight of a man in her kitchen, preparing her supper rather than demanding it, surprised her. She closed her parted lips and walked into the safety of her bedroom to change into her yellow sweatsuit.

At the table, she picked at the immense hamburger and scalloped potatoes. While she debated entering a discussion about emergencies, Sam carefully placed her cup of tea at her side. "Here. You've had a hard day," he said as though resenting it and her.

Drinking beer from a bottle, Sam sprawled on the chair opposite her. "Where were you all night?" he asked quietly, toying with the fringes of her place mat.

"At the office. Working on proposals. What did you burn?" While Dallas realized Sam had fought bears, washing machines and prepared supper, he didn't own her time.

"About a pound of hamburger." His fingers moved restlessly across the mat. "So how is the usurping coming? Anything you need to discuss?"

Dallas dismissed the thought that Sam needed her attention. It would be his style to try to get a jump on her plans and waylay them. "I'm not ready for a presentation yet. The dinner is lovely. Thank you," she added, relying on manners when she really wanted to start something dark and ugly.

"You're welcome," he returned formally, sliding a finger across the back of her hand. "You look tired. Are you all right?"

The question was spoken in his deepest Southern drawl, throwing her back into the afternoon.

She'd been out of control, needing him—giving him too much of herself. She'd done that once and ended up with enough scars to last a lifetime.

She jerked back from his touch, cleaning off the table with a flourish to disguise the way he'd upset her. As she scraped the dishes, Dallas knew she was overreacting. "Fine. I have work to do, you know. Classes and your project."

Behind her, Sam leaned close as he whispered ominously, "Any night you're supposed to be in your office, you'd better damn well be. Call me when you leave, and if you stop along the way, let me know." The tone sounded like the Mounties, the Cavalry, and the Green Berets would all be out turning over Seattle pavements for her.

Dallas was no longer tired and worried. She whipped around to face him. "If you have a problem with my life-style, you're going to have to swallow it."

Placing his hands on the counter on either side of her hips, Sam lowered his head toward her. "Lisa and the kids were worried."

She noted the lines around his eyes and the uncompromising

set of his mouth. A muscle, covered by dark skin and rough stubble, contracted in a jaw that looked like granite. She didn't feel exactly sweet herself. "Lay off, Loring. I've managed without you for years, you know. My mother and the children both know this happens occasionally—"

"*I'm not your mother. Nor your children,*" he said too quietly. "You call me."

"Sam, if you're asking for trouble, I'm just in the mood to give it to you," she returned just as quietly, lifting her chin. "Back off."

"I'll bet you don't have to tell that to Beau," he said in a nasty tone, glaring down at her.

"Don't you have things to do?" she asked sweetly, wondering if she could wrap her hands around his thick, muscular neck and squeeze slowly. "Washing? Scrubbing the bathroom floor? Picking up trucks and dolls?"

"I've done all that," he said in a different soft tone, looking at her mouth. "What do you want for supper tomorrow night?"

"Anything," she responded, thinking of his mouth on hers earlier. He had such a nice mouth, firm, and delightfully tasty when he— She nudged his chest sharply with her shoulder and surprisingly, he stepped away. The knowledge that Sam could be so easily dislodged was somehow disquieting. "I'm having another cup of tea in my room. Privately."

"Fine. You do that." She didn't trust his easy tone as she walked away from him into the sanctity of her bedroom.

Lisa called at eleven-fifteen. Lying amidst her favorite magazines, twisted in her rosebud sheets, Dallas turned off her lamp and lit her favorite scented candle while she talked with her mother. Lisa's calls were uncanny, perfectly timed for sleepless nights. Sam roamed around the house apparently doing house things; the basement stairs creaking beneath his weight.

"Sam is such a sweetheart...has he gone to bed?" Lisa crooned over the line as Dallas watched the flickering candle flame. The scent and the aura spreading over her delicate room was soothing in contrast to the whole, tense day. Especially after she learned that Sam knew how to warm carpeting.

Concentrating on the flame, Dallas tried to ignore the sound of things being moved in her basement. Big things with motors that started reluctantly. "He's playing with Daddy's tools."

"Of course, dear. I thought he'd seek them out. Real men always do. They're really just toys to men. Nothing makes them happier than puttering around...." Lisa hesitated, then added, "Well, maybe a romp in bed. Those tools...I just couldn't part with them, and knowing that you're keeping them makes me feel better. How's your work at Brice going?"

A saw buzzed directly beneath Dallas, then stopped. She took a deep breath. "I'll be working nights at the office, weekends, too. With Lettie and Sybil filling in for me at the daytime stress classes, I've got a neat margin of time—" Another, smaller saw began ripping through the silence, then ended quickly. "Mother, can I call you tomorrow?"

Dallas listened to another motor chug gently beneath her bed and groaned, tugging her pillow over her head.

Friday morning, Sam faced the board in Brice's spacious conference room. "I admit going out on a ledge without presenting the package to the board. Dallas Pendragon is doing nothing more than exploring our management techniques for stress problems. She won't find any...and when her project is completed, Brice will still stand. Things of this nature are generally too time consuming to discuss before quarterly reports."

He recognized the men's closed-door expressions. Sam nodded briefly to Edward Swearingen, a man he deeply respected, though they had business differences. At sixty-five, Edward was a burly, six-footer who moved like a dancer. One of his base life theories was that every man needed a good woman. Sam immediately had pegged Edward as being in favor of the stress-management program.

Jerry Keys leaned in his chair and folded his hands across his rounded stomach. "Pendragon is asking a lot of questions, has an architect rummaging around the place and has generally shot the way of things to hell. She's driving personnel nuts, asking about methods of testing, employee backgrounds and the like. What the hell do her 'family profiles' have to do with a workplace?"

Shifting uneasily, Sam frowned at the scars on his knuckles. He'd seen some of the worker's interviews and was stunned with the results. He drove himself harder than anyone on staff, not asking them to do anything he hadn't done himself. Big, ugly terms like "burnout," "feeling stretched" and "pressure at work is affecting personal relationships," stood out like tombstones.

The whole interviewing matter had Dallas uncapping a volcano of complaints. Sam ground his teeth together and felt the muscles in his neck tense as they did when he was about to take a hard punch to the jaw. He'd had no idea about the amount of worker discontent.

Francis Tome leaned forward, tapping his pencil. "She's real trouble, Sam. Has a nose for seeking out what might appeal to the general staff. She's got to be shut down before she does any real damage. I've heard about this stress bunk before. This fiscal period we can't afford to go rummaging around financing employee stress-free environments."

The thought that he'd been mentioned in the polls as a major cause of worker's stress caused Sam's stomach to contract. Was a "piece of concrete machinery driven by productivity charts" really how they saw him?

Looking up from his papers, Edward Swearingen noted, "Pendragon has got some good ideas. I've known her mother for years and understand that Dallas is an enterprising young woman. Her beliefs just might be valid and need attention."

Leaning back in his chair at the head of Brice's sprawling walnut table, Sam thought about Mullens, the male architect Dallas had hired to do estimates, and wanted to start punching something with bones and flesh and a California grin. Mullens was a lady's man, an aging surfer with too-tight jeans who managed to be the center of the secretaries' huddle. Dallas didn't seem to mind Mullens hovering over her, nor the way his head bent near hers.

Once, Sam had caught Dallas smothering a giggle as Mullens whispered in her ear. He had just started toward them when Dallas smiled brightly at him, "Problems, Sam?"

Of course, he had problems. A man didn't wait for a woman

every night, launder her practical cotton underwear and share her kids' sniffles without having Big Problems.

The honeymooners next door were driving him nuts, and he wanted to chew steel.

He needed to call Delilah and hire a babysitter. When a virus invaded a man's system, he took steps to waylay it.

Maybe he just needed to hear the little noises Dallas made at the back of her throat when he tasted her skin. God, they were sweet sounds—aching and encouraging.

"...We all know you're living with Pendragon, Sam. But business is business," Ben Thompsen stated, slamming his open hand on the table.

"What's that?" Sam asked, leaving the image of Dallas's pale flesh and returning to the board room. He felt slightly guilty, as though he'd exposed his woman to voyeurs. To cover his uneasiness, Sam sighted down on Thompsen.

The younger man shifted slightly, tugging at his tie.

"What's the story?" another board member asked. "I've never known your private life to interfere with business before Sam."

Emily suddenly began refilling the water glasses and coffee cups. And Sam felt as though the Indians were circling his wagon train, closing in for the kill. Or was it vultures over near-dead prey? Loosening his tie and flicking open the top buttons of his shirt, Sam glanced uneasily at her. Emily had a way of baring her fangs without changing her expression.

He explained the wager quickly, ignoring the speculative light behind Emily's glasses.

Ike Ramsey leered, nodding. "Hell of a setup, man."

"That's a new one," another man added, chuckling.

"Sweet," a third voice commented. "No wonder you've been looking like hell lately. Worn out as hell."

Emily accidentally spilled hot coffee on the man's hand and he yelped. "Sorry," she murmured without remorse, sweeping on down the table.

When Sam stood, slowly stripping off his jacket and rolling up his sleeves, the board members sat up straighter, their grins dying. Turning his back to them, Sam heard a sudden hushed round of exclamations as he looked out over the drizzle and the fog shrouding Brice's top floor.

Turning slowly back to the men, Sam leveled a hard stare at each member. "Brice has always been at the front of innovative ideas. Think of me as a pilot project," he ordered succinctly.

Max Dragonski tapped his cigar on an ashtray. His gaze returned to Sam's shirt, strolling slowly over it. "Mixing corporate business and private business are two different things, Sam. I agree with the other members. I'm uncomfortable about this."

Relying on instincts that had served him well, Sam made a quick decision. He turned to the windows again, outlining the idea silently and ignoring the hushed snickers behind him. Rubbing his jaw, Sam turned. He knew exactly how to use his height and stare to disintegrate challenging counterparts.

No one snickered about Dallas.

He surveyed the men, then spread his hands on the table and leaned on them. "I'd appreciate your cooperation in this matter. Emily, set up a time that's agreeable with the members, then contact Pendragon to see if she's in sync. Gentlemen of the board, you're welcome to meet Pendragon. She'll be willing to answer any or all questions—I suggest you stick to business."

He paused, trying to ignore Emily's pleased grimace. "Anyone having problems with my place of residence, I'll meet you in my private gym after the meeting. Meeting adjourned—"

At the door, Emily smiled toothily. "Mr. Loring, Ms. Pendragon is just outside. I'm sure she wouldn't mind an interview with the board now."

Knowing Emily's persistence, Sam nodded curtly. "Gentlemen," he said a moment later as Dallas swept into the room, wearing a navy skirt and sweater and carrying a briefcase. "This is our Ms. Pendragon."

Sam noted Dallas's tiny flinch before she smiled coolly at him. Dallas didn't want to be anyone's Ms. Anything, keeping her possession to herself. The thought irritated him mildly. He'd never wanted to fully possess a woman—to wrap himself in her warmth and take care of her. The thought that perhaps he now wanted to, which was as desireable as fleas on a hound dog's back, hurt.

Introducing the board to Dallas, Sam glanced down at her. Shooting him a quick frown, she glanced at his shirt. Why was everyone so fascinated with his damned shirt? Her green eyes darkened and her mouth tightened. "Sam," she said with quiet force.

"The gentlemen would like to ask you a few questions, Dallas. Would now be a good time?"

"Sam," she repeated more forcefully, glancing meaningfully at his shoulder.

"Ah, Ms. Pendragon. About this matter of management providing child-care centers..." a board member began.

"It would cut down on absenteeism when a child is sick and give the workers time to run down to check on their children during lunch and breaks," she answered, edging in front of Sam.

Dallas glanced over her shoulder. "Ah, Mr. Loring, would you mind sitting down and getting more comfortable?" she asked, tugging out a chair for him.

He shrugged, noting the skill with which she moved into the spotlight and arranged another meeting for a formal presentation. Pendragon knew how to pitch, he decided, watching her field a battery of questions.

"I see this whole thing as a waste of company time—"

"When a company stops trying to improve, I think it demonstrates a tendency to stagnate, don't you?" Dallas answered, smiling.

She knew how to throw out challenges, Sam decided, watching her move around the room in that long-legged stride. He wondered idly if she were wearing her weekday panties or the violet splashed ones.

"You don't think you're getting special privileges because of Sam, do you?" Brent Pennington asked slowly. "He's never allowed anything to interrupt company policy before—"

Sam tapped his thumb on the wooden arm of the conference chair. Pennington had wanted to show off from the day he arrived. "Brent—"

Dallas flashed a quick smile at Sam, stopping him from slashing the little punk down to size. She continued the interview in a light, brisk manner while pushing her theories and promising backup statistics. Then not lingering, Dallas discreetly excused herself and gave the members a chance to talk without her presence.

"She's on the ball. Quick thinker," Swearingen said later as he left the room. He grinned at Sam, glancing at his wrinkled shirt. "Better hogtie that one. If I were a few years younger..."

"Sam, I think you're coming along nicely," Emily noted when the room had cleared. "Except you really should learn to use fabric softener in the wash."

Distracted by the depth of his feeling about protecting Dallas, Sam frowned. "What the hell has laundry got to do with a business conference?"

Emily plucked a pink pair of cotton panties from Sam's back. She dropped them on top of his notes and grimaced happily. "Fabric softener stops cling."

She pointed to his shirt front and added, "Take clothes out of the drier ASAP—as soon as possible—and hang them up. I'll take care of Mr. Pennington and his remarks—*I control the switchboard hold button, you know.* Until he learns better, his calls will take quite some time to process. On Monday, I'll sneak you some recipes that are good, easy and cheap. Do all the laundry and major grocery shopping during the weekend and leave Sunday night for relaxation... Have a nice weekend."

Sam barely heard her leave as he picked up Dallas's practical underpants, crushing them in his fist. With "Monday" scripted on the cotton, they would be the same pair she'd worn in his office. Sam jammed them into his slacks pocket, the one with Billy's tiny truck, and hoped he had enough saved to pay the baby-sitter.

By the following Friday, Sam felt stretched like a rubberband between his office and household duties. If he had to admit honestly which ones he preferred, he would choose basking in the cheery warmth of the Pendragon household.

At nine o'clock, he settled down to working his way quietly through reports. Emily's voice cutting into his intercom was urgently sharp. "Billy's sick. The sitter couldn't get Ms. Pendragon. Her office says she's on a two-hour trip to a class and can't be reached—"

"I'll go. Cancel all my appointments for the day," Sam ordered, thinking that Billy had been too quiet this morning. His eyes had a weepy look—

"Morrison and Forbes are scheduled for a conference at one, Mr. Loring. They won't talk to anyone but you—"

"Those—" Sam clamped his teeth together and began stashing papers into his briefcase. "The kid is sick, Emily," he said, striding past her on his way to the parking lot. "I'll check in as soon as I see what the situation is."

Sam didn't think about Emily's quiet, pleased smirk; he worried about Billy.

The boy was hot and droopy, too easily managed as Sam carried him into the house. Though the baby-sitter said that Billy's temperature had dropped and that a doctor wasn't necessary, Sam doubted her credentials. But Billy just wanted to be held, snuggling to Sam quietly.

In an hour, Sam had dressed Billy in his Superman pajamas, served him iced orange juice and sat on the couch. Holding the small boy, his blanket, toys and Baghdad on his lap, Sam felt helpless. In his lifetime, he'd worked through rough times, but holding the listless, warm child to him, Sam knew he had never worried so much.

Dozing in his arms, Billy sniffed once and all the muscles in Sam's body tensed. Should he have taken the boy to the emergency room?

"Want macaroni and cheese," Billy mumbled against Sam's chest.

"It's not lunchtime, Billy. How about—"

"Want macaroni and cheese."

The phone rang and Sam extended a hand to retrieve it, muffling a curse. The boy was sick—didn't the world know he couldn't handle macaroni, a sick child and whatever the person on the other end of the line wanted? Forgetting for a moment where he was, he snapped, "Loring here."

Emily spoke in hushed tones. "How's Billy, Mr. Loring?"

"Look, Emily. I'm busy here. I've got my hands full—ouch!" Sam eased Baghdad's kneading claws from his thigh.

"Ah...Mr. Loring? Lisa Pendragon called." Emily smothered a sound that could have been a girlish giggle. "She's picking up Nikki and delivering her to the house. Nikki isn't feeling well. When Ms. Pendragon's office called, I knew you'd need help—"

Knowing that help was on its way, Sam took a relieved breath.

"Mm...cheese...now," Billy mumbled just before he sat up, leaned over and emptied his stomach on Sam's stocking covered foot.

"Call you back—I can make it until Lisa gets here—" Sam said, holding the boy carefully with one hand as he extended his foot and grimaced.

"Sam! Don't hang up!" Emily's imperial shout stopped him from hanging up the receiver.

"What?"

"Lisa Pendragon also said that she's got to catch a flight out right away. She'll drop Nikki by—she said the girl isn't really sick, just something about an upset stomach. She knows you can handle the sick children competently."

Sam felt sick. He knew how the Lone Ranger felt without Tonto. He knew how the captain of the Titanic felt. He knew how his foot felt. "Okay," he agreed weakly, then replaced the receiver.

Just after cleaning and changing Billy and himself, Sam reinstated the child on the couch. While he was mixing another batch of orange juice, Lisa delivered Nikki, kissed his cheek and sailed off in her red sports car.

"Glad you're aboard," Sam muttered Lisa's cheerful parting comment.

By the time he settled Nikki comfortably at the other end of the couch, Billy was looking at him with huge, haunting eyes. "Want Mom. Want macaroni and cheese," he demanded softly in a hurt tone, as if Sam were sloughing off his duties.

At one o'clock in the afternoon, Sam was exhausted. The

house looked like a tornado had passed through, and the phone rang again. Emily asked, "How are they doing, Mr. Loring?"

"Sleeping," he whispered back, removing two dolls and three tiny trucks from the couch. "What's up?"

"Morrison and Forbes are in your office, ready for a conference call. Can you handle it?"

Rolling his eyes upward for heavenly help, Sam agreed. Sitting on the floor with his briefcase opened, he conducted an entire business deal in whispers.

Sometime between two and three—between Nikki's request for juice and Billy's for a story—Sam dozed, stretched out on the floor beside the couch. He was exhausted, worried and…exhausted.

The phone rang, and he snatched it instantly. "Sam?" Dallas asked softly. "I just got the message—but Emily said you had everything under control. I'm sorry I wasn't there, but I'm driving back as soon as I can. Thanks, Sam," she added hesitantly.

"The kids are okay," Sam whispered. "They're better now. They're both sleeping and don't have a temperature. It's like the sitter said, just a passing thing."

"I have a girlfriend who comes over at times like this. If you need to get back to the office, I'll call her—"

"Not a chance. I've got everything under control," Sam whispered, glancing around the house. If he hurried, he could just clean up before she arrived and make the whole day look like a walk through the park.

In the next ten minutes, just as Sam slipped back into comfortable dozing, someone knocked at the front door. When he opened it, Emily grinned and held out papers to him. "You have to sign these today, Mr. Loring."

Glancing at the papers, Sam scrawled his signature, took another look and wiped away a crumb of the Sunbirds' Cookies. Emily vanished before he could ask her to help him clean up.

After another frantic two hours, Sam managed to clean the house, wash the soiled clothing, fix peanut-butter sandwiches and read a story to the children.

When Dallas arrived, opening the door quietly, Sam dozed

on the floor. He blinked at her as she bent over him and smoothed his hair.

"Poor Sam," she said in the sweet, hushed tones he loved to hear. He blinked again, trying to look as though the experience was something he could easily manage. But he'd lost a whole day somehow and he had paperwork to finish for a contract discussion he had rescheduled for the morning.

"Hi, Mommy," Billy said brightly, stepping over Sam's prone body. "I was sick, but Mr. Sam took care of me and now I feel great! Want to play, Mr. Sam?"

"Hi, Mom," Nikki chimed in, evidently recovered. "What's wrong with Sam? Why's he just laying there staring up at the ceiling like that?"

Seven

Monday morning, Sam threw his briefcase onto his desk. Dallas had spent the better part of the weekend at her office or in her bedroom plotting his downfall. In the three weeks since he'd met her, he'd had nothing but trouble.

He jammed his fists into his jeans pockets, resenting that he had shot Rule 2.01 of Brice's Executive Dress Code to hell. He didn't have the money for dry cleaning the suits splattered with Bertha's oil patterns. It was the first time in his ten years at Brice that he had worn a sweater over a wash-and-wear shirt.

Running a hand along his collar, he grimaced. The longish length of his hair—also because of temporary budgetary problems—was a blatant infraction of Rule 2.02.

Nikki had forgotten her favorite doll, and Billy's zipper had stuck, causing Sam to be late to the office, thus breaking Brice's rule for prompt business hours.

Sam extended a long leg, checking the length of the jeans to see if it covered the new bleach spots on his dress socks. He'd lost the appropriate mates and had found an odd assortment clinging to everything, haunting him. Dallas hoarded her clothes, and he doubted that he could handle them without hormonal distress. The thoughts of her monogrammed panties had kept him from reworking a market report due in January.

Rubbing his hand along his jaw, Sam admitted that playing working parent and house husband wasn't as easy as it had first appeared.

He'd never wanted children, but he'd miss Nikki and Billy. His past Christmas seasons seemed empty now that he'd experienced the warmth and excitement of children. While other children seemed to want enormous lists from Santa Claus, Nikki and Billy just wanted Mr. Sam.

He explored the novelty of being wanted for himself and decided it hadn't happened in his lifetime.

Someone always wanted something from him—work, money, gifts. And he'd given and taken without any remorse or lingering attachments.

Sam rubbed his hands together, chafing away the cold he felt seeping into his life.

Living with Dallas wasn't easy. Her scents filled the house; her laughter caused his breathing to change.

Thoughts of her aching little sighs had kept him from sleeping. Dallas was working too hard, looking bleak and hollow eyed. He thought of her savage, hungry expression as she lay in his arms...her body arching toward his touch...and then Sam groaned. He didn't want to step into commitments at his age, much less a relationship. Especially with a woman who was his enemy in business, proposing weird ideas about stress management.

Were they weird? he wondered, acknowledging the tension he felt trying to balance his new home life and a business. And why hadn't he some idea that his employees were unhappy before Dallas started turning over policies?

Okay, he'd been busy, fighting to keep Brice at the top and concerned about production. Of course, he cared, it was just that he had no idea—

Just as Dallas had no idea of her sensuality until lately. She'd be a man's living dream—a lady in public and responsive in bed.

Surf-boy Mullens would be waiting for her to fall into his bed. Or would Beau, the wimp, taste those strawberry lips?

Scowling at the fog bank encompassing his office, Sam noted the colored holiday lights below his office. Christmas was next week, the children were excited and he had empty pockets.

For a reason Sam didn't want to explore, he needed to give Dallas something special. A part of himself.

When was the last time he'd wanted to share any part of himself with anyone? Sam wondered.

When was the last time he'd shared the warmth of a real home, felt children snuggle against him after a really good round of bear hunting—

He caught the scent of coffee—an extravagance he couldn't afford—and turned around to see Emily placing a cup of delicious, steaming brew on his desk. "Bless you," he murmured humbly, inhaling the scent and cupping the warm cup in his hands.

She placed a folder stuffed with odd papers on his desk as he sipped the coffee. "Recipes from the staff. They're enjoying your trials as a working mother, you know. One of them said that you were almost human. Especially when you're mooning over that Pendragon woman. They think you should take her on a date, maybe dinner overlooking the bay."

Sam stopped sipping, stretching Emily's charity. "With what?"

"Limits one, doesn't it?" she asked cheerfully. "Don't forget. The gifts for the office party and donations to the needy are expected of you, like everyone else. I can't write your charity check this year," she added with a tiny drop of humor. "But, of course, I can see that the accounting branch prepares the Christmas bonuses, if you wish. Oh, and Ms. Pendragon will be here at ten for a conference with you. She has questions that need clearance before she can proceed. Mr. Mullens will be with her, the lovely man."

Emily glanced at Sam's dark expression, then winked, and before leaving his office, she added, "Lisa called. She and Edward Swearingen have been seeing each other. They're taking the children for the weekend. Sledding and marshmallow roasts at his cabin on Snoqualmie Pass. You and Ms. Pendragon will just have to make do this weekend. Alone.''

Alone. The word stopped Sam in midswallow. Dallas would be his for the weekend. *No children. No Lisa.* Sam swallowed, wondering why he felt so light-headed.

Between calls and dictation, Sam worked on his plans for the weekend alone with Dallas...candlelight dinners, low lights and Crab Louie, Seattle's famous seafood salad. Or maybe he should take her to dinner and dancing at the bay. Sam mentally rummaged through his wallet and wondered if Emily knew any romantic ''stretcher'' meals.

When Dallas arrived for her ten o'clock conference, she spread the first-floor plan across Sam's desk and pointed at it. ''This would be the best spot for a child-care center. Employees could easily drop the children off when they arrive and pick them up when they leave. That floor is also the best place to put a gym and shower system. However, if you think another spot would be appropriate, we can estimate that, too. Can't we, Carl?''

She glanced up to find Carl Mullens and Sam glaring at each other over her head. While Carl's expression was bland, Sam's dark eyebrows were jammed together, his jaw rigid. They looked like two alley toms snarling over territorial rights. Dressed in a woolen ski sweater and jeans, Sam appeared rugged and appealing next to Carl's polished carelessness.

''Ah...Carl, would you mind going on without me?'' Dallas touched his arm and felt Sam tensing at her side.

''Sure thing, baby,'' Carl mumbled, shooting one last hard look at Sam before walking his tight jeans out of the office.

''Sure thing, baby,'' Sam repeated through his teeth as he glanced at her navy, pin-striped chemise dress. ''Is that jerk really any good?''

Something went fluttering about in her when Sam's hard stare lingered on her mouth. He looked so grim, she couldn't resist teasing him a little. ''At what?''

Watching her, Sam slowly removed his glasses and placed

them on the blueprints. "I could show you what," he returned in that low Southern drawl, reaching for her.

She stepped back. For a moment they just looked at each other, breathing hard. Sam did look delicious. Wickedly masculine and sexy. There was something primitive roaming around within him, as if he wanted her more than anything in his life.

Dallas lowered her eyelids, feeling her cheeks warm. Sam's large hand cupped her chin, lifting it as he smiled tenderly. "You're blushing, Ms. Businesswoman of the Year."

When he brushed his lips across her cheek, Dallas couldn't force herself to move away. She breathed quietly, trying to sort out the emotions within her. "Shoo," she ordered weakly as he drew away.

"Are you wearing your Monday panties, Ms. Pendragon?" Sam's deep sexy drawl reached right inside her. His intercom buzzed, and Sam jabbed a button on it, clearly irritated by the interruption. "What?"

"Call on line two from Nikki and Billy," Emily crooned softly.

Holding Dallas's worried gaze, Sam took the call. "Hi, you mean, tough bear hunters."

He nodded, watching Dallas. "I know, Nikki. You're right, your doll does need a bigger crib—one that rocks. Okay, Billy, we'll go down to the mall to see Santa Claus. Uh-huh, I do have a present for your mother," he said, beginning to smile.

Sam slipped his hand around hers, his thumb caressing Dallas's knuckles as he listened to the children intently. Dallas stood quietly, absorbing the gentle strength in the same hand that ruled Brice Cleansers and dressed Nikki's dolls. Then for a moment, his thumb stilled and Sam frowned, apparently listening closely. "Thank you," he said quietly, his voice raspy. "It will be the best one I've ever had. Okay. And let's stop on the way home for ice-cream cones to celebrate, okay? You want to talk to your mother? She's right here—"

Big, tough Sam Loring definitely looked weak and pale as he sprawled into a chair. He stared off into space while the receiver dangled from his limp hand.

Taking the telephone, Dallas learned that the baby-sitter

wanted a new kitchen sponge for Christmas. When she placed the telephone in the cradle, she asked, "Sam? What's wrong?"

He stared at her blankly, and she caught the damp glitter on his lashes before he lowered his head to study the plans. When his shoulders tensed, Dallas placed her hand on his arm. Sam's muscles contracted beneath the woolen sweater. He rotated his neck as though it ached, and Dallas instinctively began rubbing the taut muscles.

Taking her hand in his, Sam raised her palm to his mouth. She allowed the intimacy because Sam looked so helpless. "Billy just called me 'Daddy,'" he managed to say unevenly against her skin. He breathed deeply. "Daddy," Sam repeated reverently. "And they're making me a stocking. God, I'm forty-six—"

"Don't let it go to your head, big guy," Dallas said softly, smoothing his hair. She'd advised Billy about the "don't-call-Sam-Daddy" matter, but apparently her son had slipped in a wayward moment.

She liked how the crisp texture of Sam's hair clung to her skin and enjoyed petting Sam in his moment of weakness. Normally he was so solid and impending, the thought of soothing him was like reaching her hand into a tiger's lair.

Because he was so vulnerable, because she was so frightened of caring again, Dallas stepped away. She rummaged through her large purse, extracted a paper bag and tossed it to him. "I brought you a present."

Opening the bag carefully, Sam shook the contents onto his desk. A Kaiser bun stuffed with alfalfa sprouts, sliced tomato and assorted lunch meats in plastic wrap looked delicious. Dallas handed him a small thermos, the scent of clam chowder filling the room when he opened it. "I know you've been skipping lunches by the way you stock up at night. This might help."

He looked astonished and very uneasy. He swallowed, and his mouth worked a fraction of time before he actually spoke. "This is very nice," Sam said stiffly, then cleared his throat.

Poor Sam, Dallas thought, watching him stare at the sandwich and hot soup. He swallowed again. "I haven't brown bagged it in fifteen years or more," he said in a deep, uneven voice. "Thanks."

Because Sam was so clearly touched, Dallas couldn't resist bending to kiss his cheek. Then his mouth turned slightly, and she stood still as Sam's lips worshipped hers, tasting and warming.

Though his hands didn't touch her, she was drawn nearer by the soft, cherishing movements of his mouth. Dallas found herself leaning into his warmth, resting against the strength of his body while Sam slanted his mouth to nibble at her bottom lip. "I've missed you, sweet pea," he said huskily against her chin, easing her gently into his lap. "Come here."

Resting her hand on his chest, Dallas looked up at his tender expression and traced a new shaving cut. "Don't mess with me, Sam," she returned shakily. "I'm really not up to any of this."

He smiled at that, nibbling on the tip of her finger and gently sucking it. "What makes you think I am?"

"You're not what I want." Why were his eyes so tender? Why did she feel so safe in his arms?

Why couldn't he have been anyone else? Someone less demanding, like Beau or Doug...?

"I haven't wanted anyone for years," he said as though to himself.

"Then don't want me," she returned, raising her lips for his kiss.

The instant their lips met, Dallas forgot to resist. She forgot to keep Sam in the T.J. category of women-using men and allowed herself to listen to the throbbing jungle drums. Running her hand behind his head, she toyed with the crisp, longish hair at his collar.

When his tongue flicked lightly at the corners of her mouth, Dallas parted her lips and drew him nearer. She wanted his mouth desperately, wanted the heat and strength of Sam wrapped nearer about her. Under her, over her— "Sam?" Dallas needed to press her mouth against the rough skin covering that throbbing vein. When she did, the jungle tom-toms began beating rapidly, unevenly.

Moving deeper into Sam's arms, Dallas forgot everything but

the way he tasted. She explored his lips with her tongue, listened to his quiet, uneven breathing as she tugged at his sweater, lifting it upward and over his head.

Fighting the heat moving through her, Dallas sat straighter and studied the way his hair stood up in peaks. The way his hard mouth had softened with her kiss. He tasted wonderful. Like tender promises and warm Southern nights scented by magnolia blossoms.

She loved the way he trembled, the heat flushing his cheeks, and the stormy gray color of his eyes. On her hip, his hand trembled, and Dallas suddenly wanted it on her, roaming, searching and finding.

Delighted in a way she had never been, Dallas reached down to grip Sam's shirt in both hands. The buttons tore easily, popping off with little, exciting snaps.

Like her taut, feminine senses.

Beneath the stained and wrinkled—but clean—shirt, Sam's chest and throat were wonderful. Exciting and waiting to be discovered like a sumptuous new dessert. Rubbing her nose against Sam's soap-scented, hair-covered muscular chest, Dallas wanted to be near him. Laminated to him.

Winding her arms around his neck, she drew him down for her kiss. Breathing rapidly, Sam tightened his arms, his large hands warming her back and hips and legs. He was moving too slowly when Dallas's tom-toms weren't waiting—too gently when she wanted him hot and close.

"Sam-boy?" she asked huskily against his cheek, feeling the underlying heat as he trembled.

"Ouch," he muttered as her hips shifted more comfortably within his hard lap. Lifting her easily with one arm, Sam extracted a tiny toy truck and a frilly doll dress to carefully place them on the desk.

He grinned with the air of a boy savoring a double-dipped chocolate ice-cream cone. "Now where were we?"

Dallas fought the heat building within her, fought the tender look of expectancy on Sam's dark face. With his hair mussed by her fingers, his eyes dark and wickedly pleased, Sam was too masculine, too enticing, too—

His bottom lip was cut, and she stared at it blankly.

Holding very still beneath her, Sam watched her closely. "You bit me, sweet pea," he said in a deep, ragged tone that reminded her of spreading a blanket beneath the stars. Near a lily pond with frogs and crickets. "And called me Sam-boy. Did wonders for my ego."

Dallas's eyes widened, meeting the dark humor in his. "Me?" She managed in a tone that sounded like a squeak.

"You." Sam kissed her sensitive mouth lightly. Then he grinned, looking down at his bare chest and her undisturbed clothing. "Sorry to take advantage of you this way," he drawled in his sexiest Southern accents. "But I just couldn't help my-self."

Throughout the week, Dallas fought cost estimates, ran her business through her assistants and suffered from a lack of sleep due to hearing Sam move about in the basement...and his sweet kiss. Dallas had heard her tom-toms every night, awakening to find herself twisted in rosebud sheets and aching with the empty promise of her dreams.

The Deons were on a sizzling, kissing rampage everywhere she looked.

Sam made coffee every morning, dressed in loose pajama bottoms. They were originally white, but assorted pinks and blues had stained the cotton. She found herself thinking how easily that knot at his enticing navel could be tugged loose....

Even after she reminded them that Sam's stay was only temporary, Nikki and Billy were calling the squatter and usurper of her hormones Daddy. Each time they did, Sam reacted in a humble, loveable way that caused her to forget her mission for a moment.

Nothing about Sam was safe, at least what parts touched her. Every morning when she had handed Sam his lunch, he'd stared down at her in that quiet way that said he knew something she didn't.

She loved handing Sam his lunch. He took it with such reverence and appreciation, as though each time was a brand-new gift that he hadn't expected.

She had scheduled a date with Beau on Friday evening. She'd badly needed a kiss to compare with Sam's unholy devastation. When Beau had come to pick her up, Sam had seemed in unusually good humor, clapping Beau on the back. "Have fun, kids. I won't wait up," he had said, returning to the contents of his briefcase beneath the snickerdoodle cookie recipes.

Beau had shuddered openly. Later—after Sam's kiss—Dallas had shuddered, too.

Without the children to consider, Sam went on a midnight binge of sawing, hammering gently and making a spine-tingling scrape-scrape she recognized as sanding.

Dallas ran cost estimates of labor for a child-care center, sniffed the new potpourri Sam had added to the simmering pot, and wondered why T.J.'s kiss hadn't moved her to tearing off his clothes.

Pulling her rosebud-splattered sheets over her head, Dallas tried to ignore the disturbing creature in her basement.

She couldn't trust Sam Loring for a moment. He was sneaky, waiting for a chance to shoot holes in her presentation. Waiting for a time when he could get her beneath his thumb and spread her failure as a woman before the world.

She was a failure in bed. Hadn't T.J. told her often enough?

Why hadn't she kept herself safe? What she'd actually done by instigating Lisa's scheme was to place the fox in the hen house. The saw buzzed merrily in the basement shop, and Dallas forced herself not to grit her teeth.

Loring was cunning. With her senses running wild and his saws buzzing all night, she couldn't possibly put together a decent proposal.

With that thought, she sat upright, turning on her bedside light. Loring's kisses and sawing wouldn't keep her from designing the best proposal the Seattle business world had ever experienced. Dragging her briefcase into the bed with her, Dallas began jotting down notes on a legal pad. If he could work all night, so could she. Dallas spritzed herself with cool rosewater she kept beside her bed, breathed deeply and began working on The Whammy Plan Designed for Business Executives.

The Whammy, a working plan to educate managers, needed

refining. The Whammy would demonstrate employee stresses created by managerial demands. It involved inverted cross-training, where managers sat at a secretarial desk and performed light clerical duties. Dallas smiled as she jotted down her notes. She doubted if Sam could fit his long legs under a secretarial desk. Let alone tactfully settle office disputes before they got out of hand.

Saturday morning she awoke to the sound of hammering in the basement. Dragging herself into the shower, then dressing in jeans and sweatshirt, Dallas left the house for her office. She intended to push the proposal into shape for the January consideration by Brice's board. By making good use of the weekend, she could enjoy Christmas with her family.

During the day, she found herself thinking of Sam.

It wasn't often a woman found a man who preferred boxer shorts to the newer bikini cut. Before Sam discovered fabric softener, his cotton shorts clung to towels and sheets, which had been folded with methodical precision. She missed finding the assortment of underwear, she admitted reluctantly.

T.J. had preferred minuscule black shorts cut across his hips for vanity's sake. Sam, on the other hand, didn't have an ounce of vanity in his hard muscular frame. He had scarred knuckles and a neck that seemed to lower into his shoulders when he was angry. He had big, gentle hands that dressed dolls and felt warm and safe when they caressed her skin—

Dallas closed her eyes and shivered. It had to be the Christmas season or midlife approaching. In the afternoon, Sybil dropped in with a thermos of seasonal cheer. She vaguely mentioned something about rum.

At five o'clock, Dallas found herself exiting her computer outline. Deeply tired and drained, she hadn't made progress for the past hour and recognized her problem easily. As a businesswoman, she couldn't afford distraction and knew she had better deal with it.

The game plan had shifted, and Sam presented an immense, personal problem to her. Driving through the cold drizzle, Dallas worked out a tentative plan to let Sam out of his part of the contract. She nodded to the swish-swish of her windshield wipers. Sam could move back into his penthouse and they'd modify his life-style from there.

Parking over Bertha's new pool of oil, Dallas smiled. Sam would buy the wager's modification and move out. Given some space, she could erase the hot, tight feeling when he pulled out his damned dimples and Southern drawl.

Feeling in control for the first time in weeks, Dallas walked up the steps and opened the door with new confidence.

Sam, seated on the living-room floor and surrounded by wrapping paper and wooden toys, glowered up at her. Particles of sawdust clung to his longish hair. A peek-a-boo hole in his T-shirt exposed a nipple circled by hair, and his muscular legs were bare from his pink boxer shorts to his mismatched socks. The scent of spaghetti and garlic bread mixed with winter-pine potpourri swirled around her as she studied him—the villain who kept crashing uninvited into her outline for the Brice proposal.

Sam's neck began to sink into his broad shoulders in a gesture she now recognized as self-defense.

He flexed his fingers—the ones trapped in cellophane tape. "I was going to clean up and have supper waiting—spaghetti. Barbara in accounting gave me the recipe for sauce. You *said* you'd call before you came home," he accused between his teeth.

"Darned if I didn't," she agreed lightly, trying to ignore the skipping of her heart.

Noting the mistletoe ball just directly over his head, Dallas longed to taste his mouth....

He rubbed his unshaven cheek against his shoulder, dislodging a scrap of wrapping paper with a smiling Santa Claus on it. "It's Christmas," he growled in his grumpy bear-in-the-cave tone. "Get lost."

Sam deserved a little irritating for creeping into her computer outline repeatedly. Dallas kicked off her canvas shoes, threw her jacket onto the couch and curled into one corner. Feeling warm and cozy, she spread herself luxuriously over the cabbage roses. "Nikki will love the doll crib," she said, meaning it as she studied the handcrafted toy. Little hearts decorated the little rocking crib. A box with a leather latch had Billy's name stenciled on it. "Billy needed a toy box."

"It's a box for special things," Sam informed her in an arrogant sniff. "Has compartments and drawers for keeper items. Every boy needs one."

"What did you make me, Sam?" she asked, enjoying the way he flexed his fingers within the masses of tape.

"I'm not telling," he returned, lowering his eyebrows at her as a muscle contracted in his cheek. "I thought I told you to beat it. Go back to the office and call me. Drive carefully—the streets are slick."

"You're not handing out orders, are you?" she asked, prodding him and knowing it. When Sam's neck sunk lower into his shoulders and he glared at her from beneath the thick line of his eyebrows, she teased, "You're a cellophane-tape prisoner."

Tilting her head, Dallas asked speculatively, "I wonder if Mr. Sam Loring, business hardhead, is ticklish."

Sam stared at her, his gray eyes stormy. "I don't know what's wrong with you...but touch me, Pendragon, and I won't be responsible."

"Tired from all that midnight sawing, are we?" she asked, kneeling down to face him. Looking disgruntled and yet rawly masculine, Sam sat there looking like her special Christmas package from Santa Claus.

"Tired enough to know that you and I are alone in the house for the first time. Tired enough to know that if you don't control your...impulses to torment me, I just might do something rash. And I've been the perfect gentleman so far," he muttered, seeking the end of the tape with his teeth and jerking it. "I've got aches to prove it."

"Oh, yeah?" she asked, heady with a breathless erotic power she'd never experienced. The thoughts of having Sam, helpless and sexy, within her touch went to her head like a rum drink.

She never touched drinks with rum in them—except for this afternoon. Once, after a rum drink, she'd danced a flamenco on a table. With the Christmas-tree lights twinkling above her, she placed her arms around Sam's neck as he watched her warily. "What are you up to?"

Dallas glanced upward at the mistletoe ball and Sam's gaze followed hers. "Trust me," Dallas urged against his mouth, needing the taste of him.

As she leaned into him, Sam swayed backward, crushing the wrapping paper beneath him. Pressuring him just a little more, Dallas forced him to the floor.

"I'm not easy," Sam said unevenly, the reindeer-and-Christmas-tree paper rustling beneath his head.

But Dallas was listening to the beat of her special tom-toms and fitted herself over him. She'd never wanted to be touched so badly in her life. She was cold and lonely while the Deons were hoarding all the heat. Midlife was waiting like a big, black chilling hole, and she wanted a memory to take with her into the abyss. She needed the heat in Sam flowing over her as it had behind his desk that day. She'd shuttled through the rocky relationship with T.J. only to discover her dreams were shattered.

A kiss from Douglas hadn't caused a ripple of heat. And Beau just couldn't manage a kiss.

But Sam knew how to make her feel as though she were desired. A very feminine, desirable woman.

When Sam walked away, she would deal with the ache. But later—

"Shoo," he ordered huskily as she nibbled at the delectable corner of his mouth. He hadn't shaved, and the rough texture of his new beard sent a fresh wave of longing over her. She stroked his taut cheeks, soothing Sam as she had wanted to from the beginning.

She could feel the ache and the loneliness of his life spread into her. Taking her time, Dallas traced his features with her fingertips and followed their trail.

Somehow Sam's hands were free then, and he was touching her, moving her beneath him and crushing the reindeer wrapping paper. Along her cheeks, his rough fingers were trembling and warm. Keeping the heavy weight of his body from her, Sam stroked her hair back from her cheeks. "Don't mess with the cook," he murmured softly, looking down at her.

Holding his dark gaze, Dallas allowed her fingers to prowl downward. They found the peek-a-boo hole and slid through it to toy with his nipple. Over her, Sam's taut body hardened as she circled the flat nub. "You're asking for it, sweet pea," he threatened in a low, Southern drawl accented with dimples.

"Oh, Sam," she murmured helplessly as he eased away from her. "Oh, Sam," she repeated uncertainly as he picked her up and carried her into her bedroom.

Eight

"Sam," she whispered a third time as he gently placed her on her bed.

In the shadows of the room, Sam stood looking down at her, his hands placed on his waist. Then he turned slowly and walked out of the room, closing the door and leaving her alone in the dark with the rosebuds.

She suddenly heard the shower running and she wanted to cry. Aching with a cold space inside her, Dallas forced herself to strip and slip into her flannel nightgown. She eased beneath the blankets with the feeling of being very old and unwanted.

Curling into a ball and turning on her side, she drew the quilt higher and fought the cold. With the children and her career keeping her busy, she'd been successful at forgetting.... Looking into the darkness beyond the window, she knew why Sam had left her alone.

You can't keep a man turned on, baby, T.J. muttered through the distance of the years.

Then the door opened, the hallway light slicing through T.J.'s demeaning growl. Outlined there, Sam's body looked tall and dangerous.

Dressed in his shorts, Sam balanced a tray filled with a teapot and a cup-and-saucer. "You need this," he said softly, crossing into the darkness with her and shutting the door.

Placing the tray on her bedside table, Sam poured tea. Taking the saucer from him, Dallas sipped the hot liquid slowly. She averted her head, not wanting Sam to see the tears chilling her cheeks.

"Scoot over," he ordered mildly, lifting the covers to slide into the bed with her.

"Shoo," she muttered unevenly, trying not to sniff. She didn't want him meddling in her private pain, searching out the weaknesses and the scars. "Go away."

"Not a chance, Pendragon." Sam's deep voice was smooth Southern honey covering the business steel—his trademark. Propping the pillows up behind him, he placed his arm around her and eased her against his side. "You *are* a virus. When I moved in here I thought I'd give you a dose of your own medicine. You've gotten under my skin and you're driving me nuts," he admitted roughly against her temple. "Maybe I should get you out of my system. If I can."

When she tried to ease away from the temptation of his warm body, knowing that she couldn't afford another dismissal à la T.J., Sam's arm held her tightly against him. He'd skim away her defenses and see everything, she thought desperately, trying to escape his warm thigh pressed up against hers. He'd see how inadequate she was.

Sam rocked her gently at his side, wriggling his toes against her cold ones. "Nice, isn't it? Two old folks snuggling in a four-poster bed while the kids are at Grandma's," he said, wry humor tinting his deep, lazy drawl. "You're even wearing a flannel nighty."

His fingers caressed her arm slowly. "Shoo," she repeated without force, knowing that if he did go she'd wither in the cold, barren loneliness.

"Hush," he murmured against her ear, taking the saucer from

her to place it on the bedside table. "Feeling better? Or are you still feeling amorous because of the rum?"

"Amorous? Rum?" She tried unsuccessfully for an innocent tone, tinged with a pinch of indignation.

When she turned to stare at him, Sam kissed her lightly. "Honey, you tasted like it. And your mother told me you're primitive if you have a drop. What I want to know is, how do you explain yourself without it...?"

He began unbuttoning her gown, lowering his head to taste the soft skin he uncovered. With his lips against her, Sam asked, "Do you know what you're doing, sweet pea?"

She swallowed, trembling as she tried to resist touching him. It was a moment for truth, and she'd have to deal with the aftermath later. The honorable thing to do, of course, was to prepare him for her lack of skill. "Yes, I know," she found herself whispering helplessly.

Poor man, she thought sadly. Nestled so sexily against her, his muscular legs tangling with her flannel-covered ones, Sam would be so disappointed.

Sam's mouth found the tip of her breast, his teeth toying with it gently as he unbuttoned her gown down to her ankles. "Do you want me, sweet pea?" he asked.

"Yesss," she said shakily as Sam stripped the gown from her. If she ever needed anyone, it was Sam. He made her feel magnolia sweet and as lickable as sugar cane. Beneath his touch, she felt dainty and feminine, almost desirable. When he shifted over her, she discovered his shorts were missing.

She began shivering, his hair-roughened body nudging and weighing down hers. Absorbing his heat, adjusting to the hard planes and angles, Dallas felt the first timid beat of a distant tom-tom. She ached to rub herself against the roughness brushing her, arch her thighs against the hardness of his—

Resting lightly on her, Sam kissed her throat. The scent of his soap and after-shave blended with a deeper, intimate musk. Dallas fought exposing her inadequacies. She curled her hands against her thighs with the need to keep from touching him. Against her throat, Sam smiled. "Like I said, a man likes to be touched."

Aching with the need to obey, Dallas forced herself not to notice how touchable Sam was. She wanted to explore him from head to foot—but then he'd see....

She was turning into liquid heat, the jungle drums throbbing rhythmically, coming closer....

Were those her moans blending with the drums?

Someone in that same distance was breathing unevenly as though in a jungle fever.

But she wouldn't touch him. She'd keep her pride intact—what little remained....

Caressing her body with his, Sam nibbled on her ear as his hands moved over her, stroking. When his tongue gently slid into her ear, Dallas gasped as the tom-tom beat quickly. "Oh, Sam," she exclaimed unevenly as he pressed against her.

He kissed a trail to her lips, running his rough palm along her ribs. He molded the curve of her waist as though imprinting it in his memory. His thumb found her navel, circling and pressing it lightly. "How long has it been?"

Looking up at his tense expression, Dallas felt his shudder against the length of her body. Sam wanted her badly, his large body taut with desire. Pressing against her lower stomach, Sam's bold shape both frightened and excited her. A funny little constriction quivered deep within her, waiting. Startled, Dallas tried to push the intimate nudging of her body aside. The stubborn little quiver repeated itself, bringing with it a frightening memory. She didn't want Sam stripping her, finding the cold inside. "It's been years, Sam...I can't."

Gently, he nudged her knees apart to fit snugly within her thighs. Sam stroked her cheeks with his thumbs, deepening the intimacy as he looked down at her through the shadows. "You're shaking, Dallas."

Dallas fought the emotions tugging at her. And she fought wanting Sam. "Shoo," she ordered faintly, her palms finding his taut, muscular back.

Smiling softly above her, Sam eased his mouth over hers and kissed her with the most adoring kiss she had ever experienced. "Shoo, yourself," he repeated against her lips.

Shuddering with passion barely controlled, Dallas gasped.

"Oh, Sam...I'm so afraid." His weight and desire frightened her badly now as she remembered the shafting pain.

Arching against his invasion, Dallas whimpered, trying to withdraw. "God, Dallas, what's wrong?" Sam asked roughly, holding himself taut above her. His thumb rubbed a fresh tear from her cheek.

"Sam, I... You... This is really a mistake," Dallas began shakily, trembling. Wanting to move into his warmth and fearing the consequences.

"Damned if it is," he muttered, drawing away slightly. Dark, primitive anger swirled inside him, his large body shaking with it. When he scowled, moving as if to leave her, Dallas poised on the brink of her choices—alone, or sharing the heat of passion with this gentle man.

She'd been alone and cold as the drizzling rain beyond the window's lacy curtains. Once after...well, after Sam uncovered her faults, she'd be alone again.

She arched her hips slightly, cradling him, keeping him locked closer to her.

Tensed above her, Sam shot her a hot look. "Look, Dallas. Don't mess with me now—I'm trying to give you some space." His voice caught as her hands slid across the hard, hair-covered planes of his chest. "I can understand..." His voice trailed off when her insoles prowled his bulky calves.

The movement brought him slightly into her, and the funny little constrictions began partying.

When he groaned wistfully, the sound slid warmly within her. For now, Sam wanted her. Yet he cared enough to consider her needs, too. She smiled and stroked the nape of his damp neck. Sam was just that sort of guy—gentle, careful, sweet, loveable, and tasty. Even when he made his disgruntled bear noises, she knew he'd never hurt her.

"Come here," she murmured, drawing his head down to hers. "Come here," she repeated, sliding a hand down his back to press his hips against hers.

"Dallas...." He protested because of her obvious fears, and that endeared this rough, gentle man to her. Feeling herself open to him, giving him the warmth he badly needed, Dallas watched him intently.

Sam held himself from her, his expression taut with agony she barely understood. "You have to loosen up, Sam," she teased against his damp throat, feeling herself relax slightly. For a moment, the funny little constrictions paused and wondered.

Sliding her hand downward, wanting to explore...she touched him.

Sam almost leaped out of her arms. "Watch it, Pendragon," he rapped out when he settled uneasily. His mouth slowly curved into a wicked grin that she found herself returning. "This isn't exactly an everyday experience for me, either."

"No?" she asked, repeating the maneuver just to feel his heartbeat pound rapidly against her hot cheek. His admission activated ideas about tying Sam to her four-poster bed and keeping him there until the tom-toms faded and the constrictions were pacified.

"Hell, no," he muttered roughly, easing into her again. His breath caught and his eyes closed when he rested within the tight passage. Sam's broad chest rose and fell unevenly; his lean cheeks were beginning to flush. Beside her, his large hands grasped her pillows, the cords on his arms standing out in relief. "I've been saving myself."

"Well, then..." She ran her fingers through the hair on his chest, prowling through it and then down to his buttocks. She touched his flat stomach, and Sam inhaled sharply.

While she knew Sam was being the perfect Southern gentleman, tender and understanding, Dallas wanted to be untethered and primitively wild.

Sam was so solid and strong, she knew he would keep them both safe as she merrily chartered hot, steamy, unknown jungles. She glanced at Sam's expression and found it so intent, she knew he would take whatever she gave and give it back to her with tender beauty.

Snuggling her hips side to side against his, Dallas found herself adjusting to Sam, who now seemed to have difficulty breathing. He didn't seem to mind as she raised her arms and legs, locking him to her with all her strength.

He held absolutely still while Dallas allowed her fingers to roam across the slightly damp, tense ridges of his back, soothing him. Her teeth found his earlobe, testing it gently. She closed her eyes, luxuriating in the hard, warm, safe feel of Sam at her disposal. She ran her fingers down his shoulder blades and his spine to seek the hollows at the base.

She lifted her hips higher, drawing him even deeper. The hot, riveting constricting, pleasure-pain waves came suddenly, spreading throughout her. Surprised by the pinpointing pleasure deep within, Dallas held Sam with all her strength, knowing that he could keep her safe. His uneven breath swirled about her as the heat rose, consuming her. He trembled as the aftershocks forced her to cry out with pleasure.

"Better?" he asked gently, soothing her breasts with his hands as she drifted through the satiny warmth back to him.

Shaking, powerless against her emotions, Dallas realized how she had acted—fierce, dominating, hungry. Setting the pace was a man's choice, wasn't it? "Oh, no," she groaned softly.

"Oh, yes." Sam caressed her hips, filling his hands with the softness as he raised her to him again. His mouth found her breasts, gently testing the sensitive flesh with his teeth. When he tugged at the peaks, the hunger came raging back full force, her body tightening around him as though it had been starved for an eternity.

A new set of aftershocks shot through her, startling her.

"My turn." Sam reached downward, touching her gently.

Dallas breathed lightly, afraid to move, wrapping herself in the utter pleasure of Sam making love to her.

She closed her eyes as he explored the taut muscles of her throat and shoulders. He tasted her slowly, as though she delighted him and he wanted to savor every inch.

She felt the sweat slick between them, waited for his revulsion, which never came. Sam licked the tip of her breast, tasting it. Experimenting with the sensation of lingering, of enjoying lovemaking, Dallas flicked her tongue along Sam's damp shoulder.

She smiled then, tasting the tang of the salt and the desire between them. Experimenting again, Dallas drew him deeper into her arms. Sam's heart thudded heavily, rapidly against her sensitized breasts. Closing her eyes again, Dallas absorbed Sam into her, unknowingly tightening and tugging him deeper within her body.

She cried out again as he held her tighter. And then there was no time, nothing but the surging joy of Sam and her flying through an endless, silky rainbow.

He held her there, poised delicately within the fire and the pleasure. She ached as she strained for an undefined goal. With a soft cry, Dallas unleased the heat within her, trusting Sam to keep them both safe.

She awoke to Sam's head resting on her breast; his heart beat slowly against her stomach. His eyelashes brushed her skin as he stroked her body lazily. Sam seemed content to linger in the scents and the warmth of their lovemaking, and she hugged the moment to her. Stroking his mussed hair, she realized how much she liked soothing Sam.

Raising up on his elbow, Sam caressed her cheek, running his hand downward to place his palm over her stomach. The gesture was strangely possessive and Dallas shifted beneath it uncomfortably. She waited for him to say something, anything devastating. Wasn't that what T.J. always did? she thought absently, running her fingers through Sam's crisp hair.

Dallas held still, wanting Sam to stay with her, yet fearing that now he had seen her inadequacies. Her cheeks burned as she remembered her shameless demands.

His finger circled the tip of her breast while he moved his thigh against hers slowly. When she looked at him, he grinned his most wicked, devastatingly sexy grin. He pulled out his dimples with all the effect of a sleepy, huggable, tamed wolf. The laugh lines deepened around his smoky eyes. "That was good for starters," he drawled in a low rich tone that started miniature tom-toms beating within her.

While Sam's big warm hand stroked her inner thighs, Dallas found herself returning his knowing, hungry grin. "Come here, sweet pea," he urged huskily after a soft, knowing chuckle. "Let me hear those hungry little purring sounds you make when we're—"

"Do not." She resisted acknowledging the prowling, stalking fingers and his rumbling, conspiratorial laughter.

"Okay. Then what about one delighted cry—muted of course—with trembling little purrs afterward? Or could you just sort of chant my name again like I've never heard it before?" he asked before his mouth hungrily sought hers.

Later she snuggled to him, savored the warmth and acknowledged with a blush that he had drawn every previously mentioned sound of delight from her.

She smiled, allowing her fingers to smooth the hair on his chest. She had caused some intriguing masculine sounds herself.

In the dawn, Sam stretched carefully, to avoid dislodging the softness wedged against his side. He breathed lightly, prolonging the moment when Dallas awoke. Catching the scent of her hair, Sam turned slightly to inhale the sweet-pea fragrance and savor the flow of her body down his.

Had he taken advantage of her rum-tinged weakness?

Sam scowled against the strand of red-brown hair clinging to his morning stubble. He'd never taken advantage of a woman before; he'd chosen ones who knew what to expect. But Dallas wasn't that type of woman. He'd known from the first that she was untutored and sweet.

Her body tightened, her breathing changed, and Sam waited.

When her eyes opened, Sam recognized the raw fear and pain scurrying around inside.

His anger surged to the surface before he could trim it.

"I want to know who did this to you," he demanded unevenly, fighting the urge to hold her down and make her answer his question. When Dallas's well-kissed mouth began to firm stubbornly, Sam knew that a field of cotton rosebuds wasn't the place to sort out his problems with the Pendragon virus.

He'd caught the puzzled frown before she'd turned away. The line of her back was tense and vulnerable. Dallas didn't want a repeat performance; he'd have to be granite not to recognize the symptoms.

"I can't have this happen again, Sam," she said quietly, and the sound of his emptiness went roaring through him.

He fought the urge to make her listen, to wrap her in his arms and coax her into loving him....

Sam's fist crumbled a spray of cotton rosebuds. Who the hell had ever loved him? "Have it your way," he said between his teeth, wanting to slip back into the soft, sweet night and her arms.

Then, because he was hurt and fighting mad, too, Sam did what he knew best—he lashed out at her. "Call me when you're in the mood again."

When her body tightened as though taking a blow, Sam felt his stomach contract painfully. She turned slowly, drawing the sheet between them. "Sam, I'm sorry."

"What the hell do you mean—sorry?" Sam wanted to tear away the past, lock onto the future and never let Dallas go!

"This is my fault. I take full responsibility and it won't happen again."

"You had a weak moment, right?" Sam demanded rawly, wondering if his heartbeat would ever return to normal.

"Something like that," she agreed, looking away into the rain dripping beyond the window.

Who was she remembering? Why should he care? He'd had her, hadn't he?

Why wasn't it enough? Why didn't he have enough pride to walk out now?

Why did he want to linger with Dallas as long as he could?

The afternoon before Christmas, Sam hid in his office. He'd avoided the secretaries who seemed to regard him in a new, endearing light. He'd sidestepped Debbie Wynbroski's attempt to snare him beneath the mistletoe ball in the employee lounge.

This morning, he'd been thinking about Dallas and had almost missed an important point in the company's new merger agreement. Sam ran his fingers through his longish hair. In three short weeks, he'd been totally absorbed by the Pendragon family. He knew exactly how Billy rubbed his eyes when he was tired; he knew exactly when Nikki decided to dig in her heels and argue.

He knew when Dallas needed a cup of tea. *And when she'd decided to back off from the relationship.* Sam wanted to free-fall into an affair, wrap himself in Dallas and her family. But Dallas skirted the issue and him with all the markings of one badly burned by an experience.

He smiled softly, remembering the way her eyes looked up at him after lovemaking. Soft and curious, wondering eyes.

Quite a feeling, he mused—Dallas's softness warming him beneath the quilt in the confines of the antique four-poster bed.

Quite a feeling knowing that memories of another man shared that bed with them. Sam found himself grinding his teeth each time he thought about Dallas's shy, tentative hands fluttering over him as though she expected—expected what?

In his lifetime, Sam had rolled with the blows and had landed a few himself. But the one thing he wasn't taking easily was that Dallas measured him against another man.

The thought hurt; it caught him in the belly with the force of a fighter's punch. For a man who'd never wanted lingering affairs, Sam found himself thinking of ways to snare Dallas.

In another week, he'd be expected to move. A cold shiver slid through him. He hadn't slept in his penthouse for weeks and dreaded the stylish, modular glass-and-steel building. It appealed to him as much as an iceberg cavern.

Running his hand through his hair again, Sam grimaced, staring into the gray cloud banks encompassing the bay. And Sam knew exactly how he would feel without the Pendragon family—exactly like Washington's Mount Rainier, alone and snow-capped in the distance.

Dallas's laughter echoed behind his office door, and Sam listened intently to the low musical sound. Sam turned, alert and tracking the sound carefully. He'd been keeping his distance, trying not to push a situation that he didn't understand himself. But there were just some things a man knew he had to do. And right now Dallas was near the Christmas mistletoe ball. For the present, problems with her past or not, Sam intended to use every mistletoe ball he could when Dallas's lips were in the vicinity....

Dallas turned, sensing someone at her back. Someone tall and warm and impatient placed a hand on her shoulder—a strong, possessive hand faintly scented like Nikki's doll. This morning,

Sam had stuffed the children into Bertha's cab in a cloud of sweet-smelling powder.

She averted her head to shield her smile. Though she was badly frightened of being hurt again, her feminine senses started humming when Sam acted like a gentleman come calling. And for all Sam's defensive ways, he treated her in a very courtly manner. With a little pang of sadness, she thought about the life without Sam that waited for her.

Sam loomed over her, a strand of hair crossing his forehead. Behind his glasses, his eyes were intent as he watched her mouth. "You're standing beneath the mistletoe ball, sweet pea," he whispered before drawing her into his arms.

"Oooh," Emily cooed in the distance before Dallas found herself responding to Sam's sweet kiss. His lips rubbed against hers gently, his breath brushing her skin.

His heart beat steadily beneath her palm as he rubbed his cheek against hers. "Don't get any ideas, Ms. Pendragon. Just take it as a gesture of Christmas cheer," he said roughly, then his arms trembled around her, gathering her against him.

"Sweet," Emily commented as Dallas moved deeper into the kiss, dismissing the rest of the party. "Any other takers?"

"My turn," Debbie Wynbroski stated firmly, edging between them.

Dallas noted the way Sam's mouth clung to hers as though he resented being detached from her. Wild, primitive glee went skittering through her when he shot Emily a low-browed, menacing look, and his neck began to sink into his shoulders.

As the women began hooting and surged to surround Sam, his eyes widened. "Do something," he whispered hoarsely from the corner of his mouth, eyeing the approaching women warily.

"It's Christmas. And you started it," she returned, perching on a desk and crossing her arms. For the first time since Sam had been so furious with her, she began to feel lighthearted. He hadn't been totally unaffected by their night of lovemaking. Sam had a way of giving her self-esteem a big boost. "You didn't say please."

"Please?" Sam gritted through his teeth, glaring at her.

"Uh-uh. You're on your own."

Catching a glance of Sam's threatening expression, Dallas grinned cheerfully. "See yah," she murmured, stepping back to let Debbie get a better grip on Sam's muscular neck. "Line forms to the right," she called, stepping aside as the first wave of women passed her on their way to Sam.

"I'm calling the accounting, packaging and shipping departments." Emily punched the intercom button with a vengeance and smirked widely. "He's been due for this for a long time."

"How many women?" Dallas asked, her grin widening as two women pressed Sam between them. With a stiff grace Sam dutifully lowered his lips.

"Forty...and every one of them has been waiting for years. Edna Fairhair is saturating her lips with vitamin E right now. You know Edna—she was a wrestler before working in loading."

They watched a mother of seven grown children bend Sam backward and kiss him. "He's okay," Emily said absently. "He's just got this thing about centering in on business and forgetting everything else. He really had no idea of the stress problems or the ways to solve them. I think it hurt him to find out how thoughtless and too busy he'd been to realize.... You've been good for him."

Later, Dallas arrived home before Sam, carrying Emily's thoughts with her. She wanted Christmas Eve to be special for them all, a memory to last when he was striding through his domain in a replay of Attila the Hun. While she wasn't magnificent in some womanly areas, she could give him a slice of Christmas cheer to remember. She had enjoyed setting the scene—from bubbling potpourri to lasagna baking in the oven. Sam's favorite double-dutch chocolate cake was topped with richer frosting and studded with maraschino cherries.

Curling on the cabbage roses, dressed in a flowing dark blue caftan, Dallas sipped her oolong tea and reloaded the camera. She wanted to capture the expression on the children's face as they opened their gifts.

And she wanted a memory to savor when Sam left her alone.

Her thoughts danced like the flickering candlelight in the dark room.... She didn't love him. She couldn't. Sam—house husband, child-sitter—was a holiday mirage.

Sam had merely risen to a challenge presented to him. When the wager was completed, he'd slide back into his comfortable, untouched mode and his Lincoln without the slightest remorse. Dallas could feel the ache build painfully, the burning of tears behind her eyelids.

He'd been there when she needed him. He'd taken and he'd given. She missed his arms enfolding her against the cold night. Her old fashioned four-poster bed really needed Sam in it to complete the picture. All dark skin covered by just the right amount of hair, he matched the rosebuds and the ruffles so well.

Dallas wiped the back of her hand across her damp eyes and sniffed. *Sam Loring could just*—Bertha roared into the driveway and honked. Nikki and Billy were laughing wildly, and Sam's footsteps sounded on the porch. The door swung open to reveal Sam carrying a squirming, giggling child beneath each arm.

"Hey, lady. Have you lost two bear hunters?" he asked, the laughter in his face dying as he slowly absorbed the Christmas scene. "I'm home," he said softly, easing the children to their feet, the light warming in his eyes.

"When can we open our presents?" the children asked, tossing their coats aside to run to the tree.

"After supper, we're going to church. I baked a chocolate cake. Then you can open your presents," Dallas answered absently, concentrating on Sam's deliberate movements. He closed the door behind him with the air of a man shutting out the world and his problems. The genuine air of a man coming home.

He stripped off his coat and walked slowly toward her. "Hi," he said as though she were his alone, tossing the coat onto a chair.

"Hi, yourself," she returned, thinking that with his hair ruffled by the wind and his dark cheeks cold and ruddy, Sam Loring was absolutely, incredibly all hers.

Hers? She echoed the thought, turning it over.

He needed her.

Oh, no, he didn't. Sam needed business and women without

children who knew when to stop loving. He didn't need a cling-ing vine.

Oh, no, she couldn't love him. Oh, no....

While the children inspected the packages for new ones, Sam knelt by her, taking her hand in his cold ones. "I'm suffering from lip burn and it's your fault," he complained softly, watching her mouth. Raising her hand to his lips, he nuzzled the warmth.

He was teasing and when he grinned, pulling out the thousand-watt dimples, Dallas couldn't resist returning the favor. "Hard day at the office, dear?" she asked, fighting a smile. Sam might prefer another sort of woman, but she really liked petting his battered-tom-cat image.

Sam looked at her as if he needed her touch, her kisses or just her spare time. He looked like Baghdad coming back after straying into the cold, uncaring alley.

"When can I have my present?" he returned silkily, rubbing her hand against his cheek. "Like a kiss when the office staff and the kids aren't watching. I think you owe me."

Could they be friends? she wondered briefly as she remembered the mistletoe mob at the office. Sam had taken the maneuver in stride and gallantly allowed the stiff image of a company boss to slip, endearing him to his staff. She patted his jaw sympathetically. "I've made it up to you with lasagna and cake."

Nibbling at her fingertips, Sam grinned. "Mmm. Real food. All this—" his gaze slid down the blue caftan, lingering on the curve of soft thigh exposed by the slit "—and she can cook, too." He raised an eyebrow and leered wickedly at her. "What I had in mind wasn't food and you know it."

"Really?" Dabbling in Sam's tastes could become addictive, she decided as she fluttered her lashes at him.

Billy crawled into Sam's lap and hugged him. "Sam and me got a secret, don't we, Sam?"

Nikki squealed and jumped on Sam's back. "Me and Mommy got a secret, too...and you don't know what it is, Billy. "Cause you're a little kid and you'd tell."

"Would not."

"Would, too."

Later, Sam sat beside Dallas in church, watching the children sing in the children's choir. With his arm resting behind her on the pew, Sam looked like any other proud father. When he smiled down at her, she felt a warm glow settle within her. They were a family, together at Christmas, caring for each other and rejoicing in the baby's birth that changed the world.

When they opened presents at the house, Sam folded Dallas's hand within his. Nikki's new baby doll fit perfectly into Sam's crib; the girl's eyes lighted each time she looked his way. Not as subtle, Billy ran into his room and began lugging out "stuff" to fill his special box.

Sam handled the children's gift of after-shave carefully, placing it on the table as he stood. "I'll be right back."

Sitting on the floor with the children, Dallas rocked the crib with her toe and helped Billy choose only the best "special stuff" for his box.

"Dallas," Sam said quietly behind her.

When she turned, he placed a walnut quilt rack rubbed to a rich sheen in front of her. Folded neatly across it was a patchwork quilt. The design of delicate stitching swirled across pieces of worn flannel, faded cotton gingham. Kneeling beside it, Dallas carefully ran her fingers across the walnut and the quilt. On the underside, a faded rose flannel had been pieced together. "Oh, Sam," she whispered, feeling her throat tighten with emotion. "This is lovely."

"It's yours," he said, lowering his neck slightly. He looked away and swallowed as though embarrassed. "The quilt, too."

Running her hand across the wood, Dallas felt her heart shift and warm. "Sam, did you make this just for me?"

He shifted restlessly, his neck sinking into his shoulders in the familiar gesture. "Of course," he said roughly. Behind the glasses, his smoky eyes darkened. "Do you like it or not?"

Rising to her feet, Dallas couldn't resist standing on tip-toe and kissing Sam's overworked lips. He'd given her a part of himself, a gift that she could cherish alone in the fields of lonely cotton rosebuds. "It's beautiful. Thank you."

"You're welcome," he returned stiffly as a dark flush crept up from his throat. For a hard-nosed businessman, Sam looked definitely embarrassed. The moment was one to be treasured.

Running her hand across the well-washed quilt, Dallas teased, "And you can quilt, too."

He shrugged lightly, widening his legs in a defensive stance. "Someone special made it. It suits you."

"Someone very special?" A little hurt twanged inside Dallas. She couldn't rest beneath a quilt created by his past lover—

"Granny Dunnaway." Sam looked away. "A hill woman who smoked a corncob pipe and blistered my backside more times than I want to remember. After my...mother ran off, Granny bribed the juvenile officer with a jug of moonshine when he came for me...made me hide in the outhouse.... She'd want you to have it."

Dallas fought the tears blurring her eyes. "Oh, Sam."

"Oh, sweet pea," he teased softly. "Granny was tough as leather. I cut and stacked three cords of wood when we didn't need any. Then she made me this quilt. She'd want you to have it."

Sam had revealed very little of his past, and Dallas hugged the insight to her, his special gift.

While the children played, unaware of the two adults locking gazes, Dallas whispered, "I've got your present tucked away."

"I can't wait," he murmured huskily, placing his hand on the back of her neck to draw her closer.

"Uh-uh." She fought the urge to cling to him. "I'll be right back. Come on, kids. Let's get Sam's present."

Minutes later, Nikki and Billy presented Sam with a huge box, gaily decorated with a red bow. "From us," Billy announced proudly.

"It's silly," Nikki said haughtily, cradling her new baby doll.

"Is not!" Billy stated with decided male arrogance. "Girls' stuff is silly."

"Open it, Sam," Dallas urged gently as Sam's large hands trembled on the box.

For a man who had made a corporation his life, Sam appeared filled with emotion. "You didn't have to—"

Because he seemed so vulnerable, needing her, Dallas sat on the arm of the couch and placed her hand on his shoulder. She rubbed the tense muscles gently. "Get with it, Loring," she urged lightly in his ear.

Sam began unwrapping carefully, his hands shaking as he discovered the engine of a toy train. The muscles and cords of his throat tightened beneath her light touch. And because Sam needed petting, Dallas smoothed his hair, feeling the crisp texture cling to her skin the way Sam was to her life.

"It's something to show you how much we appreciate you helping with the grizzly bears and the housework."

"I'm a rotten cook," he admitted quietly, running his fingertips across the new shiny red caboose. "Those were really microwave potatoes the other night. I burned the real ones. There's more to this home-and-family bit than meets the eye."

The unsteady timbre of his voice caused her to ache. Big, tough Sam Loring was honestly touched by the gift. He eased the sections of track from the box, placing them carefully on the floor.

"Do you like it, Sam?" Billy asked, sinking to the floor to place the toy caboose on the track. "Isn't it the best ever?"

"The best ever," Sam echoed, his broad shoulders shuddering just once.

Dallas spotted a suspicious moisture behind Sam's lenses, and smiled knowingly. Tough guy Sam Loring was having an encounter of the emotional kind. "Get to it, Loring," she ordered, touching his arm. "You know you want to."

"I suppose you think this lets you off the hook," he said seductively, sliding to the floor with Billy. "But to keep the record straight, it doesn't...."

He nodded, sliding a hand around her calf and caressing it gently. "Nice try, though," he said, unpacking the rest of the train set and fitting it together. "I've always wanted one...."

The tiny train chugged through tunnels and switched rails while Billy and Sam lay on their stomachs engineering the feats. "Silly stuff," Nikki said with a delicate sneer, tucking her doll blanket inside the crib. "Boys."

Later, Dallas drifted off to sleep as the little train whoo-

whooed merrily around the track. She awoke to Sam wrapping her in the quilt and holding her on his lap.

"Whatcha doin', Mr. Sam?" she asked sleepily, comforted by the warmth and strength of his touch on a cold Christmas night.

"Holding my best girl." Sam kissed her forehead and tucked her against him. "Go back to sleep. I just want to hold you. Thanks for the train, Dallas. And the visit to church. I haven't felt so...well, it was nice."

Because Sam needed her, Dallas wrapped her arm around his neck and toyed with the hair brushing his collar. "I'll cut your hair tomorrow when I do Billy's," she murmured sleepily.

Tensing slightly, Sam shrugged. "A barber can do it."

"Don't be afraid. I won't mark you for life." She sighed against his warm throat as she drifted off to sleep.

"Maybe I already am.... I don't think a flu shot is going to take care of this virus," he whispered unsteadily, holding her tighter.

Nine

"**H**old still," Dallas ordered, tilting Sam's head to one side while she combed and snipped his hair.

While the children played with the toys placed in their Christmas stockings by Santa Claus, Sam savored every touch of Dallas's cinnamon-roll scented hands. He'd never spent a time like this one, lolling in the warmth of a family filled with Christmas spirit.

Dallas wore a curious but satisfied look. Like a woman who needed to care for others—her children and himself, of course. Beneath the smugness there was also a fear that Sam knew only time could soften.

Stretching comfortably beneath her touch, Sam allowed his eyes to close. Dallas needed his protection. She needed him.

Quite a feeling, he thought with pleasure—knowing that someone needed him. A warm, fuzzy feeling that filled all the rough edges of his life. He allowed himself a small smile. Dallas didn't know exactly how much she needed him in all areas of her life, including the sensual one. She'd been shocked by herself, embarrassed by her needs. Despite the control she managed now, Dallas had once forgotten herself. With him. It was just a matter of time before he had her seeing things his way.

Thoroughly enjoying her care, Sam felt like a cat sunning on a warm window sill. With a bowl of milk waiting for him. Drifting along dreamily under Dallas's intent care, Sam wondered absently if next Christmas he could replace her plastic manger scene with a hand-carved one.

Dallas tilted his head, angling it for a better cut. She frowned, studying her handiwork. "I know you're running short on money Sam," she murmured absently, brushing a snipped hair from his chin. "I can loan you enough to get you through until the first of the month. Or I'll get the grocery bill this week and you can repay me."

"No," he said flatly, catching her wrist and jumping off his imaginary warm window sill. Dallas needed to know a few of his personal rules. "I've never had a woman support me yet."

A quick shaft of pain crossed Dallas's expression before she eased her wrist away and returned to snipping his hair. "I was offering a loan, not support, Sam."

The thoughts of discussing his deflated wallet with a woman who had stormed his body molecules like a virus caused Sam to straighten. Santa had stuffed Sam's stocking with toothpaste, razors and new black dress socks, and now the woman he most wanted to take care of was asking if he needed support. In Sam's book of rules, he did all the running.

He frowned, replaying his last thoughts. Up to now, he'd always called the shots in his relationships, never letting anyone share his problems. Letting Dallas inside him wasn't easy. Neither was admitting that he was wrong about the difficulties of a woman's working world.

Not wanting to spoil a memory he'd need to warm him later, Sam shifted uneasily as her fingers swept down the back of his neck. "So maybe I jumped the gun. I'm not used to someone else picking up my tabs," he managed stiffly.

"Our tabs, Sam," she corrected, her green eyes lighting with humor. "You know, sooner or later, you're going to have to admit that running a home with children and working isn't easy."

Running a soothing finger along his eyebrows, Dallas grinned. "Admit it. I won...say it out loud. I dare you."

When Dallas touched him, Sam had the feeling of being petted. *He liked Dallas petting him.* He also had the feeling she could wrap him around her cinnamon-scented finger. The thought startled him. Pre-Dallas, no one teased or messed with him. If he were that cat on the windowsill, he'd probably roll over to have his belly scratched. The thought of Dallas touching his stomach started Sam wondering when he'd have her alone again. "Don't rub it in...I'll give you a maybe."

When her grin widened, Sam suddenly became light-headed. "Okay, you won. I've glanced over some of your proposals and they don't seem too far out of line. We'll start working on them in the new year."

Dallas's low, delighted giggle made Sam's whole body feel light and airy. "Okay, Pendragon. Cut the gloating and finish the job," he said, returning her infectious grin.

The day after Christmas, Sam returned to work, leaving Dallas sleeping in a bed where he very much wanted to join her. Revving up Bertha, he pulled out of the driveway with a feeling of leaving a life he desperately wanted and needed.

Traditionally Sam used the after-Christmas lull to work without the interference of calls and appointments. This year, the quiet had lost its appeal. Manned by a skeleton staff for the holidays, the office seemed cold and drained of cheer. Emily was visiting her grandchildren, leaving Sam to the mercy of a replacement who needed a dictaphone.

By noon, Sam gave up working and sank into his thoughts as he watched the few people on the sidewalk below. Most of them had parcels in hand, and Sam guessed absently that they were returning gifts.

Sam switched to watching the expensive paneling on his walls. *He* felt like a returned gift, one taken out of the shop on approval that now had to be restored to the shelf. Every impulse within him said to go home and play with Billy and his toy train.

Every nerve ending said to go home to Dallas and listen for the low melodic sound of her laughter.

Was she wearing that African caftan, the one with the thigh-high slit and the embroidered neckline that shifted when she bent?

Pouring Dallas's hot vegetable soup from his thermos into a bowl, Sam wondered who would chase household bears? Who would powder Nikki's doll's rubber backside when he left? "Not that damn Beau," Sam growled, spooning out the lima beans Dallas had generously dumped into the soup.

What about Dallas's trim backside? Who would be touching it?

Who would warm his lap next Christmas Eve and snuggle against him as though he were all that mattered.

Sam had never been nestled in the warmth of a home, children and a woman who looked at him with sleepy, sexy witch's eyes. Now that he had experienced all that, Sam wanted the whole picture.

The new year without the Pendragon family loomed like a cold, dark abyss before Sam. He spooned another lima bean into his trash can and began reading Dallas's proposals intently.

Taking second place to his efforts at money-stretching casseroles and managing a family, the reports had never had his full attention. They were detailed, projected and outlined in the professional manner that Sam had expected. Sam frowned and nudged The Whammy Plan aside; he didn't like that one at all. He couldn't see himself shifting into Emily's practical chair. But the other proposals were fleshed out with backup material and costs, and could be braided into Brice's employee plan. "They're too good," Sam muttered darkly, turning to his other paperwork. "They need a few kinks to keep the cogs from turning too fast."

Sam flipped through her summary presentation and tossed it aside. The Pendragon virus had invaded his life and altered his focus on what he wanted, how he wanted to live. Dallas had unknowingly intruded into his comfortable no-strings life-style; she had filtered through his protective shell. It was too late for immunization in Delilah's bed.

Driving home that night, Sam had the sinking feeling that the house would have disappeared. But it stood against the cold drizzle, the lights in the windows. He entered the front door to inhale the scents of pot roast, apple pie and home. Dallas turned from the stove, her eyes lighting as she smiled at him. Billy called loudly, "Sam's home." And suddenly Sam felt fear clawing wildly at him. A few more days and he'd be back in the cold.

And Beau would hover like a vulture, waiting to kiss Dallas on her doorstep.

"The hell he will," Sam stated with all the possession he felt, closing out the cold beyond the small house as he picked up Billy and hefted him into the air playfully.

Over the next five days, Sam shielded his pride and his heart. He dreamed about Dallas walking toward him with her arms open. Like a miser hoarding gold, he absorbed every tiny scent and sound, the colors and texture of Dallas.

Did she ache as he did? he wondered as he'd caught her lingering gaze with his own.

Would she miss him? he wondered as she'd slid her gaze from his.

Was it reality or his dreams when her hand had brushed his and trembled? Dallas's voice had lowered and softened during the last few days of his visit, and Sam fantasized wildly that she would ask him to stay.

On the thirty-first of December, Sam moved out with promises that he would keep: He'd call and see the children often. When he glanced at Dallas as he stood in the doorway with his suitcase, she shifted and looked away. She'd be glad to not have him underfoot, he thought moodily as Nikki wrapped her arms around him. And Sam wished Dallas was waiting in line.

She wasn't. Her hands gripped the wood railing as firmly as Sam had grasped his pre-Pendragon virus life. When their eyes met, Sam drew his mouth into a smile. Unable to say anything to her, he turned away with the grim knowledge that he was leaving a big slice of himself smeared on her front steps.

He hunched his shoulders and drew up his denim jacket against the cold drizzle and the aching emptiness within him.

That night, New Year's Eve, Sam propped his worn boots on his penthouse desk. He ignored the oil Bertha had spit on his jeans and squinted at the remaining half bottle of whiskey—which he intended to drink.

On a side table, the toy train chugged merrily through tunnels and over hills, guided by Sam's switchbox controls.

The train passed two doll children and Sam grimaced. He already missed caring for Nikki's doll while he studied a cookbook.

He'd planned to sink into the paperwork crushed beneath his boots. But remembering Dallas's soft fingers as she cut his hair had sent him over the edge.

Closing his eyelids, Sam recalled Dallas's intent expression...the tilt of her head as she'd studied her handiwork. He'd never been made over in his life. Never really had a woman touch him with lingering hands as though he were her special project. As though he needed petting. Surrounded by her touch and scents, Sam had been afraid to move and had longed for the moment to stretch into eternity.

The warm little house, filled with kids and love and Dallas nestled cozily apart from his world.... Nothing lasts forever. The mirage was over.

He'd experienced a big concentrated chunk of the things that he'd never wanted before—family, love and a woman who knew how to make him feel needed and warm inside.

Wrapped in his glass-and-chrome tomb, without the potpourri scents and the children, he felt like hell. In the old days, when he'd needed to strike out at the world, he'd find some nice accommodating construction worker. One the size of a freighter and mean clear through. Slugging it out with Dallas wasn't possible.

"That's the problem with viruses. They invade your immune system. Once you're infected, you can't fight 'em."

In an effort to self-inoculate, Sam sipped from the bottle, the whiskey burning his throat. In the week after Christmas, Dallas had worked harder, the circles darkening beneath her haunted eyes. She didn't need him messing in her life, messing it up. Rosebuds and backwoods leather didn't mix. He'd slipped into her soft little loving world for a month, had let the warmth trickle around him, and had known that he'd have to leave before he hurt her.

"Hell, what do I know about keeping her safe?" he muttered, tilting the bottle to his lips.

Dallas wouldn't know about keeping the score even, about clean endings. About saying meaningless things like, "I'll call," or "See you soon."

She'd seen him with his business-suit veneer.

He'd seen her lounging in the cotton rosebuds and nothing else—

Sam groaned, needing the warmth of Dallas's soft body snuggling against him.

Dallas was as afraid of a commitment as he. Sam digested the thought with another burning sip.

He didn't want to hurt her. And he didn't need any more scars.

Hell, he didn't know the simplest thing about loving. *It wouldn't work.*

Why not?

Because he was afraid. Somewhere along the way, he'd shucked a piece of himself. Paid his dues and came out too tough for a tenderhearted woman like Dallas. Some jerk had cut her heart, and she didn't need to be hurt again.

Feeling thoroughly cold, Sam sat and stared at the little train.

At midnight, Dallas sucked the juice from a chocolate-covered cherry candy and wiped away her tears. "What's New Year's Eve for if not to cry?" she asked the feather bird nestled in the candle ring.

Nestling deeper in her four-poster bed, she tugged Sam's quilt closely around her. The crumpled empty wrappers rustled as she reached for a new box of candy.

Watching the candle flicker within its holly-and-pinecone wreath, Dallas thought of Sam. He'd be happy now, returning to his penthouse and his smooth, expensive life-style. Ripping away the box's cellophane wrapper, she ignored the fresh tears creeping down her cheeks.

She sniffed, sucking more cherry-flavored juice.

She should have never allowed herself to be drawn in by a Southern drawl and dimples. At thirty-nine, just when things were rolling along safely in her life, Sam had come along. She'd fallen for his dimples, Southern drawl and battered tomcat image.

Then he'd packed Bertha and ran for freedom, just like T.J. Except Sam had a haunted, sheepdog look about him when he walked down the steps.

"Well, more like a tomcat kicked out in the rain," she mused to the feather bird.

She shrugged, dislodging Granny's quilt, which she pulled tightly back around her. Fighting bears by herself wasn't the fun it used to be. Exploring a lump in the quilt's folds, she extracted Sam's black dress socks mottled with bleach spots. Wiping away the tears, Dallas stuck her hand in it and wriggled her fingers through the hole at the toe.

Sam Loring would admit that the working woman's world wasn't a bowl of chocolate-covered cherries.

Her proposals were perfected, including The Whammy Plan for Executives.

She'd succeeded—but she'd lost Sam. She liked caring for him. Loved the unexpected pleasure softening his hard face as the train went whizzing by him.

If he were in her four-poster bed now, she doubted that she could restrain herself. Dallas groaned again just as the phone near her bed rang. "Hello."

Nettled by the silence at the other end, Dallas sniffed. "Look you, if this is a crank call—same to you, buddy."

"Are you crying?" Sam's slurred Southern voice asked.

Dallas's fingers stopped wriggling in the sock hole. A person couldn't even get a really good cry going without interruption. Just when she wanted to wallow in chocolates and misery, Sam would choose to call. "Have a cold. Why are you calling?"

"I would like to know just what you're wearing, please," he stated in a too-proper, distinct tone.

Not wanting to give him an edge on her dismals, Dallas returned, "I'll tell you if you tell me."

Sam breathed heavily once, as though preparing for a difficult survey. Then after a long silence, he stated proudly, "Boots."

"A nightgown."

"The flannel one with rosebuds?" Sam asked in his bear growl while his train choo-chooed in the background.

"Uh-huh."

"Oh, God, I thought so," he groaned before the line went dead. Dallas hung up, feeling colder and older than ever.

When the phone rang again, Dallas jerked the receiver to her ear. Sam had disturbed her entire life, the least he could do was to let her suck chocolate-center juice in peace. "Lay off, Loring. You lost and you know it. I couldn't care less if you're wearing nothing but boots and a smile. You keep your side of the deal, and I'll keep mine. You've been listening with an open mind, and I appreciate that, no matter if the project is approved by the board or not. But I don't apreciate you trying to remind me that we...we—"

"Honey?" Lisa's soft voice crooned above an off-key rendition of *Auld Lang Syne*. "I just wanted to wish you a Happy New Year."

"Oh, Mother!" Was it the hour or the brink of a new year that caused her to say just what she meant to the wrong person?

Glasses clinked near Lisa. "Edward and I are at a party. I can hear those chocolate wrappers rustle. Are you having a bad night? And what's more important, is Sam really wearing nothing but boots? Why aren't you all together? Or in the altogether, together?"

"He packed his toy train and ran at the first chance," Dallas stated sulkily.

"Don't ever compare a man like Sam to the likes of T.J., Dallas, dear," Lisa warned softly. "Did you ever buy that peignoir set? Did you ever give Sam any indication that you wanted to play in his sandbox with his toys?"

"Mother—" She'd played with Sam, and now could she forget? Every time the Deons started nuzzling, Dallas shivered with cold...Sam's arms were so warm—

Lisa laughed softly. "He's gotten to you, hasn't he? He's just a little sweet boy beneath all those lovely muscles. Have a Happy New Year, dear. I'll call soon."

On January 2, Sam lounged behind his desk like a lion waiting for a lamb chop while Dallas spread her proposal before him. He'd returned to his gray suit and businessman's shell.

While Dallas explained the innovative child-care center idea, complete with remodeling costs, Sam tapped his pencil. "That's a big chunk of budget dollars," he said curtly when she finished.

"Think of it as an investment to cut employee absenteeism."

"You don't think the mothers will be distracted by having their children nearby?"

Dallas looked away from Sam's penetrating gray eyes, which were flicking curious glances at her as though trying to see into her. If he were able to scan her emotions, he'd get a pretty icy picture. Or maybe red-hot flames. Maybe he could pack all those December memories in a box and forget them, but she couldn't. Where did he get off, anyway?

They'd made love, hadn't they?

What was she, a pre-Christmas aperitif? Why hadn't he called again? "Less distracted than if they were worrying about their children getting good care. With a company nurse and skilled babysitters at hand, the children would get the attention they needed. Remember how you felt when Billy and Nikki were sick?"

"How are the kids?" he asked absently, scanning the stack of reports she had removed from her briefcase. He flipped through the graphs and figures she had prepared for the job-sharing proposal. "Did Nikki get over her upset stomach?"

"They're fine." *How are you?* Dallas longed to ask as she scanned the lean cheeks hiding Sam's dimples. His neatly clipped hair caught the winter light passing through the windows, now gray appearing in the black strands. "How's Bertha?" Sam looked up at her, his smoky eyes cool behind the lenses.

"Fine," he returned in that gravelly steel voice that had lost its beguiling Southern magnolia tones. "A little first-gear problem."

He's run for cover, she thought, arranging her cost-summation sheet before him. *What man wouldn't after experiencing her lack of control?*

Sam glanced at his watch. "Let's see the rest of your presentation. I've got another appointment."

Just like that: The chocolate cake was nice. Thank you for the truth. And the romp. Who needed an inflexible tyrant with a broken nose? "I can see you're very receptive to change, Mr. Loring," Dallas snapped scathingly. "If you're going to back out, I'll expect repayment for costs."

Logic told her that she wanted no part of a relationship with Sam; her heart and body were angry because he'd obviously forgotten a moment that she'd remember her entire life.

"Change isn't the problem. I admit that a working mother has a difficult time in the workplace. You've seen that I've experienced it firsthand. But Brice doesn't throw time and money around easily. I'll work with you on these programs myself, and we'll move into them slowly. I can see the business day as an easy first step. But the rest of the programs will have to be integrated into policy. It could take months, but I'm open to your suggestions now. We can start work...tonight at my place."

She didn't want to be anywhere in his vicinity. Right now, her fingertips ached to trace the deep line running between his eyebrows. To smooth that rebellious gray hair in his left eyebrow. Offices were fine...well, other than that one incident behind his desk. But a penthouse was an intimate setting. "I get the idea. A conditional trade-off."

"I'd be a fool to go half-cocked into anything this big." Sam's voice had lowered, edged in raw steel as he leaned down toward her. "You know that up front. We'll work together on this thing, smoothing out the rough edges."

He shrugged, tightening his mouth grimly. "You may have to swallow the fact that you'll have to work with me closely in the next few months. But you'll find that we can do a better job together."

Sam was the one man she didn't want near her, especially for "the next few months." Beau, by comparison, wouldn't start her nerves clipping along at too fast a pace.

"No one asked you to do anything but have an open mind," Dallas said crisply, stacking her proposals neatly into her briefcase. "I suppose you're going to take your sweet time about it, too."

"Stop bristling, Pendragon. I just don't want you to fall on that beautiful rear—"

"It's my rear, isn't it?" she began hotly. "So gallant. So trustworthy. You're—"

"I'm backing you, Dallas," Sam said slowly, watching her with narrowed eyes. "But don't get the idea that I'm putting my company at your fingertips. We have to move through the processes, blend carefully so that production and business aren't affected. Roughly, give the plans six months or so...a month for a proposal."

Sam thought her rear was beautiful. For a moment, Dallas just stared at him, digesting the thought. It was nonsense, she decided. If Sam wanted a woman, she'd know it. Like that night, she'd known well enough that Sam wanted her. Why didn't he now? Maybe T.J. was right.... "Working with you isn't easy," she said carefully. "I'd prefer an office environment."

Sam grinned slowly, wickedly. "Chicken."

"I'm very busy. We've just signed new contracts for stress schools and I'll have to train another aid." Dallas fussed with her proposals, feeling her body temperature rise as Sam leaned closer.

"For someone who goes around throwing challenges at nice men minding their own business, you're a chicken," he murmured against her neck, and Dallas jumped with the impulses rioting through her. She wanted to wrap her arms around him and—

Dallas took a deep breath. She was a professional. She could handle Sam Loring. On any terms. "Okay, what's first?" she asked, dismissing Sam's dimpled smirk.

Moving behind his desk, Sam sat down. "A meeting with the board. They've got to see this project as valuable in long-run terms, not as an expense that could be avoided. We'd better show results with the first project, and I'm recommending the job-sharing idea. You're going to have to work with the managers and the employees, Dallas. And keep me briefed. No notes, but daily conferences.''

He tapped a pen on his desk. ''I'm calling the shots from now on, Dallas. Telling me to shoo won't cut it. Since you're not comfortable with my place, we'll have to make do with the office and your place...that will work in neatly with my plans to visit Nikki and Billy.'' He smiled then, a slow full-of-confidence smile. ''See? I'm ready to modify. I'm going into this thing with an open mind. See that you do the same.''

Fighting the small flutter in her stomach, she returned Sam's predatory smile. He was up to no good!

Ten

"**S**hoo!" Sam threw a left smash into the punching bag, dancing around it. "She thinks she can shoo me away, does she? I'm taking the gloves off this time," he muttered, matching his one-two jabs with the words. "No more Mr. Nice Guy."

By the end of January, Sam's taut nerves and body needed the intense workout. He could see now that he'd blundered where nice guys didn't. He'd forced a situation before its time and now he'd just have to wade through the basics he had skipped. Dallas wasn't the kind to step out on a ledge easily and for a momentary thrill. The thought that she was alone in her rosebuds had caused Sam sleeplessness and a rough edge that Emily tagged as "...Sheer low-down orneriness. And you were coming along so nicely, too."

"Nice!" He threw a left upper cut into the bag, feeling stretched to his limits. For the first time in his life, Sam knew that one wrong move or word would cost him a future with Dallas.

He needed her in his life. So Sam had done what he knew best: he'd sketched out a ruthless plan to capture and isolate the

Pendragon virus. He didn't want it spreading to other men, acquiring them along the way.

Sam jabbed at the punching bag, circling it with an intensity he intended to use on Dallas.

Sam zapped the bag with a right cross. He'd taken down some major heavyweights in his time by seeking out their weakness and then zooming in on them.

To start his strategy off right, Sam had sent her a large box of bonbons topped by a huge red bow. According to Lisa, Dallas ate chocolate-covered cherries when she was nervous. He instructed the candy maker to keep sending the boxes. In his brand of honor, you let the opponent see you coming.

When Dallas woke up in the morning, Sam had had breakfast waiting. He'd touched base with her several times during the day. Taking Emily's suggestion, he'd occasionally popped into the Pendragon offices with a basket lunch. He'd fought household bears at bedtime, and then had waited for when Dallas had her ritual cup of tea.

He liked her cabbage-rose couch. It was just small enough to place his arm on the back. From there he could stroke Dallas's smooth cheek. Or rub the taut muscles at the back of her neck.

Dallas was too tight, too nervous. "Scared stiff is more like it. She's not the only one."

Emily opened his gym door and grinned toothily. "Nikki Pendragon on line two."

Sam pivoted to her instantly. "What's wrong?"

Her grin widened. "It sounds serious." But Sam had already brushed past her on his way back to the office.

Had something happened to Dallas? Did Billy fall down stairs or play with tools that should be locked away? Forcing his fears aside, Sam said gently, "Hi, Nikki?"

One small sniff echoed loudly through his heart, stopping the quickening beat. By the second sniff, Sam found his hand strangling the receiver, his knuckles showing white beneath the skin. "Nikki, is something wrong?" he forced himself to ask calmly.

"The Sunbirds are all bringing their dads to a special meeting. We're supposed to fix box lunches and put on plays and sing and...oh, Mr. Sam, Mom said not to bother you." Nikki's rapid burst was followed by another heart-chilling sniff.

Dallas didn't want him—Sam swallowed, his throat too tight to accept the moisture. He didn't intend to be squeezed out of the Pendragon household, no matter what Dallas's fears were. The children needed him, and if Dallas would stop fighting him long enough— "I'd love to come, Nikki. I haven't had a good box lunch in my entire life. It's a date."

"But Mom said...." Nikki protested in a tone that sounded like she'd just gotten another Christmas present.

The thought that Dallas wanted to cancel his adoption papers drew Sam's neck down protectively. He could feel himself gearing up for a fight. The odd thing about it was, he really liked fighting with Dallas as much as he liked talking over a proposal. Or loving her into the rainy night.... He'd never been friends with a woman before, and without the white-hot sensual tension running between them, Dallas just could be his first female friend. "I'll call your mother and ask for permission to date my favorite girl. How about that, Nikki?"

"Great!" After excitedly relaying the details of the gala, Nikki's voice lowered. "Baghdad hasn't come home for a long time...Daddy. Mom says old toms sometimes just find another home. I like Baghdad, and Billy's just a kid—he cries sometimes. Do you think he'll come home?"

Old toms sometimes just find another home. Sam's mouth firmed as he reassured Nikki about the cat's return and offered to join the search party.

Hell, he'd found what he'd been looking for in one short month—Dallas's soft, caring touch. "This old tom isn't going anywhere," Sam muttered after saying goodbye.

He punched out the telephone number of Dallas's office. "What's this about not bothering me, Dallas?" he asked when she picked up the line.

"Stop snarling, Sam. I don't need the stress today," she warned lightly, but he ignored the tone.

"Stress, hell! You're creating stress. If Nikki wants to ask me to the Sunbirds box lunch, she can—"

"Sam." He knew she was fighting for control and didn't feel

like giving her the edge. In his experience, once the pressure was on, it was best to keep it going.

Sam found himself grinning. Dallas shielded her base emotions from everyone else. But not from him. He'd felt her fire once, had found her fears, and he intended to make her recognize what she needed—him. "You need me, Dallas. Admit it. Nikki and Billy do, too. By the way, you viruses are all alike. You interfere with a perfectly good working system, mess around with the basics, then scoot on out without looking back—"

"What are you talking about?" Dallas's low husky voice had just the fighting edge to it that Sam wanted. The really nice thing about Dallas was that he could level with her.

Zeroing in on that tone, Sam felt himself smirking. He'd caught a cluster of secretaries talking about what excited them, and a favorite line in a movie yielded results that spanned from weak knees to hearts stopping. Deciding to give sweet-talking a try, Sam said, "I'm talking about soft sighs on my skin, sweet shy kisses, rain on the windows and rosebuds on the sheets, a demanding, sexy, witch-eyed woman with hair like liquid, silky copper and a body like I've never touched before. Of long, fascinating, silky legs that reach way up. Of low sultry whispers sweeping over me like intoxicating red wine. Of lips like fresh strawberries and arms that make me feel all new. I'm talking about sweet peas growing at the back door on an Appalachia moonlit night, of magnolias and fresh-baked bagels. Of commitments to last forever and of sharing mistletoe balls every year and watching Nikki and Billy grow up together and holding their children on our laps and of loving every single day of our lives together. I'm talking about you and me, caring for each other, needing and wanting and having it all between us.... And none of that has anything to do with T.J. McCall, Nikki and Billy or our contract. Think about it," he added lightly, cheerfully, and then he gently replaced the phone in the cradle.

Sam looked at the spot behind his desk where Dallas had first found her immunity-to-love slipping, and found himself grinning widely. "Let her chew on that," he said proudly before whistling a sexy *Blue Tango*. Dancing with an imaginary woman, Sam tangoed around his desk, bent his ladylove over his arm and kissed her soundly.

Arriving on Dallas's doorstep that night, Sam rubbed Baghdad's scarred ears with just the right roughness the cat preferred. Finding the tom wasn't difficult after he offered every child in the neighborhood a new bicycle. When in doubt, Sam followed his old rules: you have to put out to get what you want. And he wanted Dallas.

"Do your stuff, boy," he coached the purring tom as he waited for Dallas to answer the doorbell. "Slide right in there."

When Dallas opened the door, wearing her long electric-blue caftan, Sam found himself staring hungrily at her. "We're here." He managed to say before the children swooped down on the thin and grinning tomcat.

But Dallas crossed her arms across her breasts—which Sam had found himself remembering very well—and frowned up at him with all the warmth of a refrigerator. "Aren't you glad to see Baghdad?" Sam asked lightly, stepping past her and taking off his coat to hug the jubilant children.

"Of course, I'm glad to see the cat. What do you mean," she said between her teeth when he straightened to grin at her, "saying things like you did today?"

"Hmm?" Sam asked absently, settling himself on the floor to play with Billy's new dump truck. Edgy and miffed, Dallas's steamed look reminded Sam of the way she made love. Baghdad—acting his in-cahoots part—rubbed against Sam like an old, beloved friend. He purred so loudly, Dallas couldn't possibly ignore his happiness.

"I'll talk to you about the matter some other time," Dallas stated in her strictly-business-but-uncertain-about-herself tone.

Sam allowed his gaze to slowly wander up Dallas's long leg, exposed by the thigh-high slit. Wrapping his hand around her ankle, he caressed her skin with his thumb. "Let's start dating, sweet pea," he offered in a tone of honorable innocence. "Bowling, movies. With or without the children. Of course, I don't think they'll want to go to those dull plays that you enjoy so much. But I will. I'll try my best to understand the underlying, obscure meaning. I'll even let you drive Bertha to the junkyard. She's due for a new doorknob. We can scout out the wrecks together, okay?"

"Sounds like great fun," she said under her breath and in a sarcastic tone.

"Getting to you, aren't I?" he asked, scratching Baghdad's scarred ears roughly. When Dallas's cheeks began to flush, Sam lifted his eyebrows several times, teasing her with his imitation of Tom Selleck. The gesture supposedly aroused his secretaries, too.

"Sam...I can't get any more involved," she whispered unevenly, avoiding his attempt at play.

Taking his time, Sam rose to stand near her. He cupped her chin and looked deeply into her teary, witching eyes. Loving her and meaning every word, he said, "I learned a long time ago that nothing is impossible. Between us, we'll work out the problems. Just don't close any doors, okay?"

With that, Sam kissed her with all the sweetness he felt. Despite Baghdad rubbing against their legs and purring, despite Nikki and Billy cheering in the background, Dallas's lips clung and brushed and warmed his. When her hands slid to his waist and rested there, Sam thought distantly that it was enough for now.

By the middle of February, he noted that the candy maker's bill did not show returned candy credits. He also noticed a new, but definite roundness to Dallas's streamlined body. Sam added the two facts together: Dallas was under definite stress despite the successful job-sharing program. "She'd better be nervous. I play to win," Sam muttered, slamming into his punching bag viciously. "All's fair," he grunted.

Working together every day on designing the child-care center, Sam sensed her studying him. Though she managed to avoid his issue of dating, she seemed to enjoy having him in her home—and knowing his limitations just now, Sam let her. Dallas covered her soft, wounded heart with business trimmings, keeping him on his toes. She let him hold her hand, and to Sam, the gesture signified a beginning.

* * *

After the father-daughter Sunbird box lunch, Nikki's glowing report drew Dallas's slow, contemplative stare to Sam. The look held and warmed and promised as she said quietly, "Thank you, Sam."

"Thank you," he returned softly, meaning it.

"Why?" she asked in an uneven whisper as he took her hand.

Lifting it to kiss her chocolate-scented fingers, Sam said simply, "For changing my life. For warming me and caring."

"Oh, Sam," she whispered, looking up into his eyes.

Later, Sam turned her tone over in slow replay. She sounded helpless, vulnerable and too uncertain.

Dallas was as afraid of a relationship as he was.

He wanted her petting him, damn it! He wanted to take care of her even if she didn't want him around. "I want to move back in, is what I want to do," Sam muttered, slamming the bag one last time. "Hell, they adopted me didn't they? I'm not going to turn in my adoption papers without a fight. If Dallas thinks she can put me out in the cold, she's wrong."

The first of March blew gently into Seattle, at odds with the steamy, unvented feeling that Dallas carried within her. Sam knew how to cause stress. He was too sweet, too patient, too adorable, too...everything, including warm and sexy and funny. He gave everyone the impression that though he admired her business skills, he definitely thought of Dallas as his lady.

A man of Sam's size and importance wasn't easily swept aside.

She didn't have the heart to separate him from her cabbage-rose couch, Billy's trucks and Nikki's glowing adoration. Sam really seemed to need her and her family.

"Oh, of course, he knows all that and is using every ounce of it," Dallas snapped, standing up from her office desk. "He knows perfectly well how charming he can be, when to use his dimples and his boxes of candy."

She thought of how Sam had looked into her eyes, claiming her hand and placing it on his chest before she could recover from his sexy stun stare. "Every trick, no matter how low," she muttered, remembering how she'd found her fingers rummaging through the hair on his chest.

She wanted him desperately. He was nothing like T.J.—he was just Sam. Yet somehow, Dallas couldn't let him sweep her off her feet.

This time...this man deserved every bit of thought put into a relationship he obviously wanted.

Tossing the empty candy wrappers into the trash can, Dallas firmly placed the lid on the box of chocolates. She touched the huge elegant red bow, recognizing the blatant symbol of war.

Dallas replaced her pumps with running shoes. She clicked on the electric treadmill she'd had installed in her office. Eight pounds of nervous chocolate binges had lodged on her bust and hips since she'd met Sam. Dallas turned up the pace, walking more quickly. Besides the eight pounds gained she was not sleeping well.

Her mind had wandered in the middle of a class biofeedback experiment, setting up a howl caused by high emotion. Touching base with the questioning expressions of her class, Dallas had found that she had been thinking of Sam's sexy declaration.

Memories of Sam standing in front of the stove, dressed in sweat pants and a stained cotton T-shirt had sent the monitor screaming.

Then there was the hopelessly reverent way he accepted any small thing she'd done for him. Like pasting toilet paper on his untended razor cuts and baking his favorite chocolate cake. Sam never took anything for granted; he took everything personally as if no one had ever cared before.

Thoughts of his kisses started raising unpredictable little constrictions in areas she considered ultrapersonal. "Sexual frustration," she muttered, working harder to drain off her excess energy.

Dallas started thinking about Sam's version of The Three Bears— "And who's been sleeping in my bed?" But lately he'd been tracking her with his smoky eyes, telling her silent stories that caused her to tremble. Of furry navels and gentle, large hands. Of hairy chests and sweet magnolia kisses.

Of lying tangled in the rosebuds sheets while the rain sounded softly against the windowpane. Of pleasure defined by a low, lazy masculine growl.

Dallas wiped the sweat from her forehead and began jogging earnestly. She concentrated on the professional elements of the Brice project.

The job-sharing feature of her plan was a huge success. Though Sam growled about seeing different faces at the same desk every day, he reluctantly admitted liking the cheerful expressions on those faces. Sam did admit when he'd made a mistake—she very much liked that about him.

She planned to add the latchkey program to the child-care center. Sam had suggested the idea, saying he didn't think it was safe for school children to enter empty homes. His latchkey "waiting station" clause also reduced the stress on working parents.

Panting and trying to catch her breath, Dallas shook her head. Sam wanted the plans on his desk in the afternoon to prepare for dinner with the board members and their wives. He wanted her at his side to answer questions wearing "that little basic-black number." "It's good PR to show up at these soirees and push your plans. I want Billy and Nikki to be the first enrolled in the child-care center, Dallas," Sam had stated flatly. "Everyone here knows that I'm...well, attached to them. They'd qualify as my family. I'm not above pulling rank when I have to. Of course, you have the say-so. What do you think?"

She'd thought it was a good idea. Having a creative mind, Sam knew how to balance suggestions with the practical side of his business. Making it clear that he'd accept comments from the staff, Sam was possessive about the program. He did know how to present plans, Dallas admitted. He listened with an intelligent, questioning mind and respected her ideas.

It was the dark side of him that frightened her. *Because she had her own dark side, one she'd never explored until that night.*

Because as gentle as Sam could be, Dallas now feared her own primitive needs when he was near. If he tapped into that fear—Dallas hopped off the treadmill and opened the candy box.

Sucking the bonbon's juice, Dallas thought of the way Sam had been coming to dinner every evening. He often picked up the children, got groceries and had supper waiting on the table when she arrived late at night—and he swept aside her protests with a shrug, "Need to pay you back for the loan." Sam could well afford to pay her back; he was using the tiny loan as an excuse to infiltrate her home and to use her father's power tools. Sam had squashed Beau's interest and she'd never gotten that comparative kiss.

In fact, the last kiss she remembered was Sam's. The memory of it kept her awake at nights, caused her to sink into sweet, sensual dreams and wake up hugging her bed pillows tightly. Closing her eyes, Dallas admitted that Sam knew how to create memorable memories. Every time the Deons celebrated that spring was on its way, kissing in the backyard, the front yard and in the car, Dallas's midsection ached.

Sam wasn't staying at the penthouse now, she was certain of it. Sam had installed his toy train in the center of the company conference table, stating that no one used the space anyway. Judging from the evidence—aftershave on his desk and slacks thrown across a conference chair—Sam's new home was his office. The thought made Dallas's guilt barometer rise.

Sam Loring had that underfed-lonesome-stray-battered-alley-tomcat look pasted all over him. He knew its appeal to her. He knew just how to make her feel like renewing his adoption papers.

But there was more at stake. Big red-flagged, dangerous things like love and commitment and sharing her children and grandchildren. Things like letting her tom-toms riot when the children were asleep. Those were all the things she'd dreamed about at twenty-nine; she had no illusions about white knights carrying off ladies in distress. "Am I in distress?" she asked herself, then answered in a reluctant mumble, "Only when I'm near Sam."

Then there was the awful thing. Like failure looming before her. Remembering her last experience with giving a man one hundred percent, Dallas groaned.

That evening at the dinner for the Board members, Sam's tie was crooked and when Dallas instinctively straightened it, his hands wrapped around her wrists. "I like you fussing over me, sweet pea," he whispered in his sexiest Southern drawl. "Someone will think you care."

"I'm not fussing over you. Anyone would have done the same.

And why don't you use that voice with anyone else?" she demanded in a hushed whisper.

"'Cause you're special, sweet pea," Sam whispered back, pulling out his devastating dimples. "Adjusting my tie is a gesture of squaring off female territorial rights. Can't you handle being possessive of me?"

"You're not my territory, Sam. But I can handle anything you can dish out," Dallas said between her teeth.

Sam lifted one eyebrow, the one with the rebellious gray hair. "You think you can, huh?" he asked mockingly. "I can be devious and I'm loaded with chocolate-company stocks."

Recognizing the simmering beat of her tom-toms at Sam's wicked look, Dallas looked away. "Scram. Beat it. Shoo."

Sam's large hand swept down her backside, leaving a trail of warm sensitized flesh. "Not this time," he said in his deadly, means-business tone.

Dallas glanced around the dining room to find her mother watching her intently. Sam traced her frown. "Lisa likes me. The kids like me...Bertha misses her parking spot. I want to move back in. I've passed all the hard housebreaking stages now. It would be a perfect chance for you to show me that you can handle anything I can dish out," he said, repeating her words. "I dare you."

"Sam..." she warned as his hand fitted neatly into her waist to draw her snugly against him. Aligned with a lean body she wanted to hold, Dallas could feel her temperature rise. Beneath her palm, Sam's heart pounded heavily. "Stop. People are watching."

"Marry me," he said quietly, his gray eyes serious behind his glasses. "Take me away from all this stress. I dare you."

"I tried that, thank you." Dallas forced herself to swallow, moistening a suddenly dry throat.

"Big deal," he said flatly as though sweeping away a bird dropping. "So did I."

"See? We don't even know each other. I don't know anything about why your marriage failed—"

"Is it really important? But I do know a little about T.J. McCall. Enough to know that I'm not paying for another man's idiotic problems."

Sam looked down at her, the angles of his face sharpening with anger. "Lady, I'm not putting up with flack. We worked out the details of my stay at your house, didn't we? We've been working on details of this and that for four months. The bottom line is that we're a good team. And there's more to it than that."

"I'm not going to discuss this here—"

"Then you'd better agree to discuss it in private."

No matter how much she cared for Sam, she wasn't going to let him run her life nor make unreasonable demands. "I don't like ultimatums. Or you'll do what?"

"Or I'll go down on one knee and announce my feelings before this whole dull, boring bunch of desk warmers. Since meeting you, I've become loveable, you know. They wouldn't like you very much if you turned me down. You could make a bad impression that would affect your Brice program. Are you willing to discuss the matter later or not?"

"This sounds like blackmail." Dallas's hands curled into fists.

"Okay, so when I want something, I'm not always nice. I'm tired of waiting for you to give me a fair break." With that last statement fresh on his lips, Sam drew Dallas into his arms. He bent her backward, leaning over her in a Valentino-sheik pose and kissed her.

Underlying the sweetness, his kiss tasted slightly like savage hunger, and Dallas began to answer in kind. His teeth nibbled her bottom lip gently. Though his hands remained quite properly on her waist and shoulders, Dallas had the feeling that they were undressing her and seeking her previously sensitized areas. The heat between them caused her to part her lips, and immediately staking claim, Sam's tongue invaded her mouth.

Locking her arms around him, Dallas sank into Sam's offer. The tender play deepened, and she wondered distantly how anything could improve so much every time he kissed her.

When Dallas was allowed to straighten, she looked into Sam's warm, smoky eyes behind his steamy glasses. She wondered absently what they had been discussing. She stared at Sam's slightly swollen lips helplessly, wanting more—

Lisa wrapped her arm around Dallas's shoulders. "My, my. I think he's got it."

"Got what?" Dallas asked absently, still staring into Sam's flickering, promising gaze behind the steamy lenses.

Lisa laughed low and hugged her daughter. "Whatever it is

that puts stars in your eyes. You'd better watch out. Our Sam has his sights set on you. He's not the kind to let you mold on the shelf. I knew this would happen the minute I saw him,'' she crowed softly before moving toward the buffet table and Edward Swearingen.

Beside Dallas, Sam gave one small sniff. He looked down at her with his untended-battered-and-lonely tomcat look. "Sorry. Guess I'm coming down with a cold. Maybe a virus."

Dallas knew she was falling for the look. The fear from her scarred past rose up instantly and instinctively. Before her, the future loomed like an uncharted abyss. While she knew Sam wasn't her past, the thought that he could be her future badly frightened her. "Take two aspirins, drink juice and go to bed,'' she said over her shoulder as she quickly walked toward a covey of board members.

"I've got a virus—you,'' Sam stated clearly behind her. "And I'm needing an immunization shot. Which you should feel obliged to give,'' he added as he wrapped his arm around her shoulder to forcibly steer her to a forest of potted palms.

"Sam,'' she protested weakly, bound by his smoky eyes and silent promises.

"Shh, sweet pea. I want you so much.'' Holding her immobile in the dark secrecy of the shadows, Sam nuzzled her nose with his. When his large, warm hand sought just the right spot low on her spine, Dallas gasped. The wonderful heat she badly wanted to ignore raced through her. While she was fighting her body's unsubtle inclinations to repeat the behind-the-desk scene with a grand finale, Sam nibbled gently on her earlobe. In that lovely, low warm sensual drawl, he whispered, "I love you, sweet pea...I respect you for what you are—who you are—and I think of you as my best friend. I know that if I'm hurting, you'll be there, and I promise to do the same for the rest of my life.... I've never said that to another woman.... Think about it.''

Eleven

Easter morning arrived sunlit and spring fresh; Sam arrived on Dallas's front steps ready for church, egg hunting and a family dinner. In his hand was a huge bouquet of daisies and sweet peas; in his eyes was a question Dallas wanted to answer privately.

Sam clearly intended to warm himself in each minute of the day. With evident pride and reverence, he'd walked up the church steps. Later in a quiet moment at the dinner table, he looked across the sweet-pea bouquet to meet her gaze. "Thank you," he murmured quietly, holding Nikki's hand.

Dallas forced herself to look away from him, fearful that she'd throw herself straight into his arms.

Lisa nudged Edward and whispered, "I'll bet dinner that she doesn't make June."

"You're on," he whispered back.

"What's on?" Nikki asked in childishly clear tones.

"You're losing, sweet pea," Sam said quietly, forcing Dallas to look at him when he took her hand.

"Losing what?" Billy asked, carefully isolating his carrots and peas from his "good" food.

* * *

The next Thursday night, Lisa called just as Dallas wiped away a tear creeping down her cheek. "You're drowning in those chocolates, Dallas dear," Lisa noted. "Why not just admit that Sam is just perfect for you?"

"Mother—"

"I've never thought of you as a cruel person, Dallas. But Sam is someone very special who obviously adores the children and you. Your father was the love of my heart, dear, and you really mustn't waste any time away from Sam. Every moment is just too precious. Now I've rented you a weekend cottage on Dabob Bay, and I want you to take Sam down there and sort it all out. Work something out before—"

"I do love Sam, Mother," Dallas said quietly, testing the words on her lips. "It's just that I have to find my own way of telling him."

She could almost see her mother's pleased smirk. "You're not stepping through a field of landmines.... See that you do tell him, Dallas dear. Before June, if you could manage it. I like Sam. He's what I call a real man, one you can love with nothing held back. Know what I mean?"

After replacing the receiver, Dallas closed her eyes, forced herself to breathe quietly and wondered just how hard she could love Sam without frightening him. Then, with a feeling of parachuting into the unknown, she picked up the telephone to dial his office.

Sam answered in grizzly-bear tones. "Loring."

After a deep breath, Dallas said "Hello."

"What's wrong, Dallas?" Sam asked, his deep tone anxious. "Do you need me? I knew the kids were eating too much candy.... I'm coming over right away—"

"Sam?"

"What?"

"I want kisses at midnight, warm hands to hold when I'm lonely, pleased-grizzly-bear growls after lovemaking, hot-buttered bagels in the morning, someone sweet and tender holding me while the rain runs down the windowpanes, someone to take care of when he's cold and lonely, someone to take care of me when I'm down, someone to run power tools at midnight and touch me like I'm the only woman he's ever loved. I'm talking about a sweet-talking man with a Southern drawl and dimples who makes me want to never let him go. About being together in the good times and the bad. About our family going to church and Easter dinners, laundry on Saturday nights, and baking chocolate cakes for a man who really appreciates them. About fighting and making up, and trusting and sharing, and loving for years to come. I'm talking about putting a baby in a hand-crafted cradle and watching the children grow up together.... How am I doing, Sam?" she asked breathlessly.

After a long pause that caused Dallas's fingers to grip the phone too tightly, Sam said quietly, "You'd better know what you're talking about, lady."

"Meet me tomorrow night at the bay, Sam. I'll send you the directions. And we'll negotiate clauses."

"Pretty damned hard to negotiate with a virus," Sam stated roughly. "They get you every time."

Dallas quietly replaced the telephone with the definite feeling that Sam was ready to tear down doors to get to the one woman he wanted. And she was the only woman he wanted. She allowed herself a delicate, pleased smirk—to be Sam's woman was quite a feeling—his mate when all the negotiations were completed.

Bertha was already parked at the cabin when Dallas arrived. The low, gray clouds swept over the rough waters of the bay; the fine mist curled about her as she walked up the path to the cabin. She smiled softly, thinking that the weathered cabin with smoke rising from the chimney reminded her of Sam. While it appeared seasoned and cold, the cabin withstood the fierce elements, and comfort and warmth waited for her inside...just like Sam.

He opened the door, the lantern light behind him outlining his body. With the wind riffling his hair and dressed in a cream knit sweater and jeans, Sam watched her intently. He took her case and slowly placed it on the floor, still looking at her. Straightening to his full height, he said tightly, "Tell me you love me."

When she took off her jacket, nervously running her hands down her sweater and jeans, Sam demanded stiffly, "Okay. Then tell me you want me."

Dallas lifted an eyebrow at him, teasingly. "Could we go at this in stages?" she asked, knowing that Sam had his own ideas about the proper stages of negotiating a lifelong contract.

"Nope," he stated flatly, then scooped her up in his arms and carried her to the bed. "I want it all now. And later. And then more. In between, we'll sort out the clauses."

When he placed her gently on the bed, Dallas traced the fierce line between his eyebrows. "I do love you, Sam."

He sat beside her slowly, brushing her hair away from her cheek, his hands trembling. "You took your sweet time."

Carefully placing his large hands along her cheeks, Sam kissed her tenderly, making promises that would last forever. "Don't get any ideas that you can cancel this contract," he murmured unevenly against her cheek as he eased down on the bed beside her.

With trembling hands, they slowly undressed each other, making promises with caresses and gentle kisses and lingering gazes. Folding her carefully against him, Sam smoothed the line of her back gently. Dallas moved closer, raising her arms to hold him tightly, fitting herself against the man who would last through the hard times. Against his ear, she whispered a warning, "Hold on, Sam."

He chuckled warmly, knowingly. "So that's how it's going to be?"

"Yes," she managed as they became one, bound by love and the future waiting for them.

Sam moved against her hungrily, searching for her mouth and claiming it. Without fear, she gave him what he sought.

He tasted of the hunger driving her; his heart pounded beneath her hand, her own special tom-toms begging her to incite a riot.

Diving into what he offered, what he would take and give back with the honesty she demanded, Dallas drew him into the magic of a hot, Southern, sweet-pea-scented-Appalachia-air magnolia night.

Trailing kisses across her damp cheeks, Sam nibbled at her lips. She traced his mouth with hers, blending the intimacy with a rough hunger that caused Sam to growl low in his throat.

The sound quickened Dallas's internal tom-tom beat and her

hands slid down his back. Drawing Sam deeper, Dallas showed him all the heat within her, all the love just for him.

He accepted her gift, lifting her higher, and while Dallas fought the need to cry out, Sam gently bit her earlobe and whispered roughly, "I'm here. I'll always be here—I love you, Dallas."

No longer fighting, Dallas stepped out onto her private ledge and went free-falling into Sam's love.

Later, he held her, bringing her back to earth and the cabin with sweet Southern drawls and quieting hands. "Help," he teased, running a large, open hand down his newly claimed territory. "Tell me you love me again."

Knowing that Sam really worked to get his way when denied, Dallas grinned up at him, smiled widely, and said, "Nope."

"You're tough, Pendragon. But I''m determined," he returned with a matching, teasing grin. "You'll tell me—"

"No way," she murmured before his lips sealed hers in a sweet, devastating sexy kiss. "Well, maybe—" she added as he drew her over him.

Epilogue

"The kid is a demanding tyrant," Sam said in a pleased daddy tone, placing his son in his cradle after a midnight feeding.

"He'll start sleeping better once you stop showing him off," Dallas teased as Sam bent to kiss her. During the seven weeks since baby's birth, Sam had definitely leashed his kissing powers. Dallas, after shedding her candy and "new-mother" pounds, didn't want any sensual stress to cause a repeat of her chocolate-covered-cherry's eating binge. With quiet determination, she had baked Sam's favorite chocolate cake and asked her mother to take Billy and Nikki for a weekend in the mountains.

While Sam turned off the lights in their new home, Dallas plotted to seduce him. She lit candles in their bedroom, the hard-wood floor catching the glow that washed over their king-size four-poster bed. Dallas watched her husband stroll back to bed with the air of Baghdad's male this-is-my-kingdom confidence.

In the year and a half since their wedding ceremony, Sam had never complained about family life. She loved him deeply and was confident in his love. Sam really listened to her, often giving her ideas for improving her business and ideas—except for the Whammy. The really nice thing about Sam was that he did wonderful, personal things for her ego. And he demonstrated his love in any way he could.

But Sam had a tendency to be a little too careful. Especially when she'd been pregnant and he'd looked at her with such love and concern that she'd ached for him. He'd been there during Brent's delivery, then had quietly seemed to go limp and helpless after the birth.

She smiled as the candlelight softened the desire in his expression. Sam had built the new house as a gift of love, yet never was too busy for the children, who adored him. The toy train and "guy stuff" occupied a place of honor in the family room, and Sam had whittled a tiny female engineer just for Nikki.

Pausing beside the bed, Sam looked down at Dallas tenderly. "What's the candlelight occasion?"

Taking his hand and lacing her fingers with his, Dallas savored a game that she knew they would play forever. "You're going to tell me you love me tonight."

Sam frowned, a tense muscle moving in his cheek. "I must tell you that at least twice a day. I even call you at your offices—" Then his frown deepened, shielding what Dallas thought to be high hope. "Did the doctor say it was okay to...?"

She smiled wickedly, tugging lightly on his hand to urge him into the rosebud sheets and her waiting tom-tom beats.

When Sam slid into the rosebuds, she fitted her naked body to his, wrapped her arms around him and nibbled at his ear. She'd found that Sam's earlobes were definitely susceptible to nibbling. "Tell me you love me," she urged, allowing her hands to caress Sam's powerful, hair-flecked anatomy.

"Make me," he challenged, laughing up at her. "Be gentle," he whispered a moment later.

Even later, he managed to say "Okay. I love you."

* * * * *

Just in time for Christmas! Rush right back to the stores for THE PERFECT FIT, the final Tallchief title by Cait London. Next, BLAYLOCK'S BRIDE will be an April 1999 publication, and there will be another Blaylock story available in Desire before the end of the year. Be sure to check them out!

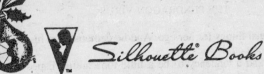

Take 2 bestselling love stories FREE

Plus get a FREE surprise gift!

For a limited time, Harlequin and Silhouette have an offer you just can't refuse.

In November and December 1998:

BUY **ANY** TWO HARLEQUIN
OR SILHOUETTE BOOKS and

SAVE $10.00

off future purchases

OR BUY ANY THREE HARLEQUIN OR SILHOUETTE BOOKS
AND **SAVE $20.00** OFF FUTURE PURCHASES!

(each coupon is good for $1.00 off the purchase of two
Harlequin or Silhouette books)

JUST BUY 2 HARLEQUIN OR SILHOUETTE BOOKS, SEND US YOUR NAME, ADDRESS AND 2 PROOFS OF PURCHASE (CASH REGISTER RECEIPTS) AND HARLEQUIN WILL SEND YOU A COUPON BOOKLET WORTH **$10.00** OFF FUTURE PURCHASES OF HARLEQUIN OR SILHOUETTE BOOKS IN 1999. SEND US 3 PROOFS OF PURCHASE AND WE WILL SEND YOU 2 COUPON BOOKLETS WITH A TOTAL SAVING OF **$20.00**. (ALLOW 4-6 WEEKS DELIVERY) OFFER EXPIRES DECEMBER 31, 1998.

I accept your offer! Please send me a coupon booklet(s), to:

NAME: _____

ADDRESS: _____

CITY: _____ STATE/PROV.: _____ POSTAL/ZIP CODE: _____

Send your name and address, along with your cash register
receipts for proofs of purchase, to:

In the U.S.	In Canada
Harlequin Books	Harlequin Books
P.O. Box 9057	P.O. Box 622
Buffalo, NY	Fort Erie, Ontario
14269	L2A 5X3

PHQ4982

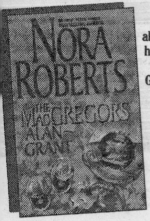